DARK DAYS

DARK DAYS

JOCELYNN DRAKE

FANTASY

NIGHTWALKER Copyright © 2008 by Jocelynn Drake
   Publication History: Eos mass market paperback, August 2008
DAYHUNTER Copyright © 2009 by Jocelynn Drake
   Publication History: Eos mass market paperback, May 2009

First SFBC Science Fiction Printing: June 2009

Published by arrangement with
Eos
An Imprint of HarperCollins *Publishers*
10 East 53rd Street
New York, New York 10022-5299

Visit The SFBC online at http://www.sfbc.com

ISBN # 978-1-61523-184-3

Printed in the United States of America.

CONTENTS

Nightwalker

To Mom and Dad
You believed in me first

ACKNOWLEDGMENTS

The road here has been long, and at times ugly. The list of people who have helped me get here is equally long, and I want to thank everyone who laughed with me, held my hand when the dark closed in, and shared their lives with me, even if it was only nervous small talk in a slow-moving line. You've shaped me and in turn shaped my words.

However, there are a few people I need to thank specifically. Thanks to my brilliant agent Jennifer Schober. Your patience, endless enthusiasm, and belief in me have meant more than you will ever know. Thanks to my amazing editor, Diana Gill, for taking a chance on a newbie and demanding that I be the writer I always wanted to be.

A special thanks to Kim Harrison, Rachel Vincent, and Joseph Hargett. For years you have been my personal cheering section, editors, friends, champions, and when I needed it, a valuable reality check. Thanks for putting up with me.

And thank you to my family. Thanks, Stephen, for reminding me cartoons and video games are still an essential part of living no matter how old I get. Thanks, Nate, for always making me laugh, even when I thought it was impossible. Finally, thanks, Mom and Dad, for pointing out that I would be much happier as a writer than a chemical engineer. You just may have saved the world.

ONE

His name was Danaus.

And what I remember most were his eyes. I saw them first by lamplight; a flicker of dark cobalt as he paused a distance from me. His eyes were the color sapphires were meant to be, a grim sparkle of pigment. I stared at those eyes, willing time to slow down as I slipped into those still, stygian depths. But it wasn't the waters of the Styx I swam in, but a cool lagoon of Lethe where I bathed in a moment of oblivion.

He stopped on the deserted street outside the edge of a pale pool of light thrown down by a wrought-iron lamp, his eyes darting up and down the empty expanse. He drew in a deep breath. I think he could sense me watching from some perch but could not peg my exact location. His right hand flexed once at his side, and to my surprise he stepped forward into the light, his night vision momentarily destroyed; taunting me with the bait he dangled before my eyes.

I slowly ran my tongue over my teeth. Not only was he impressive to look at, but there was a confidence about him that begged my attention. I was half tempted to step away from the shadow of the chimney and allow the moon to outline my slim form. But I hadn't survived for more than six centuries by making careless mistakes. Balanced on the ridgepole of the three-story house across from him, I watched as he continued down the street. His black leather duster flared as he walked, snapping at his heels like a chained wolf forced to follow its master.

The truth was, I had watched him for more than a month. He'd blown into my territory like a cold wind and wasted no time destroying my kind. In the past weeks he had killed nearly half a dozen of my brethren. Almost all had been fledglings, with less than a century to cut their teeth upon, but it was still more than any other had dared.

And these killings had not been spineless daylight stakings. He hunted each nightwalker under the caress of moonlight. I had even watched some of these battles from a hidden perch and barely kept from applauding when he knelt, bloody, over each of his prey, cutting out the heart. He was speed and cunning. And the nightwalkers were bloated on their own inflated sense of power. I was the Keeper of this domain, entrusted with protecting our secret; not protecting those who could not protect themselves.

After weeks of watching my would-be prey, I thought it was time for formal introductions. I knew who he was. More than just another Nosferatu hunter. Something wonderfully more, with a vibrant power all his own. I wanted a taste of that power before he died.

And he knew of me. In their final seconds some of the weak ones had mewled my name, hoping my identity would buy them a last second reprieve. It hadn't.

I sped silently along the rooftops, leaping over the gaps and landing with the sure-footed grace of a cat. Slipping past him and down two more blocks to the outer edge of the historic district, I stopped at an abandoned home with a widow's walk and worn red brick that would serve as a nice meeting place. Its single turret and dark windows gazed out toward the river like a silent soldier.

The night air was warm and thick despite the fact that we hadn't had any rain for more than two weeks, leaving the brown lawns struggling from yet another rough summer. Even the crickets seemed to put forth only a halfhearted effort with their chirping, burdened by the oppressive heat. The light breeze that blew in from the sea carried with it more moisture, thickening the air until it carried a weight all its own. I had come to Savannah more than a century ago, seeking anonymity, an escape from the world that had consumed me for nearly five hundred years. I loved Savannah's grace and history, the ghosts that seemed to haunt every shadowy corner and rambling house. Yet I could do without her oppressive summers. I'd spent too many years in cooler climes.

The abandoned house was half hidden behind enormous oak trees dripping with Spanish moss, as if guarded by a pair of grand dames swathed in antique lace. The front of the property was lined with a tall, spike iron fence ending in a pair of stone pillars that flanked the path up to the house. I sat on the top of the left pillar with my legs crossed, waiting for him. The subtle throb of my powers tumbled from my body. I wanted him to follow the trail until he came to me, like the pied piper trilling his merry tune for the children of Hamelin.

Danaus stopped when he reached the edge of the property to my left and stared at me. Yes, it was brazen, and maybe even a little over-confident on my part, but I didn't want him to grow too sure of him-self. He would have to work for his blood tonight.

With a slow smile, I rolled off the pillar, disappearing behind the spike fence and into the deeper shadows of the overgrown yard. I cut through the air as if I were made of the night, disappearing through an open window on the second floor at the back of the house.

Waiting in a former bedroom, I listened. Anticipation coiled in my stomach, my body tingling with the thrill of the hunt, so rarely had I the chance to pit myself against something that could actually destroy me. I'd killed my share of human hunters, but they hadn't been a real challenge, waving their silver crosses about and praying to a god they had abandoned until that moment of final judgment. After so many long centuries, there were too few ways in which to feel that rush, to dance along the razor's edge and remember, even if only for a breath, what it had meant to be alive. Danaus would help me remember.

This hunter was different. He was as human as I was. His body was only a shell, barely capable of restraining the power that seemed to pour from him like a river.

Downstairs, the front door exploded open, banging against the wall. I smiled; he knew I was here waiting for him. I strode across the hardwood floor, moving into the master bedroom, the heels of my boots echoing through the empty house. Now he knew exactly where I was, too.

Peace, Mira, I reminded myself. *No reason to rush this. You haven't hunted him for more than a month to snap his neck in a care-less moment.*

No, I would put an end to his destruction of my race and enjoy it as I did so.

Once in the bedroom, my steps quieted until I didn't make a sound as I crossed to the far side of the room. I leaned into the empty corner, letting the shadows fold around me like a cloak, falling into the darkness that had long whispered secrets of the night and death. Around me the old house creaked and sighed as we both waited.

Danaus finally appeared in the doorway, his shoulders so wide they nearly brushed the sides of the entry. I stood silent for a moment, enjoying the slow, even rise and fall of his chest. He was perfectly calm. He was tall, maybe six feet, with raven black hair that hung wild to his shoulders. His cheekbones were high and his jaw strong and hard like granite. Along the way he had shed his black coat, and his right hand gripped a six-inch silver blade that caught the moonlight.

"You are the one they call Danaus," I said. My voice slithered out from the shadows while my body remained hidden. His head jerked toward me, his eyes slits of blue in the darkness. "They say you killed Jabari in old Thebes."

I stepped forward, the shadows sliding their arms about my body, and paced across the room so he could see me clearly for the first time. In the soft light that poured through the windows, my pale skin glowed like white marble. I moved no closer to him, giving him a chance to size me up.

"But you missed Valerio in Vienna," I said, curiosity lifting my voice. "And Yuri waits for you in St. Petersburg, though he is not half as old as Jabari."

"There's still time." His voice was like a growl in the back of his throat.

I paused, staring at him for a moment. I couldn't place the accent, and I'd heard many over the centuries. It was old, very old. Not nearly as old as Jabari's Egyptian lilt, but something that hadn't been uttered in ages. It would be something to ponder, but I had more pressing queries.

"Maybe," I conceded with a slight nod. "But instead you came to the New World. While I may be one of the oldest here, I am far younger than Valerio. Why travel such a distance?"

"Aren't you called the 'Fire Starter'?"

I laughed, a deep throaty sound that curled through the air and brushed like a warm hand against his cheek. The ability to touch another with your voice was an old trick that came naturally to some nightwalkers. It had few real uses, but was great for unnerving your opponent. Danaus shifted from one foot to the other, but his expression never changed.

"Among other things." I walked back toward the opposite wall, but this time I moved a few steps closer to him. His muscles tightened but he didn't step backward. It was enough for me to brush against the circle of power that enveloped him, rubbing against my bare skin like warm silk. It also gave him a better taste of my own power. By the time I reached my original corner, something had changed in his eyes.

"You were at the Bonaventure cemetery three nights ago," he said.

"Yes." The word came out a whispered hiss.

"I killed two vampires that night." He said it as if it should have explained everything.

"So? Since entering my territory a month ago, you have killed five nightwalkers."

"Why didn't you try to stop me?"

I chuckled softly, with a slight shake of my head. *Try.* Were we both truly this arrogant? I lifted my shoulders in an indifferent shrug. "They were not mine to protect."

"But they were vampires."

"They were fledglings without a master," I corrected him. Pushing off the wall, I started to walk toward him. "A master you killed more than a week ago." Of course, I'd been planning to kill Riley myself, but Danaus beat me to it. Riley had been expanding his own little family without my permission, and a balance had to be maintained in order to preserve our secret.

Danaus moved, mirroring me as he stepped out of the doorway. He turned so his back was to the wall as we circled each other. His steps were graceful and fluid, like a dance. The knot tightened again in my stomach and my body hummed with energy.

I took a single step forward, testing him, and Danaus lashed out with his right hand. Jerking away, I kept the blade from slashing at my face. Yet, he surprised me when he immediately spun back around, lifting his left hand to reveal a Saracen blade curving up the length of his arm. His first move had been a feint to get me to expose my throat. I dropped into a spin kick, clipping one of his feet before he could move. The hunter stumbled as he backed away, but remained standing. Balanced on the balls of my feet, I pressed my fingers to the dusty hardwood floor.

"Nice sword. Gaelic runes?" I inquired, as if making idle small talk, but my eyes were locked on him. The hand holding the sword tightened. It was an exquisite blade, with a line of runes etched down the side. I couldn't read them, but I would have wagered that they were more than just decoration.

He grunted, which I took for an affirmation to my question.

"Thanks for not coming at me with a stake," I said, standing. He looked at me, his dark eyebrows briefly meeting over the bridge of his nose. "It's so cliché." The right corner of his mouth twitched before he could stop it.

"You would have set it on fire," he said stiffly.

"True." I waited a heartbeat, then crossed the distance between us, hitting him in the chest with both hands. Air exploded from his lungs. The blow threw both of his arms involuntarily forward as he stumbled back. I kicked out with my right foot, hitting his left hand. The impact loosened his grip and sent the scimitar spinning across the floor, to clatter against the far wall. Unfortunately, he recovered faster than I expected and swung his right arm forward, grazing my cheek with the dagger.

The unexpected stab of pain screamed through me, and I jerked back out of arm's reach. I hissed at him, fangs bared, my body hunched as if prepared to spring. Yeah, I know. The hiss was even more cliché than a wooden stake, but the grating sound erupted from my throat before I could think about it, let alone come up with something a little more civilized. I'm 603 years old, not an Ancient.

Again I forced myself to stand and relax. Danaus drew in a few ragged gulps of air before his breathing evened out. Breathing would be painful for a while, but at least he still could. I lifted my left hand to my cheek and then moved my fingers into my line of sight; my eyes never leaving his tense form. Blood covered two fingers. Slowly, I licked them, letting the copper taste coat my tongue. The pain in my cheek was already gone and I could feel the wound closing. In another moment there would only be a smear of blood.

That bit of blood had been enough. The taste lit the lust, sending it burning through my veins. Sure, it had been my blood, but it was all the same; vampire, human, and even whatever Danaus was. It all pulsed with power from the soul, the very essence of life, and I knew this time it would be his I tasted.

I rushed him again, but Danaus was ready. He swung the blade at me, once again going for my throat. I easily caught his hand. He swung his left fist at my face. I batted it away. Squeezing his right hand, I tried to force him to drop the dagger without breaking his hand, but despite the pain, he wouldn't drop it. Out of the corner of my eye I saw his left hand go for another weapon at his side.

"Fine." The single word escaped in a growl as I grabbed his left wrist. I swept my leg beneath his, throwing us both down. Lying on top of him, I pinned both of his hands against the floor. Sure, he was heavier than me, but even with all his muscles, I was still stronger. Vampirism has its perks. Sliding along his body, my leather pants slipped along his legs until I was straddling him. I smiled down at him, rubbing against the hard bulge in his pants. He didn't carry a gun. Unless you put a shotgun in our mouths and pulled the trigger, you really couldn't kill a nightwalker with a gun. It generally didn't even slow us down.

"I thought you were glad to see me," I purred, unable to keep the laughter from my voice. Danaus glared at me, his eyes hardening into cold gems. I knew better. The violence turned him on, not me. The thrill of the hunt.

He stared at me, his mind turning over thoughts I wished I could hear. Something about me bothered him. Sure, I was beautiful, but all nightwalkers were a pretty face and a nice body. If his attention was that easy to catch, he would have been dead long ago.

The question that flickered in his eyes was the only reason I think he had not actually tried to kill me yet. We'd taken a few nice stabs at each other, but no killing blows. The other fights I watched had been quick. Each of his attacks were precise and efficient, planned to end the battle and take down the nightwalker. Maybe we were still sizing each other up, enjoying the building tension, but it felt like there was more hanging unsaid in the ether.

With my hands still locked on his wrists, I pulled backward, lowering my face until my chin rested on his sternum, my eyes locked with his. I could feel the muscles in his body tighten beneath me, but he didn't jerk or try to throw me off. Despite the fact that my lips were barely an inch from his chest, I couldn't bite him at that angle. We both knew this, so he lay still, waiting.

Drawing in a deep breath, I let his scent fill me. I could smell sweat and that certain musky scent of man, but there was more, the wind, a distant sea, and best of all, the sun. The scent was so strong I could taste it, conjuring up ancient memories of basking naked in the midday heat.

I needed to get off of him, to put some distance between us. I was becoming giddy on his power as it wrapped its arms around my cool flesh. Giddy, along with other things I knew would serve us no good tonight, except maybe kill him a little faster. And I so wanted to do this slowly, to enjoy the fight that he offered.

"I didn't come here to destroy you," he said, his voice rolling through the silent room like a rumble of distant thunder.

A bubble of laughter escaped me as I moved forward so my face hovered above his. "And that is supposed to stop me from killing you? You come into my territory, kill my people, and then you say you're not here to destroy me. No, Danaus, I plan to dig around inside of you to find out where that little ball of power is hiding." I smiled at him, broadly enough to expose my fangs.

Danaus was moving before I even had a chance to react, rolling so he was now on top of me. But I was still holding his wrists. I pushed him backward, throwing him off me and across the room. The hunter landed on his back and slid a couple of feet. When he was standing again, I was on the other side of the room.

I leaned back into the corner, balanced on my heels, with my shoulders braced against the two walls. After letting his warm powers wash over me, I forced myself to slow down. I had never encountered a creature with powers that felt like his. We had acquired a new, dark threat. I needed to discover who or what he was, and if there were more like him. We had not spent countless centuries fighting, and finally defeating, the naturi, only to find ourselves faced with a new foe. One free to walk about in the daylight hours.

I forced a laugh, sending the sound dancing around the room until it finally skipped out the open window to my right. My laughter seemed to put him more on edge than my straddling him. Or maybe it was the fact that he had enjoyed being pinned. I doubted he'd ever allowed any nightwalker get that close to him without putting up a fight.

Staring at him now, something else caught my eye. "Where's your cross, Danaus?" I called across the distance, hooking my thumbs on the front pockets of my leather pants. "All good hunters have a cross dangling about their necks. Where's yours?"

"How can you control fire?" he demanded. His face was grim and half hidden in the shadow of his hair as it fell forward. "It's forbidden." He took a wary step forward, the gritty floor crunching under his foot.

I gracefully rolled to my feet, as if I was a marionette pulled up by my strings. There was nothing human about the movement, and I was pleased to see it still unnerved him even after all his years of hunting us. He took a half step back before he could stop himself, his frown deepening.

"Forbidden?" I repeated. "Has someone written a book of rules on nightwalkers that I don't know about?" *Information.* Could that be the reason he had come hacking and slashing into my domain? He was curious and seeking information?

"No vampire has ever been able to control fire."

"Few have ever hunted us without the protection of a silver cross," I countered.

Danaus stared hard at me. I had a feeling he would have growled at me, but I think he was leaving the animal-like noises to me. He turned the knife handle around in his hand, weighing his options. How important was this information to him? Enough that he would finally be forced to divulge some of his own? Of course, he could then kill me and that would be the end of it.

When the hunter spoke again, the words seemed dragged from his throat. "A cross cannot protect one who is already damned to Hell."

A dozen new questions rushed to my lips, but I had my answer and knew he wouldn't willingly give up any more. At least, not without my answer to his question, and I was willing to play, for now.

"We all have our gifts," I said with a shrug. "Yuri can call wolves to his side. Seraf can raise the dead."

"But fire . . ." His voice drifted off.

"Doesn't quite seem fair," I said. "The one thing that is supposed to kill us all, and I am completely immune. But it has nothing to do with being a nightwalker. I could control fire before I was reborn. Somehow, I retained the gift."

"Like the naturi," he murmured.

"I am nothing like the naturi!" My temper flared to life instantly and I took a step toward him with my fangs bared. All I saw was a quick flick of his wrist, faster than I had ever seen any human move. But that was my fault. I was still thinking of him as human.

The blade flashed for half a second in the moonlight before burying itself in my chest. I stumbled backward, my back slamming into the wall behind me as my hand closed around the knife. It was an inch below my heart, clipping the side of my left lung. With his skill, I guessed he missed my heart on purpose. Even a blow to the heart wouldn't have necessarily killed me, but weakened me enough so he could stroll over and take my head off. It was supposed to be a warning, and if I wasn't so angry, I might have heeded it.

I pulled the dagger from my chest, gritting my teeth as it rubbed against bone and sliced more muscle and flesh. Pressing my left hand against the wound, I tried to slow the flow of blood as it moved like warm fingers down my stomach. The dagger fell from my fingers and clattered to the floor. The sound echoed through the house like shot across an empty plain. I glared at him, finding he had already pulled another knife and held it clenched in his right fist, waiting for me.

This time I walked across the room. I wanted him to see me coming. The movement pulled and twisted the cut in my chest as the flesh struggled to mend. I'd worry about that later. I kept the faint smile on my face, burying the scream of pain deep in my chest.

He slashed at me with the same speed he'd thrown the knife, but I expected it as I watched the twitch and flex of muscles play below his skin. I knocked his hand away, feeling the crack of bone in his wrist as my arm connected. The knife fell to the floor as his fingers spasmed under the flash of pain. He kicked out with his left leg, trying to keep a safe distance between us, but I caught his leg with my right hand and threw him back into the wall. I grabbed his arms, slamming them against the drywall with enough force to dent the surface, keeping them raised above his head. My left hand pressed a bloody handprint into his forearm, and I crushed my body against his with enough force that he grunted. I was done playing nice.

I was shorter than him even in heels, but I could still reach his neck without tiptoeing. I smiled, displaying my fangs. His heart skipped faster, pounding against my chest with its intoxicating warmth. His scent came back to me, the sweet kiss of the wind sweeping over dark waters and the bright sun.

"What are you, Danaus?" I whispered, peering into his eyes. His lips were pressed into a firm, tight line. He was furious. I smiled and leaned into him, close enough that he could feel my words caress the tender flesh of his neck. This time he struggled, muscles straining up and down his body as he tried to rid himself of me, but he was trapped. In a battle of strength, he knew he couldn't win.

My breath brushed across his ear. "It doesn't matter." My lips dipped down to graze his neck, and I could feel a chill skitter across his sweaty flesh. "You'll tell me one day. Before I'm through, you'll even trust me."

I released him and jumped backward, landing easily on the other side of the room. No reason to give him another chance to put a knife in my chest. I had a feeling that this time he wouldn't miss. I stared into his eyes, and there it was this time: fear. A deeper look of uncertainty and doubt. I had finally shaken him down to his core; touched something no one else had. It made him infinitely more dangerous, but then again, I had just become infinitely more dangerous to him, threatening him with something far more horrible than a painful death.

"We're not finished," he said, one hand holding his fractured wrist.

"Oh, you're right. We're not finished by a long shot, but tonight's fun is over," I announced, tilting my head to the side.

"I didn't come here to kill you."

"Really?"

One corner of his mouth jerked into a half smile as he watched me. "Not this time."

"Just remember that your business is with me. Touch another nightwalker and you'll be dead before you even know I'm there." I let my hands fall to my sides, palms facing him. Drops of fire tumbled from my fingertips like water. The flames pooled at my feet for a moment, then shot out like something alive, surging toward the walls and across the hardwood floors. My eyelids drifted lower until my eyes were barely open. I could see him watching me, but my focus was on the fire that had slipped down through the floor and was quickly seeking out both of the exits.

With one last smile I darted out the open window to my right and landed in the yard. I jogged across the lawn and only paused to look back when I was in the middle of the street. The house was engulfed in brilliant orange and yellow flames. I knew he would get out. Men like Danaus didn't die so easily. I was half tempted to remain behind to see him run from the building, but there wasn't time. The night had grown old and I needed to feed to replace the blood he'd spilled tonight. I would finish killing the hunter later.

Two

The sand has run out on more than six centuries for me. I have seen the rise and fall of kingdoms, the discovery of new lands and peoples, and acts of cruelty by humans that chill even my cold blood. But across the ages and changing face of man, I have to admit that the twenty-first century is by far my favorite. In these times, people can shed their past and appearance like a snake slithering free of its dead skin. The world is covered in a new Technicolor facade that has been built over the old realm, blotting out the sky and the earth.

Now there is no need to stalk my victims through dark alleyways and gaze down from hidden rooftops. Lost souls dot the landscape like daisies, waiting for me to pluck them up with promises of release. They stare up at me with empty eyes and broken hearts like I am their saving angel. I slip into their lives to deliver them briefly from an existence that has no direction or greater meaning.

In an effort to blot out this vast void, these poor people have decided to fill it again with the primitive. In the dark corners and hidden clubs, the comfortable mask of civilization has been ripped away and they indulge in a feast for the senses. This new age of decadence has these creatures drowning in a wellspring of sensations, bathing in new tastes and smells. But my favorite is the glorious sense of touch. No matter where I go, there always seem to be hands reaching out to caress, to fondle, and to connect.

After centuries of covering our flesh from the tops of our heads to the soles of our feet, clothes have shrunk and become a type of second skin. In fact, I've never seen a people with a greater fascination with leather. That wonderful material has been cut, stretched, and stitched into so many amazing shapes that it can now cover every inch of the body or just the social essentials.

Upon waking with the sinking sun, I decided to go to one of my favorite haunts not far from the river. The Docks was an old, derelict building that had been converted into a nightclub. I strolled through the city streets, enjoying the warm caress of a late July breeze. The area hummed and throbbed with life. It was a Friday night and people were rushing toward one distraction or another. Weaving through the random herds of people gathered here and there, I listened to the steady cadence of my heels clicking against the cracked and dirty sidewalk, echoing up the sides of the flat brick buildings that lined the city landscape.

At the corner, I paused. I had been about to turn north when I sensed a nightwalker at Forsyth Park. This giant green space lies in the historical district, dominated by a great white fountain bathed in the glow of yellow lights. Among the various races, Forsyth was a type of demilitarized zone. Within the boundaries of the park, there was no hunting, no fighting, and no spell casting. Anyone who broke this truce forfeited his or her life. It was here that most of my kind requested meetings with me. Of course, I could ignore the request. Unfortunately, the young nightwalker's tension was thick in my thoughts and polluting the air. Such things were never good for keeping the peace.

Threading an errant lock of red hair behind my ear, I continued west to the white fountain that rose up in the center of the park. The night was thick with the scent of flowers that overflowed from their beds. Despite the ongoing drought, this favored spot was well-tended by city officials, determined to maintain its verdant perfection. The soft splash of water hitting stone danced in the air, nearly overwhelming the steady swish of cars headed toward the hot spots along River Street.

Joseph lounged on the low marble wall surrounding the fountain. His long legs were extended and crossed at the ankles. He wore a pair of dark dress slacks and a burgundy dress shirt open at the throat. Barely more than twenty years old, Joseph was still a baby among my kind. He had been a member of Riley's flock, but at least was brought over with my approval. Only recently had Riley begun creating nightwalkers with careless abandon. Since Riley's demise, Joseph stuck to the outskirts of my domain, determined to find his own way. He had also been wise enough to avoid me. I didn't tolerate the young well.

"This isn't your part of town," I said as I entered the park. He slid easily to his feet, but anxiety tightened like a rubber band in his frame. I could feel his emotions as clearly as if they were my own.

Older vampires learned to shut the door of their mind. Joseph was still struggling.

To make matters worse, I had surprised him. I shouldn't have been able to, but his attention was divided at the moment. There was only one thing I could think of that would drive a fledgling vampire to seek me out: Danaus.

"The symphony lets out in a few minutes. I thought I'd visit with the blue bloods tonight," he said. He shoved his hands in his pockets, trying to affect a casual stance, but his legs were spaced wide apart, ready to run or fight.

"Running low on funds?"

Other than a slight twitch of his right eye, his bored expression never wavered. We all started out that way, a mix of bloodsucker and pickpocket. Most didn't appreciate being reminded of it. Joseph's normal hunting grounds were the narrow strip that housed most of the nightclubs as well as the scattering of bars not far from the university. Aesthetically speaking, those areas were more pleasing to the eye and generally more entertaining. Unfortunately, the college crowd wasn't the greatest source of income.

"We're not all as lucky as you," he said.

"Everything comes with a price." I strolled closer, vaguely aware of the scattering of people spread about the area. However, none were close enough to overhear our conversation. The steady rush of traffic flowing past us also kept our words muffled against the curious. I stopped before him, gazing into his hazel eyes. The gentle tug of his powers teased at my mind as he tried to enthrall me. He couldn't help it. He had not yet learned to control it. Humans would fall to his every whim, but if he encountered anything else, it would most likely rip his throat out in irritation.

I ran my left hand up his chest and was starting to wrap it around his throat when he jerked away. It was an instinctive move, showing a distinct lack of trust. I had to only arch one eyebrow at him in question before he returned to my side, tilting his head to offer up his throat. Seizing his neck, I forced him to sit back on the low wall.

"You are pressing your luck." I struggled to keep from gritting my teeth as I spoke, keeping my cool, patient facade in place for any onlookers.

"The truce," he said, reminding me needlessly that we were still standing in the park.

I smiled down at him, exposing my pearly white fangs. "The truce keeps us from fighting. It does not save you from punishment." Beneath my hand the muscles in his neck stiffened as a new fear entered his mind. His hands tightened their grip on the rim of the fountain.

The life of a nightwalker was about power and control. Those at the top of the food chain had all the power and wielded absolute control over anything below. Those weaker had to bow or be broken.

Joseph had come to me, and I needed to see a little subservience if he wanted to stay in my good graces. I wasn't the type that needed an assortment of toadies following me about. But to maintain my position as Keeper of the city, I would be feared.

"Lucky for you, I have no interest in toying with you tonight," I said. "Let's get on with business. Why have you requested this meeting?"

"They say you fought the Butcher," Joseph said.

I released his throat and slid my fingers under his chin in a gentle caress before my hand fell limp to my side. "Butcher" was what many of the young ones were calling Danaus; understandable, given that he'd carved up several of us like so much meat.

"We have met." I shrugged, ambling a few feet away, my arms swinging loosely at my side. Two couples strolled across the park, their loud laughter drifting through the open area as they headed toward any one of the several bed and breakfast hotels that surrounded the park.

"But he's still in town." The poor boy sounded so confused. He obviously expected me to either eject Danaus from my domain or kill him. That was all part of the plan, but I wasn't about to burn through such a great opportunity in one quick fight. Unfortunately, Danaus had become more of a problem that just an efficient hunter. He had come to my domain specifically looking for me. Nightwalkers aren't exactly listed in the phone book. We're notoriously difficult to locate unless you are a nightwalker yourself, or a member of our trusted inner circle. Before killing Danaus, I needed to know what he was and how he came to find me. And if I was being honest with myself, I wanted to know what he knew of the naturi. There was more to his offhand comment, considering very few even knew the name, let alone anything about the race.

Pushing those concerns aside for a moment, I turned my attention back to the fledgling. "Are you questioning my methods?" My tone came out light and innocent sounding, but Joseph was no fool.

"No! Of course not!" He lurched to his feet and hurried to my side. "I'm young. I'm still trying to learn our ways. I want to understand." He took my left hand and pressed it back to his throat, offering himself to me. Smooth, diplomatic, placating, with just a hint of humility. He was good. There was hope for him yet.

He was a few inches taller than me. Pulling him closer, I pressed a kiss to his jugular vein with my lips parted so my fangs grazed the skin. Dragging my lips up his throat and across his jaw, I deepened the kiss when I reached his lips. I ran my tongue over his fangs and for a moment my blood filled his mouth, letting him taste me. A shudder ran through his frame as I stepped away, but he did nothing to hold me there. Joseph had shown me a moment of absolute trust and for that I rewarded him.

"You may not understand our ways, but you are learning quickly," I said with an appreciative smile. I walked back to the fountain and sat down. "Has the hunter killed anyone since my meeting?"

Joseph blinked twice as if waking from a dream. "No."

"Nor will he unless provoked. His business is with me."

"Yes, Mistress," he said, bowing his head.

Rising from the fountain, I stretched my arms. "Now if you will excuse me, I seek a bit of amusement for the evening. Enjoy the symphony."

"I always do." Joseph smiled and the tips of his fangs poked from beneath his pale lips. He darted away, moving so fast that he seemed to disappear. Across town the curtain was falling and the house lights were coming up. Soon Joseph's prey would be stepping into the warm summer air and his cool embrace.

THREE

I strolled toward River Street, heading slowly northwest to the Docks. The River Walk area housed the majority of the city's nightlife entertainment. For most of the year the front doors would be thrown open and the sweet sounds of jazz and blues trickled out onto the street, drawing people into the dark confines of the various bars. However, at the far western edge of the street the neighborhood turned a little darker and grittier. People shrank back into the heavy shadows that clung to the buildings and followed me with slitted, calculating eyes. They watched but never moved, as if they could sense that I was somehow *other*. Or at the very least, more than the easy prey I appeared to be.

I nodded to the large, heavily muscled man who stoically guarded the front door to the club. He nodded back, one corner of his thin mouth quirking in a half smile as he let me in ahead of the line. The Docks was one of my regular haunts, and the manager seemed to appreciate my business. Pulling my wallet from my back pocket, I grabbed a twenty and laid it on the chest-high counter as I walked in. The cover charge was only five dollars, but the little extra was part of a silent agreement that ensured the doorman wouldn't ask for my ID and they wouldn't try to put one of those silly paper wristbands on me indicating I was over twenty-one.

With a smile and a wink, I slipped my slim leather wallet into my back pocket. The entryway was open, with a scattering of tables and a large bar taking up residence against the right wall. A network of televisions hung from the ceiling, playing rare and independent music videos that no one could hear over the cacophonous roar of music tumbling from the other end of the building. A winding maze of walls and partitions blocked the main dance floor from the rest of the bar. The lighting at the front of the club was nearly nonexistent, with only the occasional spotlight and stuttering strobe cutting through the smoky haze of shadows.

Scanning the midnight crowds, I wandered toward the dance floor. Even without my powers, I would have felt the looks running up and down my body. Swathed in my typical attire of black leather pants that fit like a second skin and my matching black leather halter top that stopped at my midriff, I felt like a ghost from an SM dream. My only concession to my unnatural abilities was a pair of gold-rimmed, red-tinted glasses balanced on the bridge of my nose. My eyes had a tendency to glow in a heated moment, potentially scaring off my hard-won prey.

I was on the dance floor when I finally sensed him. Sandwiched between a pair of strong, healthy male bodies, I let the thunderous beat of the music wash over me. Their hands roamed my body, slipping from slick leather to cool flesh and back to leather. Sweat beaded on their skin and their heartbeats vibrated against my body in their own hypnotic rhythm.

And then somehow above it all, I felt a new pulse ripple through the crowd. I cracked open my eyes and scanned the darkness. Something new and strong had entered my domain. Danaus stood on the edge of the dance floor directly across from me, arms folded across his chest, legs braced wide apart, as he stared.

He was early. I knew he would seek me out, but I had guessed that it would be another night or two before our paths crossed again. I also hadn't expected him to confront me at the Docks. We couldn't try to kill each other here. Too many potential witnesses, too many people who could easily get hurt in the fight. The secret existence of nightwalkers hadn't remained intact over so many years because we fought our battles around scores of humans.

Danaus could have easily waited outside, watching for my departure—maybe this strange creature was telling the truth when he said that his goal wasn't to fight me. But I had my doubts. Unfortunately, I was still waiting for word from my contacts in Europe regarding the hunter. If someone else had information on Danaus, I could remove his head and put the whole messy business behind me. But if he represented something no one knew about, I couldn't get rid of the hunter until I had gotten a little info out of him. I would have to string him along until I heard from the Old World.

Smiling at Danaus, I leaned back into the young man who danced behind me. I lifted my left arm and lay it behind his neck, my long fingers threading through his brown hair. He put one arm around my waist, his hand grabbing my side. His warmth seeped into my body and I absorbed it like a sponge. In fact, if I spent the night on the dance floor with a man wrapped about me, I would finish the evening with a nice flush to my cheeks without ever having to feed. I could suck in their warmth, their vitality. It would give me the look of the living, but I still needed blood to sustain my existence.

When the next song started, Danaus's frown deepened. He finally caught on that I wasn't going to leave the floor just because he was lurking on the fringe. I turned my back to him as he approached, wrapping my arms around the neck of my dance partner, grinding my hips into his. Leaning into him, I ran the tip of my tongue up his neck. I had just reached his earlobe when Danaus's hand clamped on my right shoulder.

"Enough," he growled in my ear. "Come with me."

I turned my head enough to look at him over my shoulder, my eyes barely open. My wide smile had faded to one of languid pleasure. "I'm a little busy." I looked back at my dance partner and the lovely expanse of his neck when a sharp object was suddenly pressed into my back, biting through the leather halter.

"Now! I have a knife in your back and I have no problem putting it in you while on the dance floor."

"Is that the slang for it now?" I laughed. Reaching back with my right hand, I grabbed his hip. I started to slide my hand toward the front of his pants, but Danaus released his hold on my shoulder and grabbed my wandering hand. Then he thrust my hand away and turned, stalking through the crowd, which seemed eager to jump out of his way. His black leather coat flared as he walked, making me wish he wasn't wearing it. It would have made watching him storm off more enjoyable.

Curiosity demanded that I follow. I had to know what would make this man follow me not only to this lonely ring of the Inferno, but out onto the dance floor. What would make a vampire hunter seek me out for anything other than to kill me? I leaned back into my dance partner, running my tongue over the pulse throbbing against the surface of his skin, promising myself I would find this tasty little bit later.

I strolled off the dance floor, my arms swaying at my sides. My gaze casually traveled over the pockets of people gathered along the black walls and in remote corners. Some looked up, their eyes following me as I passed, but most seemed oblivious to my presence, lost to whatever escape they had sought for the evening. I paused for a moment when I entered the bar area at the front of the club, wondering

where my little stalker had disappeared to, when I felt him just behind my shoulder. Turning, I found him sitting on a bench against the
wall. He leaned back, one hand resting on the table while the other
lay on his upper thigh, inches from where I guessed a knife was
sheathed near his waist.

Biting my lower lip to keep from smiling, I walked over, placed a
knee on either side of his hips and sat in his lap. If he could have
jumped up, I believe he would have been hanging from the ceiling in
his attempt to be free of me. But all he could manage was sitting up a
little straighter, his back pressed into the wall as if he wished to
merge with the wood and gypsum.

"Did I interrupt dinner?" His low voice rumbled up from his chest.
His teeth were clenched and the muscles in his jaw strained against his
skin. Narrowed blue eyes glittered at me, catching the pulsing white
light that tripped from the dance floor.

"No, just an appetizer, as it were. Have you come to offer me a
warm meal?" I asked, wrapping my arms loosely around his shoulders. He remained silent, staring at a point somewhere behind me. I
leaned forward and lay my head on his shoulder, touching the tip of
my nose to his throat. "I'm so glad to see that you managed to escape
without being singed too badly."

"Get off."

It was a struggle to keep from saying the first crude thing that
came to mind, but I finally succeeded. "I can't. The music is too loud
in here. We'd never hear each other speaking if I moved away." I sat
up so I could look into his face.

His eyes narrowed at me, his muscles stiffening. "You could hear
me from across the room if you wanted."

"But could you hear me?"

His lips pressed into a tight, thin line of anger and frustration.
What could he do? I honestly wondered. I sat here in his lap, with his
aura wrapped around me like a fleece blanket. What could he do with
all this strength and power? Of course, he wasn't going to volunteer
the information.

The soft throb of power washing over me felt all wrong for the
typical rabble of witch or warlock. And a warlock wouldn't rely on a
sword when hunting nightwalkers when he could use magic. Lycanthrope? Maybe. He didn't have the same rich earthy scent as most
weres, or their amazing strength, but he definitely had their speed and
agility. I mentally shrugged. The quandary would be nice to figure
out, but it wouldn't stop me from killing him.

"What do you know about the naturi?" he asked.

My thoughts were a sudden train wreck, ideas and images lying broken and derailed. I stared motionless at him for a long time, my mind unable to fathom why he would bring up such a topic. While few knew of the existence of nightwalkers, even fewer knew that the naturi actually lived and breathed. The other races had spent countless years wiping away all accounts of their existence. Of course, some tales had become embedded in the human psyche, which we could not destroy. From the naturi grew the stories of elves, fairies, and many other magical creatures that could not be explained away with the cold, hard logic of science.

But the naturi weren't the only ones we attempted to erase from history. After humans were created, the old stories stated that the gods created two guardian races to maintain the balance. The naturi were guardians of the earth, while the bori were guardians of all souls. The naturi existed in five clans—water, earth, animal, wind, and light.

On the other hand, the bori existed as a single clan with their own dark side, as they worked to become the one dominant power on the earth. From the bori, the legends of demons and angels were born.

Unfortunately, the powers and strength of the two races were dependent upon what they protected. As humanity flourished, the earth weakened. So the wars started.

"Sorry," I said. "I don't know what you're talking about." No one talked about the naturi. They were gone, for the most part, banished centuries ago to another reality, similar and forever linked to this world, but always locked away, hopefully.

"The naturi; guardians of the earth. Sometimes referred to as the Third Race, the Seelie Court—the Sidhe," he corrected.

"They're nothing more than fairy tales." I leaned back down so I could rest my head on his shoulder while I ran my fingers through his dark hair. It was softer than I had initially expected, almost silky in texture. "Where do you come from?" I whispered in his ear.

He was silent for a minute, and I listened to the sound of his breath slowly enter and leave his chest. "Rome."

"It's been years since I was in Rome. Boniface IX had just been named Pope. Beautiful city, even before Michelangelo painted the Sistine Chapel. Have you seen it?"

"The Sistine Chapel? Yes."

"Is it as lovely as they say?"

"Better."

"I guessed as much." The Sistine Chapel was one of the many things that I would never see. Whether I believed in a one great God didn't matter in the grand scheme of things. I could never step foot into a church. Trust me, I've tried—it was like running into a brick wall.

"Tell me about the naturi, Mira." His voice softened for the first time to something less than a growl. It wasn't what I would call an inviting or pleasant tone, just one not honed to an angry edge. His right hand settled on my left knee for a moment before falling back to the bench, but the brief touch was enough to send a wave of heat through my leather pants. I pulled away from him so I could look him in the face, my eyebrows bunched over the bridge of my nose in surprise. It was the first time he had used my name.

"So you know about the naturi; bully for you," I said. The topic of conversation was beginning to grate on my nerves. "Vampires too much of a challenge for you, so you thought you'd go after a naturi or two?" The taunt was childish, but I didn't want to think about the naturi, let alone talk about them. I wanted to forget about that whole horrible race. A part of me wanted to get up and return to the dance floor, to drown in the warm flesh and let the angry grind of music pull me under.

"Tell me."

"Tell you what?" I snapped, but quickly got my voice back under control. "They were here, but now they are gone. That's it."

The naturi wanted nothing more than to rid the entire earth of all humans and nightwalkers. For them, protecting the earth was only possible through removing its greatest threat—mankind. But it was more than that. I had my own painful past with the naturi, memories overflowing with pain and white-gray stones splashed with my blood in the fading moonlight. And worse yet, a return of the naturi held whispers of a potential return of the bori. A tug-of-war that offered no victory. For nightwalkers, the naturi represented extinction, while the bori represented an eternity of slavery. The naturi and the bori had to remain in exile, never to be spoken of.

With his right hand, Danaus reached into the interior pocket on the left side of his jacket and pulled out a sheaf of papers. He dropped the pile on the table behind me. I twisted in his lap to look at what turned out to be a pile of high gloss, color pictures. My whole body reflexively stiffened and what little warmth I had gained on the dance floor flowed out of my body, leaving a sharp chill to bite at my tensed muscles.

I reached out, forcing myself to touch the top picture. With a little pressure, the pictures spread out across the scarred tabletop. They were all of trees with symbols carved deep into their bark. My eyes skimmed over them, vaguely noting that each curling symbol was etched into a different type of tree. It was the language of the naturi. I couldn't read it or speak it, but I had seen enough to know that I would never forget it.

A knot in my stomach tightened and I fervently hoped I wouldn't vomit in the mix of fear and horror that was replacing the blood in my veins. Somehow I managed to keep my expression bland and non-committal, but that's what nightwalkers did. We kept everything hidden beneath a mask of boredom and beauty. Danaus was watching me, peering deep, as if trying to read my thoughts.

"Trees. Nice, but not exactly my thing," I said, proud of the fact that my voice didn't crack. "I don't know why you sought me out. I don't know anything about the naturi or trees." With one hand braced on the wall to the right of his head, I slowly unfolded my body from around his and stood. Turning my back to him, I started to walk away. I needed to leave and wash down the terrible memories with blood.

Out of the corner of my eye I saw Danaus rise, his left hand locking around my wrist. "What about this?" There was an ominous thunk on the wooden table beside me. Something in me screamed, *Run*. All the survival instincts left in my brain were screaming for me to keep going, but I had to know.

In the center of the table, piercing the pile of pictures, was a dagger. It was a unique dagger—one I was sure no living human had ever set eyes upon it. Slim and slightly curved, the silver blade straightened an inch before the tip. It was designed this way so it slid nicely into the body and at the same time caused the most amount of damage when worked around the vital organs. On one side of the blade, symbols similar to the ones in the pictures were etched into the metal. The handle was wood, stained dark from the blood that had soaked in over the years.

I knew that blade. Not just its type, but that particular blade. The metal shiv had sliced sinew and carved hunks of flesh from my body. I'd spent seemingly endless hours developing an intimate knowledge of that blade and the many-faceted layers of pain it could cause.

I spun and grabbed Danaus's shirt below the collar, slamming him into the wall. The hunter grunted. "Where did you get that?" My fangs peeked out from beneath my drawn lips. I'd drain him to the very edge of death that second in order to get my answers.

Around us, people scrambled away, trying to keep a safe distance and yet still be able to glean something from our conversation. It had to be a strange sight. A woman was pushing around a man twice her weight and size like a rag doll, while a dagger stood straight and tall in the table beside them. They would have paid less attention if I'd just pulled out a gun and shot him.

"From a naturi," Danaus said. His voice was calm and even, completely unshaken by my explosion of temper.

"What naturi?" My grip on his shirt tightened and I was vaguely aware of the fact that he had released my wrist. He could have been going for another knife, but at that moment I don't think I would have felt it even if he had buried the blade straight into my heart.

"Nerian."

"You lie," I snarled, slamming him into the wall a second time. Desperation was starting to crowd my thoughts. No one could have told him of Nerian except for a select few, who would have killed him on sight. "He's dead."

"Not yet."

"Where?"

For the first time, a cold smile lifted his lips, revealing a hint of white teeth. His eyes danced with a dark light that almost made me growl.

"I'll crush you now, Danaus. Tell me where he is!"

He stared at me for a long time, obviously enjoying the fact that the tables had been turned and I was at his mercy. "I'll take you to where I have him," he said at last.

I released him suddenly, as if he had burst into flames. He had Nerian? How? It didn't seem possible. It had to be some elaborate trick.

Stepping away from him, my eyes swept over the crowd. Everyone scurried out of my line of sight, returning to his or her conversation. Their world had shuddered to a stop for a moment and stood balanced on the edge of a knife. But with a jerk it all started again, and they banished what they thought they'd seen. They weren't ready for my kind and all the others lurking in the shadows.

It was coming, I knew that. And if Nerian was still alive, it might be sooner than I'd originally thought. Of course, if Nerian were still alive, I had to wonder if I would live to see mankind's Great Awakening.

Beside me, Danaus pulled the dagger from the table and slipped it back into a sheath on his left hip. His nimble fingers swept over the table, gathering the pictures into a single pile. As he placed them back into the interior pocket of his coat, I looked toward the dance floor. One of my favorite songs had started, the lead singer promising that he would not let me fall apart. His low, whispered cry settled my nerves and I reluctantly smiled. I had often toyed with the idea of seeking out this human, with his raw emotions set loose for all the world to see. But I had learned the hard way that my kind often had an ill influence upon the artists of the world, and I liked his music the way it was. Tonight I would take his promise with me as I visited an old shade from Hell.

FOUR

The night air was thick and still, as if the city held its breath, waiting for something else dark and creepy to slip from the shadows. I stepped outside the Docks, resisting the urge to roll my shoulders and relax the tension from my body. There were a lot of questions hovering in the silence and no answers. Like how the hell did Danaus capture Nerian? The naturi fought to the death, and had no intention of ever being held captive. Was Nerian using Danaus to get to me? The hunter didn't strike me as the type to serve anyone's purpose but his own.

I tried to keep from frowning as I followed him down the street into an even darker part of town. Through the trash-cluttered and crumbling streets, we angled north, trudging farther from the heart of the city and tidy parks. The street lamps were fewer and spaced wider apart here. The houses sagged, almost leaning into each other as they sought support under the weight of years of neglect. It was only a couple hours after midnight, but the streets were deserted.

We were a few blocks from the club when I stopped. Danaus halted beside me, his hand sliding up to his waist near one of his sheathed knives.

"You pull that naturi dagger and I'll rip your arm off." Each word squeezed past my clenched teeth. Out of the corner of my eye I saw him give a quick nod before his hand shifted to the small of his back. "We're being followed."

I had sensed the poor fool when we left the club, but didn't stop until the nightwalker closed the distance significantly. No one else needed to know about the naturi just yet. I wanted to determine for myself what was going on and how bad the damage was before word spread. There were still a few naturi wandering around, lurking in the forests and jungles of the world, keeping far from humanity when possible. No reason to start a panic when this could be nothing more than a random sighting.

Not wanting to waste any more valuable time, I stretched out my senses. The power washed through the buildings, sending back slight vibrations of the people lying huddled in their beds. Throughout the city, I could feel the other nightwalkers in the midst of their nightly activities. For a breath, they paused at the slight touch of magic, then returned to their amusements. They knew I wasn't searching for them.

The second I located my prey, he sprang. He crossed the remaining two blocks between us in a heartbeat. I had opened my mouth to warn Danaus but it was already too late. The vampire was a blur of shadow and gritty color as he pounced on the hunter.

Danaus hit the ground but used his momentum to fling the vampire off him as he rolled back to his feet. The blond vampire regained his feet and would have attacked again if I had not stepped between the two combatants. I didn't have the time or patience for this nonsense. First Joseph muddled up my night, and now Lucas—I had more important problems on my plate at the moment.

"Stop!" I shouted, holding up my hands to keep the two creatures apart. Lucas glared at Danaus before straightening from his half crouched position and looking at me with a smug expression. My fingers twitched and closed into a tight ball as my hands dropped back to my sides. I longed to knock the look from his face.

Lucas stood at roughly five feet three inches, with blond hair that curled loosely around his ears and jaw. With his slim figure and soft features, there was something almost feminine and delicate about him. But this angelic guise was ruined by the cold cruelty he could not keep from his Nordic blue eyes.

"So, the rumors are true," he said with ill-concealed amusement, unable to keep his smile from widening to reveal fangs. "You've abandoned your own kind for the hunter."

Damn, the grapevine was fast among vampires. But then again, we were telepathic. I should have expected this. Every nightwalker in the city knew of my confrontation with Danaus. I had enjoyed it too much to not share flashes of the encounter with my kind, letting them savor the emotions and the violence like a fine wine. Yet, two nights had passed since that introduction, and many of the young ones were surprised to find the hunter walking the streets of the city. I had been waiting for more information from the Old World before killing him, having learned to be cautious over the years. Information was its own power, and held more value than a quick snap of the neck when all was said and done.

Furthermore, I'd watched Danaus long enough to know that he had enough of a sense of honor not to hunt further in my domain until our business was completed.

A weary sigh escaped me as my shoulders slumped. "You're mad."

"Then stand aside and let me enjoy my kill," he said, making it sound like we were arguing over who got the last piece of chocolate cake.

"He belongs to me. His life is mine to enjoy when I so choose." My voice hardened to the cold, hard edge of tempered steel. I took a step toward the vampire, but he held his ground, the smile crumbling from his face. Lucas was always a bit of a fool. "The other nightwalkers of this city know not to touch him unless he attacks first. And you can't kill him. If I didn't have more pressing matters, I would stand aside and let him cut your heart out."

I was standing so close our noses nearly touched. In my boots, I was four inches taller than him, just enough for me to look down at him. Lucas's eyes darkened with anger, his irises expanding, nearly blotting out the pale blue of his eyes. A ripple of his power washed through me like a cool breeze and remained trembling in the air. I had nothing to fear. This blond-haired monster with the angelic face was only a few centuries old and had more ego than real strength.

"Why are you here?" I demanded when he finally took a step back.

"I was sent to check on you," Lucas said. The smug smile returned to his lips, while his irises shrank to let the sky slip back into his eyes.

"Why haven't you presented yourself before now? You've been in my city for more than a week."

He gave an indifferent shrug of his shoulders as he slipped his hands into the pockets of his black slacks. "I am the Companion of Macaire. I go where I please."

I crossed the distance in a single step and grabbed the front of his red silk shirt, twisting it slightly around my fist so I could be sure I had a good grip on him. A bubble of laughter nearly escaped me when I saw the brief look of surprise that flooded his handsome features before I threw him across the street and into a dark alley. I wandered across the street, following the sound of the metal trash cans colliding with Lucas. He had just picked himself up off the ground, a low growl rumbling from the back of this throat at the sight of me. He roughly brushed bits of trash and rotting food off his slacks.

It was a while since I'd had the opportunity to fight something that could take a good beating. Danaus had been fun, but extremely brief. Lucas, on the other hand, could go a few rounds and still come back for more.

The vampire lunged at me, his fingers out like claws. I caught him by the throat with one hand and slammed him into one of the brick walls that lined the alley. Behind me, Danaus entered the alley, his footsteps nearly silent on the trash-strewn concrete. Under normal circumstances I would have worked Lucas over until he was nothing more than a quivering ball of raw flesh in the corner. Unfortunately, I had other tasks to complete tonight. Naturi business and preserving the secret always came first.

"I don't care if you are the newest toady for Macaire. I am still Keeper of this domain and you will give me my due." I raised my free left hand, cupping it slightly with fingers spread. My pale flesh was bathed in the glow of dancing blue flames.

Lucas immediately began to struggle, shrinking away from the fire as his fingers clawed my hand holding his throat. *"Per favore, Mira! Mia signora!"* he said, unconsciously slipping into Italian. Lucas wasn't Italian. I hadn't a clue as to what he was other than his slight accent, which seemed vaguely Slavic. However, the Coven was based in Italy, and eventually all nightwalkers learned to beg in Italian. "I—I was sent by the Elders. They're concerned."

"About what?" I asked. Did they know about the symbols as well? A sick fear twisted in my chest. Coming to the attention of Ancients was never an enjoyable experience.

"The humans—they're beginning to ask too many questions."

"They've always asked questions. That hasn't changed." Mankind had speculated about the existence of nightwalkers for centuries, but never truly believed the tales to be true.

"But they have proof now," he said, falling back into English.

An uneasy feeling added to the weight of my earlier fears and I went still. "Proof? How?"

"Bodies were found in California two nights ago, and another in Texas last week."

"I heard."

"The Daylight Coalition is claiming it's proof that we exist."

"They're just a fringe group." I extinguished the flame from my hand but didn't release Lucas. "No one believes them. The police claimed it was a hoax."

"It doesn't matter. They are winning over more followers. The number of hunters has more than doubled during the past few decades. The Elders think we're running out of time."

"So why come here?"

Lucas stopped trying to pry my fingers loose and went still. "They want to know who left the bodies. You're one of the oldest in the New World."

"I didn't come here to babysit, nor will I clean up after every kill." My grip on his throat tightened and I leaned closer. "I don't know who made the mess." Releasing him, I paced over to the other brick wall in the narrow alley. There were already more pressing matters on my mind. I didn't need to worry about the Elders and their flunkies invading my territory.

"They will find out who has caused this ripple among the humans." Lucas said. "If he or she is still in the New World, it will be your job to mete out the punishment." His hand absently rubbed his throat.

"I do not jump for the Elders." But even I knew that statement was only partially true. I was stronger than most nightwalkers my age, and it was more than just my ability to use fire, though that unique gift kept many at a distance. I had destroyed more than my fair share of Ancients, earned every bit of my dark reputation through centuries washed in blood and death.

I didn't feel the need to jump for the Elders, because of Jabari. He acted as a buffer between me and the rest of the Coven, giving me my freedom. The oldest and most powerful member of the Coven, Jabari had earned my unwavering loyalty. He had only to ask and I would perform nearly any task for him. But Jabari was missing now, my buffer gone.

"You will obey if you wish to keep your domain and your life," Lucas said, his eyes narrowing to thin slits.

I stared at him, willing myself not to rip his head off. He was a pathetic creature. Less than three hundred years old, I knew he probably wouldn't survive to see another century. Those who served as Companions to the Elders rarely lived long lives, but the reward during those short years was the ability to bask in the amazing power the Elders wielded. Once you were selected as a Companion, other nightwalkers could not touch you without risking the wrath of the Elder. Of course, if you failed your caretaker, which inevitably happened, your existence was forfeit. And from what I'd heard, your death was always slow and painful.

"Leave here, Lucas. Return to your master and tell him what you have found."

"Like your defense of the hunter?" His gaze flicked over to Danaus at the mouth of the alley then back to me.

"Like how I spared your life," I said with a smile that was all fangs and menace. "You've delivered your message. Be gone before the sun touches the earth or I shall introduce you to a whole new realm of pain."

Lucas glared at me for another second before turning and walking down the alley, back toward the street. I watched him go, his body nearly brushing against Danaus, who didn't flinch. A vampire like Lucas was easy prey for Danaus and not worth such worries. Of course, Lucas was also the mouthpiece for something much larger and scarier.

From the entrance to the alley, Lucas turned back to look at me. "The Elders are not the only ones concerned. The others are watching as well," he called, then disappeared into the night.

"Shit," I whispered into the darkness when I was sure Lucas couldn't hear me. I had enough to worry about without having the Elders and all the others breathing down my neck. I doubted Macaire would come after me for roughing up Lucas, but I certainly didn't need to be on his bad side if the Elders suddenly decided to hand over a sacrificial lamb to the humans.

In the nightwalker hierarchy, we kept things simple. The top dog was Our Liege, who ruled all nightwalkers. Below him was the Coven, which consisted of four Elders. Below the Coven, it was just whoever was the strongest and the smartest. Of course, Ancients—any vampire more than one thousand years old—were their own special bundle of trouble. And I was asking for trouble.

It was one thing to talk big while standing in a dark alley in my own domain, but I had never faced all of the Elders at once. I had maintained a comfortable distance from the group. I'm sure some of my actions caught their notice and made them frown on more than one occasion, but I'd done nothing to endanger our secret.

Unfortunately, on more than one occasion I had flaunted my total disregard and general lack of subservience for the group. So far they'd let it slide, and I knew I had Jabari to thank for it. Yet, if things started to get out of hand here in the New World, the Elders would use it as an opportunity to either bring me to heel or serve my head up to the humans.

I saw Danaus put his dagger back in its sheath in the small of his back. Of course, this creature was yet another problem to figure out before I had the Ancients on my soil.

"Nerian," he said in his usual deep growl.

And back to the more pressing of the problems. Lucas and the Elders could wait. So could Danaus's death.

FIVE

My teeth were clenched when my gaze fell on the two-story house with the peeling, pale blue paint three blocks from where we encountered Lucas. I frequently hunted in this part of town. The inhabitants here struggled to eke out a living, and the air smelled thick of sweat and despair. Their lives were simple and harsh, with hopes that stretched no further than thoughts of food and warmth. Not so different than the village where I'd been born more than six centuries ago.

The street lamps at the top and the bottom of the road were out. Danaus had most likely seen to the darkness when he moved in. Thick, velvety night oozed around the houses and filled the street like heavy tar, making it easier to slip in and out of the neighborhood without being noticed.

A light breeze stirred from the south, rustling leaves on a sickly scattering of trees. The harsh, dry summer left them covered in only thin foliage that had already begun to brown. Most of the broken-down houses crowded on the street were dark except for a handful that leaked a blue glow thrown down by television sets. A high-pitched whine stole down the block as the wind blew open the gate of a sagging chain-link fence.

As I mounted the crumbling stone steps, I reached out again with my powers, running my senses through every inch of the house. Danaus was the only other creature I could pick up. Unfortunately, I couldn't sense the naturi. I could be walking into a house full of them and wouldn't know it until the dagger was already in my back.

The hunter looked back at me, his hand on the doorknob. He felt me use my powers as well.

"Open it," I said with a nod of my head, relieved that my voice didn't betray my concern. For all the world, I sounded as if I was actually looking forward to seeing Nerian, like a reunion of old friends. Hardly. My only hope was that I didn't kill him on sight, but I had serious doubts as to whether that was a realistic thought.

Danaus pushed open the door, which moaned in angry protest. The hunter stepped inside first and moved so I could follow while he closed the door. Once inside, I turned to face him, keeping my back to the wall. I didn't trust him or this situation. With his hands open at his sides, he walked in front of me down the main hall. The floorboards creaked and screamed under the weight of our footsteps. The walls were cracked and crumbling, and the scent of some long-dead animal lingered in the air. A dark staircase ran along the left side of the hall, leading to a silent second floor.

Stopping halfway down the hall, Danaus pulled open a door under the staircase. He flipped on a light, revealing a set of plain wooden stairs that led into the basement. I was surprised. Most homes in Savannah didn't have basements, due to the height of the water table. I had one in my own home, but it was added at great expense. Of course, underground was the only safe place to be during the daylight hours.

A single bare bulb dangled from the ceiling above the stairs, fighting to push aside the shadows that inhabited the dark corners of the subterranean room. I followed him down the stairs, my heels echoing like gunshots off the wood. Neither of us was trying to be quiet. The scent of blood on the damp air brought me to a sharp halt on the landing. It was the first bit of proof that someone else was in the house, but I still couldn't sense anyone. I continued down the stairs, my eyes quickly scanning the room.

The walls were made of gray concrete, covered in a spiderweb of cracks and fissures that now leaked water from the ground outside. The floor was the same cold concrete. It was completely empty except for a furnace squatting in the far corner and a network of pipes and wires overhead. The air was musty and damp, filled with mold and the faint tang of blood.

It took me a couple seconds to actually see the hunched form. Maybe it was because my mind didn't want to see him, didn't want to know that he actually was still alive. But once I did see him, rage flooded my senses, blotting out all rational thought. The muscles in my body involuntarily clenched and knotted as if I'd been hit. When I looked at Nerian, I didn't see him standing against the wall, his wrists and ankles chained in iron manacles. I saw him standing over me more than five centuries ago, with that dagger covered in my blood. I heard him laughing in my mind and my scream.

And then I realized I really was screaming. I kept screaming, clamping my hands over my ears as I tried to push the memories from my mind. The sound only stopped when the rawness of my torn throat finally overcame the images. The silent night air had been shattered by the wretched sound and was left cringing in some dark corner.

I blinked, my screams still echoing in my brain. Both Danaus and the naturi were staring at me. Nerian was smiling with that same horrible smile, basking in my pain.

"You remember me!" he exclaimed. He tossed his head back and laughed, the sound somehow managing to be both musical and maniacal at the same time. I shivered, clenching my teeth against the sound as a fresh onslaught of memories danced through my brain. My knees turned to jelly and for a moment I thought I would fall, but the wave passed.

"Thank you, human," Nerian continued. "Seeing this parasite again is a real treat. Though I'm surprised she had the sense to stay alive this long. But even cockroaches are known for their resilience."

"I see you managed to pull yourself back together," I said. My voice was choked and rough, failing miserably to portray my usual bravado. I finally descended the last couple of wooden stairs and stood in the basement. "I imagine it was difficult to get your intestines back inside your skin."

At Machu Picchu so many years ago, Jabari had given me the gift of killing Nerian. We fought and I eviscerated him, leaving him curled on the ground, clutching his stomach and intestines. But the sun was rising. My own strength was failing me in the growing light. I was forced to run to find shelter before the sun finally broke above the horizon. If I had thought it was at all possible that Nerian would survive, I would have stayed and finished him, meeting my own end.

"Unshackle me and I will happily show you how difficult it was." His tone was still light and full of amusement. There was some veiled enticement lying hidden between his words as his voice tried to work a spell over my will.

"No." The silence settled back between us for a moment as my eyes ran over his blood-encrusted wrists, battered face, and stained clothes. "I think I like you better this way; trapped by a human."

Nerian was of the animal clan, resulting in his shaggy mane of brown hair and the hard, aggressive bone structure of his face. His vibrant green eyes were vertically slitted, like that of a cat. The iron manacles were the only thing keeping him from calling for assistance from any other naturi or animals. The old tales of iron and its harmful effect on the fey were actually true. It kept the naturi from performing any kind of magic.

His taunting smile crumbled from his face. "Hardly a fair fight."

"What do the naturi know of fair?"

"What do we care of fairness when dealing with vermin?" His voice had changed from one of enticement to that of a cold, hard glacier. "Both vampires and humans are beneath contempt. You should never have survived so long, but at least humans have their uses. Vampires are just parasites."

With my teeth clenched and fists at my sides, I closed the distance between Nerian and myself. I felt more than saw Danaus take up a position behind my right shoulder. His arms were folded over his chest, his legs spread wide.

I stared at Nerian, only inches between us. In all this time, he hadn't changed. Yet, it felt like something should have been different. He should have been scarred in some way. When I'd last seen him, both his legs were broken and he was struggling to keep his intestines in his body. I had left him for dead. He should be dead. But instead he stood before me, his wrists bloody from pulling against the iron manacles. His brown leather jerkin was splattered with blood. His sharp, wide face was smudged with dirt and blood, his thick brown hair dirty and matted. And still he smiled at me, dark amusement glinting in his green eyes.

I don't know how long we stood there staring at each other. It could have been hours or seconds. Time had become a thing that existed outside this small, damp basement, twisting and contorting into something I no longer recognized.

"Has the seal been broken?" I demanded at last. I had no more energy for verbal sparring with him. My voice sounded rough, as if it had been dragged along the lower levels of Hell before finally reaching my ears.

I didn't think it was possible, but his smile widened, revealing a perfect set of white teeth. "Rowe has spoken with the sun," he said in a lyrical voice. Without words, it whispered of clear streams and green woods. That voice had bewitched scores before the slaughter. "The dawn is coming."

There was no clear thought after that. My body throbbed with rage and all I felt was anger and fear. Enough fear that I could taste it in the back of my throat. Enough that I was drowning in it. A kaleidoscope of brutal memories flashed through my brain. The naturi held me captive for two weeks at Machu Picchu, torturing me each night until I finally escaped consciousness with the rising sun. Their hope had been to wear me down until I agreed to serve them as a weapon against the nightwalkers. They wanted me for protection as they opened the door between the two worlds, freeing the rest of their kind. But I knew they could never be free. It would mean the destruction of everything I loved.

My hand shot out and closed around his throat, squeezing until I felt my fingernails tear through skin and muscle. I squeezed until my hand was filled with his warm flesh, and then I pulled. He gave one last gasp as his throat was ripped from his body. I dropped the squishy clump of flesh at my side, but chunks of it remained buried under my nails. I stood there, letting his warm blood spray over my face and shoulders, closed my eyes as the blood ran down my arms and coated my bare stomach. A scream rose up in my throat again, but I stood silent, listening to the gurgling sounds he made as he struggled to breathe without an esophagus.

When I could no longer feel his blood raining on me, I opened my eyes. Nerian sagged forward, held up by his arms, which were still chained to the wall. His head had fallen against his chest and his body was now covered in blood. Stepping back, my mind stumbled out of the blinding haze of anger. I could taste his blood in my mouth, and a part of me panicked. Naturi blood was poisonous to nightwalkers. I spit and raised my arm to wipe it off my lips, but my arm was covered with his blood as well. A little taste wouldn't kill me, but it was enough to send an anxious chill through me. It didn't taste like other blood. It was more bitter and unnatural.

Turning, I suddenly found myself facing Danaus. For a moment I had forgotten he was there. He stood in a crouch, the naturi dagger in his hand. I don't know if he'd purposefully drawn that dagger or instinctively reacted when I tore out Nerian's throat. It didn't matter. My emotions were still too raw and violent for me to think clearly. I lunged at him, my hands going for the dagger. He swung it at me, causing me to jerk backward. Screaming, I slashed and kicked wildly. There was no holding back anymore. I wanted death; his, and maybe even mine. Anything so I could be free of Nerian's smile. Backing Danaus against the wall, I finally kicked the dagger free. It spun through the air and crashed against the cinder-block wall.

The monstrous piece of metal held me in its bloody thrall, and I had to be rid of it . . . for good. I turned my back on Danaus, heedlessly, and stalked over to the blade. With my right hand, I threw a ball of blue fire at it. I encased the dagger in flames hot enough to cause the cement to sizzle and pop. The room grew uncomfortably hot, but I poured all my anger and hatred into the fire, willing the metal to bend and melt.

Exhausted, I sank to my knees, extinguishing the blaze. Then I stared at the naturi blade and started to laugh, high-pitched and a little mad. The blade was completely untouched. For a moment the metal had glowed red, but it was unchanged. I could do nothing to it. The charms on the blade would keep it from ever rusting, chipping, or melting. As long as the naturi existed, so would this blade.

Turning my head, I narrowed my gaze on Nerian. I might not be able to get rid of the dagger, but I could wipe his existence off the earth. Instantly, his body became engulfed in beautiful yellow and orange flames. The stench of burning flesh and hair filled the air, but I didn't care. I kept the flames on him until the body crumbled to a small heap of white ash on the floor. The smoke filtered up through the warped boards of the ceiling to fill the upper part of the house. I didn't care if anyone noticed. I'd be gone from this place soon enough.

Nerian was gone, but his memory would never leave me. For the first time in centuries I longed for Jabari. He had saved me from Nerian and his kind once. He had helped to keep the horrid memories at bay. Now I longed for the feel of his strong arms around me and his calm, cool presence in my brain, cradling my thoughts.

But Jabari was gone; dead or just absent, I didn't know. It also didn't matter. Nerian was dead at last. I had stood on my own two feet for more than four centuries. I would continue to do so no matter how weary I became.

The sound of a foot scraping along the cold concrete floor drew my attention back to Danaus. Gazing at him over my shoulder, a soft sigh rose from me. I felt a little freer than I'd been in a long time. A ghost had been sent back to Hell where it belonged; where I knew it would wait for me. But that wasn't now.

I was more than a little surprised that Danaus had not tried to kill me when I attacked him. He'd defended himself, but nothing more. He had not needed me to kill Nerian for him; the naturi was at his mercy. To keep me alive, Danaus must have still needed something from me. However, I was coming up with fewer reasons to leave the hunter alive. Right now I only needed to know how he captured Nerian and if there were any more naturi.

"What do you know of the naturi?" I inquired, turning to face him. I held up my right hand and a small yellow flame danced on the palm.

Danaus stood against the far wall, a bead of sweat running from his temple down along his hard jaw. His dark blue eyes were narrowed in the faint light. With his right hand, he grabbed the right side of his leather coat and held it open. He reached over with his left hand and pulled a folded piece of paper from the interior pocket. With a flick of his wrist, he sent the paper across the room, to land less than a foot away from me. Extinguishing the flame, I leaned forward and picked up the paper. It was another high-gloss, color picture.

This one was distinctly different from the others. It was of a woman lying naked on reddish-brown paving stones. Her arms were thrown over her head. The skin on her chest had been peeled back and all of her organs removed. The little piles of black ash around the body had been her various pieces. Her blood pooled beneath her, but on the ground several feet away from her, symbols similar to the ones carved into the trees were drawn with her blood. Her face had been turned toward the camera, her mouth forever frozen in a scream that no one would ever hear. She had been alive during the ceremony. I imagine she was kept alive and lucid right up until her heart had been removed.

"When?" The single word floated through the room like a white wraith. The momentary peace I'd found with Nerian's death had shriveled up in the pit of my stomach.

"Three months ago, night of the new moon."

I nodded. I understood enough about magic to know that you started new magic under the new moon for the maximum potency. The full moon was used for breaking old spells, curses, and for binding. The naturi were just getting started.

"Where?"

"Konark."

My head snapped up, eyes locking on his grim features. The muscles in my body clenched painfully. "Where?"

"Konark. The Sun Temple in Orissa, India."

"I know it's in India," I said irritably, straightening up. My brain was struggling to take in this information. They had started making the necessary sacrifices in order to break the seal and open the door between the worlds. There were twelve sacred locations scattered around the world that could hold enough power for the naturi to perform the necessary spells. But how could they be doing this now? It didn't make sense. It had been roughly five hundred years since they had last attempted this. Why now?

"There will be more," Danaus said. It was more of a question than a statement.

I looked up at him, weighing my options. "Two more." My earlier relief slowly leaked from my soul and I tried to organize my thoughts.

"You asked about a seal. What did you mean?"

My gaze fell to the floor for a moment as I thought back to the stories my maker, Sadira, and my beloved Jabari had told me. My own memories of Machu Picchu were sketchy and fragmented, but I knew the old "ghost stories." I'd read our histories and the journals written by other nightwalkers detailing all we knew of the naturi.

"Centuries ago, before my time, before the time of any night-walker that still exists, the naturi lived on Earth. Vampires forced them to another world. One that was similar and connected to this world, but different. A nightwalker triad closed the door and fashioned a seal on this side to bar them from returning. It's like an elaborate magical lock."

"So, the seal has to be protected."

"That's only part of it. The naturi have other locations they can use to make the other two sacrifices. We have no idea where and when they will strike."

"I might."

Wiping off a drop of blood that was running down my cheek, I narrowed my eyes at Danaus. "How?"

"I am part of a large organization, spread around the globe. We will know if something is happening." The hunter dropped his hands into the pockets of his leather duster, a faint smile tugging at the right corner of his mouth.

"Like you knew about Konark? Or the symbols on the trees?"

The would-be smile disappeared instantly. "We didn't know we should be watching for something at the temple. We know there will be at least two more sacrifices and that they will likely happen around certain phases of the moon. We can watch for signs."

"It's more than the moon phases," I grumbled, shoving my right hand through my hair, trying to ignore that it was now cold and sticky. "They could also use seasonal holidays or even any of the holidays from the dead religions. It's hard to say when they will attempt the second sacrifice, or even where."

"But vampires are limited to only night surveillance. My people are not."

I frowned. I hated to admit it, but he did have an edge in that arena, and help in this matter was necessary. We couldn't call in the lycanthropes for daytime assistance because they would be too easily enthralled by the naturi, their former masters. And working with witches and warlocks was always sketchy at best and never particularly reliable.

"You seem to be very well informed," I said, cocking my head as

I took a couple steps closer. Danaus removed his hands from his pockets and bent his frame as if preparing for an attack. "You knew of the naturi, you knew of the symbols in the trees, you knew where to find me and even some of my past."

"The organization is very well informed. We have spent many years watching your kind."

I shook my head, placing my hands on my hips. "Oh, this is more than just watching. Someone has been giving you information about nightwalkers and our world."

"We are well informed, but not strong enough to directly take on the naturi. I was sent to find someone who defeated them at Machu Picchu."

"Yes, I was at Machu Picchu, but the triad defeated the naturi."

"Where is the triad?"

I just smiled in return. Did he honestly think I was going to tell a known hunter where to find three of our most important nightwalkers? But in truth, one was already dead and a second was missing, possibly dead. I didn't have a lot of good news to offer on this front.

"I thought I had earned it. I gave you information on the symbols and the sacrifice. I also gave you Nerian," he continued, taking a step closer.

"It's a good start."

"We're also offering to watch the other sites for you."

"Mmmm . . . yes, very altruistic of you."

Danaus snorted, closing the distance between us. "I would love nothing more than to see both naturi and nightwalkers wiped from the earth. However, I realize that the naturi are the bigger threat, and we need your assistance. But you also need our help. I am offering a temporary truce. We eliminate the threat of the naturi and then we can get back to the natural order of things."

"Back to killing each other?"

A smile danced in his eyes. "Exactly."

I nodded once and took a step back from him. "I need to think about this. Meet me at Orleans Square at Hull Street and Jefferson tomorrow night at ten o'clock." I turned to leave the basement, but paused as another thought occurred to me, my right foot resting on the first stair. "Before coming, drop that in the river," I said, pointing to the naturi dagger against the opposite wall. "It will not help you."

I headed up the stairs and outside without looking back. A breeze rushed from some secret hiding place, rubbing against my body. I suppressed a shiver as it chilled the blood still coating my skin. I was a mess, but no one noticed me as I walked down the street. It was a weak entrancement spell that all nightwalkers could perform from the moment they were reborn. It worked on most, though witches, warlocks, and psychics were somewhat problematic. At that moment I really didn't care. I was covered in the blood of a naturi, something I never expected to happen again. With the exception of a few dozen left in hiding, the naturi had been wiped from the earth and sealed away.

Yet, on the silent street in the middle of my own domain, I wondered how many naturi were lurking nearby. Was there one hiding in the shadows, watching me, waiting for the opportunity to strike? Or worse, follow me back to my private lair, where he would stake me during the daylight hours? And who was this Rowe that Nerian had mentioned? Was he the one who sought to free the long-lost queen of the naturi? Too many questions . . . and there were no easy answers to be had.

But the path was clear. I had to discover who this Rowe was and stop him from making any more sacrifices. And the only way to do that was to locate the triad, or at the very least, what was left of it.

SIX

My plan for the rest of the night was simple. I would return home, shower, and then hunt. I could even hunt first, and then return home to shower. I was flexible. But those plans were pitched out the window. The acrid smell of smoke tainted the air a couple blocks away, along with a rising wave of fear. This was worse than a random house fire in the early morning hours that claims the lives of the unwary. Something had stirred up the natives in an ugly way.

I ran the last blocks to the fire, to find a trio of bright red fire trucks positioned outside the Docks. Firefighters were pouring water on the flames, which were still jumping out the front door. The hoard of people standing beyond the trucks was covered in smoke and soot and blood. Women were weeping hysterically, while more than a few men were pacing, pulling at their hair in a sort of impotent rage. And others stood still, eyes staring blindly forward in numb shock, their minds refusing any further information.

This was more than just a fire cause by a carelessly dropped cigarette. I dipped into one scarred mind after another to find that several people had been murdered. Someone had come among this hardened, jaded group, cutting down people at random before setting fire to the place.

Turning my attention to the fire, I closed my eyes and quickly extinguished the flames. In a matter of a couple minutes the last tongues of fire were completely gone. It would have looked a little odd to the experienced firefighters, but no one would question their sudden good luck. I needed to get in there to find out what happened, and the fire was destroying evidence.

Pulling aside one stunned man, I convinced him to give me his shirt. Without his eyes ever drifting from the blackened building, he pulled the T-shirt over his head and handed it to me. I wiped off the naturi blood that still covered me and scanned the crowd for a familiar face. Off to one side stood Jonathan, surrounded by a small contingent of friends. His black tights were torn and his plaid skirt and white button-up blouse blackened with soot and splashed with blood. His blond wig was missing and his face was streaked with mascara-tinged tears. He would have made an attractive woman if he weren't built like a linebacker.

With the man's shirt waded up in my left hand, I walked over to Jonathan, who had been attending the Docks for years and knew all the regulars. His friends stepped aside at my approach, their lost gaze seeming to hold me for only a moment before drifting back to the building.

"Hey, Little John," I said when he looked up at me. "What happened here?"

"Oh, MiMi," he sighed, rubbing his left eye with the heel of his left hand. "There you are. They just started killing us." His voice was surprisingly soft despite his large barrel chest, but it held a mountain of sorrow.

"Who? Who did this?"

"I—I don't know," he said with a shake of his head. "I had never seen them before. Two men came in. No, it was two teenagers with long brown hair and green eyes. They were . . . they were . . ." Jonathan paused and stared straight ahead, blinking rapidly for a moment as if trying to clear his vision, or maybe just his memory. "They were looking for someone. Nathan somebody, I think. We didn't know this person, so they started—"

"It's okay," I said, taking his large hand in mine as his voice cracked. I could guess at what happened, but there was no way a pair of teenagers could cause this kind of damage and create this level of fear. Not even if they walked in with Uzis, and not once had I picked up the image of gunfire in anyone's thoughts.

There was more to this tale. I didn't think Jonathan was lying to me. His mind was just struggling to make sense of what he'd seen. Carefully, I slipped into his thoughts, reviewing his memories. Two slim, graceful figures waltzed in. Their longish blondish-brown hair fell around their faces, but I could see their almond-shaped green eyes and catch glimpses of high cheekbones. It was a safe bet that Jonathan's mind had already blurred the sight of anything else that didn't quite make sense to him. Naturi, possibly from the wind clan, from their graceful movements. However, their use of fire to consume the place made me wonder if one of them was from the light clan. If members from either of the two upper clans were out searching, this was serious.

"Nerian," I whispered.

Jonathan's hand jerked in my grasp and his gaze jumped back to my face. His brown eyes widened. "Yes, that's it. Nerian. Do you know him?"

"He's dead."

Jonathan took a step away from me, pulling his hand from my grasp. "They'll be pissed, Mira!"

"I'll handle them."

As I slipped away from Jonathan, I raised the enchantment back around me and wiped his memory of our conversation. Weaving through the crowd of onlookers, firefighters, medical workers, and police, I slipped unnoticed into the Docks. The walls and ceiling in the main bar were blackened by the fire, but the worst of it appeared to be toward the back.

Around me, bodies were strewn about, their limbs lying at strange angles. Some had died quickly with their necks broken. Others had been stabbed and left to bleed to death. More than a dozen were killed. It appeared that after the naturi failed to get the information they wanted, they set fire to the room that held the dance floor, and several had died in the chaos and ensuing stampede.

Walking back toward the dance floor, I paused at the table Danaus and I had sat at only an hour ago. It was blackened but unburned. Around the scar in the wood from the naturi dagger, several symbols were written in blood. More symbols from the naturi language. I was willing to bet they were tracking down Nerian through the blade.

By now they would know that he was dead. If Danaus was as good as he seemed, he would be able to take care of a couple of naturi. Besides, the naturi had been gone for a while now, and the night was wasting away. The hunter was on his own.

Turning away from the table, I slowly gazed around the room. Faces I had seen on a regular basis during the past few years were being covered with white sheets. For so many, I didn't know their names or histories, but they had been a part of my domain, a part of my home. The naturi had stolen them from me.

Destruction, death, and fear; that was all the naturi had to offer both nightwalkers and humans. I knew vampires weren't a great alternative, but at least we had learned to coexist. If the seal was broken and the door opened, the naturi would reduce the world to a blackened shell much like the Docks. From that, they would build their world, one exclusively for the naturi.

As I walked back toward the front door, the table burst into flames. No evidence could be left behind of their existence. When I returned home, I would burn the T-shirt I'd used to wipe off the naturi blood. Things were beginning to spiral out of control and it was all starting in my domain—this I would not allow. I had to make plans fast if I was going to crush the naturi once again.

SEVEN

The Dark Room was more than a mile south of my current location, within the confines of the Victorian District, with its elegant stained-glass windows and gingerbread trim. It was the only nightclub in the region. It was also the only nightclub that catered almost exclusively to the *other* races, and for very good reason. When the various races got together, accidents tended to happen. During my reign in Savannah, I had burned down two other incarnations of the Dark Room because of fights and human deaths. We had finally learned to play nice together, as well as come up with some rules that worked, which included allowing the lycanthropes in the club except during the week of the full moon. Humans were allowed inside, but they had to be accompanied by nightwalkers.

I quickly walked to the Dark Room, where I knew I would find Knox. Along the way, I made several calls on my cell phone, making preparations as best I could before arriving at the club. Turning the last corner, I found a long line standing outside the club, consisting mostly of humans. Two large men with black T-shirts stretched across their muscled chests guarded the front door. One was a werewolf and the other a vampire, there to make sure that both races were treated fairly and allowed into the club.

As I approached, the eyes of the nightwalker flared slightly in surprise and he stepped away from the door to let me pass. "Mira," he whispered. "It's been quiet, I swear."

I swallowed my rude comment and walked wordlessly past him and the crowd, which was now grumbling at my entrance ahead of them. Regardless of whether it rankled my nerves, I understood the bouncer's comments. The last time I'd shown up at the Dark Room, I had to dispose of two nightwalkers who broke some of the more basic rules of the club—no feeding immediately outside the club and no turning a human on the premises.

I quickly passed through the narrow hall that held two empty coat check rooms and paused before the main floor. The Dark Room was a sanctuary of decadent luxury within the city. The main floor was dimly lit with small sconces around the room, casting a thick red light. The walls were lined with deep booths partially hidden by thick velvet curtains. The center was a massive dance floor, where creatures now swayed and writhed to the low, almost hypnotic music that swelled in the air. Where the Docks had been filled with fast and hard beats that created an almost frantic need within its occupants, the Dark Room was a slow seduction of the senses. The Docks was made for humans who wanted to pretend to be dark predators; the Dark Room was made for predators who didn't want to hide what they were.

My eyes skimmed the room while I lightly reached out with my powers to search for Knox. The small bar on the left side was relatively empty, but that was normal. The only ones who ever used it were the lycanthropes and the human companions of the nightwalkers. Alcohol consumption was not what kept this place open. It was an exclusive club. All nightwalkers and lycanthropes that entered the club were on a members' list and paid annual dues. Furthermore, if they ever brought in guests, there was a second set of dues that had to be paid. Attending the Dark Room was a status symbol, a sign that you had not only achieved *other* status, but also acquired some wealth. And the more guests you brought, the more money you had.

Of course, paying your dues didn't guarantee you admittance on any given night. If the place reached capacity—which was relatively low, in an effort to avoid confrontations—you couldn't be admitted. Also, if you had recently pissed me off, you were on the no-admittance list until I said otherwise.

I stood at the entrance to the main room for only a moment before a tall, lean nightwalker stepped out of a shadowy booth and stared at me. I hadn't told Knox I was coming, so my presence at the nightclub naturally surprised him. He tilted his head to his right before turning and walking in that direction. I cut across the dance floor, weaving through the crowd, to meet him as he opened a door at the back of the building. There were several private rooms in the club that were used for feeding and other activities. However, feeding was the only thing specifically outlawed in the main room.

As I stepped past Knox, he ran an index finger down my bare

arm, wiping away some of the blood I had missed. "Looks like you've had an interesting evening," he slowly drawled. "The Butcher?"

I roughly seized his wrist as he raised his finger to his mouth, halting him in the act of tasting what he assumed to be a very messy meal. "Naturi."

Knox stumbled backward from me, jerking his wrist from my grasp. He frantically wiped his hand and wrist on his dark slacks while a string of low German curses escaped him. I gave him a few moments to collect himself.

At just under six feet, Knox had a lean, narrow build, a mix of bone and hard muscle. He was nearly two centuries old, still somewhat young, but very powerful and intelligent for his age. But that was no great surprise considering his maker. Valerio very rarely converted a human, but when he did, it was always with a great deal of care.

Knox moved into my domain less than two decades ago, and has served as my nightwalker assistant almost that long. While we had no official name for it, he served as a type of second-in-command. His mere presence helped to maintain the peace. Yet, I never used him as an enforcer. While he was more than strong enough for the task, I preferred to handle such things personally.

"The Butcher is in league with the naturi?" Knox asked when he was finally calm again.

"Actually, the naturi was a gift for me," I said with a light shrug. I turned and walked past the black leather sofa and matching chair to the far wall. Putting my back against the wall, I slid down until I was seated on the floor with my knees bent before me. I was tired and needed a few moments to think.

Knox pushed the ottoman closer to me with his foot and sat on the edge. "He comes into your domain, kills five nightwalkers, and then gives you naturi as a gift. Forgive me if I'm slow, but what the hell?"

"It's more complicated than that," I murmured, dropping the blood-stained T-shirt I'd been carrying next to me. I threaded my fingers through the thick charcoal-gray carpet that stretched through the room and helped to muffle our conversation.

"I sincerely hope so," Knox said.

Resting my head against the wall, I looked up, watching him brush some sandy blond hair from where it fell across his forehead. I had grown accustomed to his dry wit and calming influence during the past few years. It took a great deal to rattle him, but it appeared that the naturi was one of those things, given the lines of strain around his mouth. I was grateful Valerio had at least taken the time to educate Knox on that dangerous bit of history.

"I have to leave town for a while," I said, pulling my fingers into a loose fist. I hated not being here if the naturi were running around my domain, but they had to be stopped, and the answers I needed could not be found here.

"Are you leaving because of the Butcher or the naturi?"

"Both. While I am gone, spread the word that I want everyone pulled close to the city. No one is to hunt alone until I return or send word that it is safe. And do not mention the naturi. I don't want a panic."

Knox rubbed his temples and forehead with one hand, staring off into space for a moment. "This will make things . . . difficult."

I knew what he meant. While we frequently congregated at the Dark Room, nightwalkers were solitary, independent creatures by nature. Forcing vampires to stay within close proximity for an extended period of time was asking for trouble. But telling them that the naturi were close would only make matters worse.

"I hope to get this taken care of as quickly as possible. Where is Amanda?"

"Concert at SSU," Knox quickly replied, referring to Savannah State University. The college was relatively small, but frequently played host to a variety of bands, both known and unknown. The college also made for a great feeding ground for nightwalkers. "Do you want me to summon her?"

"No, talk to her after the concert, fill her in. Get her to help you keep the peace."

While they looked nothing alike, I frequently referred to them as my Doublemint Twins because they both had the same shade of blond hair. Amanda wasn't quite fifty years old, but had taken to vampirism like a fish to water, seemingly without the struggles many her age went through. I had no idea who her creator was. She had simply appeared in my domain ten years ago and seemed to instantly fit in. Of course, her sunny yet positively brutal personality won a special place in my heart. Despite her youth, she managed to keep a tight rein on some of the younger nightwalkers. If Knox was considered my second-in-command, then Amanda had managed to quietly attain a type of sergeant-at-arms position.

"What about the Butcher?"

"He will be gone from my domain before I leave." I hadn't yet decided how I would take care of the hunter, but I would not leave him here while I was away. Right now, he was balanced between too dangerous to leave alive and too important to kill. I was still waiting for the scales to finally tilt in one direction.

Knox opened his mouth to say something, but the words were halted by a knock at the door.

"Show him in," I called, quickly pushing to my feet. I had sensed the approach of the bouncer and knew he would come to that room for only one reason—my invited guest had arrived.

"Use your best judgment." By the finality in my tone, Knox knew he was being dismissed. The blond vampire nodded once and then left the room as Barrett Rainer entered.

Given his broad shoulders and somewhat stocky build, it was no surprise that Barrett Rainer was a werewolf. The man was more than 250 pounds of pure muscle, but he moved with a subtle grace, dancing between animal and man. What was surprising to most was that he was the head of one of the most powerful packs in the country. The Savannah pack wasn't the largest—that honor belonged to a pack in Montana—but its members had been carefully bred, trained, and in some cases selected for their strength, speed, and intelligence.

And at the top of the heap was Barrett Rainer with his burnished gold hair and copper-colored eyes. Like his predecessors, Barrett had been groomed since birth to assume his current role. Of course, the Savannah pack was unusual in that since its very beginning, it had always been run by a member of the Rainer family.

It was this steady consistency over the years that had enabled me to strengthen the relations with the lycanthropes in the area. In most cases, nightwalkers and shapeshifters didn't generally play well together, as each side attempted to carve out a territory of its own. Only through steady negotiations with Barrett, his father, and his grandfather had I been able to work out a stable peace. That's not to say we didn't have our occasional scuffle, but at least it wasn't the secret wars and strained truces found in other regions around the world.

Barrett dragged his stubby fingers through his short hair, leaving it standing on end and slightly disheveled. He wore a gray suit, but his tie was missing and the top two buttons of his shirt were undone. It was nearly two in the morning. Judging by how quickly he had gotten there, I was willing to guess I'd caught him as he was leaving his restaurant, Bella Luna, on the other side of town.

"You look like hell," he said after Knox shut the door, leaving us alone.

"Nice of you to notice," I replied with a smirk. "You're looking a little ragged as well."

"It was summer high moon a few nights ago. We're all still trying to bounce back." Barrett gave a little shrug, but even that motion seemed somewhat stiff and slow.

I wasn't particularly clear on the details, but summer high moon was the full moon that fell between midsummer and autumn harvest, and tended to pack a little extra punch for all the lunar shapeshifters such as werewolves. From what I understood, it was a three-night frenzy of hunting, fighting, and sex. I used to tease Barrett that night-walkers didn't need the moon to tell them when to have an orgy, we were always ready. However, I didn't feel like joking tonight. I needed the pack at peak strength.

"How's the family?"

"Sated," he said, his voice sounding heavy as he rubbed the bridge of his nose. "What's going on, Mira? You generally don't feel the need to check on the shifters at two in the morning."

"Several humans were murdered at the Docks tonight. The club was partially burned before I arrived," I began, carefully weighing each word. Barrett said nothing as he nodded, but I listened to him draw in a deep breath. He abruptly halted in the midst of drawing in air, his thick brows snapping together over his nose. He quickly released the breath and drew in another, scenting the air, but confusion was still written across his face. He smelled Nerian on me but couldn't identify the scent. I doubted if his father could have. There were so few naturi left, and it had been years since the last one was seen in the area.

I paused, not even wanting to breathe the word that could potentially shatter his world, but I had no choice. I had brought him here so he could at least try to protect his people. "The naturi struck—"

"That's what I smell!" he snarled. His nose crinkled, Barrett took two steps toward me. His wide eyes glowed slightly as they swept over me, his hands were open at his sides, with fingers curled like claws. "You reek of naturi."

"A hunter is in town. He gave . . . he gave me a naturi from my past." I paused again, licking my lips. I mentally sorted through the intimate details of my captivity at the hands of the naturi, trying to decide if there was anything that he needed to know. "That naturi is dead, but there are at least two others searching for him or the hunter. They are the ones that struck at the Docks."

Barrett paced away from me to the opposite wall, the heels of his palms pressed to his temples as if he were suffering from an intense migraine. "Mira." My name escaped him in a low growl.

"Do you have an emergency plan?" I asked, trying to keep my voice calm.

Barrett whipped around to face me "An emergency plan?" he repeated. "That's like me asking if you've got an emergency plan for a day when the sun refuses to set. Of course not! I don't know of any pack that has faced the naturi. Hell, I only know of them because of you and my great-grandfather."

I could feel the anger rising in him, but he fought back the panic and won. To the naturi, the lycanthropes were little more than slaves, foot soldiers in their war against the bori and mankind. Trapped between animal and man, the lycans had no choice but to answer the call of the naturi and obey.

"Pull your pack together, hold them, and make them fight this. I—I have to leave town for a little while."

"You're leaving now? This is your domain! The vampires are the only ones who can fight the naturi," Barrett shouted as he closed the distance between us with a few long strides. I barely resisted the urge to put my hand on his chest to keep a semicomfortable distance between us. I didn't want to feel crowded. My nerves were already frazzled from Danaus and the naturi; an irate werewolf didn't exactly put me at ease.

"I have to stop this from growing worse, and I can't do that here," I snapped. I didn't want to leave. I didn't want to leave my people seemingly defenseless. Unfortunately, I'd heard nothing from the Coven regarding Danaus. I couldn't sit there on my hands, waiting for them to send word regarding the naturi. What's more, I was not only one of our strongest fighters, but I also had experience dealing with the naturi. I knew I would be of more use in the Old World than in the New. I had to leave.

"Worse?" Barrett said.

The left corner of my mouth twitched as my eyes darted away from his direct gaze. I didn't know what the lycans knew of the seal or what happened at Machu Picchu so many years ago, but it was a rule that nightwalkers didn't speak of it to anyone outside our species. We might have all been on the same side when it came to the naturi, but nightwalkers by their very nature were all about power, and information was the richest form of power. We didn't tell others more than they absolutely had to know. And regardless of how much I respected and trusted Barrett, I couldn't fight six hundred years of conditioning.

"There are trying to return," I quickly said. "I'll tell you more when I know more."

My only warning was a low growl that rumbled deep in his chest before his right hand swiped across my midsection, his fingernails replaced with long black talons. I jumped backward, my shoulders slamming into the wall behind me. While I was fast, the wall kept me from escaping him. Four furrows slashed across my ribs and down my stomach. My leather halter top kept the cuts from running too deep, but my stomach had been completely bare.

Before I could slam Barrett with a few blistering comments, I saw him stare at his trembling hand, now flecked with my blood, and then turn confused eyes up to my face.

"I'm s-sorry, Mira. I—I don't know what happened," he said, his voice low and rough. He blinked once, his eyes glowed a deep copper, and then he blinked a second time, erasing the glow. A knot twisted in my stomach.

"Barrett?" A part of me wanted to reach out and lay my hand on his shoulder, but my body was still pressed against the wall as I balanced on the tips of my toes, struggling for those few extra centimeters of space. It didn't feel safe to move.

"I—I think they're here." And then his eyes glowed again. The naturi were here and they had Barrett, the Alpha for the Savannah pack, under their control.

"Shit!" I hissed between clenched teeth.

As he reached back with his right hand to take another swipe at me, I jumped forward, throwing all my weight into his left shoulder. I knocked us both to the floor, but quickly rolled to my feet. I squared off against him, putting my back to the only door in the room. Barrett returned to his feet and crouched in an aggressive stance. Beside his glowing eyes, his face was completely expressionless. He had no idea what he was doing. He would destroy me because that was the command implanted in his head, regardless of what he felt about me.

"Barrett, can you hear me? You have to fight this," I said in a hard voice, while I scrambled for a way to subdue him without hurting him too much. Other than the fact that I didn't just kill for the sake of killing, I needed him alive to help preserve the local pack.

In the main room, faint sounds of fighting drifted to me. Quickly sifting through my memory, I could recall seeing only two werewolves in the bar when I walked through, not counting the bouncer at the front door. I could only hope that Barrett had not brought more when he arrived. Unfortunately, I couldn't afford to divide my attention between scanning the area and watching him. I would have worry about it after I managed to take care of the Alpha.

My gaze darted around the room, taking in a quick inventory. Leather sofa, chair with ottoman, floor lamp, two end tables, two iron wall sconces. I didn't have a lot of choices. I needed to knock his ass out so I could settle the main room and take out the naturi.

Barrett lunged at me with a snarl, both hands now tipped with long claws. I sidestepped him, ducking under his outstretched hands. As he passed me, I kicked out with my right leg, knocking him into the wall. I needed some distance between us. Barrett wouldn't shift. It would take too long and it would give me a chance to attack. But it wasn't as if human form would leave him at a disadvantage. He was extremely fast and strong.

He pushed off the wall and threw himself into me. I was a half second too slow. We fell to the floor in a tangled heap, his elongated teeth instantly clamping onto my throat. I felt his teeth sink in, sending pain screaming through my frame. Yelling, I jerked my left arm free from beneath his body and punched him in the side. At least three ribs snapped beneath my fist, but I held back enough to keep from punching straight into his chest. He groaned, but clamped down harder, teeth sinking deeper into my throat.

My vision swam. I reached back and hit Barrett again, but this time I hammered his kidney. He yelped, finally releasing my throat. With a soft gurgle, I shoved him off me, sending him skidding a foot across the floor. Tapping down a fresh swell of pain, I pushed to my feet and grabbed him by the lapels of his jacket. His handsome face was covered in my blood and his eyes radiated with an eerie copper light. His large hand clamped on my wrists, threatening to snap them, but I didn't give him a chance. I slammed him into the wall, trying to knock him out.

It didn't work. Either his head was too thick or his lycanthropy made him too strong. I pulled him back and slammed him into the wall again, partially pushing him through the wooden studs. A third time left him dazed but conscious.

Dropping him to the floor, I grabbed an iron sconce off the floor and clocked him on the back of the head. He collapsed like a sack of dead fish. Blood immediately began to ooze from his scalp and trickle down his temple. I had cracked his skull, but I could hear his heartbeat. He would live.

Gritting my teeth, I took a step away from him, still clutching the sconce. Blood was still leaking from the wound at my throat that was struggling to close. A low roar had begun in my chest and was echoing through my brain. It wanted blood. It wanted Barrett's blood, and it would only be satisfied when I'd finished draining him dry.

I took another backward step. It took everything within me to turn my back on him and walk to the door. The blood lust was lit and would only be satisfied when I finally made a kill, or at the very least, fed deeply.

Slowly opening the door, I peeked out into the main room. Chaos ruled. Curtains were shredded, tables overturned, and I could see at least five dead bodies. I immediately identified two of them as night-walkers. Blocking the entrance were two naturi. Why were they there? Danaus wasn't here.

The quickest way to end this struggle was to take out the naturi. They were the greatest threat. Reaching out with my power, I quickly located Knox but hesitated making my presence known. He was fighting a werewolf. I could feel his building anger, but a cool, under-lying logic still guided his thoughts.

Please, don't kill them, I whispered in his thoughts.

Thank God! Knox sighed back, relieved to find that I was still alive. *Barrett—*

The naturi. Kill the naturi and the werewolves will stop, I directed.

Tried that. Irritation filled the comment. *They've killed Roland and Adam.*

I've got it. Keep the lycans off my back.

I silently walked the last couple of steps down the hall to stand on the edge of the main room. And the battle instantly shifted. The two naturi saw me and smiled. One of them was obviously from the ani-mal clan. He had the same wide bone structure to his face as Nerian and dark, shaggy hair. With a wave of his hand, the four lycans I could see on the dance floor looked over at me. At once, they all attempted to disengage from their opponents so they could come after me.

Unconsciously, I took a step backward, my mouth falling open. The naturi had come after me. Not Nerian. Not Danaus. They were looking for me.

Before the lycans could move more than a couple steps, the vam-pires surged, bringing them down. Sickly sounds of tearing flesh and breaking bones barely rose above the earth-shattering screams of pain. Knox was willing to follow my orders up to a point. He had di-rected the others to keep the lycanthropes busy, but as soon as it be-came apparent that I was the main target, the order had changed to protect me at any cost. The four werewolves were dead, outnumbered and overwhelmed.

Swallowing a scream of frustration, I conjured up a fireball in my left hand and hurled it at the two naturi who were slowly approach-ing. It never reached them. One of them gracefully lifted one hand. The fireball flowed to him and then disappeared. I looked carefully at him for the first time. Tall and thin like a delicate willow, his skin was snowy white and his hair fell about him in silken waves of gold.

If the sun could ever cry a tear, he would have been formed from it. He was from the light clan, and I knew I was seriously screwed. I wouldn't be able to use my ability to conjure fire as a weapon against them as long as he stood.

I smiled. He would just have to stop standing.

"I've already killed Nerian tonight," I called to them from across the dance floor. There was no missing the laughter in my tone. "We've killed your poor foot soldiers. This will be your one chance to leave my domain while you can still walk out of here." As I spoke, I conjured another fireball in my left hand.

Once again the naturi from the light clan captured the fireball, protecting them both. "You're mistaken, Fire Starter. This is your one chance," he replied. His voice was light and warm, like the early morning rays from the summer sun. "Come with us now, and we won't destroy every vampire in your domain."

My smile faded. Bright fireballs consumed both my hands this time. Quickly, I launched them both at the naturi from the light clan. With a wave of his hand, he easily dispersed the fire, but it did nothing to stop the iron sconce that had been engulfed in the second fireball. The heavy piece of iron struck him in the middle of his chest, throwing him backward as it embedded itself. I had no doubt that he was dead the moment his lithe body slammed into the wall.

The remaining naturi growled at me for only a second before darting out the open front door. Without the added defense of someone from the light clan, he didn't stand a chance against fifty nightwalkers and the Fire Starter. It had been the only way the naturi could hold me during the first week. With a member of the light clan constantly hovering in my shadow, I'd been unable to use my ability against them. By the second week I was too weak to even light a candle.

Now, with the threat finally gone, I took a step onto the dance floor and surveyed the damage. I tried to shove both my hands through my hair but stopped when I encountered the dried blood left from Nerian. My body trembled in pain, exhaustion, and blood loss. But the faces of the nightwalkers watching me were worse. Haunted, confused, and frightened, many clung to each other or knelt beside the dead. The two nightwalkers I could identify as Roland and Adam had gaping holes dominating their chests where their hearts once were. Two more bodies lay in awkward positions on the ground, headless.

The bodies of the four werewolves were badly mangled and covered with blood. No one stood next to them. The lines were already being drawn, but they were the wrong lines.

"Mira?"

My head jerked up to find Knox standing next to me. His navy shirt had been ripped in several places and there were several superficial wounds healing on his arms and chest.

"What's the count?" I murmured, my gaze returning to the bloody scene before me.

"Six nightwalkers and five lycans, unless Barrett is—"

"No," I said sharply, then drew in a deep breath, softening my voice. "No, he'll recover."

"Why?" I heard someone whisper in a broken voice.

I lurched into action, my heels clicking ominously on the cold tile floor. "You know why they did this, don't you?" I demanded. My gaze slowly swept over the assembled mass, making sure that I briefly held the stare of every nightwalker. "They had no choice! That was the naturi," I said, pointing over my shoulder toward the dead naturi. "Certain naturi can control the lycans. The lycans have no choice but to obey the naturi when they are close. This is not their fault."

"But how do you stop this?" a female asked in a tremulous voice.

"Kill the werewolves," another answered in a cold, dead voice.

I surged across the open space, grabbing him by the throat as I slammed him into a divider between two booths. "No! You kill the naturi! You kill the naturi and the lycans are free. You kill the naturi and we are free." Releasing the nightwalker only after he gave me a faint nod, I turned to face the others again. "If you kill the lycan, you still have a naturi waiting to rip your heart out."

Walking over to one of the booths that was still covered with a tablecloth, I pulled it off and draped it over one of the dead werewolves. Donald Moreland. He'd been the bouncer at the front door. "Spread the word. If anyone attacks a lycan after tonight, I will stake you out in the sun myself," I said in a low voice. "No one is permitted out into the marshlands or any other known lycan territory until I give the word. You remain in the city. No one hunts alone."

"What about the naturi?"

I looked up, my eyes locking on Knox. "I leave tomorrow to tell the Elders about what is happening. The naturi will follow me."

While the remaining vampires disposed of the various bodies, I took Barrett to my town house a few blocks away and waited for him to awaken. Distraught and heartsick after hearing everything that had occurred, the Alpha left my town house an hour before sunrise. He and Knox would attempt to maintain peace while I was gone, but we both knew the damage was done. The memories of nightwalkers did not fade. Generations of werewolves would come and go through my territory, but the trust between the two races would never be the same again. We both knew that tempers would run high during the next few years. And despite the fact that the werewolves were as much victims in this mess as the nightwalkers, someone would use the attack at the Dark Room as an excuse to lash out.

Damn the naturi! And damn Danaus for bringing them into my domain. Intentionally or not, he had destroyed a delicate balance I had spent decades building.

Settled in my hidden lair beneath earth as the sun edged closer to the horizon, I finally allowed my mind to drift back to the thought I had been avoiding. The naturi had come looking for me. Tabor was dead and Jabari missing; dead or not, I didn't know. Sadira was the only member of the triad I was confident was still alive. Of course, she was my maker. I was sure I would have felt it if she'd been destroyed. Outside the triad, there were only a few other nightwalkers that had survived the battle at Machu Picchu centuries ago. Were the naturi hunting them down in an effort to make sure we couldn't stop them again?

Danaus knew about the naturi. Danaus knew about the sacrifice in India. Danaus knew that I was at Machu Picchu and how to find me. Danaus knew too much. I would take him with me. I would discover how he knew these things. And when I was sure that I knew everything he knew, I would kill him.

EIGHT

The black limo glided out of the flow of traffic and pulled up to the corner just after ten o'clock. We were in what I lovingly thought of as the theater district, even though there was only the Johnny Mercer Theater in the vicinity. It was an enormous building with tall arched openings that adjoined the Civic Center Arena. The whole area was lined with beautiful parks and tall oak trees draped with Spanish moss.

Beside the historic district, this narrow strip was yuppie central. All that glittered, glowed, and drove a BMW strolled through this area. And the hunter stuck out like a dirty street urchin at the queen's diamond jubilee.

I hadn't actually meant to make him stand out so much, though a part of me wished it had been a conscious effort. The corner of Hull and Jefferson was near the edge of the historic district, and everyone knew the Civic Center. It would be easy for him to find. That had been my only concern.

Danaus stood on the corner outside the lamplight, still in his black leather duster. It was far too hot for the jacket, but was clearly the only way he could walk around the city with his assortment of weapons. A black duffel bag lay at his feet, and I had a feeling that it held a great deal more than clothes. It was nice that I didn't have to tell him we would be going on a journey. Of course, we both knew that the next sacrifice wouldn't be here. We had to get moving so we could pull the triad back together.

The driver alighted from the limo and circled around to open the door for Danaus. The hunter's eyes darted from the car to the man, his grim face expressing his confidence that the man had lost his mind.

"Mr. Smith?" the driver inquired, motioning with one hand toward the interior of the car. I had informed the poor man that we would be picking up a dark-haired gentleman by the name of Mr. Smith at the corner of Hull and Jefferson.

Struggling to keep from laughing, I called to Danaus from the shadows of the limo. "Come along, Danaus."

The driver picked up Danaus's bag and placed it in the trunk, all under the dark gaze of its owner. When it was carefully stowed, Danaus climbed into the limo and took the seat across from me.

When he was comfortably seated against the soft leather bench he got a good look at me. I laughed when his eyes flared and frown deepened. Anyone else's mouth would have been hanging open, but Danaus seemed to be the king of composure. He would have made an excellent nightwalker, but I had a feeling vampirism might not actually be an option for him.

I lounged in the seat wearing a pair of black slacks and a matching black blazer over a deep purple shirt. My dark red hair had been carefully twisted and pinned to the back of my head, showing off my high cheekbones beneath pale white skin. A pair of lilac sunglasses sat balanced on my nose. In our two other meetings, I wore my usual attire of leather, and very little of it. Unfortunately, I had to make these travel arrangements through my human assistant, and she needed the reassurance that her employer was a normal, human businesswoman. Though her mouth did fall open when Danaus took a seat beside her in the limo.

As his gaze moved over me, my hand drifted up, my fingers briefly dancing over the faint scar that now stretched along my collarbone and the base of my neck on the right. Barrett's bite had only partially healed since last night. It was rare for nightwalkers to scar, but lacking adequate rest and blood, it was possible. I'd lost too much blood during the battle and hadn't left myself enough time after leaving Barrett to hunt. The lines on my neck weren't the first scars I had acquired since being reborn, and considering my lifestyle, I knew they wouldn't be the last.

"Mr. Smith . . ." I started then paused. Toying with Danaus was too easy, and I struggled to keep from smiling and exposing my fangs. After the unexpected debacle of last night, I need something to lighten my mood. "This is my assistant, Charlotte Godwin," I continued, motioning toward the petite woman seated next to him.

Charlotte extended her hand, but Danaus only nodded at her then turned his glare on me.

"We are dropping Ms. Godwin off a couple blocks from here.

She decided to tag along in an attempt to get me to look over some papers before our trip."

"It's just that you are so hard to pin down for a meeting, Ms. Jones," chided the slender brunette with chocolate-colored eyes. Her words slipped through the limo with a sweet, Southern drawl. She wore a mint green suit, very composed and professional, and her long fingers grasped the stack of papers in her lap.

My gaze drifted back to Danaus, and he arched one eyebrow at me when she mentioned my surname. So they were obvious fakes; that was half the fun. It gave sweet little Charlotte something to sweat about when she lay awake at night.

With an indifferent wave of my hand, I attempted to brush off the topic. "It's completely unnecessary. You have everything well in hand."

"But the investors are demanding to know why you won't approve the mining expedition in Peru," Charlotte countered.

"They want to go digging in the Sacred Valley, and I won't have it. If they want to load up on the sweat of the sun, tell them to pick another country. Try Chile," I said. Gazing out the window, I watched as the city slid by in a motley of lights and color. I was part of a consortium of investors that ran a gold-mining company. We had made a great deal of money so far, and now they wanted to venture into the heart of the Incan empire. They had set their sights on some mountains in the shadow of Machu Picchu. I wanted nothing to do with it.

"They won't be happy." Charlotte's soft voice intruded on a set of less than happy memories.

"Tell them to take it up with me."

Charlotte quickly broke eye contact, looking back down at the stack of paperwork in her lap. Luckily for her, the limo pulled over to the sidewalk again in front of a set of office buildings in the heart of downtown. Charlotte maintained offices both in Savannah and Charleston, where she generally reigned supreme until she had to check in with me.

It had to be frustrating. She had her own assistants and made multi-million-dollar decisions on a daily basis. Most of it was my money, though she did run a few other partnerships that I was involved in. But for all she accomplished, she was still forced to jump when I asked. Last night, I'd called at four in the morning from my town house as I waited for Barrett to awaken, and demanded that she make arrangements for the trip. And I knew that Charlotte had most of it completed by dawn. No matter how high she rose or how much money she acquired, she would still be my flunky.

The delicate brunette with the pale rose complexion tidied up the papers, drawing in a deep breath. "I hope you have a good trip. I have often wished to see the pyramids." The words escaped her in a rush of air.

"Thank you," I said. "I will contact you in a day or two to arrange for travel."

Her head snapped up to meet my eyes again. "Back home?"

"Hopefully. You'll hear from me." She nodded and nearly leapt from the limo when the driver opened the door. My soft laughter followed her out of the vehicle and onto the street.

Danaus waited until the driver shut the door before speaking. "She doesn't know?"

"No, she doesn't know what I am. Her only fear is losing her job."

"It's more than that," he corrected.

"Really?" I leaned back into the corner of the seat and stretched out my legs, crossing them at the ankle. Draping my left arm along the backseat, my index finger drew a lazy infinity sign on the slick leather. "What else does she fear?"

"Losing her soul."

I laughed, letting my powers flare out from my body. It was like relaxing a muscle after holding it tensed for a long time. I tried to rein my powers in when I was in close quarters with Charlotte. Being human, she might not have been able to sense them, but that extra bit of self-preservation that all humans possess would have picked up something. She would know that something was slightly off about me.

Danaus flinched against the unexpected wave of power, his right hand flexing at his side. Being a hunter, I suspected he would have felt infinitely more comfortable with a dagger in his hand, but he'd kept up the act of being civilized in front of sweet Charlotte. In the front of the car, the sound of the driver climbing back behind the wheel snapped me from my amusement. I pulled my powers back into myself and sighed. While the pane of glass muffled our words, it would not have stopped power from eddying out beyond it.

We pulled back out into traffic and headed out of the city. I saw brief flashes of the river as we passed through wide intersections. I had scanned the area intermittently since awakening that evening, pushing my powers as far as they would reach. By sunset all the lycanthropes were outside the city limits and settled in the surrounding countryside, while all the nightwalkers were in the city. Barrett had even changed the hours of the restaurant temporarily so it now closed before sunset. As much as we both hated it, the boundaries had been drawn. When the naturi were once again defeated, Barrett and I would begin rebuilding the trust between the shifters and the nightwalkers.

"We're going to Egypt?" Danaus asked.

"I had hoped to keep it a surprise." I let the silence sink into the car for a moment, trying to see if I could get him to demand more information, but he was proving to be a very patient creature. "We are flying to Luxor with a brief layover in Paris. From there, we take a barge down the Nile to Aswan."

"A car would be faster from Luxor, or why not fly straight to Aswan?"

"True." I nodded, my gaze darting back to my restless fingers and their infinity sign. "But you are now traveling with a vampire, and certain . . . rituals must be observed. I am entering the territory of an Elder and must move slowly as a show of respect. You never go directly into the known domain of an Ancient. It's a sign of aggression."

"I thought you said Jabari was dead?"

My eyes jerked back to Danaus's face, studying his intent expression. "So you didn't kill him. I doubted the rumors."

"I was in Egypt briefly, but I have never seen Jabari." His shoulder-length hair hung close to his cheek, casting dark shadows about his eyes.

"I don't know what to expect," I said with an elegant shrug, as my eyes strayed to the window. After you reach a certain age as a nightwalker, you can make almost any gesture seem elegant. It's part of the package. "Jabari has disappeared. I don't seek him, but I think he may have left some valuable information behind; journals describing the seal and the triad. It's a starting point. However, I think it would be wise if we proceed with caution. If he does appear, I would prefer to remain in his good graces."

"My presence will not help that endeavor."

"No, it will not." There was no reason for me to tell him that I intended to hand him over to Jabari and/or the Coven if necessary. Let them extract the information his brain held. I would have preferred to handle it myself, but there was no time to waste on my own interests. My domain was beginning to tear at the seams.

I looked down to find that I had unconsciously begun to fiddle with the silver band on my ring finger. The ring had been a gift from a lover years ago, etched with what looked like ocean waves. The Greek design whispered of old, half-forgotten memories.

Danaus let the conversation drop and stared out the window. I wondered what must be going through his head. He was willingly walking into the den of the enemy. Why? He could have left after showing me the pictures, leaving it to the nightwalkers. Of course, I doubted he trusted us to handle it. I wished I knew exactly how much he understood of this whole horrible mess. Yet, any question I asked might give the vampire hunter valuable and even deadly insight into my world.

Stretching my legs, I relaxed against the seat. I would leave it for now. If I found Jabari, he would handle it. If not, I would find Sadira. I hadn't seen her since that night at Machu Picchu, and wasn't particularly looking forward to the reunion. Our relationship had never been a happy one during the century we spent together. We both wanted control over me, and only one of us could win. It resulted in some ugly battles, and there were some wounds that even five centuries couldn't heal.

"Did you encounter the naturi last night?" I asked, forcefully redirecting my thoughts away from my maker.

"No. Did you?"

My teeth clenched so tightly my jaw ached. Before I'd left the Dark Room, the final body count was seven nightwalkers, six lycans, and nine humans, against the death of only two naturi. What did we face if the naturi returned to this world en masse? "A pair attacked the Docks, killing several people. They appeared at the Dark Room later. Several nightwalkers and lycanthropes were killed."

"I'm sorry."

"Yes." Surprised by his solemn comment, I finally looked over at him. "So am I."

We traveled in silence to a nearly empty airstrip almost a half an hour outside of the city. My private jet was fueled and waiting for us. I preferred to travel this way. Items could be loaded and unloaded from the plane outside the glare of a large airport and prying eyes.

The limo stopped a few yards away from the plane and the driver hopped from the car, leaving the engine running. I was his only task of the night, and I could feel his eagerness to have it done. Picking up and dropping off strange people at deserted airfields was not a part of his normal chores. He opened the door for me and bowed his head, as if he could feel my power. I smiled and slipped a fifty dollar bill into his fingers; I liked it when my servants were quick and efficient. A brooding Danaus followed silently behind me as the driver rushed to grab our bags.

A few steps away from the limo, Danaus reached for one of the knives at his side. I laid a restraining hand on his shoulder and smiled. He had just caught sight of the two large men flanking the short staircase that led into the jet. They wore shoulder holsters with a pair of lovely guns over their tightly stretched black shirts plus a thigh sheath for a knife.

"Down, boy," I said, patting his shoulder. "They belong to me."
He stopped walking, his hand resting on his knife. "I don't like to
travel without protection."

He released his hold on the knife at his side and continued to
walk a step behind me. I smiled at my two bodyguards and let my
hand run across the chest of the one on the right as I started to climb
into the jet.

"Wait," Danaus said. "We're being watched."

I turned, my right foot on the first step, my hand on the shoulder
of my bodyguard. Stretching out my powers, I searched the area.
Deep black night stretched in all directions for several acres, hemmed
in only by a thin line of trees. All the humans nearby were employ-
ees, and the closest nightwalker was almost fifteen miles away. I
sensed no one else, which sent a chill up my back. Was Rowe hunting
me now?

"Let them watch," I announced. "Let's go." I forced myself to
climb the rest of the way into the jet causally, turning my back to the
darkness.

Once inside, I stripped off my blazer and tossed it over the back
of one of the white leather chairs. An exquisite piece of machinery,
the plane always made me wish I traveled more. The front had two
long benches in soft white leather along the sides of the plane. A pair
of chairs faced the benches in the same white leather. The floor was
covered in thick, creamy white carpet, muffling the footsteps of the
passengers. Toward the back was a bar with a fridge and microwave,
along with another set of chairs. I never used it, but my bodyguards
found it nice for the long trips. Behind all that was another room with
a bed and a door that locked.

I stretched out on one of the benches while Danaus took the bench
opposite me. It allowed him to keep an eye on my assistants and me.
For the first time, he looked uneasy. I doubted it was a fear of flying. I
think maybe everything was sinking in. He was in a dire situation and
would have to fight his way out of it. And to make matters worse, he
was forced to rely on a vampire to guide him through this maze of
snarls.

After shutting the door, the pilots fired up the engine. My bodyguard, Michael, walked over and knelt before me. He was a handsome man of less than thirty with beautiful blond curls brushing his
shoulders. They made him look younger than he was. He had served
me as a bodyguard for the past five years.

Yet for the past three he had helped to keep the loneliness at bay.
He gave me laughter and diversion when the nights seemed to stretch

out before me like the vast Siberian tundra. But that's all there was for us. No matter how I tried, I could not give my heart to a creature I knew needed protection from me and my kind. Some nightwalkers could. The tale was older than I was . . . a centuries-old vampire falls in love with a human, and then turns him or her so they can spend eternity together. Yeah, right. Humans can't make a marriage last more than a few decades. Do you honestly think a pair of vampires can stay together for centuries? I've yet to see it happen.

Biting back a weary sigh, I smiled down at Michael, my right hand smoothing back his hair and idly touching his cheek. He reached up and pulled my hand down so my fingers rested against the pulse at his neck. My eyes drifted shut as I let its siren song beat through me for a couple of seconds. My lips parted slightly and I touched my tongue to my fangs. A hungry longing rose up in my chest, but I smothered it, lifting my hand back to his face.

"Not now, love," I whispered, opening my eyes. "When we reach Aswan, I will need you." Michael turned his head and pressed a kiss against the palm of my hand before rising to his feet. He turned, walked toward the back of the jet and took a seat across from my other guardian. Brown-haired Gabriel had served as one of my bodyguards for more than ten years, but he still could not keep the look of envy from his eyes. I'd fed off both men in the past and neither had uttered a complaint.

Danaus's dark growl drew my attention back to the hunter. "A donor?"

"I thought I'd pack lunch," I said. "It will take us nearly twenty-four hours to reach Aswan. I don't want to walk in weak and hungry."

"They both know?"

"They have both assisted me in the past when I was in need." I watched Danaus as his forehead furrowed with this bit of information. He seemed genuinely surprised. "What has confused you? That any human would do such a thing?"

He sat forward, balancing on the edge of the seat, his elbows braced on his knees. "You can feed without killing?"

"Of course,"

"I thought it was necessary for you to kill for your survival."

"If that were true, we would have completely wiped out humans long ago." I shook my head and then threaded a loose lock of hair behind my right ear. I had thought we finally put that old superstition to rest, but apparently it still lived on in Danaus, and maybe within this group that he was a part of. "Few kill, and most of the time it's an accident. In this day of DNA and fingerprints, it's too hard to kill and then deal with the body. We have a secret to keep so we feed carefully."

"But some still kill for sport." Fresh tension seemed to hum in his frame as his hands clenched the edge of the bench.

It became a fight not to clench my teeth. "Yes, and we take care of them." I had personally taken out more than my share of fellow nightwalkers who went out of control. I might like to poke the beehive of the Coven Elders, but knew better than to stir up the humans. I liked my comfortable lifestyle.

Staring at my new companion, I was surprised by the new thought that occurred to me. "You've not actually spoken with many of us, have you?"

Danaus snorted and shook his head as he sat back against the seat, resting his hands limply in his lap. "Why? So you can try to convince me that you're not soulless killers, spreading evil by converting humans? Nerian was right—you're parasites, feeding on humanity, your only drive to fulfill your own desires."

My head fell back and I laughed, my right hand covering my eyes. "How is that any different from humans?" I dropped my hand back to the leather seat, where I tapped my nails softly on the bench. "Haven't you just described humanity? Creatures surviving off the lives of others, driven to fulfill their own desires?"

He remained silent and I let the subject drop as the plane lifted into the air. We both had our own issues to work out, but I was still curious about him, and he was at my disposal for several hours.

"What are you, Danaus?" I asked. His eyes darted over to the bank of windows over my right shoulder, avoiding me. "I've been turning that question over in my head for more than a month now," I continued, as if he'd spoken. "I've known several odd creatures in my time, but nothing like you. You have all the trappings of a human—wrapped up in your very human anger—but at the same time you sit over there pulsing with power. Are you even aware that you're doing it? Your powers are so warm and alive, so wonderful. And the angrier you become, the stronger the pulse." He still hadn't looked at me, but I knew he was listening. His jaw hardened as he clenched his teeth and his eyes narrowed. I wondered how much he understood of himself.

"You know, you smell of the wind and of some distant sea. Sometimes I think it's the Mediterranean, but it has been too long since I stood where it lapped the shore. You also smell like the sun."

The description made the corner of his mouth quirk. He was suddenly fighting a smile. The description was strange, but it was the image conjured in my brain when I breathed him in.

"If you will not tell me what, then tell me how old you are."

He stared at the windows hard, and I had about given up when his lips finally parted. "I served as a guard under Marcus Aurelius." The accent I had heard when we first met flared to life again, teasing at my thoughts.

My brain shuffled through the card catalog of names in my mind, digging deeper for a time and place. It took only a moment, and when I placed it, my mouth fell open. Several minutes passed before I could organize my thoughts enough to form a coherent sentence. "You're nearly three times my age," I whispered, bringing a smile to his lips as his eyes finally returned to my face. "You look good for an old man." The smile faded. "It also means you're Roman in the truest form of the word. You watched the fall of the empire."

"I had left already," he volunteered in a low voice. While his expression never changed, the light in his eyes seemed to dim. Had the fall of the great empire bothered him? I think I wanted it to—it made him seem a little more real.

"Where have you been?" The question escaped me in a whisper of wonder and awe. I was just over six hundred years old, but it always filled me with a childlike giddiness when I encountered a creature older than me. I envied the knowledge their brains held, the sights they had seen that were now forever gone from this earth.

"Everywhere," he replied, his own rough voice sinking into softer tones. His eyelids drifted low, as if he were reliving some old memories. "Rome, then west across the Carpathian Mountains, through Russia and south through Mongolia into China. I came back through India, the Middle East, Africa, back through Europe, where I lived with monks." His eyes flicked back to my face and his voice hardened. "And across all those countries and through all the religions, one thing held true. Vampires are evil."

"How did you capture Nerian?" I asked. He blinked at me, his mind seeming to stumble over the abrupt change of topic. There was no discussing my species' right to live. Words would not be what convinced this man: only actions would accomplish that feat. Of course, I didn't expect him to live long enough for that.

Danaus pressed his lips into a thin line as his expression hardened. I was beginning to recognize that expression; his "I don't have to tell you anything, bitch" look.

Sitting forward on the leather sofa, I balanced my elbows on my knees. "You'll be asked that again, by those who have a lot less patience than I do. You can tell me now and we move on, or we can wait and let them drag it from your lips using pain. Whether you've realized this or not, I am the only buffer between you and them."

I sat back again, draping my left arm over the back of the sofa. Danaus was a rare gift. He was strong, powerful, and intelligent. I wanted the pleasure of picking apart his secrets, and then I wanted to hunt him. The challenge he offered was worth a little work, a little risk.

Minutes ticked by with only the roar of the wind outside the plane filling the tense air. He stared at me, as if weighing his options. They weren't great and I couldn't promise to protect him even if he did deliver the information. If an Elder stepped in, I would have to back off.

"Luck," he said at last.

"Luck?"

"He was following you. I caught him off guard and knocked him out."

I smiled and shook my head. I don't know whether I completely believed it, but only Nerian would be so cocky as to not pay attention to a human that close to him. Of course, I was beginning to wonder how badly I was underestimating Danaus as well.

"How long did you have him?"

"A week."

I nodded, rising to my feet. I stood in front of him for a moment, hands on hips, my legs spread against the slight turbulence. He tensed but his hands didn't move toward the knives concealed on his body. I didn't know how much, if any, information he had dragged out of the insane naturi, but a week was enough time to get some juicy tidbits. I was going to have to kill Danaus soon. His interesting qualities would be outweighed by the fact that he was becoming too dangerous to leave alive.

"Have you learned anything about Rowe?"

"Nothing yet. My contacts are still digging," he said.

I couldn't begin to guess at whom he was in contact with or how they would acquire information about the naturi. While nightwalkers stuck to the shadows and were diligent about maintaining our secrecy, the naturi were mere ghosts in this world.

With a sigh, I walked to the back of the jet and curled up in Michael's lap. He wrapped his large arms around me and held me against his chest. I placed my ear against his heart, letting the steady rhythm soothe my mind. My right hand restlessly played with the hair at the nape of his neck while the other rested on his shoulder. My thoughts calmed as I lay in his warmth.

I didn't want to be a part of this. I wanted to live in my city and seek pleasures where I found them. My great deed had been done more than five hundred years ago, and I walked away from my kind after that, never seeking a nightwalker companion for more than a night or two. But now I was being pulled back down into their ranks, sucked deeper into the mire. I could struggle all I wanted, but there would be no escaping.

NINE

I awoke to find myself locked in a box. For a brief moment a wave of panic surged through my frame and I nearly screamed. I thrust my hands against the top, which sank against the cool, silk lining. With eyes closed and teeth clenched, I willed the wave of fear to subside. It had been a long time since I'd done the old coffin bit. Most of the time, I slept in a windowless room on a king-sized bed covered in silk sheets. I had forgotten about traveling to Luxor, about Danaus, and Nerian. By now we should be drawing close to Aswan, home to the Tombs of the Nobles, the island temple of Philae, and the doorway to the old Nubian kingdom and Jabari.

With my hands on my stomach, I relaxed the muscles in my arms, waiting for the calm to sink back into the marrow of my bones. If I was going to steer myself out of this mess without getting killed, I needed to be calm and thinking clearly. Resisting the urge to sigh, I reached over and flipped the interior locks to the coffin. I call it a coffin, but it was actually a large box made of a nearly indestructible, lightweight alloy. The interior had been lined with red silk cushions, not that it really mattered. When daylight hit, I could sleep just as comfortably on a bed of broken glass. There was a pair of locks on the interior, ensuring that no one could open it from the outside. It went with me whenever I traveled, and I kept a spare at my private residence.

Pushing open the lid on its silent hinges, I sat up, grateful to find that no one was about to see my "rising from the dead" act. The quaint little room with walls made of dark wood was empty. The box rested on a full-sized bed covered with a colorful hand-stitched quilt. The curtains on the small windows were pulled back, revealing dark skies. Beyond, I could hear an engine running and the lap of water. We were traveling down the Nile. A ball of excitement tightened in my stomach and I struggled to keep from biting my lower lip like a giddy schoolgirl. It had been centuries since I last saw the sand dunes of Egypt.

I was climbing out of my private resting spot when someone knocked on the door. A brief stretch of my powers revealed that it was Michael, right on time. "Come in." He stepped into the room, wearing the same black shirt and pants from the previous night. His shoulder holster was missing, but I could feel Gabriel taking up his post at the door.

The young bodyguard was his usual handsome self, blond hair tossed by the wind. He already smelled of Egypt, with its exotic spices and history. His sharp blue eyes swept over the room as he cataloged his surroundings before settling back on me. He was good at his job, taking my protection very seriously. It was a nice feeling to have someone who wanted to see me rise every night. Sure, it was his job, but most of my own kind would rather shove a stake through my heart.

Prior to taking up the position as my bodyguard, Michael had briefly served in the Marines, accounting for most of his training. I didn't know how he came to be recruited by Gabriel and I'd never asked. My guardian angel had his connections and I left it at that.

At first, guarding me was just been a job for Michael; a well-paying job, but still just a job. After a couple of years that changed. For him, I became a source of strength and intense pleasure. I also fulfilled his deep need to protect.

For me, he became both a comfort and a distraction when my thoughts grew too dark. There was still something strangely innocent in his eyes and an eagerness to please me that was endearing. He treated me as though there was something still human in me. To him, I was never a monster, no matter what he saw me do.

I extended my hand to him, needing the physical contact. "Is all well?"

He wrapped his long fingers around my hand as he walked over to me, his intense gaze never straying from my face. "Yes."

The sound of the engine dulled and I concentrated on the steady throb of his heart. Its pace quickened the closer he came, causing his face to flush. "Was there any trouble in Luxor?"

"No, everything went as Ms. Godwin instructed. We have just come within sight of Aswan. The captain says we should dock in another fifteen minutes."

When he stood only inches from me, I released his hand and slid my palms up his arms and across his shoulders. I had taken my boots off before dawn, putting me at a flat-footed five feet six inches at best; rather tall considering people six hundred years ago were much shorter but still roughly a foot shorter than my guardian angel.

His warm lips brushed against my temple in a gentle caress. "I missed you." He lifted his hands and lightly placed them on the sides of my waist as if he was afraid he would break me with his touch.

"I guess I should travel more," I whispered, threading my fingers through his hair, enjoying the feel of his silky locks.

His lips moved down from my temple and along the line of my jaw. "We could meet outside of work."

A low noise similar to a cat's purr rumbled from the back of my throat, and I rose up on the tips of my toes so his soft lips could reach more of my flesh. I needed Michael. I needed his warmth and vitality. It reminded me of my own shredded humanity. It also fought back the darker urges that screamed for me to throw him to the ground and drain him dry.

"I think something can be arranged." My lips brushed against his throat as I spoke, teasing me. So close. Less than an inch and my fangs would be embedded.

"Yes." There was more air in the word than actual sound. His hands tightened on my waist. I could feel the trembling need in the muscles stretching up his arms. He was fighting the desire to crush me against his body, molding me to him. From past encounters, he knew I liked to prolong the moment when time allowed, basking in all the sensations flooding my mind.

"Lay on the bed," I said, stepping back from him. Michael moved around me and pushed the box to the far side of the bed. He stretched out his long body and for a moment I stood at his side, admiring his peaceful expression. I had spent the first few centuries of my existence hunting down my prey, wrestling them to the ground, and it always felt a little strange when my meal came to me with arms open. Some of the rush spilled from the moment, but my thirst was already starting to make itself known, petty thoughts pushed to the back of my mind.

Crawling onto the bed, I straddled his narrow hips. I was beginning to see a distinct pattern when it came to the men in my life, but the position made feeding easier. It also allowed me the pleasure of pressing the full length of my body against his. I leaned forward with my forearms on each side of his head and pressed slow kisses against each eyelid, his nose, and along his left jaw. Beneath me, I felt him sigh as if the tension was unraveling from around his soul. I pressed a long, lingering kiss to his lips, carefully drawing his tongue in my mouth, enjoying the taste of him. His strong hands slipped under my shirt and slid up my bare back, pulling me more tightly against him. His body hardened beneath me and I suppressed my own frustrated sigh. There just wasn't enough time for everything.

Pulling reluctantly away from his mouth, I slid my lips down his jaw to his throat. The tip of my tongue ran over the heavy pulse that throbbed there before I finally sank my fangs deep into his flesh. He stiffened against the sudden pain then relaxed again. Drawing the sweet blood into my body, I sent a warm, tingling wave of intense pleasure through his body. He moaned as it swept into his limbs. I drank deeply, pulling his life into my thin frame until I could taste his heartbeat, feel it vibrating down in my own chest.

His hands slid down over my rear, kneading my body, keeping me pressed against him. He moaned my name; his hips shifted and rose off the bed. Except for our clothes, he would have been inside of me. The thought sent a shudder through my taut body, and I twisted the blankets in my fists. The feeling of his warm blood filling my veins was already quite satisfying, but the desire to have all of him was coiling tighter in my body. I ground my hips against him, a pure animal growl rumbling in the back of my throat as I reveled in the hardness of his body.

Releasing my grip on the blanket, I slipped my left hand under his shirt, running it up along his ribs. My thumb grazed his nipple before heading back down to his flat stomach. His skin was so warm and enticing, an intoxicating combination of hard muscle and soft flesh.

My hand brushed against the button on his pants as my fingers skimmed along the soft flesh just below the edge of his underwear. His hips lifted again, pressing into me, his body demanding entrance. With every last ounce of self-control I had, I put my hand back beside his head, wrapping my fingers in the blanket. I wanted him so badly I could scream, but I wouldn't be happy with a quickie. It had been too long and I wanted to linger over him. And Michael was worth the wait.

I lifted my mouth from his neck with great reluctance and nuzzled his ear for a moment. Focusing my powers on his neck, I closed the wound, leaving behind only a slight redness in the area. "We cannot, my angel. Not this time." Leaning up on my forearms, I looked into his face. He watched me with wide, heartbroken eyes. "If sunset had come but an hour sooner I would happily linger over you, but time will not allow." I ran my tongue over my bottom lip, drawing in the last bit of his blood, and he sighed, moving his hands up the back of my thighs, keeping me pressed against him.

I laughed and shook my head as I got off the bed. "But you are a temptation," I said, unbuttoning my shirt.

"Not enough of one," he said with a little bit of a pout. He watched as I stripped down and walked over to my bag of clothes, which lay at the foot of the bed.

"Sorry, but this is not a pleasure trip. There are serious matters I must handle."

His eyes greedily followed me as I pulled on a pair of red silk panties, then a black cotton skirt that fell to my ankles. Then came a red lace bra and a black button-up shirt with short sleeves. Michael sat up, resting his back against the headboard when I sat on the edge of the bed next to his hip. He was a little paler than he had been when he came in. I never took so much blood that his life was in danger or that he couldn't fight, just enough to take the edge off of my hunger. With any luck, I would begin the return trip home tonight and hunt again in my own domain tomorrow night.

"Are you sure you don't want Gabriel and me to accompany you?" he asked as I drew on a pair of socks.

"No, I'll be fine."

That was a lie. I was anxious and confused, but telling him my fears wouldn't have made him feel any better. His job was to protect me when I could not protect myself, which was only during the daylight hours. Michael and Gabriel protected me against humans only. They were no match for any of the other dark creatures that lurked in the night. How could they hope to protect me against Danaus or the naturi?

I shoved my feet into a pair of black boots with a low chunk heel that laced up to nearly my knees. These were built a little better for the terrain than my usual high-heeled leather boots. I ran my hand through my tousled hair, wishing I had time and access to a quick shower.

"But he will be going with you," Michael said. There was something sharp and bitter in his tone that startled me, breaking my mind free of the last lingering tendrils of desire that had clouded my thoughts.

Turning my gaze back to his handsome face, I was surprised to find lines of anger and jealousy furrowing his brow. "I do as I please," I quietly reminded him.

"I'm sorry, Mira," he said, hesitantly touching my shoulder. A look of fear flashed through his pale blue eyes. We both knew this budding relationship was a strained and uneasy thing as we sought out each other's boundaries. "I didn't mean anything."

I sighed, placing my hand against his cheek. He relaxed instantly and pressed a kiss to my palm. "I know. Danaus is part of the matter that I must take care of. Rest for a while. I am going up to the deck. I will meet you and Gabriel at the hotel before dawn."

Walking up to the main deck, I ran my hand across Gabriel's shoulder as I passed him. He followed me at a discreet distance, hanging back toward the shadows as I strolled over to the railing of the barge. The dark night sky was filled with glittering stars. It had been a while since I'd seen so many stars, but they were quickly being overwhelmed by the growing brightness of Aswan. When I had last appeared in the town, it was only a scattering of huts, low buildings, and a single wooden dock. While it was nowhere near the size of Cairo or Alexandria, it was swelling in its own right. The tourists were starting to grow weary of the pyramids and were traveling farther down the Nile to see the mysteries of Philae and the beauty of Abu Simbel.

The wind played with my hair, tossing it about my back. I closed my eyes and slowly reached out with my senses. It was like running my hands over the people in the city, gently touching each mind for less than a heartbeat then moving on. I let my senses reach out as far as the Tombs of the Nobles and down through Abu Simbel before pulling my powers back into my body. I could not feel Jabari, though I'm not sure if I was expecting to find him.

The battle at Machu Picchu five centuries ago had not gone well, despite the fact that we were the victors. Two weeks earlier I'd been kidnapped from Sadira's care in Spain and taken to the Incan city in the sky. Surrounded by members of the naturi light clan at all times, Nerian tortured me by moonlight while all-too-sweet voices promised that the pain would stop if I only promised to protect them from the evil vampires. If not for my constant thirst for blood, I would even have forgotten, under the weight of the unrelenting pain, that I was a vampire. For two weeks there was only pain and hunger.

And then Jabari arrived. The rest of the triad was with him, as well as a great nightwalker army, yet looking back, I recalled only him. His white robes seemed to glow in the firelight, his dark skin almost as black as the night itself. He had saved me and fought the naturi. But still, only the triad and a handful of others escaped that wretched mountain, while some of the naturi disappeared into the surrounding jungle.

While Jabari hunted the naturi, he left me a wounded Nerian to finish. I broke his legs and slashed his stomach open, but dawn was coming. I was out of time. I left Nerian to die while I ran from the mountain. In the jungle, I buried myself deep into the earth to escape the sun's rays, confident that Nerian had died on the mountaintop.

The next night, Jabari returned for me. Held tightly in his strong arms, he carried me off to the safety of his home in Egypt. I remained with the Ancient for one century. He helped to keep the nightmares at bay during both the night and the day, when I should have been able to escape my battered psyche.

Jabari gave me something I had managed to find only briefly during my human years and never as a vampire: a home. Within his domain, I was always welcome. I was viewed as a beloved child, a talented protégé to be taught and encouraged. Sadira had taught me to read, to play instruments, and even various languages. But with Jabari, I gained true knowledge. He taught me the history of our kind, of the naturi and the bori, and the war that consumed all of the races before the bori and naturi were finally exiled.

While I was with Jabari, he encouraged me to explore my ability to manipulate fire. For the Ancient, it wasn't about being a weapon, but honing a skill, becoming better at something. Under his guidance, I took back control of my life, no longer a pawn for Sadira or the naturi.

Opening my eyes, I frowned, a chill encasing my lungs. There were no other nightwalkers within the area. Egypt had always been sporadically populated with my kind because of Jabari's presence. No one wanted to risk catching the attention of an Elder. Yet, it had been a long time since I walked into a region that didn't have several nightwalkers lurking in the shadows. I might not seek out another nightwalker, but there was something comforting in knowing that he or she was there. That I wasn't completely alone in the darkness.

I turned my head, catching sight of Danaus out of the corner of my eye. He had approached while my focus was on the city and surrounding area. The leather duster was gone, but he still wore his black cotton pants and black sleeveless T-shirt. There were several knives strapped to his waist, wrists, and thigh. He was prepared for battle.

"I see you've fed," he said as he stepped closer to the railing. I resisted the urge to run my finger over my lips. I generally wasn't a messy eater. "You're . . . pink," he continued, filling in the silence. The word stumbled and tripped from his throat as if he struggled for an appropriate description.

Throwing my head back, I laughed, the sound drawing the attention of several deckhands. I always looked a bit flushed after a good meal, my skin taking on a pinker, more lifelike color for a few hours, but I hadn't expected him to notice. He wasn't looking particularly happy with me; not that he ever was, but his glare seemed more censuring than usual.

Leaning back, my elbows rested lightly on the rails. "Have you eaten?" He nodded, his gaze directed at the dock as we pulled in. "I bet something died for your meal."

His narrowed eyes jerked to my face. "It's not the same." His jaw was clenched and his lips pressed into a hard, thin line. Hot, angry power bubbled within him, pulsing against me in waves that would have rivaled the midday sun that baked the Egyptian landscape. "Why not?" I turned and walked toward the bow, my eyes on Aswan. I didn't expect an answer or want one. There shouldn't be a difference. I didn't care what he thought. We both did what we had to in order to survive; it was as simple as that.

It wasn't long afterward that we docked at Aswan, our little boat skirting several larger cruise ships to settle at a less crowded berth. I jumped down to the wooden dock, not looking back to see if Danaus had followed. But I could feel him a few steps behind me, his anger simmering. I was irritated with him. At least, I think he was bothering me. It could have been that I was forced to cut short my time with Michael, or that I didn't know where the hell Jabari was. It could have even been the fact that the naturi were once again threatening and I didn't want to face them. It could have been any or all of these things, but right now Danaus was an easy target.

I paused on the Corniche el-Nil for a moment, gazing up and down the road as I tried to get my bearings. The road ran north-south along Aswan closest to the Nile, housing a variety of travel agencies, which in turn managed the various motor launches and feluccas that ferried tourists to the islands that dotted this stretch of the Nile. We had landed farther south in Aswan than I'd anticipated. Directly in front of me was the Nile and Elephantine Island, and beyond that, Kitchener's Island, with its exotic botanic gardens. One block over behind me, the rich sounds of the souq could be heard. Vendors would be at their trade for another few hours, hawking their wares to anyone who passed close enough to be considered a potential customer. Vibrant Nubian music filled the air, played on pear-shaped guitars called ouds and shallow douff drums. The sun had set, but the city was just coming alive as people finally escaped the oppressive heat of the day.

During my stay with Jabari, we had passed most of our time farther north, in Thebes and occasionally in Alexandria. Because I needed to feed more frequently than he did, the Ancient thoughtfully lingered near populous areas, though I suspected he would have preferred to move to a more remote, secluded location. On two occasions we took trips up the Nile to Aswan, where we stayed within the local Nubian villages; Jabari's true home.

Just prior to moving to the New World, I encountered Jabari in Venice during one of my infrequent visits to the Coven. He spoke of moving south to Aswan to oversee the construction of the first Aswan dam. It would flood the areas that had once been the heart of the Nubian empire. While I never had a chance to ask him decades later, I was confident that the Ancient Nubian had also overseen the construction of the High Dam and the careful moving of Abu Simbel and Philae to a safer, drier location.

Walking north along Corniche el-Nil, I weaved my way through the crowds as they stepped off their feluccas and headed back toward their hotels, with Danaus following like a dark rain cloud. The people barely looked up at me as I passed by. The city had a feeling about it that whispered of darker things than me. Jabari had spent his entire existence in this part of the world. He had ventured elsewhere, seen the green lands of South America and the cold tundra of Russia, but he always came back to his beloved Egypt. I think the people of Aswan could feel him when he was there. They never understood what it was they were feeling, though; perhaps assumed it was one of the old gods lingering in the temples or a pharaoh's ghost.

I wondered if they felt his absence. The people hurried down the streets with their heads down, careful not to make eye contact. The Middle East had always been rife with civil unrest, but now there was an edge to the people that I couldn't understand. Maybe they knew their god was missing.

After a few blocks I finally found what I was searching for. Unfortunately, the ferry to the West Bank was closed for the night. Aswan lay on the East Bank, overflowing with rich vegetation, hotels, and shops. The West Bank was mostly desert, with only a few monuments visited by tourists throughout the day. However, all those monuments closed by 5:00 P.M., so there was no reason for the ferry to remain open past that hour.

Shoving my hand through my hair, I turned where I stood, gazing up and down Corniche for an open felucca. It was only a guess, but I truly doubted that Jabari would have settled near the busy heart of Aswan. There were two types of nightwalkers: those that ran from their past, such as myself, and those that still embraced their human history, like Jabari. I knew where he would have gone. I just had to get there.

A smile lifted my lips as my eyes fell on a young man with skin like rich coffee as he was tying up his small felucca. It couldn't have held more than six people, smaller than most used by tourists, but he could have easily advertised it as a more private excursion.

I bargained for the price of a quick jaunt across the Nile to the landing for the Tombs of the Nobles. He was polite enough to at least ask if I was aware of the fact that the Tombs were closed, but he didn't push the matter. What did he care? He would get paid whether I was turned away at the entrance or not.

Danaus and I boarded the small boat and the captain pushed off from the dock and immediately unfurled the white sail. Between the brisk wind and the swift flow of the Nile, we were able to cross to the West Bank in only a few minutes. Something in me wished for more time, though. I would have liked to head farther up river to see the Temple of Philae in her new home, bathed in the glow of golden floodlights. Or even gone down river to Edfu and the Temple of Horus. While a Roman replica of ancient Egyptian architecture, the temple still outdated my lengthy existence and was magnificent to see. But for now, I sat in a tiny boat with a vampire hunter while I searched for an Ancient vampire that might or might not be dead.

TEN

anaus said nothing until we hired a pair of camels and started riding northwest into the desert, past the Tombs of the Nobles. I looked over my shoulder once as we topped the massive hill to see Aswan spread out before me, glittering in the night, with the Nile gliding like a black asp toward the north. We were leaving behind the last signs of civilization.

"Where are we going?" the hunter called from his camel behind me.

My gaze remained on the rock formation to the west that was steadily growing in size. It was the western quarry. "Seeking the key to the triad."

"Which is?" he prompted after a few seconds of silence.

"Who is, you mean."

"Mira . . ."

I smiled. There weren't too many creatures that could reduce my name to a low warning growl, but Danaus was quite successful. "Jabari."

"I thought you said he was dead."

A warm wind swept across the desert from the south, carrying with it the faintest hint of the Nile. The only sound in this vast wasteland was the muffled footsteps of the camels as they steadily maneuvered through the soft sand. There was no life out here beyond the snakes and scorpions. Not for the first time, I wondered if I was gazing at the reason why the Ancients of my race were dwindling. As time passed, Jabari spent less time in the company of the living, preferring the solitude of the vast desert terrain he ruled. And while Tabor had been barely more than half Jabari's age when he was murdered, I knew he had taken to spending more time in Russia's icy tundra than in the western cities of Moscow and St. Petersburg.

While we never aged and were completely immune to disease, my species struggled to last more than a few millennia at best. What was the point of immortality if you couldn't live for more than a couple thousand years?

I bit back a sigh and absently patted my camel's neck, running my finger over its coarse hair. "I don't know. Jabari was always the strongest of the triad. If he is gone, I would like to know if the naturi are responsible."

I didn't know what had happened to Jabari. I suspected that I should have gone straight to the Coven, but I wouldn't have been able to keep the hunter at my side, and for now, I didn't want him out of my sight. Besides, my interaction with the Coven had always been through Jabari. I didn't know how to directly contact Macaire or Elizabeth, the two other members of the ruling vampire body. I didn't think anyone in the Coven would have tried to destroy Jabari. He was one of the oldest and strongest of the Elders, just below Our Liege. Besides, getting any kind of answer from the Coven was proving to be a waste of my time. And for the first time since becoming a nightwalker, I had a feeling that time was in short supply.

After a thirty-minute ride through the desert, we finally reached the great rock outcropping that rose up around us. An anxious knot tightened in my stomach as I dismounted from the camel. The wind had stopped and the desert seemed to hold its breath as the shadows created by broken slabs of rock watched us in silence.

Danaus started to walk around me and enter the quarry, but I placed my hand in the center of his chest, stopping him. One last time I stretched out my powers, scanning the area. I reached out into the desert and back toward the Tombs and to Aswan, searching for any sign that a nightwalker was near. There was nothing, and it hurt. It hurt more than I wanted to admit. There was no Jabari. Only something dire would draw him away from this area for so long. Maybe he already knew about the naturi and was with the Coven, but for some reason, I didn't believe it. I'd left messages with every contact I had with the Coven and heard nothing. I'd even checked one last time when I awoke in Egypt, but no one responded. With a slight shake of my head, I headed into the quarry with the hunter close at my side. We were on our own.

Slowly, we picked our way around giant boulders and slabs that had been smoothed with ancient hammers and chisels but never taken to the monuments they were intended for. I paused beside an unfinished obelisk. Three sides had been smoothed and carved with hieroglyphics and other images. The fourth side was still unfinished after countless centuries. Abandoned.

"Why here?" Danaus said, standing beside me. "Of all the places in Egypt, why would he be here?"

My hand slid over the unfinished obelisk, images of the last time I had walked through this quarry flashing through my brain. I could recall it as if it had happened only moments ago. I'd been feeling restless then, in no mood to be around the peoples of Alexandria while memories of the naturi haunted my daylight rest, and Jabari brought me down to Aswan. We'd wandered up one side of the Nile and down the other, allowing the quiet to seep into our skin. Walking beside me, Jabari had explained all that went into creating an obelisk of this size.

"Jabari was one of the chief architects for Amenophis II. He designed parts of Karnak," I told Danaus, pride bringing a wavering smile to my mouth as I stared into the emptiness. Jabari had told me of a trip he made to Aswan when he was human, and to two of the quarries here to inspect the stones that would be shipped back to Karnak. Though he never spoke of it, I always got the impression that he never had the chance to finish his life's work at Karnak because his human life had ended somewhere between Aswan and Luxor.

"What are we looking for?" Danaus asked.

Holding out my left hand, I conjured up a small flame, which flickered in the breeze that begun to stir once again. "A sign." Closing my hand around the flame, I tossed it out into the night before us. The flame split into six separate balls of fire and shot out into the deep reaches of the quarry. Shadows danced and retreated around us, revealing their secrets. If Jabari had fought the naturi here, there would be signs of a battle. The rock wall would have new scars, the earth gouged, but above all I would have been able to sense Jabari's death. I was around when nightwalkers were destroyed, had even killed a couple Ancients myself. I knew that a ripple of magic was left in the air when a nightwalker was destroyed, and it lingered for years. The older the nightwalker, the thicker the mark. If Jabari had been destroyed here, I would see it and feel it.

"This is unexpected," stated a deep voice from behind me. We both spun around to find Jabari standing at the top of the unfinished obelisk.

At just over six feet, he was an impressive figure in his traditional robes. Even for a vampire, his skin was still dark, midnight hair cut short on his head. His almond-shaped, mahogany eyes watched me, questioning. He hadn't directed his gaze at Danaus yet and he wouldn't. To recognize Danaus's presence was to give him importance.

Despite the fact that he was standing just a few feet away from me, I still could not sense him. It was like he wasn't really there. I hadn't moved from the base of the obelisk, couldn't even drag my voice past the lump that swelled in my throat. It was like staring at a ghost.

His eyes softened and he raised a hand toward me, beckoning me to his side. It was all the encouragement I needed. I scrambled up the obelisk until I nearly collapsed against him. Wrapping my arms around him, I pressed my cheek to his shoulder. My teeth were clenched so hard my jaws ached as I swallowed the sob that had knotted in my throat. He hadn't been destroyed. He was real and right here.

For a moment my world threatened to crumble. Centuries had passed since I last stood with him in his beloved Egypt, held in his benevolent arms. He had helped me recover from horrors I thought would plague my dreams for all eternity. And then one day I left and never looked back. I stood on my own two feet. But now I stood there holding him as if he were my last tie to sanity.

"Welcome home, my little one," Jabari whispered as he pressed a kiss to the top of my head. His beautiful accent skipped to my ears, seeming to caress my frazzled nerves. He wrapped his strong arms around me, holding me tightly against his chest. "The Old Kingdom has missed you."

Jabari represented more than just a mentor. In many ways he was also the voice of the Coven when Our Liege deigned to remain in the background. During the past few decades, I had been absent from Europe and the Coven, preferring to direct my focus to establishing a steady, consistent balance in my own domain. While nothing negative was ever said about my choice, a dark undercurrent had started to form, strengthened by the growing silence I was receiving from Venice. I needed Jabari to protect my back.

"I feared things must be bad to drive you back here, my desert flower," he murmured, running one hand down the back of my head, smoothing my hair.

I shuddered, struggling desperately to pull myself back together. Jabari was the only vampire in this world that I trusted. He was all I knew of safety and love among my own kind. "Why can't I sense you?"

"I did not wish to be found." There was no censure in his voice, just a statement of fact.

"Forgive me," I said, reluctantly releasing him. "I had few options."

Taking a few steps away from him, I ran a trembling hand through my hair to push it back from my face. My thoughts were coming back into focus. With a wave of my hand, I extinguished the balls of fire that flickered around the quarry. I hadn't expected to find the Elder. Hoped and wished, but never expected it. Yet, he was here now, and he would fix everything.

"You are forgiven," he said, bowing his head in a single, regal nod. "What has brought you to my lands?"

"The naturi."

Those two words sounded flat and dead to my ears. Something seemed to die inside of me every time I mentioned them. I watched Jabari's face, but there was no change in his expression. There was nothing to reveal that he was surprised by what I'd said, or that he had known the naturi was once again threatening to return.

"How?"

"Their symbols have begun to appear on trees, and there was a sacrifice at the Indian Temple of the Sun, Konark." I paused and licked my lips, forcing myself to hold Jabari's piercing gaze. "Nerian was also following me. The naturi attacked us—"

"How is that possible?" Jabari interrupted, though his voice remained even and calm. "You were to kill Nerian more than five hundred years ago."

I took a hesitant step forward, holding both hands out to him. "I thought he was dead."

"Thought?"

I never saw Jabari move. One second he was standing still more than three feet away, and in the next I was flying through the air. My back slammed into the wall of broken rocks. Stars exploded in front of my eyes as my head hit half a breath later. I slid down the wall, my left shoulder striking the ground. Blinking, I looked up to see Jabari step off the obelisk and walk toward me. His expression was still calm and emotionless, but the air tingled now with his anger.

"You were ordered to kill him."

"His legs were broken and his intestines had spilled onto the ground. I didn't think he would survive." I pushed myself off the ground. In my haste, my hand slid in the dirt and rocks, tearing at my palm. Pain screamed through my shoulder and down my spine as I moved.

"The naturi held you captive for two weeks," Jabari argued. "We never could discover all that they did to you. You were a threat to all nightwalkers and were only permitted to live because Nerian was dead. You should have made sure."

"It was dawn!" I screamed. Panic fluttered in my stomach, begging me to run. It was only years after Machu Picchu that I discovered Jabari had defended me from the rest of the Coven, which demanded my destruction. He had saved my life not only from the naturi, but from my own kind as well.

"That's not an excuse." Jabari's right hand lashed out, grabbing me around the throat. I didn't even have enough time to claw at his hand before he tossed me against another outcropping of rocks like a rag doll. "You failed me."

Pain slashed like lightning through my back as I hit the wall and fell to the floor. "He's dead now," I whispered, doubting I had the strength to rise before he attacked again.

"Centuries too late." His sweet features hardened and his brown eyes had darkened to black clouds in a midnight storm.

My eyes fell closed, holding back the tears that started to gather. I had failed him. Jabari had always been able to depend on me for any request, no matter the task. He had given me so much, and I'd failed him. And now he was going to destroy me just like any other night-walker who failed to live up to his expectations. A part of me welcomed it, an escape from the pain, but a faint brush of Danaus's power quickly reminded me why we had traveled to Egypt; the naturi. If Jabari destroyed me, no one would be able to protect my home, my people. It was enough that I had failed Jabari, I wouldn't fail all those who had come to rely on me.

I opened my eyes at the sound of a foot scraping in the dirt. Danaus suddenly stepped between Jabari and me, the blade of an eight-inch knife glinting in the faint starlight. My body was sore and protesting, but I pushed to my feet. This was not the wisest decision on Danaus's part nor could I even begin to understand it. Jabari would destroy him before the poor creature could draw a breath, and I still needed Danaus alive.

"This does not solve the problem of the naturi," Danaus said, his hard voice calm.

"Not only do you fail me, one whom I trusted above all others," Jabari began, finally beginning to shout, "but you bring this . . . this human into my domain!"

Standing beside Danaus, I tried to edge in front of him and keep Jabari's attention on me. "He was the one who captured Nerian. He showed me pictures of the symbols and the sacrifice."

"You betrayed me!" Jabari closed the distance in a blur, grabbing Danaus by the throat. He pitched the hunter a hundred feet across the quarry as if he were tossing garbage out to the curb. Danaus crashed into a smooth wall of rock, cracking and crumbling stone. I winced, gritting my teeth. The impact alone should have shattered the man's spine and broken at least one of his shoulders. I started to drag my eyes back to Jabari, the muscles in my body tensed and waiting for the attack, when I saw Danaus pick himself up off the ground. He rolled his shoulders as if shaking off the momentary pain.

Something in my blood froze. After that bone-crushing impact, Danaus should not have been able to move, let alone stand and prepare for yet another attack from Jabari. My thoughts tripped over themselves as I tried to understand how he was now standing. I didn't know of any creatures other than nightwalkers that might be able to shrug off such a blow. Even a lycan would have been slow to regain his feet.

I think the realization also alarmed Jabari, because I felt the power in the area increase until it was a physical pressure weighing against my chest. The hunter had been upgraded from "bug to be squashed" to "threat that must be eliminated," regardless of Danaus's potential uses. I wanted the hunter dead as much as any other nightwalker, but we needed to get some information out of him first.

Jabari lunged at Danaus again, but despite the Elder's alarming speed, Danaus managed to sidestep him so that the nightwalker's attack was reduced to more of a glancing blow. However, it was still enough to knock Danaus back a step, sending him down on one knee, his knife clenched in one hand.

I balled my fists at my side. What the hell was going on? Danaus wasn't using his knife. He was doing what he could to defend himself without attacking Jabari outright. I didn't know if Jabari had noticed or if he just didn't care. At least Danaus had realized that we needed the information from the Elder, and so wasn't trying to kill him. Yet, if this continued, he would have no choice and one of them would end up dead.

While Danaus was still kneeling on the ground, glaring at Jabari, I rushed over and stood in front of the hunter. Rage now burned on Jabari's face, and I knew I had only seconds to get through to him.

"Jabari, I have not betrayed you," I said, no longer trying to keep the fear out of my voice. My hands trembled uncontrollably and my knees threatened to buckle. "I made a mistake with Nerian, and if you wish to kill me for that, I accept my fate, but bringing Danaus here was not an act of betrayal. I want you to see how desperate we are. The naturi are coming again. If the seal is broken, they will destroy not only the humans, but the nightwalkers as well."

"Do not lecture me!" Jabari's upper lip remained pulled back, and I fought to draw my gaze from his long fangs. He was going to tear my throat out if I didn't think of something.

"Danaus is a hunter, and yet he came to me looking for a way to stop the naturi. I remember so little of that night, and I don't want to remember. I came here hoping to find you, needing you to reform the triad that stopped the naturi the last time."

Behind me Danaus had risen and took one step forward, as if trying to move around me. He apparently wasn't the type to let anyone protect him, but he was going to get himself killed before I could get any more information out of him. I sidled so that I was standing directly in front of him. Reaching back, I grabbed a wrist in each hand. He stiffened at my touch, but I could still move his arms. I pulled his right arm around my waist, his knife still clutched in his hand. I drew up his left arm between my breasts so his left hand was holding my right shoulder. If Jabari was going to kill Danaus, he would have to go through me first. I wasn't completely sure that it would stop him, but I was hoping to buy us a couple more seconds.

The muscles in my body spasmed for a second when Danaus's left hand closed over my shoulder like a circuit closing, wrapping me in his powers. Between the weight of Jabari's powers and the tense strength charging through Danaus, a hand seemed to clench around my soul. A sharp little cry broke from my throat as I struggled to pull my thoughts above the flow of power. A second later I managed to surface and blink, focusing my thoughts again.

Jabari stared at me, his lips pressed into a hard, thin line. The anger had not completely ebbed from his eyes, but something else had distracted his thoughts. He took a half step backward, his brow furrowed. I could only imagine he was shocked to find I was willing to risk my life for a hunter; someone who would cut out my heart before saving me. I couldn't blame him. I was more than a little surprised myself, but the threat of the naturi had put us in an awkward position.

"It does not make sense to kill him when he has information that could be useful," I said. "I came to you because you were at Machu Picchu. You have always been the strongest of the triad. I came to you because I trust no one else."

The silence stretched and twisted in the quarry, the wind dying back down to nothing as the Ancient stared at me, his expression dark and unreadable. "You defend him as if he means more."

Something jerked in my stomach, a new, dark fear springing to life. This was bad. Had Lucas already been whispering to the Coven about me? Were rumors spread by Lucas the reason why I had heard nothing back from the Coven during the past couple of nights?

"I defend him because it is the wise thing to do. I will not throw valuable information away because I do not like its messenger." I definitely didn't like where this was going. If I had learned anything in my six centuries, it was to never prick the ego of a vampire. And the older they were, the worse it would be. I had managed to calm Jabari, and I thought he might have even begun to see the wisdom of what I was saying, but that didn't change the fact that a creature well beneath him in age and power had corrected him. He still had to exact his retribution.

"Would you turn on your own people to protect this hunter?" His deceptively calm voice wrapped around me before sliding into my brain. The peaceful tone of the question belied the underlying menace that lurked in the shadows.

"My loyalty belongs only to those who have earned it."

"Has he? A destroyer of our kind?"

An overwhelming urge to take a step backward trembled in my limbs, but with Danaus behind me, it was difficult to move. "I protect him to save our kind from the naturi, nothing more."

"And when the naturi are gone?" His voice had become calm and even. So much so that we could have been discussing the weather. He had straightened from his previously aggressive stance, his thin body perfectly erect.

"Then I will deliver his life to your hands. I will deliver us both if that is what you wish." Behind me, I felt Danaus stiffen, but he never made a sound, leaving me to my desperate pleading. "You have been both a friend and protector, Jabari. If it is my life you want, then it is yours, but I do not think it will save us from the naturi." I wanted to reach out and cup his face with my hands, to kiss his neck and swear my complete devotion to him, but I couldn't move. I knew I had already lost him.

Jabari approached us, each step careful and precise. He stopped less than two feet away and his voice was barely over a whisper. "It is not your life I want, my Mira." His words were coated so thickly with ice, I shuddered and closed my eyes. Danaus tightened his arms around me, pulling me harder against his chest. His warmth seeped into me through my bare arms and the cotton material of my shirt. The panic faded, enough so I could speak.

"Do not say it, Jabari."

"It is my right to ask."

But that was the big joke; it wasn't a request. When an Elder asked to make you a Companion, you had no choice but to accept. Refusal only meant death. Most would not hesitate to accept such an offer. Though the position was dangerous, it was prestigious. But it also took away all independence, all individual will and rights. This was the punishment Jabari had chosen. Not death. He would wear me down until I was a pale shadow of my former self, driving me to the point where I lay down in the dawn light.

"You know my answer," I said in a low voice. My hands tightened on Danaus's arm to the point of my nails digging into his flesh.

"Mira—"

My head snapped up and I knew my eyes were glowing, a strange blue-purple like bittersweet nightshade. Death in battle held its own honor, and I could face that. What Jabari offered was slavery. My power welled up inside my chest until it was pressing against the inside of my skin, desperate for release. "Do not place us on this precipice," I warned, my tone taking on a hard edge. "I will destroy us both; to hell with the naturi."

Without actually conjuring the thought, a deep blue flame sprang from the earth at my feet. It quickly circled Danaus and me, then rose in intensity until the flames reached my chest. Never had I created a fire against Jabari, but I would not become his slave.

He stared at me through the flickering blue flames, holding his ground. He would never forgive me for this, I knew it. Anger had made his face pale and drawn.

"Let us save our race now," I bargained. "We have all eternity to destroy each other."

The tension was making me a bit hysterical, and the power in the quarry was crushing my brain. My thoughts were scattered and broken at best. I needed to put some distance between these two men or it would drive me mad.

A frigid smile grew on Jabari's face, and he bared pristine white teeth at me. "This is not over."

"I have no doubt," I snapped.

Jabari nodded once and then turned his back on us. He walked over to the end of the unfinished obelisk, his hand running reverently along its smooth surface. The flames shrank back down to the ground and disappeared. Danaus released his steely grip on me and I fell forward to my knees. A chill ran up my arms and I felt as if I'd been dragged through the street behind a runaway carriage.

I forced myself to stand. My knees threatened to give, but I didn't sway as I turned to look at Jabari. He was staring down at the obelisk, a fragment from his past. His face was once again calm and completely unreadable.

"I will think on what you have told me. We will talk again tomorrow." He reached up and ran one hand over his close-cut hair, his gaze out into the night. I had been dismissed.

"May I find rest in your lands?" I asked. A new fear twisted in my stomach as he remained silent. I was a stranger in his domain and I had to ask his permission to remain. All vampires had to present themselves before the Keeper of the domain. If he refused, I had to leave his lands before the sun rose. This would be particularly difficult considering that Jabari's domain encompassed most of Northern Africa and a scattering of islands in the Mediterranean.

"You may rest here," he slowly said, as if he doubted his decision.

"Thank you." I looked over at Danaus and motioned for him to leave. He hesitated a moment, his eyes darting from me to Jabari. Then without a word he slipped past me and headed toward where the camels had settled.

I stared at Jabari, his body straight and almost painfully erect. I wondered if he hurt as badly as I did. Tonight my heart had shattered in a way I hadn't thought possible after all these long centuries. He still thought I had betrayed him, and whatever wonderful thing that once existed between us had died. He would never forgive me.

"I love you, Jabari. I have loved and trusted you above all else," I whispered. "And even after what has happened tonight and with the knowledge that you will one day kill me, I still love you and will never stop." I don't know if he was listening or if he even cared. I had to say the words. I had to release them into the air so I could be free of the terrible weight on my heart.

Turning, I walked out of the quarry. I wanted him to call for me. I wanted to hear him say that he had loved me too, or that he forgave me, but he didn't make a sound; didn't move as I walked away from him. As I exited the quarry, I conjured up a small flame on the palm of my hand against the overwhelming darkness. I watched it wriggle and dance for a moment. Staring at that tender bit of light, I realized why I had retained this power even after death. If there were such a thing as fate, I had been put on this earth to destroy and not to create.

ELEVEN

The moon hung pale and swollen overhead in the night sky. Clouds crept over the stars, blotting out their glittering light and holding in the oppressive heat of summer. I stood in the main square, the low gray-white stone walls circling about me like the sun-bleached bones of an extinct monster. Farther away the mountains rose up, great monoliths of stone and earth that had survived dynasties and would still be prodding the sky when my body had turned to dust. The air smelled thick with vegetation, and the faint tang of blood was carried by the wind. I followed that wonderful scent up the stairs, passing through an arch into another temple.

I paused, my heart lurching in my chest. A woman lay stretched out across a low, large gray stone. Her head was tilted back so her long black hair flowed from the stone and brushed the ground. Her brown eyes were wide, trapping me in their liquid gaze. Standing over her was a man clutching a knife in one hand. I hadn't made a sound, but he knew I was there. He looked up at me and I saw Nerian smile.

I tried to take a step backward, but hands grabbed my arms, forcing me to stay where I was. Struggling, I attempted to look around me at the people holding my arms, but I couldn't see them. Footsteps echoed through the silence of the night, rising off the stones; more were coming to hold me. I looked back up and Nerian was walking toward me, dagger still in hand. I jerked and twisted, fighting my captors, but I couldn't escape. Cold sweat slithered across my skin. Panic was throbbing in my chest faster than my own heartbeat.

Beyond, I could hear the woman repeating, "You betrayed me," in a soft voice that held an accent long dead from the earth. I pushed backward against my captors, digging my heels into the stones, trying to catch on the small crevices between the bricks, but I couldn't gain any leverage. I pushed, but I couldn't move. Nerian kept coming. His white teeth gleamed in the darkness.

I screamed and jerked but could find no release. He stopped inches from me, his laughter cutting into my skin like little razors. If I looked down, I would find that I was bleeding. He was supposed to be dead. I knew I had killed him. I had incinerated his corpse, leaving behind only a small pile of white ash in Danaus's basement. But he stood before me now, smiling. I could feel the heat of his body, smell his woodsy scent. He pulled back his arm, his laughter rising, growing almost frantic in its pitch. As the dagger plunged into my stomach, my eyes opened and I screamed again.

The sound filled the box, but I couldn't stop. I kept screaming, my hands clawing at the red silk lining the top of the box until it was shredded. I screamed until I choked on a sob lodged in my throat.

With my fingers clenched around the torn silk above my head, I lay still in my protective little box. The muscles in my arms were painfully tensed and my jaw was starting to throb. I was gritting my teeth, trying to keep from screaming again. Bloody tears streaked down the sides of my face. I swallowed a second sob and forced myself to relax. It was just a nightmare. Nerian was dead and I was safe.

Releasing my death grip on the silk ceiling, I roughly wiped the tears from my face with the heels of my palms. It had all felt so real. I could remember smells and the feel of their hands biting into my flesh. Worst of all, I could remember the beating of my heart. I laid my trembling right hand on my chest, pressing against my sternum, but felt nothing. Things like breathing and a heartbeat were tricks, illusions used by vampires to give the appearance of life. But things like that took power and energy, so we rarely bothered with it unless we were trying to fool humans. I never resorted to such tricks, but lying there now, I wondered if my heart had been beating while I dreamed.

I had not had a nightmare about Machu Picchu in a very long time. They once nearly drove me mad, but Jabari helped me, protected and guided me from my nightmare. After I'd left Egypt centuries ago I thought I also left his protection, but now I feared that I had been wrong. Maybe he helped me during my daylight sleep during all these years, and now that we'd parted ways, he had lifted his protection. Did I now face an eternity of waking with a scream on my lips?

Or worse, had Jabari sent the dream? Would he torture me until I was finally broken and came crawling back to him? I closed my eyes and folded my shaking hands over my stomach. I forced my thoughts away from the rising panic. The nightmare could be nothing more than what it was: a nightmare. I was upset about Jabari and the naturi; both had invaded my rest.

I lay there, fatigue creeping into my frame. Nightwalkers generally didn't dream during the daylight hours. We had no memories of those hours when the sun hovered above the earth. It was dangerous for me to dream. It used up energy that I was supposed to be conserving for the night, for the hunt.

It wasn't impossible for nightwalkers to dream, but it was extremely rare. As far as I knew, it only happened to those of us known to as First Bloods. They were rare simply because most nightwalkers couldn't be bothered with spending several nights to several years carefully working a spell to bring over a human. First Bloods rose stronger and more powerful than our more common brethren, those lovingly referred to as "chum." While crass and insulting, the nickname fit. Chum was quickly made and little more than bait for a true predator.

As my thoughts calmed, drifting away from the nightmare, a deeper sense of foreboding seeped into my bones. Hesitantly, I stretched out my senses, but I didn't have to go far. Michael was leaning against the box and he was hurt. Someone else was in the room. I unlocked the box and threw back the lid, sitting up. My eyes easily located Michael, who was sitting on the floor near my feet, clutching his right arm to his chest.

Jumping to my feet, I turned to find another man, standing near the wall, a gun in one hand. My muscles tensed at the sight of Omari and I bit back a low growl. The dark-haired, dark-skinned man who served Jabari lowered the gun to his side but didn't put it in his shoulder holster.

"He came to protect you," Michael said in a rough voice before I could lunge at the human. I hadn't told him about what occurred with Jabari, but I had no doubt that my astute assistant could easily read my tense posture.

"What happened?" I said, pivoting slowly on a heel as I gazed about the room. We had been lucky enough to secure a corner suite at the Sarah Hotel on the southern edge of the city. I took a couple steps forward, glass crackling under my feet. The pretty little room had been turned into a war zone. Furniture was broken, pictures pulled or knocked off the wall, and curtains torn. There was also a splatter of blood against one white wall, while the others were peppered with bullet holes. The hotel was located on a clifftop overlooking the city. With any luck, the distance had helped insulate us from drawing the attention of other city dwellers. However, I knew that both the hotel owner and the police had to be taken care of financially before we left the city.

"Four men attacked a few hours before sunset. They were well-trained hunters," Michael said. He reached a hand over and closed the lid of my coffin. In the center was a deep dent, as if someone had taken an axe to it. I gritted my teeth as I stared at it. The dent was over where my heart would have been.

"I arrived shortly after them," Omari stated, his words rolling to me like a low rumble of thunder.

My narrowed gaze snapped to his tense frame. "How did you know?"

Dressed in a pair of jeans and a plain, white button-up shirt, he had the polished look of an executive on holiday. Of course, the splatter of blood on his shirt and the tear in his jeans near his right calf destroyed the effect.

"Jabari doesn't trust the one called Danaus. He sent me to watch over you, and Jamila was to follow Danaus if he left the hotel during the day," Omari said, finally holstering his gun under his left arm.

"Where is the hunter?" The muscles in my shoulders tightened into a hard knot. Danaus had not been there when I was attacked.

"He left the hotel about an hour before the attackers arrived," Michael said. "He hasn't returned yet."

I stared down at my protector, relieved that the scent of his blood wasn't clouding my mind. After reaching the five-century mark, I discovered that I could go several days without needing to feed. With the meal Michael had provided for me the previous night, I was still feeling quite sated.

"Where is Gabriel?" I demanded, suddenly realizing his dark form was missing from my chambers.

A frown pulled at the corners of Michael's full lips. "He's following the men to find out who they are and where they have hidden themselves. I haven't heard back yet." He was worried, and I couldn't blame him. Gabriel was good at what he did, but four against one was a little much even for him. I gazed out the window, taking in the murky gray sky. I was awake earlier than usual. Quickly, I mentally searched the city for Gabriel.

"He's safe." My voice sounded as if it had crossed a vast distance before reaching my ears. "He's returning to the hotel." I reached out a little farther and discovered Danaus was several blocks away toward the northeast but had not yet begun moving toward the hotel.

"If I'm not needed, I'll return to my lord," Omari said, drawing my gaze back to his face.

"Is Jabari near?"

"Yes, he keeps a residence within Koti."

I nodded, recognizing the name of one of the Nubian villages on Elephantine Island. "Will you take Michael with you; tend his wounds?"

Omari stared at my bodyguard then looked up at me before briefly bowing his head. "Yes, I will take him with me."

I pressed my lips into a firm line as I looked back over at my angel. "Take Gabriel with you. I will come to Jabari after I deal with the hunter."

"Are you sure you will not need us?" Michael said, wincing as he pushed to his feet. He was hurt, but Omari and Jamila would see that he was properly stitched up. I needed to travel fast and I did not want them in my way when I faced Danaus.

"I'll manage," I said, failing to keep my fangs from peeking out when I spoke. "Go now."

I walked over to the small balcony that looked down on the city and the Nile. Nearby was the first cataract with the outcropping of stone that had once caused a series of rapids in the Nile. With the addition of the High Dam in the seventies, the rapids had been largely tamed. I waited until I sensed Gabriel meeting Michael and Omari in the lobby before putting one hand on the balcony railing and vaulting smoothly over it. Before I hit the ground four stories below, both my invisibility and cloaking spells were in place. I could not be seen by humans nor sensed by other magic using creatures. I didn't know what Danaus was capable of, but I wasn't taking any chances. He had been conveniently gone while someone attacked me while I slept and endangered the lives of my angels. I struggled to believe that he might have been kidnapped while this all occurred, or that it was coincidence that he just happened to be away from the hotel at that moment.

Cutting down the road that led back into the city proper, I ran toward the north, slowly working my way east. I slowed my gait every few blocks to check Danaus's location, but he hadn't moved yet. The city streets were still crowded with a mix of locals and tourists, enjoying the cooling temperatures now that the sun had set. After less than a mile, the tall white buildings and shorter tan square homes gave way to a vast expanse that looked like the ancient ruins of a forgotten city. It was Fatimid Cemetery. The old Muslim burial ground was filled with small, square mausoleums with domed tops and arched entries. However, the sun, wind, and sand that had ravaged the country over the long centuries took its toll on the monuments here. Names and inscriptions chiseled in the stones were worn away. Stone paths into the cemetery were broken and mostly covered by sand and dirt.

The sounds of the city died off here, falling to a soft hum of noise. Pausing at the entrance, I reached up and brushed some hair from my eyes. The wind had picked up, carrying with it the smell of the Nile. It wasn't all that pleasant a smell, but it carried good memories with it. Some nights Jabari and I would follow the winding river north, walking along as close to the banks as possible. He would tell me tales of when Thebes was the capital city of the Egyptian Empire and how he designed great monuments for the pharaoh.

Danaus was on the move finally. He had been with a group of three humans. I sensed him headed in my direction, with the other humans headed northwest, back toward the city and the river. With a smile, I silently darted over to the shadows of a large mausoleum. After I dealt with Danaus, I would go after the humans.

Leaning one shoulder against the smooth white stone wall, it surprised me that I was amazingly calm. I knew I was going to kill Danaus. I was going to put my hand into his chest and pull out his heart. It was all quite simple. It might not be his style to stake vampires during the daylight hours, but he apparently had no problems sending in others to do the job. None of it made any sense, but that didn't matter. He wasn't there when I was attacked. That was damning enough for me.

Barely five minutes passed before Danaus finally walked past me. "Where were you?" I said, dropping the cloaking spell at the same time. I tapped down the urge to sink my teeth into his throat as I watched him skillfully spin around to face me while pulling a dagger from a sheath at his side.

"Out," he snapped. He straightened his stance when he realized it was only me, and put the knife back in his sheath. That was a mistake, I mused.

"Where were you?" I repeated, pausing between each word. I was still lounging against the side of the mausoleum.

He stood only a few feet away, his feet wide apart and his hands hanging at his sides. Despite the fact that he'd put away his knife, tension ran through his frame; alert and ready. "Seeing the city."

"While you were *conveniently* gone, attackers appeared." I pushed off the building and stepped away from it into the open. Danaus took two steps to the right, maintaining a comfortable distance between us. "Four hunters, well trained. Just . . . like . . . you. Did you send them?"

"No."

"Did you know they were coming?"

"No."

I launched my body into his, and we crashed into the side of another worn mausoleum with a heavy thud. "Lies," I snarled, my fangs bared. I might not be hungry, but I would happily drain him before ripping his heart from his chest.

Danaus pushed me away and drew his knife again, narrowing his eyes at me. We had danced this before, but now there were no more games.

"I didn't know they would come."

"But you know who they are, don't you?" Kicking out with my left foot, I clipped his hand, but he held tight to his knife. I wished I had changed from the previous night. While the skirt was slit on both sides up to the knee and provided ample ease of movement, I never liked fighting in a skirt. "You know them because you're one of them. They knew how to find me because you told them."

"I didn't know they would attack." He edged away from the wall so he had more room to maneuver, but it wasn't easy. The ground was uneven, filled with graves and large cover stones, not to mention random chunks of rock broken off from other monuments.

"You sold me out!"

I grabbed him. His knife sliced my upper right arm, but it didn't stop me from throwing him into the wall. The impact knocked the air from his lungs, and I was there before he could suck in the next breath. My hand locked around his throat, pressing into his esophagus. He struck at me with his knife again, but I caught his wrist. With few options left open, he kicked at me. The force pushed me backward, but I used the momentum of my falling body to pull him with me to the ground. Danaus landed on his side next to me.

Frustrated, I released my hold on his throat. I needed a better approach. Rolling back to my feet before he could, I kicked him below the chin, snapping his head back as he got to his knees.

"I defended you from Jabari!" Circling him, I could barely hear the crunch of rock and sand under my feet over the pounding fury in my head. "I defended you and now I have lost him forever." Stopping in front of him, I grabbed his shirt in both hands. I pulled him to his feet so he was staring me in the eye. "My life is forfeit because of you. My domain is lost, *because of you*."

"I didn't send them," he repeated, his eyes narrow, glittering slits. "Why would I send someone else when I'm looking forward to cutting your heart out?"

I tensed the muscles in my arms, preparing to slam him into a nearby pile of jagged rocks, when something shot through the slim distance separating our faces. I jerked my head backward, my eyes widening. We both looked at the mausoleum wall beside us to find a small arrow shivering in the tan brick wall. A bolt from a naturi wrist crossbow.

Danaus reacted before I could, throwing his body into mine. We landed in a heap on the ground behind the tall sides of a grave cover stone. He lay on top of me as I heard three more arrows ping against the stone and bounce off. The naturi had found us. I loosened my grip on his shirt and slid out from beneath him, trying to edge around the side of the grave enough so I could see around the cemetery.

"How many are there?" I demanded, as another arrow whizzed over the top of the grave. I lay flat on my back in the dirt, straining to hear any indications that they were close. I looked back at Danaus, who was regarding me with a confused expression. "In case you haven't caught on, I can't sense them."

"How has your kind survived so long?" he said with a slight shake of his head.

Glaring at him, I pulled back my lips enough to angrily expose my fangs. I was in no mood to exchange barbs when I had the damned naturi trying to kill me and I still had to kill him before the night was over.

The wind shifted and I caught a light smell of trees and water, the green smell of the rich earth after a rainstorm, all scents that had no business being in Egypt. They were close. I reached over and pulled a sword from a sheath on Danaus's back. Facing a member of the naturi unarmed was never a wise choice.

"Seven," Danaus said. "Four are in the cemetery, approaching fast, and three are on a rooftop outside the cemetery."

I nodded. The three outside the graveyard were to keep us pinned down until the ones in the cemetery could reach us. I rolled to my knees at the same time I heard the ultrasoft footsteps of the approaching naturi. We had visitors.

Leaping to my feet, I raised the blade so it was in front of my heart. Two naturi stood a couple dozen yards away with their arms raised toward me. Bolts sped across the expanse, aimed at my chest. I deflected them, wishing I had something with which to return fire. I didn't carry a gun. No nightwalker carried a gun. There had never been a need until now. With any other creature, it would have been a matter of knives or our bare hands. It had been five hundred years since we'd had a series of encounters with naturi before this, and guns hadn't been the models of efficiency and accuracy that they were now. I was learning the hard way how to deal with the naturi. If I survived this, Gabriel would have to give me a quick lesson on how to fire a gun.

Without bothering to reload their crossbows, both naturi drew short swords and rushed me, clearly realizing that a gun would be relatively useless. The blade I held had more reach, but I knew they would waste no time coming in close to make good use of their steel.

"Nerian?" demanded the one closest to me, his hazel eyes narrowed. He had the same bushy hair and thick frame as Nerian, indicating that he was probably with the animal clan as well.

The smile grew across my face before I could stop it. It was a smile similar to one I'd seen on Jabari's face in the past, one of peace and joy and malice. "Ashes," I replied in a voice that could have frozen the Nile. "And you will join him soon."

They both attacked at the same time, forcing me to dodge the blade of one while blocking the other. Across the cemetery I could hear the sound of steel clanging against steel. Apparently, Danaus had made some new friends. I kicked one of my attackers in the chest, sending him tumbling backward over a raised grave, while I blocked two more slashes from the naturi aiming to take off my head.

I would have to get rid of one of my attackers if I had any hopes of incinerating the other. Unfortunately, creating and controlling fire took a great deal of energy and concentration, particularly with the naturi. With houses, and sadly with vampires, all you had to do was start the fire. Humans took a little more work, but for some reason the naturi were the worst. Something about these creatures didn't want to burn. That's not to say they couldn't, with the exception of a conscious naturi from the light clan. Overall, the naturi made nice kindling; it just required extra effort. And with one aiming to cut me into multiple pieces, I couldn't be distracted with cremating my foes.

I turned, careful to keep my back to the wall of one of the larger mausoleums. If Danaus lost his battle or if one of his attackers abandoned him and attacked me, I didn't want him to suddenly appear at my back. The naturi thrust his blade at me. I blocked it. As he drew it away, he flicked the tip so the edge grazed the bottom of my arm. A long red line appeared, sending a sharp, burning pain up my arm. It was a sensation I had forgotten about. All the naturi weapons were charmed, a special poison that screamed through the body.

I kicked at him, but he sidestepped my blow. What he didn't expect was my fist landing on his nose the next second, snapping his head backward. Beneath my knuckles I felt bone break and flesh give. He staggered a couple steps backward, blood pouring down his face. He cursed, which always sounded strange to me. Their language was so beautiful and lyrical that curses came out sounding more like compliments, which is how I took it.

Across the graveyard a groan broke above the sounds of fighting. I couldn't chance a look over, but it wasn't Danaus's voice. The hunter rid himself of one of his opponents. I attacked my bloody opponent before my other foe returned. Lucky for me, pain from his broken nose clouded the naturi's judgment, and it was only two seconds later before my sword was buried in his chest. Grinning, I drew the blade upward, ripping through his vital organs and snapping bone until it broke through his collarbone and shredded the muscles and tendons in his shoulder. His eyes glazed over and his short sword clattered to the ground. Before he could collapse, I slashed my sword through the air, freeing his head from his neck.

I looked up to find my other playmate coming at me, rage glittering in his green eyes. His anger gave him more strength and speed than his companion, but I still had an edge. Nerian haunted my thoughts enough that I knew I had to kill this naturi or I would be in their hands once again—a fate I would not repeat. The brown-haired creature slashed and blocked with ease, forcing me to circle away from the wall, exposing my back. I tried to circle around so I didn't have to worry about anyone plunging a blade in my back, but he was good.

We exchanged glancing blows so that after a couple of minutes we were both bleeding small streams from half a dozen little cuts. My body burned and my arms trembled from the pain. The naturi's leather jerkin was soaked with blood and sweat, but his eyes were narrowed and keenly focused on me. Clearly, his goal was to kill me.

Gritting my teeth, I blocked another series of blows aimed at my heart and slashed at him, backing him up a couple feet. With a little space between us, I lowered my eyelids until my eyes were reduced to narrow violet slits. He took a step toward me with his sword raised but lurched to a sudden stop, eyes widening. His irises seemed to be swallowed up by the whites of his eyes and his mouth opened as a low, strangled cry echoed through the strangely quiet graveyard. I lowered my sword, focusing all my energy on his body. It took only another couple seconds for the flames to peek through his flesh, blackening it. The sound of sizzling skin and tissue hissed in the air, while the smell of burning hair and leather overwhelmed any lingering scents of the Nile and the city. I stepped back as his clothes ignited and he crumbled to the floor. He never screamed and it was a bit disappointing, because it had been such a painful way to go. But what do you expect when you start a fire in someone's lungs?

When the naturi was reduced to a clump of blackened pieces, I withdrew the power, extinguishing the fire. Exhausted, I crumpled to my knees in front of the corpse. The sounds of fighting had died off and I could vaguely feel Danaus nearby. I needed to rest for a moment before turning back to my dilemma with him. Summoning a little power, I pushed out and touched the minds of any humans who had wandered close at the sounds of fighting or the sight of the brief fire. It took a little effort, but I erased the image, convincing them to turn around and return to their homes. Our secret was still safe.

"There's the little princess," announced a bold, mocking voice into the growing silence.

Spinning around, I landed on my butt in my haste. The last naturi had forced me to turn, leaving my back to the vast expanse of the cemetery. The last three naturi from across the street were cautiously drawing closer.

Seated on the ground with my back pressed to the sand-worn wall of one of the crumbling, red brick tombs, my eyes were locked on the center naturi, who was staring at me. I had never seen a naturi like him. Well over five feet, he had hair so dark that it looked black, where all the naturi I had ever seen before were either blond or light brown. His right eye was covered with a black leather patch, while his right cheek and jaw were crisscrossed with rough, jagged scars. The naturi healed from nearly everything, their warm beauty seemingly protected for all time.

The one-eyed naturi took a step closer, edging around the dead bodies of his companions with his sword tightly clenched in his right hand. "Time to go."

"Not a chance." Something in his voice teased at my memories, as if I should remember him, but I could not recall ever seeing a naturi like him.

"But I have such plans for you." He took another step closer. Digging in my heels, I prepared to leap to my feet. Out of the corner of my eye I saw the other two naturi turn toward Danaus. They would keep the hunter occupied while this naturi took care of me.

Yet, again his voice and words haunted me, bringing back images of Nerian and our final conversation. "Are you Rowe?"

His grin widened and he threw open his arms in a shallow bow. "At your service." His dark red button-up shirt was open at the collar, and when he bent forward, I got a clear look at the scars that streaked across his muscular chest. As he straightened, he paused and his grin faded. "You don't remember me, do you?"

"Nope."

"We'll fix that." Rowe brought his sword down, but I blocked it with my own. Seated on the ground, I was at a definite disadvantage. I was too tired and hurt to try to burn him. I needed to get to my feet.

Rowe was about to bring his sword down again when a pair of high-pitched screams rent the air. A chill went up my spine and I flinched against the sound as if it were slicing through my skin. We both looked up to find that the other two naturi had dropped their short swords and were clawing wildly at their arms and face, pulling at their skin while screaming. I didn't have a clue what was happening to them. They collapsed to the ground then, their lithe bodies jerking and arching in pain. Suddenly, the tanned skin split and blood poured out, hissing and bubbling. Their blood was boiling. If I hadn't seen it, I wouldn't have believed it to be possible.

"I'll catch you soon," Rowe said, pointing his sword at me. The sole surviving naturi then darted across the graveyard and down into the shadowy street.

My stomach twisted as it tried to turn itself inside out, my eyes falling back on the dying naturi. It was only then that I felt the enormous press of power filling the graveyard, pushing against my skin like a hand on my chest. My gaze jerked around the area and I found Danaus focused on the two naturi. He was on his knees, one hand outstretched toward them. He was doing it. This creature I had threatened and taunted was boiling the blood of his enemies from inside.

There was a brief moment of awe as I sat there watching their blood cool in the night air. My trick was good, but his was better. And what was to keep him from doing the same to me and the rest of my kind?

TWELVE

When the naturi stopped writhing on the ground and were silent except for the occasional pop and hiss of melting bone and tendon, Danaus lowered his shaking hand. In the light from a distant street lamp, sweat glistened on his hard face and ran down his arms. The power he had called forth flowed out of the cemetery and a cool breeze swept in. He looked exhausted and a little pale. That unique ability obviously took a lot out of him.

He looked up at me and our eyes locked, both thinking the same thing. Did I have enough strength left to kill him before he could kill me? We were both exhausted, but if it meant our lives, I knew we both had the energy to crush one another. I had felt his power, let it wash over me when we were close, but it never occurred to me that he could do something like this. He could kill nightwalkers without ever getting close. And yet I'd never heard anyone mention such a unique gift. Of course, the hunter would have quickly become the hunted if we had known he was this dangerous. The Coven would have sent scores of vampires after him and we would not have rested until his existence was wiped from this earth. We could not afford such an enemy.

I don't know how long we sat there staring at each other, waiting for the other to flinch first. Time seemed to stretch and twist in that graveyard filled with naturi corpses. We both had these horrible powers, which created a great amount of fear in those around us. For centuries Jabari was the only thing that kept me from being crushed by the Coven. And now I knew Danaus's secret. One word from me and he would be hunted by vampires from all over the world until he was dead . . . if he didn't kill me first.

Yet, sitting there in the dirt in that lonely Egyptian cemetery, I wasn't sure I would ever speak of what happened. He saved my life when he had absolutely no reason to. I didn't think it was possible, but I was even more confused than I'd been twenty-four hours ago.

"Who are you?" My voice sounded rough and ragged to my own ears. The various cuts and strains were coming back into focus, until I was nearly drowning in the pain. My grip on the sword in my right hand relaxed and I let it slip from my limp fingers. A breeze stirred, sweeping up from the river and weaving its way through the city before finally reaching us. Rich spices mixed with the thick smell of humanity drifted toward us, freeing us from the pall of death that had blanketed the graveyard.

Danaus sat down and was swallowed up by a deep shadow thrown by one of the mausoleums, becoming little more than a dark figure. A nightmare.

"I am a member of a group called Themis." His breathing was still labored and his arms trembled. There was a long cut across his left bicep, leaving the arm nearly covered in blood. Something in me stirred at the sight of the blood, but after what I had seen him do, I would not try for the temptation.

"The same as the men who attacked before sunset?"

"Since leaving the U.S., I haven't had a chance to get a message to them. Tonight, I finally met with my contact at the Officers' Club at the far north end of the city." Each word that passed his lips was slow and hesitant. He looked down at the ground, his brow furrowed. I suspected he didn't want to tell me anything, but knew that if we were going to move forward I had to know more. "I didn't know they were sending anyone here. When I met with my contact, I discovered they thought I had been captured and was being held against my will. There are some in Themis that don't ask questions. They were to rescue me and kill you."

"And now?"

"They have been informed that we are . . . working together." A wry, almost bitter smile quirked one corner of his mouth. His deep blue eyes flicked up to my face briefly and I had the impression he was fighting a laugh.

"I'm sure they are pleased with that." A faint noise jumped from the back of his throat that almost sounded like a laugh. Apparently, I wasn't the only one skating on thin ice at the moment. "Is that who you were meeting with here?"

"Yes, I caught them as they headed back north."

"Has Themis called off its dogs?" I inquired, idly picking up a small rock and turning it over with the tips of my fingers.

"The hunters will be on a plane out of Egypt within the next hour."

"Smart."

I would hold off from killing Danaus for now. He had used his power to not only destroy the naturi attacking him, but also successfully scared off Rowe, incidentally exposing his unique ability and saving me from a fate potentially worse than death. However, I wouldn't mind taking a chunk out of the hides of those who had hurt Michael. Nothing could light my temper faster than the thought of being attacked while I slept. I had no respect for cowards who attacked a person while he or she was defenseless.

I rose to my feet, wincing and gritting my teeth as I moved. My body hurt, and it would continue to hurt until I either fed or slept for the day. Both possibilities were still a way off, unfortunately.

"Who was your friend?" Danaus asked, slowly pushing to his feet as well.

I shook my head as my eyes danced over the remains of the naturi. "The naturi Nerian had mentioned, Rowe."

"They want you again?"

"So it would seem," I whispered. I wanted to make some witty remark about how they should have learned their lesson the first time, but I couldn't form the words. Something inside me was screaming in mindless terror. *Not again.* I couldn't let them take me again.

"Drag the bodies over to this mausoleum," I said, motioning with my head toward a large, crumbling building with its dome roof still intact. The arch opening was cracked and broken: the years had not been kind, but I was hoping the neglect meant that it was abandoned by the owner's family. Grabbing the arm of the headless naturi, I bent down and picked up the head by the hair, then pulled them into the tomb.

Danaus followed my lead and pulled over the bodies of the two naturi he managed to boil from the inside. After wrestling a little with limbs, we got the mangled remains of the six bodies piled inside the tomb.

I stumbled backward a couple steps out of the mausoleum, my vision blurring as I struggled against growing fatigue. Danaus caught my arm and steadied me.

"You're still bleeding," he said as he took his hand away and looked at the dark blood smeared across his fingers.

"Charmed weapons," I said in a low voice. "It takes longer to heal."

"You need to feed."

"You offering?"

Danaus took a step away from me and shook his head once. "No."

With a slight shrug of my shoulders, I looked out across the graveyard. The air was silent again, no one wandering close to this resting place for the dead. "I am going to Jabari's. I can manage until then."

"I'll get a car—" he began, his footsteps heading toward the graveyard entrance.

"You're not going." I shook my head, trying to clear the fog. Jabari was waiting for me. I needed my wits about me. Hiking up the left side of my skirt, I grabbed my cell phone from the garter that kept it strapped to my thigh. I had put it on the previous night upon our return to the hotel. I wanted to keep it close after Michael and Gabriel decided to do a little exploring in the city. Danaus looked at the thing like I had just pulled a rabbit out of my ass.

"We are not all fearful of this century's technology." I grabbed his wrist and slapped the phone into his palm. "Call Charlotte. Her number is programmed into the phone. Tell her I need to see if she can get my plane down to Aswan tonight. We're leaving."

"Where are we going?"

"Tell her home. I'm done. Jabari knows of the naturi. He will take care of it." I paused for a moment and stared at the hunter. I couldn't believe what I was about to say, but he'd just saved me from the naturi. Staring up at Rowe tonight, I realized that I'd been spending much of my energy blaming Danaus for everything that had gone wrong recently. In truth, it was a fair mix of my own stupidity and the naturi. Danaus didn't bring back the naturi. He was just the poor schmuck that got stuck with the job of telling someone about it. "You can hitch a ride with us back to the States. After that, you're on your own." I knew I couldn't leave him here with Jabari.

Danaus arched one eyebrow at me in mocking question, but I imagined that was all he could manage. We were both exhausted. I ignored the expression and pushed on.

"When you get back to the hotel, settle up our rooms. If Charlotte can't get the plane here in the next few hours, tell the hotel manager that we need to rent or buy a truck. We have to drive to Luxor tonight and be on a plane before sunrise."

"That may be difficult."

"I know, but I can't travel without my box," I said. While my jet was specially designed for me and could afford me some protection, I couldn't be sure the other places I might be forced to stay would be enough protection. "Money is no object. At the foot inside the box is a leather case. There's cash inside. It won't take long to find someone who can help."

"And you trust me not to double-cross you?" he asked, shoving his hands into his pockets.

"Not really." I shrugged, taking a step closer. "But if you steal the cash, my phone, and dispose of my box, that won't destroy me, just slow me down. And before I come after you for that betrayal, I will hunt down those men that attacked me tonight and hurt Michael. Help me now and I'll forget about that attack and even get you out of Egypt alive. I think that's a pretty fair trade considering the attack made by your little Themis friends. Agreed?"

Danaus stared at me in silence for a full minute before he finally spoke. "Agreed." And even then, the word escaped him in a low grumble.

I smiled. I still had an even better bargaining chip in my pocket, but I was saving that one for a rainy night.

"And speaking of your friends," I started, strolling even closer to him. "I want you to call Themis. I want a meeting." While I was more than willing to hand the naturi problem over to Jabari and the Coven, I wanted to know more about this little group that had made a hobby of hunting nightwalkers.

His eyes snapped back up to my face. "They won't do it."

"I don't care what you have to say to arrange it. Before the sun rises, I want a promise that I will meet with a member of your little group," I said, unable to stop myself from clenching my teeth. My anger was building, which was good because it was giving me a little burst of energy. "I still have to meet with Jabari and I haven't a clue as to what I'm going to tell him. I want to know what the hell is going on. I want a meeting or you're not getting any more information out of me. I am tired of my ass being the only one in the fire."

Frowning, I swept past him and stalked toward the entrance of the graveyard. Yet, I stopped only a few yards away from Danaus. It galled me to ask, but I was exhausted and unarmed. "How many naturi are left in the city?"

Silence stretched between us for a few seconds, but I refused to look back at him. It would do him no good to get me killed now after he had expended so much energy to save me earlier in the night.

"There are two more near the river, heading north." His voice was quiet and low, like distant thunder.

If I were lucky, I would have enough time to get to Jabari and return with my angels before I ran into Rowe and his companion. "How far did you search?"

"All of Aswan, from the High Dam to the Tomb of the Nobles."

"Can . . . can you sense Jabari?" My insides clenched and twisted as I waited for his response.

"No."

I nodded once, a part of me relieved. I didn't want him to be able to sense the Elder when I could not. "I should be back inside of an hour."

Thirteen

Rock crunching under my boots, I headed out of the cemetery to the northwest and the heart of the city. Pain swept through every movement, as my body attempted to heal the array of wounds and poisons left behind from the naturi blade. After only a few blocks I was weaving through the crowds on the street. I expended just enough of my powers to make myself invisible to the people passing by, but Jabari would be able to sense my approach. I could feel Gabriel and Michael across the river on Elephantine Island. They would be at the home the Ancient kept there.

It was relatively early in the evening, and the local souq was still open and would remain so into the late evening hours. Colorful fabrics danced in the spice-rich breeze. A knot of eight boys ran by me with a burst of excited chatter. The leader of the pack carried a scuffed and worn soccer ball under his right arm. Just one quick game in the fading evening light. I briefly walked through the souq, noting the pyramids of fruits carefully stacked in brown baskets and arranged according to color. Colorful signs were written in Arabic, drawing the eyes of the evening shoppers. There were a few women in the souq, but they were either accompanied by a man or traveled in tight knots of three or four women to a group. It was a different world from the one I had inhabited in the States or even in Europe during the past centuries.

Some of the tension eased from my shoulders as I watched the early night life of these people go on. The air was filled with their animated chatter, and someone softly picked out a melancholy tune on a stringed instrument, a counterpoint to the harder murmur of noise created by cars. Here, at this point, the naturi had not touched humanity yet and my kind was just a silly myth no one actually believed anymore.

Slipping down to the Corniche el-Nil, I directed the felucca captain to take me across the river to Elephantine Island. The poor man never even saw me. I slipped into his mind before even stepping onto the small white boat with matching white sail. Sinking down in a seat at the bow, I closed my eyes, listening to the creak of the wooden boat and the splash of the water as we cut across the Nile. The wind dropped to kiss the water before rising again to sweep past me, carrying with it secrets from the Nubian kingdom from the south and other stories from deep in the heart of Africa. I listened to the wind and water, wishing I could understand them, wishing they had the answers to this dilemma.

Stepping off the dock, I instructed the captain to wash off the smear of blood I had left on the white paint of his boat before heading toward the southern tip of the island and the village of Koti, near the Ruins of Abu. The path was compacted dirt, and trees and broadleafed plants crowded the lane. I stared into the darkness that filled in the open areas, wondering if the naturi had followed me across the Nile to the island.

I relaxed slightly as I walked past the seven-foot rock wall that surrounded the village of Koti. The naturi could still follow me into the village, but I was closer to Jabari. At least, I hoped the Ancient was in the village, but I still could not sense my old mentor.

At the end of a narrow alley flanked by two tall buildings that rose up like yellow tulips was a two-story square building painted bright blue. All the homes in the Nubian village were painted bright, cheerful colors—sunny yellows, cool blues, and sweet pinks dotted the landscape like stone flowers in an enormous garden for the gods. As I approached, the ornate door opened and Omari stood in the doorway. He couldn't see me, but I suspected that Jabari had alerted him to my approach. I removed the invisibility when I was still a couple yards from the door, startling Omari, who then moved out of the doorway and motioned for me to enter.

The main chamber was bathed in the warm glow of candlelight, a hint of burning incense in the air. Jabari looked up when I entered, his gaze hardening when he took in my appearance. I sensed Michael and Gabriel also jumped to their feet from where they lounged on a pile of cushions on the floor to my right.

"Naturi!" I shouted, the word exploding from my chest.

"Here?" Jabari demanded. He leapt smoothly to his feet, his face furious, white robes swaying around him.

"No, they attacked me at Fatimid Cemetery. Seven of them. None appeared here?" I thought going after me had merely been a pit stop on the way to Jabari. The Ancient had to be their main target. He was the strongest of the remaining members of the triad.

"No one has come but your protectors and you." The Ancient shook his head in amazement. "How?" The word was one of the few I knew in Ancient Egyptian, despite both our efforts, but his meaning was clear: How had I survived? Even a vampire as old and powerful as Jabari would have been hard pressed to come out with his head still attached.

"Just barely," I said with a weak chuckle. Two on one had been a close match, but seven on one would have been impossible. "Danaus saved my life. I don't know why and at the moment I don't care. We need to get out of the city. There's one called Rowe—he's been in contact with Aurora. He tried to take me, possibly to make sure they would have a clear shot at you."

"I've not heard of this Rowe," Jabari said with a shake his head. He stared at the ground in thought for a moment, potentially digging through volumes of old memories.

"I hadn't heard of him until Nerian mentioned him. He's scarred and wears an eye patch. He pretends to know me, but I don't remember him."

"Not from Machu Picchu?"

"No. I would remember a one-eyed naturi that dresses like a pirate," I said, a smirk briefly twisting on my lips before fading away.

"Maybe you are the reason he possesses only one eye," he said, lifting his gaze back to my face.

"No, I would remember him."

"And his goal was to capture you?"

I shoved a shaking hand through my hair and nodded, unable to say the words through the tremor of fear that sapped my strength.

"You're right," Jabari said. "The naturi felt they had to get you out of the way so they could destroy the members of the triad. They were successful in destroying Tabor. They will also go after Sadira. You must go to her, protect her."

My brows bunched over my nose and I could not stop myself from shaking my head. I didn't want to leave him unprotected, even if he still wanted my head on a pike. "What about you?"

"I will go to the Coven. They must know what is going on. I shall be safe."

"But—" The words died on my lips as the room swayed. Whatever energy I'd scraped together to get me from Fatimid to Koti had run out and my vision was growing black. I put my hand out to try to steady myself on anything I could find and came in contact with a soft, warm shoulder. Blinking, I found myself looking into Michael's concerned eyes.

Jabari's deep, soothing voice floated into my ears and wrapped itself around my thoughts. "The naturi poison is still inside you. You have to feed to cleanse yourself."

My stomach twisted and knotted, attempting to turn itself inside out in hunger and pain. The muscles in my legs quivered, demanding I sit down.

Michael took my hand and placed it against his neck, once again offering himself to me. A weak smile lifted my trembling lips, but my eyes were closed again. "This will hurt, my angel," I warned. "I can't spare the energy."

"You need me."

That was enough. In a surge of raw need, I pulled him down to me, sinking my fangs deep into the vein in his throat. A rough cry escaped his parted lips as the pain tightened the muscles in his body. His hands grabbed my arms, but he didn't struggle. Forcing him down to his knees, I leaned over him and slipped my fingers into his blond hair, holding him captive.

Fear exploded in his chest and ran through his bewildered thoughts, speeding up his heart, pumping his wonderful blood into my body that much faster. His fear was almost as intoxicating as his blood, awakening something that lay curled up in a dark pit in my stomach. The creature unwound itself and swam up the river of blood. It roared inside my head, demanding more, demanding I take it all.

The hand entwined in Michael's hair tightened and a small whimper escaped him, sending fresh pleasure skipping through me. I kept his neck pressed to my mouth even as his heart began to grow sluggish. I didn't care. There was only the warmth flowing into my cold limbs and the ball of energy swelling in my chest. My fear and the pain were finally gone. I felt alive and powerful.

"Mira." Jabari's firm voice somehow broke through the haze of blood and power, but I tried to ignore it. "Release him, Mira." Instead, my free hand gripped Michael's shoulder, locking him to me.

"Release him, Mira, or you will kill him."

I jerked my mouth away from Michael and loosened my death grip. My guardian sank back to sit on his heels, blinking in a desperate attempt to stay conscious. I had taken more than I had planned to and yet the creature inside still howled for more.

When I finally looked up, I found Jabari standing beside his wooden, high-back chair. His right hand rested on the back, gripping it so tight his knuckles were turning white. His brown eyes seemed an eerie yellow in the flickering candlelight. He had heard the creature's cry inside of me, felt the same blood lust. The Ancient blinked once, releasing his grip on the chair.

Michael touched my hand timidly and flashed me a crooked smile, searching for the reassurance that everything was okay. Smiling back at him, I gently ran my fingers through his thick blond hair before pressing a kiss to his forehead. My right hand slid down to cover the bite mark on his neck. With a brief swell of power, I healed both this fresh wound and the one from the previous night.

Something inside of me trembled when I looked down at my angel. A quick search of his thoughts revealed he had no idea how close he came to dying. But Gabriel knew. When I released Michael, I felt a wave of relief wash from Gabriel as he put his gun back in its holster. A bullet from Gabriel wouldn't have killed me, but would have succeeded in loosening my hold on my bodyguard and saved his life, at least until I reacted.

It had been a long time since I last succumbed to the blood lust. A well-fed vampire was a vampire in control. But the pain and poison had shattered that hard-won control and nearly cost me my angel.

"You must go to Sadira," Jabari said in an even voice, as if we hadn't just been interrupted by my desperate need to feed.

"I can't." Shaking my head, I took a step back, away from Jabari. "Send someone else; someone older and stronger than me. Have the nightwalker escort Sadira to rest with the Coven. They can protect her." I walked over to a low bookshelf and picked up a small statue of a man seated on a throne. By the arrangement of the hands and the facial structure, I determined that it was a piece of Nubian art, though very similar to some of the pieces of work that came out of the Middle Kingdom.

I think I would have said anything at that moment—not only to avoid Sadira, but also the chance of meeting the naturi again. My good deed was done. The Coven now knew of the growing threat. Hell, I'd destroyed four naturi in as many nights, and I was willing to wager it had been centuries since the last nightwalker could make such a claim. Now, I just wanted to go home.

"Protect Sadira while I hunt this Rowe. You failed me once with Nerian. I am willing to give you a second chance. Will you fail me in this request as well, my Mira?"

A string of curses in three languages exploded from me as I slammed the stone statue on the bookshelf and stomped away from

Jabari. It was a mix of gutter nonsense, but it didn't matter. The Elder's deep laughter rumbled over my curses. He'd won and he knew
it. He was the only one who could convince me to face the naturi yet
again.

"Where is she?" I said, unable to keep the distaste out of my voice
as I turned back to face him. Jabari stared at me a moment, surprise
filling his dark brown eyes. "I won't do it," I snapped. "I won't reach
out for her."

"She is in London. I imagine she will come to you after you arrive," Jabari said after letting me twist for a moment in the silence. I
had not seen or talked to Sadira since Machu Picchu. I didn't want to
see her now, but I didn't have much choice.

However, I couldn't stop the instant curiosity that furrowed my
brow at his answer. "England?" I asked before I could stop myself.
The British Isles were a hotbed of magic, which nightwalkers tended
to avoid. We had our own problems without heading to a place beloved by witches and warlocks. "Has she moved from Spain?"

"No, her main residence remains in Spain. I do not know why she
has gone to the island." His tone was neutral, but something in his
eyes made me think Jabari was laughing at me.

Shaking my head, I turned around the room again and stared at
my angels. Gabriel had helped Michael onto the pile of cushions.
My wounded bodyguard was a sickly shade of white and his arm
was wrapped in a white bandage. I knew this was part of their job;
protecting me meant that they put their own lives in danger. However, the past few years had been quiet, each of my random trips
without incident. The relentless peace had made us all soft in a different way.

"Omari," Jabari called, breaking the silence that had stretched
in the room. "Take Mira's companions down to my felucca. I will
bring Mira down in a moment, and then you will take them back to
Aswan."

I nodded when Gabriel glanced up at me for direction, and then
watched as he and Omari helped Michael back to his feet. Michael
would bounce back from this encounter soon enough, but I knew it
was weak and stupid of me to take so much blood. Such behavior
only endangered both our lives.

"Walk with me, Mira," Jabari said, extending his hand toward me
after Omari and the others disappeared out the front door.

I hesitated a second, stunned by the gesture. The pain of the fight
from the previous night was still fresh in my mind. My body was still

recovering from the fight with the naturi too, and I didn't need any more fresh wounds. But it was Jabari who reached for me. With my lips pressed into a tight line, I took his hand.

There was no warning. The world around me slipped away and was consumed by complete blackness. I tightened my grip on his hand and felt him pull me to him until I was pressed against his strong chest. One second there was only blackness, and in the next the world rushed back, golden sand and towering walls bathed in a warm yellow light. We were at Philae, several miles south of Elephantine Island and just north of the High Dam. Not far away, a large chattering group of people gathered for the nightly light and sound show.

Jabari tightly gripped my hand, threading his long fingers through mine before turning his back on the crowd and leading me toward the Temple of Augustus. It was darker in this area, and it appeared that the nightly tour would stop at the Temple of Isis before winding south back to the Hall of Nectanebo and the boat landing.

I gazed around, admiring the way the lights and shadows washed over the high walls. The regal faces of gods and pharaohs watched as we passed by in silence. "They did a good job," I ventured as we neared the temple hidden in darkness. "I really can't tell the difference."

Before the High Dam was completed, the government had been forced to move the Temple of Philae from its original island to Agilkia Island, to the north, or it would have been permanently submerged beneath the deep blue waters of the Nile. They had obviously been careful to reconstruct the temple and the surrounding flora almost exactly as on the original island.

"Hmmph," Jabari snorted. "The island is too small. The temples are too close."

"Better too close than underwater," I softly said, but instantly regretted it. When had I become so careless with my comments? Valerio. I blamed Valerio. He had been a bad influence, and too many years at his side made me careless when it came to speaking to other nightwalkers. "I'm sorry, Jabari."

"No," he snapped, and then stopped. He sighed heavily, running his free hand over his head as he stared at the Temple of Augustus as it rose up before us. "I am the one who is sorry, my young one." He pulled me into his arms, releasing my hand so he could wrap both arms around me. I flinched at the contact, but relaxed a moment later when he brushed a kiss across my temple.

"Last night I overreacted when I saw you standing in the quarry with the human. Egypt was always our home until you left, but then you returned . . . with a hunter of our kind and word of the naturi. I didn't mean to . . ." His voice drifted off as I let his words soak into my brain, completely stunned. I don't know which part took me more by surprise—that he referred to Egypt as "our home" or the quiver in his voice when he spoke of me leaving. There had been no question of me leaving Egypt centuries ago. I told the Ancient that I wanted to return to Europe, and he made no move to stop me. I had no idea that he was bothered by my choice to leave.

Taking a step back, out of his arms, I reached up and cupped his face with my hands. I brushed my thumb over his lips, loving the feel of his smooth skin beneath my fingertips again. "It was time for me to leave," I whispered in a choked voice.

Jabari took my right hand and laid it on his chest. "I know you are right, but my heart did not wish for you to leave." There were no heartbeats beneath the palm of my hand, but I understood the gesture.

Leaning forward, Jabari kissed me. At first it was just a light brush of his lips against mine, soft as a baby's breath, as if he were testing my response. I instantly went up on the tips of my toes, pressing closer to him. He deepened the kiss as I wrapped my arms around his neck. The kiss quickly became hard and possessive, claiming me back from the hunter, my domain, and the wide expanse of years that had separated us. He tasted me, as if trying to relearn me.

I pressed close to him, welcoming him. As he deepened the kiss I also felt him slip into my mind like a finely sharpened blade. For the first time in so long, I could finally sense him. I could feel the presence of his soul, and some tension I hadn't been aware of eased around my own soul. Jabari was everywhere, everything, for a brief span of time. The world slipped away and the years rewound. I was home and safe.

And then it was over. Jabari slowly pulled away, slipping out of my mind. Yet, my lips tingled and something in my chest burned. I felt as if he had branded me, marked me for all the nightwalkers to see. It screamed, "Mira belongs to Jabari." Not a Companion, never that, but something . . . different.

The Ancient reached up and touched my cheeks, wiping away tears I hadn't realized were falling.

"What is going on, Jabari?" I inquired, unable to completely purge the fear from my voice.

"The naturi have found a way to weaken the seal." His voice was calm again, the emotion wiped away as if it never existed. Our world had been put right and we were back to the business side of our relationship.

"How?" I asked, struggling to hit the same unemotional calm that he possessed. "It can't be because of Tabor's death. That was more than fifty years ago. Why would they have waited so long to strike?"

"I do not know how they have done it. It is one of the reasons that I go to the Coven. Our Liege may know something." For some reason, I wasn't sure that Jabari believed it. There were other things troubling him, something dark and grim enough to make my beloved mentor shield himself even from his own.

"How do we stop them?"

"We will reform the triad and destroy Rowe."

Oh, yeah. Just like making the bed or tying my shoes. "How?" I countered, frustration rising in my voice. Damn it, I was starting to sound like a bad fifties cowboy and Indian movie. *How? How? How?* "Tabor is gone."

"Your task is to protect Sadira and reform the triad while I speak with the Coven and Our Liege. The three were chosen by bloodlines . . . find someone of Tabor's bloodline and the triad will be reformed."

"None of this makes any sense," I complained, wandering a short distance away from Jabari, back toward the south. I could see the golden lights shining up at the tall walls that comprised the Temple of Isis. A soft breeze picked up, stirring the trees that ringed the island.

"It does not have to make sense to you." His voice lashed at me like a whip, halting my complaints. "Leave now with your people. I will contact you soon in London."

This was the other reason why I left Jabari, more than the need to finally take control of my own life. No matter how much I loved him, I would never be viewed as an equal in his eyes. Jabari loved me in his own way, but I would always be his subordinate, beneath him even if I earned his respect. I couldn't live like that. It would have broken my heart.

With the long-lived, there were various hierarchies and layers of discrimination. For some, it was the Old World versus the New, or the discrimination of First Blood versus chum, or man versus woman, or ancient versus fledgling. But with Jabari the only creatures above him were Our Liege and his gods. And those not by much.

"As you wish," I said, bowing my head stiffly. I had forgotten myself—he was an Ancient and an Elder. Regardless of what had occurred between us, I still owed him my respect, and in many ways my life. For now, it didn't matter if I understood what was going on. All I needed to know was that I had to keep Sadira alive and find a replacement for Tabor. After that, I was done and headed home. The Coven and the triad would handle the naturi.

"What about Danaus?" I asked, looking up at the Elder again. "He knows about the naturi and he knows about Machu Picchu. He also knew where to find me. Sometimes I think he may be a spy for the naturi, and then other times . . ."

"Yes?" Jabari prompted when I drifted off in thought.

"I have seen him kill at least four naturi, and he has stood by while I killed several myself. He saved me from the naturi tonight when he had absolutely no reason to. I—I don't know what to think about him."

"Keep him close, Mira," Jabari said, putting a strong hand on my shoulder. I suddenly felt very small next to his ancient height. "I do not think he is with the naturi, but we have other enemies. He may lead you to them."

A half smile lifted one corner of my mouth as I looked up at my old friend and mentor. "You make him sound like a bori spy."

A ghost of a smile slipped across Jabari's face, but it could have just as easily been a trick of the light. "At least we know *that* is impossible. I do not know what secret he holds, but he needs to be watched for a time."

"But will it be safe for him to be with me while I protect Sadira and search for the third member of the triad?"

"What better way to draw out our enemy?" Jabari asked, titling his head as he gazed down at me. "Besides, you will not fail me a second time by not protecting your maker."

I resisted the urge to touch my neck, searching for the noose I swore I felt tighten there. I nodded, trying to smile up at Jabari but not quite succeeding.

He gathered me close again and I felt the world fall away. I closed my eyes against the darkness and only opened them again when I heard the splash of the Nile. Michael was being helped into the felucca by Omari. We were gone only a few minutes, but it felt like hours. I gave Jabari's hand one final squeeze and then boarded the felucca behind Gabriel.

I didn't know any more now than when I had first arrived in Egypt, but at least something was being done about the naturi. It was a start. Maybe not much of one, but at least there was the promise of progress.

I also had the possibility of a meeting with Themis. And while I might still be their enemy, we were both threatened by the naturi. The old "an enemy of my enemy is my friend" routine. This little shadow group might know more of what was going on with the naturi, and I needed any information I could get my hands on.

Fourteen

We made our way slowly back across the river. Less than two hours had passed since sunset and the streets were still crowded, but no one took notice of us. Usually I'd be rising from my daylight nap about now, but my nightmares had woken me early that evening. Or perhaps some deeper sense of self-preservation allowed me to wake as soon as the sun slipped below the horizon.

"So, we're off to London now?" Gabriel asked.

"And we get to meet your maker," Michael said with a wide, playful grin. "I always wondered what she would be like."

"She didn't birth me." The words came out sounding sharper than I'd intended. I didn't want them to meet Sadira. She was evil and I was not like her.

"No, but without her, we would have never met you," Michael said, drawing my wandering gaze back to his face. I looked down at his bandaged arm resting in a sling fashioned from a black silk scarf.

Without Sadira, Michael and Gabriel would not be here in Egypt, fighting hunters and the naturi. But I shook off the thought as quickly as it appeared. They had made their own choices. They knew what they were getting into and were free to leave at any time.

"We go to London and protect Sadira," I repeated, as if saying the words over and over again would give me courage. "I wonder if we could lock her in a box for a few days. Just until the Coven destroys Rowe and the rest of the naturi." Sadira would never go for it, but I was sorely tempted to try.

The smile died on my lips before it had a chance to grow. We had gone one block in from Corniche and were walking past the giant souq in search of a private taxi to take us back to the hotel toward the south when I looked up to find a naturi staring dumbfounded at us. His hand rested on the knob of a door leading into a flat-fronted, two-story building. By his stance, he had been in the process of either entering or leaving the building when we turned the corner and caught him by surprise.

Muttering something under his breath, he pushed open the door and disappeared inside, slamming it shut behind him.

"Stay here," I ordered, grabbing the knife from the sheath on Gabriel's waist. I would have preferred the gun, but it didn't have a silencer and any shots would catch the attention of the crowds still lingering in the market. I couldn't afford to divide my attention between fighting the naturi and trying to cloak the fight from the humans.

"Was that . . . ?"

"Naturi."

"But—"

"Walk down through the souq. Stay in the more crowded area." I laid a restraining hand on Gabriel's shoulder, pulling his gaze back to my face. "Protect Michael. He's weak. Keep one eye on the door. There should be two in there. If one slips past me, I will need you to tell me which way it went."

Frowning, Gabriel nodded. He didn't like the idea, but he would follow my directions. I wanted to flash him a cocky smile to ease his concerns, but I couldn't. For the second time tonight I was going to be outnumbered by naturi. Sure, I could torch the building, but without going inside, I couldn't be sure that I'd gotten both the naturi Danaus sensed earlier in the evening.

With the knife tightly gripped in my right hand, I kicked open the door. The scent of blood, death, and excrement smacked me in the face, causing me to hesitate. Humans were inside. At least, they had been at one time. I rolled inside, followed by the sound of darts hitting the wall where I'd just been seconds ago. I paused behind a chair. The spindly thin naturi I followed in was shouting something to Rowe. I couldn't tell what they were saying, but I was willing to bet it had something to do with the vampire crouched behind the hideous patterned chair.

Pushing to my feet, I was prepared to hit both naturi with fireballs. No fighting. No taking chances. But I froze when I finally saw the room. I was standing in what had been a living room, but it looked as if hosed down with blood. There once were four humans in that room; maybe more, maybe less. Their appendages had been hacked off and strewn about. By the smaller torsos, I could identify at least two children.

Rowe was in the far corner, up to his elbows in a man's chest. The human's head was still attached, his eyes staring blindly up at the ceiling. The black-haired naturi was drenched with blood, his red shirt sticking to his narrow frame. I lurched forward when the blond naturi I had followed in leapt onto the chair I was behind. With one foot braced on the back, he used his weight to topple the chair, attempting to bring it down on top of me. A short sword was raised in his right hand, ready to take off my head.

Stumbling backward, I fell away from the chair. My right shoulder slammed into the end of a table before I hit the ground, sending a shockwave of pain through my back. The naturi tried to fall on me, the sword aimed to bury itself deep into my chest. With the pain slowing me, I only managed to get my knees up between us. Dropping the dagger, I grabbed his wrists.

"Come now, vampire," he said. "I only want your tongue." The naturi struggled, trying to break my grip.

With a grunt, I shoved him off me. He flew across the room, hitting the door and slamming it shut. "How funny." I pushed into a sitting position and raised my left hand. "I only want your life." With a thought, the naturi was engulfed in flames. He lurched about the room, waving his sword about in a last desperate attempt to kill me. For a moment it looked as if wings were sprouting from his back, but the fire quickly consumed them. Had I finally met a member of the elusive wind clan?

I would get no answer from him. Flailing, the naturi slipped on the blood-soaked tile and fell, cracking his head. He stopped moving.

The sound of crinkling plastic caught my attention. I looked up in time to see Rowe darting across the room with a black, plastic garbage bag tucked under this arm. I tried to hit him with a fireball, but it struck the wall as he disappeared into the next room. I could only set him on fire if I could see him.

Muttering a cruse, I climbed over the overturned chair. I slid across the blood-covered floor, knocking limbs out of my way until I hit the opposite wall. So much for catlike grace. Pushing off the wall, I ran through the tiny kitchen and out the open back door. We wove our way through a maze of garbage-choked alleys and narrow streets that fluttered with laundry overhead. I couldn't see Rowe, but I followed the scent of the blood that still coated him.

Coming out of one alley, I skidded to a sharp halt. The alley opened into the busy souq, several blocks down from where I'd left Gabriel and Michael. The crowded marketplace hit me with a barrage of scents, spices, cooking food, coffee, tea, and the redolent scent of men smoking sheesha. A brisk wind swept down the street from the south, carrying with it cloves, cinnamon, ginger, and the sweat of man, all mixed together to mask the scent of blood. A quick scan of the thoughts of the gathered people revealed that no one had noticed a blood-covered, one-eyed naturi carrying a garbage bag filled with human organs. Like a vampire, he had cloaked himself from their sight. And now he was gone.

Biting back a scream, I jogged back to the house. Without Danaus, it would take me hours to track down Rowe. Time I didn't have. I shut and locked the back door before trudging back into the living room. The scent of burnt flesh mingled with the blood, leaving a rancid taste in the back of my throat.

It took every bit of willpower I possessed to walk over to the body Rowe had been digging in. Squatting down, I tried to ignore the fact that my skirt was growing heavy with the blood. A quick examination revealed that the man's tongue and lungs were missing. Scanning the room, it was hard to miss that the chest cavities of all the humans were cut open.

I'd walked in on a harvest. I hadn't seen one in centuries. Jabari and I stumbled across one a few years after Machu Picchu, in which nearly twenty humans had been slaughtered. But back then the naturi were greater in number and desperate to free their captured queen. Typically, they relied on earth magic for their spells. Yet, with time, they learned to use magic based on blood and the soul. It was just as powerful. Of course, their attitude was always, "Why kill a flower when you can kill a human instead?"

Standing, I leaned against the wall and closed my eyes. When I finally succeeded in clearing my mind of the horror around me, I reached out and touched Gabriel's mind.

Gabriel?

Mira! Are you hurt? His thoughts rushed into my brain, hot and frantic. Through his eyes, I could see him, across the street, staring at the door of the building I was in. Michael was leaning against the wall beside him. Gabriel wasn't telepathic, but after several years of training, I had taught him to focus his thoughts into precise sentences so I could read his mind and project into it my own response. It took us a while to perfect, a task I had not yet begun with Michael.

I'm not injured. Something in my soul had been hurt by what surrounded me, but I was not physically hurt.

Should I come in?

No! I paused until I regained my composure. *No. Start walking toward the hotel. I have to burn the place. I'll catch up to you in a couple blocks.*

Be careful.

I waited until he pushed off the building he was leaning against and started down the street with Michael at his side. When I opened my eyes, my gaze fell on the blood-streaked face of a girl with long, black hair. She couldn't have been more than six. I set her on fire first, wishing the flames would erase her wide brown eyes and tender face from my mind. But I knew better. I always remembered their faces.

Lingering in the house only long enough to see the bodies blackened and shrivel in the fire, I left through the back door, cloaked from human sight. I walked along the alleyways until I caught up with my angels. With a single touch on Gabriel's shoulder, I made my presence known, but no one spoke. We managed to grab a private cab another block away, and took it the last few miles to the Sarah Hotel.

In front of the hotel, we found Danaus working with a short, thin man as they attempted to strap my coffin to the roof of a dilapidated taxi that looked as if it could have been around during the time of the pharaohs. At the sight of him, I sensed a rush of anger fill both of my guardians. Danaus might have saved my life from the naturi, but he was still the cause of the attack prior to sunset.

I laid a restraining hand on the shoulders of both Michael and Gabriel before I stepped between them. Their protectiveness was warming, but a fight on the street would not speed us from this city. "I don't think this will make it to Luxor," I said as I walked up to him.

"It doesn't have to," Danaus replied without looking up at me. He tested one of the ropes to make sure it was properly secured. "Your assistant contacted the pilots and they are bringing the jet to Aswan. It should be landing within the next half hour."

"Excellent." Charlotte was good at her work. I had thought it might be too difficult to get the pilots ready in time, but apparently she'd left them on standby. The vast majority of my trips were short, and she must have grown accustomed to my desire to leave quickly. "And the hotel owner?"

"Happy to be rid of us," Danaus said in a low voice, finally lifting his eyes to meet my searching gaze. He returned my leather case, which felt significantly lighter. With an amused smile, I tossed it over to Gabriel. I was still in my skirt from the previous night, leaving me short on pockets.

"And my meeting?"

"Later." His eyes darted over to the driver, who was staring at me with his mouth hanging open. He had noticed me when I started talking to Danaus, breaking the spell. The little man in the stained cotton shirt looked terrified, but I couldn't blame him. My clothes were full of cuts and tears, and what could be seen of my flesh was covered in dried blood and black soot. Of course, Danaus looked the same as I did, with an assortment of cuts that were healing much faster than would be considered normal. His face and arms were smeared with blood and ash.

"The airport," I said in badly accented Arabic, a jaunty smile directed at the driver. The little man bobbed his head and jumped behind the wheel. He was muttering under his breath as he went. I couldn't understand it, but I doubted it was complimentary. I motioned for Gabriel to precede me into the backseat so I could sit on his lap. Michael took the front seat while Danaus was forced to sit in the back with me. It was a quick, twenty-minute ride across town to the airport, and we didn't speak again until my coffin was safely loaded into my jet. I paused at the bottom step and gazed across the airstrip. The black night sky was dotted with the dark shadows of looming palm trees. I could still smell the Nile and the hint of foreign spices. I wished I wasn't leaving like this. Despite the fact that I had escaped death and aided in the destruction of seven naturi, it felt like I was running with my tail between my legs. Rowe was still out there, hunting me and killing humans.

I was running, and time was nipping at our heels. I'm not sure how or why I knew, but I could feel it bearing down, threatening to crush us all.

After bitterly informing the pilots that we would need to land in London instead of heading home, I moved to the private room at the back of the jet. Danaus followed me back while my two guardians settled into the comfortable leather chairs near the door. During the night hours, they were generally off duty. Besides, I was in better shape than either of them at the moment, though I know I didn't look it.

Flipping on the light in the tiny bathroom, I winced at my reflection. For once I didn't look pale—my skin was covered with ash and blood. My blue-violet eyes looked nearly black and my hair was a matted mess. Turning on the faucet, I rubbed the cool water over my hands and up my arms. I wouldn't be able to properly wash until tomorrow night, when I was in my hotel room. For now I just wanted the grime off my hands and face.

"What did you find out?" Danaus asked, not venturing far from the door that led to the rest of the jet. He didn't look much better than me, with his soot-streaked body, assorted cuts and bruises, and sweaty, matted hair. He was tired as well. I doubted he was sleeping much since joining me on this little escapade either. At night he was surrounded by nightwalkers, who would rather drain him dry. During the day he was faced with my angels, who would rather see him dead than threaten me. And then there were the naturi, who could come out to play whenever they wanted. The shadows around his cobalt blue eyes had deepened and his movements were a little slower. There was now a thick growth of black whiskers on his chin and filling in the hollows of his cheeks.

"Not much," I said, splashing some water on my face. "I am to locate a nightwalker and protect her while Jabari hunts Rowe."

"Where are we going?"

"London."

"Directly?"

"Yes. Tell Michael to contact Charlotte on my cell. She'll have the hotel arrangements made before we land. We'll be in the city for a couple days." I rubbed my skin hard in a vain attempt to scrub off the blood. All my wounds had healed, but my body was covered in long lines of dried blood.

"What's going on? You look worse than when you left the hotel."

"Just give me a minute. Give the phone to Michael."

"Mira—"

"Please, Danaus!" My voice jumped and trembled in the tiny room as my composure splintered.

Danaus stepped out of the room for a moment, and the soft murmur of his voice drifted back to me as he relayed my wishes to Michael. Charlotte wasn't going to be happy with all these interruptions, but I was trying to keep her kind alive. Sure, I was trying to save my own skin as well, but my survival would benefit her. The hunter returned to the room, shutting the door behind him. He walked over so he was standing near the bathroom door.

"Did he attack you again?"

Looking up, I caught my reflection in the mirror. I hadn't summoned my powers, but my eyes glowed. I closed my eyes and shoved my newest set of memories away as I gripped the edge of the sink.

"What happened?" His deep voice was soothing, a gentle hand massaging my frazzled nerves.

"Have you ever seen a harvest?"

"No."

"I have, a couple of times. The naturi will attack a family or a small village. They kill all of its inhabitants and harvest certain organs and body parts for the magical powers they possess." The words slipped from me, dry and quiet, but the explanation failed to numb the pain and horror.

"In Egypt?"

"Four people. Two children."

"Mira . . ." Danaus's voice drifted off under the weight of the images I painted.

"They were butchered. Innocent people. Just a means to an end."

"And we'll get them."

A derisive snort escaped me before I could stop it. Turning my head, I was halted by the sadness in his eyes. "Then what? I know what you think of my kind, and you're partially right. We are capable of that kind of brutality, but not all of us."

Danaus reached for me and I jerked out of his reach. If he touched me, I would crumble and the tears burning behind my eyes would break free. I refused to cry on the shoulder of a man who planned on killing me at the first opportunity.

"It doesn't matter. What of my meeting?" Releasing the sink, I grabbed a creamy white towel that lay folded on the counter. I wiped off my arms and face, feeling a little cleaner than before.

"When and where?"

"Tomorrow night. Your contact can pick the place, but this person must appear alone," I said, tossing the rumpled hand towel back on the counter. I leaned against the sink, folding my arms loosely over my stomach.

"He won't meet you alone." He shoved both of his hands through his hair in a restless gesture, pushing it out of his face. The movement pulled his body into a single long line, flexing muscle and sinew in a tempting picture. I had been so focused on peeling his skin from his bones that I'd almost forgotten he was a man. An attractive one. Danaus was all muscle and tanned skin, telling tales of a long, hard life. I wondered about this ancient creature that walked around in the shell of a virile man.

"You can come too, but no one else," I said after a moment. "And trust me, I'll know. The naturi are the only ones I can't sense."

"Anything else?" Danaus folded his hands, resting them on the top of his head. With his black shirt tucked in, the fabric pulled against his chest, accentuating his flat stomach. If I hadn't known better, I would have said he was trying to distract me on purpose.

"Just that it may be a good idea to make the place private. I don't mind an audience, but I imagine your little group doesn't want to be a part of a scene."

Shaking his head, I saw a smile playing on his lips as he turned and left the room.

"Get some sleep, Danaus," I called after him. "I promise Michael and Gabriel won't bother you."

"They think I tried to have you killed," he replied, looking over his shoulder at me, his hand on the doorknob.

"They also know you saved my life." I shook my head and frowned. "Even if you hadn't, my angels only defend, never attack. They also won't harm a creature when it's defenseless."

Danaus turned around to face me, his brow furrowed. "A vampire with a sense of honor?"

"There are a few of us," I whispered. "There are some ideas that not even death can kill."

The hunter nodded once to me and left the room.

Kicking open my metal box, I lay down with one booted foot still on the jet floor. I wasn't tired and it was still hours away from dawn, but I didn't want to join the others. It had been a long time since I last spent this much time surrounded by humans. Of course, there were my nightly trips to the clubs, theaters, and other amusements, but when I had my fill of them, I was always able to walk away. I could return to my quiet sanctuary and let the silence fill me. Now I was up to my ears in vampires, humans, naturi, and whatever the hell Danaus was.

To make matter worse, I still didn't understand what was going on. The naturi were attempting to break the seal and open the door between our two worlds. I didn't know how they were doing it. All I knew was that I had to reform the triad and keep Sadira safe. Not a particularly enjoyable task, but it wouldn't last long. Jabari would find Rowe and kill him. There would be no need for the triad. Soon it would all be over. I would go home and try to forget about it.

I ran my hands over the red silk that lined the side of the box, enjoying its smoothness. A part of me wanted to call for Michael. I wanted to feel his warm arms around me, reminding me of home and my life before this nightmarish escapade began. I wanted to make him moan and to erase the memory of the pain I'd caused him earlier.

But I couldn't. I couldn't even raise my voice to utter his name. I had come so close to killing him. I hadn't drained a human during the act of feeding since I was a fledgling. Yet my fear of the naturi and the taste of Michael's blood fueled something in me. It had given me back a shred of power and control when it all seemed to be slipping from my grasp.

I could tell myself I would have stopped in time, but that did nothing to erase the knot of doubt in my stomach. No matter how much I cared for him, I would always be a threat to him.

With a sigh, I pulled my leg inside the coffin and stretched out. I needed to sleep. I would need my strength for London, and I wasn't completely healed from my encounter with the naturi. And truthfully, I didn't want to think anymore.

Fifteen

Danaus was near me. It was the first thing I thought of when consciousness slipped back into my brain. He was in the same room, somewhere close. I moved my left hand, feeling for the side of the coffin so I could unlock it, but instead my hand came in contact with a thick velvet cover. My eyes snapped open, a snarl lunging forward behind clenched teeth. I was lying on a large bed in a luxurious bedroom, with dark, heavy furniture and thick curtains pulled across the pair of windows on the wall to my left. I sat up, my fists grasping the wine-colored comforter. Danaus sat in a chair set against the door, his arms folded over his chest. He was staring at me; his intent gaze taking in my expression, the movement of my muscles beneath pale skin. Wrapped in his blanket of power, he sat there like some reluctant guardian.

"Why was I taken out of my box?" I was as angry with myself as I was at my companions. I had fallen asleep with the lid open, so it hadn't been locked from the inside. But I had been moved. *Someone had touched me while I slept.* A cold chill of fear gripped my frame in a tight fist. No one saw me during the daylight hours; not servants or guardians. The complete vulnerability during that long stretch of time was the only thing I loathed about being a nightwalker.

"Michael said you don't sleep in a coffin when you are home," Danaus said. "He also said you were screaming when you awoke last night."

"It was a nightmare." My eyes darted back to the subdued pattern on the comforter. I'd had a blissfully empty day this time, but I could clearly recall the nightmare from the previous day. Pushing the thought aside, I looked back up at Danaus. "Who moved me?"

"I did," he said, holding my gaze.

"Why?"

"I wanted to see you sleep." His eyes never wavered from my face. There was a strange intensity to him that set me ill at ease. "You never moved. You're just a corpse." His eyes seemed to harden as he spoke but he sounded confused. It was as if he couldn't reconcile the fact that moments ago I was cold and stiff and now I was sitting in bed talking to him. "Can you awaken during the day?"

"Not yet. Someday, maybe. The Ancients sleep less, but we all lay down when the sun rises in the morning. Vampires are remnants of an old war," I explained. This line of questions was unexpected.

"What war?"

"The eternal battle between the sun and moon."

Danaus nodded and rose from his chair, which he pulled to one side. "I don't harm creatures while they are defenseless."

"A hunter with honor."

"One of the few. The meeting is in an hour," he announced, then left the room. I stared at the closed door, feeling him moving about the hotel room. He was uneasy as well, some part of him simmering. I couldn't read his thoughts, but I could pick up on his emotions. So much anger and turmoil stewed in his chest. He also had questions with no answers, and I was at their center. He had spent years of his life killing my kind, but I think he was beginning to question his choices. Maybe a part of him was starting to see we weren't all mindless killers, and it bothered him.

Grinning, I sauntered into the pale yellow bathroom off the bedroom and turned on the shower. I might be able to use this to my advantage. I wasn't sure how, but it was an interesting development. Hell, at that point I was happy to have anything resembling useful information.

Scrubbing off the layers of blood and soot, I hummed an inane little tune to myself, glad to finally be free of the last remnants of naturi. After blow-drying my hair, I pulled on a pair of black leather pants and a long-sleeve silk shirt. This one was a brilliant blue, nearly matching the shade of Danaus's eyes. It would establish a subtle tie between us. I wasn't confident my new friend from Themis would pick up on it, but I had plans for this evening. As a finishing touch, I added a pair of rectangular sunglasses with blue lenses. I turned in front of the large mirror, taking in my appearance. A warm meal, a good day's sleep, and a hot shower had left me feeling upbeat. I could finally see an end to this winding road. After my brief meeting with this Themis character, I would locate Sadira and find a replacement for Tabor. When that was done, I was headed home and the Coven was on its own. I was back in control of my life and it felt good.

My intrepid companion didn't give me a second glance as we left the hotel and climbed into a taxi. We were silent as the little car swept us across the city to Mayfair. My trips to London had been infrequent over the years, but I'd been here often enough to recognize the various boroughs regardless of what century it was. And for as long as I'd known, Mayfair was the posh center of the universe for the monied elite. Alighting from the cab, I paused and looked up at the beautiful brick town house with its flower boxes overflowing with blooms. This was not what I had expected. I thought we would find ourselves in a seedy part of town, the back room of some disreputable bar or grimy warehouse with its family of oversized rats.

Directly across from us was Grosvenor Square, with its old trees reaching up at the night sky. The landscape was dotted with old brick facades and black iron fences, keeping the common rabble at bay. Matching black lamps stood at the corners, attempting to beat back the fog that had already begun to roll in from the Thames as the temperature dropped for the night.

The city felt vastly different from Savannah. Old Europe was quieter, more subdued, as if its dark history demanded that a hushed silence be observed in the dark hours of the night if you were out on the street. As if, otherwise, any one of the ancient myths of the fey or even my own kind might creep out from the shadows and strike. Europe held onto her old tales and superstitions longer, weaving them into the histories they had witnessed as if they were truths as well. The New World proved to be vastly different, with her shorter memory and fast-paced lifestyle that wouldn't slow down for anyone, not even an old ghost story like a vampire.

Shrugging, I followed Danaus up the front stairs and into the house, trying to ignore the way the air seemed to tingle around me. Too much magic in the air, too much old magic in this hallowed isle.

I noticed that he didn't bother to knock, but walked into the foyer. Without pause, he continued down the hall to a door on the left of the stairs that led to the second floor. He had been here before.

The building was the typical English town house, with shining hardwood floors and Oriental rugs. The paintings on the walls were of hunting scenes and wild gardens set up against dark woods. There were no photographs of family and friends. I reached out and found only one other person in the house; a man, extremely nervous. I couldn't stop the smile that lifted my lips, leaving the tips of my fangs poking out just below. Danaus paused with his hand on the brass-handled double doors and looked back at me. He felt the slight sweep of power as I searched the house, and frowned. I like to think he knew better than to ask me to behave.

Pushing open the two doors, we stepped into a brightly lit library. The man sitting behind the desk jumped at the sound of the doors opening but quickly covered it up by rising to his feet. He was wearing a dark brown suit with a creamy white shirt and brown patterned tie. A pair of gold-rimmed glasses was perched on his sharp, straight nose.

I laughed. I laughed so hard and deep that I leaned forward on Danaus's shoulder, my hand pressed to my stomach. This was not what I had expected. My experience with Themis was Danaus and hunters like him. I had naturally assumed this was a trained group of assassins; cold, hardened mercenaries. The confused man standing behind the large desk looked like a librarian. Still laughing, I watched him out of the corner of my eye. He sucked in a harsh breath as the power layered beneath the laughter brushed against him like a cat wanting affection. Interesting. He shouldn't have been able to feel that unless he had some experience with magic.

Then I stopped laughing. It was like I flipped a switch. One moment my laughter filled the room, and then it was gone. There was no gentle ebbing of the sound, just complete silence, except for the man's harsh breathing. I glanced at Danaus. No frowns. No glares. No unspoken warnings. In fact, his face was completely expressionless. I almost started laughing again. In his own way, he had given me the green light to have some fun. He, of course, would try to rein me in if I went too far, but until we reached that point, I had carte blanche.

"Enough games," I announced with a weary air, still leaning on Danaus. "I've had my laugh, but we don't have time for this. Where is the contact from Themis?"

"I –I am from Themis," the man, still standing, stammered, lifting his chin a little higher into the air.

"I don't want to talk to its accountant."

"I am a full-fledged member of Themis and have been for almost ten years." His voice gained strength as anger crowded his words. His brown eyes flicked to Danaus for half a breath before jumping back to me, as if urging the hunter to speak up.

"Really?" My gaze swept over the room. The library was a nice large room, with floor-to-ceiling dark wood shelves running the length of two of the walls. Floor lamps with beaded fringe shades stood guarding the four corners, beating back the darkness to its hiding place behind the sofa and under the large desk at the opposite end of the room. What little could be seen of the walls revealed a deep hunter green that was also in the Persian rugs that covered the hardwood floor.

I stepped around Danaus and approached the desk. Behind me, I heard the hunter step out of the line of fire to the plaid-patterned sofa that rested near the back wall.

The librarian tensed, but he didn't back up, as I strolled closer. "In what capacity do you serve Themis?"

"I'm a researcher, like most members of Themis."

"Most?" I turned sideways so I could look at Danaus, who was watching me. "What about Danaus? It was my impression that you were all like him."

"Oh, no," he said. He shook his head as a condescending smile lifted his thin lips. "Danaus is part of a small group of enforcers within Themis."

"Don't you mean trained murderers?" I corrected, my words cracking across his chest like a whip. This time he flinched. He tried to take a step backward, but ended up falling back into his chair. He paled and struggled to form words. His eyes darted over to Danaus as if seeking protection, but his enforcer never moved.

"We have to protect ourselves," the librarian said at last.

"You've had creatures killed that were no threat to you," I said evenly. I paused beside one of the pair of chairs positioned in front of his desk, my hand resting on the back.

"You've killed humans!" he said.

"Humans kill other humans every day in order to survive." I shrugged my slim shoulders as I strolled closer, my hand slipping off the chair.

"But you feed on us."

A smile flitted across my lips as images of Michael danced through my thoughts for a moment. "Only those who permit me."

"But—"

"In two days, she's fed at least twice." Danaus's presence and his deep voice almost cast a shadow over the room; a part of me wanted to step back into that bit of darkness. "No one has died."

"That's impossible!" the man said, jumping to his feet and slamming his palms on the empty surface of the desk. His eyes were wide and glittering in the bright light. "You just haven't seen the bodies. It has been well documented that vampires must kill their prey to sustain their existence. It's not really the blood they survive on, but the death that gives them power."

I laughed again, shaking my head. He sounded like he was quoting from a textbook. "How long have you studied my kind?" I inquired, wiping a tear from the corner of my eye.

"Themis has watched vampires for almost three centuries."

"And how many have you spoken to?"

"Personally? None." His voice lost some of its confidence and he sat back down again, seemingly shaken. His brows were gathered over his nose and his lips were pressed into a thin frown. "Until now."

"What about the others?"

"We don't talk to vampires. It's . . . too dangerous. You . . . kill," he said, struggling to find the words.

Smiling again, I paced around the desk until I was standing behind his chair. He twisted around so he was looking at me. Folding my hands on the back of his chair, I rested my chin on my hands. His fear was so thick and heavy I could taste it. My eyelids drifted closed and I drew in a deep breath, letting his fear swirl around me like an expensive perfume.

"So, you've decided to slaughter my kind based on myths and false information."

"But—But you kill," he said, as if it was the answer to everything.

"So do you," I whispered, staring deep into his eyes before I continued the circuit around to the front of the desk. Walking over to Danaus, I removed my sunglasses and hooked them over the top button of my blouse. I could feel the librarian relax in his chair as I moved away from him. Putting my right knee on the sofa next to Danaus's left hip, I sat down beside him, throwing my left leg across his lap. His hands remained limp at his side. He didn't touch me, but, more important, he didn't push me off away either. I leaned close, putting my left arm across his chest, resting my hand on his shoulder. Out of the corner of my eyes I could see the other man watching us closely, his forehead furrowed with a look of absolute confusion and shock.

Luckily for me, Danaus had bathed and changed into a clean set of clothes. He had rid himself of the smell of the naturi, reminding me again of a warm summer breeze dancing across the whitecaps in the Mediterranean. His chin and cheeks were free of dark stubble and he looked as if he'd actually caught a few hours of sleep.

I leaned in so my lips lightly brushed Danaus's ear. His muscles tensed. "Does Themis know what you can do?" I whispered. His powers flared around me in response to some emotion I couldn't quite place. I don't think it was the question that bothered him, but some deeper thought. I could understand that. We all had something to hide.

"No."

"So I thought," I murmured. I started to lift my left leg from his lap when Danaus grabbed my calf with his right hand, holding me in place. His touch was warmer than I'd expected, almost burning through my leather pants. Shocked by his sudden willingness to touch me, I went completely still.

Turning his head to look at me, my lips brushed his cheek and we both froze. Danaus exhaled slowly and I found myself drawing in his breath, holding it inside me. If one of us moved less than an inch, our lips would meet. But we sat like two stone statues.

"Jabari?" he finally asked, his whispered question deep and husky.

I stared at the hunter's chiseled profile, nearly drowning in his deep sapphire eyes. I hadn't told Jabari. It hadn't even occurred to me to tell the Ancient. Of course, if I had, Danaus would not have left Aswan alive. Why hadn't I told Jabari? If he didn't kill me over the whole Nerian fiasco, my existence was definitely forfeit for this little oversight.

Why didn't I tell him? Was it because I didn't like to share? Jabari would kill Danaus and that would be the end of it. He wouldn't appreciate the challenge the hunter represented. Or was it that Danaus was like me, an outcast among his own kind? Of course, I didn't know what he was, so that line of logic was a dead end.

"No," I said, unable to keep from coating that single word with my obvious surprise.

Danaus arched one dark brow at me, mocking one of my favorite expressions. Yeah. I was just full of surprises.

"Lilacs," he suddenly said. When my only reply was confused silence, he continued. "You smell like lilacs. No matter what you've been doing, you smell like lilacs."

Moving my head slightly, I brushed my lips across his chin. Every fiber of my being was screaming for a kiss, just a taste of his lips and his mouth. My hand tightened on his shoulder and I pressed my body a little closer. "Like you smell of the sun and sea?"

"Yes." His hand squeezed my calf again, but it wasn't a warning. His strong fingers kneaded the muscle in a deep massage, keeping me pressed tightly against him.

"Is that a bad thing?" My lips rose, skimming across his jaw to the corner of his mouth.

"No. Just . . . unexpected." With the speed of a glacier, Danaus turned his parted lips toward mine, his hot breath caressing my face.

A pen clattered to the hardwood floor, jerking us apart. We had forgotten about the gawking librarian. My head swung to the man behind the desk, a low growl escaping me. Danaus tightened his grip on my leg while his other arm wrapped around my waist, holding me in place.

"Let me throw him out the window," I said in a low voice.

"Mira . . ."

My eyes jerked back to his face, searching his gaze for any sign of frustration. I couldn't see it in his eyes, but the evidence pressed against my thigh, which was still draped over his lap. "I'll be gentle."

"With me or him?" I don't think he meant to say it out loud because his eyes widened with surprise. I leaned in to finish the kiss that had been rudely interrupted when he said, "The naturi." The only two words that could instantly kill my libido.

My head fell forward and I rested my forehead against his shoulder. "Bastard," I muttered softly. Danaus rubbed his hand up and down my back once, as if trying to soften the blow. Now was not the time.

I turned my gaze back to our spectator behind the desk, my cheek grazing Danaus's jaw. The librarian shifted in his chair, attempting to square his shoulders. I slid my hand back across Danaus's chest as I rose from the sofa as if pulled by marionette strings.

"What are you called?" I asked, strolling back over to the desk.

"James Parker."

"I am Mira." Taking one of the seats in front of his desk, I put my right heel on the edge of his desk and crossed my other foot over it at the ankle. He frowned at my feet.

"The Fire Starter," he said, dragging his eyes from my boots. His long, nimble fingers snatched up a fountain pen that had rolled off the ink blotter.

"Perhaps not all your information is bad, after all. Your group seems to be relatively well informed about the naturi—tell me what you know."

"About the naturi?"

"Start with your opinion of them," I commanded, inspecting my fingernails.

"Well, they are nothing like the fairy tales that are based on their race; all that nonsense about elves and fairies," he began. Withdrawing a small square of cloth from this pocket, James removed his glasses and started to clean them. I had a feeling that this was more of a nervous habit than any actual need to remove dirt. "They are cold, ruthless, and view humans as a plague on the earth. Their power lies with the sun and the earth. We have evidence that says the naturi are the reason for several lost civilizations through time, up until about five hundred years ago."

"What happened five hundred years ago?" I tried to keep my voice bland and uninterested, but my eyes flicked back up to his face. His hands stilled for a moment as his brown eyes met my deep violet orbs.

James licked his lips and drew in a deep breath before speaking again. "Our information is sketchy at best, but I was under the impression that you were there," he replied. "I was hoping you would be able to tell me."

"I want to hear what you know first," I hedged, smiling wide enough to reveal my fangs.

"Not much." His hands started to work over the glasses again. "We interviewed some Incan descendants a long time ago. It's all legend and myth now. They said children of their sun god came down to Machu Picchu one day. They were holding captive a daughter of the moon god. The people of the sun were preparing to sacrifice several of the Incans in the Sacred Plaza when more than a score of the children of the moon god arrived, and freed the captured moon daughter. The Incan descendents mentioned a great battle.

"We've not been able to make that much sense out of it. It was obviously a battle between vampires and the naturi. After that night, the door between the naturi world and this one was closed, defeating the naturi. I was hoping that you would be able to tell me more." James inched forward a little to sit on the edge of his chair, glasses forgotten in his hands.

"I can't." And it was the truth. I couldn't tell him because I wasn't sure. I couldn't remember any of the other nightwalkers at Machu Picchu. I knew others had been there; the greatest gathering I had ever seen, but even now I couldn't recall a single face beyond the triad: Jabari, Sadira, and Tabor. "The naturi were never defeated." Putting my booted feet back on the floor, I restlessly pushed out of the chair and paced over to one of the bookcases that lined the wall. "The queen of the naturi still lives. The final battle was simply postponed."

My eyes flitted over the various leather-bound volumes, reading the titles. They were all books on the occult. Books on vampires, lycanthropes, magic, and obscure bits of history lined these shelves. It would have taken a lifetime to accumulate this extensive a collection. I glanced over at James for a moment, taking in his clean-shaven face and eager eyes. He looked like he might be in his late twenties, early thirties at the absolute latest. This either wasn't his house or this was a family occupation. Curious.

"But you will find her in time?" he asked, rising from his seat again.

I turned back to the shelf and pulled down a large volume on nightwalkers. I opened it in the middle and let my eyes scan over the page. With an angry growl, I pitched the book over my shoulder and picked up another.

"Stop!" James said before he could stop himself. "That one's rare."

Ignoring him, I opened another book on vampires. I tossed this one aside before reaching the bottom of the page. Overriding his fear, James came around the desk to my side as I was grabbing a third book. I dropped it over my shoulder, but he caught this one.

Turning, I grabbed his jacket lapels as he cringed. Behind me, Danaus's powers brushed against me, warning me. "Is this what you have been reading about us? Has all of your kind been soaking in these lies?"

"They can't be. These journals were written by people who have survived encounters with vampires," he said. "You can't deny that you kill; you treat us like cattle."

"You paint us as mindless killers, monsters in the darkness." I released him suddenly as if he were something dirty. "Humans are remembered for more than the wars they wage and the lives they take. We create things of beauty as well." I took a step closer to James. He inched backward but was stopped when his back hit the bookshelf. I smiled at him, careful not to reveal my fangs. Lifting my hand, I held it barely an inch from his face. He flinched, his wide eyes darting between my face and hand. Lowering my hand with infinite care, I drew my fingers across his forehead to his temple and into his hair. "We feel pain and joy. We feel sadness and love just like you," I whispered, my voice like a caress. "We can give and take exquisite pleasure."

"E-Even with humans?" he asked, stumbling over the words.

I chuckled, pulling my hand back to my side. "Some of my favorite lovers have been human males. You're very . . . attentive."

Turning, I walked away to the other side of the room. As I passed Danaus, I shoved my hands into my back pockets and winked at him. He looked back at James's desk, but I caught the slight quirk of one corner of his mouth. He knew the game I was playing, and at the moment, after the questionable information they had supplied him with, he was not pleased with Themis.

"But there is one thing I am confused about." I turned back. "Despite all the horrible things you believe about my kind, Danaus was sent to find me. I don't think he was sent to acquire my assistance, just information. Why?"

"If the stories are to be believed, vampires stopped the naturi once. I thought you could do it again," James said, still clutching the book to his chest.

"I? Not we?"

"Some of the others . . . did not see the wisdom in this idea."

"And do they know about this meeting?"

He looked at Danaus, then back to me. "No." His grip on the book pressed to his chest tightened, as if it could protect him from the wrath of his superiors.

"You are a brave one. Of course, you do have Danaus here to protect you from me, but I have a feeling your little friends aren't going to be too happy about this. Interesting."

"What are you planning?" Anxiety spiked his voice.

I strolled back over to the chair I'd been sitting in and plopped down, propping my feet up on the edge of this desk. "Nothing at the moment. It's just interesting information. Do you have anything else interesting to tell me?"

"A-About what?" he said, walking back over to his chair behind the desk. He sat down and reluctantly laid the book down on the surface.

"About the naturi."

Pulling open one of the drawers to his right, he withdrew a manila folder and handed me what looked like a thin stack of photographs. I had to force myself to reach for it. The last photograph I'd been handed had sent me on this fool's errand. Gritting my teeth, I took the glossy pictures and nearly screamed in frustration when I saw more naturi symbols, each smeared in blood.

I lurched to my feet, struggling to keep from igniting the picture in my hands. "When?" I heard Danaus stand and walk over, his heavy steps echoing off the hardwood floor. I handed him the pictures, my eyes never leaving James's pale face.

"They've started appearing during the past couple of days."

"Where?" I needed him to confirm my suspicion.

"I—I'm not completely sure. I think one was in Spain," he said, running a nervous hand over his tie.

"The Alhambra," I confirmed. "Where else?"

"Another was in Cambodia."

"At Angkor Wat." I grabbed the pictures out of Danaus's hands and laid them out across the top of James's desk. "There are six pictures here. We have Angkor Wat and Alhambra." I put the two that I was sure had been identified aside. I knew these places. Jabari had drilled them into my head. I picked up another with rose-colored stone and added it to the pile with Angkor and Alhambra. "That's Petra and this is the Palace of Knossos on Crete." I added the fourth picture to the pile, flipping it over and laying it down with a slap. I'd known that place before Jabari. I'd been born in Crete.

"Oh, I remember this one." James picked up a picture of a plain dark brown sign set against a backdrop of trees. "They said it was on the back of a sign in Yellowstone National Park."

"And the last one?" Danaus asked, picking it up.

"Mesa Verde, Colorado." I recognized the stonework. Turning my gaze back to James, I fought back a knot of panic that was starting to twist in my stomach. "What about the other five sites? Have your people checked them?"

"Other five?"

"The holy cities of the naturi. I assumed you were checking those." I turned my gaze on Danaus, clenching my teeth. "You said your people were watching potential sites for the sacrifices. Did you lie?"

"We are watching them," he snapped, taking a step toward me.

"All twelve?"

"Twelve?" He looked genuinely puzzled for a moment. "There has to be more than twelve. We're watching all the ancient temples and structures that have been linked to ancient myths."

I shoved both of my hands through my hair, swallowing a scream of frustration. I knew I should have asked for more clarification sooner. He seemed to know so much when we met that I assumed he knew all about naturi history. I was wrong, and it might just cost us.

Drawing in a deep breath, I turned back to the desk and picked up the pictures. "A quick lesson on the naturi," I said, then looked up at James. "You might want to take some notes."

The Themis member immediately plopped back down in his chair and pulled out some paper and a pen.

"There are twelve so-called holy sites for the naturi spread around the world, based on the energy that culminates in the area. In North America, there is Old Faithful and Mesa Verde. In South America, it's Easter Island and Machu Picchu. In Europe, we have Stonehenge, Alhambra, and the Palace of Knossos. In Africa, there's Petra, Dead Vlei, and Abu Simbel. And in Asia, there's Konark and Angkor Wat."

Danaus shook his head, frowning. "That doesn't make any sense. Some of these places aren't that old, and Abu Simbel has even been moved from its original location. The naturi are older than all of those structures."

"It's not the structure that makes a place holy to them, it's the power emanating from the earth in an area that makes it special." I grabbed the pictures again and spread them out across the desktop. "Humans have created amazing structures at these locations. Why? Because they are drawn to these places. Some part of their brain senses something, even if they can't recognize it."

"Abu Simbel was moved."

"Only two hundred meters. It's still close enough to the original location, which is now underwater and only of use to the water naturi."

"What about the marks in the trees," James said, his head snapping up from the paper where he was furiously scribbling notes. "They weren't anywhere near these locations."

I shook my head, nibbling on my lower lip. I was getting into shaky territory. Nowhere in the histories I'd read of the naturi did I encounter tales of them making marks in the trees like the ones I'd seen. "Those feel different than the ones at the holy sites. More permanent, but I have no idea what they are for."

Danaus leaned his hip against the edge of the desk and folded his arms over his chest. "And the blood marks?"

"They weren't made from human blood," James interjected before looking back down at his notes. "We had it tested. It was all animal blood."

My gaze drifted back down to the pictures. "They're testing sites," I murmured.

"What do you mean?"

A half smile lifted one corner of my mouth. "It's old magic. You'd think you would know a little old magic, Danaus," I teased. "The next sacrifice is to break the seal, and they will need as much power they can get. With Aurora stuck in the other world, they'll need to draw as much power as possible from the earth. To do so, they have to locate the site that has the best charge. So, the naturi are testing sites with minor spells, looking for the best location."

"But Danaus said there would be a total of three sacrifices," James said, his brows meeting over the bridge of his nose.

"There will be if we don't stop them. The first was sort of priming the pump, pulling the power up from the earth. The second will break the seal, and the third will open the door."

"And you don't think they will use any of the sites that had the marks?"

"No, they would have covered their tracks. Cleaned off the blood and immediately ended the spell. Konark has been used and the other six marked."

"So, there are just five possibilities: Stonehenge, Machu Picchu, Dead Vlei, Abu Simbel, and Easter Island," James read off his list.

"Contact Themis," Danaus ordered. "Get people to those locations now."

The hunter then turned his grim eyes intent on my face. All lightness and entertainment for the evening had been sucked from the room.

I sighed. "We have to find Sadira now." We couldn't sit by and hope that Jabari located Rowe. We were nearly out of time. If the naturi were actively searching for another site, it meant that they were likely to complete the next sacrifice soon. But it didn't make any sense. The next new moon was nearly a week away. I had a dark suspicion when they planned to strike, but I needed to confirm it, which meant I needed Sadira.

"Wait!" James said, hurrying around his desk. "I can help."

I paused at the door, my hand resting on the doorjamb. "Go back to Themis, James Parker. Go back and warn them." My voice suddenly sounded very tired. I pitied this young man who had devoted his life to studying the things that crept by in the shadows. That was one of the greatest differences between the naturi and nightwalkers. Unlike the naturi, we could feel pity on occasion.

SIXTEEN

We grabbed a taxi back to the hotel. Huddled in the darkness with Danaus beside me, I reached out into the city and for the first time in almost five hundred years searched for Sadira. It should have been an easy task. With any other vampire, I would have had to search slowly, letting my powers creep over the earth until I finally reached him or her. But Sadira was different. She was my maker. My connection with her would always be strong, no matter the distance or time. I should have been able to find her immediately, like lightning being drawn to a lightning rod. Yet, it felt as if she didn't exist. But I would have known it if she was dead; I would have felt it. Something was wrong. First Jabari, and now Sadira. I could feel the nightwalkers in the city, but not these important two.

"Are there naturi in the city?" I asked. Silence filled the dirt-encrusted taxi, broken occasionally by the scratchy, distorted voices from the cab radio. I stared out the window at the assortment of town houses and shops as we headed back toward the Thames and the Savoy Hotel, near Charing Cross.

"Not in the immediate area." Danaus's voice rose, as if we were waking from a dream. "I think near the outskirts of town."

"You're not sure?" I turned my head so I could see him out of the corner of my eye.

He grimaced in the darkness, his features drawn in concentration. "It's hard to tell. It's like trying to see through a thick fog." Frustration edged his voice and hardened the line of his jaw.

"It's this island." Sinking back into the dirty backseat, I leaned my shoulder against his strong arm. I was sure he'd run into other magic-related problems while staying in Great Britain in the past.

There was too much old magic in these lands. Too many old gods had been born and died on this island; too many powerful warlocks had stretched their arms here. Magic doesn't just die—it fades into the air and seeps into the earth. After centuries, this ground was saturated. Many magic users came to Great Britain because they could tap this well of power.

"Who's Sadira?" he asked, changing the topic.

"She was one of the three to form the seal centuries ago."

"Jabari and Tabor were the others?"

"Yes."

"Were you a part of it?"

"No, just a recovered prisoner." I was barely a century at the time, still a child among my kind. I had been captured two weeks before and tortured. The naturi wanted to use my unique ability to control fire as a weapon against the nightwalkers.

"Do you think the naturi will come after her?"

"Yes. Enough naturi were left behind in our world who would be able to identify the members of the triad." I just didn't understand how they would find her, when we couldn't sense them and they couldn't sense us.

Leaning my head back, I placed my right ankle on my knee, which brushed against his with the movement. Neither of us stirred for a moment, almost as if we waiting to see who would flinch first. What did it matter? I had crawled all over him on more than one occasion. And right now I wanted the reassuring warmth that washed off of him . . . it was better than the cold reality of the naturi.

"Is this how you expected things to progress?" He turned his head to look at me, his blue eyes catching a shaft of light as the taxi lurched into motion again.

"No." I slumped in the seat and crossed my arms under my breasts. "Finding Jabari was supposed to improve the situation, not make it worse. I should be home looking after my domain, not searching for Sadira. It's all a mess." Beside me, I could hear the steady rhythm of his heartbeat while his powers brushed against my cheek. His power might not feel human, but his heart did. I had been out of contact with Knox for several nights now, and a part of me was desperate to know how things were progressing with him and Barrett. I needed to be home to help suppress any fires should they spring up between the nightwalkers and the shapeshifters.

"Is this how you planned it?" I asked. Sitting so low in the seat, I was forced to tilt my head up to meet his gaze.

"No."

"Oh, really?"

Danaus leaned toward me as he whispered, "You should be dead."

I chuckled and threaded my arm through his. He stiffened but didn't jerk away. "But we work so well together," I said, earning a soft snort. "We worked quite well together in Aswan."

"You mean when you stopped trying to kill me."

Leaning my head against his shoulder again, I let my eyes drift shut. "Well, I thought you tried to kill me while I slept. I was understandably upset."

"It's my job."

"Get a new job, like being a florist." I snuggled a little closer, trying to irritate him now. The night air was warm and we had our windows down, allowing the fresh breeze to circulate through the stale car. Yet, the warmth and strength rolling off Danaus would have been comforting no matter the season.

"I can't."

"Why?"

"You're evil."

My whole body stiffened at those two cold words and my eyelids lifted. I stared blankly at the back of the front seat. "Prove it."

"Come into a church with me tomorrow night."

I couldn't, which was the point. "Why haven't you caused my blood to boil? If we're so evil, why haven't you destroyed us all that way?" I asked, attempting to dodge his question as I sat up, pulling away from him.

"The same reason you haven't set me and every naturi you meet on fire," he said. He shifted in his seat so he could pull his wallet out of his back pocket.

"Because it lacks style and finesse?"

Still balanced on his left hip, Danaus leaned over, his mouth hovering just a few inches above my face. "Because it's exhausting. If you don't kill everyone, you're left vulnerable. In a fight, our powers are a last resort."

As the taxi pulled over to the curb, he sat back in his seat and began to shuffle through his wallet to pay the driver. I slid out of the car, grateful to be back out in the night air. There was nothing to say. He was right. With time, I gained more strength, more endurance, but the use of my unique ability would always be exhausting.

We walked up to my hotel room, lost to our own dark thoughts. I was only vaguely aware of the looks that we were earning from the other guests. Charlotte had picked the Savoy, with its palatial elegance and gilt ornamentation. Its guests were the upper crust of society, and I was wearing leather pants, silk shirt, and blue-tinted sunglasses. I think I looked like a rock star, which was amusing. Clinging to that rationale, the observers naturally assumed that the heavily muscled, darkly handsome man at my side was either a body-guard or a lucky lover. Danaus had wisely decided to leave the scimi-tars in the room, and instead had an assortment of knives concealed about his body. Walking around armed in Aswan was one thing. Lon-don at least kept up the pretense of being a little more civilized.

When we reached the double doors that led to my private suite, I stopped sharply. Something was wrong. A brief touch of Gabriel's and Michael's minds revealed that someone else was in the room with them. They were tense and anxious. However, a light scan of the room turned up only my two human angels.

With a playful smile, I threw open the two doors and walked in. But all playfulness was ripped out of my body as my eyes fell on Sadira. I hissed at her, my lips drawn back to reveal a perfect set of white fangs. My hands clenched into tight fists, my nails digging into my palms until I was drawing blood.

"Such manners," she chided with a shake of her head. Her soft sweet voice was hypnotic, seeking to burrow down into my brain. She sat with her back ramrod straight and her chin up, as if she were a regal princess on her throne.

I straightened my shoulders, sending a warning look to the night-walker. I knew my first encounter with her after all this time wouldn't be good, but I hadn't expected to react with such uncontrollable hos-tility.

"Why couldn't I sense you?" I demanded, failing to unclench my teeth.

"Jabari contacted me. He said to hide myself, and that he was sending someone for my protection. I had no idea it would be you." Her voice was calm and cool. Nothing seemed to ruffle her perfectly groomed feathers.

My skin crawled as I stared at her. Everything about Sadira seemed to be one great lie, and I hated her for it. At just under five feet, she looked like someone's sweet little mother. Her long dark hair was streaked with gray and pulled up into a bun. Her features were soft and rounded, leaving nothing alluring or threatening in her ap-pearance. She wore a long black skirt and a pale yellow shirt with pearl buttons. She looked prim and proper, safe and almost fragile.

But it was all a lie. I had seen her tear out a man's throat while she fed, the blood dripping down her chin. I had seen her plunge her hand into a woman's chest and pull out her heart so she could drink

the blood directly from it. Yet, even when she was killing these people, she never looked like a predator. Just a hideous nightmare.

"Who is your dark shadow?" she inquired, smoothing over the
silence that filled in the places where the tension had yet to reach. Her
accent was haunting, an exotic flavor no longer on this earth. Ancient
Persian. After more than a thousand years, Sadira had come no closer
to shedding her accent. Most of us relinquished our old ties, preferring to blend in. Even Jabari's accent faded when he was away from
Egypt. But Sadira kept hers.

"He's not your concern." I took a step to my left so I was standing
directly in front of Danaus. "The naturi are coming. They're planning
to break the seal."

"How?" Surprise lifted her thin eyebrows and extended the wrinkles that stretched from the corners of her almond-shaped eyes. Her
pale hands clenched in her lap, twisting her slender fingers.

"The usual way—blood and magic. Jabari said I am to protect
you and reform the triad."

"Has he been selected to protect you, then?" She refused to drop
the issue of Danaus, intrigued by the fact that I was traveling with
this stranger.

She never questioned the assistance of my daylight warriors, Gabriel and Michael. When a nightwalker acquired a certain level of
power and frequently traveled into the domain of other powerful
vampires, he or she would enlist the services of such guardians. Danaus, however, was distinctly different from these protectors. It wasn't
that he stood there exuding his own dark power. It was his confidence
and the fact that he seemed completely at ease in a room with two
nightwalkers. He had also been out with me at night, so keeping him
at my side meant that he carried a different kind of importance to me.
He was an equal, not a servant.

"I do not need nighttime protection," I told her.

"Oh, my Mira," Sadira said, her voice filled with warmth and
concern. "You need protection more than me or Jabari."

"I can take care of myself. I was never as weak as you liked to
pretend."

"I never thought you weak, my dearest child." Pushing smoothly
to her feet, she took a couple steps toward me, but I stepped away
from her, the two of us circling in the small living room. I wouldn't,
couldn't, let her lay a hand on me.

Sadira stopped, a look of patience filling her warm brown eyes. "I
feared you would grow to be too confident in your powers. I didn't
want to see you hurt. I wanted to protect you."

I blinked, and images of her castle in Spain sprung to life. She was in my head again, manipulating my thoughts like the early days. Mentally, I reached for her to shove her back out, but it was like grabbing smoke. The memories blurred, and then abruptly focused. I was back in the dark dungeon with its damp, crumbling walls. I was lying on the cold slab, hovering somewhere between life and death, with only the sound of Sadira's voice to guide me back from madness.

Most nightwalkers are made in a night. A kiss of death, an exchange of blood, and the deed was done. But Sadira had wanted something more than when she made me. She wanted a First Blood, and thus she spent ten years—night after endless night—nursing me into her world and bringing me into the darkness. And when she was done, I was her greatest creation.

Our years together were ugly. She wanted absolute control over me; the same control she had over the other dozen vampires that resided in her castle. She had created a few others, but I was her only First Blood. They all flocked to her, clinging to her image of the caring, protective mother, but I never believed those lies, and only stayed because I thought I had no other option.

Now, however, I was free. Clutching that thought, I finally shoved Sadira from my mind and threw up as many metal barriers as I could. I pushed her back until she was just a vague shadow at the edge of my thoughts.

"I did not come here to fight with you, my Mira." Sadness tinged her voice. "When I felt your presence, I thought you had come to talk."

"Did you think I had come back to you?" Dragging my eyes back to my maker, I shook my head. "How could you believe such a thing?"

Sadira smiled at me, her head tilted to the side. The look a parent gave a foolish child; one of infinite patience and love. "Why do you still harbor this hatred for me?" We were circling each other like cats, waiting for an opening. "Does it chase away the nightmares? Does it help you to forget about Crete . . . and Calla?"

"I warned you to never speak her name." My low voice crouched in the shadows, watching. I stopped circling, my whole body painfully tensed.

"You left her and now you find it easier to blame me for your regrets. You can't run from us both forever," Sadira said, taking a step toward me. She lifted her hand to touch my cheek, but I raised my hand, just an inch from her face. Flames danced over my fingers and slithered down to my wrist. Her eyes widened.

Before Sadira, I had a life. It was a short, fragile human life, but it was my life nonetheless. I'd had a family that I loved and a place in my small corner of the world. My world didn't include nightwalkers or torture. It didn't even include my own powers, since I'd chosen to hide that unique ability and start fresh.

But Sadira slipped into my world one night centuries ago and stole me away, threatening to kill all those I loved if I did not remain at her side. So I stayed through the humiliation, pain, and seemingly constant fear. She kept me at her side as a human for roughly four years. During that time, I discovered that I would make a better vampire than I could ever be as a normal human. The nightwalkers surrounding her feared me, feared my powers. And for good reason: Sadira had taught me everything she knew about torture and manipulation. When the Black Plague swept through Europe, she offered to make me a nightwalker in an effort to save my life. I agreed, walking away from any hope of returning to the life I'd lived before.

I hated Sadira for stealing me away. I hated myself for saying yes, because I could not be what I wanted—normal. Human.

Lifting my open hands, a pair of flames danced on my palms, flickering yellow and orange. I lowered my hands again, but the flames remained hovering in midair like little balls of light. Sadira took an uneasy step back, unable to drag her eyes from the flames. She had seen my tricks with fire before, even commanded me to perform, but I'd learned a few things since I was last with her. She had never seen me burn the air itself.

With the barest nod of my head, the flames streaked toward her. Less than a foot from her chest, they split in two different directions and started to circle her. She pulled her arms against her chest, her head jerking from one side to the other, desperately trying to keep the fire in sight at all times. She was terrified . . . and with good cause.

"I left her because I had no choice. You would have killed her," I said, unable to even speak Calla's name. I hadn't thought about her in centuries, but Sadira's cruel mention brought a fresh rush of pain, as she'd no doubt intended. "I left you because I would have killed you had I stayed. You made me, so I spared your life as an act of gratitude. I owe you nothing now."

Sadira lifted her eyes to my face, and I could see a mixture of anger and genuine confusion in their depths. A part of her honestly could not understand my hatred. She did everything in the name of protecting her children, but that also meant controlling them. And no matter how hard she tried, she could not completely control me. In the past, she could make me bow under the pain and anguish she caused, but it was always short-lived.

Danaus purposefully entered my line of sight, standing behind

Sadira's left shoulder and frowning. He didn't have to say anything. This argument was wasting time we didn't have. I would have to add Sadira to my list of unfinished business. If naturi didn't kill me first, I would finally deal with Sadira and my past.

"Enough of this." Waving my hands in the air, the flames vanished with a puff of smoke. I paced away from Sadira, over to the windows that looked down on the city. Pushing aside the gauzy white curtains, I looked down on the busy street as a steady flow of traffic rushed below us.

When I turned back around, the tableau looked exactly as it had when I entered the room. The moment had been erased. Sadira's face was expressionless, but that did not mean I'd been forgiven. A vampire never attacked another of her kind that was twice her age. And you never attacked your maker unless you were sure you could kill them. While Sadira worked under the pretense of love and protection, she was no different than the others. She would strike out at me at her first chance, but I wasn't particularly worried. She could hurt me but would not try to kill me. I was a valuable pet, and she wanted me at her side, broken and obedient.

"One sacrifice has been completed at Konark, and the naturi have attacked me twice," I said, trying to boil down everything that had happened recently into a concise description. It wasn't easy. Was it fair to leave out the dead in my domain or the fear that seemed to burn in me every time I stepped outside? "We think they are going after anyone who survived Machu Picchu."

"We?" Sadira said, cocking her head to the side as he eyes slid back to Danaus.

"Jabari and I," I sharply corrected her assumption. "Tabor is dead. That leaves you and Jabari as part of the triad. I don't remember who else was at the mountain that night, but not many of us survived."

Sadira's dark brown eyes narrowed on me as she frowned. Resting her right elbow on the arm of the chair, she settled her narrow chin in the palm of her hand. "What do you remember of that night?"

"Not much after you arrived. I remember Jabari rescuing me, holding me, with you and Tabor standing nearby. And then nothing . . . just light and . . . pain." I struggled to pull the memory loose from the jumble of thoughts crowding that night. "Why can't I remember? What happened after you arrived?"

"Have you asked Jabari?"

"He said he would tell me later." Frustration and anger crept back into my tone. I shoved my right hand through my hair, pushing it from my face.

"Then I will leave it to him," Sadira said quickly, with a relieved look. She was obviously glad to wash her hands of the ordeal. "I don't wish to talk about that night."

"Why? What happened? It couldn't have been that bad if we won." Taking another step closer, I moved around the coffee table in the center of the room in front of the sofa.

"No, Mira, please. You may doubt me, but I do love you. Even after all these years, the sound of your screams still haunts me at night. It is a sound I know I shall never forget."

"You never heard my screams," I said in a low voice. "The naturi had stopped torturing me before you arrived." Her eyes darted away from me, locking on a point somewhere over my shoulder. A heavy knot twisted in my stomach as my mind pushed against the dark shadows that crowded my memories of that night. "How could you have heard me screaming?"

"It's not important right now. There is nothing we can do until the triad has been reformed." Her voice wavered before she could bring herself to meet my gaze. I stared into her brown eyes for a long time before I spoke again. She'd made her decision and I couldn't move her.

"Fine." I shoved my hands into my back pockets in an effort to keep from sending another fireball at her. "Jabari said to reform the triad I needed to find someone of Tabor's bloodline. I don't know Tabor's maker so I guess we need to find one of his children."

"And there you are in luck, though I wish one of his other children were closer," Sadira announced, a light frown pulling at her full red lips.

"Why?"

"His name is Thorne. He is a little . . . different from what we have known. He appears to be a part of a new breed of nightwalker. He's rather open about his condition," she said delicately.

"Whatever. I'll deal with him," I said with a dismissive wave of my hand.

"He's not likely to come with you."

"I'm sure I can handle him." And I was sure. "Have you met him? If he's going to be difficult, I would prefer it if he didn't know I was looking for him."

Searching the area for a nightwalker I had never met before would take time and be invasive—rather like bending every vampire over and checking the initials in their underwear. If Sadira or I had met Thorne before, I could feel for him more discreetly.

"We have not been formally introduced, but I recently tracked him down to a bar on the outskirts of the city called Six Feet Under."

"I'll find him," I bit out. Turning, I was about to stalk out of the room, happy to finally be leaving Sadira, when Danaus moved toward the door as well. "No, you're staying," I told him, placing a restraining hand on his chest, ignoring his dark looks. "Someone needs to stay here and protect her."

"What about the naturi?" he asked.

Fear lurched in my stomach, wrapping itself around my heart. "Are they close?"

"Not that I can tell, but you wouldn't know it until they were standing next to you."

I glanced over at Michael and Gabriel seated on the sofa. If our enemies attacked as they had at Aswan, they wouldn't have a chance. They were no match for the naturi.

But by that logic, I also couldn't drag Sadira behind me through the bowels of London. She would be too much of a distraction if I were forced to try to protect both her and Thorne. I was trapped. I couldn't imagine how Jabari had expected me to manage this. He could have just commanded Thorne to appear using his telepathic abilities, and Thorne would have appeared. Easy as that. Unfortunately, I wasn't that intimidating yet.

I paced away from the door, desperately trying to find a new solution. I didn't know any other nightwalkers in London I could call on and trust them to defend Sadira with their lives. And Danaus wasn't about to stay behind when we both knew I needed him at my back to tell me if the naturi were closing in. I was about to give in and have Sadira accompany me to the pub when I felt someone else.

My hand flew to my mouth, but a chuckle still escaped. It was crazy and desperate, but I was completely out of options. I spun around sharply, facing Danaus. He jerked back a step, surprised by my quick change of direction. "Could Themis protect her?" I asked. His dark brows snapped together and he looked at me as if I had suddenly gone mad. "Do they have the firepower here in London to protect her?" I repeated a little slower.

"Yes, but—"

"We don't have any other choice. I'm not thrilled about the idea, but I can't be in two places at once."

A long, heavy silence stretched through the room as Danaus stared at me. When he finally spoke, it sounded as if he'd ground up the word with his back teeth before releasing it: "Agreed."

"Great. Now go fetch James. He just came up on the elevator," I said with a laugh at his surprised look. "He followed us to the hotel and has been searching for us."

Danaus hurried out of the room, a dark look filling his eyes. I don't know whether he was upset that James had followed us or because he hadn't noticed earlier. I had a feeling Danaus was so focused on the nightwalkers that surrounded him and the naturi that he forgot to pay any attention to the humans lurking on the fringe.

He reappeared a minute later, dragging a flustered-looking James in by the arm. He gave the young man a shove into the center of the room as he slammed the door closed again. It was nice to see Danaus angry with someone other than me. James ran his hands over his jacket as he eyes quickly surveyed the room. He stiffened at the sight of Michael and Gabriel, but when his eyes fell on Sadira, he stumbled backward a few steps, running into Danaus. Stepping away, he found himself that much closer to me.

"This was what you wanted, wasn't it?" I said, taking a step even closer to him, my hands lightly clasped behind my back. "I felt you bumbling through the hotel. You had to know I would be aware of your presence." I circled behind him as I spoke. I gave him credit for not trying to run as I heard his heart thudding like that of a cornered hare.

"I—I want to help," James said, struggling to keep his voice from breaking. He wasn't wearing his glasses now and I noticed his eyes were more copper than an ordinary brown; an odd shade with an almost red highlight in their brown depths. Trapped in that room, surrounded by monsters, he was younger than I initially thought; definitely mid- to late twenties.

"And so you shall," I whispered in his ear. I quickly moved away, then stepped in front of him again. "James Parker, may I introduce Sadira," I grandly announced with a flourish of my hands as I bent in a mocking bow.

"A pleasure and an honor," he said with the kind of grace and aplomb everyone had come to expect of the British. He gave a slight bow of his head out of respect, but nothing more. I was impressed.

Sadira smiled at him, a picture of sweetness and gentility. "It is good to meet you, James Parker." Her soft accent made it sound like she was almost purring. She then looked at me, and the warmth was replaced by a look of extreme caution. "What games do you play, my daughter?"

"No games. I have a task to be completed and I cannot drag you along, yet I can't leave you behind either. My new friend James will see to your protection while I am gone."

"I beg your pardon." His eyes widened until I feared they would roll from their sockets. "How can I possibly hope to protect her?"

"Take her to the Compound," Danaus responded, his deep voice sweeping unexpectedly through the room like a bitter winter wind.

James spun around to look at the hunter. "Have you lost your mind? No vampire has ever been permitted inside the Compound."

Danaus just stared at the young man. He obviously didn't care about precepts and traditions.

"James, she is one of the three nightwalkers that can stop the naturi," I said, placing an arm around his bony shoulders. He stiffened at the touch but didn't try to pull away. "I must go fetch one of the others and cannot protect her at the same time. So it is in everyone's best interest that she remains alive and well guarded. Your little group can do that." I leaned close so he could hear me when my voice dropped to a whisper. "Besides, after all the damage your group has brought on my kind, you owe us this one."

James turned his head to look at me. I smiled, letting him get a good look at my fangs. He jerked violently backward, stumbling into Danaus again. "But what if—I mean, if she—" he started, but halted each time as he struggled to form the sentence without completely insulting Sadira in the process.

I chuckled, shaking my head. I'd put him in an awkward position. Less than two hours ago he had never spoken to a nightwalker before, and now they surrounded him.

"She'll behave herself."

"Mira!" Sadira gasped, sounding appropriately scandalized.

My name only earned her a dark chuckle.

"Where are you trying to send me?" Sadira demanded, her hands tightening on the arms of her chair. There was no threat or warning in her voice, but it held none of its usual sweetness either.

"The safest place I can think to put you." I paused, stepping away from James, to stand directly in front of her. "In a den of hunters."

Sadira came out of her chair instantly, her body rigid. "Are you mad?" Her eyes were wide and sparkling in the pale yellow lamplight.

"I have no other options. They won't harm you as long as you don't attack them."

"Can you promise that?"

"No," I admitted with an indifferent shrug. "But it's in their best interest that you remain alive since you're key to stopping the naturi. Of course, if you threaten them, I'm sure they have ample stakes lying around."

"You can't do this, Mira!"

"Do you have a better idea?"

She stared at me, impotent rage and fear blazing in her eyes. Her small hands were balled into fists at her side.

"I didn't think so. I'm sending Michael and Gabriel with you as well, to help act as protection and a buffer between you and Themis. Don't think to strike at me through them . . . you have your own string of pets that I can go through too."

Sadira sat back down, lifting her chin a little higher. "You'll regret this."

I laughed at her. "You're not the only one who wants my head on a pike at the moment. Take a number and get in line." I turned my back on her and walked over to the windows, still shaking my head.

"Themis will never let them in." James's voice was fragile, as if he was terrified I would rip his throat out at any second.

"Call Ryan." Danaus said before I could speak. The two members of Themis just stared at each other.

"Use the phone in the bedroom," I said, pointing toward one of the doors in the two-bedroom suite. "I'll have my limo brought around to the front while we wait."

Finally, James frowned and left the room, closing the door behind him. Michael had already risen from the sofa and was calling down to the front desk for a limo, while Gabriel sorted through weaponry.

"Take it all," I said. His head snapped up, lines of confusion digging furrows in his forehead as he looked at me. "You may not be returning here again. I want you and Michael prepared for anything. Set up sleeping shifts when you arrive at this Compound. I want one of you awake and with Sadira at all times."

"But at dawn . . . ?" Gabriel started before the words seemed to die in his throat.

"I'm not sure where I'll be. Hopefully, I'm being overly cautious." Gabriel frowned, his gaze darting over to Danaus for a moment. I noticed that his hand tightened on the dagger he'd been about to place in a belt sheath. "He will not kill me while I sleep," I told him.

"But will he protect you?"

"Yes, I think he will." The idea was amusing, lifting my mood a bit. I looked over at Danaus, who stood stiff and expressionless. He was completely unmoved by Gabriel's glares and our conversation. "I think he would much rather kill me himself than allow someone else to do it."

"That is not much comfort," Gabriel said, a wry smile briefly touching his lips.

I looked away from my guardian, my eyes falling on Sadira. She had been closely watching the conversation, a smug smile lifting her lips. "Now you have your own," she said. I had always mocked her about her need to be surrounded by pets and puppets.

"It's not the same." My momentary amusement drained from my body. "Their job is to guard me when I cannot protect myself. Nothing more."

"Really?" Her smile grew as her eyes slid over to Michael sorting through the pile of weapons at Gabriel's side. She could tell that I had fed off of him. The faint mark we left behind was a warning sign to other nightwalkers. If I did not feed off of him again in a week's time, the mark would fade.

"Only when I travel," I said. "And they are still human. When they return home, they have other lives in the sunlight. For your *pets*, there is nothing for them beyond you."

James picked that exact moment to come out of the bedroom. I hadn't wanted to continue this conversation with Sadira anyway. She had a knack for twisting things, and I didn't need to justify my actions when it came to my guardian angels.

"We can go," James said, his shoulders sagging a bit. "They are expecting us."

"Good. The limo is waiting. With any luck, Danaus and I should be no more than an hour behind you."

"Wait!" Sadira suddenly cried, drawing my gaze back to her face. "If I am to go to this Compound, you must fulfill a request for me."

"We don't have time for this, Sadira," I growled.

"You know you have no choice. They cannot keep me where I do not want to stay," she reminded me with a small smile.

She was right. She was an Ancient nightwalker who would be surrounded by humans. If she didn't want to stay at Themis, she could leave regardless of the fact that she would be risking her own life. "What do you want?"

"There is another nightwalker traveling with Thorne; tall, brown hair with blue eyes. Tristan belongs to me. Bring him back with you as well."

"If he belongs to you, why is he with Thorne?"

Sadira dismissed the question with a wave of her slender hand. "Just a little misunderstanding. Bring him back to me and I promise to behave."

I stared at my maker, my teeth clenched. I didn't like this. Why was this nightwalker with Thorne if he actually belonged to Sadira? Was I about to step into a battle between two Ancients? Or was Sadira playing some other game? Damn it, I didn't have time for this nonsense, but if I didn't protect Sadira and reform the triad, Jabari was going to have my head.

"Very well," I snapped, looking away from her.

"Thank you, my daughter," Sadira purred. I wanted to shove a fireball down her throat.

I turned my attention to Danaus again. "Anything?"

With his arms folded over his chest, he closed his eyes, his thick eyebrows drawn over his nose in concentration. His powers filled the room like warm sunlight, but no one's expressions changed, not even Sadira's. Was I the only one who could feel the wonderful wave of power bathing the room?

Out of the corner of my eye I saw him lift his head, his eyes opening. "No naturi in the immediate area. They should be able to make it to the Compound safely."

"Go now," I said, resisting the urge to shake my head in an attempt to shed the last tendrils of warmth still clinging to my brain. James led the way out the door, and Sadira didn't look back as she followed. Michael and Gabriel both nodded to me once, then left without a word. A part of me wanted to hug both my angels. I wanted to hold them and then send them straight back across the ocean. Their job was to protect me during the day, with the expectation that it would only be against any human that found me. My intention had never been for them to face anything like the naturi. It was more than either had ever bargained for, and I had not wanted this for them.

Biting back a sigh, I followed my angels down to the lobby with Danaus at my back. I had just handed Sadira over to a pack of vampire hunters while crawling through the bowels of London looking for Tabor's replacement. I doubted this was what Jabari had in mind when it came to protecting Sadira.

SEVENTEEN

Every city has a section that police seem hesitant to enter, even ultracivilized London. In my own beloved Savannah, these dark streets, which housed the Docks, were among my favorite to stroll down. In London the dark section was far from Mayfair and Hyde Park. It grew out on the fringes of the city, filled with tightly packed, brick tenements. The air was thick and heavy in the summer heat, filled with ghosts and old, grim memories. I doubted there were many psychics in that part of town; the dead would have given them no rest. But the air pricked my skin and tingled with anticipation. You came here to get problems taken care of, one way or another.

Our taxi driver seemed grateful when he let him drop us off a couple blocks from the pub. He snatched up Danaus's money and turned his car around, heading back to the bright lights and busy hum of traffic. We continued the rest of the way to the pub in silence, our eyes scanning the area for anything that might offer a potential threat. Beside me, I could feel the gentle throb of power emanating from Danaus. It pushed and brushed against my skin, probing as if it were trying to figure out exactly what I was.

Trying to ignore it, I felt outward with my own powers. While I couldn't sense the naturi, in this small, six-block region I counted more than a score of magic users, even a couple of full-fledged warlocks and witches. They took note of me in the sense that they were aware of something powerful passing through their part of town, but nothing more. There were only a handful of nightwalkers in the area, all significantly younger than I was. As vampires go, I wasn't particularly old, but finding those that had walked the earth longer

had become more difficult recently. There was something very un-
settling about that fact.

Six Feet Under was a dive in the truest sense of the word. It had
once been a mortuary with its own crematorium, but apparently the
previous owners had moved on. A neon sign flickered over the entrance of a corpse clutching a lily to his chest, a tombstone resting at
his head. A bit cliché for a vampire hangout, but who was I to scoff?
One of my favorite haunts back home was a vampire-owned bar
called Alive One. Its clientele was almost all human, with a few of us
stopping by for laughs. Pickings were better next door at a nightclub
called Purgatory. Alive One was a place to warm up for an evening of
feeding and debauchery.

With a name like Six Feet Under, I expected the normal goth
scene of black clothes and pale skin. What I got was wall-to-wall
London punk.

We elbowed our way through the crowd outside the club to the
front door, where I cleared the mind of the bouncer. I wasn't about to
spend the next hour waiting in line to get into a club while the naturi
were lurking. Just inside, I'd pulled my leather wallet from my back
pocket when it dawned on me that I was only carrying American dollars. I'd had Charlotte procure me some Egyptians notes before leaving
but no other currencies because I wasn't sure where I would end up.

Before I could say anything, Danaus reached over my shoulder
and handed the bored-looking doorman with purple hair a folded
twenty-pound note. Enough to get us both in with no questions.

"Don't worry. I'll pay for our next date." I walked into the bar
before he could retort.

He and I paused just inside the pub, gazing over the crowd. The
people were packed so tightly it was amazing anyone could breathe.
It looked as if all the walls had been knocked out of the place, making it into one huge room. A long bar dominated the right wall, with
customers lining the edge more than three deep. On the back wall
stood a stage where a band was currently screeching and a pale waif
of a man screamed into the microphone. I'll admit I'm no great fan of
punk, but fan or no fan, this was just noise.

I let my eyes dance over the crowd, looking for any sign of our
prey. Before entering the pub, I had picked up the presence of two
nightwalkers, but I didn't try to identify them. Yet, in this crush, I
knew I would have to use my powers to find them. There were too
many people here to try to pick out Thorne and Tristan quickly by
sight. Stifling a sigh of frustration, I reached out a little. It took only a
second and I didn't like what I found.

"Damn it," I said through clenched teeth. I couldn't catch a break.

"What?" Danaus said, turning to look at me. "Did you find him?

"Yeah, I found him." Tristan had been easy enough to locate. The pale brown-haired vampire was seated in a circular booth off to the left of the stage. He was also the only one I could see in this place who was fashionably dressed, no doubt thanks to Sadira's tastes for expensive things.

But the other nightwalker was just as easy to spot; I had no doubt that the pale singer clutching the microphone was Thorne. How was I supposed to get him now? I could push my way through the crowd, jump onstage and throw him through the nearest window, but I was trying not to make a scene.

"We wait," Danaus announced in a low voice after I pointed out the singer in disgust. He muscled his way through the crowd along the back wall. Ignoring the fact that the floor crunched beneath my feet, I followed in his wake, watching the dislodged people look up angrily then sidle away when their eyes touched his face and bulging form. It was an interesting twist. For me, brute force was saved for my own kind. When it came to humans, I needed only sensual allure and a slight threat of something dark and powerful to get them to do what I wanted. But Danaus could stand in a room, and its occupants would begin to squirm. He had become what the humans equated to the grim reaper: walking death.

Ensconced in a shadowy corner, I leaned back against the poster-covered wall with my arms folded across my chest and watched our prey. It was all wrong. I checked again and again to the point that Thorne stuttered in mid-song and scanned the bar. He felt me but hadn't pinpointed my exact location yet.

A vampire singing on a stage in front of a crowd of screaming fans. How could this have happened? From the moment we are re-born, we are all taught one thing: *Stay in the shadows. Never draw attention to yourself.* The longer the humans look at you, the more they will see and sense that there is something different about you. They will know you're not human. They might not be able to comprehend what you are, but they will know.

At the end of the song, Thorne leaned forward, balancing some of his weight on the microphone stand, and hissed at the crowd, pulling back his lips and flaunting his fangs. I lurched forward, but Danaus's hand stopped me from getting more than a couple steps away from the wall. The crowd went insane, their cheers rattling the windows and pushing me back a half step. They knew what Thorne was and they loved it. I scanned the spectators, taking in their expressions. There was no fear; just excitement and pleasure. It would have been intoxicating if it didn't seem so wrong.

"They know?" I asked, turning to look at Danaus. The hunter stood beside me, continuing to stare up at the stage as he dropped his hand from my shoulder.

"They think it's just an act," he said, nodding to the undulating crowd. I looked back, my stomach twisting. If they knew the truth— that three real nightwalkers stood in their midst—would they still be celebrating? Or would they run screaming from this place that still smelled faintly of death under the layers of sweat and alcohol?

We hung back as Thorne stepped down from the stage. Followed by the rest of the band, he waded through a surge of the crowd, laughing as they ran their hands over his body and reached for him. He settled into a circular booth next to Tristan, surrounded by his fellow band members and a smattering of female groupies. I took the lead this time, threading my way there, with Danaus following close on my high heels. I needed to have this done now.

Standing in front of him, it was still hard to believe Thorne was a nightwalker. Without the slight flow of power leaking from his body, I would have said he was only a sad, thin human. He looked like someone had animated a skeleton and then carelessly thrown a draping of skin over his bones so that they would hold together. His flesh was almost a powdery white, nearly matching the bleach-blond hair that stuck out in all directions on his head. He wore a pair of skintight leather pants that only accentuated his thinness. His chest was bare, revealing every rib and bone.

He wasn't even bothering to breathe. Any other human would have been winded after singing a full set, but he didn't even pretend, and the people around him didn't question it. It was like momentarily slipping into someone else's dream. A vampire sat, open about what he was, and no one noticed or cared.

On the other hand, Tristan was what I'd come to expect a nightwalker to be. He appeared to have barely escaped his teens when he was reborn. His dark brown hair hung down to brush against his thin shoulders and his pale blue eyes watched the crowd, but his gaze seemed distant, as if his thoughts were somewhere else. He was nicely dressed in Hugo Boss, Ralph Lauren, even a little Armani, in the luxury Sadira swathed herself and those around her. Looking at him, I wondered if I'd had the same grim and unyielding appearance near the end of my first century.

"Bugger off," snapped one of the band members. My eyes never left Thorne, who had yet to notice me. He was too busy whispering sexual promises to the pink-haired girl sitting next to him. Tristan had looked up and was closely watching me, but no expression had yet to appear on his handsome face.

"Are you Thorne?" I demanded, preferring to ignore everyone else.

The nightwalker reluctantly pulled away from the woman and looked up at me. A broad smile lit his face, revealing his fangs again, as his eyes slid down the length of my body. "For you, I can be anybody," he said in a thick, cockney accent.

The line would have been far more effective delivered by the likes of Pierce Brosnan or even with a lovely Scottish burr, like Sean Connery's. From Thorne it was just pathetic.

"Are you Thorne, child of Tabor?" I demanded. That definitely caught his attention. He stared at my face, his eyes narrowing as he concentrated. There was a faint surge of power from him for only a second before his eyes widened.

"Bloody hell, another vampire!" He laughed, throwing his head back. Everyone at the table looked at me in a new light, questioning. They were weighing me, wondering what Thorne had meant. The tension around the table grew slightly, but not enough to indicate any real concern. The bassist narrowed his gaze on me then looked over at another band member, trying to decide if they should be worried. To them, I was another imposter.

"We need to talk," I said over his laughter. "Now."

"As you can see, I'm a mite busy." Lounging insolently in the booth, he linked his hands behind his head and stretched out his legs beneath the table. The pink-haired woman in the ripped white T-shirt leaned over and placed her head against his chest, wrapping her arms possessively around his waist. She shot me a dark, warning look. I wanted to laugh. How could I want some toothpick when I had Danaus hovering in the shadows? Of course, my "plaything" could boil my insides with a thought. But that play date would come only if we survived the next few days.

"Send them away."

"Who the hell do you think you are, you damn wanker?" he demanded, sitting up.

I leaned forward, slamming my hands down on the dirty tabletop with enough force to rattle the pints of beer. The amber liquid sloshed a bit on the table and everyone jumped backward. "I am Mira, and your better." He jerked back suddenly, his heels digging into the floor as he half stood. He was trapped between the booth and the table, looking like he was about to start climbing the wall to get away from me.

"Fire Starter," Tristan whispered in a tone that sounded a touch too much like awe. His eyes widened and his pale lips parted slightly as he stared at me with new interest. I ignored him for the moment. My main concern was that I now had Thorne's attention.

"My reputation precedes me," I said tightly. "Get rid of them before I throw your bony ass through the wall."

"You wouldn't dare," he snickered, his eyes darting off toward the huge crowded that danced and screamed behind us. Sticking to the creed of remaining in the shadows would not include throwing a person through a brick wall, but what Thorne didn't know was that I had a penchant for pushing the limits of the shadow dance we maintained.

"She'll do it," Tristan said evenly, his wide eyes never leaving my face.

Thorne hesitated a moment, staring at me through narrowed, beady eyes. "Get out of here," he grumbled in a low voice. I glared at him, resisting the urge to grab for his throat when he looked over at his companions. "Get out of here!" he repeated. He gave the woman at his side a hard shove, sending two people to the floor. The others scrambled out of the booth, grabbing their drinks as they pushed their way into the crowd.

EIGHTEEN

I slid into the seat to Thorne's left while Danaus walked around the booth and sat across from me, trapping Thorne and Tristan between us. The faded maroon plastic seat sagged in certain places and had been mended more than once with silver duct tape. The music spun by the DJ crowded the dance floor with scantily clad people. It was a good turnout and would have been a nice place to spend a few entertaining hours if I wasn't already previously engaged.

Thorne stared at Danaus for a long time, his eyes pinched and narrowed. He sniffed the air, then jumped backward, hissing. He tried to stand in the booth, but I grabbed his arm and jerked him back down.

"I know your smell. You're the hunter." His voice was choked as he slid closer, his haunted gaze then slamming back, confusion twisting his features into an ugly knot as he picked up Danaus's scent on me. "But . . . why are you traveling with him?"

"Not your concern," I said, but the sound came out sounding more like a growl than actual words. "Why didn't you try to protect Tabor when he was attacked? Wasn't that your job?"

"I wasn't there," he said, wrenching his arm out of my grasp. He picked up the mug of beer in front of him and emptied the contents before slamming it back on the table. It was sort of strange. He didn't expend the energy to breathe but would use the energy to digest alcohol. As far as I knew, no vampire could digest solid food, but we could do liquids. Unfortunately, no amount of alcohol would intoxicate us, but drinking the blood of a drunk human would give you a nice though extremely temporary buzz. Intoxication for nightwalkers had nothing to do with alcohol.

"Where were you?" I laid my hand on the table, then quickly lifted it in disgust when I discovered that the surface was covered in a sticky film.

"I was on loan." The right corner of his lips twitched as if in a suppressed smile. I nodded, while Danaus stared hard at me, expectant.

"I'm always surprised at how little you know," I said, setting my hands back in my lap. "It is a common practice among nightwalkers to loan out their pets to others of similar strength. It's called being polite."

"And they let themselves be used like that?" There was a curl to his lip as he spoke in distaste. Resting on the table, his left hand tightened into a fist.

"You make it sound like we have a choice," Tristan softly interjected.

A sharp, bitter laugh escaped before I could clip its wings. "When you are young and weak, you go where you are told and do what you are told. If you're lucky, you survive the encounter and return to your maker."

"And if you are killed while you were *on loan*?" Danaus's hard blues never wavered from my face.

"Then your maker gets to kill one of the other vampire's pets. A fair trade," Thorne said with an indifferent shrug.

"Why? Why do this?" Even as Danaus shook his head, his gaze still never left my face. He watched me closely, as if seeing me or my kind for the first time. I think whatever little bit of respect I had earned was dying before my eyes.

"Why else?" My laughter spiked higher, trying to hide an unexpected stab of pain and embarrassment. "Pleasure and entertainment." It was time Danaus understood us a little better; the good and the bad.

I looked over to Thorne, who was staring out at the crowd, dancing to the music. His gaze was distant, a smile teasing at his thin lips. His thoughts were lost to another place and time.

"Who did you go to? Claudette?" I prodded. She had a reputation for sampling the children of the Ancients. I'd had the pleasure of visiting with her once. Luckily, it was a brief visit.

"Macaire." Thorne blinked twice as if trying to free his thoughts of some old memories. "I was sent to help break in his newest Companion." A smile blossomed on his thin, angular face, his fangs poking a little against his lower lip.

"Lucas is a fool," I muttered under my breath.

"True," he chuckled. Thorne stretched out his legs again, toying with a stray bottle cap on the tabletop. "He won't survive long. He thinks too much on his own."

It was a sad but true thought. Good servants did exactly what they were told and nothing more. You start thinking and trying to predict the needs of your master, and you'd get crushed when you made a mistake.

"Of course, Tabor said the same of you," he continued.

My eyes jerked back to his face but I kept my expression blank. "That I think too much?"

"No, that you wouldn't survive." Thorne's brown eyes seemed to dance with malicious glee for a second in the faint undulating light. "He said that without Jabari, the Coven would have killed you centuries ago."

I had suspected this for a while, but to actually hear the words sent a chill down my spine. "I'm no threat to the Coven." I tried to sound as if none of this made any difference to me.

"So you say, but Tabor is dead and a seat is still open on the Coven. I may be in London, but even I hear the occasional whispered thought or rumor." He leaned forward, his chest nearly brushing the edge of the table. "Everyone is watching, waiting for you to make your move."

Sitting up in the booth so my nose was mere inches from Thorne's, I tightly gripped the edge of the table for balance. "Well, tell everyone that I don't want it."

"No, you just want the colonies." He snickered, flopping back against the booth, his amusement unbroken. He elbowed Tristan once in the ribs, flashing him a wide grin that the other nightwalker didn't return.

The colonies had become the last refuge for my kind. The Coven and the Ancients dominated Europe, Asia, and even down into Africa. South America had been abandoned by nightwalkers because of what happened at Machu Picchu . . . the death and pain that still lingered was too unpleasant, even for my kind.

That left the United States. It was an enticing place, with its lax morals, hypocritical philosophies, and fast lifestyles. In the West, all was still new and precious. It was an exciting place to be, especially when there was little to no threat of encountering an Ancient. I had been part of the wave of young ones to leave Europe in search of my own home, moving out from beneath the thumb of the Coven.

But the newness of the colonies was a curse as well. It lacked the history and long memory of Europe and Asia. The colonists didn't realize that there were dark corners that should not be illuminated and questions that should not be asked. There was no doubt among my kind that when the Great Awakening arrived, it would start in the New World.

The nightwalkers in the States were different from those in Europe. We were younger on average, and quiet. The families were fewer and smaller in size. We did what we could to safeguard our secret. But our numbers were growing, and the Coven knew it. It didn't help that I was one of the oldest among those across the ocean. There was some speculation of a coup, and my stubborn silence didn't soothe any of the frayed, anxious nerves.

"I'm surprised the Coven has not come down on your head," I said, desperate to change topics. I sat back in the booth and let my hands fall back into my lap. It was one thing to open the door to our world to Danaus; it was another to let him see into the politics. I didn't want anything to do with the Coven. And I certainly didn't want to play Keeper for all of the States. I just wanted my little city with its cramped alleys, trendy little bars, and quiet, tree-cloaked neighborhoods.

"For what?"

"Your little show." I waved my arm to encompass the dimly lit pub filled to the brim with waiting victims.

Of course, I was sure part of the reason Thorne had been overlooked so far by our kind was because he'd settled in London. Between the wellspring of magic that had soaked into every inch of the island and the constant flow of witches and warlocks passing through the city, the whole place was a powder keg waiting for a careless match. No vampire stayed in the city long. If anything went wrong here, we all knew a vampire would play the scapegoat. Few older vampires would hang around, and definitely not long enough to bother with him.

"You know it's our law to stay in the shadows and never reveal yourself to more people than necessary," I continued. "I'd wager this crowd is a little more than necessary."

"Why?" Sitting up, Thorne crushed the bottle cap between two fingers and dropped it on the table. "Why keep hiding? These humans have seen more horrible things in their lives than us. I've seen monsters in their movies and on their newscasts that were ten times worse than what I've done. It's time they knew."

"It's not for you to decide."

He hit his fist on the edge of the table, knocking over his empty mug. "Then who?"

"I don't know. It's coming, but not yet. There is more at stake than just the nightwalkers. There are things these humans aren't ready to face."

"I don't think they'll have much choice. Besides, they accept me."

"They think you're a fraud," I reminded him. Slouched in the booth, I tried to avoid kicking Danaus in the shin, but the booth was crowded with long legs.

"Not for long. It's time we stepped forward. Let them bask in our power. I'm tired of hiding."

"But it's what we are, what we've always been. We are just shadows and nightmares to these creatures. Nothing more." I recited words I had heard a hundred times over. I sounded old even to my ears. My rationale was a tired one, clinging to the ways of my kind. I had seen this longing in many of the younger ones as they walked among the humans. Movies were made about us, with only small nuggets of truth permeating their depths. Humans gobbled up books about nightwalkers and magic users, looking for an escape from the mundane. But what if they woke up one morning and realized those things that thrilled and secretly enticed them were real and living next door? Would they still look at us with the same interest, or would we become vermin to be exterminated, like rats or cockroaches?

"Yeah, but it's like you said. It's coming."

"Enough!" I shouted, scratching my nails on the table, picking up a gooey layer of grime underneath them, causing me to grimace. Watching Thorne peripherally, I began to clean out my nails with a matchbook lying in the center of the table. "None of this matters. It's not why I've come. What did Tabor tell you of the naturi?"

At the mention of the naturi, Thorne stiffened beside me.

"He rarely spoke of them and only when he was in a black mood," he said, his voice barely more than a whisper as he gripped the edge of the table. "It was always at the same time of year; new moon in the middle of summer. He would stay locked away in his private rooms for several nights on end." His accent had grown thicker and older again.

I paused. "What did he tell you?"

"Nothing that made any sense. Just that if I ever saw one, I was to run. Don't try to fight. Just run." He raised haunted eyes to my face. I understood his fear. Tabor was not only his master and creator, but had been an Ancient and an Elder on the Coven. Thorne knew that for something to unnerve Tabor so thoroughly, it had to be bad.

"More than five centuries ago, a triad sealed most of the naturi from this world. They are trying to break through. We need your help to seal them again."

"My help?" A nervous laugh escaped him and skittered under the table to hide. "What the hell can I do?"

"Tabor was part of that triad. He's gone, but he made you. As part of the same bloodline, we think you can take his place in the triad."

"And do what? Tabor was more than three thousand years old when he made me." He stared wide-eyed at me, confident that I had lost my mind. I couldn't blame him. Even though I'd said it, I was having trouble believing it myself. Thorne wasn't a particularly strong nightwalker. He had probably stayed alive this long only because of Tabor's protection and his own smarts.

"I don't know. This wasn't my idea. Jabari sent me to find you," I admitted, frowning.

"Bloody hell," he muttered. Slumping back in the booth, he pushed the overturned mug with his index finger, making it rock. Any hopes he might have had about escaping me dissolved to dirty slush. He might have hoped to talk his way out of my grasp, but if an Elder had sent me, there was no escape. I would hunt him until I expired. And in a fight, he had no chance.

At that moment, a waitress in a tight black tank top brought over a tray laden with three mugs of ale. It was the dark type that reminded me more of motor oil than any liquid a human might actually want to imbibe. She leaned forward as she placed the mugs in front of each of us. Around her neck dangled a pentagram; she wasn't the first one I'd seen in London wearing such an item.

"I thought you might want another pint before going on again," she said, picking up Thorne's empty glass. She shuffled away, squeezing between the band members who had come back over to the table.

"We got another set," announced the man with a purple mohawk who had been playing the drums when we walked in. His brown eyes shifted to my face in an appraising manner, but I could also feel his anxiety. I was threatening his meal ticket.

"We have to go," I said, drawing Thorne's gaze back to my face.

"Y'got me," he snapped. "I can't outrun you. Let me finish this set before you take me to Hell."

Frowning, I looked expectantly over at Danaus. He knew what I wanted to know, and I was getting sick of asking. The sooner the naturi were taken care of, the sooner I could go back to trying to kill him instead of depending upon him to watch my back. Danaus shook his head at me, his eyes narrowing.

"Fine. Go. Just a couple songs. It's late," I said, irritation clipping my words as I slid to my feet so I could let him out of the booth.

Avoiding Danaus's gaze, I watched as Thorne quickly downed half of his beer. He slammed the glass mug down on the table, his face twisted in disgust. "Blast, that's a nasty brew," he groaned, then said nothing more as he slipped out of the booth. But as he turned to follow his band mates up to the stage, Thorne grabbed my right wrist. He gave my arm a little jerk, but I didn't move. "Come on," he said, motioning with his head for me to follow him up to the raised platform.

"I can't sing." A swell of panic rose up in my chest and I pulled against his grip, but he didn't release me.

"You call this singing?" He laughed, his smile widening. Around us, the crowd was screaming and jumping as the other members of the band picked up their instruments. The shouting throbbed and crashed against the walls, threatening to topple the place. Their excitement was a live thing in that large room, pushing against me. Thorne stepped close, pressing his cool, bare chest against my arm. "Come up there. Show them what you are. It's the next best thing."

I looked down at his brown eyes, which were now glowing, the irises overwhelming all other color. He was riding the wave of their emotions, and for him it was the next best thing to actually feeding on them. The idea of standing on that stage and screaming into the microphone, purging all the anger I had carried around during the past few days, was tempting. But it would be more than that. I would bare my fangs to them, and those humans would scream for more. They would love me for being a nightwalker. Deep down, they would think I was a phony, but for a moment I wouldn't be hiding.

"What were you before?" I asked suddenly.

Thorne cocked his head to the side, the glow vanishing from his eyes at the strange question. "Before Tabor?" I nodded. "I walked the boards at Drury Lane," he said, smiling. For that sentence, the cockney accent disappeared. It was still British, but cultured and precise. Tabor always had snobbish tastes, so I imagined that Thorne had been born to a life of privilege and luxury. I wondered what his companions would think if they knew where he came from. Of course, that would all be moot once they discovered he was roughly two hundred years old.

"Go now before I change my mind," I said, stepping away from him as I pulled my arm free. Sitting back down in the booth across from Danaus, I watched Thorne jump back on the stage. I wasn't surprised. He'd been an actor before Tabor turned him. He had been accustomed to being the center of attention, pretending to be something he wasn't. Watching him now, I wondered if I might have seen him during my brief visits to London during the late eighteenth century. At that time, there were only three theaters: Drury Lane, Haymarket, and Covent Gardens. On several occasions Drury Lane had played host to Edmund Keane, the preeminent actor of his day. And now the emaciated Thorne stood shrieking before a crowd of disillusioned teenagers.

I looked up to find Danaus watching me, his expression again unreadable. A part of me wished I could crawl around in his brain, wrapping myself around his thoughts. The longer he stayed with me, the more he saw of my world, and I wanted to look at it all again with the eyes of an outsider. There was so much I had grown numb to during my long existence. Before Sadira changed me, I'd marveled at her strength and power. I sat in awe of her, amazed at the sheer number of nightwalkers that came to her side and bowed to her. Even before I was reborn, I grew inured to the killing and torture. I had been a gift to those who pleased her and an instrument of torture for those who disappointed her.

With my maker still lingering in the background of my thoughts, I looked over at Tristan, whose interest was starting to make me extremely uncomfortable. He was younger than Thorne, maybe a century, at best, judging by the quiet throb of power that rolled off of him.

"So, where do you fit into all of this?" I asked, dropping my hands down to my lap.

"I don't," he replied with a faint shrug of his shoulder.

"Why are you here?"

"I came for the entertainment. Thorne said it would be interesting."

Danaus snorted and looked back out at the crowd. Interesting. That was an understatement. The screaming crowd wasn't so much dancing as it was writhing in a giant mass. The array of clothes and colors bore no resemblance to anything I had ever seen in nature.

"Why does Sadira want me to take you to her?" I asked.

Tristan flinched at the mention of the Ancient and lines of tension tightened around his eyes and mouth. "You've spoken with her?"

"I saw her less than an hour ago. I came here for Thorne, but I will be taking both you and Thorne back with me to where she is hiding."

"No," he whispered. Some of the light that seemed to burn in his eyes when he discovered who I was had died, and a knot twisted itself around my soul. When he spoke again, his voice had hardened with a mix of anger and fear. "No! You can't! I won't go back. Mira, please." He leaned forward and held my gaze when I would have looked away from him. "You know what it's like. You remember. I can't go back."

I sat back against the booth and closed my eyes as it finally dawned on me. "She made you," I murmured softly to myself. Sadira had made Tristan, and he ran away after being her pet for roughly one century.

"I've known about you since almost the beginning," Tristan said. He reached under the table and grabbed my left wrist, forcing me to open my eyes and look at him. "You were the one that got away. You escaped our maker and have lived your own life. That's all I want."

I gritted my teeth and swallowed the snarl rising in my chest. That bitch! That manipulative, evil bitch! I didn't want to shove a fireball down her throat now. It was too kind a death for her. I wanted a baseball bat. A baseball bat and one endless night.

In one swift move she would accomplish an amazing coup over both Tristan and me. I had no choice but to retrieve the wayward vampire for her. Sadira wouldn't believe any excuse I gave for not bringing him, and she would disappear from my grasp, putting my head back on the chopping block with Jabari and jeopardizing all the people in my domain. However, if I brought Tristan back to her, it would not only crush his one shining hope of ever escaping her, but prove to everyone that I was still a servant to my maker despite my "escape."

"I didn't escape Sadira. I was with Jabari," I said, but quickly stopped. It wasn't an escape. Jabari just took what he wanted and that was that.

"So you escaped an Elder?"

"No, it wasn't like that." I shoved my hand through my hair and looked around as I quickly scrambled for a way to explain this. Danaus smirked, watching me with his arms crossed over his chest. I wasn't sure if he fully understood what we were talking about, but he could tell that I was digging myself in deeper.

Dropping my hands back down to the table, I turned back to Tristan, who was watching me with desperate eyes. "This isn't about me. I can't help you. Right now, the naturi are making a mess of things. I need Sadira cooperative if we're going to stop them, and that's only going to happen if I bring you back to her. And conscious or not, that's what I'm going to do."

"Mira—"

"The naturi are my concern right now, not a nightwalker that hasn't learned to take care of himself," I snapped angrily, hating Sadira and myself more with each passing second. I wasn't made of stone. I remembered what it was like living with Sadira. The nights of screams, fighting to stay in her constantly fluctuating favor, abandoning all semblance of pride and dignity just to survive until the dawn. But now wasn't the time.

"What about after the naturi are defeated?"

A part of me wanted to smile at his innocence. To him, there was nothing so strong that could defeat our kind. Of course, he had yet to face any member of the naturi.

"If I stand with you against Sadira, I would be claiming you," I said with a weary shake of my head. "I don't keep a family."

"But you have a domain."

"That's different, and you know it." Ruling a domain, you were the peacekeeper and arm of the Coven for a specific area. The head of a family was more than that—in general, a family unit protected each of its members against other nightwalkers or families, and none more so than its head. Of course, the family itself could be more dangerous than any other vampire outside the family. There were several families within my domain, and they all answered to me if there was a problem.

I didn't want my own family. It was enough that I watched out for a large group of nightwalkers within a single area. A family evoked a certain type of intimacy and dependence I continued to eschew. Anyone you took into your family generally lived with you and looked to you for direction. I was still able to keep a distance from the nightwalkers in my domain. Sometimes, weeks passed between my meetings with Knox.

"Tristan, I can't fight this fight for you," I replied. But even as I said it, I wondered if I should. Hadn't Jabari fought for me in his own way when he took me to Egypt and away from Sadira?

I was snapped from my thoughts when a scream tore through the air above the shouts of the crowd, one of flesh-searing pain. My head jerked back up to the stage to see Thorne stagger backward, his left hand grabbing at his chest. His sharp fingernails left a trail of jagged lines in his flesh. Dark blood oozed from the wounds, leaving almost black streaks down his pale white skin. His gaze darted back over to me, filled with pain and confusion. Around us, the crowd went wild. They all thought it was part of the act.

Lurching to my feet, I took a step forward, but was stopped by the press of screaming fans as they crowded the stage. Danaus stood behind me, his body humming with tension, ready for action. Unfortunately, I didn't have a clue as to what we were fighting. My eyes never left Thorne, who had crumpled to his knees with another scream. His face was now streaked with dark, bloody tears. The cuts on his chest were not healing. By now they should have stopped bleeding and started to close, but the thick liquid continued to seep down his chest.

Reaching out with my powers, I scanned the bar. There were a couple magic users, but not one of them could have taken down a vampire, even one as weak as Thorne. I couldn't understand what was killing him.

"Naturi?" I shouted over my shoulder at Danaus.

"None near," he replied without hesitation. Apparently he'd had the same thought and had scanned the area. "How?"

"I don't know." My voice sounded dazed and lost as I watched Thorne fall to the stage with a thud. He was dead. I couldn't sense him anymore. The end had come quite suddenly, as if it had crushed his very soul. He was dead before his head hit the stage.

"We have to go," Danaus said as the rumble of the crowd started to change to fearful questioning. The act had finally gone a little too far for them, and they could sense that something was off. We had to go before they started to think about with whom Thorne had last been talking. I turned and started to walk past the table when my eyes caught on the mugs of beer. My right hand snaked out and snatched up Thorne's half-empty glass. Dipping a couple fingers into the dark liquid, I dabbed it on my tongue. I spit the vile liquid back out and threw the mug against the wall with enough force that it shattered in a starburst of glass and dark amber beer.

"Poisoned!" The drink had been laced with enough naturi blood to poison Thorne. Thanks to my lengthy captivity with the naturi, I would always be able to recognize that wretched taste. However, most nightwalkers wouldn't. The naturi were too few in number, and it had been centuries since I last heard of a nightwalker being poisoned.

"The barmaid," Tristan snarled as he slid around the booth to stand directly behind me.

The barmaid with the pentagram stood behind the bar looking in my direction. I wasn't sure she could see me, but she didn't have to. She knew she had succeeded. Growling, I launched myself into the crowd, tossing people out of my way as I waded through the sea of flesh. Bodies flew through the air, limbs askew as they crashed into the undulating hoard. I was halfway across the room when Danaus finally caught up with me.

"There isn't time!" he shouted, grabbing my arm.

My gaze never wavered from my prey. Jerking free of him, I roared, "She's dead!"

"We're leaving now." Danaus wrapped one of his arms around

my waist and lifted me off my feet. Balanced on his hip, he turned and carried me toward the door. Tristan was right behind us, looking unsure about whether to follow Danaus or go after the barmaid. I screamed in frustration and clawed at Danaus's arm, but he wouldn't release me. I was stronger but couldn't get the leverage I needed to free myself.

Looking up, my eyes met with the blue-haired woman that had killed Thorne. She was smiling triumphantly at me. I should have let the naturi she served have their fun with her, as I knew they would. But I couldn't. I smiled back at her, my eyes glowing in the semidark. Behind her, dozens of bottles of alcohol exploded in a wall of fire. Glass and liquid fire rained across the bar, raising the volume in the pub to hysterical levels. Thorne's killer shrieked, her body engulfed in flames.

As Danaus pushed his way toward the double doors, I grabbed the edge of one of the square columns that rose up to support the second floor, abruptly halting him. I pulled my body back into the crush of people running for the exit. We were being pushed and elbowed, but we managed to shrug most of it off. We'd both be a little sore for a while, but I had bigger fears.

"The body!" I shouted above the thunder of cries and screams. Danaus carried me back in so we were pinned against the column, ignoring the angry cries of confusion. "Lift me up!"

Without question he boosted me up so I was sitting on his shoulder. If not for his strength and my superior balance, it would have been an impossible task in this crowd. I looked over the writhing wave of bodies to the stage. Thorne had not been touched and his band mates had disappeared. I still had to see what I was burning if I couldn't specifically sense it. Frowning, I focused on his body and it was instantly bathed in dancing flames.

Flames were already starting to eat at the walls and lick at the ceiling. In a few minutes the fire would consume this place, but I couldn't take any chances. I had to be sure the body was destroyed before the local fire department managed to extinguish what I started. They'd have trouble discovering why the fire started, but I was more concerned with Thorne's corpse. Jumping down from Danaus's shoulder, I grabbed his forearm and pulled him out the exit door to the left of the stage, bypassing most of the people who crowded the exit at the front of the building. I looked back once to find Tristan following us, thankful that he wasn't trying to escape in the chaos. At the moment I think he was too shaken up by the attack and death of a fellow nightwalker to be concerned with his own freedom.

In the distance, the high-pitched whine of approaching police cars and fire trucks echoed in the night. We weaved our way through the crowd and down the dark streets, then ran for blocks until we were bathed in the bright lights of Piccadilly.

NINETEEN

Darting down one of the few dark, empty alleys I could find, I stopped running, letting the shadows wrap their arms around me. At the back of the narrow passage I howled into the night. The horrible sound bounced off the brick and stone walls before finally flying free into the black sky. My hands were shaking with frustration and fear. The one person that was supposed to fix all of this, that was supposed to make the naturi go away, was now dead. To make matters worse, it was because I had failed to protect him. I should have expected the naturi to pull such a trick. I should have grabbed Thorne and dragged him out of that place. I couldn't fathom how they knew to kill him, that he would be the one I would need. It didn't matter. It could have just been my usual rotten luck. It didn't make Thorne any less dead.

Silence consumed the alley again until all I heard was Danaus's labored breathing. Our run had left him winded. It was a strange reminder that I was still dealing with a human, or at least someone part human. I walked back toward the hunter, who was leaning against the wall, struggling to catch his breath. My gaze briefly tripped over Tristan, who stood against the opposite wall, shaken by the unexpected turn of events.

"What happened?" Danaus demanded between ragged breaths.

"The waitress poisoned Thorne. She spiked his beer with naturi blood. She probably spiked all the beers she brought over," I said. My anger flowed from my tensed muscles, leaving behind only the cold, lead weight of fear in my stomach.

"Why?"

"She was a pagan. They're usually naturi sympathizers." Frustration crept back into my tone as I paced to the back of the alley. "They believe the naturi are sweet and peace-loving like all those asinine fairy tales. They've struck out at my kind before, but most don't have access to naturi blood."

Jerking my head around, I turned my narrowed gaze on the young nightwalker. He was squatted down with his elbows on his knees, his fists tightly clenching his hair, as if trying to hide from me or the naturi. "How long had Thorne been going to that pub?" I asked.

Tristan flinched and then turned his face up to look at me. "I— I'm not sure exactly. He knew a lot of people there so I think he had been appearing there for a while."

"I wasn't looking for a damn insider!" The comment escaped me in a low growl as I paced a couple steps away and then returned.

"How did she know to go after Thorne?" Danaus's breathing had returned to normal. He was recovering from our little run a lot faster than he should have. But that was my mysterious Danaus. The long scratches I'd left on his arms were long gone and there was only a light crust of dried blood running across his tanned skin.

"I don't know." I threw my hands up in the air as I approached him. "Less than a dozen people would have known about my search for Thorne." The moment those words drifted past my parted lips a horrible thought dawned on me. I stared at him. "And you're the only outsider in this whole mess."

Closing the distance between us in a flash, I slammed him back against the wall. His arms were pinned between our bodies, keeping him from drawing any weapons. Of course, he didn't need his arms to kill me, but that was the least of my concerns at the moment. Jabari was going to rip me in half, if the naturi didn't get to me first.

"You knew about the naturi first. You knew I was at Machu Picchu and hoped I would give you more information about the nightwalkers. Once you learned that we could rebuild the triad, you alerted your people to Thorne's existence," I snarled, my words lashing at him.

"Then why did I save you in Aswan?"

"Because you need me to lead you to the other members of the triad so you can finish them off." I felt a sickening lurch in my stomach as my mind continued on that line of thought. "And I put Sadira right into your hands."

"What?" Tristan gasped. Despite his desire to escape his maker, the reflex loyalty was always the hardest to get over.

Releasing my hold on Danaus, I stumbled backward. "I left Sadira with his people as protection," I told him. "I couldn't protect Sadira and come after Thorne at the same time." I could care less if Sadira lived or died, but I couldn't keep burning through triad members if I wanted to defeat the naturi. "Why?" I asked, looking back at Danaus. "Why would you help them? Is that what you are? Part naturi?"

"I'm not helping them," he said, taking a step away from the wall toward me. I sidestepped him, keeping a comfortable distance from him. "Think, Mira. They tried to kill us both in Aswan."

"Of course they did. It's what the naturi do—kill anything that is not their kind. Surprised that they would betray you?" I cried, still circling him. My foot kicked an empty aluminum can, sending it skidding around the dirty alley. "Your connection to the naturi also explains how you got Nerian. He would have fought you and you would have had to kill him. You can't capture the naturi."

"Nerian was insane," Danaus said, his voice edged with what was beginning to sound like desperation. "While I had him, he ranted endlessly about you. He spoke of Machu Picchu and things that had been done to you. Even if less than half the things he spoke of were true, how could I help monsters like that?"

I shivered, breaking eye contact for a moment. Pacing back down the alley, I ran my left hand along the rough brick wall to steady myself. Danaus had dredged up thoughts that had no place in that dark alley. I didn't know whether to believe him. I had absolutely no reason to believe him. But I was also desperate and running out of time.

"I would love nothing more than to see all vampires wiped from existence," he said, "but right now vampires are the only ones who can stop the naturi from destroying mankind. I can put my hatred aside for now. Can you?"

"Mira?" Tristan's questioning voice was little more than a soft whisper, searching for a little direction, reaching for something he could cling to in the swirling maelstrom that was sucking us in.

My gaze slid around the deep shadows of the narrow alley as I reviewed Danaus's actions during the past few days. When we weren't bickering, he had proven useful. Had he actually put his hatred of my kind aside? I didn't want to believe him.

"How?" I whispered. My voice was on the verge of shattering. "It's like they're one step ahead no matter where we go."

"I don't know," Danaus said softly. I looked up. He sounded tired for the first time. His shoulders were slumped and his voice soft, almost fragile. I watched him for a couple seconds. He was worried, and maybe even a little scared. I still didn't trust him, but I believed his fear. We were all about to get crushed by this army that was grinding away toward oblivion. I didn't know whose side he was on, but we were all in its path regardless.

None of it mattered, though. I needed to get to Sadira. After that I would figure something out.

"There's the little princess." Rowe's voice danced down the dark, narrow alley, shimmering out of nothingness. I spun around, my eyes scouring every inch of the alley before shooting up to the rooftops. The naturi couldn't use glamour against nightwalkers; we could see through it. At least, we always had before, but I couldn't see him.

"Danaus?" My right hand fell to my hip, searching for a weapon, only to discover that I was unarmed. Danaus wouldn't allow me to attend my Themis meeting armed, and I hadn't thought about grabbing anything before leaving to fetch Thorne. Walking around armed was no longer a normal occurrence for me.

"Who was that?" Tristan demanded, pushing away from the wall. He circled past Danaus, looking around the area, though he had no idea who he was looking for.

"Rowe, a naturi," I bit out. My hands were out to my sides, ready to attack.

"I can't sense him," Danaus said, slowly turning as he peered into the deep shadows.

"What?" My gaze jerked to his face, but he wasn't looking at me.

"I can't sense any naturi in the immediate area." The hunter's jaw was clenched and his power beat in thick, heavy waves against me. He was pouring everything he had into locating the owner of that voice. A knife was gripped in his right hand, ready.

"Maybe he's not here. He might have projected his voice from another location to scare us," Tristan suggested.

Danaus paused for a moment and looked over at me. "You think so?"

"Not really, but I'd rather not stick around to find out," I muttered. "Let's just get going."

"Not yet, princess," Rowe said with a chuckle. This time his voice sounded as if it was coming from behind me. I turned to see the brick wall quiver as if made of water, and then Rowe stepped through, smiling at me.

"Shit!" Turning, I tried to run. He was less than a foot away from me, too close. It would be too easy for him to stick a blade through my heart before I had a chance to act. I needed distance, but there wasn't time. Rowe grabbed a handful of my hair. With a quick jerk, I fell backward, my shoulders slamming into his chest.

He didn't waste a second. He released my hair and his left hand snaked around my waist, up between my breasts, to roughly grab either side of my lower jaw. Tilting my head back, he pried my mouth open with his fingers and thumb. I blinked once and my eyes focused on the open vial filled with red liquid. Rowe held it balanced over my open mouth. If I jerked or moved, its contents would dump straight down my throat.

"Hold, all of you!" he commanded, his light voice hardening for the first time. "Or we find out if the little princess can survive a heavy dose of naturi blood. We've already proven that the albino couldn't."

I jerked my head in anger without thinking before I reacted. He had killed Thorne. However, my rage was overwhelmed by fear once again when a drop of blood fell on my lower lip and slowly ran down my chin. A faint trembling started in my limbs that I couldn't control and slowly spread through the rest of my body. I couldn't move or he would destroy me.

A low growl rumbled from the other end of the alley and I could feel the cool breeze of Tristan's powers as he stood poised to attack. I prayed that he wouldn't move, as I was in no position to start shouting orders.

Rowe leaned his head down so I could feel his hot breath against my neck. "Tell me you remember the taste of my blood, Mira. Tell me. Of course, you've tasted more than just my blood." A strangled cry erupted from the back of my throat as he ran the tip of his tongue up my neck to my earlobe.

"Let her go!" Danaus shouted, taking a step forward. Dragging my eyes from the vial over my head, I looked at the hunter. His face was twisted with rage and his heartbeat pounded in the silent alley. But the knife pointed at Rowe was steady.

"Go on, misfit. Kill me like you killed the others. But can you do it before I drop this down her throat?"

"What do you want?" Danaus bit out each word, holding his ground.

"I've got what I want." Rowe chuckled, his grip tightening on my jaw. My blood filled my mouth as my teeth dug into the sides of my cheeks. "She goes with me."

Rowe pulled me backward as if he meant to go back through the wall. I dug my heels into the concrete as best as I could and stiffened my whole body. My hands grabbed his pant legs near his knees, holding him trapped. If he tried to jerk me backward again, he would either stumble or be forced to drag me, causing the blood to tip into my mouth. If he moved, he'd kill me. So be it. I would rather die a relatively quick death than be held captive by the naturi again. I wouldn't go with him. I wouldn't let him have me.

"Move, princess, or I dump the blood down your throat." Rowe brought his face close again, his cheek pressing against mine. "I want you alive purely for my own pleasure, but you are just as useful to me dead. Either way, I win."

My gaze darted from Danaus to the vial. The hunter could do nothing without killing me. The angle of my head made it impossible for me to see Tristan, but he was still a way off, closer to the entrance of the alley. His low growl had stopped, but I would sense his powers.

I would not go with Rowe. Death was a better option. Closing my eyes, I forced my shaking hands to release Rowe's pants.

"Mira, don't." Those two words drifted from Danaus, nearly breaking the thin barrier that held back my gathering tears.

As Rowe took a step back, I focused my powers on the naturi blood within the vial. The liquid and glass ignited in Rowe's hand. Screaming, he attempted to tip it into my mouth when the vial exploded from the extreme heat, raining down glass and boiling blood. The distraction allowed me to pull from his grasp. My knees slammed into the concrete, sending a shock wave of pain through my legs.

Glass and blood were splattered across my face and eyes, blinding me. I threw a fireball behind me, hoping to hit Rowe. At the same time, I heard metal clatter against brick.

"He's gone," Danaus said as I prepared another fireball in my hand.

Extinguishing the fire, I raised my hands, trying to wipe away the blood burning my face and eyes. I cried out, jerking away my trembling hands. The shards of glass had cut both my fingers and face. "I can't get it off! I can't get the blood off!" I screamed, panic taking over.

"Stop, Mira," Danaus commanded, his voice closer now. "I'll help you." A whisper of cloth and the scrape of his shoes revealed his approach. I put my hands out, feeling for him, not sure if I wanted him close since I couldn't see him. Danaus took my left hand in his and squeezed it. My other hand brushed against warm skin, his bare chest. I froze, my mind stumbling. To my right I felt Tristan approach. He knelt beside me, his cool presence brushing against me while one of his hands came to rest on my knee.

Danaus released my left hand and placed his hand under my chin, gently tilting my head up. "Hold still. I'm going to wipe your face off." A soft cloth slowly swept over my face, wiping away Rowe's blood and the bits of glass. Danaus's scent filled me. I could smell smoke from the fire at the club, his sweat, the soap he used, and deep down I could

smell him now on my skin. He had taken off his shirt and was clean-
ing my face with the same gentle care one would show a baby.

When he was done, he swept his shirt over my hair, smoothing it
back from my face, shaking out any remaining bits of glass. Blinking
a few times against the last of the blood that had seeped in, I lifted
my eyes to his face. His emotions were clear—fear and anger. Beneath my hand, his heart still pounded like a jackhammer.

"Better?" he asked, his voice deceptively calm.

I tried to speak but the sound cracked before I could form a single
word. Jerking from him, I attempted to crawl away from him and
Tristan. I couldn't let them see me cry. They couldn't know that terror
still hummed in every muscle and screamed like a madwoman in my
brain.

"No!" Danaus grabbed my wrist and pulled me back. Seated on
the ground in the middle of the alley, he held me in his lap, his strong
arms forming a protective cocoon around me. Burying my face in his
neck, I sobbed. It felt as if my very soul had shattered. All my strength
and power had been stolen away the moment Rowe touched me.

"I can't go with them again. I can't do it again. Not again," I
pleaded mindlessly, as if Danaus could save me in some way. Images
of Nerian and Machu Picchu danced through my head. The memory
of my screams and Nerian's laugh rang in my ears. And now there
was Rowe. His scent, the feel of his skin, the heat of his breath, were
all imprinted in my brain. *I couldn't escape them.*

"Never," Danaus whispered, his voice breaking through the barrage of memories in my brain. "Never again. I won't let it happen.
The naturi will never touch you again."

I believed him. From Danaus, it was a vow. If it was within his
power, he would not allow the naturi to capture me again. Regardless
of what happened between us as vampire and hunter, he would not
allow me to fall into the hands of the naturi.

The silence of the alley crept into us as we sat on the ground.
With one hand over Danaus's heart, I pressed my head to his chest with
my eyes closed. Tristan sat beside us, his long fingers now entwined
in the fingers of my right hand. His presence was a cool, calming
balm, while Danaus's warmth acted as a safety blanket. Listening to
his heartbeat, I let its steady rhythm wash through me, cleansing me
of the fear and the pain. Danaus rubbed his jaw against the top of my
head as his hand ran down my hair and back in a soothing caress.
Surrounded in their combined power, for a brief moment I felt protected. But it couldn't last. The night was dying and we still had to
reach Sadira before Rowe found her.

"Thank you," I whispered, rubbing my cheek against his warm chest before slowly pulling out of his embrace. I gave Tristan's hand a quick squeeze before pulling my fingers free. My knees shook as I stood, but I managed to keep from falling on my ass.

I walked over to where Rowe had held me. Behind me, I heard Danaus rise and pull his shirt back on. Tristan stood beside me, a soundless shadow. I kept my eyes on the ground. Shards of glass sparkled as they caught some distant shaft of lamplight.

"How was he able to sneak up on us and walk through the wall?" Danaus asked.

"Spells," I murmured. "I think it's why he risked a harvest in Jabari's domain. Certain human organs are needed for some extremely powerful spells. Rowe knew he'd need these spells if he was going to succeed in grabbing me." Lifting my eyes, I reached out, my fingers hovering mere inches from the brick wall he had come through, but I couldn't bring myself to touch it. The wall appeared solid, but I half expected to see Rowe's hand reach out and pull me in.

Danaus walked up beside me and picked up his dagger, which lay on the ground next to the wall. He'd apparently thrown it at the naturi at the same time I blindly threw my fireball. "When you broke the vial, you expected to die," he said, drawing my gaze. His hair hung down around his face, cloaking his features. "I saw it in your eyes."

"Yes." I couldn't lie. I hadn't wanted to die, but death was preferable to being held by the naturi.

"Don't ever do that again." Anger vibrated in his tone. A long, heavy silence settled between us, holding us still before he finally spoke again. "I will not let you escape me so easily."

Biting back a smile, I bowed my head slightly. "As you wish."

I glanced back at the brick wall one last time, my would-be smile fading to a frown. I was tired of being the prey in this little game of cat and mouse. It was time to turn the tables on the naturi.

"Was it just Rowe you couldn't sense or can't you sense the naturi at all now?" I asked, cocking my head to the side as I looked at my semihuman companion.

Danaus's warm powers swept out of the alley and pushed out through the city for almost a full minute before they finally dissipated. "I can sense the naturi, but I cannot tell if one of them is Rowe."

"How close?"

"Outside the city," he said with a shake of his head. "To the north."

"You have any more weapons?" The naturi were killing my kind, killing people in my domain, and Rowe was trying to kidnap me. It was time to strike back.

"We don't have long until sunrise, Mira," Tristan interjected.

I nodded, glancing over my shoulder at the young nightwalker. I wanted revenge, but I wasn't about to get caught out in the open without a safe place to go to ground during the daylight hours. "How far away is this Compound?"

A half smile tugged at one corner of Danaus's mouth. "Less than two hours away. To the north."

"So, you're saying it's on the way . . ."

"Possibly. I won't know until we get started."

We had time. Not a lot, but there was a window. We could strike quickly, cut down some of their numbers, then make a run for the Compound. It wasn't much, but I just needed to reduce their numbers. Hopefully, I would get another shot at Rowe.

Danaus nodded and led the way out of the alley. If I had any shred of luck left in this pathetic existence, Sadira was still alive and staying out of trouble. But I wasn't betting on it at this point.

"Mira." A catch in Tristan's voice stopped me from following behind Danaus. The nightwalker didn't need to say anything. I could feel his fear. "I can't fight them. I mean, I've never—"

"I need you," I said, laying my right hand on his shoulder. I needed every spare hand I could find when it came to taking on the naturi. Right now all I had was Tristan and Danaus. "We have to stop them or they're going to make living with Sadira look like a Sunday garden party."

His large blue eyes darted away from my direct gaze and he stared down at the ground. I was losing him. "Stand with me now, Tristan." I paused for a moment, searching for some words of encouragement. I knew what I needed to say, but it took a moment to finally force them out. "Stand with me now, and I swear, I will help you find a way free of Sadira."

His gaze snapped back up to my face, questioning and distrustful. I couldn't blame him. We both had the same manipulative maker. "I swear. I don't know how, but I will help you," I repeated.

Tristan nodded and turned to follow Danaus out of the alley. I was still cursing myself when I fell into step behind them. I don't know whether he had just manipulated me, but it didn't matter. I needed his help, and there was a good chance both of us weren't going to survive this little escapade, making my promise moot.

Pausing at the mouth of the alley, I glanced up. The night sky was a murky midnight blue in the lights of the city. Dawn was just a few hours away. I could sense it like an old man could feel a storm brewing by the ache in his bones. From the first second we are reborn, nightwalkers can sense the night. After the sun set, I could feel the night swelling around me, oozing into every crevice and dusty corner. The burgeoning night flourishes toward its midpoint, which is so rarely midnight, and then it wilts. As the night dies, time crumbles around me. I can feel it waning like the steady flow of sand in an hourglass.

And now that I was desperate for time, I felt it slipping that much faster out of my grasp. I clenched my fist at my side and swallowed a curse for the sun. Even immortal, I was still a slave to time.

TWENTY

Less than two hours later I was kneeling with Tristan in the outer fringe of a thin copse of woods just northwest of London. There was a scattering of farmhouses close by, their fields outlined by spindly wooden fences and stone walls. According to Danaus, we weren't too far from Stonehenge and less than thirty minutes from the Themis compound.

For a July evening, the air was crisp and heavy, as if the skies would soon open up with rain. Beside me, Tristan drew in a deep breath, relying on his hunting skills to track his prey, but they wouldn't help him with the naturi. They smelled of the earth, holding none of the musky scents and pheromones found with other living creatures. I bit down on my lower lip as I watched the woods through narrowed eyes, trying not to think about Tristan's inexperience. But that kind of inexperience was rampant among my kind. It had been five hundred years since any of us faced a serious battle against the naturi. Since Machu Picchu, we had been content to fight among ourselves, with only occasional incursions against the lycanthropes and the warlocks. But even those amounted to little more than beating chests and gnashing teeth.

"Remember what I told you," I whispered. "Shoot them in the head or in the heart. Once they go down, take off the head as a precaution." I looked down at the gun tightly clutched in my right hand. Danaus had supplied us both with handguns and, when we both looked lost, a quick lesson in using them. Vampires didn't use guns. Up until now, the old ways were always more efficient . . . and more fun.

"Do you honestly trust the hunter?" Tristan hissed, turning his head to look at me. Danaus had dropped us off near the entrance to the woods and then drove on a couple more miles. He was going to circle around and find a perch on higher ground. He had a rifle and planned to pick off some of the naturi from a distance while Tristan and I attacked.

"No, but he's had more than one opportunity to kill me and hasn't taken it. It doesn't make any sense to do so now." I scanned the area, picking up nothing but small flashes of wildlife. Danaus was about a quarter mile away to the east, no longer moving. It was time. I couldn't sense the naturi, but he had said he would attempt to put them directly between us. All we had to do was walk through the woods toward him and we should trip over them.

"Let's go," I murmured, standing and silently walking deeper into the woods, ignoring Tristan's soft comment under his breath. Something about me pushing my luck. Yeah, that went without saying.

I wasn't counting on the element of surprise as we moved soundlessly through the woods. While the naturi couldn't sense us, they would know something was approaching as we unavoidably disturbed wildlife along the way. Furthermore, after our time in the pub, we smelled of smoke and human sweat, which would also give away our position. But with Danaus playing sniper, I was hoping to at least keep them confused, earning us a slight and very brief edge.

We moved in the woods, picking through the underbrush. What little noise we did make sounded like the wind running its fingers through the leaves. While nightwalkers preferred the city, we all spent a little time out in nature. It was a good way to hunt; to stretch our powers, our senses, our bodies to their limits.

And tonight we were hunting naturi.

After a few minutes we stopped at the low murmur of voices in quiet conversation. I couldn't make out any of the words but seriously doubted they were speaking any language with which I was familiar. Their comments were quick and sharp. I had a feeling they knew we were close.

Crouched low in the dirt, Tristan and I crawled closer, sticking to the thick undergrowth in an attempt to remain hidden as we got as close as possible. I paused for a second as a branch snagged the left arm of my silk shirt. My leather pants afforded me some protection from the rocks and dirt, but this wasn't exactly the best attire for crawling through the woods. Neither were my leather boots. My heels had sunk into the soft earth and small holes on more than one occasion.

We finally halted a few yards from a small clearing in the woods. There were ten naturi scattered before us, four from the animal clan. Other than those from the water clan, with their blue-green hair and gills, the animal clan was easiest to identify. They wore their dark brown hair long and shaggy. The structure of their faces was wider and harsher, with sharp cheekbones and a hard jaw. At least two more were from the earth clan. They seemed the exact opposite of the animal clan, with their tall, willowy frames and dark, earthy skin. Their hair color was a broad array—purple, blue, yellow, green—all the colors of the flowers.

What had me worried was the other four I couldn't identify. Their height and build varied, as did their hair color. They could have been from the wind clan, which I had little experience dealing with, or the light clan, which would take away my special gift as an advantage.

Of course, I was coming after the naturi on their own turf. If we were going to survive this, we had to strike fast—the longer the fight lasted, the more chances the naturi had to take advantage of their surroundings.

I was also worried that I had yet to see Rowe. The pirate wannabe had been so good at finding me so far, I just assumed that he'd be with the nearest group of naturi. Or that he'd come to me.

Looking over at the white-faced Tristan, I flashed him a broad smile full of fangs and joyful menace. It was time to go. I just hoped Danaus stuck to his end of this bargain.

As I stood, I flicked off the safety and widened my stance while holding the gun with both hands. I would have only enough time to get off a few shots, and I'd never used a gun before—I had to make each bullet count. Tristan rose smoothly beside me at the same time, a low growl rattling in his throat.

We squeezed off six quick rounds, and the two naturi standing closest to us went down. The report of my gun and Tristan's was almost immediately answered by a shot from farther away. Danaus took out one of the earth clan and two of the unidentified naturi. In less than three seconds we had taken down six naturi with guns. From there, it got hard.

Overcoming their initial shock, the four remaining naturi scattered. Tristan and I continued firing, but they were on the move and our aim wasn't that great despite our superior reflexes and speed. The last remaining member of the animal clan lunged at Tristan, while I saw the earth naturi simply sink into the ground as if she'd stepped into a quicksand pit. I couldn't see the other two naturi, and in the distance the mournful cries of wolves were raised in chorus. The damned naturi had already called for backup.

I snarled as I turned on a heel to grab for the naturi wrestling with Tristan. But I never got there. Vises wrapped around my wrists, jerking my arms over my head. I was dragged backward into the center of the clearing before being pulled into the air.

Looking up, I found the two missing naturi. There was one holding each arm as they pulled me higher in the air. Given their enormous iridescent wings, I assumed they were members of the wind clan. Where the hell humans got the image of six-inch, half-naked pixies with a golden trail of magic dust I'll never know.

"I guess Rowe missed the Fire Starter," giggled one of the naturi in English, for my benefit.

The other gave an inelegant snort, tightening her grip on my right wrist, her long nails digging into my flesh. "She wasn't so hard to catch."

I tried to jerk free of their grip, but their fingers were like metal shackles that tightened until I was sure my bones would soon break. Narrowing my gaze on my two captors, I summoned up my powers, preparing to set their lovely wings on fire, but something else grabbed me, shattering my concentration. Twisting as best I could, I looked down to see what had grabbed my right ankle. A long, thick vine had wrapped around it and was snaking up my calf.

"If he is so fond of her now, won't he love her more if we make her taller?" chuckled a third, saccharine-sweet voice to my left. I looked around to find the earth naturi standing on a tree branch, her shoulders propped against the tree trunk as she did her best "Tarzan meets Jane" impression. Out of the corner of my eye I saw her wave her hand, a second vine wrapping around my left ankle a moment later.

"Or he might love her twice as much if there are two of her," suggested the first wind naturi. Meanwhile, the wind naturi continued their ascent, and the vines attempted to pull me back down to earth. A scream erupted from my throat before I could stop it. My body was being stretched and pulled in two separate directions. Their nails dug into the soft part of my wrists, sending tiny rivers of blood down my arms while the vines tightened around my ankles. I vainly attempted to twist in their grip, but neither the naturi nor the vines loosened their hold.

Closing my eyes against the rising pain as my shoulders threatened to dislocate, I focused on the creatures I could feel holding my arms. Heat built in my limbs, crawling up to my fingertips. My eyes flew open and I directed the fire at their wings. The tissuelike substance went up in a bright ball of orange flames before jumping to their lithe bodies. They instantly released me and we all plummeted back down to the earth.

There wasn't time to scream. Pain ripped through my body as I came to a sudden halt. Something plunged through my back and tore through muscle and organ before finally punching through my chest. The world swam. The darkness crowded my eyes for a moment, and I fought back against the wave threatening to consume me. Clenching my teeth, I looked down, ignoring the fact that my feet were dangling in the air, to find a piece of wood sticking out of my chest. I had been staked from the back by a branch. The naturi had staked me. The only reason I was still alive was that she'd managed to miss my heart, barely. Blood was pouring out of me at an alarming rate, soaking into my clothes and running down my legs.

Discovering that I was still alive, the earth naturi screamed in frustration. A second later the vine tightened around my ankles and resumed its attempt to pull me back down to the earth. I screamed as the branch pulled on muscles and tore at organs. My weight finally overwhelmed the branch and it broke, sending me back to the earth with a heavy thud. The impact sent a shock wave of pain through my tortured body, further loosening my hold on consciousness.

A gunshot cut through the night then, and I heard something fall near me. The air carried with it a puff of earth and wind. The naturi. Either Danaus or Tristan had shot the naturi. One less thing to worry about, but it didn't matter. I was running out of time. I couldn't lift my arms to try to push or pull out the branch. I couldn't move.

My eyes fell shut, riding the next wave of pain that threatened to swamp me. I had to think of what I needed to tell Danaus or Tristan. Someone had to tell Jabari, Sadira, the Coven, about the attacks. Someone had to tell Knox that I was gone and that he needed to watch over the nightwalkers in my domain.

"Mira!" Danaus barked my name.

My eyes fluttered open again and I saw the hunter kneeling next to me. One of his hands was cupping my cheeks, tilting my head so I could look up at him, but I couldn't feel it. My entire world floated in a sea of pain.

"Tristan?" I roughly whispered.

"I'm here," he said, suddenly coming into my line of sight. He was a mess of cuts and scratches, and bloody matted hair.

I closed my eyes, trying to find the strength to continue talking. Some of the pain was beginning to recede, and that worried me. The branch was still embedded in my body. "Naturi?"

"They're gone. Dead."

"Wolves?"

"Mira, we have to get this stake out of you and get you somewhere safe to heal," Tristan said, a soft waver running through his voice.

"Wolves?" I knew they were coming. Even with the last of the naturi dead, they would continue to come and attack, clinging to the last command shoved into their brains.

"Damn it!" Tristan snarled when the air was once again filled with the forlorn cries of the approaching wolves. "Hunter, take care of the wolves. I will help Mira." I saw Danaus nod at Tristan before carefully lowering my head back to the ground, then disappearing from my line of sight.

Tristan moved behind me and knelt behind my head. Over the pain, I felt him grip my shoulder, his thumb sweeping back and forth a couple times in a gentle caress. "I'm sorry," he whispered, then jerked the branch out of my body. Every muscle in my frame clenched and I screamed again. I hadn't thought the pain could get any worse. My thoughts were scattered to the wind, swirling around me in ragged fragments.

". . . losing blood . . . need to feed . . ." Tristan's words were coming to me in bits and pieces. I tried to focus. There were things I needed to tell him, but I couldn't concentrate, couldn't remember anything that had seemed so important just minutes ago. Or was that hours? Time was slipping away from me.

Danaus's name suddenly popped up in Tristan's diatribe about me needing to feed. I fought back the wave of pain and managed to open my eyes. Tristan was still behind me but was leaning over so I could look him in the face. He was pushing something into my back, keeping the pain screaming through my body.

"Danaus?" I murmured.

"Fighting the wolves," Tristan confirmed. "When he comes back, you will feed from him so we can get you somewhere safe."

That's what I thought he had said. "No," I choked out, letting my eyes fall shut again.

"Mira, we have no choice. My blood won't help you."

I licked my lips and gathered up my energy again. I was in no mood to die, but drinking from Danaus seemed like a very bad idea. Even as I appeared to be facing my final hour, the hunter didn't seem the type to give such a donation. "No . . . dangerous. Bad blood."

"What? What are you talking about?"

"His blood is dangerous . . . Don't feed from him." I didn't have the energy to explain it, but I was still conscious enough to know that until I knew what he was, drinking from the hunter was a bad idea. While there was a chance his blood could heal me, there was also a good chance it could kill me faster than the hole in my back and chest.

"Mira—"

"No, Tristan," I bit out around clenched teeth.

The young nightwalker heaved a heavy sigh, looking away from me. "We need to get you to Sadira," he muttered. As much as I hated it, he was right. Our maker was the only one who had a chance at keeping me alive.

"Leave me now," I whispered, "and not even death will stop me from collecting your head."

A fragile smile played with the corners of his lips as he looked back down at me. "Very frightening, Fire Starter," he murmured, smoothing some hair from my face.

I wanted to smile and say something reassuring, but I was just too tired and had no doubt that I looked as threatening as a half-downed kitten.

"Is she dead?" Danaus's voice intruded in the growing silence.

"Asshole," I grumbled.

"We need to get her to Sadira," Tristan said, his hand tightening on my shoulder.

"Take her to where I dropped you off. I'll bring the car," Danaus instructed.

"How do I know you won't abandon us?"

"Because I need her alive," Danaus growled, stepping away from me.

I wanted to think about that comment, turn around what he meant, but I didn't have the chance. Tristan picked me up, sending a fresh wave of pain through my body, and then the world went dark.

TWENTY-ONE

The world slowly swam back into focus, and I instantly wished it hadn't. Pain washed through me in sickening waves, threatening to pull me back under into the thick darkness. I resisted the desire to let unconsciousness sweep me under again. Tristan and Danaus were arguing about something, but I couldn't quite catch the thread of their discussion. I could make out the low growl of the car engine. A window was open, and a breeze slipped across my skin, chilling the blood that was drying on my arms and stomach.

Cracking my eyes open, I found myself lying across the backseat of a small car. I was on my side, my head in Tristan's lap. He was still pressing what I guessed was his shirt into my back in an effort to slow the flow of blood, while his other hand was pressed to my chest.

"How the hell should I know?" Tristan angrily snapped, his voice finally pushing through the fog of pain slowing my thoughts. "The Ancients never talk about Machu Picchu. We don't talk about the naturi. The naturi are gone. They were gone . . ." His voice faded toward the end to a low whisper.

I closed my eyes again, his words echoing through my brain. He was right. We didn't talk about this ugly part of our past, running from the horror, the moment that brought my kind to the very brink of extinction. We ran from it, afraid mentioning it would conjure up our enemy once again.

"Why? What happened there? Why is it so important?" Danaus fired back from the front seat, where he was driving. "They've killed Tabor and they continue to go after Mira. Both were at Machu Picchu."

"Machu Picchu is important because it was the last battle," I said in a low voice. I felt Tristan flinch beneath me, surprised that I was conscious again. "It was the last in a long series of battles against the naturi."

"What happened?" Danaus inquired, his voice softening somewhat.

"I don't remember anything about that night."

"It's understandable," he murmured under his breath. The words had nearly been stolen away by the wind, but I caught them before they flew away.

"Why?" I tried to turn my head to look up at him, but it felt as if it weighed the same as a baby elephant and I gave up the attempt.

"Sometimes the mind forgets things to protect itself."

A chill slithered across my skin that had nothing to do with the wind. I wished I could fold my arms over my stomach, fighting back the black memories of the naturi. "What did Nerian tell you?"

"Enough to haunt me."

The truth was, I didn't want to hear the details about that night. I still remembered the naturi with startling clarity, as if the memories had been charmed so I could never escape the pain. And now there was Rowe, with his voice teasing at my brain as if I should remember him.

"I remember Nerian." My words barely inched over a breathy whisper. "I remember what the naturi did to me. They held me for almost two weeks. They wanted to use me to kill the nightwalkers when they arrived at Machu Picchu. We had been battling them off and on for several centuries. Prior to Machu Picchu, they managed to break the seal using the energy at Petra. They had come to Machu Picchu to open the door between the worlds and finally free the remaining host along with their queen, Aurora." I paused for a moment, trying to force my eyes open so I could look around, but it just took too much energy. I felt lucky to be talking.

"I remember seeing the nightwalkers arrive, but I can't recall their faces, except for Jabari. It was the first time I had ever seen him. And then, nothing. I can't remember anything after seeing them appear."

"What is the next thing you do remember?"

"Standing over Nerian. Sunrise was near and he was dying. I escaped into the surrounding jungle for the day. The next night Jabari came for me."

"What about Rowe?"

"I had never seen Rowe before the attack in Egypt," I said with a sigh.

"He seems to know you."

"I know, but I don't know him. I'm pretty sure I'd remember a one-eyed elf." It didn't make any sense. I had dug through my memory during the past couple days but couldn't recall anything about a naturi named Rowe, or any naturi that resembled him. "At Machu Picchu, I remember feeling Sadira, though I can't recall seeing her. I also remember hearing Tabor's voice. Before leaving, I heard him speaking with Jabari. He sounded tired . . . and angry."

"Where are we going?" Tristan abruptly demanded. I could feel the tension running through him increase. Unable to move, I gathered up what energy I could and dipped into his mind. It was relatively easy since he was holding me, but I didn't have the strength to maintain the link for long. I managed to pick up flashes of trees from his mind, edging closer to the road. The area seemed desolate and lonely, perfect for an attack.

"The Themis Compound. Sadira is there," Danaus said.

"What's Themis?" Tristan asked.

"Vampire hunters," I muttered.

"That's not the goal of Themis," the hunter snapped.

I didn't try to stop the snort of disbelief that escaped me, despite the fact that I was currently in no shape to pick a fight. "Enlighten me. From what I've seen, it doesn't make much sense. There's you—a nightwalker hunter—and James, a bookworm who seems to be completely out of touch with reality."

A deep silence settled into the car, and I sat patiently, feeling it gently take each dip and curve in the road as we headed closer to the Compound, which housed more humans that had hunted my kind.

"The goal of Themis is balance," Danaus volunteered at last. "Most of the members of Themis are like James Parker, scholars who study the occult. They watch from a distance, cataloging events and creatures. And then there are those who are hunters. They are sent when your kind threatens mankind. We are trying to keep your secret, and the secret of all the others, from leaking over into the world of man."

"And are you sent to destroy my kind by wise, knowledgeable men like James?" I demanded, sarcasm dripping off my words.

"No, the leader of Themis is the only one who can dispatch a hunter."

"Ryan?" I asked, recalling the name that Danaus had tossed out earlier that evening when persuading James to take Sadira to the Compound.

"Yes."

"I look forward to meeting him," I said, trying to sound confident, though my blood was soaking through Tristan's shirt and into the cloth car seats.

An odd sound came from Danaus. It sounded broken and rough, as if his voice were dragged over sandpaper. He was laughing at me. I tried to smile as well, though it was a struggle to get all the right muscles working. It didn't matter. The sound helped push back some of the pain for a brief moment. It was like catching a shaft of sunlight between shifting thunderheads, and I wanted to bask in it before the black clouds stifled the golden light.

"You will not be able to intimidate and manipulate Ryan like you did James," he said in an amused voice.

"How about seduce him with my feminine wiles?" I asked in a low voice. Tristan let out a rough sound that could have been a laugh, but he quickly covered it up by clearing his throat. I knew there wasn't much attractive about me right now. If I didn't get to Sadira in the next few minutes, there wouldn't be anything left of me but a blood-covered corpse.

"Doubtful," he said.

I sighed dramatically, my eyes managing to flutter open for a moment before I gave up the fight. "I guess I shall just have to figure out what he truly wants."

"How will you do that?"

"I haven't a clue," I admitted, which earned me another chuckle.

"And you're not concerned?"

"It's less than one hour until sunrise, and I'm riding in a car with a hunter toward a conclave of hunters. The naturi are breathing down my neck, literally, and my last hope for defeating them was killed while I stood watching. Just supposing that I survive the next hour, I still have Jabari, who will rip out my throat because I failed to protect Thorne. At this point, I think the least of my concerns is a human with his own agenda."

There was a soft creak of plastic as Danaus tightened his hands on the steering wheel. "I hope you're right."

"With my recent track record, I doubt it. But what have I got to lose?"

"True," he conceded in a low voice.

As the silence slipped back into the car, I felt Tristan shift beneath me. I knew why. I could feel it too. We were running out of time. If Sadira didn't have enough time to properly heal me before the sun rose, I would not reawaken when the sun set again. Both the blood and life would drain completely from my body and I would be dead.

"How much farther?" Tristan asked.

"Not far."

Dawn was drawing too close and I didn't like the options Tristan and Sadira would be left with if I didn't make it. Would Danaus defend them against his brethren? It wasn't an issue I wanted to contemplate.

"How long have you been with Themis?" the young nightwalker asked, trying to redirect his thoughts.

I managed to move my right arm enough so my hand came in contact with Tristan's left leg. I touched his ankle, rubbing it in an attempt to ease some of the tension that flowed through him.

"A few centuries."

"Why did you join them? You don't seem to be the type to fall in with a cult," I teased, my hand falling away from Tristan.

"They're not a cult."

"Answer the question."

"Because I seek balance," Danaus said, to my surprise. He rarely answered my questions about himself, but apparently I had not dug too deep. I wondered if his powers had kept him out of balance.

"And what did you do before Themis?" I wanted to know about the shadows that lurked in his beautiful eyes. What horrors had he witnessed, and had he ever been the cause?

The steering wheel creaked again. "I hunted and destroyed evil."

"That's rather vague." Tristan stirred beneath me. "Whose definition of evil are you going by?"

"God's."

"Great. So you've spent your life hunting nightwalkers because some human decided we were evil." Whatever momentary warmth there had been between the three of us shriveled and froze as I balled my right fingers into a fist, my nails digging in my palm. For a time we had forgotten who we were.

"You kill," Danaus snapped.

"You're beginning to sound like James." For a time, I think we forgot that we were still on opposite sides; that we were working under a temporary and fragile truce. "Humans kill. You kill. So do we. It may not be right, but we do what we must to survive."

A tense silence hung heavy in the air as Danaus turned off the main road and the car seemed to grow darker. I opened my eyes and peripherally could see only flashes of sky through the trees that thickened around us, blotting out the remaining half of the moon.

Before me, Danaus's powers flowed out from his body, bathing me in its warmth, easing my tension. "There are no naturi here."

"Are you sure? You couldn't sense Rowe," I said, wishing I could sit up and look around.

"There are no naturi here," Danaus repeated calmly.

"Why can you feel them while I cannot?" Tristan demanded.

Loosening the tension from my fingers, which had been balled into a fist, I forced myself to relax. I needed to conserve my energy if I was going to make it through the next few minutes. The darkness was crowding in again, and I could no longer hold my eyes open. My body had tried to heal itself, but without more blood, it was hopeless. As it was now, I was using up most of my energy just to stay alive.

"Because they are the essence of life itself and you are no longer alive."

"But I can sense you and other living things," I whispered.

"You can sense all things that are human, or at least started human, because a part of you is still human. The naturi world is closed to you." His voice was strong, like a hand massaging the tension from my shoulders.

"Then how is it that nightwalkers can seal them away from this world?"

"That, I do not know."

"Just keep working on that, will you?" I said, my words fading toward the end.

Danaus parked the car and turned off the motor. I gave up trying to look around and slipped back into Tristan's mind. He was terrified but was holding together for now. He looked up at the enormous mansion that loomed before us. Every window was filled with light despite the late hour. Apparently, their unexpected guests were causing a bit of a stir.

Tristan had already scanned the manor, easily finding both Michael and Gabriel. While Tristan had never met either human, I knew both extremely well and could recognize them in his thoughts. The other humans were a hive of chaos; anxious, fearful, but also curious. Sadira remained hidden, and Tristan was reluctant to step out of the car.

She has been told to hide herself, I said softly in his mind. *She is here.*

Are you sure?

Positive.

I slipped out of Tristan's mind but still felt something else humming in the air. For a moment I thought it was Tristan or Danaus, but the signature of the power was different. There was a magic user inside, a very powerful one.

Danaus heard me softly chuckle as he opened Tristan's door. "What?" he asked. He probably thought I'd finally lost my mind.

"Some interesting occupants. I look forward to meeting them," I replied. Of course, that was assuming Sadira could put me back together again.

TWENTY-TWO

Blinking against the bright entrance, I tried to raise my hand to cover my eyes, but it was too heavy to move. Instead, I pressed my head into Tristan's bare, blood-smeared chest as he carried me into the great manor. It seemed they had flicked on every light in the place, much like James had earlier in the evening, attempting to protect themselves against the dark creatures entering their sanctuary. Before closing my eyes, I caught a glimpse of the enormous marble and wood staircase that dominated the main hall. On both the left and right of the hall, doors were pulled open and footsteps scraped and echoed off the hardwood floors as people stepped out to inspect Tristan and me.

"Sadira," I murmured softly against Tristan, my lips lightly brushing the cool skin of his chest. I wasn't sure if anyone could actually hear me anymore. The world was fading away—the pain had dimmed and I could no longer feel Tristan's arms holding me.

"Mira?" Tristan's worried voice demanded an answer, but I simply didn't have the energy to reply. "Sadira! Where is she? We're losing Mira."

The young nightwalker's question was answered with a horrible sound, a mix of scream and snarl. It was Sadira. I knew her voice, its every tone, pitch, and nuance. For years it had echoed through my brain, a singsong chant I could never escape.

Soft hands touched my face, turning my head. "Mira! Open your eyes and look at me now!" Sadira commanded.

My eyelids fluttered for a brief moment before I finally gave up the attempt. Licking my lips, I drew in a slow breath. "We had . . . problems," I whispered.

A snarl of low curses escaped Sadira in a rough voice, but she was very gentle when she pressed a kiss to my temple before resting my head against Tristan's chest again. "I need somewhere to work undisturbed. There. In there."

My thoughts drifted away for a while. I was vaguely aware of Tristan carrying me somewhere followed by a flurry of angry voices and some slamming doors. A soft whimper escaped me as Tristan set me down on a hard surface that I could only guess was a long tabletop. The bright lights were banked at last and I was able to force my eyes open a crack. Tall bookshelves lined the wall to my right, broken only by portraits of grim-faced men with gray and white hair.

"They found us . . ." I forced out as my eyes fell shut again. There was no more time. I had to tell Sadira what happened so she could tell Jabari. The Elder would fix it; he'd be able to stop the naturi. "They killed Thorne. N-Need another."

"I know," Sadira whispered. I could only guess that Tristan had caught her up on the evening's events while I drifted in and out of consciousness. She was standing beside me. Her small hand swept over my forehead, pushed hair away from my face. "But we need to heal you now."

"Triad—"

"None of that matters. None of that matters without you." Sadira pressed a kiss to my cheek and then my forehead. "I need you to relax your mind."

"Tired. So . . . tired." I was exhausted. Tired of fighting, tired of the pain.

And then something stirred. Swamped within the pain, I felt something faint shift in my thoughts, but as I tried to focus on it, it slipped away, pulling back into the swirling mist that consumed my thoughts. I reached out again, searching for the movement, and then the pain was gone.

My eyes flew open and I screamed. My thoughts came to a screeching halt as I looked around me. The wall of books and stern-looking men was completely gone. The gleaming hardwood streaked with my blood was gone. Around me were cold stone walls and wooden torches held in wrought-iron sconces guttering with firelight in the large room. It was a dungeon. It was the dungeon below Sadira's castle in Spain. It was the room where I'd been reborn.

Another scream of panic rose up in my throat as I sat up and twisted around to thoroughly scan the room. It couldn't be the same place. When I closed my eyes, I'd been dying on a boardroom table in England. Sadira didn't have the ability to instantly flit from place to place like Jabari. It couldn't be real.

"It's not real." Her disembodied voice floated through the air for a moment before she came through the stone wall to my right and stood beside where I sat on the long stone slab. "The pain was taking you away from me. I needed to take you away from the pain so I could heal you. The damage is . . . extensive. Organs have been shredded and your heart has been punctured. You're dying."

"I guessed as much," I sighed. Anxiety crawled up my spine, digging claws into my back. I could tell my brain that it wasn't real, but rising panic wasn't buying it. It looked real, it felt real, it smelled real. "But why here?"

"I need you to trust me," Sadira said with a soft smile, tilting her head to one side. "This is the one time in your life you trusted me completely."

A snort escaped me as I swung my legs over the side of the stone table and dropped to my feet, putting the table between us. "I have never trusted you."

"That is an interesting lie," she chided. "You lay helpless night after night for ten years, completely dependent upon me to keep you alive. I was in your mind; you never doubted that I would return each night to you."

I stood with my left hip pressed against the stone slab, my arms crossed over my chest. Out of the corner of my eye I could see Sadira watching me, waiting for my response. I knew she was right. I had trusted her to bring me into her world, not to abandon me. But at that point my only other option was death.

For a moment Sadira's image wavered, and I turned to face her, automatically reaching for her, but my hand passed through her. "So much damage . . ." Her voice whispered through the air, but her lips never moved. She was having troubling repairing the damage and maintaining the fantasy world. Pain cut through my chest, doubling me over, my forehead pressed against the stone table before me. I felt nothing but the pain for several seconds before it faded again like a wave pulling back out to sea.

When I stood again, Sadira was before me. Her face was strained and pale, but she was with me again. "There is so much damage. I wish I could reach Jabari," she absently said. She wasn't looking at me, but down at the table that stood between us. "But then he may use that as an excuse to take you back."

Something twisted in my stomach that had nothing to do with the wound she was fighting to close. Jabari couldn't help her. Only Sadira could heal me. She was the one that made me a nightwalker, and only her blood could repair the wounded flesh she'd helped to create. I hesitated to ask. Sadira was very careful with knowledge, well-aware that controlling the flow of information was the easiest way to control her children. Despite her distracted demeanor, she didn't drop that information without a very good reason.

"Only you can save me." Even if it was all an illusion, the words tasted bad on my tongue as I said them.

Laughter danced in Sadira's eyes as she looked up at me. "How I wish that were true." She chuckled even as the light seemed to die from her expression. "Jabari has watched you from the moment I found you in Greece. I was *allowed* to keep you only if I promised to bring you before him whenever he commanded. And when the time came to bring you into the darkness, it was agreed that you would be a First Blood."

"What do you mean 'agreed'?" The statement implied that others were involved in the discussion about my fate, but there was never anyone but Sadira and her children around. As a human, I was occasionally brought before the Coven and other Ancients as a form of amusement, but Jabari had never been around then.

"Jabari and Tabor discussed it." Sadira reached across the table and took my right hand in both of her hands. Turning my arm over, she ran the fingers of her left hand down the inside of my arm. "My blood runs in your veins—shaped your organs and gave you an immortal life—but so does Jabari's and Tabor's."

"No!" I jerked my arm out of her grasp and took a step back. "I don't remember either of them."

"You were barely alive. It was easier to manipulate your memories then."

"I don't understand," I said, pacing away from the table. There was no sound in the room, not even my footsteps on the stone floor. There were only our voices, because that was the point of bringing me here, not helping me to escape the pain. There was something she needed to tell me regardless of whether I wanted to hear it. "Why?"

"You were different, Mira." Sadira walked to the end of the table and started to come around it but stopped when I backpedaled, trying to keep some distance between us. "There was no human like you. It was more than your ability to control fire. We could sense an energy in your soul that we had never felt before. So, we decided to make you into a nightwalker, but we knew you would have to be a First Blood if we were to have any chance to preserve this energy."

"So you made me into a First Blood. That was part of our agreement. What about Jabari and Tabor?"

"Do you think Jabari would allow me to make a creature that could potentially destroy him?" Sadira demanded, incredulous. "Of course not. But if his blood flowed in you, he was sure you would feel bound to him, protecting him from your temper. It would also enable him to know your location at any time."

I turned my back on Sadira, a chill sweeping through me as a slight pain throbbed in my chest. It was nowhere near as intense as before, but was a subtle reminder that there was another world I had to return to. I stared down at my bare arm, my pale, white skin unmarred and unbroken. The reality of my raw and bruised wrists did not bleed into this illusion. It wasn't important. My focus was on the blue veins below my skin. Jabari's blood filled my veins in some way, had helped to give me this life.

"Yet things did not go how he had hoped."

Sadira's words jerked my head up. She had silently walked around the table and now leaned back against it. Her small slender hands were folded before her stomach.

"What happened?"

"You remained . . . you," she said with a smile, while an odd glow grew in her eyes.

"What the hell is that supposed to mean?"

"It means he assumed that you would be easier to control as a vampire because you could be subjected to more intense forms of punishment without being killed due to your human frailties. But you refused to obey me. You refused to obey any Ancient that crossed your path. Also, I refused to give you up, so you were stolen."

I forced out a sharp little laugh. This was where her little story took a wrong turn and I was no longer buying it. It was a good try up until then. "I was kidnapped by the naturi, and we both know it."

A look of pity crossed her pale face as she shook her head. I longed to smack that look off her face but remained standing where I was, my fists clenched at my sides. "Think, my Mira. Before you were stolen, we were traveling west, heading back from Vienna. It was only you and me. We had gone to ground just before sunrise in a tiny village just west of the Pyrenees. No one knew where we were. The only ones who could have found you were those who made you."

"No!" I shouted, flinching at the faint echo that seemed to bounce around in my brain. I knew what she was saying and it was impossible. Jabari could have handed me over to the naturi five centuries ago. And he could have done it now. After the battle at Machu Picchu, I collapsed in his arms for a century, leaning on his strength. Then, centuries later, the naturi found me in my own domain and again in Egypt, driving me into Jabari's waiting arms.

The pieces fit, but I didn't trust them. Jabari hated the naturi. He wouldn't use them against another nightwalker. He didn't have to. If he wanted something, he simply commanded and the nightwalker obeyed. Except for me. I didn't accept a direct order from anyone . . . but Jabari, and that was only because he had saved me from the naturi.

Gritting my teeth, I shoved both my hands into my hair and paced away from Sadira. My thoughts were swirling in an endless circle. Was she telling the truth? I knew she couldn't be trusted.

"Why are you telling me this?" I growled, refusing to look at her.

"Because he's searching for a way to replace you," she whispered.

I dropped my hands back to my sides as I turned back around to look at my maker. "How?"

"The same way we made you," she said, shrugging her slim shoulders. "I have helped with ten others, and I know there have been some I was not a part of. Not one has survived beyond the first year."

"Why? What happens?"

Sadira shook her head, her eyes dropping down to her folded hands. "That's not important. The fear is that he may succeed one day."

"And then you think he will have no further use for me." My voice was dead. Was any of this true? I didn't know what to believe anymore. My eyes wandered around the room that was my home for ten years. It had been my entire world and Sadira my only contact with life. She had been warmth, and compassion, and love for those years. Had that been a lie too? Or was it the only thing during those years that had been the truth?

"I know you feel no love for me, but you are my child, my beloved daughter. I do not want him to end your life because he feels you are no longer useful to him," Sadira murmured.

I didn't want him to end my life either, but I wasn't about to seek shelter in Sadira's open arms. It wasn't exactly an enticing alternative. "Why have the others died?"

Sadira shook her head and her image wavered. At the same time, the pain in my chest increased. "It's near sunrise. We will speak more later."

Before I could stop her, pain stabbed through me and my eyes popped open. The library with its tall bookshelves and grim men surrounded me again. Candlelight flickered, casting shadows around the room. Sadira sat on the edge of the table beside my hip. She was using a delicate white lace handkerchief to wipe blood from her wrist.

Her skin was so pale she was nearly translucent, and her eyes seemed more sunken and shadowed. I could taste her blood in my mouth, but it hadn't been enough. The worst of my wounds had closed using her blood, but I still needed to replenish all that I'd lost.

Just the taste of Sadira's blood sent up a dull roar inside my chest. The monster that wound itself around my soul was awake and screaming for blood. I clenched my teeth and tried to push it back. I would likely kill anyone I tried to feed from right now if I couldn't get a handle on my hunger.

Gabriel.

I whispered his name in my mind, sending the soft plea out to his brain. A wave of his emotions pushed back through me; fear, relief, worry, and joy all came rushing back in the wave of my mental touch. I wrapped my mind and heart up in his concern, holding them close to me as he entered the room and pulled me into his arms. I used those emotions as a way of protecting him from me as I sank my fangs into his throat and drank deeply.

The monster roared and clawed at my soul until I was sure there were only jagged shreds left, but I refused to give in to its demands that I take it all. I drank only enough to get me through the day. When I awoke at sunset, I would have enough strength to hunt and replenish all that I'd lost.

Lifting my mouth from Gabriel's neck, I instantly healed the wound and rested my head against his chest as he continued to hold me. His heartbeat was strong, seeming to vibrate through my weakened frame. He smelled of spice and cotton and steak. A smile teased at my lips and I relaxed in his arms. Themis had been kind enough to supply my angels with dinner. At least they'd been safe here.

"That was too close, boss," Gabriel murmured, rubbing his chin against the top of my head. He tightened his arms around me, keeping me pressed close but still trying to be careful of my tender wounds.

Tipping my head back, I pressed a quick kiss to his cheek before gently pushing out of his arms. The room spun slowly and my limbs trembled. I was weak and my whole body hurt. Hunger still roared in the back of my brain, but I had pushed it down so it was now little more than low white noise mixing in with all my other aches and pains.

"Sunrise," Sadira murmured, and I nodded as I swung my legs over the edge of the table. We were running out of time. Sunrise was less than fifteen minutes away and we needed to find a secure location to sleep.

I looked down at myself for the first time. My silk shirt was a mess. Both sleeves were shredded and the front was torn open from the waist down. What remained of the cloth was soaked in my blood, as were my leather pants. In fact, my blood was everywhere; my hands, face, the table, Sadira, and now Gabriel. It had been too close.

As my feet touched the ground, I felt my knees give out on me, but Gabriel grabbed my elbow, helping to steady me as he came to stand behind me. This was going to be tricky. I needed rest.

The sound of footsteps on the hardwood floor was my only warning before the door to the library swung open. Tristan stepped into the room, followed by Danaus, Michael, and James. Sadira extended her hand to Tristan. The young nightwalker hesitated a moment, his eyes darting to my face before he finally walked over to her, allowing Sadira to wrap her arms around him. Stiff, he stood with his arms lightly around her waist, his eyes closed. She was in his mind, not mine, but I knew she had already begun the task of drawing him back to her side. I had a promise to keep, but not now. I was in no shape to help anyone right now.

Michael stepped around Danaus to approach me. His handsome face was heavily lined and pale from worry. He wrapped his one good arm around me, pulling me as close as he possibly could to him. His large body shook slightly as I touched him, a shiver of relief running through him. Unfortunately, I was forced to release him almost as soon as he touched me. I was still too starved. I needed to feed, and his heartbeat combined with the sound of Gabriel's was slowly driving me mad.

Stepping away from my two angels, but keeping one hand on the table for balance, I looked over at Danaus, who was watching the little reunion from the doorway. "Sunrise is close. We have no choice but to stay here. We need a windowless room, preferably in the basement with a door that locks from the inside."

"I have something," he said with a nod.

James stood just behind Danaus's shoulder, his eyes dazed as he surveyed the room.

"James, could you fetch some food and drinks for my guardians?" I said to him. "They will be locked with us for the daylight hours. I don't want them becoming weak."

The Themis member nodded, snapping from his trance at the sound of his name. "I will go prepare something," he said before hurrying from the room.

Sadira, Tristan, Gabriel, Michael, and I followed Danaus out of the library and down the hall toward the back of the manor. As we trooped slowly through the house, I was vaguely aware of the people lingering in doorways and down long hallways, watching our progress. My gaze swept over them, causing a frown to pull at the corners of my lips. Most were older gentlemen in their late forties and fifties, looking the same in their drab suits and neckties. There were a smattering of women, but they looked equally bookish, with their pale skin and pulled-back hair. I was beginning to wonder if these people saw the sunlight as infrequently as I did.

"You let me leave Sadira with a convention of librarians," I groaned, shoving both my hands through my hair in frustration. I swallowed a whimper as the movement pulled on the newly mended tissue and skin that stretched around my stomach and chest. I had lost my mind.

"She was safe." Danaus glared at me over his shoulder, his jaw clenched.

I looked back at the others, who remained in the doorways staring at me, their faces a mixture of fear and curiosity. "Don't you people sleep?" I snarled, then stalked off down the hall after Danaus, trying to ignore the spots that passed before my eyes. I needed to go to sleep before I fell over.

But beyond the pain, an odd feeling crawled over my skin. I had never been gawked at like that before. These civilized British librarians were watching me like I was a sideshow curiosity, or a monster. Or an evil miracle, considering the slow dance with death I had just survived.

The basement was unlike most I had known—dry and lacking an overwhelming smell of mold. Floor-to-ceiling bookshelves covered most of the walls, overflowing with books and ancient scrolls. I would have liked to linger down there, looking over the various stories these people had collected. Most of it was probably biased and terribly misguided, but it would have been interesting to see how humans viewed the other creatures surrounding them. I kept walking, my heels echoing off the tile floor as I followed Danaus.

At the end of the room was a wall with a thick, heavy wooden door held together with iron bands. The type of door that would lead to a dungeon. Danaus pulled the door open, the muscles in his arm jumping and dancing under the strain. Running his hand over the right wall on the inside, he flicked on the overhead light to reveal a single bare bulb glowing in the darkness. Inside, I saw several dusty crates and boxes, no doubt holding whatever strange artifacts these people valued. The room was used for storage and was obviously not visited often. Sadira stepped inside, frowning.

"It's just for one day," I wearily reminded her.

"Do you need blankets or anything?" Danaus asked awkwardly.

"No," I said with a soft chuckle. For all purposes, Sadira, Tristan, and I would be dead when the sun rose. We had no need for such comforts, though they were always nice to wake up to. "Just the food for Michael and Gabriel; I would appreciate it. This isn't the best way to spend the daylight hours."

He stared at me for a long time, his eyes weighing me. "You actually care for them," he murmured, as if his brain couldn't comprehend the idea.

"Very much," I half whispered, my gaze following my angels for a moment. "I'm not a monster from your nightmares. As you said, a part of me is still human." I was too tired to pound my fists against his stubborn misconceptions about what a nightwalker was supposed to be.

James appeared then, scurrying to the door of the basement room, an enormous basket on his arms. I stepped out of the doorway and allowed Gabriel to take it from him. James stepped back, running one hand through his hair. It had grown somewhat disheveled from the long night's adventure, and his tie was now missing.

"If you want, we can rotate in others so they can have a break," Danaus offered, instantly regaining my attention.

"No!" I said sharply. The fresh surge of fear snapped me awake. "No one else comes in or out of here." I turned my gaze over to Michael and Gabriel, who were inspecting the room. "And you do not open the door for anyone besides Danaus. No one!" Both gave me a slight nod before resuming their inspection.

I hesitantly stepped inside and turned to face Danaus, who had moved back out of the room. He pulled the heavy iron key out of the door and handed it to me so I could lock the room from the inside. I didn't ask him if it was the only copy. I didn't want to know the answer or to see him lie to me if it wasn't.

"Sweet dreams," I said. I tried to smile but knew it never reached my eyes.

Danaus reached up and slowly moved a lock of hair from where it had fallen in front of my eyes. His beautiful sapphire eyes caressed my face as if he were trying to memorize my features. "You too," he finally said before closing the door.

My hand was trembling when I put the cold key into the lock and turned it, the metal grinding against metal. It had been a while since anyone bothered to lock this door. Moving into the room, I tossed Gabriel the key. In one corner, Michael was already sifting through the large basket of food. It had been a long night already, and I hoped they could catch a little sleep in shifts, having no idea what tomorrow would bring for any of us.

On the opposite wall, Sadira and Tristan lay on the dusty floor, wrapped in each other's arms. Their eyes were closed, already giving over to the daylight sleep. We could sleep at any time but had no choice when the sun rose. It was the tradeoff we all had to face. During the long night hours, we were practically gods among the humans, with abilities beyond their comprehension. But as the sun touched the earth, we were reduced to helpless husks, completely unable to protect ourselves. I sat on a crate against the wall and stretched out my legs. With my arms crossed over my chest, I waited, staring at the opposite wall. I didn't want to close my eyes regardless of how tired I was. I didn't want the dawn to come and take away my ability to defend myself.

But it came despite my protests. I could feel the night give one last feeble gasp, clawing at the earth as it finally shriveled up and died. The light crept steadily toward the horizon, the gray sky giving way to the warm yellows and pinks that I had watched paint the clouds in my youth. Despite the fact that I had not been reborn until I was twenty-five, all my memories of the dawn came from my youth. I could recall walking down to the shore to watch the sun lifting into the sky, its delicate rays jumping and dancing on the waves. The cries of the gulls filled the air as they left their nighttime perch.

As the light broke across the sky, my body clenched, struggling to hold my powers locked within this poor frame. Yet, no matter how hard I tried, still it slipped through my skin and down into the earth. As my eyes fell shut, the last thing I recalled was the feeling of Danaus. Strong and powerful, his warmth washed through me, protecting me as he stood guard outside the door. I tried to reach out with the last bit of my powers to touch his warmth. The hunter was still protecting. He could have so easily left Tristan and me in the woods, allowing me to slowly die while he returned to Themis to destroy Sadira. Despite his angry protests about my kind being the root of all evil, he had saved me twice from Rowe and now stood guarding me from his own people during my weakest moment.

TWENTY-THREE

A scream erupted from my throat as my eyes snapped open. Machu Picchu rose up around me and Nerian stood close with knife in hand. This time I had been lying on Intihuatana as he prepared to remove my heart. It took a moment for my vision to clear. Blinking again, I found Michael standing before me, his warm hands cradling my face. I pulled away, moving out of his grasp, and pressed my back into the cold stone wall. The weight of Sadira's worried gaze pushed down on my tense shoulders. I couldn't blame her for her fears. I was supposed to protect her, and I was slowly being driven mad by nightmares that I shouldn't have had in the first place.

"I thought you had escaped the nightmares," she said, her voice a soft caress that reminded me vaguely of flannel pajamas. She was standing near the door. Tristan hovered close by, his arm around her slim shoulders. His body and face had become as still and stiff as a marble statue as he tried to mentally remove himself from Sadira, but I saw a flicker of concern flash through his eyes before he could squash it.

"They're back." I was only mildly surprised that she'd asked Jabari about me. I jumped down from my resting spot on top of the crates, wincing at the movement. My body was mostly healed, but I was still sore. "It's nothing. It will pass. What time is it?"

"Two hours past sunset."

I barely stifled the curse that had risen to my lips. I was a late sleeper, but I'd never slept that late. The nightmares combined with the injuries were draining me, forcing me to sleep later into the night. That left me vulnerable not only to humans and naturi, but also to other nightwalkers.

"Let's get out of here." I held my hand up and Gabriel tossed me the key. He looked rumpled and a little weary, but otherwise fine. Michael wasn't wearing his homemade sling and seemed to move a bit easier. Both of my angels had also regained their color from my previous feedings. I unlocked the door and pushed it easily open, the metal hinges groaning in the silence. My little band trooped across the basement and up the stairs, where James met us. I was surprised to find him wearing a pair of jeans and a hunter green T-shirt. It was a little disconcerting to see him looking so casual, even though his hair was still perfectly arranged and his shirt neatly tucked into his pants. His brown belt even matched his dark brown shoes.

"Nice outfit," I said with a half smile.

James flushed, his hand absently reaching for a tie that wasn't there. "I had a feeling I was a bit overdressed for assisting you."

"No doubt."

"Are you leaving now?"

"Soon. Where's Danaus?"

"Resting, I believe. He stood guard in the basement all day." My stomach muscles twisted and knotted at the thought of him sitting outside my door while I lay helpless. Yet, instead of fear gripping me, I was surprised to feel my cheeks flush. I felt important . . . almost cherished. I hadn't expected the hunter to stay all day.

"Do we need him anymore?" Sadira asked from behind me, shaking me from my thoughts and reminding me that she was the valuable commodity here, not me. I was just part of a game Rowe was playing.

I turned my head so I could see her out of the corner of my eye. "No, I guess not," I said, disappointment threading itself through each syllable. I had become accustomed to having him there, someone protecting my back—even though he meant to stick a knife in it the first chance he got. "We need to find Jabari and a replacement for Tabor. We might as well stay while you search."

"And then where?" Sadira's soft voice was edged with fear and doubt.

"Back to London. My jet is still there, and we can take it to the Coven. If Jabari is not there, one of the other Elders will be. It's also the safest place I can think of. You can stay there while I fetch Tabor's replacement or search for the location of the next sacrifice."

"I will show you to a comfortable room you may use," James said, leading us down the hall. He opened the door and my two guardians entered first, sweeping the room, one hand always on the butt of one of their guns. They were good at what they did and I felt a small swell of pride as I watched them. I entered only after Gabriel gave a single nod, indicating that it was clear.

Sadira settled in an ornate chair in one corner of the room, allowing her to survey the entire room and keep her back to the wall. We hadn't survived this long without learning to be cautious. Of course, in my case it also helped to be lucky.

I looked around the cozy room, taking in the pale yellow striped wallpaper and antique furniture with its slightly faded flower print. Lamps dotted the room, casting the area in a soft, warm glow while sweeping back the shadows to the far corners. There were a few landscape portraits and bookshelves set into the walls.

"Is there anything I can get you?" James inquired, drawing my attention back to him. He was so eager to be involved, to help in some fashion, even if it was only fetching food, that I wanted to smile. By the sheer fact that we hadn't drained him dry yet, he was willing to give me and my kind a chance. I wished more humans could view us with the same open-mindedness.

"Do you have any more hunters lying around?" I asked, knowing Danaus couldn't be the only hunter lurking around this rambling old house. "I'd like at least a pair at the door."

"Of course."

"And a meal for my companions."

"Food for Michael and Gabriel will not be a problem, but . . ." He hedged nervously, his gaze darting to Sadira, who smiled. While she would never admit to it, she was enjoying James's discomfort.

"Sadira and I will hunt outside of the Compound later this evening," I said, then looked over at Tristan. He was still young and I had no doubt that last night's confrontation had left him feeling like he could use a bite. I didn't want a half-starved nightwalker on my hands when I was having trouble myself, particularly around this many humans. They were hell to control and extremely dangerous.

"I'll feed later as well," Tristan volunteered, his voice soft but firm.

"Very good," James said with a quiet sigh of relief. "Anything else?"

"Yes, a shower."

"I beg your pardon?"

Pushing him back out the door, I rolled my eyes toward the ceiling. "I'm a vampire, James, not a self-cleaning oven," I said. I turned my gaze to Sadira for a moment. "Find me another Tabor. I'll be back soon." Closing the door, I looked at James again, who was blushing.

"Forgive me, I just never thought . . ." he stammered, resettling his gold-rimmed glasses on the bridge of his narrow nose.

"Yeah, all us undead don't need to bathe. Our magic keeps us clean." Laying my hands on his shoulders, I gently turned him so he was pointed toward the main hall. "Find me a shower and then fetch the food. If you're lucky, we'll be out of your hair in less than an hour."

James silently led me up the stairs to the second floor. Down the hall to the left, he opened the third door, revealing a beautiful bedroom decorated in mint green and gold. A large four-poster bed dominated the room, and a heavy walnut desk lounged against the far wall. The room was neat and clean, with its books properly arranged. I paused at the bureau to look at the row of pictures, all of smiling family and friends.

"This room belongs to Melanie Richards. She's currently in the States visiting family," James explained. "I would give you a spare room, but we're a little crowded at the moment."

"Had to call in reinforcements?" I teased. His mouth bobbed open and closed for a moment, but I had pity on him. There was something a little endearing about this poor human. Maybe it was just the fact that he didn't resemble a librarian at the moment, like all the others. "I don't blame you," I whispered, with a secret little smile.

I turned my gaze back to the pictures, wondering if any of the females was the room's owner. "I bet she's going to be upset to discover she missed out on seeing the vampire circus sweep through."

"That's an understatement," James muttered, earning a light chuckle from me.

"You'll just have to tell her that I used her shower. Maybe that will placate her," I said, feeling supremely absurd. I walked into the bathroom off the bedroom. It was small, with a set of green towels hanging on the towel rod. Most of the personal items had been removed, but I was relieved to find some shampoo and bath gel. I smelled of smoke and felt grimy, coated in a thick layer of my own blood.

"Is there anything else I can do?" he offered, his hand resting on the white marble sink.

"No, I can handle this, unless you want to stay and wash my back?"

This time James smiled and shook his head. I think he was beginning to catch on to my teasing. "I shall leave you and take care of the other items." With that, he headed out of the room.

I closed the bathroom door and looked at myself in the mirror. I looked like a nightmare. My red hair hung about my face in matted clumps, filled with dried blood, leaves, and dirt. My face and body were streaked with blood and dirt. I looked like the hideous, blood-sucking monster vampires were proclaimed to be. And yet none of my own fear was showing beneath the blood and dirt. The world couldn't see that I didn't have a clue about what I was doing. Most of my decisions were made on the fly, and the fact that I was still alive was a testament to my own stupid luck.

Turning away from the mirror in disgust, I turned on only the hot water and stripped out of my clothes. I climbed into the tub and sighed as the steaming hot water heated my cold flesh and turned my complexion pink. It was the quickest way to gain warmth without feeding. The feeling was always short-lived, but I enjoyed it while it lasted. Relaxed again, I washed my hair and scrubbed off last night's encounters at the pub, in the alley with Rowe, and in the woods.

With my hands braced against the tile wall, I let the hot water pour down on my head and over my body, rinsing off the dirt and soap. I closed my eyes and stretched out my senses. I started on the first floor, pausing for a second. While I couldn't feel Sadira, I could pick up the swell of power emanating from her. So much for hiding. Hell, let her blame it on me. Jabari had plenty to be angry with me for. Why not add one more thing? I had a few things I was eager to discuss with the Elder.

The members of Themis were still anxious, running about the large mansion like a hive of angry bees. There was a large group meeting at the opposite end of the second floor. I didn't pause to hear what they were discussing. I didn't care. We'd be gone soon and I'd never have to deal with these people again.

On the third floor, I located Danaus. He was so calm and at peace, I could only guess he was asleep. He was more difficult to read than humans and other nightwalkers. Much like most magic users, his powers seemed to muddy things. I could pick up on emotions but not specific thoughts. I lingered over him, soaking in his calm the same way I had soaked in the warmth of his powers. Reluctantly, I moved on and was about to pull away when I picked up on the other strong magic user in the house. He was on the third floor in what felt like a large room. He was calm as well, but there was a deeper sense of concern and anticipation curling around him. This had to be the illustrious Ryan.

With a shake of my head, I closed the connection and turned off the shower. Wiping off the excess water, I towel-dried my hair as best as I could. Reluctantly, I pulled on my pants, shoes, and bra. The shirt was ruined. I would have to borrow something from Miss Richards for now. If we had time, I hoped to stop at the hotel in London and pick up my things before we flew out. Locating a brush under the sink, I ran it through my hair, getting rid of the tangles as best as I could. When finished, I at least felt like I carried the semblance of average humanity.

Reaching for the doorknob, I suddenly stopped. Michael was waiting for me in the bedroom, his heart thudding fast in worry. I jerked open the door to find him pacing the room, clenching and unclenching his hands at his sides.

"What's wrong?" I demanded in a harsh voice, making him jump.

"Nothing," he quickly answered, his hand automatically reaching for his gun in his surprise. A spastic smile jumped across his lips as his hands returned to his sides.

"What are you doing up here?"

"I didn't think you should be here unprotected."

"I'm fine. Your job right now is to protect Sadira. I can manage," I reassured him, running my fingers through my damp hair. Fear unknotted in my stomach, leaving the muscles trembling for a moment.

"Do you need anything?" His eyes were wide as he watched me.

"No, I'm fine."

Something about him was making me ill at ease. He seemed nervous and extremely tense. I could only guess that it was the constant traveling and the threat of the naturi. While I'm not sure he completely understood the danger, he'd overheard enough conversations to catch a solid glimpse.

He walked over to me and placed a trembling hand on my cheek. "I'm worried about you. You nearly died last night and you're still in danger here," he murmured, pressing a gentle kiss to my temple. "This place is wall-to-wall vampire hunters and God only knows what else. You know I'll do whatever it takes to protect you, but . . ." His strong voice drifted off, suffocated by his doubts.

"But you and Gabriel are outgunned," I finished, running my hands up his strong chest. Lacing my fingers behind his neck, I pulled him down so his forehead touched mine. Michael wrapped his arm around my waist, enveloping me his warmth. "Right now, these hunters are not the threat that concerns me. Besides, they seem to follow Danaus, and he needs me alive."

He pulled away so that he could look me in the eye. "He tried to have you killed in Egypt," he reminded me, with barely caged anger.

"He claims it was a misunderstanding. They were trying to rescue him."

"And you believe him?"

"No." I laughed, pulling his head down to capture his soft lips in a quick kiss that lasted a bit longer than I initially intended. Michael's arms tightened, pressing me against his strong body. His skin was warm and his heart pounded against my breast, proclaiming his life and strength to my own cold form. I started to break off the kiss, telling myself that I had too many things to take care of, when Michael deepened it, running the tip of his tongue along the seam of my lips. My own body instantly responded, my mouth opening so his tongue could dart in, tasting me.

French kissing a vampire was an art form that Michael had mastered during our years together. He could kiss me without pricking his tongue on my fangs, but there was never anything hesitant or careful about it. He explored my mouth, opening up senses and feelings within me I hadn't realized were laying dormant, waiting for him and his touch. In his hands, I felt almost human again.

I moaned softly against his mouth, my fingers threading through his hair. With a little pressure he guided me backward until I felt something pressing against the back of my knees. Running his hands up and down my back, he slowly pulled his mouth away and smiled down at me, his eyes sparkling with some kind of mischief. It was on the tip of my tongue to ask what he was thinking when he gave my left shoulder a little shove, pushing me onto the bed.

"Make time stand still, Mira," he murmured in a low, husky voice that sent a shimmer of warmth over my body. "Give us tonight."

Parting my knees so he was standing between my leather-clad legs, I sat up and grabbed a fistful of his shirt. As I lay back down, Michael crawled onto the bed, placing his elbows on either side of my head as he leaned down and reclaimed my lips. My eyes fell shut as he wrung another moan out of me, my body instinctively arching against his. I wanted to feel all of him. I needed to feel all of his soft, warm skin pressed against the length of my body, but I would follow his lead. Michael was in control and I was enjoying every second of this escape while I could.

Moving his lips along my jaw, Michael shifted his weight onto his left arm, allowing him to slip his right hand between our bodies. His nimble fingers slid over my ribs and up to cup my breast, his thumb rubbing over my nipple through the rough lace of the bra.

"Have you missed me?" he asked in a harsh, breathless whisper, running his lips over mine.

"Very much." My hands fumbled for a moment, searching for the edge of his shirt. I finally found it, allowing me to run my hands up his back. His muscles flexed and danced beneath my fingers. He kissed me again as his fingers pulled down the bra, freeing my breast for his teasing fingers.

"Not nearly enough, I think." Changing directions, he ran the tip of his tongue along my flat stomach from my belly button, up along my ribs, skirting along the edge of the red scar left from last night's wound before finally settling on my bare breast. His tongue swirled around my hardened nipple, his teeth grazing it.

My eyes fell shut again. My fingers dug into his blond locks, twisting to get a better hold. I arched against him, my heels digging into the edge of the bed. I needed to be closer, to become a part of him.

"You're driving me mad."

Michael chuckled, his hot breath dancing across my damp flesh from where his mouth had been just moments before. "That's the point." My angel moved back up to my lips, kissing me deeply.

Wrapping his arms around my waist, he rolled over onto his back, pulling me on top of him. "Bite me, Mira," he said, moving his lips to kiss down my jaw to my neck.

"Not tonight, my angel," I said, lifting my face so I could kiss his lips again, but he kept his head turned so his neck was before me. The main artery throbbed at me, beckoning. The darkness stirred inside me, but I struggled to push it back down again. I was still half starved, needed to gorge myself on blood not only to heal but to regain my full strength. But I wouldn't feed off Michael. I had taken too much of his blood too often. His warmth and laughter kept any lingering pangs of hunger at bay.

"Please, Mira. Bite me. I need this." His words escaped him with a harsh, desperate quality that sent a chill through me.

I sat up so I could look down at him, my desire suddenly cooling. "Please, don't push me, my angel," I said wearily. "I need you strong."

"I can handle it." His right hand cupped my cheek. He tried to pull me back down but I wouldn't budge.

"No. You should go back downstairs." I moved so I was now sitting beside him, my hip pressed against his.

"Please, Mira," he said, his voice wavering. Something in his tone finally caught my attention and I stared into his eyes. They looked a little glassy, as if he was sick. Frowning, I pushed into his thoughts. Jumbled and fragmented, it took me a couple seconds to make sense out of them, but there was one repeating one; the need for the pleasure my bite brought him.

I pulled loose of the tangle of thoughts in his brain and smacked him hard enough to snap his head sideways. "Enough!" I was more frustrated with myself for letting this happen than at him. Michael had become addicted and come begging to me for his next fix. His interest in sex had nothing to do with me and everything to do with my feeding off of him.

He looked at me like a wounded puppy and I bit back a groan. "I need you to be focused. I can't get Sadira out of here safely without you," I continued in a soft but firm voice, resisting the urge to cup his cheeks with my hands. Pushing off the bed, I got to my feet and paced away from the bed, readjusting my bra so my breasts were covered again. A horrible, hollow ache throbbed in my chest. I had fooled myself into thinking that I'd held his interest.

When I turned back, Michael was standing beside the bed, straightening his clothes. His eyes still looked hurt, but he had pulled himself back together. At least for now. Maybe he wasn't too far gone yet. It didn't matter. I was done with him. When we reached the Coven meeting place, I was putting Michael and Gabriel on the next plane home. They would be of no real help after that, and keeping them at my side would only put them in unnecessary danger. I wouldn't ruin what was left of Michael's life.

"Go downstairs. I'll be down in a minute," I directed, forcing the words up my raw throat. Michael nodded again and left the room. I sat on the end of the bed and followed him with my mind. He did as he was told and went directly to the room that held Sadira and the others.

Putting my elbows on my knees, I leaned forward and rested my forehead in the palms of my hands. I was destroying Michael by being in his life. Why had Gabriel's mind come through this so unscathed? He was always a solid rock at my back. I had fed from him in the past and yet his mind suffered none of the damage I apparently had wrought with Michael.

But there was no answer. Michael was crumbling before me and it was my fault. I'd thought I was someone important in his life. I would never be so foolish as to describe the emotion as love, but at least some emotion that would be used to describe a person. But to him, I was just the source of intense pleasure, like a drug.

Being addicted to the bite of a nightwalker was a common enough occurrence, but it was also easy to avoid. If you never fed from the same person more than once, or if you did and always wiped his memory, the problem was avoided. But eventually we all ended up with a human companion that we drifted back to for a long span of nights in the name of pleasure and companionship. In time we drained them. We drained them of more than just their blood, but their willpower, their dignity, and their lives.

My thoughts were scattered again when someone knocked on the door. I looked up at the mirror over the bureau to find my face blissfully blank. It was nice to look so unaffected when I felt like screaming.

"Come in," I called, rising from the bed.

"Sorry to disturb you," James said as he entered. A deep flush stained his cheeks when he saw me standing by the edge of the bed without a shirt. He quickly averted his eyes.

I walked over to the closet door and pulled it open. "I was just heading downstairs," I said, riffling through the clothes I found hanging there until my eyes fell on a plain black button-up shirt.

"If you have a moment, Ryan has requested a meeting with you before you leave," James said, obviously expecting me to turn down the invitation.

I paused in the act up buttoning up the shirt, grateful that Melanie and I were roughly the same size. "Just me? Not Sadira?" I was surprised. Sadira was the oldest of the trio of nightwalkers in the compound, making her the natural superior.

"He asked only for you."

"I guess I can spare a few moments," I said with an indifferent shrug as I attached the last two buttons. I was going to finally meet the big boss man. I wasn't sure how much new information he would be able to provide, but so far Themis had been most helpful. Far more helpful than Jabari and Sadira, who were working very hard to keep me out of the loop, while someone was trying to kill me. And this time it didn't appear to be a hunter.

TWENTY-FOUR

Ryan was a warlock. I had suspected it before arriving at the Compound, but it was blatantly obvious when I walked into his private office on the third floor. He leaned against the front of his large walnut desk, his long legs stretched out before him and crossed casually at the ankle. He had been expecting me. Of course, I'm sure he could feel every move I made in his manor without straining himself.

He was a handsome man, standing just over six feet, with a long, lean body that somehow managed to exude a beautiful grace rather than being awkward. He wore a dark charcoal-gray suit with a black undershirt. Unlike his brethren, he wasn't wearing a tie, and the top two buttons of the shirt were undone, revealing an expanse of nicely tanned throat. In fact, his tanned skin and dark-colored suit stood in sharp contrast to his long white hair. Falling somewhere past his shoulders, it was pulled back with a narrow, black ribbon; a throwback to an era long past.

His face had a strange ageless quality to it. There were no wrinkles or deep lines, making him seem to be in his early to mid-thirties at first glance. But his gold eyes held a depth that one could only earn through years of experience. He was old; older than any human was meant to be.

Magic had a distinct effect on a human's physical appearance. And the deeper and more skilled a warlock or witch became in the use of magic, the more profound the effect. His power was etched into his features and imbued every inch of his being. It sizzled in the room like a current of electricity, making my skin crawl.

Most humans that used magic did it by accident. Events sometimes happened in their favor and the human simply chalked it up as a run of good luck. Only the ones who actually studied magic and attained some basic understanding were called witches and warlocks. And then there were those like Ryan, who made the study of magic a life's pursuit. *They* were simply called dangerous.

After James wordlessly shut the door, leaving me alone with this strange man, Ryan rose to his feet without pushing off the desk. He stood in the same, seemingly boneless manner that vampires could. I had known a few warlocks in my time, but never saw a human pull a trick I always thought exclusive to nightwalkers.

"Impressive." I said, lightly applauding. "I guess pulling a rabbit out of your hat is too mundane."

He smiled back at me; a warm, friendly smile that seemed open and guileless. That was almost more impressive that his earlier trick. How could someone who wielded as much power as he did seem so nice? The same way the naturi seemed so harmless—centuries of practice.

"My name is Ryan," he said, extending his hand toward me. I stared at it a moment, admiring his long fingers, but never touched him. It was a good, strong hand, the type of hand that could comfort as easily as it could punish.

Stepping around him, I looked at some of the bookshelves that lined his wall. I glanced over the old spines, but my attention was still completely on the room's only other occupant. I preferred to keep a little space between us for now. "I know your name," I replied blandly. "I also know what you are. My question is: Do your associates know?"

"They know I'm a warlock," he said, drawing my eyes back to him. His smile grew a little wider. "However, I imagine your assessment of my powers is a little more accurate than theirs."

Arching one eyebrow at him, I smiled. "So you've purposefully kept them in the dark." There was no anger or accusation in my voice. Just honest curiosity. I wanted to understand his motives and the situation I had walked into. I also desperately needed to understand the players in this little farce before it cost me my existence.

"My abilities aren't important to their cause."

"That's not what I meant," I corrected. "You've not only kept them in the dark about yourself, but also the truth about vampires. I've heard and read some of the things these people believe about my kind. Why do you allow them to perpetuate such lies?"

"For their own safety," he said. His wide smile faded a bit but still

lingered on his lips. He shoved his hands in his trouser pockets, reminding me of a corporate executive after hours.

"What about mine? You've been sending hunters after my kind."

"Both of our worlds are changing; much faster than I expected, I
must admit. A couple centuries ago some of the things written about
vampires were true. Most were ruthless hunters that killed every time
they fed, but now I have found they are using some discretion. You're
still very dangerous, and without some fear of you, I worry humans
will run blindly into your inviting arms."

"I may have disillusioned poor James of some of these archaic
notions. Will you silence him to keep him from infecting the rest?"

"No, of course not," he said with a shake of his head, looking
amused. "I won't suppress the truth within Themis. However, I want
them to find it on their own."

"And the hunters? Were they your creation? Another attempt to
protect your flock?" I slowly paced back over toward him, my footsteps muffled on the thick Persian rug.

Ryan had yet to move other than to turn on a heel so he was continuously facing me. "The hunters were created long before I ever
joined Themis."

"But you've done nothing to get rid of them since joining this
little cult, despite your enlightened view of my kind."

"What makes you think that my view of nightwalkers is so enlightened?" he countered, arching one brow at me.

"I'm here and still alive," I said, holding out my hands, palms up
at him. I stood directly in front of him, only a couple feet of empty
space separating us. "You could have ordered Danaus to stake me
and the others during the daylight hours, but you didn't. I also know
that you couldn't have attained the kind of power I feel in this room
without running into things far worse than me during your long
years."

"What could be worse than a nightwalker who can control fire?"
he said, his smile finally returning.

"Danaus."

Ryan's smile instantly vanished and a shadow seemed to pass
over his eyes as he stared at me, weighing my answer. We were both
now standing in a field of land mines, each wondering how much the
other person knew. His hands shifted in his trouser pockets, his eyes
narrowing in thought. I had never run across such an eye color in any
creature before—not yellow, but the true, deep luster of gold.

"Danaus is an interesting . . . person," he said, pausing for a breath before continuing. "He's had a particular interest in you during the past several years."

"How long have you known about the naturi's plans?" I demanded, my voice hardening. My hands balled into fists at my sides and I resisted the urge to take a step closer.

"His interest in you had nothing to do with the naturi." Ryan's broad shoulders slumped as he seemed to relax. He moved back to lean against the front of the desk and motioned for me to take a seat in one of the leather chairs resting before it. I was feeling indulgent, so I sat to his right, crossing my legs as I waited for him to continue.

"Before arriving on Themis's doorstep," he said, "I understand that Danaus spent many years living with monks, who taught him that good and evil was a black-and-white issue in this world. Humans were created by God and were innately good. By that logic, everything else was evil and had to be exterminated. You were an interest of his because you seemed to embody the ultimate evil. A nightwalker, a human that has turned from God, that can control fire, directly linking you to Satan and all that is evil.

"You're somewhat of a mythical creature among your own kind. It took him almost a decade to track down your given name. Most still just know you as the Fire Starter."

" 'Mira' doesn't strike the same kind of fear," I said with a shrug.

"Danaus became quite determined to find and destroy you . . ." Ryan paused, staring at me. A dark shadow seemed to passed over his face as he regarded me with his too perceptive eyes, sending a chill up my spine. I suddenly wished that I wasn't seated so close to the warlock.

"And then something changed for him. In all his searching and digging, not once did he hear a tale of you killing a human. Of course, there were numerous stories of you slaughtering your own kind, particularly those who had carelessly killed humans."

"But he thought I killed when I fed," I interjected, recalling our conversation during the plane ride to Egypt.

"True, but I think he was beginning to have doubts about that old myth as well. Before we discovered the naturi's sacrifice, he had stopped his search for you. You were beginning to raise some uncomfortable questions . . . I think he was even contemplating leaving Themis. When I sent him to look for you in the States, he had regained his resolve to destroy you." Ryan paused, staring thoughtfully. I knew he must have made sure that Danaus once again had ample motive to go after my head. "But something has changed for him." Ryan said the last softly, as if thinking aloud rather than talking to me. I knew his thoughts as though I'd read them. He was wondering about that change. Danaus had more than enough opportunities to kill me but he hadn't, and protected me on more than one occasion.

"He's learned that Themis doesn't have all the right answers," I said stiffly. "He's not pleased with your little group at the moment. Danaus has been misled and used. You've lied to him."

"I never lied to Danaus," Ryan said. The warlock frowned at me, shifting his weight from one foot to the other. "If he asked, I would have told him all I knew of your kind. He had his mind made up about nightwalkers long before I was born."

"You could have told him."

"He had to discover it on his own."

"Nice excuse," I said snidely. "You had your own agenda, and the fact that you could use Danaus's misinformed conclusions to your advantage provided you with no moral dilemma." I leaned forward in the chair, tightly gripping the arms.

"Don't we all." He shrugged his wide shoulders. "I wish you would not think so ill of me, Mira. We have the same goal."

A dark smile lifted the corners of my mouth as I stood. "I doubt that."

"I'll give you that you probably have more fun at it than I do, but our goal is the same: maintain our secret as long as possible."

"Is that your goal?"

"I'm not the villain you want me to be. We've both done things to keep the humans from discovering what surrounds them. You've killed numerous nightwalkers that jeopardized the secret. I've done the same with the hunters. We're both guardians, protecting that fragile wall that separates our world from the world of the humans."

Ryan stood a step forward, closing the distance between us to less than a foot. He slowly raised his hand, with his finger bent, and held it beside my cheek. "May I?" he whispered.

"May you what?" I watched him through narrowed eyes. Warlock or not, I could still be on the other side of the room before he moved.

"I just wish to touch your face."

I stared, confused at him for a second, my brow furrowed. It seemed an extremely strange request coming from him, but I didn't think it was necessarily a trick. When a witch or warlock casts, you can feel the building of power in the air. Of course, Ryan was more powerful than any I had known before. There was enough energy in the air already that I might not notice any specific shift. But I nodded, regardless.

Noticing my wariness, he inched his hand forward until the back of his fingers gently caressed my check, sliding down from my cheek-bone and along my jaw. His skin was warm and I felt only a slight jolt of energy from the contact, but nothing more. It was his voice that actually held me entranced briefly. "Forgive me," he murmured. "You're not as cold as I expected."

"I find it hard to believe that you've never touched a nightwalker before," I teased, tilting my head up so I was looking him in the eyes.

"Once before," he said, a grim smile touching his lips. "And that was only after he was done feeding off me."

"Yes, a meal tends to warm us up."

"But you've not fed tonight?"

"No."

"And you're still not . . ."

"Cold as a corpse?" I supplied. The darkness that had briefly clouded his expression lifted at the comparison and his smile brightened. "Under normal circumstances, I can go several days without feeding and retain some warmth. A hot shower also helps."

"Do you retain such warmth because of your ability?"

"To control fire? No. Fire does not burn or warm me. In fact, if I use the ability too much, I grow cold because it requires energy."

"I hadn't known."

"No human ever has."

"Why do you trust me?" he asked, sounding surprised.

I laughed deeply, the sound filling the room, shoving aside some his energy. He shifted at the sudden intrusion, resettling himself against his desk. "I don't." I slumped into the chair behind me, throwing one leg carelessly over the chair arm. "Call it a gesture of good faith. I give you a little something . . ."

"Because you want something," he finished.

"Doesn't everybody?"

"What is it you desire?"

My voice and expression hardened instantly. "Information."

"An expensive commodity."

"Perhaps, but what you get in return is valuable as well," I said, my eyes never wavering from his face.

"And what is that?"

"Your life."

"So we've come to threats," Ryan announced, sounding amused.

"Not at all. Just a statement of fact. The naturi are a threat to both human and nightwalker. You have information that may help my kind. We are the ones risking our lives to protect you."

"Very noble of you."

"Hardly," I said with a snort. "And you know better." I looked up at him and his expression turned serious again. We had enjoyed our brief moment of levity, but time was wasting away.

"What is it you think I know?"

"I don't know, but considering that I know nothing, it has to be more than me," I admitted. "You discovered the first sacrifice in India before we even realized anything was happening."

"Are you sure we were the first?"

"No," I whispered.

Before the disaster in London and Thorne's death, I would have emphatically said yes, but now I wasn't sure of anything. The naturi knew too much, finding me far too quickly in Egypt and again in London. Someone was betraying me, and I didn't like my options at the moment. Of course, I wasn't about to voice those thoughts to a human. And if I had my way, I'd be holding the creature's heart in my hand before the naturi attempted the second sacrifice.

"But at the moment," I continued, pressing through those dark thoughts, "it doesn't matter. How did you discover the body?"

"Konark has long been the center for heavy magic use," he explained, "though it hadn't been used for a very long time. I felt the surge in power that night. I had researchers on a plane before dawn touched the Indian sky."

"What about the trees?"

"That, I fear, was just luck. One of the members of Themis was on vacation in Canada. He caught sight of a carving while hiking and took a picture. He thought it was some new branch of Wicca springing up. After that, I sent out every available operative to find more carvings."

"How many did you locate?"

"Twelve."

"Do you know what they mean? Can you read their writing?"

"Not really," he said with a sigh. "The markings on the trees mean nothing to me, but I can make some educated guesses with the blood markings surrounding the sacrifice at Konark."

"Do you think you found all the carvings?"

"Yes. I've checked every day since the first sacrifice but detected no other places I think might have the markings. Do you know what they mean?"

"The carvings? No," I said with a shake of my head. "This isn't the first time they've attempted to break the seal, but I have never seen or heard of the carvings before."

"I had thought they were used as a way of activating the twelve holy sites," Ryan speculated. With his right hand, he picked up a crystal paperweight about the size of a baseball. It looked like a crystal ball, but instead of being clear, red veins ran through the orb. He rolled the crystal between his two hands, a nervous gesture that revealed his worry, unlike the more guarded and planned expressions that crossed his face.

"No, the first sacrifice accomplished that. The carvings mean something else," I said, shoving my hand through my hair, pushing it back from my face.

"So, now we just wait for the second sacrifice."

"It will be soon. Very soon," I whispered.

Ryan put the paperweight back on his desk and stood. "Are you sure? How do you know?"

"They've begun checking the other eleven sites. Once they locate the right one, they have only a small window of time to use it. The pool of power is constantly moving. I've never heard of anyone being able to tell when it will move or where it will go to. Maybe Aurora can, I don't know."

"But the next new moon isn't for another five nights," Ryan said with a shake of his head.

"The naturi are not bound to the key phases of the moon, though it helps," I replied, fighting the urge to get up and pace. I forced a tight smile onto my lips as I tilted my head back to look up at a warlock. "You know magic. It's more than just the moon, and the seasons, and the alignment of the heavens."

"Magic is also about circles and balance," he finished. His brows drew together slightly, as furrows ran through his smooth forehead.

"And the anniversary of when the last seal was created is upon us," I murmured. The thought had first occurred to me when I was talking to James last night. I too thought they would stick to phases of the moon, since it would provide them with the most power to break the seal. But destroying what the nightwalkers had wrought on the anniversary would not only be a powerful blow magically, but deal a heavy blow to the morale of my kind. "The naturi will be making their attempt either tonight or tomorrow night."

"And if they were to succeed . . ."

"Then they would be able to open the door in five nights, lining up perfectly with the new moon."

"And the pagan harvest holiday."

"We're running out of time," I said with frustration, pushing out of the chair. I paced over to the wall of books on my left and back to Ryan, my arms folded over my stomach.

"But you have everything you need," he argued, looking at me with confusion filling his face.

"No, I don't," I replied, turning to walk back toward the bookshelf. "A triad of nightwalkers stopped the naturi five centuries ago. One of the three, Tabor, was killed by the naturi several years ago. With him gone, we have to reform the triad. Unfortunately, the replacement I found was killed while I stood there watching."

"But the triad has already been reformed," the warlock said, his voice a gentle caress in the silence of the room.

I spun on my heel to look at him as my stomach attempted to turn itself inside out. "What?"

"I could feel it as soon as you entered the compound. All the pieces needed to seal the door again have been found," he said confidently.

My legs threatened to buckle beneath me when I heard this horrible pronouncement. I was supposed to be the third? It couldn't be. Sadira was my maker, putting us in the same bloodline. And if Sadira's story was to be believed, so was Jabari and Tabor. I didn't want to be a part of the triad. My job was to find a replacement for Tabor and protect Sadira. After that, I was returning to my city across the ocean and never looking back. They didn't need me for anything else.

"You're wrong," I said, nearly choking on the words. "I can't help them."

"You have no choice," he sadly said. "I—" Ryan abruptly broke off as his gaze darted toward the door and cocked his head to the side as if listening to someone whispering in his ear. "Something is coming."

"What do you mean 'something'?" I snapped. "Is it the naturi?"

"No, something else. I don't know what. It's powerful," he said, pushing away from the desk to stand.

"Great," I muttered, already moving toward the door. "You better get your people to cover. I'll do what I can." I didn't know what I was facing, but I assumed it was at the Compound because of me and my traveling troupe of vampires and misfits.

"Thank you," Ryan called.

"Don't be too grateful. I may still need to pick your brain."

"As long as I'm alive for it," he joked, though the laughter no longer reached his golden eyes.

I paused, holding the door handle, and looked over my shoulder at the warlock. "Did you order my death?" I inquired, wondering if I would ever have another chance to ask. I needed to know exactly where I stood with this creature.

"Recently?" he asked.

"Ever."

"Yes."

TWENTY-FIVE

I walked down the main staircase toward the first floor, my feet sinking into the thick carpet that covered the stairs. Apparently Ryan had sent out some kind of mental warning to the proper people because I heard doors being thrown open around me and hurried footsteps across the hardwood floors. I needed to get these people out of my way. If something not good was headed to the compound, I didn't want to concern myself with the stray gawker trying to collect a little valuable data.

A part of me was aching for a fight. A couple of naturi to deal with, something to rip apart; their flesh squishing warmly between my fingers and collecting under my fingernails. While I'll admit that I was still extremely hungry, more than a rising blood lust clouded my thoughts. I craved just the sight of blood. I wanted to see it splashed across the skin and soaking into torn and shredded clothing. I needed the violence, an outlet for the frustration and the fear. In the brief moment when you are struggling to stay alive, you convince yourself that you're actually in control of your life and destiny. And when you kill that which was trying to kill you, you bask in a moment of true power. I wanted that moment, even if it was an illusion.

Unfortunately, I couldn't afford a fight right now. My job was to protect Sadira, and the best way to do that was to avoid confrontation altogether. Sadira's skill lay not in physical strength, but in the horrible ways she could destroy a creature's mind. She cultivated fear and obedience in her own special way but was not a fighter. Furthermore, neither she nor I were at our top strength after last night's healing session. We both had to feed, and I still needed a couple more days of rest.

A familiar voice halted my descent at the second floor, jerking me from my frantic thoughts.

"What is it?" Danaus called from behind me. I turned on the stairs to find him buckling the last leather wrist guard on his right arm as he descended. His hair was damp and hung heavy about his broad shoulders. To my surprise, he was wearing a pair of dark blue jeans instead of his usual black cotton pants. His navy T-shirt was untucked and strapped down with a pair of sword sheaths crossing his back. I guess now that he was home, he felt he could go casual. Or maybe it was the fact that his mission was technically over. I had a tendency to forget how handsome he was when I was plotting how to peel his skin from the network of muscles and sinew that danced as he moved.

"I don't know yet," I said. "Get your people somewhere safe. I'll handle it." I continued down the stairs at a slower pace, reluctantly serious.

"They're being moved to the basement, and all spare hunters are going to stand guard down there," he replied, walking down one step behind me.

"Any naturi?"

"None that I can sense."

I think Danaus was about to say something else when the heavy front doors crashed open against the walls. Splinters flew through the air and I barely had enough time to raise my arm to shield my face. There had been no warning, no surge of power. I stayed, unmoving, on the third step from the bottom, a gust of cold air trying to push me back up the stairs. Lowering my arm from my eyes, I saw Jabari step across the threshold, the wind dying away to a whimper.

I've heard humans say someone looked like the wrath of God. To me, Jabari looked far worse. Bare-chested, the nightwalker stared at me, his eyes glowing a wicked pale yellow, like so many fires I had conjured in my past. His cheekbones seemed more prominent than usual and his cheeks were hollows. For the first time since I'd met him, Jabari looked like the walking dead. He reminded me grimly of Charon, the ferryman for the underworld. Indeed, I believed Jabari had arrived to usher me from this life.

Some part of me still loved him, but even I was beginning to question who it was that I loved. The questions were piling up, and the one person I'd been willing to trust was holding a stake over my heart. Sadira's tale replayed in my head as I stared at him, dragging up painful questions as a knot of betrayal and anger rose in my throat. I had seen Jabari manipulate and use other nightwalkers like pieces on a chessboard, moving them about and sacrificing others when necessary to accomplish his ultimate goals. Somewhere along the way I'd convinced myself that I was different, that I truly mattered to the Ancient. Had I been wrong? Would he dangle me before my greatest fear in an effort to control me? *Yes.*

"Jabari!" I cried, throwing my arms up in sham surprise. "It's so good of you to join us. Please, come inside." If it had been at all possible, his gaze would have set me ablaze at that moment. I only widened my smile, my teeth clenched so hard my jaw ached.

"You were ordered to protect Sadira," he snarled, his voice crackling through the air like lightning.

"And so I have." My tone was still light and mocking. I had nothing to lose any longer and was tired of being pushed around.

"Here?" He threw open his arms to encompass the manor. At the same time, half of the little globes in the overhead chandelier exploded, dimming the light. Shadows lunged from the corners and clawed up the wall to slink across the ceiling.

"They've hunted us for centuries. It's time they protected us for a while."

"You go too far."

"No, not yet," I said with a sigh. "But don't worry; I will." To his obvious surprise, I came down the last three steps to the main hall, drawing closer to him. "Would you like to see Sadira?" Extending my right arm toward the hall along the left side of the staircase, I motioned for him to walk with me. His body was so stiff with rage, he could give only the barest of nods. I don't know why he didn't rip me in half then, beyond pure curiosity.

I preceded him down the long, narrow hall, keeping a slow pace, as if I didn't have a care in the world. What did I have to fear other than the rabid vampire at my back? The pair of hunters flanking the door headed toward the basement with a jerk of my head. No need for an audience. In a fight between nightwalkers, humans just ended up being props.

Opening the door, I saw the same tableau I'd witnessed before leaving to take a shower. Sadira was seated in her chair like a queen, her back to the wall. Tristan stood dutifully behind her with a blank expression, while another pair of hunters stood near the door and window. My own pair of guardian angels, pacing the room, paused as we entered.

"All humans out!" I announced as Jabari, Danaus, and I entered. The two hunters quickly left the cheerful, buttercup-colored salon without another word, but Michael and Gabriel didn't move. "My angels as well," I added, my tone softening. Both frowned, but left without another word. I think instincts alone told them to put some distance from this lethal gathering.

I turned to shut the door behind them and found that Danaus was still in the room. My eyes moved from him to the door in a silent question. A grim half smile lifted one corner of his mouth for a couple of seconds. "I don't fit either of those categories."

"You may regret this," I muttered, shutting the door.

"Wouldn't be the first time where you're concerned."

That I believed. If he wanted to remain, so be it. My only worries were Jabari and my neck.

"He leaves," Jabari ordered, snapping my attention back to the Ancient. "He is not one of us." I flinched at the sharpness of his voice, but I tried to not let it show. The Elder wanted me groveling before him, cowed and obedient. Not this time.

"No." I stepped away from the door, to stand next to Danaus. My face was blank, devoid of servitude. I wasn't taunting or particularly begging for a fight, but I wanted Jabari to know that I was finally drawing the line in the sand.

I sensed more than saw it when the Ancient's arm snaked out with the intent of grabbing Danaus's neck. Gritting my teeth, I caught his wrist and shoved him backward, nearly throwing him across the room. Jabari slid across the polished hardwood floor and caught himself before he slammed into the opposite wall. In the far corner, I heard Sadira gasp and Tristan hiss softly at my unexpected response. Both seemed to shrink as Jabari growled, the sound resembling a tiger's warning more than anything that would emerge from the throat of something that had once been human. His powers flooded the room, nearly choking me. I mentally clawed my way back to the surface, refusing to be swamped by him. Truth be told, I would rather have been killed by Jabari than face the naturi again. But either way, I'd go down fighting.

"Is this what shall finally destroy us? This creature, I will not let you kill," I spat out, my lips drawn back to reveal my fangs. My posture was hunched as I waited for him to attack again, every muscle pulled taut and ready. The wound in my chest and back screamed in pain, but I pushed it back. The darkness deep inside of me began to rise up, swelling until it started to slowly blot out what was left of my humanity. It was the blood lust, the driving need to feel another creature's life clutched in the palm of your hand. I remained in front of Danaus, making it clear to the Elder that he would have to go through me first.

"There is always your failure to kill Nerian as I ordered," Jabari reminded me.

"He's dead now. Just a few centuries late."

"You also failed to protect Tabor's replacement," he continued, his body completely still. The quiet before the storm. Apparently, Sadira had succeeded in reaching him with the news that evening.

"The naturi knew where we were. They knew." Rowe always seemed capable of finding me easily. My voice dropped down close to a whisper. "I wonder how."

"What are you implying?" Jabari's fingers curled into fists, and the glow in his eyes flared, as if he was using all of his energy not to crush me. He knew exactly what I was saying.

"Not implying. Just curious," I hedged, trying to give myself some room to maneuver. "The naturi seem one step ahead no matter where I turn. They can't sense us, but Nerian knew where to find me. They knew to kill Thorne before I even knew who the hell he was. Rowe has come hunting for me twice now. Someone is betraying me." I moved a step closer.

"So you turn first on your own kind, when the enemy stands at your back," Jabari bellowed, pointing at Danaus. The nightwalker took a step to his right, moving away from the wall and closer to me.

"Not first. I've talked to them. I don't think Themis has been in contact with the naturi, and they're not the ones keeping me in the dark." I'd reached the point where I preferred to see both Danaus and Jabari dead than give either of them another chance to carve out my heart.

"You've been told everything you need to know. You do as you have been instructed."

"Bullshit!" I screamed, taking another step closer. "I stopped taking orders a long time ago, and I won't put up with your secrets when it's my life on the line. I was the one they were trying to kill in Aswan, not you."

"How do you know he didn't send for them? His people attacked you while you slept."

"Because the naturi don't follow orders either," I hissed. "Not from humans or nightwalker. Or am I wrong?"

Jabari's eyes widened before he lunged at me. I barely had enough time to jump out of the way. Pain flashed up my arm as his fingernails ripped through the sleeve and slashed my skin. I landed in a crouch and launched myself into him, colliding with his chest. He fell back with a heavy thud. Siding across the floor, he crashed into a pale blue sofa with me on top of him. A small end table went over and a ceramic lamp was smashed, sending small shards skidding across the hardwood. I sat up, hissing at him, my fangs bared. Jabari backhanded me, snapping my head around. To him, I was nothing more than an annoy-ing fly. I tumbled backward but quickly rolled to my feet, to find him standing as well.

"You've been hiding for a couple of years now," I said before he could attack again. "Why? Why hide when the naturi can't sense you? Afraid of someone else finding you?"

"I want to be left alone."

"Did you know about the naturi?"

Instead of answering, Jabari threw himself at me again. The haze of anger clouding my thoughts also slowed my reflexes, allowing him to catch me before I could move out of his grasp. His momentum car-ried us into the wall, and a grunt escaped me as my spine dug into it. Lifting my legs as soon as I hit, I placed my feet against Jabari's chest and kicked out with all my strength, pushing him off me. Then I pushed off the wall and lunged. Jabari was just getting back to his feet when I hit him, reaching for his throat. Once again he brushed me aside.

"Did you know?" I asked again, jumping to my feet. I shoved against the sofa, sending it skidding across the room, its wooden feet screeching against the floor. I didn't want anything in my way when I went after him again. The Ancient stood unmoving, watching me. "Did you?" My scream rattled the glass in the window.

"Mira, stop," Sadira said. I could barely feel her tension and fear over Jabari's angry powers. She'd stopped cloaking her presence when he appeared. Now I could feel all of her chaotic emotions, even hear some of her thoughts.

"Then tell me I'm wrong," I demanded, never taking my eyes off Jabari. His blank expression never changed. "Tell me."

"You are wrong," he said, carefully enunciating each word, as if talking to an addled child.

"I don't believe you." The words came out choked and broken.

"That is not my concern."

"It will be," I whispered, straightening my stance. I was no longer poised for the attack, but I wasn't relaxed either. The fight was over for now. "I don't know who you're protecting, but I hope they're worth it."

"It should be your life you worry over. You are the one who has failed to reform the triad. You are the one who has brought your sire to this haven for hunters," Jabari said, his lips pulling back in a sneer.

For a brief moment I wondered if he was referring to Sadira or himself, but I let the thought drop. If it was true, Jabari obviously didn't want me to know, which gave me a slight edge for now. "You gave me an impossible task," I snapped. "I couldn't protect Sadira and fetch Thorne at the same time. Not with the naturi running around. She had to be put somewhere safe and this was my only option. She has come to no harm. If anything, they've treated her like a queen since she stepped foot on their grounds." Reaching up, I shoved a lock of hair that had fallen in front of my eyes behind my ear.

"You should have taken her with you. She could have saved Thorne."

"Maybe, but I doubt it," I said with a shake of my head. "I couldn't have properly protected them both. But none of this matters. The triad has been reformed."

"What? How?" Sadira demanded, springing from her chair. I could feel the hope blossoming in her chest. I clung to that light emotion against Jabari's drowning anger.

"Me. I will be the third," I said, my eyes darting from Sadira back to Jabari. I didn't want to be, and if we could find someone else, I would happily hand over the position, but that didn't seem to be an option.

Jabari laughed, the dark sound crawling across my flesh like a hundred tiny spider legs. "Where would you get such an idea?"

I glanced over at Danaus, who was standing near the door. He was returning his sword to the sheath strapped across his back. I hadn't even seen him draw it. He paused in the middle of the act for half a breath, his eyes narrowing on me. "I spoke with a warlock," I continued, returning my attention to Jabari.

"And what does he know about the triad?"

"Apparently a lot. At the very least, he knows more about what is going on than I do. He said that the triad has already been reformed."

"He said you would take Tabor's place?"

"Not exactly, but it's not like there's a lot of other vampires hanging around. He could have meant Tristan, but I didn't think so since he's still cutting his fangs."

Jabari's gaze never wavered from me as his smile widened and I saw his beautiful white fangs. It reminded me of Nerian's smile, with all the grim, painful promises it held. "You fool," he said, the words encased in a chuckle. "You believe the word of a human over your own kind."

"I'm just trying to survive, and you've done nothing to help that cause recently."

"Mira, my child, you can't be the third," Sadira whispered, as if trying to soften the blow. "It's impossible."

"Why? Because we're of the same bloodline?"

"You've turned on your own kind," Jabari snarled.

"Not yet, but I see little reason to defend them at the moment. Why can't I be the third?"

"You're not strong enough."

"Bullshit. I'm stronger than Sadira, and I'm stronger than Thorne was. Why can't I?"

"Mira!"

I turned on my heel, startled by Danaus's voice. His presence had been pushed from my mind by Jabari's attack, and now I stood so I could look at both him and Jabari, not wanting to put my back to the Ancient I no longer trusted.

"They're coming," the hunter said.

I read it in Danaus's face before he could speak. Tension had crept in around the corners of his mouth and pulled his lips into a worried frown. A thick, heavy silence pushed into the room, and it was all I could do to keep from drowning in it.

"How many?"

"Enough."

My throat suddenly constricted and I'm not sure what kept my knees from buckling. Either it was too many to bother to count or it was better I didn't know.

"Do we have time to leave?" I asked, wondering how long it would take to get everyone out of the compound.

"No, they're too close."

"Who?" Jabari interrupted.

"We'll have to make a stand here," I said, desperate to get hold of a situation that continued to spiral out of my control. "Your people safe?"

"Safe as can be expected." Danaus reached up and withdrew one of the swords strapped to his back. His deep blues flicked before he tossed it to me.

"Who's coming?" Jabari demanded again, his shout filling the room.

I slashed the air a couple of times with the sword, testing its weight and balance, purposefully ignoring Jabari for a moment. It wasn't the same one I had borrowed in the Aswan cemetery. It seemed of a higher quality. Maybe something from his private collection, kept for only special occasions? *Lucky me.*

At last I looked up at Jabari and smiled. "The naturi."

TWENTY-SIX

The naturi were coming. My fingers tightened around the sword and I closed my eyes for a moment, drawing the anger and tension into a single ball that resided in the pit of my stomach. I was done running.

Turning to look at Jabari, I resisted the urge to point the sword at his chest. No reason to antagonize him any more. We had enough problems. "Are you with us or against us?"

"And who exactly is this 'us'?" he sneered, his hands clenched into fists at his sides. "Humans? The hunters?"

"Anyone who wishes to stand against the naturi. I welcome both hunter and nightwalker. We can settle the question of my allegiance some other time."

The nightwalker drew up to his full height and straightened his shoulders. "I harbor no love for the naturi."

"Great. Stay here," I said, trying not to think about the fact that I was giving orders to an Elder. I had no doubt I'd pay for it later, assuming there was a later for me. Desperate to keep the situation in hand, my attention flashed to the other two vampires in the room. Tristan stood with his arm around Sadira's delicate shoulders, as if trying to comfort her, but the fear in his wide blue eyes told another tale. He had faced a small group of naturi with me last night and I barely survived. He was in no hurry to push his luck any further.

"You are expendable. Jabari and Sadira are not," I said, pointing the sword at him. "Protect them no matter what."

"Where are you going?" he asked, his grip tightening on Sadira.

"To see if I can find more help," I called over my shoulder as I marched out of the room with Danaus following on my heels.

I paused in the hall, trying to assess the battlefield, as Danaus closed the door. There were too many rooms, too many doors and windows. "How many entrances are there on the ground floor?" I asked.

Danaus stood beside me now, his eyes also scanning the terrain. "Three; front door, back door off the kitchen, and a garden entrance."

"Not to mention windows in every room," I murmured, talking mostly to myself.

"We can move to the basement," he suggested. "There are no windows down there and only one entrance."

"We would be trapped." I shook my head, my hair falling around my face. "They could wait us out until dawn, then come down and slaughter everyone. Besides, they are only after us. I'd rather keep the naturi away from your librarian convention downstairs." I continued down the hall to the front doors, which were shut again, my heels hitting the hardwood floor the only sound in the silent manor. "Where's Ryan?"

"I'm here." A weary voice drifted down the stairs toward us. I looked up to see the warlock seated at the top of the stairs on the second floor. He'd shed his jacket, his shirtsleeves were rolled up past his elbows, and sweat slicked back the hair at his temples. His powers filled the air like an electric current looking for an outlet. I hadn't noticed the power crackling around me until I saw him, my focus having been centered on the coming horde.

"How long have you been holding them off?" I asked, unable to keep the note of awe out of my voice. The air sizzled with whatever spell he was working, but even now I could feel it weakening.

"You don't think I called them?" he asked in surprise.

"You're not that stupid."

"Thanks." His mouth quirked in a half smile. "I'll do what I can to hold them off, but I won't last much longer."

"Save it," I said, waving him off. The spell he'd worked had left him nearly exhausted and he would need his strength. "Go to the basement with your people. The naturi are after my kind, but I can't promise they won't slaughter humans just for the fun of it."

Danaus walked up the stairs past me and helped Ryan get to his feet. The warlock descended to the first floor with his hand on the hunter's shoulder. Ryan still looked a bit shaky, but appeared to be catching his second wind.

Seeing the two men standing side by side for the first time, I realized that I liked Danaus's eyes better. There was something more human in those cobalt depths than Ryan's glittering gold; something that still whispered of hope. It was missing from Ryan's eyes, creating a strange juxtaposition. Danaus was a man who said he was doomed to hell, and yet hope still flickered faintly in his precious blue orbs.

On the other hand, Ryan was a fraction of Danaus's age, with a smile perpetually haunting his lips, but he'd lost that flicker of hope that seemed to haunt all creatures. I don't know what a human had to endure to become a warlock, but was it truly worse than what Danaus could have seen in his centuries of life?

"Do you have any more magic users lurking about?" I asked, snapping back to the problem at hand.

"A few, but they're no match for what is coming," Ryan said as he reached the bottom step.

"Have them charm the door and any weapons you can dig up," I instructed. "Iron hurts the naturi. A bullet to the head or heart will work. Otherwise, you generally have to cut off their head or remove the heart to kill them."

"A lot like killing vampires," Danaus interjected.

"Or humans," I said, glaring at him. "Get Ryan downstairs and lock the door behind you."

"I stay up here," Danaus stated, earning a startled look from me.

"Apparently I'm not the only one with loyalty issues." The smile slipped from my lips before it could fully form. "You need to protect your people."

"I can do that best up here. Ryan will be in the basement should we fail." He paused, smiling when I could not. "Besides, we have unfinished business."

Yes, our great showdown. Misfit versus misfit. I had forgotten somehow. Couldn't let something else kill me before he had his shot.

"Very well," I said with an indifferent shrug. Looking over at Ryan, I bit back a sigh of frustration. "I'm sorry. I had no desire to endanger your people."

"I knew the risk when I agreed. All I ask is that you win." He turned and started down the hall toward the basement, the fingers of his right hand trailing along the wall as if to steady himself should he suddenly falter.

"You were wrong earlier," I called after him. "The triad hasn't been reformed. It can't be me."

Ryan looked over his shoulder, his palm pressed flat against the wood-panel wall. He stared at Danaus for a couple of seconds, then at me. I didn't feel any stir of power. He was just thinking, as if reassessing his earlier conclusion. "No, you have everything you need," he said at last.

I nodded, though I'm not sure I actually believed him. If it wasn't me, then it meant Tristan was seriously holding out on me. It had been a long time since I'd last underestimated the power of another vampire. It was a mistake one generally didn't have a chance to make twice.

As Ryan disappeared down the stairs, he was quickly replaced by both of my guardian angels. I shut my eyes and clenched my teeth as I bit back a curse in rough Italian. Somehow I'd managed to forget they were here. I should have sent them home as soon as we hit London.

"Where do you want us?" Gabriel inquired, a gun clenched in each hand.

"Back down in the basement," I said, waving my sword toward the hall they had just come down.

"Our job is to protect you, not these people," Gabriel replied, not moving from where he stood.

"Your job is to follow my orders, and I'm ordering you to get back downstairs!"

"No," Michael said, standing stubbornly beside Gabriel.

"I can handle things up here. I haven't survived six hundred years depending on the protection of humans. Now get back downstairs before I drain you both."

"We—" But the sound of cracking wood and shattering glass halted Gabriel's rebellious words. I was beginning to see serious drawbacks to this whole loyalty thing. Unfortunately, now was not the time to discuss some of its finer aspects. Our guests were knocking.

"Danaus!" I shouted, turning my attention back to the entrance to the manor. Facing the front doors, I gripped the sword he'd given me in my right hand, my legs spread apart as I awaited the attack.

"They're surrounding us," he said, standing beside me with a weapon in each hand. "Six at the front door, another dozen coming in through the windows."

"They're already in the room with Jabari," I told him. I couldn't sense the naturi, but I could see them through Sadira's eyes. Fear had ramped up her powers and in turn strengthened our natural connection. There was a strong link between us after I had taken in so much of her blood last night. We could share thoughts and emotions with no effort. We could also see and feel things each other felt, introducing a potentially dangerous distraction into the mix.

"Gabriel, you're in with Jabari and Sadira. Keep them alive no matter what," I shouted. "Michael, you've got my back." I didn't look at them, but kept my eyes trained on the door. Their footsteps echoed down the hall as each took up their new positions. Their fear filled the air, teasing me with its thick, heady scent. There was nothing that could excite the senses of a vampire faster. Except maybe the scent of fresh blood and a woman's silence-shattering scream, but that was on the hunt.

Twisting my right wrist once, I impatiently slashed the air with Danaus's sword. I was eager to start this dance at last. It was my turn to lead.

As if in an attempt to be courteous of my wishes, the doors exploded open. I have to give them their due. Where Jabari had thrown them open, the naturi blew them completely off their hinges. Both large oak doors flew through the air, spinning like an out-of-control windmill. I dove sideways, knocking Danaus to the floor. As I fell, I grabbed the front of Michael's shirt with my free hand, pulling him down with us in a large heap. I rolled off Danaus, careful that the dagger and sword he held didn't accidentally relieve me of my head.

Behind me, arrows whizzed through the open doorway and thunked heavily into the wooden staircase. They were trying to clear the entrance. I was on my feet when I felt a shift in the wind.

A loud cacophony of noise filled the air, a grating mix of wings, claws, and calls. Raptors of all shapes and sizes filled the large entryway, making it suddenly seem small. We remained trapped on our knees against the wall as ravens, owls, hawks, and falcons flew through the halls, heading up the staircase and then back down again. Few bothered to attack us, but that wasn't their goal. The naturi had sent the birds in as a distraction to buy them some time.

Michael lifted his gun and squeezed off a couple of rounds, picking off a couple of the larger birds when they got too close. I covered his wrist with my hand and forced him to lower the gun.

"Don't waste your ammunition," I shouted over the noise. I jerked my head to the side as a brown owl dove close enough to drag its long talons across my cheek. Pain slashed through me and I fought the urge to press my hand to my cheek. If I lifted my arm, I'd only end up with a series of scratches.

"Mira, we can't stay like this!" Danaus snapped.

With a growl, I grabbed a vase off a nearby pedestal and threw it across the room toward the largest clump of birds as they fought for space in the air. The porcelain shattered on impact with the chandelier, sending it wildly swinging overhead. Shadows lunged and stretched in a gruesome dance around the room. Several birds were knocked from the air, hitting the hardwood floor with a heavy thud.

As the birds scattered, I lifted my left hand and focused on anything that was flying. Feathers instantly caught on fire, filling the room with a horrid stench. I killed only a few, though I wished I hadn't been forced to kill any of them, but it was enough to clear the air. The birds of prey scattered, with some heading out the open door while others flew up to find sanctuary on the third floor.

With the birds preoccupied, I turned my attention back to the entryway in time to see a naturi edge forward, his wrist crossbow aimed at me. In a single, liquid movement I pulled a knife from Danaus's belt and flung it at my adversary. The blade buried itself in his throat and nearly severed his head. He fell backward, the shaft firing harmlessly up at the ceiling. The dead naturi from the animal clan disappeared into the dark doorway, out of sight.

"Come out and play, blood drinker," sang a melodious voice outside the door.

"You come in. I'll reunite you with your brother, Nerian," I replied, tightening my grip on the sword. Some part of me was relieved to find that it wasn't Rowe once again calling out to me.

To my surprise, the naturi stepped into the doorway, short sword drawn. Danaus raised his gun, but I put a restraining hand over the top of the weapon. "Take care of our other guests, and cover my back," I said, motioning with my head toward the opposite end of the hall and the back door as I rose to my feet. The telltale sound of claws clicking across hardwood indicated that several wolves had found their way into the manor. Danaus and Michael had their own set of problems while I took care of the naturi in the doorway.

Barely topping five feet, he looked like a slender youth, more akin to a young willow than the human he was supposed to resemble. His long blond hair was pulled back, revealing a face similar to that of a fifteen-year-old boy, with its fresh sprinkling of freckles and wide green eyes. But his appearance belied the years of experience that hummed through his thin frame and filled his narrowed eyes.

"I thought we'd see Nerian together. I understand he had some special plans for you." A malicious grin split his young face. A chill crawled up my skin, sinking sharp fangs into my muscles. He was from the light clan, I had no doubt. Neither us could summon fire to destroy the other.

Closing the distance between us, I swung my sword with enough force to cleave his body in two. He sidestepped the blow for the most part, and deflected what he couldn't escape with his blade. He was quicker than most naturi I had encountered so far, each movement precise and fluid like a dance. Was he another form of Danaus? A creature that had studied the fine art of hunting nightwalkers?

The chaos around me dulled and the sounds trickled into my ears now as if enveloped in cotton. There was only the naturi standing before me in a pair of worn blue jeans with the left knee torn out. Hatred burned in his almond-shaped eyes.

Our swords scraped and clanged, searching for an entrance into the soft, meaty parts of the body. Dodging a thrust aimed to place his blade between my ribs, I brought my own sword down. He backpedaled, moving smoothly out of danger. With teeth clenched, I tossed my head, moving a lock of hair from where it had fallen in front of my eyes. The creature tried to use the momentary distraction to his advantage, slashing at my stomach. I was ready, catching his blade with mine and pushing him back toward the opposite wall.

I screamed. A searing pain splintered throughout my left shoulder, like someone had shoved a red-hot knitting needle into it. Someone had put a naturi dart in my shoulder. The pain slithered under my shoulder blade, slinking down through my muscles like liquid fire. I barely managed to block the naturi's next two attacks as my mind struggled through the fog of pain.

"Danaus!" I shouted, kicking my blond adversary back against the front doorjamb.

"We're being overrun from the back!" His deep voice boomed over the sound of singing steel and breaking furniture. "Hurry up!"

"Fine," I growled to myself. My left arm was starting to go numb and was nearly useless. I couldn't close my left fingers around a weapon if I had to.

"You look tired," the naturi mocked. "Want a drink?" He tilted his head to expose the long line of his throat. I feinted with my sword for his neck, then abruptly switched directions and plunged the blade into his heart up to the hilt.

"I'm not into junk food," I said as I slowly withdrew the blade and slashed it through the air, removing his head from his neck. The unattached member bounced and rolled away, his wide, gemlike eyes staring up at the ceiling, lost and unfocused. "Tell Nerian I said hi."

Spinning around, I found my companions barely holding a mix of naturi and wolves at bay at the opposite end of the hall. Inside the salon that held Sadira and the others, I could still hear the constant crash of furniture and gunfire. Sadira's thoughts were muffled but her fear was still riding high. However, that was matched by anger, which was encouraging. Sometimes the only thing that kept you moving was raw anger and hatred.

Gritting my teeth, I lifted my left arm. A low groan broke from my throat as the pain threatened to overcome my fragmented thoughts. I ignored it as best as I could and focused on a collection of creatures drawing closer to Michael and Danaus. It took only a couple of seconds for each one to explode in a glorious ball of fire. Only when they thumped lifelessly to the floor did I finally extinguish the flames. I'd taken an ugly risk using my powers. If I used them too often, it would leave me exhausted and vulnerable. Not a good combination when battling the naturi, particularly since I wasn't at full strength before this battle even started.

My left arm dropped back down to my side and I swayed on my feet. I opened my mouth to ask for a naturi count from Danaus when Michael rushed toward me. Stunned, I didn't think to move when he turned his shoulder into my chest and sent me back toward the open entryway. I stumbled over the body of the naturi I'd killed moments ago and landed hard on my butt. My left hand fell in a cool, wet spot on the Oriental rug. Glancing down, I discovered I was sitting in a spreading pool of blood that was leaking from the dead naturi. I frantically wiped it on my shirt and pants, desperate to be clean of the stuff. I imagine there is truly no stranger sight than a vampire wiping blood off like it carried the plague.

With fangs bared, I tore my gaze from the blood back to Michael, a vicious curse on the tip of my tongue, when I instantly stilled. He stood over me, his face slack. His blue eyes were staring blindly at some distant point I could not see. Something cold slipped down into my bones and knotted in my throat. A small, damp spot in the middle of his chest was growing by the second across his shirt while his skin paled to a gut-wrenching gray.

Behind him I heard the soft, liquid squish and suck of a blade being pulled from muscle and flesh. I noticed then that the door to the first room off the hall was open, when all the doors had been closed moments before.

I lurched forward on my knees, catching Michael's limp form as he fell forward. Lowering him to the ground, my eyes never wavered from my angel's pale face. Beside me, I felt more than saw Danaus attack the one that had stabbed my guardian. With a trembling hand, I smoothed his golden locks from his forehead, inadvertently smearing some of the naturi's blood across his perfect skin.

Michael's eyes drooped closed and his full lips briefly formed my name.

"Sleep, my angel," I whispered, my voice as rough as concrete. I bent down and pressed my parted lips to his. "You've done well."

The tension and lines slowly disappeared from his handsome face, as if time was kindly erasing some of the wear and tear he had suffered through his long years. He was moving away from the pain and the fear. Peace was settling inside him.

Something inside of me screamed in pain. I should have sent him home. I should have never included him in my life. Michael was a breath of fresh air. He had glowed with light and vitality, and I'd seen to its destruction.

Holding him, I could feel the life draining from his body, his heart slowing to a thick, torpid beat. His soul was pulling loose of its bonds, struggling to be free. I couldn't heal him. With all my power and abilities, I couldn't heal the human body beyond the closing of puncture wounds from my fangs. The best I could do was try to turn him into a nightwalker, but I wouldn't. His soul wanted to be free like a kite on a string. I knew I had to let him go no matter how badly I needed him to stay.

TWENTY-SEVEN

The pain in my left arm was gone. I stood without actually using my muscles. I just pushed out with my powers until I was lifted to my feet. Around me the sounds of battle dimmed and the world faded. Time ground to a crawl, edging along the floorboards like a multilegged insect. I paused long enough to grab both of Michael's guns and my sword. Tucking one gun in my pants at the hollow of my back, I kept the other in my left hand while the sword remained tightly clutched in my right hand.

To say that I was angry would have been an understatement. I wanted to send a wall of fire through the entire building, cleansing it of every moving creature, breathing or not. Michael was gone and I wanted a gallon of naturi blood for every drop spilled of his. I wanted them dead.

Striding into the front parlor, I paused long enough to assess the scene. Furniture had been overturned and the lighting was dim as one small lamp in the far corner fought back the darkness. Danaus battled two naturi at once, a scimitar in one hand and a short sword in the other. A flicker of light danced across the steel that had yet to be smeared with blood. Three more naturi stood near the window where they had come in, watching the show. I would have normally let Danaus have his fun, but I just wanted them dead. One of them had killed Michael.

Stepping forward, I lifted the gun toward Danaus's assailants. Without hesitation, I squeezed off several rounds, putting one into the forehead of each naturi before they could turn on me. The recoil sent a shock wave up my arm and I hissed in pain, but it didn't slow me as I swung around and fired the last three rounds at the remaining naturi. Only one found its mark, briefly pinning the brown-haired creature to the blood-splattered wall before he slid to the floor.

Out of bullets, I pitched the gun at the closest naturi, shattering his nose and left cheekbone. He screamed and stumbled backward, holding his face. I closed the distance, rage bubbling in my veins. His companion stepped forward to protect him, and I left his head rocking on the floor seconds later.

The wounded elflike creature lashed out, swinging his sword wildly, half blinded by the pain. In a flash of movement I was standing behind the creature. I grabbed a fistful of brown hair and jerked his head back before running my blade across his throat. I was careful to slice the main arteries and open his windpipe. It's a subtle art; something learned through years of torture and death. If I had left him like that, he might have drowned in his own blood. Unfortunately, I wasn't sure how quickly he would heal so I lopped off both his hands. I didn't want him coming back to stab me later. This way he would at least bleed to death. He would suffer awhile longer than if I'd just decapitated him like his companion. I wanted his death to be a slow one.

Danaus grabbed my right arm as I started to leave the room, halting my progress. "He's not dead," the hunter growled. His hand bit into my flesh while his powers beat angrily against me.

"He will be." Danaus didn't release me, his gaze burning into my cold eyes. I knew what he wanted. He didn't believe in torture. "Remember, they did far worse to me. At least he knows he's going to die. I had no such guarantee." I wrenched my arm free of his grasp and continued to the hall.

I was relieved to see he followed directly behind me instead of ending the naturi's suffering. Maybe he knew this wasn't the best time to cross me. I paused in the hall, careful not to look down at Michael's cold body. Instead I gazed up the hall to find three more naturi heading toward the room holding Jabari and the others, looking to attack the small group from behind. I pulled the second and last gun from my pants and plowed through the three that were now coming after me.

"Are there any more coming?" I stepped on the body of the nearest naturi, indifferent as to whether he was dead yet, as I walked toward the closed door.

"Yes, but we have a couple of minutes," Danaus said, following close behind me. "The last of them are in with the others."

I shoved open the door and for a second my confidence slipped several notches. The room looked like a cyclone had blown through.

All the furniture had been destroyed. Exquisite landscapes were ripped off the walls, their heavy frames used as weapons. The walls were pockmarked with bullets and gaping holes created by flying bodies. Corpses littered the floor, broken and torn.

Sadira stood in one corner with a wounded Tristan behind her. One of the legs of the chair she'd been sitting in was tightly clenched in her fist and her fangs were bared. Other than the fangs, she still didn't look like a vampire, just a mother protecting her child. Of course, we're talking a half-crazed, bloodthirsty mother with her blood-splashed yellow shirt sticking to her thin frame and dark hair flowing down her back.

My Gabriel still stood strong beside her, a knife in one hand and a naturi short sword in the other. I didn't want to contemplate how long he had been without ammo. His right shoulder and left thigh were bleeding, but he didn't waver, so I hoped the wounds were superficial. I couldn't lose him too.

And in the eye of the storm stood Jabari. His energy pulsed in violent waves through the room. At least a dozen bodies circled him, torn apart in various ways. The nightwalker stood empty-handed, covered in the blood of his enemies. Jabari didn't use a sword or knife. He preferred to take apart his enemies with his bare hands. It was a lost art.

Watching him face down the five naturi that currently circled him, I remembered why I had always loved him. I loved his strength and his power. I loved that I only felt anger radiating from him, no fear, no doubt, no indecision. With little effort and no hesitation, Jabari pulled the heart from a naturi's chest. He tossed the two objects carelessly aside and moved onto his next prey.

And deep down I knew I was standing in that line, no matter what happened from here on out.

"Shall we?" I said, looking over at Danaus as I tried gauge the best place to enter the fray. Relieving Sadira and Gabriel would probably be the wisest place to start. Jabari was doing fine on his own.

"After you," Danaus said, motioning for me to precede him. I was beginning to think he was enjoying himself. He was splattered with blood and a line of sweat ran from his temple to his hard jaw. His narrowed eyes were keenly focused on the naturi in the room, weighing their skills. But there was also a glitter of amusement there, soaking in the thrill of the battle and the rush of adrenaline. At that moment, Danaus was more of a predator than the naturi could ever be. He was a dark stalker riding the wave of blood and death, his human side obliterated.

With a slight shake of my head, I jumped in, lunging at the naturi that was backing Gabriel toward the wall. After a couple of exchanges he was dead, his head rolling across the room. In the spare moment between adversaries, I tossed Gabriel the gun I'd been carrying. I wasn't sure how many bullets it still had, but it was better than nothing.

"Keep back and make sure nothing comes through the door," I said over my shoulder as one of the two naturi attacking Danaus rushed me. We crossed swords, circling each other the best we could considering the floor was thick with miscellaneous body parts and slick with blood. Poorly balanced with my left foot on someone's chest while my right foot rested on another's hand, I blocked an overhead blow aimed to split my skull. I finished by swinging my blade down, cleaving my foe in two.

Half stumbling off the dead body, I looked up in time to see Danaus skillfully finish off his opponent with a neat spinning slash that not only lifted and threw the naturi across the room, but cut him clear to the spine. While I was skillful with a sword, watching Danaus was like taking in the Russian ballet. I could feel more than see the ripple of muscle and sinew dancing beneath his tanned skin. Every movement was precisely timed and balanced for the maximum effect. The light throb of his powers tumbled from him to wash through me.

I glanced around the room. Jabari was down to his last two naturi. Sadira knelt beside Tristan, her bloody hands cupping his pale cheeks. Gabriel leaned against the wall near them, struggling to catch his breath.

"How bad is it?" I inquired, looking down at the young nightwalker. We were all covered in blood, making it hard to tell who was actually bleeding.

"The cut isn't deep, but the sword was charmed," Sadira said, flicking worried eyes over to me. There was a smear of blood across her forehead, and her blood-soaked clothes clung to her slender frame, making her look even frailer.

"It slows the healing. It's more pain than actual poison. He'll survive," I said, turning my attention to my guardian angel. He stood staring down at the gun in his hand, a frown on his full lips.

"He died saving my life," I volunteered, struggling to keep my voice steady as an image of Michael lying in my arms flashed across my mind. I should have been paying more attention. I might not have been able to sense the naturi, but I should have heard the door opening or the footsteps.

Gabriel nodded. "Then he died happy." His fingers tightened

around the handgun, his expression hardening. He'd said the words as much for me as for himself. My brown-haired angel had outlived three bodyguards now. The other two had been brash and careless, picking a fight when they should have known better. Michael, in contrast, had been smart. He knew when to keep his head down and how to follow orders. In the end, I was just bad for him.

Forcing my attention back to Danaus, I pushed those regrets aside for now. They would only distract me and get me killed. Later, I would cry bloody tears for my fallen angel. The hunter was staring toward the broken window, his expression intense and drawn. It wasn't good.

"Here they come."

I was already moving before the last word crossed his lips. Jabari had just ripped the arms off his final opponent and was standing in the open in the center of the room. Much like Michael had with me earlier this horrible night, I put my shoulder into Jabari, throwing us both to the ground as a barrage of arrows entered the room through the window. These bastards were starting to become predictable.

Frowning, I looked down to find Jabari staring up at me with a stunned look in his wide brown eyes. I guess I would have too, had I been in the same position. Less than an hour ago we'd tried to kill each other.

"It's been years since we had fun like this," I said, lying across his strong chest.

Jabari gave a weary sigh, his eyes suddenly turning sad. His face had lost its walking dead look. He looked almost human, or at least a little less like a corpse. "I still do not understand you, desert flower." He reached up and tucked a dirty, wet strand of hair behind my ear. "But things have not changed between us."

"I don't expect them to. You are just one of the many people who wish to kill me right now," I reminded him as I rolled off his chest and to my feet. I remained squatting down as another barrage of arrows soared through the room. I could smell his blood now that we were so close. He had been cut. It was impossible to tell how many times or how deep. As an Ancient, he would be able to tolerate the pain better than most, but without rest or a meal, he was going to slow down. We all were.

"Promise me something," I continued, my eyes locked on the window.

"What do you desire?" He knelt beside me, his long body tensed and ready for the attack. His soft accent rippled across me like a soothing hand rubbing my back.

"I love it when you say that," I teased in a dreamy voice. He said nothing, but his expression hardened in warning. I was pushing my luck. "When the time comes, let it be between us. Don't let the Coven send one of its flunkies. I deserve better than that." I looked over to find him smiling, white fangs peeking out beneath his lips.

"As you wish." His voice was deep and solemn.

Not quite. I wished to walk away from this mess and go home. I wished that I could push the naturi, Themis, Danaus, and this whole nightmare to the farthest reaches of my mind. I wished for my fairy godmother, the good witch of the north, or some other bitch with a wand to glide in here and zap these arrow-shooting assholes. But I wasn't counting on it.

"How many?" I called across the room. Danaus frowned at me, his grip tightening on the short sword in his hand. He knelt behind some broken furniture near Sadira and Tristan. The naturi blood was beginning to darken and dry on his skin. His cobalt blue eyes glittered in the weak lamp light.

"You don't want to know."

"Tell me."

"Thirty—more or less."

I nodded, my expression carefully blank. I wanted to scream that it was impossible. I didn't think there could have been two dozen naturi on the entire island. Unfortunately, one nightwalker was already down and another was starting to weaken. Sadira could hold her own better than I'd previously thought, but Gabriel wasn't going to last much longer. I was tempted to call for Ryan, but his own people would need him. We were on our own.

As if on cue, naturi started leaping through the open window. Danaus was nice enough to take out the first one from across the room by carefully placing his knife in the creature's forehead. It was enough to startle the naturi standing next to him, buying me an extra second as I jumped to my feet. The first few fell quickly, but our little group was soon pushed back by their sheer number.

I was only vaguely aware of my companions. I just kept moving, blocking, and slashing. Yet, it seemed for every one I killed, I was forced back a step as two more took his place. Frustration and fatigue finally got the better of me. The naturi I faced now wasn't a better swordsman, only lucky. I raised my sword to block a swing aimed at my neck and missed the dagger he plunged into my stomach with his free hand. I removed his head with a scream of frustration and pain, but the damage was done.

Crumpling to my knees, the naturi poison surged through my body, adding to the renewed throbbing ache in my left shoulder.

Desperate, I did the only thing I could think of: I created fire. It was all I had left. The flames leapt up from the floor in front of me and quickly spread down the line until it separated the naturi from our little group. The naturi stepped back, watching us, possibly wondering what I would do next or waiting for a member of the light clan to appear so he could remove my final weapon.

"Burn them, Mira!" Sadira screamed from some distant point off to my right.

"I can't." The words escaped me as a hoarse whisper, but I know she heard me over the crackling flames. My sword clattered to the floor and I pulled the dagger from my stomach. The pain was already beginning to crush my thoughts, and I knew I wouldn't be able to keep the flames going much longer. Still weak from the previous night's battle, I had too little strength left to call upon.

"Burn them, Mira!" Jabari commanded angrily. "Destroy them all."

I wanted to say no, but I was too tired to even form the word. I looked up to find Danaus standing beside me, his hand extended, offering to help me to my feet.

"Let's finish this together," he calmly said. "Your life is mine to enjoy when I choose."

I wanted to laugh. Danaus would choose now to make a joke, repeating what I'd said about him days ago to Lucas. I think I smiled. I'm not really sure since I could no longer feel my lips over the pain in my abdomen.

But most important, he was making a deal with me; one last push with us both using our powers to destroy the naturi that stood watching their prey. If we survived, we'd both be exhausted and at the mercy of whoever was left standing. Unfortunately, we were out of options.

Slowly, I lifted my bloody right hand from my stomach and placed it in Danaus's hand. And I screamed. Whatever pain I'd felt from the naturi poison was a mere bee sting compared to the power flowing through my body now. It surged down my arm and through my limbs, threatening to peel my flesh from my bones. It kept building, trying to rip me apart.

Burn them.

I blinked and found myself standing somehow, but the room was growing black. "I—I can't see them," I said in a choked voice. Panic was crowding in where the pain had yet to sink.

Yes, you can.

This time I realized the voice in my head belonged to Danaus. I wanted to curse and scream at him, but something strange caught my attention. I suddenly realized the room was more crowded now. A split-second search revealed I could now sense the naturi.

I picked through the occupants of the room as the pain built to a point where it seemed I was hanging onto consciousness by a thread. As I reached out, there was only one thought left in my brain—to kill them. I mentally tried to grab their hearts and set them on fire. It was a trick I'd used in the past that had proved effective, but something would not let me. It pushed me toward this almost wispy throb of energy in each naturi. Too weak to fight it, I gave in and wrapped the powers building in me around that bit of smoke.

Another scream ripped from my throat, louder than the first, as the energy flowed out of me. My knees buckled and I fell, still tightly clasping Danaus's hand as if it were my last anchor to sanity. As the pain ebbed, I heard the thought again.

Kill them all.

My focus cleared and I felt more naturi. Without hesitation I pushed outward, past the walls of the manor, into the trees surrounding the compound. I set aflame every throb of naturi energy I ran across, pushing the power out until I finally encountered a different feeling of power blocking my reach somewhere miles from the Compound.

Then the energy stopped. Beside me, I heard Danaus drop to his knees, my hand slipping from his to thud against the cold, sticky floor. The room was silent except for his ragged breaths. My body still hurt with an intensity I never thought possible, but my thoughts were clearing, and I wished they hadn't.

I realized with a startling clarity what I had done. I'd destroyed their souls; wiped them completely from existence. Previously, I had just set their bodies on fire. Yes, I killed them with a certain amount of glee, but their souls had been free to pursue whatever afterlife they believed in. This time there was nothing left. My eyes were closed but I could smell the charred bodies and burned hair. I had destroyed them completely. And not just the ones attacking us. I had obliterated every naturi within several miles of the Themis compound.

TWENTY-EIGHT

The silence was overwhelming. After the heavy pound of footsteps, clang of steel, and screams of pain, the quiet was suffocating. Even Sadira's thoughts were now hushed. I could still feel her in the room, but there was only a muffled confusion. Did she know what I had done? I hated the naturi with every fiber of my being, but had I known I was capable of such utter destruction, I would never have committed the atrocity. Taking a life is one thing. The body ceases, but something of the creature still lives on somewhere. I had stopped that, done something I didn't think possible.

But how? It didn't make sense. I had never done such a thing before. Even at my peak, I should have been able to only flambé the occupants of the room, if even that. There were so many, and I was exhausted.

Something happened when I touched Danaus. Not only had I been able to sense them, which is unheard of among nightwalkers, but I could also destroy their souls.

Slowly, I opened my eyes and turned my head to the right to look at Danaus. The ebony-haired hunter sat on the floor beside me, his body hunched over. His head was bowed, leaving his face hidden behind a curtain of long dark locks. He had been affected as much as I, his breath still ragged and uneven. When he finally looked over at me, I saw my horror mirrored in his blue eyes.

Danaus reached out to touch my arm, but I lurched across the floor, pushing away from him. "Don't touch me!" I shrieked. I cringed, nearly curling into a ball as a fresh wave of pain washed through my body. It was blinding, but my fear of what had happened was greater. I know it didn't make much sense. I had crawled all over the man on more than one occasion and nothing had happened, but the memory and pain were still too fresh.

"Mira?" Sadira said, her voice a fragile shade of its normal strength.

"They're gone." My words had been reduced to a pathetic whimper. The raw ache was starting to subside at last and my thoughts were coming together in a more logical fashion. I lifted my head and reluctantly gazed around the room. It was a disaster, something from a nightmare, with body parts strewn haphazardly around the small area. But to me, the most garish of these grisly sights were the bodies of those I'd destroyed. After their souls were incinerated, their bodies had been reduced to gray and white ash. Most had collapsed into large heaps, but a few still stood like thin, dirty snowmen. Because of me, the island was dotted with dirty snowmen, empty shells waiting for a breeze.

"Then it's done," Sadira said. She was sounding strong, more sure of herself. "The triad has been reformed."

"So you believe me now," I said, trying to force a smile on my lips. But it fell short. What I really wanted was to vomit. My stomach twisted in a desperate dance to purge itself of the violence I had been responsible for, but I'd lost too much blood during the past couple nights.

"No!" Jabari roared, his angry voice an explosion in the silent room. "It can't be him."

"Him?" My head jerked up to look from Jabari to Sadira, but both of them were ignoring me.

"He's not even one of our kind," Jabari declared.

"Apparently that does not matter," Sadira said matter-of-factly. "You felt the power in this room as much as I did."

"No!"

"You'd pick Danaus over me to be in the triad?" I demanded. While I was never one to discriminate according to a person's race, there was something that irked me about asking Danaus—whatever it is that he was—to be in an all-vampire triad of power. Particularly after he'd spent so much time killing us.

Unfortunately, it might not have been the wisest decision to call attention to myself, considering that I could barely remain in an upright position. I wanted to lie down, but the pools of cooling naturi blood and assortment of body parts made the idea unappealing.

"You're still blind to the truth?" Jabari asked incredulously. He walked over to me, his face twisted with rage. "You can never be a part of the triad, no matter how old you become or how strong you grow." Kneeling down so he could look me in the eye, he sneered. "You are just a weapon, nothing more than a sword or a gun, a tool. Your true power is in how another can use you."

"No," I croaked, but my mind was already turning over the idea. The voice in my head had been a command and I obeyed. I had no choice, couldn't have stopped what happened no matter how hard I tried.

"The triad focuses its power in you. We used you like a key to lock the door between this world and the naturi," Jabari explained.

"If I was so important to what happened, why can't I remember that night?" I asked through clenched teeth. The thought of being controlled by another twisted in my chest, numbing the pain still throbbing in my body. It seemed that from the moment I took my first gasping breath on this earth, I'd struggled for my independence, my ability to control my own fate.

"To protect you."

A snort of disbelief escaped me as I narrowed my eyes at my old friend and guardian. "I'm beginning to think that nothing you've ever done for me was for my benefit."

Jabari smiled at me, and it was unlike any other I had ever seen cross his face. It was like a mask had finally been lifted, one I hadn't even realized I'd been staring at for the past five hundred years. I had seen him smile in pleasure and in hatred, but now he seemed formed of ice, cold and unyielding. He put a finger under my chin and titled my head up. I tried to jerk my head away but I found that I couldn't. The leak of power oozing from him through his finger into my skin was slight, but it was enough to cause my already sore muscles to tense. There was a new presence in my head claiming dominion, but he had yet to speak or command me. For now, he was just staking his claim, proving he had control over me.

"You can't remember because we didn't want you to remember," Jabari stated.

"We?"

"The Coven. We needed to know who could control you. You can be quite an effective weapon."

I gritted my teeth and tried again to move my head away from his touch, and again I couldn't, which made his smile widen.

"Sadira can control you," Jabari continued. "Tabor could, and so can I. Surprisingly, a couple of Tabor's children could as well, so we naturally assumed that it was a matter of finding the proper bloodlines."

"There were others?" A new horror dug its claws into my flesh.

There were no memories to drag up, but I could easily imagine the scene: me playing the puppet for the amusement of the Coven and its lackeys.

"A few. We ran some experiments. Unfortunately, most of those we found who could control you had to be destroyed. We couldn't let our little secret out. We also had to make sure you didn't know. There would always be the chance of someone reading your mind and discovering your unique ability."

"So I've been allowed to live this long so the Coven could pull my leash at any moment," I said. Something flashed in Jabari's eyes for half a second, a random thought I wasn't supposed to know. "What?" I snapped. "Something about the Coven?" I watched him as his expression hardened, and I smiled back at him. "Not everyone can do it," I slowly said. "Not everyone on the Coven can control me." My smile widened and his expression went purposefully blank. I was right. "That must be an ugly sticking point for someone." My mind quickly rifled through the other members of the Coven; Macaire and Elizabeth. Tabor, my other leash holder, was gone. Could I have been the reason for his final demise?

"You're very lucky to have survived so long," Jabari said. "Wisely, you chose to fulfill the requests of the Coven, giving you a purpose and the illusion that you would obey our wishes."

"All the Coven asked of me was to keep the peace and protect our secret. Not an entirely unreasonable request," I replied, with a slight shrug that made me instantly wish I hadn't moved my hurt shoulder.

"And now we have this problem," Jabari growled, his eyes sliding over to Danaus, who was closely watching the exchange. The hunter pushed to his feet, wincing at the movement, but at least he was standing. I still wasn't sure I could.

"We naturally assumed that you could only be controlled by your own kind," Jabari continued. "That's not good, my desert flower; particularly since there are questions about your loyalty."

"There are few who have done anything to earn my loyalty," I replied, causing him to frown. I liked it better than his smile at the moment. "But it doesn't matter. You will only let me live until you find a way to create another like me."

"If you live that long," Jabari said, moving his finger from beneath my chin. If I still breathed, I think I would have sighed with relief. The Ancient stood before me, staring down as if weighing something. "The naturi know you are the key to stopping them. Enough of them survived Machu Picchu to know that you were the one who sealed the door. You were right. They were trying to kill you in Aswan, not me. I believe they were also trying to kill you in London, but they killed Tabor's child instead. You have always been their target."

"If I'm so damned important, why send me to protect Sadira? Why not send someone else?"

"We needed bait."

"Bait?"

"To draw out Rowe. We knew he would come after you again. The chance to kill you is too much of a temptation."

I closed my eyes, trying to ignore the knot of tears that had grown in the back of my throat. It seemed I was becoming everyone's favorite target. "And killing Rowe would end this? It would stop the naturi?" My voice trembled as I fought for control of my emotions.

"Rowe is the last known leader of the naturi," Danaus volunteered.

My head snapped up to look at him, meeting his glittering blue eyes as he watched me. "You used me too," I whispered.

To his credit, he didn't look away, but continued to hold my horrified gaze. "Yes. When he tried to take you in Aswan, I realized that you must have some other importance that you either were not telling me or didn't remember. I thought he would make another grab for you."

"Well, you both missed your chance to end this. Rowe had me in London, threatening to kidnap me," I said bitterly. "It would have meant destroying me, but I can only guess that you both have other plans for me still."

"Mira . . ." Sadira began in a placating voice.

"I've heard enough!" I shouted.

"So have I!" mocked a horrible voice from behind me. I didn't need to look around to see who had spoken. I knew by the sound, the tone, the look of complete shock on the faces of the others who had spoken. With a burst of sheer terror, I tried to lurch forward, but he grabbed me by the hair, wrapping it around his fist. Jerking me backward, he pulled me into the darkness and out of the Compound in less than a heartbeat. Rowe had finally caught me.

TWENTY-NINE

The darkness gave way suddenly to a moonlit plain hugged by a desolate ribbon of road. I slowly pushed up into a sitting position so I could look around. Rowe took a few stumbling steps away from me before finally collapsing to his knees in the grass. Bent over, his fingers clutching the grass, he struggled for air. His whole body was trembling, his shirt sticking to his narrow frame as if he were sweating profusely. All this flitting from place to place was taking its toll on him.

Digging my nails into the dirt, I started to pull my legs beneath me so I could rise. My whole body screamed in pain and the world swayed slightly. I was too low on blood to pick a fight and expect to win, but at least Rowe was in ragged shape as well.

"Watch her," Rowe bit out without looking over at me.

Until he spoke, my gaze had not drifted beyond him. Now, I lifted my eyes to see six naturi of various size and clans approaching us warily. And beyond them rose the pale monoliths of Stonehenge. They were attempting the sacrifice tonight, and for some bizarre reason, Rowe had decided he needed me on hand to witness their triumph.

"Shit," I hissed, lowering my head. I was in no shape to take on seven naturi alone.

A wheezing laugh escaped Rowe. He was kneeling on the ground with his forearms in the grass in front of him. His head was turned toward me, his black hair partially obscuring his face, but I could still see the smirk twisting his lips.

"Oh, like you're in any better shape than me," I snarled.

"At least I have someone to protect me," he said, pushing into a sitting position with pain-filled slowness.

I looked back at the naturi standing before us. A female with pale blond hair that fell to her waist stepped forward. She extended one hand and flames danced over her fingers. Naturally, one of my keepers was a member of the light clan.

"It doesn't have to be like this, Mira," Rowe said.

"Go to hell, Rowe," I snapped, my gaze never wavering from the six naturi standing before me.

A harsh clutter of words jumped from Rowe that I couldn't understand. Several of the naturi briefly expressed surprise and confusion, but after a moment they backed away, returning to the inner circle of stones.

Silence crept back over the plain. The air was still, waiting. It was only after the naturi retreated back into the shadows of the stones that I noticed the soft sounds of a woman crying. The naturi had their sacrifice waiting in the darkness, surrounded by great bluestones. Where the hell was Jabari? He could move from place to place in an instant. He should have been able to locate me wherever I was. Why hadn't he appeared yet? If he were there, I knew we could stop this now. I'd even have settled for Sadira or Danaus, but I knew it would take several more minutes for either of them to reach me.

I dragged my fingers through the earth, digging narrows furrows in the soft dirt. The grass was moist, as if it had rained recently. Beneath me, I could feel the strange hum of power beginning to build. Had they begun the sacrifice already? I couldn't see most of the naturi, as they remained hidden behind the giant stones, but I could hear the faint sound of movement; breathing, the soft swish of clothing.

"You can feel it, can't you?" Rowe said. The weight of his stare was a physical pressure on my shoulders, but I refused to look over at him. "You could feel it while you were at Machu Picchu. In those last days, Nerian didn't need to touch you, the power in the mountain was enough to have you writhing in pain."

I shook my head. I wasn't going to let him play mind games with me. "Just stop. You weren't there," I replied.

"I was there," he murmured. My gaze jerked over to him at the sound of movement. He crawled a couple feet closer but remained out of arm's reach. "Every day and every night of your captivity, I was there. You just don't remember because I looked a little different back then."

"Years not been kind?" I mocked.

His face twisted into a look of anger and hatred for a split second before he could wipe it away. "I'm sure the years have scarred us both in interesting ways."

"Why bring me here? I could still stop your sacrifice, destroy all your plans." I smiled at him as I sat up. I rubbed my hands together, knocking off the dirt.

Rowe sat up as well, seeming to move with a little more ease and less obvious pain. We were both slowly regaining our strength. "Because the reward is worth the risk."

A laugh escaped me before I could stop it. "Killing me is worth that much to you?"

Rowe shoved his left hand through his hair, threading some of it behind his left ear so it no longer fell in front of his one eye. A white scar ran along his jaw and seemed to glow against his tanned skin in the moonlight. "My goal is not to kill you."

I snorted in response, and Rowe said something under his breath in his own language, frustration filling his voice. He looked over at the arrangement of stones for a moment before turning back to me again.

"It doesn't have to be like this between us."

"What? The naturi have graciously decided to stop killing night-walkers?"

This time he was the one to snort. "No, nightwalkers are vermin. They need to be exterminated. I meant between you and the naturi."

"I am a nightwalker, asshole."

"But you were never meant to be," he said, leaning toward me as his voice dropped to an urgent whisper. "You never should have been made into one of their kind. Your powers reach beyond their limitations. You could have been more. You still could be."

I leaned back, trying to keep some distance between us. With him sitting this close, it was hard to resist the urge to take a swipe at him, but I didn't stand a chance with his compatriots just a few yards away. "Let me guess, you can help me become more," I sneered.

"You can feel the power here, and no other vampire can. When they swarmed Machu Picchu centuries ago, not one of them reacted the way you do. You can still feel the earth despite being a night-walker," he explained. "It's still a part of you because it's more pow-erful than anything you've gained through becoming a nightwalker. You belong with us, not them."

A slow chuckle built until my head finally fell backward, my laugh-ter filling the plain, silencing the soft plaintive cries from the woman doomed to die tonight. "Save your breath. I've heard this speech be-fore, though it was more interesting the first time. At Machu Picchu, you guys were just trying to convince me to kill my own kind. Now you want me to believe that I belong among you."

"Can you honestly tell me you feel you belong among your own kind? Hmmm, Fire Starter?"

The laugh died inside of me. "It doesn't matter."

"You can end the war tonight," Rowe softly said.

"By killing you?"

"By completing the sacrifice."

My brow furrowed as I stared at him for a long time, letting the silence grow between us. "What are you talking about?" I asked, my voice dropping to match his softness.

"If you complete the sacrifice, the seal will be broken *permanently.* You made it. If you break it, the nightwalkers will never be able to recreate it again. We end this battle forever."

"And if I don't?"

"I kill you now."

"And if I do?"

"You walk away. The naturi shall never bother you again."

"But I will be branded a traitor and will be hunted by my own kind until the end of my nights," I said with a shake of my head.

"Then break the seal and remain with us," he offered, stunning me. "I am consort to the queen, and you will be under my protection. The naturi will never harass you and the nightwalkers will never touch you."

I turned my head to look back at Stonehenge for a second before letting my eyes fall shut. In the hands of the naturi, I was a weapon against the nightwalkers. And while among the nightwalkers, I was a weapon against the naturi. Without ever knowing it, I had managed to dig a heel into both worlds.

Planting both of my hands into the dirt, I pushed off and rose to my feet. Beside me there was a soft rustle of clothing as Rowe stood. He stuck close to me as I slowly walked past the first circle of stones and into the inner circle. The other six naturi circled the woman lying on the ground. Her wrists had been bound together and then tied to a stake in the ground above her head. Her ankles were also bound together and staked so that she was stretched out, her body running east to west. She had short, dark brown hair and her round face was streaked with tears. The smell of her blood filled the air, as her wrists were rubbed raw from her struggles.

"What do you need me to do?" I asked, staring down at her.

Rowe stepped in front of me and gently grabbed my chin, tilting my head up so I was forced to look him in the eye. "You will do this?"

"It's time to end this war."

A half smile lifted one corner of his mouth briefly and he nodded. "You must cut out her heart and place it on the ground. Her blood must saturate the earth before we burn her heart."

I had to be sure. I couldn't make any mistakes now. As Rowe stepped back to my side, I took a step closer to the woman. She stared up with wide eyes, pleading silently with me to free her. But I couldn't. She was the only human in the area. As long as she lived, she could serve as a sacrifice for the naturi whatever I did. The best I could do for her was make it quick.

Staring down at her, I focused on her heart. The slender woman gasped suddenly, shattering the silence in the night air. Her body arched off the ground and all the naturi took a step backward. The woman jerked again, this time screaming.

"What's happening?" someone demanded.

"It's the nightwalker! She's killing the woman," another voice snarled, but I didn't look up. I remained focused on the woman's chest until her pale blue shirt with pearl buttons finally started to blacken and catch on fire.

"Stop her!"

Rowe grabbed me and threw me backward into one of the enormous stones, breaking my concentration. I fell back to the ground, my eyes clenched shut as I waited to see if I'd hit the stone with enough force to knock loose the other stone balanced on top of it. When I wasn't immediately crushed, I opened my eyes, trying to ignore the pain throbbing to life along my spine and in the back of my skull.

"Can we still use the woman?" Rowe demanded, looking briefly over his shoulder at the woman, who was no longer moving.

"The heart has been destroyed," someone else confirmed.

The naturi with the eye patch turned back to me, a knife clutched in his right hand. "Then we will try it with her heart," Rowe proclaimed.

I dug my heels into the earth and tried to scoot backward, but I was halted by giant stone sticking up from the earth. I had used the last of my powers to kill that poor woman, and now I had nothing left to save myself.

My only warning was a slight building of pressure, a shift in the powers that filled the circle, and then Jabari was standing beside me.

Rowe and the other naturi jumped back, gathering on the other side of the circle, the woman's corpse between us. The knife in his hand trembled as he stared at the Ancient, his breath hissing between clenched teeth.

"You cannot have her," Jabari proclaimed.

Rowe hunched forward, then a low growl escaped him as giant

wings exploded from his back. As black as a moonless night, the fully extended wings were more than nine feet long from tip to tip and resembled those of a bat. "You cannot keep her forever," he snarled, pointing his knife at Jabari.

I looked up at my onetime mentor and protector to see a wide grin split his handsome face. He extended his arm so his hand was nearly over my head. Power immediately surged through my body, ripping a whimper from my throat. It was as if strings had been attached to various parts of my body and I was pulled back to my feet. There was no voice in my head commanding me, but I could feel a presence, a subtle push of power. There was nothing to fight. Nothing to push or struggle against. I was merely a spectator in my own body. Reduced to a mere marionette.

A second wave of power pushed through my body, nearly blinding me with pain. My left arm lifted and three of the naturi exploded into balls of fire. I could feel the member of the light clan trying to extinguish the fires, but she was no match. She was engulfed in flames next.

With a single flap of the enormous wings, Rowe launched himself into the air. "See you with the dead," he bit out, and then he was gone, leaving behind the last two naturi to be burned alive.

When the last of the naturi were reduced to ash, Jabari released me. My knees buckled and I collapsed back onto the ground. Pain seemed to be a living, breathing entity within my body. I didn't seem to exist anymore. There was only pain and horror.

I blinked a couple of times, trying to clear my vision, and saw Jabari extend a hand toward me, offering to help me back to my feet. I jerked away from him. "Don't touch me," I snapped.

His dark laugh rose up in the silence, wrapping itself around me like a noose. "I don't need to."

A shiver rippled through me and I clenched my teeth to keep them from chattering. No. No, he didn't need to touch me to control me.

"We go to Venice. It is the best way to protect you from the naturi," Jabari announced.

I certainly didn't want to admit it, but he was right. Venice was the one place I would be safe from them. They never set foot in the city. The old tales said that one of the naturi's gods had died in what is now the city of Venice, creating the canals that wove their way among the tiny islands. The naturi supposedly couldn't enter the city. Unfortunately, Venice was also the home of the Coven. I didn't want to be anywhere near another Ancient, let alone near at least three of the most powerful nightwalkers in existence.

I frowned, realizing I had no options. I didn't have the strength to fight Jabari, and even if I did, I didn't know how. The bastard could control me like a puppet. And if I slipped away from him, I had no doubt that Rowe would cut my heart out the first time he caught sight of me. At least Jabari needed me alive for the time being. I had stopped the second sacrifice, bought us a little time. The naturi would strike again.

But the triad was reformed, even if it now included a vampire hunter. And the triad still had me, a weapon that could kill or bind them.

The sound of a car engine jerked us both from our thoughts. It was Danaus. I knew it without using my powers. It was the hunter.

"You will travel to Venice and you will bring the hunter with you," Jabari ordered. "We will be waiting for you."

I nodded, my eyes darting away from his face. "Sadira?"

"She has already left for Italy. She asks that you bring her child." My gaze jumped back to his face, to find a mocking smile lifting his lips. She would demand that, keeping both Tristan and me on a short leash. As the car drew close, Jabari stepped backward and disappeared.

My eyes fell shut and it was a struggle just to remain upright. For the first time, I wondered if I'd chosen the right side. If I'd sided with the naturi, I would have been forced to kill nightwalkers and stand by while the naturi killed the humans. If I'd sided with the nightwalkers, I would have been forced to kill the naturi. And regardless of which side I might have chosen that night, the innocent human woman would still have died by my hand.

The car engine stopped and I could hear the sound of heavy footsteps running across the field. I opened my eyes in time to see Danaus come between a pair of large stones, a long knife in his right hand. His eyes quickly swept the carnage, pausing briefly on the woman that lay to my left, before he finally put his knife back in its sheath at his side.

I slowly pushed to my feet, but my legs buckled again. Danaus crossed the short distance separating us, grabbing my arms and keeping me from hitting the ground again.

"Jabari?" he asked.

"Come and gone already," I said. My voice was harsh and rough as I forced it past the lump in my throat. "We go to Venice." A fragile, mocking smile slipped across my lips. "We did it. We reformed the triad and even have a weapon that can stop the naturi."

I flinched as his large hands cupped my cheeks, but the power that filled him didn't try to push inside of me. It swirled around us, forming a warm, comforting cocoon.

"Don't let him beat you," Danaus ordered, forcing me to meet his glittering gaze. I knew he was talking about Jabari. He didn't know about Rowe yet, and I wasn't sure I would ever tell him. I was already enough of a danger to the world around me; no reason to up the ante.

"He already has," I murmured. "I'm a tool. A weapon."

"No, you're the Fire Starter. A walking nightmare to both vampire and naturi. We'll find a way to beat him."

I didn't even try to keep the skepticism from darting through my eyes as I stared up at the hunter. I couldn't imagine what kind of miracle he expected me to work.

"You've eluded me for the past few decades. What trouble could a few old vampires offer?" he continued, arching one thick brow at me.

Danaus was being ridiculous, but I understood his point. We had to find a way if we hoped to survive. Our fates were linked now.

"We'll find a way," I whispered. "I always do."

Danaus leaned forward and brushed a kiss against my temple, sending a wave of peace deep into the marrow of my bones, helping to ease some of the pain. "And then we'll kill each other as God intended."

Dayhunter

To Nate
Thanks for all the laughs

Acknowledgments

A special thanks to my editor, Diana Gill, for making me a better writer, and to my agent, Jennifer Schober, for working so hard to keep me sane.

ONE

We needed to feed.

Tristan's hunger seared my senses, burning through me in a hot, angry wave, until I was pressed against the rough brick wall that lined the alley. My nails dug into the palms of my hands, leaving bloody crescent moons as I hung onto the last tendrils of control over myself and the young nightwalker. Slowly, the consuming desire for blood subsided as the vampire struggled against the red haze. The wave pulled back, dragging across my bare flesh like a bouquet of stinging nettles.

Leaning back, I closed my eyes and drew in a steadying breath in an attempt to get a better grip on myself, but instantly regretted it. The narrow alley was filled with stale, fetid air, laced with rotting meat, mold, and what I could only guess was the smell of a decaying rat or two. Gagging, I lost my hold on Tristan's mind and the next wave of hunger swamped us both, knocking me to my knees.

Across the dingy expanse, Tristan's blue eyes glowed with a light that had nothing to do with heaven or the glory of God. His long fingers were like claws and his nails were dug into the wall behind him as if in one final, desperate attempt to keep himself from attacking the first creature to cross his path. There was little left to him that was human beyond the slender frame that held him. His beautiful features were drawn and lean; a fierce collection of bone and muscle possessed with the need for blood.

Mira.

Tristan's mind reached out and touched my own, but it wasn't his usual soft voice. It was deep, rough, and darkly seductive; matching the rumble that echoed against the ragged remains of my soul. The same monster lived inside of me, craving blood, longing for the feel of my fangs slipping into flesh. It was the monster that demanded I drink so deep I felt the soul of my prey brush against the back of my throat.

The voice in my brain faded, replaced by the cacophony of man. Sweet London, teaming with humans and the thunderous pound of their hearts. The night was so young and fresh, like a fragile girl on her way to her first ball. Tristan and I had escaped to a dark, seedy corner of the old city that overflowed with life calling out in a steady drum beat.

We both needed to feed, desperately. The battle had gone badly, leaving Tristan and me wounded and drained of the very substance that had sustained our existence well beyond what should have been our natural end. We needed blood and we knew I was the only thing keeping him from killing his prey when he finally sank his teeth in. He wouldn't mean to; we didn't need to kill. But there was no moral fiber guiding his decisions any longer. There was only the red wave of blood lust and the need to survive.

At the other end of the block a man with graying brown hair shuffled out of the night and paused at the corner. Cupping his hands before his face, he lit a cigarette and looked around, his heavily lined visage apparent in the lamplight. He gazed up and down the street, the hand holding the cigarette trembling, the little bud of fire twitching in the darkness.

A low growl rose from Tristan's throat as his eyes locked on this prey. I launched myself across the tiny alley and crushed him against the wall. The young vampire snarled at me, fangs bared and blue eyes reduced to narrow slits. He no longer saw me or cared that I could rip him apart without straining myself. I was older and stronger, but he needed blood and nothing was going to stand in his way.

"Wait," I ordered between clenched teeth, my fingers biting into his muscular arms. His clothes were ripped and splattered with blood from our struggle with the naturi earlier in the evening. My thoughts stumbled as the smell of Tristan's blood and that of the naturi mingled in my nose, conjuring up images I didn't want to recall just yet. The battle had been a success only in the sense that we both survived and had the energy to hunt, a failure in that my beloved bodyguard Michael lay cold and dead back at the Themis Compound.

With a grunt, I turned my attention to the man standing on the distant street corner. I had to exert only a little effort to touch his drug-addled brain and draw him over with the misconception that a potential customer had beckoned him, interested in viewing his wares. When the man was standing within the shadows of the narrow alley, I released Tristan and slipped silently back to the opposite wall.

"Don't kill him," I whispered as the nightwalker lunged.

Tristan's prey heard my words and managed a half step backward, his fear spiking so I could feel it cut through the dark alley and the haze of blood lust, but it was too late. I stepped back, pressing against the brick wall as the nightwalker wrapped his arms around the man like a pair of steel bands. I couldn't tear my eyes away and found myself sliding to my knees as Tristan fell to his.

Slipping into the nightwalker's mind, a wave of sensations washed over me, pulling me under. Tristan drank deeply, sucking the intoxicatingly warm blood into his cold body. I could hear his throat muscles convulsively working, sending the thick liquid down into his stomach. To make the feast that much sweeter, he left the man conscious. The drug dealer's heart was pounding in his chest, a single piston hammering away but getting him nowhere. His fear filled the narrow alley, overwhelming the scent of rotting garbage and damp mold, dragging a soft moan across my parted lips. Kneeling on the ground with my hands clenched into fists, I listened to the man's heartbeat start to slow. He had passed out.

"Release him," I said in a hoarse voice. Tristan hesitated but did as I commanded. Laying the man against the wall, he turned to look at me, balanced on the balls of his feet. His blue eyes glittered and danced, rare gems in the darkness.

For the first time since I had met him, Tristan seemed truly alive. At the nightclub with Thorne, he had been on the run, hiding from Sadira, his personality muted by the constant fear of discovery. But now, something within him finally pulsed with new life. It was my promise to help him gain his freedom from our maker. A promise he knew I would do my best to keep.

The scrape and shuffle of footsteps intruded into our dark, bloodsplattered corner of the world. Both of us froze, waiting to see who approached. From the moment Tristan sank his fangs into his meal, I had been cloaking our presence; a natural reflex at this point in my existence rather than a conscious thought. The veil protected us from the sight of any and all nonmagic users. In other words, normal, everyday humans.

At the steady cadence of footsteps, the young nightwalker had thrown up his own protective veil, which was instantly interwoven with my own. He felt stronger now and his thoughts were sharp and clear. I could sense the nervousness that worried the frayed edges of his mind, but he remained as still as stone, and I was confident that he would follow my lead.

A man with short brown hair started past the alley. His walk was brisk and confident. He turned his head toward the alley and his eyes quickly swept the narrow expanse. Tristan and I remained unmoving, waiting. For a moment I felt as if I was somehow both predator and prey. Yet the man's gait never faltered and his gaze returned to the street before him. He didn't see us.

But the witch and werewolf did. Following two steps behind the man with the square jaw was a witch in worn jeans and a lycanthrope in khakis. Her easy walk skidded to a rough halt and her shoulder-length brown hair swung forward to crowd her narrow face. The lycan stopped beside her and frowned, causing heavy lines to furrow his hard face.

"Shit!" The explosive whisper escaped her as she stared at us.

Tristan and I remained frozen, waiting for the intruders to make the first move. Tristan's dinner was still unconscious and mostly hidden behind the young nightwalker. However, we were both covered in blood and our clothes were torn from our fight earlier in the evening. Not one of our most attractive moments. Of course, when it came to the other races, we had all developed a kind of "to each his own" attitude. So we waited. If the witch and lycan resumed walking, we would all pretend we didn't see each other.

We weren't that lucky. The human spun on his heel at the witch's exclamation, grabbing a gun from the small of his back. It had been hidden beneath his loose-fitting, button-up shirt with a garish dragon print. His eyes and gun swept the alley again, but he still did not see us.

The witch reached over and laid her right hand on his broad shoulder. She whispered, *"Specto,"* and I felt a small ripple of power move through the air. The spell could have been performed by nearly any novice with a basic knowledge of Latin, but it was enough. The man blinked once and instantly paled as his grip tightened on the gun. Now he saw us.

"Keep walking," I said in a low voice. I couldn't risk a fight. The need to feed was nearly overwhelming, and if I was forced to fight, there was a very good chance that someone would end up dead. The monster inside me roared and hammered against the inside of my chest like a frantic heartbeat, demanding blood.

Tristan turned his head to look at me, waiting for my direction. Unfortunately, our new friend was trigger-happy. Jerking the gun over to point at the young nightwalker, he squeezed the trigger. With the soft click of the firing pin, Tristan and I were already in motion.

The young vampire fell to the ground, but the bullet slashed across his upper right arm.

Darting across the alley, I grabbed the man's hand as he swung around to point the gun at me. Stupid humans. Even if he shot me in the heart, he wouldn't have succeeded in killing me. Guns couldn't kill a nightwalker. Shotguns could be troublesome, but then the shooter had to get lucky as well. With fangs bared, I slammed his hand into the nearby brick wall, crushing bones. The man screamed as the gun fell from his limp fingers and clattered to the ground. Still holding his hand, I tossed him like a bag of trash over my shoulder into the alley. He hit the wall and crumpled to the ground unconscious.

"Watch him," I growled to Tristan as I turned my attention to the witch and the lycan.

There was no chance to slow down and talk it out. And in truth, I was no longer in the mood for polite conversation. With an ugly snarl, the werewolf launched himself at me, his eyes glowing copper red. He slammed me into the brick wall, pinning my arms between our bodies, but his arms were free. His right first slammed into my left side, cracking at least two ribs. The shock wave of pain that rippled through me cut through the haze of blood lust and fatigue. His left fist followed, hammering my right side, bruising organs still tender from my earlier fight with the naturi.

Grunting under the pain, I jerked my head forward. The top of my forehead connected with his nose, breaking it. He fell back a step and I lifted my knee, slamming it into his groin. The lycanthrope howled in pain, stumbling away. His hands moved from his broken nose to his groin, holding himself as if it would ease the pain. The scent of his blood instantly hit the air.

Any thought of restraint evaporated. I was on him before he could draw a breath. My fangs sank into his throat, tearing the flesh. The blood rushed into me and sweet relief swept through my entire body. It was thick and warm and carried with it the lycan's strength. He fought me, pushing, punching, kicking, and clawing desperately, but I could not be removed. With each swallow, he grew weaker and I grew stronger, slowly draining his life away.

"Mira!" Tristan shouted, finally causing me to lift my head. I let the lycanthrope fall unconscious at my feet. Tristan rushed forward to stand between me and the witch in an attempt to protect me, but she must have assumed he was coming after her.

"No!" she screamed, her small, narrow face a ghostly white. She hadn't moved during my brief scuffle with her companion. I doubt she even breathed. Her wide brown eyes skipped from me to Tristan.

Raising her right hand, she began murmuring an incantation under her breath. I had taken a single step toward her, trying to get in front of Tristan, when her right hand was engulfed in a ball of yellow and orange flames. I paused, a tiny smile toying with my lips. She was smart. Normally, the sight of fire in the hands of a witch would send any nightwalker running for shelter. However, I wasn't just any nightwalker, I was the Fire Starter. Controlling fire had been both my gift and curse since I was a human child. Poor witch.

With a grunt, she hurled the fireball, aiming for Tristan. Reaching out with my right hand, the fire curved toward me and settled in the palm of my open hand. Smiling broadly, I closed my fingers and extinguished the flame, plunging the narrow alley back into darkness.

The witch frowned, confusion clearly written across her pale face. Refusing to admit defeat, she lifted both hands and repeated the spell. This time I could feel the pull of energy in the air. She was putting everything she had into this one. I stepped in front of Tristan as she threw a pair of large fireballs at me.

My eyelids drifted nearly closed and time slowed. The smell of the rotting garbage and the sounds of the people within the city ceased to exist. There was only the fire as it roared at me. With my palm out, I waved my left hand before my body. The flames once again followed my pale hand. They gathered around it for a moment, then slithered up my arm and down my chest like a well-fed python. I could not be burned.

Yet something was off. While my focus was on the fire, I could hear the monster inside me screaming, but it wasn't the roar of hunger I had listened to for more than six centuries. It was a shriek of anger and pain. Suddenly confused and fearful, I redirected the flames to wash down my legs like water. However, the second the fire touched the ground, my senses exploded. The earth was consumed in a blinding white light, scorching my brain. Beneath my feet I could feel an enormous well of power flowing like a river, and the fire was returning to it.

And then nothing. The fire was gone and cold silence crowded around me. The new connection had snapped off before I could even begin to guess at what I'd tapped into. The white light faded. Even the growling hunger inside of me had gone still, possibly with the same wary confusion.

The telltale scrape of a shoe across concrete drew my attention back to the witch. Her arms were tightly wrapped around her middle and she was slowly shaking her head. "Oh, God," she moaned in a hoarse voice. "The Fire Starter. Here."

Before I could take another step toward her, the woman reached into the front pocket of her jeans as she took a step backward and disappeared.

"Damn it," I whispered, fighting back the chill that swept up my spine. She knew who I was. It was one thing for a nightwalker to recognize me on sight. Fear was useful when it came to controlling those who would try to control you. But I didn't like it when the other races discovered my presence. There was no telling who was pissed at me at any given time.

Now the questions became: Where did she go, and was she reporting my presence to someone stronger and meaner? Judging from her age, spell choice, and amount of power used, she wasn't a particularly experienced witch. Furthermore, transportation spells like that were extremely advanced. When she'd reached into her pocket, she must have touched a locator charm, probably created by someone much more powerful.

Frowning, I bit back a curse. This was all idle speculation. I knew a fair amount regarding magic because I had suffered through enough run-ins with witches and warlocks to learn a few things. I needed to talk to Ryan and get his thoughts. Unfortunately, the white-haired warlock was his own bundle of trouble, and I was in no hurry to deal with him again just yet. I would have to manage with the witch's unconscious companions for now.

Turning to approach Tristan, my knees buckled and then I found myself kneeling on the ground. I blinked once to clear the growing fog from around my thoughts. Using fire had sapped the last of my strength, and my body was demanding that I feed again and rest. What strength I had gained from feeding off the werewolf was gone.

The young vampire appeared at my side, a firm hand resting beneath my elbow. I gazed up at him, a worried expression twisting his handsome face. "Has she done something to you?" he inquired. For the first time since meeting him, I heard a soft accent in his speech. French maybe, but different. A remnant of his human life. Slowly, he guided me back to sit on the ground, my back pressed to the brick wall.

"No," I replied with a weary smile. "Just tired. I need to rest a minute." I jerked my head toward the human who had pulled the gun. "Is he still alive?"

"For now," Tristan grumbled, the hand on my elbow tightening as his eyes drifted over to the body of our gunman.

Laying my left hand beneath his chin, I forced him to look at me. "And he'll stay that way. I need you to discover the identity of our attackers without killing him."

Frowning, Tristan rose and returned to the man's side. He stood over the man, his fists on his hips. I couldn't tell whether the nightwalker was stalling out of distaste for the task or if he had begun rummaging through the man's mind. Some nightwalkers had to physically touch their prey to enter his or her mind, especially if the person was unconscious.

"David Perry," Tristan suddenly said, a faintly far-off quality to his voice. His mind was half with me, half with the human. "Thirty-six. Ex-marine. From Birmingham, Alabama. He's—" His words were broken off with a harsh hiss and his eyes glowed pale blue when he looked over at me. "He's a member of the Daylight Coalition."

"Tristan!" I barked, lurching to my feet as the nightwalker started to reach for the unconscious man. He halted, but still growled in the back of his throat, and I couldn't blame him. I would have been happy to rip the human's throat out at that second too.

The Daylight Coalition was a group of humans within the United States who knew of the existence of nightwalkers and sought our total extermination. Humanity believed them to be a cult of insane fanatics and didn't take them seriously. Of course, that didn't erase the fact that members of the Coalition had staked a number of nightwalkers during the daylight hours. Regardless of whether you resided in the United States, all nightwalkers knew of the Coalition. We all feared they were the future we faced if we came "out of the coffin," so to speak.

But for now my concern was not the little zealot at my feet, but the witch and lycan he traveled with. All our information said that the Daylight Coalition was exclusively human, wisely avoided by the other races. In fact it was against our law to work with the Coalition. One turncoat could result in all out war. This was not a good development when we already had a war brewing with the naturi.

"Focus," I snapped, standing beside Tristan. "Who was the woman?"

Tristan stared down at the man, radiating a lethal mix of anger and fear. "Caroline . . . Caroline Buckberry, but he wondered if it was her real name . . ." The anger started to ebb as his focus tightened on the man's thoughts, causing his eyes to drift closed. "He didn't know her. He was sent by the Houston branch to fetch the woman and the man. Harold Finchley. That's all." Tristan opened his eyes again and looked up at me. "He was told to go to London and bring them back to Houston. I don't think he even knew what they were."

"He didn't have to know," I murmured. "Perry is just a foot soldier. He follows the orders he's given."

"Do you think they were to be plants by the witches and lycans?" Tristan inquired. I didn't miss the hopeful note in his voice.

"No," I replied with a slight shake of my head. "The witches and warlocks have no business with the Coalition. Either one of them could have said something to explain their association with the human. But instead they attacked because they know the law."

"But—"

"Forget what you saw," I said, cutting off his next comment. "We have bigger problems."

"The naturi." His hands curled into fists and the muscles in his jaw tightened.

Yes, the naturi were coming and they would destroy us all, human and nightwalker, if given half a chance. In comparison, the Daylight Coalition was nothing; a fly on a rhino's ass.

Standing, I propped my right shoulder against the alley wall and let my eyes drift shut for a moment. I hardly recognized my world anymore. A few nights ago I had been standing in my own domain back in my beloved Savannah, the warm summer air filled with the scent of honeysuckle and lilacs. It had been five hundred years since that night on Machu Picchu. The naturi were a distant memory, a dark nightmare from my past that could no longer touch me. The Daylight Coalition was just a fringe group with no contact with the others. But now both were threatening. My world was crumbling at an alarming rate and it all started with the hunter, Danaus. But there was no need to kill the messenger . . . yet.

Thoughts of him brought a faint smile to my lips as I pushed off the wall and opened my eyes. Tristan was watching me intently, waiting. He needed me alive to fulfill my promise to him. There was still time.

Briefly, I looked around the alley until I located the gun the human had used. There was no hesitation. There was no gray area in this law. Standing close, I fired a single bullet into the head of the lycanthrope. He had betrayed not only his own kind, but all the other races. He endangered our secret. And now he paid the cost with his life.

But his death didn't dissolve the cold knot in my stomach. The Daylight Coalition's main target had always been nightwalkers, but we were all confident they would attack any nonhumans eventually. Had Harold Finchley been a wolf acting alone, or was he part of a larger movement against nightwalkers?

"Wipe the memories of both men," I said, motioning toward the drug dealer Tristan had fed from only minutes ago. Walking over to the Coalition member, I wiped the gun off on his shirt and dropped it by his body. "Then return to my hotel room." Danaus would already be waiting there for us. From the hotel, we would head to the airport and grab my jet to Venice. If we were to have any hope of stopping the naturi and the coming war, we would need to first go to Venice and meet with the nightwalker Coven. They would know the best way to deal with the growing threat. They were the only ones who could summon an army.

"Where are you going?" Tristan asked.

A broad smile lifted my lips, revealing a pair of long white fangs. "To hunt."

TWO

I ran several blocks, merging with the shadows until I was nearly a mile from Tristan. A horrible trembling had started in my limbs and began to vibrate through my entire body. I throbbed and ached with a mixture of fresh wounds sustained during the past few hours and old wounds not completely healed from the night before. The world was an angry swirl of pain and noise and glaring lights. Pushing it all aside, my focus narrowed to a single pinpoint of finding prey.

Hunting had been a solitary act almost from the moment I was reborn. For me, it was a personal moment. Most nights I was particular about my prey, choosing him or her based on history or personal philosophy. I would listen to my prey's thoughts until something finally enticed me to move. And then there were nights like tonight, where I grabbed the first poor fool to cross my path.

She was nineteen, and for a second she thought I was a rapist. Grabbing a handful of her dark brown hair, I jerked her into the deep shadows of a doorway. She pushed against me, tears gathering in her wide hazel eyes. I sunk my fangs into her throat as a scream rose to her lips. Out of some latent kindness, I pushed her thoughts down into a deep sleep as I drank. Swallowing her blood, I let its warmth and life fill me, and I drank until my memory of the night grew blurry and distant. The monster in my chest, hiding behind the remnants of my soul, was briefly appeased by the offering.

Reluctantly, I released her as her heart slowed to a lethargic beat. Holding her in my arms, I stared down at her smooth young face. I didn't know her. She could have been a college student or a young mother on her way home. I hadn't taken the time to sift around in her thoughts, learn her hopes or her fears. I didn't know her dreams for the future and I felt cheated. Hunting and feeding were more than a power rush. It was my last contact with humanity, the last thing that kept me bound to a race I had once been a part of. While I felt rejuvenated, a more subtle ache had started in my chest. A type of weariness that might have worried me if I allowed myself to dwell on it, but there simply wasn't time.

I gently sat her against the doorjamb and healed the wound on her neck. It was a gift of evolution, I think. We could heal the puncture wound caused by our fangs so we could remain hidden. Unfortunately, I couldn't heal knife or bullet wounds, forcing me to watch more than one injured human companion die in my arms.

Before leaving, I wiped her memory clean. It was better that my kind not be remembered just yet. But it was more than a need for our own protection. She didn't need to recall the momentary horror of being held in my arms.

On my way back to the hotel I fed twice more, using the same care as with the young woman. While I never bother to learn their names, they would never remember that they had been stopped. I walked down the winding London streets, angling back toward the river as I slipped through the crowd of people. Those few remaining on the lamplit streets were oblivious to my presence. My bloodstained appearance would have caused a panic.

The night air was thick with moisture, as if the skies were preparing to open up in a late night summer shower. A slim mist hovered just above the ground and wound its way around the occasional tree. Thin and wispy, it seemed little more than a ghost, or maybe the forgotten soul of this old town.

Wandering the streets, I let the warm summer air dance around me as I thought of my home in Savannah and walking along River Street. After a night of entertainment at the bars in the area, I would stroll through one park after another that dotted the neat little city, heading back toward Forsyth Park. I would smile at the scantily clad young people as they hurried to and from the row of bars, restaurants, and nightclubs, oblivious to me even if I wasn't using an enchantment. Their laughter and voices lowered to rough, giggly whispers skipped about me like leaves caught up in a breeze, bringing a twinkle of amusement to my eyes.

At Forsyth Park, I would pause at the enormous fountain bathed in yellow lights. Seated on the edge, I'd close my eyes and listen to the steady hum of traffic as it swirled around me. The leaves would rattle and the Spanish moss sway in the breeze, whispering to me old tales of love and death and loneliness. From there I could feel the pulse of the people in my city.

But trudging along the streets of London, covered in dried naturi blood, I couldn't hear my city or the soft murmur of laughter from her people. For the first time in a very long time, I was homesick. I missed my city's streets, dotted with old oak trees and tidy little parks. I missed her fountains and the river that caressed her banks. I would have liked to see her one last time; to stroll along the historic district and gaze up at row after row of vintage homes restored to their pre–Civil War beauty. To enjoy just one last dance at the Docks, where the music pounded in loud, angry beats and the air was thick with the scent of sweat and blood.

Just days ago I had been queen of my little mountain, or as we preferred to say: Keeper of my domain. Then Danaus waltzed in and destroyed my world. The vampire hunter brought news that the naturi were threatening to escape their bindings and enter our world for the first time in centuries. While Danaus obviously held no love for nightwalkers, he at least understood that the naturi were worse.

Guardians of the earth for centuries, the naturi had finally decided that the only way to truly protect the earth was to destroy all of mankind. So a war was waged over countless years, resulting in the deaths of hundreds of naturi, humans, and nightwalkers. We finally succeeded in locking most of the naturi in another world, separate from earth but forever linked. But it was temporary. With naturi on both sides of the seal working to open the doorway, we knew it would be a constant struggle to keep them contained. A triad of nightwalkers kept the seal protected, but all went strangely quiet for roughly five centuries, and despite our long memories, we forgot to pass along information to the fledglings we created.

The end result was a series of deaths that should have never occurred. After nights of struggling to reform the nightwalker triad that sealed the naturi host away, I not only failed to protect Thorne, who was to join the triad, but also lost my precious bodyguard. Michael, my guardian angel with golden locks. Adding to my worries, I discovered that I was to be the weapon wielded by the triad, which now included a vampire hunter.

With a sigh, I looked up and found myself standing in front of the Savoy. It was time to return to the task of saving the world. I was tempted to say the hell with it all, but I would be losing my beloved city as well. And if I didn't protect it, who would?

Smiling grimly, I slipped inside the hotel and rode the elevator up to my room, where Tristan and Danaus were patiently waiting for me. Well, one more patiently than the other.

When I opened the door, Tristan was lounging on the sofa, hands behind his head, ankles crossed. His cheeks were flushed and he radiated blissful satisfaction. He had fed again after I left him and was obviously feeling quite pleased. It also probably helped that he'd showered and was clean of all the blood that once covered him. He was still wearing his bloodstained clothes, but I knew he couldn't care less. There was something about having a full stomach that made a nightwalker much more tolerant and amiable. It also didn't hurt that Sadira, our controlling maker, was already in Venice, giving him an extended break from her.

The vampire hunter, on the other hand, was standing at the window, arms folded across his chest. He was still in his torn, bloodstained clothes, but like Tristan, the blood had been washed from his skin. His dirty hair was pulled back from his face, revealing high, strong cheekbones and vibrant eyes of deep cerulean blue. His chin and jaw were covered in a shadow of dark stubble, giving him an even grimmer appearance than usual. I imagine he wasn't used to patiently waiting around for anyone, much less a nightwalker.

Shaking my head at him, I wordlessly darted through the suite to the bathroom. I quickly stripped out of my clothes and turned on the hot water. I had just stepped under the spray when I heard the bathroom door open.

"We have to leave," Danaus said irritably.

"I'm not traveling like this," I shouted over the noise of the falling water. "Five minutes."

Danaus grunted, leaving me to assume that he accepted my decision and was going to wait "patiently" in the other room. The hunter was a puzzle I was positively itching to work on, particularly with his informative, monosyllabic replies guiding me. Yet, for all his irritation and threats, I was becoming accustomed to his presence.

"Wait!" I called out when I heard him turn the door handle to leave. With my left hand, I grabbed a handful of the mauve shower curtain and pulled it back just enough to poke my head out. I cracked one eye as water ran down my face. Danaus stood half turned toward me, with the bathroom door partially open so he could beat a quick retreat if he needed to.

"What do you know about the Daylight Coalition?" I asked, running my right hand over my face to get some of the water out of my eyes.

Danaus released the door handle and gave the door a little push shut. Folding his arms across his broad chest, he leaned his hip against the white marble sink. "Just humans hunting vampires. Sounds like a good cause to me." His hard face was expressionless but his sharp eyes were intent upon my face.

Throwing one last scowl at him, I jerked the shower curtain closed and moved back under the water. As I grabbed the washcloth to resume scrubbing, Danaus laughed. Actually, the hunter didn't make a sound, but I could feel him laughing on the inside. He was teasing me, trying to get under my skin.

Earlier in the evening he had touched my hand and sent his powers through me. Our connection was still strong when we were in close proximity. We had killed the naturi and survived, but we were still working out all of the repercussions. I couldn't quite make out his thoughts, but his emotions flowed easily to me. And I had a feeling he could just as easily pick out my emotions.

"Bastard," I grumbled, scrubbing my right forearm. I did not doubt that he heard me over the water. I didn't know what Danaus was, but he wasn't human. At least, not all of him. He felt human, but his hearing appeared to be as keen as any nightwalker's. He had the speed and agility of a lycanthrope, but not their strength. He couldn't cast spells like a warlock, but had a dark ability that allowed him to boil a creature's blood within its skin. At the very least, this combination had taught me to be wary of him.

"They're fanatics," Danaus said after a moment. His voice sounded tired, worn down to a smooth murmur. "They've killed as many humans as they have actual vampires. Why?"

"Tristan and I encountered a trio tonight," I said. I soaped up the washcloth again and ran it over my stomach, relieved to find the hideous gash I received that night was completely healed. "No, that's wrong. We encountered a member of the Coalition, a lycan, and a witch."

"Traveling together?"

"Yes. The man had been sent to fetch the witch and lycan."

"Did you kill them?"

"Danaus!" I shouted, my fist tightening around the wet washcloth.

"Did you?"

Throwing down the washcloth, I turned and pulled back the shower curtain again so I could look at him. "Does it matter that they attacked us first and they were trying to kill us?" I snapped.

"No." While his face and voice were calm when he replied, I felt the flutter of something else in his chest. A flash of anger and frustration.

Maybe a bit of fear. But he had his emotions back under tight wrap before I could clearly identify any of the swirling maelstroms within his mind.

"The human is still alive," I said between clenched teeth, jerking the curtain back into place, the metal rings holding up the divider letting out a little squeal. "I broke the man's hand and knocked him out. The witch disappeared after trying to flambé Tristan and me."

"And the werewolf?"

"The lycan is dead," I bit out. Werewolves can heal from a lot of things, but a bullet in the head while you're low on blood isn't something you come back from. "He broke our law. If I hadn't, he might have told the Coalition about us all." I said the words and believed the rationale, but something knotted in my stomach for a second time. It was my complete lack of remorse. The fact that I hadn't even hesitated in my decision to kill him. Knox, my assistant in Savannah, once called me a mindless killing machine. The description had been kind.

I stood under the hot water, trying to wash away the memory of the encounter and Danaus's words. Our occasional teasing and joking meant nothing to him. My respect for his skill and his sense of honor were worthless. In the end he wanted all of my kind dead. He wanted me dead because he saw me only as a killer

"Damn it, you're missing the point," I said into the water.

"No, I'm not." His words were softer than they had been. "A witch and a lycan were traveling with a member of the Daylight Coalition. I'll call Ryan and see if he knows anything. Do you know the name of the witch?"

"Caroline Buckberry," I sighed. "That might be an alias, but I'd wager she's a local. Or at least, her mentor is."

"Why?"

"I think she used a charm to disappear, and judging by the amount of power I felt in the air, I'd guess she didn't travel far. She's a novice."

"I'll check with Themis. Ryan might know something."

"Thank you," I whispered, not caring if he heard me over the water.

"I understand why you did it, Mira," he said. I hadn't heard him move, but he sounded closer, as if he were just on the other side of the shower curtain. "You did it to protect us all. I understand it, but I don't have to like it."

I listened to the sound of the door opening and closing, a frown pulling at my lips. Bracing both of my hands against the wall in front of me, I closed my eyes and put my face into the water, wishing it could drown out my thoughts.

But I couldn't. It was the "us" that caught my attention. It was the first time I had ever heard Danaus include himself with the other races, admitting for a brief moment that we were linked in some strange way. The knot in my stomach eased.

With a sigh, I returned to the task of washing off a layer of dried blood from the earlier battle at Themis and Stonehenge.

In the grand scheme of things, the Daylight Coalition was a minor annoyance. For now, I would leave it to Ryan and his people at Themis to investigate—that was what they did. Themis was a bunch of gray-haired librarians who studied all the races that were different from humans and wrote down their findings in thick, leather-bound volumes.

Of course, Themis also had its group of hunters; trained assassins dispatched for the sole purpose of killing my kind and anyone else who stepped out of line. Ryan had smiled at me and said that it was all in the interest of maintaining the secret, protecting mankind from the knowledge that vampires and werewolves were real. But I trusted the warlock about as far as I could throw him. Probably less.

With a frustrated groan, I turned off the water and quickly dried off. Rubbing my hair to dry as much of the water as possible, I stepped out of the bathroom and into the master bedroom, where I pulled open my bag. Clean clothes. Sometimes it's the little things in this life that can pick up a person's mood. I had worn my last outfit through my meeting with James Parker at the Themis town house, Thorne's death, my fight with Jabari, my fight with the naturi, and the naturi encounter at Stonehenge. I tossed the pants and shirt into the trash can, resisting the urge to set them on fire. Burning the clothes wouldn't purge the memory of the past two nights.

Quickly, I pulled on semiclean clothes and shouldered my bag. Dawn was only a few hours away and we had to be in Venice before the sun rose. The Coven was demanding we make an appearance. And the ruling nightwalker body would not be denied anything it wanted.

THREE

I hesitated at the bottom of the stairs leading up to my little jet. Instead of winging me back across the ocean toward home, it was carrying me into the dark heart of the nightwalker empire, the Coven. Jabari would claim it was for my own protection; I had no doubt that the Elders had some other dark scheme in mind. Of course, I had no say in the matter. Running would only make it worse. And I still had to figure out a way to protect Danaus and Tristan.

With a grimace, I climbed on and came face-to-face with the young nightwalker. Tristan stood in the middle of the plane, his hands resting on his slender hips as he looked around the pristine white interior. His eyes settled on me after a moment, with one brow arched in question.

"White?" he inquired, amusement cavorting through his voice. I swept past him, ignoring his comment. What could I say? I thought the black clothes were enough of a stereotype.

"Contact Sadira," I snapped, noticing the way his smile slipped at the mention of our maker. Neither of us was in any great hurry to see her again. I had escaped her "tender care" nearly five centuries ago only to find myself faced with the controlling vampire once again. Tristan had recently escaped, but was recaptured by me as I'd been unwittingly manipulated by her.

"Tell her to have a taxi waiting when we arrive," I ordered as I dropped my bag on the floor. "We're going to be cutting it that close." Lounging on one of the long benches that lined the interior of the plane, I tried to keep up the appearance of being completely unconcerned with the fact that we were flying to Venice, with sunrise only four hours away.

"Anything else, Mistress?" he asked with an elegant bow. I frowned at the nightwalker. Get him away from Sadira and he turns into a sarcastic ass, I thought. Just what I needed. I already had my hands full with Danaus, the Coven, and the naturi; I didn't need to worry about a young nightwalker now that he was away from his master. But I also had a sickening feeling in my stomach that he was confident I would find a way to free him from Sadira's grasp. Desperation made me promise to help him. At the time, I'd been sure that one of us wouldn't survive the encounter. I was wrong, and now I was stuck.

"Go to the back and take a nap," I grumbled.

I watched him as he took a couple steps toward the back of the jet, where a tiny bedroom lay behind a door. But he paused before reaching the door, seeming to hesitate.

"Go ahead," I called. "Say it."

"Why go?" Tristan's voice was barely over a whisper when he finally spoke, as if fearful of some kind of punishment for questioning me. He turned and his eyes held that same haunted look they had just a couple nights ago in that London alley. Fearful. Hopeless. "We've got a jet. Let's go west. As far from the Coven as we can get."

"And spend an eternity running from the Coven? From the naturi?" I rose to my feet and slowly approached him. His narrow shoulders curled inward, his body tensing for an expected blow. "There is nowhere to run. Jabari will hunt us down. The naturi will hunt us down. If we go to the Coven now, they can raise an army and we can finally stop the naturi from freeing their queen."

"What about the Coven?"

I smiled at him and brushed the tips of my fingers along the side of his face. "Others have survived facing the Coven. It just takes a little finesse."

"The Coven needs you alive."

"And I promised to keep to you," I said with a shrug. "So, if I live, you live."

A cynical smile twisted on Tristan's lips, failing to lift any of the doubt from his eyes. But he nodded once before turning and disappearing in the tiny back bedroom. He knew there was no escaping our destination. We would go before the Coven. If we were to defeat the naturi, we would need their assistance.

I bit back a sigh as I returned to the bench I had been sitting on. It wasn't a great plan, but at least it was something. As I stretched out my legs and tried to relax, Danaus stepped onto the jet.

A surprised smile tweaked the corners of my mouth as he sat on the bench across from me. It was only a few days ago since we

boarded the jet together for the first time. He had been tense and uneasy as we headed off to search for clues as to how the naturi were
attempting to break free of their cage. Now he seemed almost relaxed. I was no longer a threat. At this point we both had darker
things to worry about than what we could do to each other.

"What?" he asked in a wary, near growl.

"You're still here," I replied. His blue eyes narrowed. I waved one
hand at him, brushing off his dark look. "I didn't mean it quite like
that. I thought we would have parted ways by now, whether through
your death or not."

One thick dark brow quirked at me. "I've thought the same." I
think he was taunting me. It was hard to tell. His thoughts and emotions had grown distant and hazy again, while his expression retreated
to its usual unreadable stone. The link we had established through
our combined powers had faded to almost nothingness. My aware-
ness of him was now obscured by the cloak of energy that wrapped
around him.

"So I've heard. Ryan said you've been itching to cut my heart out.
Do you plan to keep it as a trophy?" That finally earned me a frown
while my own smile widened. "Regardless of your plans for my various body parts, we'll have to keep working together if we hope to
survive the next few nights. Trust me, I'm not pleased. You're giving
me a bad reputation."

Danaus chuckled quietly, and for a brief moment his features
softened. Through that slim window of time, I glimpsed sight of a
beautiful man. His weariness and shadow of worry melted away. Normally, with his glares and frowns, he was a virile creature exuding
strength and power. Yet when he smiled and laughed, his humanity
shone through a break in the clouds. It was a strange combination.
Danaus had somehow found a way to be human without all the usual
human frailty.

And then I realized I no longer wanted to kill him. Lurching to
my feet with none of my usual grace, I paced to the back of the jet, a
curse on the tip of my tongue. Was I going soft? Had I lost my edge?

But just because I didn't want to kill him didn't automatically
mean I saw him as a comrade in arms. He was a strong fighter, and it
was nice having someone at my back who could take care of himself.
Danaus wasn't as frail as my beloved angels, but he also didn't have
their warmth and compassion.

Stretching my arms above my head as best as I could in the jet, I
shook off the strange realization. Danaus was probably still in my
head, mucking up my thoughts. It would pass, I tried to reassure my-

self. So he wasn't on my to-kill list anymore. That could change easily enough, and probably would during our stay in Venice.

"Can he hear us?" Danaus suddenly inquired, motioning with his head toward the closed door at the opposite end of the jet.

I paused as I paced back toward the bench opposite him, my brows bunched over the bridge of my nose in confusion. "Why?"

"We need to talk." Those ominous words rumbled in his chest before finally finding an exit from his lips. I could guess at what he wanted to talk about and I was in no rush, but it had to be done. Mentally reaching out, I brushed Tristan's mind and found him stretched out on the bed in the back of the jet. With a little shove, I pushed him deeper into sleep, where he would stay until the jet landed.

"Tristan is asleep. He can't hear us," I said, sitting on the bench across from Danaus. I stretched out my legs and crossed them at the ankle, trying my best to affect a relaxed posture when all the muscles in my body seemed to be tense and waiting. "What is it that we're keeping quiet?"

"What happened. Have you ever done that before?"

I didn't have to ask what he was talking about. Hours ago Danaus, Tristan, Jabari, Sadira, and I had been at the Themis Compound, surrounded by naturi. It seemed that we were dead. There was no escape, nothing to swoop in and save us. In a last desperate attempt, Danaus and I agreed to use our powers: boiling blood and fire. If we survived, we'd be exhausted and at the mercy of our "comrades." Instead Danaus somehow pushed his powers into me, his deep voice echoing through my brain as I destroyed them all. And not just the ones at Themis. I had killed every member of the naturi within several miles of the Compound.

"Incinerated someone? Yes," I said, purposefully vague. I wanted to hear him say the words. I needed to know that I wasn't alone in what I felt.

"That's not what happened and you know it," Danaus snarled. He flinched at the loudness of his voice as if afraid he would wake Tristan. He couldn't, but I wasn't about to disillusion him. I didn't need him yelling at me. I had enough on my mind without an irate vampire hunter to worry about. "We destroyed their souls," he continued in a low, heavy voice.

I remained silent. Was there anything I could say that wouldn't sound lame? Not really. Maybe a part of me was hoping I'd been wrong. But I wasn't. Danaus had felt the same thing.

"I'm assuming you couldn't do that before," I finally said.

"No!" he shouted, lurching to his feet. His hands opened and closed restlessly at his sides twice before he finally returned to his seat, his emotions once again under control. "No, I haven't. I can't do that. I've never heard of any creature doing that." His voice was a little calmer than before, but it was a forced calm. Panicking would solve nothing, not that I wouldn't have enjoyed the brief luxury.

"Then why did you force me to do it?" My own voice turned even harder and colder than I meant it to. I hated the naturi with every ounce of my being, but even so, destroying another creature's soul? It . . . it was an unspeakable act, something that smacked of true evil.

"I didn't force you to do anything!" he said, jerking his eyes back to my face.

"I heard your voice in my head. You told me to kill them. You told me to kill them all."

"Not like that."

"I tried to crush their hearts or set them on fire but you wouldn't let me." I shifted uncomfortably, placing both of my feet flat on the floor as I moved to the edge of my seat.

"I didn't stop you from doing anything." Danaus shoved one hand through his thick black hair, pushing some strands away from his exquisite blue eyes. I could almost sense the frustration humming through his muscular frame, building in him as he recalled events from earlier in the evening. "The moment I touched your hand, it felt like my powers had been amplified. Considering we were outnumbered and about to die, I didn't think this was a bad thing."

"And that's all?" I asked, failing to keep the skepticism from my voice.

Danaus took another deep breath and held it for a moment. "I could hear your thoughts," he finally admitted, his voice near a whisper. His eyes moved away from my face, dropping down to his hands, which rested half open on his thighs. "You were scared and in pain. I just kept thinking, 'kill them. Kill them and the pain will stop.' " He paused and I could feel his anger starting to ebb. The faint smell of the sea filled the cabin, seeming to cleanse the air. Danaus's unique scent. My eyes drifted closed, letting his voice brush against my cheek. "I didn't tell you to destroy their souls. I didn't think such a thing was possible and I would never have asked that."

"I didn't think so, but this is all new to me. I wanted to be sure." My head fell back against the bench. I didn't want to think about this anymore. There were no answers for what had happened or for what I knew would happen again.

Danaus let a deep, heavy silence slip back into the little jet, holding us together in the gathering darkness. It was several minutes later before he bothered to speak again. Neither of us wanted to think about this anymore, but certain questions had to be answered before we reached Venice and the Coven.

"How is it that I can . . ."

"Control me?" I finished the statement that seemed to get stuck in his throat; whether because he had a sudden concern for my feelings or just a distaste for the ability, I didn't know. Despite my own carefully crafted facade, I couldn't keep the bitterness from my tone. Jabari could control me. Sadira could. While he lived, so could Tabor. The original three members of the triad, and my makers. And now Danaus.

"I've been around enough vampires throughout my life. What I felt when I touched you . . ." Again his voice died, and I let the sentence wither away before I spoke.

"I can answer only part of that question. Jabari and Sadira and potentially other nightwalkers can control me because I was . . . made differently." I paused, nearly choking on the word. This story was not supposed to go this way. All the popular tales told of a chosen one, a child born under a particular star that was supposed to rise up and lead the downtrodden to redemption and victory. Well, this so-called "chosen one" was a tool, a weapon, a nightmare that could just as easily destroy my kind as lead them to salvation, and I hated it.

Frowning, my eyes darted around the interior of the plane as I tried to frame my explanation. "There are two ways to make a nightwalker. The first is quick, easy, obviously the most common. A nightwalker drains a human of his blood and replaces it with the nightwalker's blood at the exact second of death. The next night the human rises a nightwalker. It takes a few centuries for these vampires to gain any significant powers. These humans are reborn as nightwalkers to serve as a form of entertainment for their master. They're not expected to live long existences and rarely outlast their masters."

"Why?"

A grim smile skipped unchecked across my face, causing the hunter to stiffen. "Because many of our entertainments are lethal, even for nightwalkers. Among my kind, these quickly made nightwalkers are commonly referred to as chum."

"Is Tristan . . . chum?" Danaus asked, the term falling from his lips like something distasteful.

"Yes, but I wouldn't call him that to his face."

"I guessed as much," he murmured under his breath.

"Most nightwalkers are made this way. It takes little effort and dedication to the task."

"Have you ever . . . ?"

"No." My hands gripped the edge of my seat for a moment as I sat straight up. "I have never made a nightwalker, nor will I." With a shake of my head, I relaxed again and sat back. There were enough of us roaming the earth.

Closing my eyes, I listened to the steady rhythm of Danaus's heartbeat, the sound barely rising about the dulled roar of the jet engine. The beat was soothing, wiping away my momentary anxiety. I didn't create nightwalkers.

"But I wasn't made that way, and up until a couple nights ago I thought that Sadira was my only creator." I paused again, licking my lips as I searched for the words. "There are three stages of death. The first is that the body stops breathing, then the heart stops, and then finally the soul leaves the body. When I was made, the transformation was started before my soul had left my body. Sadira worked slowly and carefully to make sure my soul never escaped from my body.

"The process takes years—sometimes decades—to complete, but when the nightwalker finally awakens, he is stronger and more powerful than those newly born chum. Some believe that by retaining the soul throughout the whole process, the nightwalker attains a higher level of power. In general, those made this way are stronger, more powerful, and harder to kill. They are called First Bloods."

"So Tristan doesn't have a soul?"

"He does," I growled, lurching to my feet. I didn't like to hear those words uttered. It was a very old myth that vampires were soulless creatures, a myth that many humans still believed. And they would use that archaic belief to hunt us down when they discovered we existed.

Staring down at a tired Danaus, I forced myself to relax. He had meant nothing by the question and I knew I'd overreacted. My nerves were growing rawer the closer we got to Venice. Flopping back down, I bit off a sigh. "When the body is reanimated with the vampire blood, the soul is called back to the body. But when the sun rises, he dies again and the soul leaves. Of course, this is all theory."

"And you?"

"They speculate that I don't technically die like the rest at sunrise. Sadira thinks it's why I'm able to dream when the others cannot," I said with a shake of my head.

"Why did she make you like that?"

"If she is to be believed, it was what Jabari wanted," I replied. "I was kidnapped centuries ago because of my ability to control fire. When they feared the plague would take my human life, they decided to make me a nightwalker. However, Jabari wanted to see if I could retain my ability, and the best chance of that was to make me a First Blood."

"Jabari's blood is in your veins."

"And Sadira's. And Tabor's. The original members of the triad." And two of the four members of the Coven. Some of the most powerful nightwalkers in existence, then and now. "They believe they and some of their progeny can control me because their blood is a part of me."

"But I'm not a nightwalker. Never have been, never will be," Danaus said.

I bit back a comment about how there was still time. There was nothing to be gained by antagonizing him right now. He had enough problems in the form of the Coven and every vampire in Venice wanting a piece of his nightwalker-hunting hide. "You? I have no idea. Since you refuse to tell me what you are, I can only guess you're a freak of nature like me and that must give you some kind of strange edge."

"Do the others know what really happened?" Danaus demanded, deftly changing the subject. He wasn't going to tell me yet, but I liked to think I would have the truth out of him before his last breath.

"I don't think so," I said with a sigh on my lips. "If they had, I don't think we would have made it out of Themis alive; naturi or not. It would be best if we kept the full extent of what we can do to ourselves. We are about to head into the heart of the nightwalker hierarchy. It might be a good idea not to give them any more reasons to crush us into the dirt."

"You don't think they will when we arrive in Venice?"

"At the moment, they might be kind enough to wait until after we stop the naturi," I said with a frail chuckle, lifting my head to look at him.

"Lucky us," Danaus grimly said. "You expect to survive the next few nights?"

"Not really." A carefree shrug lifted my slim shoulders. "But that doesn't mean I'm not going to try."

"Then you have a plan for when we hit Venice," he prodded.

I smiled back at him, extending my legs out in front of me with my ankles crossed. The leather seat crinkled and crackled beneath me. "I have some ideas, but no specific plan. I work better off the cuff," I said, causing his expression to grow even darker. I couldn't blame him. We were in yet another situation in which he would have to trust me to protect him from my kind. Not a comfortable position, considering he had killed many of us during his extremely long career as a hunter.

"You're going to try to talk your way out of death?" Danaus guessed, sounding incredulous as he sat forward on the edge of the bench.

"I plan to bluff, cajole, grandstand, and outright lie if necessary to save my skin," I said, and laughed, throwing open my arms. One of the most powerful nightwalkers in existence wanted me dead. I had nothing to lose any longer.

"And sacrifice me when the opportunity presents itself," Danaus finished, shoving to his feet. I rose as well and stepped closer so only a couple of feet of empty space were separating us. It felt odd being that close without weapons drawn.

"I bear the Elders no love," I said. "Jabari was the only one who once resided in my heart and he crushed that before departing Themis. "On the other hand, you've saved my life on more than one occasion. I don't know your rationale behind it and at the moment I don't care," I quickly finished, holding up my hand before he could interject any of his reasons for prolonging my life, which I'm sure were on the tip of his tongue. It didn't look good for a hunter of his caliber to go around saving nightwalkers. "We will walk into Venice together and we will walk out together, I promise." I held out my hand to him. Danaus stared into my eyes for a long time, weighing my words before he finally took my hand and shook it, sealing the bargain.

"And after?" he demanded, his hand still tightly gripping mine.

"After Venice? Assuming we both actually survive, we get back to the business of trying to kill each other like nature intended," I mocked, releasing his rough, callused hand. A half smile briefly lifted one corner of his mouth as he sat back down.

"All I ask is that you keep your mouth shut and trust me," I said, looking down at him. "It's not an impossible task. You're a hunter. I have no doubt that you've slaughtered countless nightwalkers. You're not exactly winning over many friends."

"It's not my goal in life," he said, sounding grumpy.

"I believe that," I muttered as I returned to my seat. Draping my body over the bench, I listened to the roar of the engines. Even if I did live long enough to finally gain the ability to fly, I would still use my pretty little jet. Besides the obvious comfort, I liked listening to the moan of the air rushing past the windows and the roar of the engine.

As the plane carried us closer to Italy, Danaus bent down and started digging around in the large black duffel bag near his feet. I could hear the clang and ping of metal striking metal as he sifted around in his trusty bag of weapons. I was sorry that I'd left the sword I used at Themis behind, but my hands were full of Tristan at the time. My mind hadn't been on proper weaponry for our trip to Venice. Lucky for me, Danaus remembered to grab his bag of tricks from the hotel. He might have even made a pit stop for extra toys at the Themis town house where we met James Parker.

After a moment he sat back with a gun in his hand. He quickly checked the magazine before standing and walking over to me. My eyes briefly flit from the gun he was holding out to me and back to his face questioningly.

"Guns seem to be effective against the naturi," he said when I had yet to move. I stared at the gun for a second, frowning. I didn't like guns. They were so impersonal. They were also ineffective when dealing with nightwalkers. Being shot just pissed vampires off and didn't slow them down much. We also hadn't fought the naturi on a regular basis in several centuries, so most of us never bothered to learn how to use a gun.

With a frown, I finally took the weapon from him, holding the grip between two fingers away from my body like a piece of rotting garbage. Growling in frustration, Danaus took the gun back and sat down next to me. "It's a Browning Hi-Power loaded with 9mm bullets," he explained, letting it rest in the palm of his hand. "The magazine holds fifteen bullets." With a couple of deft motions with his fingers, he showed me how to load the magazine and turn off the safety. My knowledge of guns didn't extend much further than pointing and squeezing the trigger. I had no desire to learn any more than that, but if I was faced with another naturi, the Browning was going to feel a whole lot better in my hand than a knife.

"I'm guessing you can manage that," Danaus taunted, trying to get a rise out of me.

"I'll manage," I almost growled, the two words squeezing between my clenched teeth. "Holster?"

He returned to the opposite bench and pulled a leather double shoulder holster out of his bag. He tossed it across the jet and I caught it with my empty hand. It was made of a supple, dark brown leather and was adjustable so I didn't have to worry about it being too bulky. Unfortunately I wasn't wearing a belt so I wouldn't be able to use the belt-securing ties. While I was strapping on the shoulder holster, Danaus brought over a second gun.

"It's a Glock 17 with 9mm rounds," he said as I accepted the gun and placed it in the right holster. The Browning went in the left. I looked down at myself and frowned. A nightwalker carrying guns. It seemed almost sacrilegious, if that was possible. We were graceful creatures from the Old World. When we killed, it was either with our bare hands or a blade.

"Is it wrong that the refrain from 'Janie's Got a Gun' keeps running through my head?" I moaned. Danaus made a noise in the back of his throat as he quickly looked away, but not before I saw his lips quirk in a half smile. "What? You don't like Aerosmith?" I asked.

"No! I—" He halted and shook his head, no longer fighting the smile. "Aerosmith is fine. I was thinking of another song."

"Which one?"

When he looked up at me, his smile was gone, but laughter danced in his eyes. " 'Sympathy for the Devil,' " he answered.

"Ha ha. Real funny, hunter," I said snidely. "At least it's the Stones."

"Nope. Guns N' Roses," he corrected, one corner of his mouth quirked in a grin. I snorted in disgust but couldn't stop the smile that settled on my lips. However, when I looked back down at the guns hugging my frame, a sigh escaped my lips and the smile disintegrated.

"It's not that bad," Danaus said, interrupting my thoughts.

I just glared at him. He had no idea how bad it was.

His weary sigh seemed more show than exasperation as he returned to his bag one last time and quickly withdrew a long sword and scabbard. With a deep chuckle, I snatched the weapon from his hand and clutched it against my chest. The hilt and grip were of simple design, with an onion pommel and slightly curved cross guard with a flat ricasso. I pulled it out of the scabbard a little and discovered that it was a double-edged broadsword in exquisite condition. Actually, it was a sort of hybrid, with an elongated hilt common to a hand-and-a-half sword. The strap on the scabbard was designed so I could secure it across my chest and draw the sword from over my shoulder. I looked up to find him shaking his head, a smiling haunting his lips.

"I'm not the only one who prefers the old ways." A smirk twisted my mouth and I raised both eyebrows at him. Danaus rarely used a gun, and the way he held a sword made me think he'd been born with one in his hand.

"But to survive, you learn to adapt," he said grimly.

"True," I whispered, looking back down at the pistols resting on either side of my chest. I didn't like them, but they would stop a member of the naturi faster than I could cut them into pieces with my sword. "Thanks."

Danaus grunted and returned to the white leather bench. I carefully removed the shoulder holster and laid it on one of the empty seats with the sword. I stretched out on the leather sofa again, grateful to be rid of the guns.

A deep silence settled in the jet. Only the sound of the screaming wind could be heard. I relaxed against the upholstery with my eyes closed, both of us lost in our own worlds. I blotted out thoughts of my wounded Gabriel, reassuring myself that he was safe with Ryan and James. I tried not to think about the Coven, Jabari, or the naturi. I tried not to think about the fact that I had lived with Jabari in Egypt for nearly a century. For almost one hundred years he ran his little experiments, letting other nightwalkers try to control me, and I couldn't remember a moment of it. The years were a blur, but they weren't a gaping black hole in my past. I remembered nights in Jabari's home near Karnak where we would sit talking about the things we had seen. We discussed what it meant to be a nightwalker and others who had come before both of us. The Ancient nightwalker had given me a sense of history and a philosophy. He'd been a mentor and guide in the night.

I pushed those thoughts away, plunging deeper into the blackness of my mind, only to have images of Michael swim to the surface. His soft, golden locks rose up before me, and I ached to touch the smoothness of his skin as it stretched over miles of thick muscle. I remembered his wonderful smile and how it was always unsure and crooked when he struggled to read my moods. Yet tainting those good memories was the feel of his body in my arms as he died, a lead weight pressing down on my legs and awkward in my arms. The brush of his soul still chilled my skin. It beat against his chest, battling for freedom when I desperately wanted him to stay. I left him when consciousness abandoned him at last, unable to bear the final moments when his soul broke free and left me forever.

Leaning my head back, I rested one elbow on the back of the bench and threaded my fingers through my hair. A lump rose in my throat and my eyes burned with tears fighting to slip down my cool cheeks. I had killed Michael as surely as if I plunged the blade in his back myself. I had seen him slowly sliding deeper into my world, slipping further away from his own kind. The descent was slow and I had convinced myself that he could handle it. Gabriel had, after all. My remaining angel had served me as a bodyguard for more than a decade with no ill effects.

But Gabriel was always careful to maintain a normal life away from me. I had dipped into his mind on numerous occasions and saw the things he enjoyed. Gabriel looked forward to watching football on Sunday and drinking with friends at a local bar. He dated and kept lovers. I never saw such things in Michael's mind. There had been only me.

Humans did not last when they became involved with my kind. For a while it was fun, but after a time there were only two paths for their fragile minds and bodies: death or rebirth. I could have saved my guardian angel at any time from his fate, but I could not bring myself to release him. A naturi may have wielded the blade that freed Michael's soul, but I had set the trap and baited it with myself.

FOUR

Venice. Europe's ultimate tourist trap, with its clichéd gondola drivers and pigeon-filled piazzas. Venice was like watching a grand dame of society slowly wither and die. She was filled with chatty, boisterous tour groups and their little clicking cameras as they crowded San Marco Piazza and oohed at the basilica. Then it was down to the Rialto and the open air market. Did any of them bother to cross the Guidecca Canal or wander through the quiet beauty of Campo Santa Margherita? Or even venture into some of the finest restaurants in San Polo?

When I'd traveled with Jabari, I spent many nights wandering the narrow streets of La Serenissima. I loved the vibrant nightlife in Dorsoduro, populated with its college students from the nearby universities. I loved the thickly populated island of Burano with its vibrantly painted little buildings. But my favorite was taking a water taxi to Torcello in the northern part of the Lagoon. This was where Venice had been born centuries ago, but now it was little more than a ghost town, its inhabitants shrinking from twenty thousand to fewer than thirty. Torcello's streets were only dirt and broken cobblestone, while most of her buildings had been torn down so the materials could be used elsewhere. However, those fragmented shells and the desolate, overgrown land offered up a quiet respite from my world. I had even lingered on this nearly forgotten island during the daylight hours, sleeping in a dark, quiet corner of an empty building.

But I doubted I'd be able to wander along her ancient sidewalks this time. When we stepped off the plane, an escort was already waiting to greet us. Tall and lean, the nightwalker stood not far from where our jet had taxied to a private section of Marco Polo Airport. I had seen him on my last few trips to Venice. The vampire was picking pieces of lint from his dark Armani suit, looking supremely bored with the task at hand. I knew better. A toady of the Coven was a tenuous position, one that you were careful not to screw up.

Climbing off the jet, I glanced nervously at the sky. Dawn was less than two hours away and we still had to deal with the formalities of landing in Venice, *the* nightwalker playground. If not for the time constraints, I would have been happy to wait until sunset tomorrow to leave for Venice.

The nightwalker in Armani gracefully strolled over as Danaus came to stand beside me. I had given him the guns and sword. I'd take back the Browning and Glock if forced to hunt the naturi again. For now, I didn't have a clue about the Coven's plans, but I knew that Rowe wouldn't give up on his plan to break the seal just because I had thwarted him once. The naturi was going to try again, and I suspected the Coven would "request" that I be the one to stop him again.

Tristan descended the stairs last, carrying both of our bags with ease. He was lowest on the totem pole so he got to play the part of pack mule. It wasn't fair, but we were protecting him and that task was more easily done without a bag on your shoulder.

"Benevenuto a Venezia," the vampire greeted in flawless Italian, bowing deeply to me. *"Il mio nome è Roberto."*

"Mira," I said, biting out my name through clenched teeth, fighting the urge to use Italian as well. "Danaus. Tristan." I completed the rest of the introductions with a quick wave of my hand toward my companions.

Roberto smiled at me, his eyes flickering with amusement. "The Elders are glad that you have arrived safely," he replied, slipping into heavily accented English.

A snide comment nearly tumbled from my lips, but I bit off the words at the last minute. No reason to start a fight just yet. There would be plenty of opportunities for that later.

"We are losing moonlight. Shall we go?" I stiffly said in quick, sharp Italian. The language came easy for me. Sadira had insisted that I learn it even before I was reborn, and it was all Jabari had spoken while attempting to teach me Arabic. But I didn't want to speak Italian; each syllable carried with it an echo of grim memories and dark pleasures I had left behind.

"Do you have any other baggage?" Roberto asked, his eyes darting to the jet.

"No. I assumed the Coven would see to my needs," I said.

"Naturalmente." With a wave of his hand, he turned sharply and started walking toward the canals. He had been inquiring about my customized coffin. The five-and-a-half-foot box with interior locks was my sanctuary from the sun. I'd left it in London with instructions to ship it to the States. It had become too impractical to keep moving the coffin around with me, but I hated traveling without it, though it could be done. If necessary, I could sleep in the Lagoon. Nightwalkers didn't breathe, and the silt and algae made the water murky enough to block the sun. Now, I'm not saying the experience was enjoyable—there are few things more repulsive than waking covered in dirt and algae—but at least you wake up again.

Our little trio followed Roberto to a waiting boat. Once we were seated, the nightwalker deftly maneuvered the sleek speedboat from the dock and across the Lagoon. Yet, something seemed off. Instead of heading toward the southeast side of Murano, Roberto passed the southwest side of the island and soon entered the winding canals of Venice. This didn't make any sense. Typically, we traveled southeast toward the Lido before heading back north to the remote island that housed the Coven. This way would take longer, as we would be forced to travel at a slower speed while within the narrow confines of the Venice canals. There wouldn't be much time if we were to appear before the Elders before sunrise.

After a few moments darting down one narrow canal after another, Danaus touched my arm, drawing my eyes to his face. Silently, he held up three fingers and then tilted his head toward the rooftops. We were being watched, which wasn't surprising. I had felt them as we stepped onto the tarmac at the airport. However, the hunter had miscounted. With a wink and a smile, I chuckled deeply, catching Roberto's attention.

"What has amused you?" he inquired, glancing over his shoulder at me.

"The hunter is honored by the Coven's thoughtfulness to send an escort of four nightwalkers," I replied. Danaus's expression remained unreadable, but I'm sure those were not the words he would have used.

"He can sense them?" Roberto asked, his eyes briefly shifting to Danaus. His hand swept over his slicked-back, dark brown hair.

"Naturalmente," I purred.

Roberto looked over at Danaus one last time, the tip of his tongue nervously flicking across his lips before he turned his attention back to the canal. "The Coven is eager to meet him," he softly said, his voice barely carrying over the rumble of the boat's motor and the splash of the waves.

I was sure they were, but I wisely kept my comments to myself. Instead I watched the passing buildings and the shimmer of lamplight reflecting in the waters in the canal. We had briefly cut across the Grand Canal and were now moving down the Guidecca Canal. The nightwalkers watching us kept their distance and did nothing to provoke the passengers of the speedboat. They were there to make sure we didn't attempt anything stupid, though I'm not sure exactly what the Coven thought we might try.

After about thirty minutes Roberto slowed the boat and carefully docked in a beautiful landing on the Guidecca side of Venice. I frowned, my gaze and powers sweeping the immediate area. This wasn't where the Coven held court. That was still another ten minutes away on a lonely island in the Lagoon.

"Are we not going before the Coven?" I asked Roberto when he turned off the motor.

"Because of the late hour, the Elders have graciously decided to allow you to rest first. You are expected to appear in court an hour after sunset tomorrow," he explained.

"Alone?" I stood, my legs braced apart against the rocking of the boat. I doubted it, but it was always good to know exactly where you stood when you went before the Elders.

"All are to come," Roberto announced, his eyes sweeping over Tristan and Danaus before returning to my face.

I looked over at Tristan, who was still sitting. His expression was blank, but his knuckles were growing white from the death grip he had on my bag. After living with Sadira for more than a century, I was confident that he was as well versed in the romance languages as I was. "Have you appeared in court before?" I demanded, switching back to English.

"No," Tristan said with a shake of his head, peering up at me with wide eyes. A wave of fear from the young nightwalker rippled through me, skimming along my arms like a cold chill. The court of the Coven was a place of horrors and nightmares, particularly for the weak. It was there that the term "chum" had been coined.

I turned my gaze back to Roberto, who was watching Tristan like a predator sizing up his prey. "Relay a request to the Elders for me," I said, my words falling gracefully back into Italian. "Tell them I humbly request to be allowed to leave Tristan behind. He knows nothing of the matter we have come to discuss and will only waste valuable time."

Roberto smiled at my delicate choice of words. I had never been humble about anything I did. "He has come into their domain. He has to show proper respect," he reminded me, his dark gaze sliding back to my face.

"They've already given their approval for the day's rest. If they refuse, I can still send him back to London after the sun sets. No harm done."

"I'll relay your request," Roberto said stiffly, his lean face twisting with his displeasure.

"*Grazie*," I said, smiling at him wide enough to expose my fangs. It wasn't a threat; more of a friendly nudge not to cross me. Coven toady or not, I'd ripped apart stronger vampires than him for less, and he knew it. Besides, the noose was already around my neck, so what did I have to lose?

We climbed out of the boat and walked up to the hotel. I paused and watched Roberto pull from the dock and drive out into the Lagoon. He was headed for the Coven. The other nightwalkers remained around the hotel, watching. They'd hold for a little while longer but would have to find a suitable resting spot as the night crumbled around us. As I turned to continue into the luxurious hotel, I found Tristan standing before me, a look of gratitude on his face.

"Why?" he whispered, his voice seeming to catch on something in his throat.

"You wouldn't survive the night," I grumbled, stepping around him and striding toward the hotel. The look on his face, a sickening combination of gratitude and awe, was making me uncomfortable. It was the same look I had seen on his face when we first met in London at that punk bar. To Tristan, I was a legend and a beacon of hope—I had "escaped" our maker and gone on to live my own life away from her. And when he saw me for the first time, he assumed that I would help him do the same. Unfortunately for him, I wasn't the type to come rushing to the aid of a weaker nightwalker. In fact, I was frequently an exterminator of fledglings when they endangered our secret.

"Sadira won't let anything happen to me," Tristan argued, following on my heels.

"I will try to get Danaus to smuggle you back onto the jet before sunset tonight," I said, ignoring his comment. "You can be back in London or in the States before they awaken."

He grabbed my arm, stopping me. "What if they summon me and I'm not in Venice?"

"I'll tell them I shipped you away without your knowledge." It was a considerable risk. I had never defied the Coven before, but then I'd never had a reason to try.

"No," he firmly said with a shake of his head. "I'm staying." He repositioned our bags on his shoulders, completely at ease with their awkward weight. My brow furrowed as I stared at him. Earlier that evening he had wanted to run, to flee the Coven.

"I thought you wanted to be free of Sadira," I snapped. Exhaustion and fear ate away at the last of my patience. There wasn't time for this discussion.

"We both know shipping me to another country or continent won't free me from Sadira's grasp." Tristan stepped forward and placed a hand on my shoulder. He leaned in and our cheeks nearly brushed as we spoke. "Sending me away will only antagonize the Coven and Sadira. And while you may be the great Fire Starter, I don't think you are strong enough to take them both on and succeed."

My own words come back to haunt me. And he was right.

I stepped back so I could look him in the eye. "Very well." He was young, but determined. For now, he would stand by his mistress and endure the gaze of the Coven. If he were lucky, they would be so preoccupied with Danaus and me that he would be overlooked.

With a nod, I led my two companions into the opulent Hotel Cipriani. When I'd scanned the area upon our landing, I sensed Sadira on one of the upper floors waiting for us. Neither Tristan nor I had any desire to see the manipulative old nightmare again, but we were running out of time and I had something to accomplish before the night drew its final breath. As we neared the private suite, Sadira threw open the white double doors, smiling at her young ward.

"At last," she said, sounding deeply relieved. There was a slight flush to her pale cheeks, revealing that she had fed recently. She was wearing a pale pink shirt and long black skirt. The night's battle had been erased from her appearance, except for the lines of nervous worry that still clawed at the corners of her eyes. Stepping around the two nightwalkers as they held each other, I rolled my eyes in disgust. I knew Tristan was obediently relaying the night's events to his mistress through his thoughts. I didn't care to review what had happened since we parted ways. For now, I turned my attention to our accommodations. I'd deal with Sadira later.

The main sitting area was coldly elegant, decorated in smoky gray and black marble with creamy white walls. The furniture was covered in an interesting black and gray fabric and perfectly coordinated with the large area rug in the center of the room. The area oozed luxury, offering an enticing mix of beauty and comfort. Yet, the windows troubled me. The far wall was comprised of a massive bank of windows looking out at the canal. Frowning, I quickly peeked into both bedrooms to find large windows spanning the far walls. Even the bathroom looked out onto the canal. At night the view was stunning. By day it would be a death trap as the sun slowly crept through the room, searching us out.

"How are we supposed to meet them tomorrow if we burn up during the day?" My voice exploded in the suite as I stalked back out into the living room.

"The curtains are thick in the master bedroom," Sadira said. "It will be enough to block the sun." Her seemingly eternal calm was unshaken by my lack of emotional restraint. The night had been too long already, with bitter revelations nagging at me from both my beloved Jabari and my enemy Rowe. There had been no time to sit alone and think over what I'd learned, to formulate my next plan for survival. Always moving forward, toward the next destination, closer to the next creature that wanted to control me or kill me.

I wanted my metal box with its double locks on the interior. I wanted my one sanctuary in this world that was unraveling faster than love after betrayal. Traveling without the box was insane. I hadn't taken any trips outside of my domain without it in centuries. It had saved me on more than one occasion. Unfortunately, I currently needed to travel light and fast. I had to find other options. Hell, for half a second I actually thought about sleeping in the Lagoon, but quickly pushed the idea aside. The Elders were having a little fun. If they wanted to kill us, they would have done something far more creative and painful. This was just a joke; a death trap draped in exquisite luxury.

The panic ebbed and I redirected my thoughts toward my primary concern as I felt the nightwalkers move away from the hotel. It was less than an hour from dawn, and they were seeking their own resting place. They assumed I wouldn't be up to any trouble this close to sunrise. Furthermore, their human guardians wouldn't be in place to keep an eye on Danaus for another hour or two. They would have to be sure their vampire masters were safely stowed for the day before leaving. It was a window of opportunity, albeit a very small one, and I wouldn't have a second chance.

"Come with me," I commanded, pointing at Danaus as I headed for the doors.

"You're leaving?" Sadira gasped, horrified that I was heading outside when dawn was already beginning to lighten the sky.

I threw open the doors and stepped back to let Danaus precede me. "I have a question that needs answering before tomorrow's meeting."

"But the sun—"

"Don't wait up," I said, and laughed, following Danaus out of the room.

We jogged down the hall and through the hotel as silent as the wind. I might have been laughing, but I could feel the night struggling as it entered the final throes of death. No matter how hard I clenched my fist, the sand was slipping through my fingers. I was going to cut this one close, but I had to know. Rushing back outside, I hurried down to the dock, the rubber soles of my boots silent along the worn stone sidewalk. I untied one of the speedboats resting there, fighting the urge to glance up at the sky.

"Can you hotwire it?" I called as Danaus jumped onto the boat.

Wordlessly, he walked over to the wheel and knelt before it. I was stepping onto the boat when I heard the sound of breaking plastic as he ripped the panel off. He fiddled with the wires for a moment, causing the motor to sputter and cough. I was skilled with some mechanical items, but had yet to learn the fine art of hotwiring a vehicle. When I needed to go somewhere, I usually hijacked a driver as well, saving myself the trouble. Unfortunately, most people were still asleep at this hour and I didn't want to try to track down a private taxi driver.

An impatient remark nearly leapt from my tongue before the motor suddenly roared to life. Danaus rose to his feet and shifted the boat into reverse. As he dropped it into drive, I pointed toward the Lagoon and he launched us into the darkness, moving me away from the safety of a resting place for the daylight hours.

"Where are we going?" he asked after a couple minutes. We had left the Guidecca Canal and entered the Lagoon. The dark waters opened around us, the gentle waves rising and falling in a hypnotic dance. Lights danced in all directions, cold and distant, as if taunting me with promises of protection from the sun that was rising closer to the horizon. The immediate area was a thick, inky blackness, a swamp of night created by the waters—a sanctuary that was chosen only as a last resort.

"Head for that island, San Clemente," I said, pointing toward a swath of land another ten minutes away. A large hotel rose up out of the darkness, a handful of its windows glowing against the slate-gray sky. A neat row of lamps lined the sidewalks, wrapping around the island. "That's where the Coven resides most of the year. It started as a monastery but was converted into a hotel in the past century. There are other buildings on the island, including the main hall for the court."

"Why are we going there now?" Danaus asked, turning the boat and putting on more speed. His eyes jumped up to the sky for a second, possibly judging the time left until the sun officially rose.

"We're not," I replied, forcing back a smile. "Turn off the engine."

His head jerked toward me, his brow furrowed in confusion, but he also wordlessly slowed the boat to a stop before killing the engine.

Standing next to him, I spread my legs as wave after wave rocked the small craft, lapping at its sides. "I want you to scan the area for naturi."

"Now?" he demanded in surprise. His eyes darted again to the sky, which was growing lighter by the minute.

I gripped the seat in front of me, my nails biting into the plastic. "Yes, now. Just do it. We don't have time for a debate."

With a frown, Danaus stared out at the Lagoon. His powers surged out from his body, ripping through me as if made of nothing more than smoke. I flinched but didn't move. Its warmth wrapped around me in a snug cocoon, holding me tightly, but it lasted only a few seconds before it dissipated.

"I can't search all of the city," he said at last. "That island is cloaked in some kind of magic. Everywhere else is clear, but I can't verify the island."

"I suspected as much," I murmured. I could sense the creatures through the barrier. Even without using much of my powers, I could tell there were more than two dozen nightwalkers on San Clemente, not to mention the nearly three hundred humans. However, I couldn't sense the naturi. No nightwalker could, as far as I knew.

But I could with help from Danaus. I had been able to sense them briefly when we combined our powers at the Themis Compound. This was stupid and extremely dangerous, but I had to know. I had to know what we were walking into tomorrow.

"I need your help," I slowly said in a low voice that barely reached above the sound of the breaking waves. "I have to know if there is a member of the naturi on that island. When we were linked in England, I could sense the naturi. We have to do that again. I'm the only one who can push through their protective barrier."

Danaus nodded and held out his hand to me. Hesitantly, I lifted my hand, but I still didn't take his.

"We can't kill anyone on the island. We can't even try. Don't think it, Danaus, or I swear I will destroy us both," I warned. "Let's just take it slow."

It took a great deal of effort to force myself to take his hand. The pain for our last joining was still fresh in my mind, and while I had recovered, I was in no rush to experience it again.

Lucky for me, it was different this time. The power didn't run screaming into my body, but slowly flowed in like a small woodland stream. It trickled up my arm and into my chest. The warmth seeped into my bones, filling my body. But then it changed. The power expanded in my bones until I thought they would splinter and break.

"Too much," I whimpered, struggling to keep to my feet. I tightened my grip on the chair before me but could no longer feel it. There was only Danaus's hand and the steadily increasing pain.

"I can't slow it any more. Focus," he said. His voice sounded distant, as if he were on the other side of the Lagoon. The sound of the water hitting the side of the boat had faded.

Focus on the island.

This time the words came as a command in my head. Thoughts about the pain starting to rip through my limbs ebbed and my mind focused on the island that bobbed ahead of us. It took only a moment, but I found what I was looking for. A member of the naturi lay sleeping on the island. By the size, I was willing to guess that it was probably a female, maybe of the light or wind clan. I made one quick scan of the buildings but knew I wouldn't find another. It didn't matter. One was enough for me.

"Stop," I said in a hoarse voice, struggling to release his hand.

I felt Danaus hesitate, his hand still tightly gripping mine. His thoughts were a jumble, but I understood the feeling. Frustration. One order from him and I would torch every nightwalker on the island. He wouldn't get another opportunity like this one.

"Stop!" I cried, my voice cracking. I jerked my hand but couldn't break Danaus's grip. I was fighting the power burning in my body, trying to halt its progress as it raged through me.

Angrily, Danaus released my hand and I dropped to my knees. He was breathing heavily, leaning on the steering wheel, but he looked to be in better shape than during our first attempt at this little trick.

My bones ached and my muscles burned and throbbed with a pain that I was becoming well acquainted with. Yet it wasn't as bad as earlier in the evening. I'd recover soon enough.

"You would have been tempted too," he breathlessly said, struggling to straighten.

"But I wouldn't do it," I croaked, leaning against one of the seats in the boat. "We made a bargain." I put my head down on the seat and closed my eyes, listening to the sound of the water hitting the side of the boat. "Don't worry. You'll get another shot at them, I promise."

Something had died inside of me, leaving a small, heavy corpse curled up in the pit of my stomach. I never had much respect for the Coven, but I'd always believed their ultimate goal was to protect my kind. I believed they would protect us all.

Countless centuries ago the Coven had been created by Our Liege to help establish some kind of control over the growing number of nightwalkers that were filling the earth; to establish order in the chaos. Four ancient vampires were handpicked by Our Liege to hold court and pass judgment when Our Liege chose to be absent. During the centuries, Elders were killed in power struggles and evil schemes, but the feel of the court never changed. It was a place of horrors and dark fantasies. The Coven was about power and control.

But in the end I also believed it was about the protection of our kind. The Coven was created to protect all nightwalkers as much as it was to protect humans. The naturi had slaughtered nightwalkers through history like animals. For nearly countless ages they hunted down and destroyed thousands of humans and vampires, believing both races to be a pestilence on the earth. Nightwalkers had sealed the naturi from this world, and we have protected that seal. Why would the Coven suddenly turn its back on that history?

Danaus stared down at me, a look of surprise filling his blue eyes. "Let's get out of here," I whispered. "I'm running out of time."

With a nod, he started the speedboat again and turned us back toward Cipriani. I pulled myself up into the seat and stared up at the pale gray sky. Dawn was close. The night was drawing in its last gasping breaths, its weight pressing down on me as it if were my job to support its lifeless frame.

"There's a very specific reason why we chose Venice for the seat of the Coven," I slowly began. "There are no naturi here. There never have been. Members of the water clan won't even lurk in the canals. They call it the Dead City. I'm not sure why. I think one of their gods supposedly died here. They've never set foot in the city."

"Until now," Danaus interjected.

"Not only is a naturi deep in nightwalker territory, but it had to have been invited. All magically inclined creatures have to be invited onto the island."

"How do you know it's not a prisoner?"

"Because it wasn't afraid or in pain," I said. My bitterness left a nasty taste in the back of my throat. I didn't know how I was sure of that fact. Something in me just knew it. When I sensed other creatures, I could get an emotional imprint. Something in me said I would have known if that naturi had been tortured or afraid for her life.

I'd suspected that my kind had been betrayed somehow. During my travels the past few days, the naturi remained one step ahead of us, always knowing exactly where to find me. The only way they could have managed such a feat was if someone were informing them. I'd suspected it, but I didn't believe I would actually be proven correct.

Silence settled back between us as we entered Guidecca Canal and drew close to the hotel. The area was still empty of nightwalkers, and most humans nearby were sleeping. The only ones who were awake were members of the hotel staff—not that they couldn't be servants of the Coven as well. I wasn't worried. The Elders knew I had been out in the Lagoon, but they couldn't know why.

By the time Danaus was tying up the boat, I was struggling to keep my eyes open. I climbed onto the dock, lacking my usual grace. I was hanging onto consciousness by a thread. My body was sore, fighting every movement. Danaus tried to pick me up, but I growled at him, lurching away from his touch. I had enough strength left to drag myself into the hotel.

"Promise me you won't go near San Clemente during the day," I mumbled as I entered the elevator. I leaned heavily against the wall, fighting to keep my eyes open. "They'll know. You'll put us all in danger. Just wait until sunset."

"But I—"

"Just promise," I snapped. "We're in their domain. We have to play by their rules."

"I promise," he grudgingly said, obviously less than thrilled with my request.

"Wait. Wait for me. We'll get them," I whispered.

The elevator doors slid open with a soft hiss and I lurched forward, hurrying into the suite. The sun was nearly up. I wasn't going to be awake much longer, and if I wasn't hidden, I'd be fried to a crisp. Throwing open the door to the master bedroom, I stumbled inside and slammed the door shut behind me. I didn't bother to lock it. If Danaus or someone else wanted in while we slept, they would find a way in. The room was pitch-black, as the heavy curtains had been pulled across the windows. Sadira and Tristan lay stretched out on the bed, his arms wrapped around her. I tripped across the room and slid onto the king-size bed next to Tristan. Exhausted, I was drifting off to sleep when I felt Tristan roll over and wrap his arms around my waist. He snuggled close, his long body curving against mine. And then there was nothing.

FIVE

The fog lifted from my thoughts the next night and I returned to consciousness to find Tristan stretched out beside me on the bed. He was leaning on his elbow, his brown hair hanging down around his eyes as he watched me. A faint smile played on his pale pink lips, but his blue eyes were worried. He was afraid, and for good reason. We had survived the day but still had to face the Elders.

Tristan lifted his hand to touch my cheek, but I jerked away from his fingertips and frowned. "I thought you might enjoy some company," he said gently. His open hand remained hovering in the air near my cheek, waiting for my permission to resume its descent. For a second I honestly wished I could accept his proposition. The curtains were still drawn and the room was quiet as a marble mausoleum in February. But a few stolen moments of bliss in his arms wouldn't chase away our fears regarding the Coven.

"No," I replied, though the word lay between us like a dead fish.

Lowering his hand, he wrapped his long fingers around my wrist when I sat up. "I wanted to thank you . . . for what you said yesterday." His words were hesitant. I understood what it cost him to say them. I remembered what it was like to be young and weak. You never wanted to feel as if you owed anyone anything. It gave them power over you, a little bit of leverage saved up for a special occasion.

"I don't want your thanks," I grumbled. Rolling to my feet, I ran my fingers through my hair, pushing the long red locks from my face. I didn't want his gratitude when we had yet to escape Venice. "Return to your mistress."

"She said that I am to see to your needs," he said, lounging across the bed. I turned to look at him, but what I saw only deepened my frown. He lay bare-chested, a smile haunting his handsome features. His lower half was in a pair of leather pants, while his feet remained bare. Tristan was an enticing mix, naughty with just a dash of nice. He extended one hand toward me, his gaze softening. He was hot, but I felt no real temptation. I was standing in Venice and was about to see the Coven, which had a naturi in their midst. There was no escape this time no matter how much I longed for it.

"Get out of here, Tristan," I sighed. "Tell the others I will be out in a few minutes."

I didn't wait for him to rise, but grabbed my bag and stalked into the bathroom, slamming the door behind me. After a quick shower, I dug through my bag for some clean clothes, only to discover I was running low. I hadn't thought to pack for more than a few days. I thought I would be handing this matter off to someone else not long after arriving in Egypt, not globe-hopping while I ran from the naturi.

With a grimace, I finally settled on a black halter top. I pulled the black leather pants I had worn the previous day back on, but chose the leather boots with the three-inch heels. They weren't great for fighting in, but the height would add to my presence. I was hoping to do more bluffing than actual fighting tonight.

I brushed out my damp hair and piled it on the back of my head, holding it in place with a pair of silver clips. By pulling it back, it opened my peripheral vision and still gave me the appearance of sophistication and class. With one last look in the mirror, I stifled a sigh. I looked good, but I didn't feel the confidence I needed to pull off this farce.

Leaning forward, I gripped the cold black marble sink with both hands. How the hell was I supposed to do this? A naturi was waltzing around the home of the Coven, Jabari could control me like some weapon sent from Hell, and somehow I was slowly building a contingent of creatures dependent upon me to save their collective hides. Not only had I promised a vampire hunter that I would get him out of Venice alive, but it was also becoming clear that both Sadira and Tristan were expecting the same.

I couldn't beat the Coven. While I might be able to last a little bit, Jabari would pummel me into bloody paste eventually. My odds against Macaire or Elizabeth weren't any better. How could I have been so careless as to promise to protect these poor creatures when I could barely protect myself?

But the Coven had to be stopped. My fears in London had been confirmed with the appearance of the naturi in the Coven. Too often the naturi knew exactly where to find me. They knew how to track me when only the Coven should have known my ultimate destination. Someone within the Coven was trying to kill me, and that person was using the naturi as the assassin.

A knock at the bathroom door shook me from my dark thoughts. I forced my fingers to release their grip on the sink and I straightened. "Come in." My voice was firm and steady, though I didn't feel it.

The door swung open to reveal Danaus standing on the other side, his expression even darker than usual. He was back in his typical black shirt and black pants, but gone were his wrist guards, assortment of knives, and sword strapped to his back. In fact, he was completely unarmed. Of course, he could destroy us all without even lifting a finger, but there's nothing like the feel of a trusted weapon in your hand.

"Ready?" he inquired.

"Would it make any difference if I said no?"

"No."

"Then, yes, I'm ready. Can't wait!" I said brightly, pasting an extremely fake-looking smile on my mouth.

A sharp bark of laughter jumped from Danaus's throat, surprising us both. I think the tension was getting to us. We were starting to crack. With a shake of my head and a wobbly smile, I stepped around him and started to walk through the bedroom when I felt a sudden sharp shift in his mood. In fact, the jump to violent anger and horror was so extreme that my fingers curled into claws and my lips pulled back, exposing sharp fangs. I twisted around, searching for our would-be attacker, but I found myself still alone with Danaus.

"What?" I demanded, my gaze still scouring the room for the enemy that had retreated to the shadows. The curtains had been pulled back to reveal the glittering expanse of the Lagoon and the glow of San Marco Piazza against the night sky.

"Your back," he replied, his voice harsh and almost breathless. I straightened, relaxing instantly. I had forgotten he had never seen the scars on my back. I'd worn that shirt for the exact purpose of showing them off, but they hadn't crossed my mind when I walked in front of the hunter.

Turning back around so he could see them, I remained standing in the center of the room. "I thought Nerian told you," I said. The name twisted briefly on my lips as an image of the naturi flit through my thoughts. My old tormentor was dead now, but memories of him still had the power to haunt me.

I heard Danaus edge closer, his movements slow and cautious, as if he was afraid I would lunge at him. "He did, but I didn't think vampires could scar. I thought you healed from everything," he said, his voice dropping to near a whisper. Danaus had held Nerian captive for a week before I finally destroyed the naturi. It was ample time for the hunter to pull all kinds of interesting information from my enemy. The idea set me ill at ease around Danaus, fearful of the things he knew about me during my weakest moment. I was flaunting the scarring, but the rest of the painful and degrading things I endured over those two weeks were something I wanted no one to know about.

"If we don't feed soon enough after being injured by a naturi weapon, our bodies cannot heal completely," I said stiffly, trying to push back the flood of memories. "I wanted to remind the Coven of what they were dealing with."

His fingertips lightly grazed my back, tracing some of the marks. I flinched at his touch but didn't move. His anger brushed across my bare skin like a warm breath, and it was almost soothing despite our topic of conversation. "Some of these are symbols," he said in surprise. "They wrote on your back."

"I never learned what it said. Nothing good, I'm sure."

Danaus was silent a moment, his emotions a jumble as the anger started to ebb. He was studying the designs, his thoughts churning as he tried to place the symbols with matching words. "Kick me."

I twisted around, my mouth falling open in wordless shock. The hunter stared at me, the corners of his mouth twitching. Laughter, for one brief crystalline moment, shimmied through his cobalt eyes. Dear heaven, the dark vampire hunter was developing a sense of humor.

I laughed, letting the sound well up from my toes and soar through my chest. Shaking my head, I wrapped my arms around my stomach as the sound filled the room. Danaus chuckled softly too, the sound bouncing off me like a drunken monk trying to right himself in a swaying room. It was more than a minute later before I was able to finally stand straight and stifle the last of the giggles.

"Why is there a naturi within the Coven building?" Danaus asked, killing the last of our laughter. There was no harsh accusation or censure in his voice. I could almost hear the unspoken question, "What are we going to do?" in his tone.

"The Coven had struck some kind of bargain. I think it's the reason why the naturi have been able to track us so easily," I said, sitting down on the edge of the bed.

"Maybe. But they haven't gotten us yet."

"Rowe grabbed me the last time," I reminded him, trying to keep the bitterness out of my tone. Rowe had swept me away to Stonehenge to witness the sacrifice to break the seal, and offered me a chance to change sides. I didn't, and at the time I thought I had made the right choice. Yet, with the appearance of the naturi at the Coven Great Hall, I now had my doubts.

"Each time they attack, we get closer to stopping Rowe," Danaus countered.

"He always has the element of surprise."

"He's lost it." Danaus stood before me, forcing me to sit up straight so I could look up at him. "We know now that the naturi are after you specifically. We can watch out for them. Even if the naturi have struck a bargain with the Coven, their numbers are going to be limited here. We're safer here than anywhere else."

It was on the tip on my tongue to remind him that we were due before the Coven. We weren't safer. We just faced a different kind of danger.

Danaus knelt before me, wrapping one of his large strong hands around my thin wrist. "I will not let Rowe touch you. He will not kidnap you again. The naturi cannot have you," he vowed, bringing a shaky smile to my lips. Seated in a dirty London alley, covered in naturi blood and glass, he had made a similar promise to me. I could feel his anger now as he held my arm. He blamed himself for me being grabbed at the Compound. He felt angry and ashamed of his failure to keep his promise to me. But I didn't blame him. No one could have stopped Rowe at that moment.

With my free hand, I cupped his cheek, rubbing my thumb across his strong cheekbone. His pain and frustration beat at me, weakening the smile I was forcing onto my lips. How had we come to this point? Protecting each other from the threats that crowded us on all sides when we were supposed to be killing each other.

"Danaus, I don't expect you to keep such a promise. You would have to be close to me at all times. It's a step in our relationship I'm not ready to take," I teased, trying to lighten the weight in his chest. To my surprise, he didn't move. Usually when I teased him, the hunter would growl at me and stomp off. Danaus simply squeezed the wrist he was holding and shook his head slightly, his lips gently grazing the palm of my hand.

"I stand by my promise. The naturi will not have you."

"Thank you," I murmured, dropping my hand back into my lap. No one had ever anyone vocally sworn to protect me. Others had physically, but then it had the feeling of a piece of property being protected rather than a living creature.

Danaus pushed back to his feet and took a step back. "We should get going," he said, extending his hand to help me rise.

"Do you think other races know about the deal?" I asked as I slipped my cool hand into his warm one. The appearance of the witch and the lycan with the Daylight Coalition member seemed to take on a whole new frightening meaning.

"Let's hope not," he said, pulling me to my feet. "I can only fight one war at a time."

And I could already guess at which side he would fall on if the races went to war against the nightwalkers.

Six

When Danaus and I entered the main living room, we found Roberto lounging against the wall near the doors, hands shoved in the pockets of his trousers. Dressed in another black suit, he looked like a careless Italian playboy out for an evening of reckless pleasure. The deep red shirt he wore was open at the throat, his dark brown hair perfectly slicked back. Roberto was a few centuries old; closer to my age than Tristan's, but still far from being an Ancient. My encounters with the Coven flunkies were few and far between. My patience was thin and I had a tendency to burn through them. My orders had always come directly from Jabari, and occasionally from Tabor.

Tristan stood expressionless behind a seated Sadira. He'd pulled on a deep blue shirt, but had yet to button it. They were all awaiting my arrival. How nice.

"The Elders are waiting for you," Roberto said.

"And Tristan?" I asked him, stopping the nightwalker as he turned toward the doors. Roberto turned back, his eyes sliding over to the young vampire as a dark smile lifted his red lips.

"He may stay behind. He has not been invited to court."

I looked from Roberto over to Tristan, who was watching me with a desperate look in his eyes. Had I just put him in even greater danger? The Coven had granted my wish, but they never were so generous without a specific reason. If Tristan remained behind, he would be unprotected, vulnerable to any other nightwalker lurking in the city. Of course, he would have been in the same danger if he was coming with the rest of us. But someone feared that I might interfere with tonight's planned entertainment if I was around, so I was effectively removed from the equation. If I was with the Coven, I couldn't protect Tristan here.

I cursed myself and my stupidity. I had tried to outmaneuver the Coven in an attempt to protect the young nightwalker and only made an even bigger mess. He wouldn't survive an encounter with the court, but I also doubted he would make it through the evening alone in the hotel room.

While I was never an official member of the court, I had seen what it was capable of, played a part in its games as both prey and predator. Nightwalkers were resilient creatures who could survive all manner of physical torture for hours on end. But it was more than the physical pain that left a creature curled in a pool of its own blood, spewing an endless litany of pleas and prayers for mercy or death. They played with their prey until its mind shattered like a stained-glass window, so there was nothing left. No sense of self or reality.

My eyes jerked to Sadira as she stood and walked over to us while Tristan remained standing by her empty chair, one hand tightly gripping the back as if it were his last lifeline of safety.

"Say it," I growled at Sadira. My narrowed eyes followed her as she slipped by me and stood near the double doors.

"I don't know what you're talking about," she said, but she wouldn't meet my gaze nor would she look back at Tristan.

"Say it! Do what you would never do for me," I shouted, pointing at the young nightwalker. But she didn't look at him. She didn't speak. She lifted her chin slightly and continued to stare at the wall.

Against my better judgment, my eyes fell back on Tristan. I could still remember his smell from when he lay in bed with me, the sweet mix of heather and blood. The feel of his smooth skin pressed to mine and the memory of how he spooned me last night filled my brain.

I kept telling myself that he was just chum, entertainment was his purpose for being, but the words were bile in the back of my throat. A couple of nights earlier he had gone into the woods with me and attacked the naturi. He had fought beside me when we were outnumbered and destined to die horrible deaths at the hand of our enemies. He had stood beside me because he believed I would keep my word and save him from our maker. He had faith in my sense of honor.

Rage pumped through my veins, pushing aside the blood. I hated him. I hated myself. I hated the fates that had bought us to this precipice. There was no escaping the promise I had made nor living with myself if I even tried to.

Ignoring Sadira and the rest of the occupants of the room, I marched over to Tristan. Roughly grabbing a fistful of his hair, I pulled him toward me. "No!" Sadira's desperate scream echoed through the silent room. She had suddenly realized what I'd been about to do.

I had enough time to release Tristan's hair before she crashed into me, crushing me into the wall while knocking Tristan out of my reach. I tried to shove her off me but her nails were digging into my bare arms and I couldn't get a solid hold on her.

"You can't have him," she snarled.

"You're giving him up to the court," I countered, finally getting a grip of her thin bony shoulders.

"For a night of entertainment."

"They'll kill him!" I shouted, pushing her away. She immediately came at me, but I backhanded her, snapping her head around as the blow sent her to the floor.

"You don't know that," she argued.

"I do. And so do you."

Tristan is my child. The statement came as an insidious whisper across my brain, causing me to flinch as if Sadira had struck me. *Just like you will always be my child, my Mira. You can't have him.*

"I claim him," I snarled, balling my hands into fists as I tried to fight her claim on my will. Every fiber of my being screamed to obey her. Everything within me demanded that I kneel down and crawl into her waiting arms. But I couldn't. I had promised Tristan.

To my surprise, I was able to lift my arm to Tristan, beckoning him over. Sadira had the ability to manipulate my thoughts and emotions, but she wasn't as strong as Jabari. She couldn't control me physically like a puppet on a string.

Again I roughly grabbed a handful of Tristan's hair and pulled him close. Sadira increased her presence in my brain until the pain was positively excruciating. Tears streaked my cheeks, escaping from my clenched eyes. Not caring about the pain I was causing Tristan, I sank my fangs into his throat and drank deeply. It didn't require much, only a couple of swallows. The blood also seemed to wash Sadira's presence from my brain.

In those few seconds, I pulled all of Tristan's history and emotions into my brain. In a flash I saw his childhood home in Geneva, the beautiful face of his dead wife, the promise of a daughter who never survived, and a horrific slide show of events that comprised his years with Sadira.

Lifting my mouth from his neck, I pushed him down to his knees in front of me. "You belong to me now. You are mine until I choose to free you," I said in a shaky voice, my narrowed gaze capturing his wide blue eyes. Releasing him, I turned back to the others who were closely watching me and focused my attention on Roberto. "He is mine," I declared. Those three words hung like a worn hangman's noose in the center of the room for several seconds, daring anyone to argue with my decision. "Anyone touches him and I will know. Harm him and they will answer to me."

"But the Elders have already promised—" Roberto began, but I didn't let him finish that statement.

"No one touches him," I warned, my voice dropping to a low growl. "Tell the others."

Roberto nodded stiffly, his anger trickling through the room. The Coven might have granted the right to play with Tristan, but anyone who came near the young nightwalker would have to deal with my wrath. A vampire then had to decide if he thought the Coven would protect him from me, and there were no promises to be found there.

My gaze drifted over to Danaus, to find him frowning darkly at me, his brow seemingly furrowed in confusion. I could sense his disgust for what I had done. In his mind, I'd taken a slave. There was nothing redeeming in the ownership of another sentient creature. However, sometimes you had to do distasteful things to protect those weaker than you. If I were lucky, I had extended Tristan's life, if only by a few hours.

Unfortunately, it meant that I'd done the one thing I vowed I would never do—I had started a family. Tristan was mine for as long as I claimed him. He was mine to guide and protect. In my domain of Savannah, I was the Keeper, but that meant I preserved the peace and protected our secret. No nightwalker belonged to me or based his or her daily decisions on my wants and desires. Knox and Amanda acted as my assistants, but they were free to leave Savannah and pursue their own lives at any time. Tristan could not. And I could not leave without Tristan.

Anger bubbled in my chest, and I had yet to leave the confines of our hotel room. This was not going to go well. At least Tristan was a little better protected than he had been a couple minutes ago. But I'd crossed a major line, and stolen Sadira's plaything from her while she watched. It happened occasionally among nightwalkers, but never had the child of a vampire stolen another one of her maker's children. It reflected very poorly on Sadira. If she was going to save face at all, she would have to challenge me for Tristan.

And at the moment, I welcomed the chance to tear into her. Beyond our own dark history, she had been willing to leave Tristan to the tender mercies of the nightwalkers who hung around the Coven. She had done the same to me years ago, and my strength and ability to control fire were the only things that kept me alive. Tristan would not have lived to see the sunrise if I hadn't stepped up. He still might not, but at least he now had a fighting chance.

"Let's go," I said, glaring briefly at Sadira as I swept past where she still half lay on the floor and out of the room. Hatred burned in her eyes and her fingers hooked into claws. We would have words later, I had no doubt, but now we had other things to worry about. Silently, we filed down to the waiting speedboat, while Tristan remained alone in the hotel room.

Around us, people crowded the canals and sped across the Lagoon, headed out for an evening of entertainment or returning home from a long day of work. A warm summer breeze caressed my bare skin, holding me in its embrace. The air was laced with the salty scent of the Adriatic Sea. Ahead of us, the island of San Clemente loomed, its large hotel bobbing as the boat bounced and cut through the waves created by some of the larger shuttle boats. It took less than fifteen minutes to cross the Lagoon and dock at the island. It was both the longest and shortest fifteen minutes of my existence.

As I stood to disembark, I glanced over at Danaus, who had sat beside me on the trip over. His eyes briefly darted to my back and then back to my face. He silently mouthed the words *Kick me,* bringing a reluctant smile to my lips. That's pretty much what it all felt like, but for this ugly moment in time, he was with me in this endeavor.

"I assume you know the way," Roberto said, his lips curling with distaste. It was somewhat amusing. Where he had been gracious yesterday, he was equally snobbish and critical today. I had obviously put a crimp in the night's planned entertainment. Fine, let him take it up with the management. I already had a few choice words for them.

"I know it. Have fun tonight," I mocked, wagging my fingers at him as I stepped onto the dock. The nightwalker said nothing as he put the boat into reverse and backed away from the landing. I almost pitied his next meal.

Frowning, I led the way down the dock to a path that wound past the hotel and deeper into the island. Even if I hadn't been to the court before, I would have been able to find my way. Power throbbed from deep within the tiny island, and the concentration of nightwalkers grew thicker the farther we walked.

I stayed in front as we strolled down the path, Danaus behind my left shoulder while Sadira hung back on my right. Tension jumped and crackled through my frame. The fine hairs on my arms and on the back of my neck suddenly stood on end when I sensed one of the nightwalkers break off from the rest of the hidden pack and start to approach. I couldn't see him yet but I could feel him.

"Remain calm," I murmured to Danaus, but I think I needed to hear the words as well. My stomach twisted with anticipation like a snake winding itself into a tight coil. My focus had been completely on facing the Elders. I had not anticipated the long walk to the main hall. Every time I'd traveled to the island since leaving Sadira, I was under Jabari's protective wing, removed from the rigors of the horde of flunkies and courtiers who hung on the various Elders.

I stopped walking when the nightwalker stepped into the glow of a nearby street lamp. Valerio. We had traveled together for a time years ago. He was older than I was, but not yet an Ancient. He was close, though. Too close to that thousand-year mark for me to feel any kind of comfort.

"Did you leave Vienna for me?" I inquired, keeping my tone light and playful. "I'm flattered." I slipped my hands into the back pockets of my pants as Valerio strolled to the edge of the light.

He bowed graciously to me, his arms thrown open wide. It must have been a signal because I felt several other nightwalkers move closer, but they remained hidden in the shadows cast by the trees that dotted the island, creating a tiny forest.

"I come to court occasionally for a bit of entertainment," he said with a slight shrug of his right shoulder. "When I heard you would be appearing, I thought I'd pop in so we could catch up."

Valerio was the typical handsome vampire, with his blond-streaked brown hair and lovely dark brown eyes. He had a dreamy, movie-star kind of look about him. More of a romantic but sadly misunderstood lead, rather than the dark villain. His heritage was something of a Spanish-Italian hybrid.

"How thoughtful!" I laughed. I was trying my best to keep my posture relaxed, but it wasn't an easy task with so many hostile nightwalkers edging closer. Tension hummed in my frame, tightening the muscles in my shoulders.

"But I've heard that you've taken away some of our entertainment for the night."

"I see Roberto has been kind enough to spread the sad news." Ahh, the vampire grapevine strikes again. Telepathy among my own kind had its benefits as well as drawbacks. This once it might work to my benefit, not that I was particularly counting on it. "Yes, Tristan has been removed from the menu. He's too young to be of any interest for this group."

"Fortunately for us, that young one was not the main course," purred a female voice from the shadows. A curvy brunette slunk out of the darkness to my left. At just over five feet, the vampire was an attractive creature in her breezy skirt with its soft, floral pattern and pale rose shirt that left her slender shoulders bare. While we had never been formally introduced, I knew she was called Gwen. She wasn't particularly nice. I could guess who the main course was, and so could Danaus, because the tension in his body ramped up considerably when she started to slink closer.

"The great Mira has returned to us," Gwen mocked. "And not only can she command fire, but she has tamed the hunter."

My eyes slid briefly to Danaus, but his gaze never wavered from the female nightwalker. "Tamed" was hardly the word I'd use, but now was not the time to quibble over semantics. I was sure Danaus would have something to say about this if we survived.

"I look forward to tasting him," she continued. Gwen reached up to touch his face, but I caught her wrist in a flash of movement and shoved her backward a few steps. Her eyes glowed with outrage but she managed to keep from hissing. She was a toady for Elizabeth and long used to having her way. We were close in age, but she had been reborn chum, giving me an advantage. Of course, challenging her directly would be seen as a challenge to Elizabeth, and I was trying to cut back on the number of fights I picked with Coven Elders.

Around us, more nightwalkers closed in. They were now leaning against the trees that lined the sidewalk and lounging in the grass. A quick count revealed sixteen vampires of varying age; more than the usual welcoming committee.

"He belongs to me," I said in a low voice, though I'm sure they all heard me.

"You've gotten greedy, Mira. First Tristan and now the hunter," Gwen said, taking a couple slow, cautious steps toward me again. "You've been away for too long. Forgotten your place. We've been promised a taste of the hunter."

"I don't share." My soft voice was filled with enough lurid menace to give her pause in her steady approach.

"You will if the Coven commands it," Gwen replied with a smug smile. The nightwalker was attractive enough, but her mouth bothered me. It was a large, shapeless thing, as if it were simply a giant slash across her face. And every time she spoke, an ugly wound reopened, marring her lovely features.

"Consider yourself warned," I said, matching her smile with one of my own. "Touch him or Tristan and you will face me. There will be no hiding behind the skirts of your mistress."

A haunting glow returned to her hazel eyes and her fangs glinted briefly in the lamplight. "You wouldn't dare." There seemed to be something hesitant and unsure in her expression, but she couldn't back down with everyone watching.

"No?"

I dropped my hands to my sides with my palms open. Out of the ground sprang two dozen snakes made of bright orange fire. The horde slithered around us once then shot out along the ground in all directions, chasing away the nightwalkers. No one was caught by my fiery serpents, and I extinguished the flames when the other nightwalkers were a comfortable distance away. Only Valerio remained behind. He had jumped onto the street lamp, with his feet braced against the pole while one hand clasped the top. Fury contorted his handsome features and the light reflected in his eyes.

"You're forbidden to use fire here!" he shouted. A fire snake slowly slithered around the pole, waiting for its prey to descend. I extended my right leg so that only the tip of my boot touched the ground. The snake instantly changed directions and came back to me. It wriggled up my leg and wrapped around my waist once before disappearing.

"We've been betrayed. All bets are off," I replied in a hard, cold voice.

"Yes, we have," he said, his dark gaze locking on Danaus. His words cut through me. I knew it looked like I was betraying our kind to the one who had hunted us for centuries. I could have told him that Danaus had protected Sadira, Tristan, and even Jabari in England, but I would have been wasting my words. Actions were the only thing these creatures believed. Words were just neatly packaged lies.

"When the day comes that you have to choose a side, ask yourself who will be willing to protect you," I called back, drawing his grim gaze back to my face. Tonight alone, I had sworn to protect not only another vampire, but a human, from the Coven. Any protection offered by the Coven was a flighty, mercurial thing at best, which seemed to change each time the sun set. I still hadn't been forgiven by Valerio, but at least I'd given him something to think about. It was a start.

We traveled the rest of the way to the main hall unmolested. That's not to say we weren't surrounded by a sizable group of very pissed-off nightwalkers. At the moment, however, they were content to let the Elders work me over first.

SEVEN

The Great Hall of the Coven was near the opposite side of the island from where we docked but still a distance from the shore, so that any one landing would be forced to walk at least a few dozen yards before reaching the main doors. The large three-story building was made entirely of dark gray stone and resembled an old fort with its long, slender windows reflecting the pale moonlight. It rose up from the interior of the island like a cold, silent guard refused eternity's rest. There were no lights leading up to the building, nothing to welcome the curious if someone happened to be on a leisurely stroll around the island.

Walking up the main stairs, a pair of heavily muscled men pulled open the massive wood and steel doors. There were other humans about the large building, a collection of servants and pets. And when the need called for it, food readily on hand. It was better than worrying about grabbing a bite from the nearby hotel when dawn drew close.

The two doormen barely earned a glance as I strode past them and down the long, dim hall to another set of doors. A heavy pounding echoed through the entryway as the front doors were closed, the sound bouncing off the walls as it flew up to hammer against the high ceiling. A chill skittered along my spine but I said nothing as I suppressed the old memories that attempted to crawl into the forefront of my mind. Clenching my fists at my side, I forced myself to take a step through the open doorway leading into the main throne room. I didn't let myself look back at Danaus for any kind of encouragement, though I wanted it. I just kept moving, my eyes never wavering from the trio sitting on the slightly raised dais at the other end of the room.

The cold, uneven stone that comprised every inch of the entryway gave way to jaw-dropping opulence in the main hall. Shiny black marble floors gleamed in the candlelight as if a lake of liquid night stretched out before us. The three-story ceilings disappeared in the darkness, as the flickering candlelight could not penetrate the inky blackness overhead. The Coven had found a way to cage the night itself, but had yet to find a way to stop the passage of time.

There were no windows in this room, making it a safe hiding place from the dawn if necessary, but the main sleeping chamber was several meters below ground. The walls were covered in exquisite paintings, tapestries, and flags—a collection of art almost as old as man. From the ceilings hung gold and crystal chandeliers that flickered and twinkled with candlelight. Yet as beautiful as it was, it was also cold and silent. The room somehow managed to have the feel of both an elegant ballroom and a dusty mausoleum.

At the end of the hall, three small steps led to a raised platform that held four intricately carved gold-leaf chairs. In the middle sat Jabari and Macaire, while Elizabeth rest in the chair to the far left. The chair on the far right next to Jabari remained empty. It had belonged to Tabor. That vacancy seemed all the more ominous now that I'd walked in with a nightwalker hunter. While no one on the Coven had said anything to confirm it, some believed that Tabor was killed by Danaus, while others believed he was killed by another Ancient who refused to step forward, fearful of crossing Jabari. I'd begun to wonder if the slaying had been completed by the naturi. What better way to ensure that we couldn't protect the seal than to destroy the triad that had created it? Yet now, with the presence of the naturi in the main hall, an even darker theory began to take shape in my mind.

Behind the set of four chairs was another set of three stairs and a smaller dais. On this platform rested just one chair, made of wrought iron with a red velvet cushion. That chair belonged to Our Liege. It was empty as well. I stared at that empty spot for several seconds before finally dragging my eyes down to the Elders. I had yet to meet Our Liege, and while I wasn't particularly comforted by the fact that he was missing now, I was glad that I would not meet him for the first time under the current circumstances.

At the center of the room, I stopped walking and bowed my head to the Coven. It was polite but not overly subservient. I was treading on thin ice already. Jabari was more than a little pissed at me if he was looking to create my replacement, and I had never gotten around to playing nice with Macaire or Elizabeth, so there was no help to be found there. My goal was to not slit my own throat in the first five minutes, while I tried to keep the others around me alive. Danaus wisely remained a step behind my left shoulder and did not move. In fact, I wasn't even sure he was still breathing. However, by remaining behind me, I felt reassured that he was willing to follow my lead in this intricate tango. Well, at least for now.

Sadira, on the other hand, came around to stand next to me on my right. She was willing to stand with me, but her placement opened the door for her to jump ship if things got too ugly.

Macaire shifted in his chair, reclining while stretching out his left leg. His eyes paused over each of us before he finally drew a breath to speak. "*Benvenuto,* Sadira. It has been a long time since you were last in Venice." His Italian was smooth and flawless, as if he were a native.

"*Grazie,*" she murmured as she bowed to the trio. "It is rare that I leave my home, but it is always good to look on the loveliness of Venice." Despite the anxiety I could feel washing off her in small waves, her tone remained its usual calm, as if nothing could disturb her tranquility.

I thought I was going to gag, but I kept my mouth shut and my face blank.

"Please, come sit near us. It seems we have much to catch up on." The silver-haired Elder motioned with a careless wave of his right hand for her to take a seat on the stairs before him.

Macaire was not the leader of the Elders, not even the strongest of the three. That was and always would be Jabari. However, Macaire loved to play with his prey. He liked to toy with their minds, break their spirits before he broke their bodies. It was a trait Sadira shared with him, one many nightwalkers shared.

"I am honored, but I would like to remain beside my daughter," she said, lifting her chin slightly. I raised one eyebrow in surprise before I could catch it. Macaire had given her an easy out, an extremely generous opportunity to save her own skin. She wouldn't get a second chance.

"Yes," he hissed. Macaire's eyes slid over to me and his gaze narrowed. "Mira. It has been a long time."

"Not since that last little job in Nepal," I said with a pleasant smile. It was a little nudge, a friendly reminder that I had fulfilled the requests of the Coven in the past. One of the Coven toadies had contacted me several years ago to eliminate a vampire who was causing some problems in a small village in Nepal. He was leaving behind a large trail of bodies. It was raising too many questions, and a major media organization was starting to look into it. I destroyed the nightwalker and it was covered up as a rare disease sweeping through the remote area. After the job, I stopped by Venice as a way of politely checking in before returning home. At the time, only Elizabeth had been in residence on the island.

"Yes. Well, it seems you were quite busy in England recently." I opened my mouth to argue, taking a step forward, but Macaire raised a silencing hand. "Jabari told us of how you were attacked by a horde of naturi not far from London. Nasty business." Macaire shook his head, while resting his elbows on the arms of the chair. He folded his hands over his stomach and watched me for a moment as if thinking. "We are grateful that you saved the lives of Sadira and our Jabari. It would have been a dreadful loss." He paused for half a second, and I thought I saw something in his eyes, but he quickly pushed on. "But it seems your little display has caused some problems that need dealing with."

"What problems?" I flinched, the muscles in my shoulders tensing. What new horror was I opening myself up to? I took a small step forward, wishing I could push Danaus and Sadira behind me a little better, but I could offer only so much protection.

"I'll let our visitor explain," Macaire blandly said.

At the same time, a door to the left of the dais opened and a woman walked out. She was African American, with rich black hair that poured past her shoulders and large, lovely brown eyes. She walked across the room with a natural ease and seductive grace that could bring men to their knees. I'd seen her do it. Her name was Alexandra Brooks and she was a werewolf. I'd known her for nearly five years, but I doubted that the Coven was aware of it. During the long centuries, lycans and nightwalkers had learned to tolerate each other. On rare occasions, nightwalkers and shapeshifters would team up for some mutual fun, but the peace never seemed to last long.

We had held a contest once. It was Valerio's idea. We grabbed a poet and made him decide which race was more alluring: vampires or lycans. Poor fool. It really was a no-win situation for him, but we found it entertaining. After more than two weeks of allowing his senses to feast on a handful of vampires and a choice selection of weres, he made some interesting comments. For this poet, vampires could be extraordinarily sexy just standing still, quietly occupying space like the white, slender beauty of the Venus de Milo. On the other hand, lycans seemed to come alive with sexual allure the moment they moved. Their energy flared and filled the room, brushing against its occupants; an exquisite blending of animal and man.

To my surprise, we released the poet after he made his comments. Both sides seemed content with the assessment, and Valerio's interest had wandered elsewhere. I later heard that the man committed suicide a few months after escaping our collective clutches.

Behind Alexandra, a prime specimen of male beauty strolled in. At well over six feet, he looked as if he were built of pure muscle with a hint of granite. A seeming child of the sun, the stranger possessed thick blond hair and bronze skin. His features were soft, with full lips and small cleft in his determined chin. He was also a lycanthrope. His movement was too liquid to be human, and with him came the scent of nature. Not the same as you would smell when the naturi were near, but definitely woodsy with a musky hint of man.

If the circumstances had been different, I would have happily taken the time to get to know the shifter. Unfortunately, my main concern then was making sure Alexandra didn't say anything to reveal our friendship.

I smiled coldly at the woman, my fangs peeking out. "I never thought I'd see the day when the Coven let a mongrel loose in the main hall."

Alexandra sharply halted and glared at me, but said nothing. She and the male lycan were outnumbered in the court of nightwalkers. As an emissary, she expected a level of protection from the Elders, but that didn't mean the members of the court couldn't mock her in an attempt to get her to attack. If she attacked, a nightwalker had every right to defend herself.

I walked over, drawing closer with each circle I closed around her. The sharp click of my heels on the marble was the only sound in the enormous room. The blond man stiffened when I slipped between him and Alexandra, but he didn't move, didn't even change his even breathing pattern. "Tell me, Alexandra, are you still an Omega or did a Beta finally have pity on you and make you his bitch?"

Alexandra growled low in the back of her throat at me, and I saw a subtle shift in her eyes for a second. Her brown eyes had faded to liquid copper as the wolf in her fought for control on the swell of anger. Lucky for us both, she caught it in time. She wouldn't risk changing here—it was too dangerous with this many vampires hanging about; she wouldn't survive the night.

Of course, after my last comment, I was asking for her to rip my throat out. There were three grades to the werewolf pack. There was the Alpha male and female; leaders of the pack. Everyone else generally filtered down to the Beta class. And then there were the Omegas hanging on the periphery of the pack, not exactly a part or accepted, just barely tolerated. They were permitted the scraps of the kill after everyone else had eaten, and they served as the whipping boy for the family. The only thing lower than an Omega was dead.

"Arresto, Mira," Macaire said mildly with a vague wave of his hand. There was no censure in his voice, only a note of boredom and maybe a hint of amusement. "It seems you have already met our Ms. Brooks," he continued, switching to English for Alexandra's benefit.

"She came sniffing around my domain a couple years ago. I sent her on her way," I said, turning my back on the lycan as I walked back over to Danaus and Sadira.

"How nice," he said with a false grin. "That does not matter. She's brought word from her people in England."

"It seems you have made quite a mess, Fire Starter," Alex said, smiling broadly at me. It was now her turn to make me twist, and I had a feeling she was going to come out of this meeting looking a lot better than me. "All throughout the southwestern territories of the U.K. people have found heaps of ashes accompanied by items like knives, swords, bits of clothing. The humans are smart enough to figure out that these ashes were from living creatures. They are going to automatically assume they were humans. Some very uncomfortable questions are being asked, and there is only so much we can suppress."

"Get our press out there," I argued, looking over at Macaire. "Start feeding the tabloids tales of aliens or solar flares at night." Shoving my fingers into the front pockets of my pants, I tried to affect a look of indifference, though that was a horrible lie. This was a turn I had not considered or anticipated.

When Danaus and I used our powers to destroy the naturi, we hadn't limited ourselves to those at the Themis Compound. We destroyed the naturi in all directions for several miles. I was just grateful to have them gone and my life intact. I hadn't thought about what the humans would find. My focus was so entirely centered on the naturi and stopping them from breaking the seal that I had not thought about protecting our secret. Hell, what was the point? If the naturi were free, we'd have bigger things to worry about than a few people discovering that nightwalkers existed.

"Some of the Wiccans have already mobilized and are posting items on the Internet. They're claiming that the creatures were once members of the naturi and that they were killed as part of ongoing war between them and vampires."

"And we're concerned about that? Don't you realize how ridiculous this sounds?" I said incredulously, pinning the lycan with my narrowed gaze. Sure, it was the truth, but no one believed the truth anymore. "Most humans don't know what a naturi is. They've never heard of them."

"Your lack of control has thrown off our timetable," Alexandra snapped, pointing one slender finger at me as she lurched forward a couple steps. However, she quickly came to a stop when she realized the sudden movement could be seen as an act of aggression. "The Great Awakening isn't supposed to be for another fifty years at the earliest."

"And what about Rowe? Don't you think he could throw off the precious timetable?" I replied, my gaze darting back to the Elders. I didn't know how much the lycans knew of the current naturi threat, which was growing with each passing night, but I didn't care anymore. I wasn't going to be the only one in the fire. It was time to up the ante.

"That is already being considered, Mira," Elizabeth said in a calm, placating voice. She was telling me to shut up. I took the hint.

"Thank you for your valuable information, Ms. Brooks," Macaire said. "We will not need to speak with you again." Alex bowed slightly to the three Elders, then left the main hall without looking back at me. The silent blond man followed close on her heels, but I could feel his dark eyes on me before he disappeared through the side door.

I waited until after the door on the left was closed before I opened my mouth again. It was time to take the gloves off and get messy. I had been purposefully dressed down by someone the Coven saw as an inferior regarding something that was supremely trivial at this point, considering the problems that loomed and their own betrayal. I'd had enough.

"Shall we bring out your other guest?" I demanded, taking another couple steps forward so the Coven's focus would be completely on me. My hands fell from my pockets and hung limp at my sides, but I was ready for any kind of an attack.

"Other guest?" Macaire repeated, tilting his head to the side. A nice act, but it wasn't all that convincing. The other two Elders hadn't moved, didn't even blink at the question. In fact, Jabari hadn't moved a muscle since I entered the room. We still had other issues that went beyond the Coven.

"The naturi," I supplied in a voice that could have frozen the Lagoon. Macaire smiled at me in his usual condescending manner and opened his mouth to say something, but I cut off his words. "Don't insult me! There was a naturi sleeping here last night less than an hour before dawn. Bring her out."

Macaire blinked at me once in surprise and then looked over at

Elizabeth, who was regarding me with new interest. The Elder turned his cold gaze back at me, a calculating look crossing his face as frost-bite sank its teeth into the marrow of my bones. *"Impressionate,"* he slowly said as he slipped back into Italian. However, this time an old accent flavored the single word before he could catch it. Something of who he truly was snuck past his defenses while he was distracted with a new thought. "We were wondering what you and the hunter were doing out in the Lagoon so close to dawn. We knew he could sense the naturi, but we didn't think he would be able to sense them through our web of spells."

"He couldn't, but *we* could," I corrected. Macaire's eyebrows jumped at that bit of information, and even Jabari cracked. Actually, it was just a twitch of one corner of his mouth, but it was something.

"Molto impressionante. It explains how you were able to inciner-ate the naturi far from your location. It was my understanding that you could only burn that which you could see," Macaire said. The fingers of his right hand restlessly moved on the arm of his chair, and he was now sitting up a little straighter.

"Yes, well this is all very new to me considering that my memory was wiped," I sneered. My fingers balled into fists and it was all I could do to keep from lighting the tapestries hanging about the room on fire. "I thought the Coven would know exactly what I was capable of, considering it spent nearly a century experimenting on me." My words dripped with sarcasm so acidic I feared they would soon eat through the marble floor.

"That was Jabari's realm," Macaire said with a dismissive wave of his hand, but the motion was stiffer this time and there was some-thing that flickered in his eyes again. There had always been a certain amount of tension between Macaire and Jabari. While they never openly attacked each other, they had no problems pitting their vari-ous flunkies and followers against one another. I would have been willing to wager that either Macaire couldn't control me or had never been given the opportunity to try.

Again the door on the left swung open, halting the conversation. Into the room stepped a female naturi. She wore a simple homespun dress and her long blond hair was braided down her back. There were five clans of naturi—earth, wind, water, light, and animal. She was too slender and willowy to be a member of the animal clan, which were typically dark, swarthy creatures rippling with muscles. A water clan member couldn't be out of water, and her coloring was all wrong for what I had seen of the earth clan, as their hair and skin pigment had the same variety as a summer flower garden. So that left only wind and light. If she was a light clan member, I was in trouble if I attacked, as she would be able to use fire as easily as me. But I couldn't imagine the Coven allowing a light clan member in their midst. Of course, I would never have imagined seeing a naturi walking free in the Great Hall.

With her hands folded in front of her like a nun going to prayer, she walked quietly into the room. Keeping her eyes on the Elders, she bowed her head to them, but ignored our trio completely.

"What is she doing here?" I demanded, each word struggling up my throat and past my lips. My whole body was clenched with rage. I had thought my reaction to seeing Sadira for the first time in five centuries was bad. This was infinitely worse. The sight of the slender creature with her sharp features instantly made me want to rip her apart with my bare hands. I wanted to hear her scream and plead for her life. And then I wanted to hear her plead for me to kill her.

Nightmarish memories of my two-week captivity at Machu Picchu centuries ago came screaming back with a flawless clarity. She reminded me of the starvation and the pain that flooded all of my senses so that there was no escape. The naturi had captured and tortured me in hopes of breaking my mind. They wanted me to use my powers to destroy my own kind. As I stared at her now, the scars on my back burned anew.

Danaus stepped forward so he was standing beside me. His right hand reflexively reached for a weapon that wasn't there. Frustrated, his hand fell back to his side, clenched in a fist.

"You asked to see her," Macaire said with laughter in his voice.

"Why is she on the island?" My voice cracked across them like a whip snapping at the air.

Macaire stiffened and moved to sit on the edge of his chair. "We have business together," he briskly replied.

"The only business we have with their kind is their total extermination!" I took a couple slow steps toward the naturi, my hands before me with my fingers curled into claws. I didn't have any weapons, but I would happily have killed her with my bare hands. The naturi turned frightened eyes on me and stumbled a couple of steps back, edging closer to the raised dais and the Elders.

"Macaire!" she cried in her soft lilting voice.

"Stop, Mira!" Macaire shouted, jumping to his feet. "She has the protection of the Coven."

Those words stopped me cold. My body froze as if my mind had suddenly lost the ability to command it, had forgotten how to work my limbs. With infinite slowness I turned my head to look at the Elders. "What?" The word barely made it past the lump in my throat.

"Stop," Macaire commanded.

I ignored him and dragged my eyes to Jabari's face, who sat watching me. "Say it," I snarled, my voice harsh and rough.

Jabari rose from his chair, his head held high. "She has the protection of the Coven," he said loud and clear. His words reverberated through my chest until I was sure I would shatter into a million jagged shards.

Wrapping my arms around my waist, I nearly doubled over in horror. "How could you betray us?" I moaned. "They killed hundreds of our kind."

"The same could be said about the man that stands beside you," Jabari replied. A cold smile slithered across his broad lips, stretching his dark skin to accentuate his hard cheekbones. I reached back one hand, unconsciously trying to move the hunter behind me as if it would better protect him from the Coven.

"They tortured me for two weeks in hopes of using me as a weapon." I flung the words at him, even though some part of me knew not one of them cared about the pain I had endured to protect my own kind. "They slaughtered nightwalkers in my domain."

"Looking for you," Elizabeth coolly interjected.

"They killed Thorne in London," I said, but my voice had lost some of its earlier strength and venom. I didn't like where this was going.

"In an effort to get to you," Elizabeth replied. Her lovely face was blank of expression but her blue eyes seemed to sparkle and dance in the candlelight. "Our Jabari and Sadira were attacked, all in an effort to get to you."

"Times have changed, Mira," Macaire stated, drawing my wide-eyed gaze to his aged face. "It would seem as if the naturi would have no business with nightwalkers if you were not around."

"The naturi don't change. Not ever," I snarled, straightening from my wounded stance. *They would not pin this on me.* But even that bitter declaration seemed to carry with it a whimper of pain. I wasn't the reason so many of my fellow nightwalkers had been slaughtered. I wasn't the reason the naturi hunted and killed both humans and nightwalkers. This war started long before I was ever reborn, and I was sure it would continue long after my bones had been reduced to dust. *I would not be the Coven's scapegoat.*

"Unfortunately, we cannot rid ourselves of Mira as of yet," Jabari announced in a weary voice, as if reluctantly granting me a pardon.

I snapped. There was no more clear thought, just raw, horrible rage. The Coven was protecting our greatest enemy and threatening my life when I had done everything within my power to protect my own kind from the naturi.

Stretching my arms out on either side of my body, I started calling up great amounts of energy. Without making the conscious decision, I summoned enormous waves of power to me, pulling energy from every living creature within the region. I could feel it coming to me not just from San Clemente, but from all around Venice. At the same time, grim images of Michael's and Thorne's mangled remains crowded in my brain. Memories of my horrific nights with Nerian swamped me, threatening to weigh me down and deter me from my path. The Coven had to be destroyed. It didn't matter that they were the Elders, or even if I had the ability to do it.

Overhead, the candles in the chandelier flared, awakening the shadows lounging in the far corners of the hall. The shadows lunged forward and back, reaching out from under the dais chairs and crawling up the cold stone walls. The flags and tapestries waved and rippled as if a fresh breeze had rushed in through an open window.

You can't destroy me, desert flower. Jabari's dark voice whispered through my brain, threatening to shatter my concentration. *If you attempt this thing, you must be able to kill them both. Destroy the Coven, Mira. Destroy them both.*

The command was little more than a faint whisper among hundreds of fragmented thoughts and painful memories. I tried to weigh the command in that second. It's what I wanted, but now I was forced to wonder if I wanted the same thing that Jabari wanted after all his lies, betrayal, and manipulation. But I couldn't afford to pause.

Before the thought was completely formed in my head, I was stopped by the last person I thought would ever do such a thing. Danaus came up behind me and wrapped his strong arms around me, locking my arms against my body.

"No!" I screamed, my ragged voice bouncing off the high stone walls. I already felt his power swamping me, struggling to form a cocoon around me before seeping into my skin. He was stealing away my ability to choose. Jabari hadn't been forcing me. It was almost a test to see what I was capable of.

"Calm," Danaus whispered, his hot breath brushing against my ear. I also heard the word repeated in my brain like a thought, blanketing my rage, suffocating the fire. He was trying to use our connection in reverse. Instead of commanding me to draw in the power and destroy, he was using his own powers to control and calm me.

"No!" I screamed again, but even my voice had begun to weaken. The power I had drawn in was seeping from my body back into the air. I wasn't sure if he could hear me, but I tried to push my own thoughts into his brain. *Help me, Danaus. Together we can crush them like we defeated the naturi. Together we can destroy them.*

But all I heard was silence. I could still feel him in my brain, his will sapping my strength. "They have betrayed us; betrayed my kind," I whimpered pathetically, feeling as if the remains of my soul were shattering into sharp shards of glass.

"How dare you say that while you stand there in the embrace of a vampire hunter!" Jabari raged, his calm finally cracking. But I knew now it was an act after his attempt to have me destroy the other Coven members.

"He saved you in England!" I shouted, my eyes locking on his twisted face. "He protected you and Sadira when the naturi attacked. He protected you."

"He's protecting us even now," Elizabeth proclaimed, gracefully rising from her seat. There was a look of open surprise on her pale heart-shaped face. "Look. She was trying to kill us all, but he stopped her." Her voice was haunting, like a half-remembered dream drifting through my brain.

All three Elders were now standing and staring at us with a mixture of wonder and confusion. Something strange had happened, and everyone was individually working on the implications. A renowned vampire hunter who had killed countless other nightwalkers had potentially saved the lives of the Coven. Not exactly something that happened every day.

"Send the naturi away," Danaus barked, his arms still locked around me.

Macaire wasn't happy with the order, but he could see the wisdom in it. I obviously couldn't control myself when she was around. The Elder nodded, and the terrified female naturi ran from the room and slammed the door behind her. With her gone, Danaus released me. He had effectively sapped all my strength, and I fell to my hands and knees. I glared wordlessly up at the Coven. I hated them. You didn't do business with the naturi. You didn't talk to them. You didn't make deals with them. You killed them.

Jabari and Elizabeth had returned to their seats, lost in thought, but Macaire remained standing, his sharp eyes never leaving my face. I could almost hear the cold, steel wheels in his mind churning away, examining each angle of what had happened.

"That is enough for today," he suddenly announced, his voice taking on a weary tone. "You may go now. We will talk more to-morrow."

"What about the seal? And the triad?" I cried, slapping my hand angrily against the marble floor. Nothing had been discussed and yet he was calling an end to court for the night.

"We have much to think about," Macaire said, returning to his seat. "We will talk more tomorrow."

I was about to argue again. I had obviously lost all common sense the second the naturi entered the room. A smart person would have picked herself off the ground and left, grateful that she was still alive. But I got off lucky. The moment I was about to speak, I heard Macaire's voice in my head. *We will speak again later.* I got the point. Macaire wanted a private meeting. So be it. The scheming had begun anew.

EIGHT

Danaus tried to help me off the ground, but I jerked out of his grasp and less than gracefully pushed to my feet. I was livid with him and the Coven. Had he done the right thing? Had he saved our lives because I lacked the ability to control my temper? Had he pulled me away from whatever game Jabari was playing? Yes, but I was still angry. In the boat the night before I chose our joining, let him control me. But minutes ago he'd taken away my choices and forced me. I didn't give a damn right now if it was for our own good.

I wanted to tear his throat out, to see him crumpled and bleeding at my feet. My body had been used and abused, first by my own brethren and now by my enemy. I felt dirty down to my very core. I had become a thing worse than chum. I couldn't even fight my fate, only obey.

To twist the knife even further, I couldn't lash out at Danaus. The Coven and its dedicated court were watching closely. If I were to strike out at him, any one of them might take it as a green light to have some fun, and I was too weak to fend them off. And I'd made a promise to get him out of Venice alive. For now, we were one big happy family.

Silently, our little group—Danaus, Sadira, and I—trooped out of the main hall and across the island back to the dock. The other night-walkers kept their distance, but were closely watching our progress. I had no doubt they'd sensed my display of power. I was sure that creatures all over Italy had felt it. You don't create waves like that and not draw attention.

"Out of the boat," I snapped at Roberto, who stood behind the wheel. He frowned at me but said nothing as he stepped on the docks.

We jumped on the little speed boat and I threw it into reverse. I had some business to take care of and I didn't want to have a nightwalker following me. The Coven would give me a little space for now. I had a bit of interesting information, but it wasn't going to do me much good at the moment. No one would believe me if I said the Coven was plotting something *with* the naturi. Not only was it ridiculous, but it would also be coming from a nightwalker traveling with a vampire hunter.

"What's going on?" Sadira softly asked when we were halfway across the Lagoon.

"I don't know yet," I said, refusing to look at her. I directed the boat down the Guidecca Canal, narrowly dodging a shuttle bus as it trudged across the narrow waterway, sending up a spray of water on some of the passengers. The driver's curses barely rose above the rumble of the boat's engine. "But I'll know before we leave here."

"There was a naturi, Mira!" Sadira said, her voice jumping in pitch. The sight of the naturi had left her shaken, crushing the last of her composure. "A naturi in the Great Hall!"

"I noticed." I shifted the boat into neutral and let it glide into the hotel landing. I looked up at the large, elegant Hotel Cipriani. Tristan was pacing in front of the windows, waiting for our return. No one had bothered him, but that had not lessened his anxiety. Since marking him, his thoughts came clearly to me when I wanted them. I would have known instantly if a vampire had laid a hand on him. But it also worked in reverse. He could feel my own concerns and anxiety, though my exact thoughts were shrouded.

"Go up to the suite and calm Tristan," I ordered, gripping the steering wheel. I needed to be away from her. I needed some space from Sadira, the Coven, and this whole damned situation so I could think clearly. "But do not harm him in any way. You know that none of this is his fault. It's between you and me."

"And what are your plans for him?" she inquired from her seat, her voice hardening to rusty steel. After our encounter in the room and with the Coven, she had once again grown wary of me. During our last years together, Sadira had been a constant shadow in my brain, fearing my powers. The fear had left her a hollow shell, resulting in the death of many of her other pets.

I spun on my heels, my fists clenched as I looked down at her. A loose tendril of hair fell against my cheek, tickling my neck. "I have no plans for him! I don't want him. He's your pet, and you should have taken care of him. You know they would have torn him apart tonight."

"He has to learn to protect himself," she said in such a matter-of-fact tone that I longed to smack her. "You were younger than he when you first appeared before the court."

"I was also ten times stronger, and even then I barely survived." I took another step closer to her, clenching my fists so tight my nails began to cut into the palms of my hands. "You only let him go because you are too much of a coward to stand up to the court."

"How dare you call me a coward after I stood with you before the Elders!" she said, surging to her feet. Her sudden movement caused the little boat to rock and lurch in the water.

"You stood with me because you were confident that I would protect you. That is beginning to wear thin."

She smiled back at me, her usual beatific smile of peace and supreme confidence. "I'm your mother, my Mira. You will always protect me."

"Get out of here," I growled, pulling back my lips to expose my fangs. Her smile never wavered as she alighted from the boat and walked gracefully up the landing into the hotel. She sacrificed Tristan to save her own skin, and she knew that I would step forward and protect both of them from the Coven. I wanted to scream. My decisions weren't wrong. I needed the triad intact, which meant protecting Sadira, though I longed to rip her throat out. It was insane to fight her, because winning would be finally killing her, and I couldn't.

Jerking the boat into reverse, I backed it into the waterway again. Shifting roughly into first, I headed to the Grand Canal. It was a short trip, but I wasn't in the mood to bother with water taxis or shuttles. I docked in an opening on the island of Dorsoduro, almost directly across from Piazza San Marco.

Danaus jumped to the ground right behind me as I secured the boat. I almost forgot he was there, having become so accustomed to having the dark rain cloud on my heels. Of course, I was also a little preoccupied with thoughts of the Coven and their special guest.

"Mira—"

"Don't talk to me yet, I'm still angry with you," I bit out as we walked down the winding streets, slipping past the locals on their way to the bars and restaurants for a few drinks and light conversation.

"You left me with no choice." His deep voice slipped around me like a pair of strong arms.

"You could have let me kill them."

"Could you?"

I didn't say anything, but marched down the street, my teeth clenched. I didn't know. Maybe, but it was doubtful. The past few days had been strange, and I wasn't sure what I was capable of anymore. Of course, *we* could have most likely destroyed them, but he had hesitated. Last night when we were alone on the boat, I knew he thought about killing every nightwalker on the island. But today when we stood before the Coven, the opportunity spread out before us, and he stopped.

"That's what I thought," Danaus said grimly.

"You don't understand!" I shouted, whirling around to face him. "I've worked all my life to not have to answer to another creature—human or vampire. And then one night I wake up and find I'm wearing a choke chain and an untold number of people have the ability to jerk me to heel." I stepped closer, until he was backed against one of the buildings lining the sidewalk, and rose up on the tips of my toes so I could look him in the eyes. "To make matters worse, my enemy can do the same. I've become a threat to every thing on this planet. Do you have any clue as to what that feels like?"

We stared at each other in silence for several seconds. His face was unreadable, but I could feel the turmoil in his chest. Our connection was still strong from that night's brief contact. I could feel sadness, but it was cluttered with something else. I couldn't tell if it was sympathy, regret, or maybe even pity. For a second I was afraid we had more in common than I wanted there to be. He seemed to understand too well.

I softly growled in the back of my throat as I turned away from him. The sound was a strange mix of anger and frustration. It wasn't all his fault, no matter how hard I tried to pin it on him. Danaus just kept getting in the way. "You owe me," I muttered as I walked down the street.

"What?"

"I haven't decided yet. You owe me something. I'll get back to you."

"I'm on pins and needles," he said in a voice so dry I expected to see a puff of dust. I smiled despite my struggles to remain angry at him. It was becoming annoying that he could snap me out of my grim moods. Of course, dark ruminations were more of his forte than mine.

"That can be arranged," I said irritably, but he knew better. If I could sense his emotions, then he knew I was no longer angry. Frustrated and irritated, but not necessarily pissed.

NINE

We stopped at a small square flanked by some cozy restaurants and narrow shops. It was a quaint neighborhood that generally escaped the crowds of tourists, even during the high season. At night the area twinkled with guttering candles and little white lights. The air was layered with the tangy scent of spices and rich sauces with a hint of melted cheese. It almost made me miss the taste of food, but not quite.

"What are we doing here?" Danaus inquired as we came to stand in the center of the square. He turned and looked at the fountain at the opposite end, its falling water dancing in the faint yellow lights that flowed along the stone structure.

"Meeting a friend," I replied as Alex stepped out of the entrance of one of the small bars. There was an almost hypnotic sway to her hips as she closed the distance between us, her lithe body dancing to its own natural rhythm.

The lycanthrope was strong and independent, chasing after those things she wanted most in life. She cherished her existence as a were-wolf, seeing her enhanced abilities as a gift rather than a curse, like so many of her kind. But even if she hadn't been a lycan, I think she would have reveled in all of her natural abilities as a normal human being. Life for her was a drink to be gulped, sipped, and always savored.

Alex had helped me escape myself and my past when my thoughts grew too dark. In return, I did everything within my power to foster amiable relations between her kind and mine. Not the easiest of tasks.

Her powers brushed briefly past me as she scanned the area. She was making sure we were alone. I had already checked. The closest nightwalker was stalking a tourist on the other side of the canal in

San Marco. We had time. Besides, since dropping off Sadira on Guidecca, I had been cloaking Danaus and myself. We would need the privacy.

I opened my arms and was about to greet her when her fist connected with my jaw, snapping my head around. One of the benefits of being a werewolf was speed. The other was strength. I stumbled backward a step into Danaus, who tensed. I had seen her swing half a second before she hit me but was so surprised that I didn't try to dodge it.

"Bitch!" she spat at me.

"What are you doing? We're alone," I said, pushing off of Danaus. But even as I said it, I noticed the second lycanthrope stepping from the entrance of the bar. His broad shoulders briefly blocked the square of golden light pouring from the open doorway. He was either a member of her pack or assigned to her as backup should she run into any problems when dealing with my kind. Either way, I wasn't overly concerned. He was of her race and thus would protect her.

"That was for what you said," Alex told me, giving my shoulder a little shove with her index finger. Her narrowed eyes glittered in the faint light from a nearby pub but otherwise remained brown. "That Omega comment was a low blow and you know it."

I shrugged. "It had to be convincing. I'm not particularly popular at the moment and I didn't want any backlash to hit you if they thought we were friends."

"Yeah, you always had a way with people," Alex said. Her full lips eased from a hard, angry slash to a reluctant smile. "Who's this?" she asked, jerking her chin toward my dark shadow. I turned and put an arm around her slim shoulders.

"Alexandra Brooks, this is Danaus, the hunter," I said, introducing her. She twisted out of my grasp so she could look up at me, her eyes widening to the point I thought I would have to catch them when they fell from their sockets.

"Are you crazy, girl?" she gasped. She looked over at Danaus then back at me. "There've been some rumors, but I didn't believe them. What's going on?"

"I'll explain soon," I said with a slight shake of my head. "Who's your golden companion? Pack member?"

Alex looked at me strangely, her brows drawn together over her pert nose. "I thought you knew," she softly said. "He belongs to Jabari."

"What?" I gasped. "No." The growl of frustration rumbled in my throat a second before I started moving, but my nails never made it into the lycan's bronze throat. Danaus quickly wrapped a strong arm around my waist and held me close, keeping me from ripping the man's throat out before a crowd of humans.

"Not here," Danaus snapped, tightening his arm around my waist, nearly cracking a rib.

"He's going to tell Jabari that I spoke with Alex. He'll know . . . he'll know we're friends," I said. Both my hands gripped the arm around my waist but I'd stopped struggling, my eyes never wavering from the lycan's face. He stared at me with a look of such sympathy and compassion that I could almost believe he cared for my plight.

"I don't understand," Alex interjected, drawing my gaze back to her troubled features. "I thought you and Jabari . . . Well, you've never made any secret of your—"

"Jabari wants me dead," I said in a rush. "He wants my head on a pike and my heart on his mantel." Saying the words out loud suddenly made me feel very tired. My body went extremely still, as if I were made of stone, and I leaned back into Danaus, letting his warmth seep into me, calm my mind. Jabari had been my beloved mentor and guide through the night for nearly five centuries. He had been a companion when the emptiness threatened to consume me. And now he accused me of betrayal while he stank of it. I had been his puppet, his toy, his own personal assassin and servant. I had believed he would protect nightwalkers and that he would do what was right for our race.

But I'd been wrong about him; about a lot of things. Unfortunately, my blindness and ignorance were getting people killed. It couldn't continue.

"I won't say anything to the Coven about your meeting with Ms. Brooks," the man said, his deep voice like a distant drum beat waking me from my growing lethargy. "I may belong to the vampire, but my loyalty will always be to my own kind."

"Thank you . . ."

"Nico," he supplied.

"Nico?" I repeated, crinkling my nose at him. He definitely didn't look like a Nico. He was more like a John or Bruce. Maybe even Adonis, but that was guessing he looked as delicious naked as he did standing there in his cotton slacks and soft, hunter green button-up shirt. The sleeves of his shirt were rolled up past his elbows, revealing strong tanned arms covered in light blond hairs. I was willing to bet naked was better.

"Nicolai Gromenko," he replied, crushing the name with his clenched teeth.

"You're not Russian," I snapped, sounding equally irritated.

"Fourth generation. Nicolai is a family name. I'm from Phoenix. Anything else? Shoe size? Boxers versus briefs?"

"Don't worry," I purred, a grin slinking across my mouth. "There's always time to find out." The comment instantly erased the irritation from Nicolai's expression, causing a surprised smile to brighten his handsome features.

Danaus suddenly released me, a snort of disgust escaping him while Alexandra laughed. My attention snapped back to my companions and I winked at my old friend. I couldn't help myself.

"Lord! You had me worried for a minute," Alex said as she gave me a quick hug. "Between the hunter and Jabari, I seriously thought you were losing it."

"She has," Danaus grumbled.

My eyes darted from Danaus back to my friend, who noticed the smile that was crumbling from my face. "We have to talk," I said. Threading a loose strand of hair behind my ear, I swept my gaze over the area. This was going to take a while, but it would be worth it. "Hungry?" I asked, my eyes snagging on a pleasant-looking restaurant with a scattering of tables on the rim of the square.

"Starved," Alex said with a half sigh. She tilted her head toward Danaus while plopping her hands on her hips. "He need babysitting while you hunt?"

"She's eaten already," Danaus interjected, oozing disapproval.

Alex arched one eyebrow at me and threw a "What's his problem?" look my way. She had long ago adjusted to the fact that I drank of the blood of humans and thought nothing of the hunt.

Threading my arm through hers, I guided her over to the restaurant, with Danaus and Nicolai following close behind. I motioned to the maître d' that we would be taking one of the tables in the courtyard. He nodded, then disappeared inside the building to find a server.

When we were all comfortably seated and our drink order taken, I relaxed in my chair, staring out across the quiet square. A pair of lovers walked arm in arm, whispering to each other. Three young children chased pigeons, their squeals of laughter skipping ahead of them. From inside the restaurant, loud boisterous Italian tumbled into the plaza. It was all pleasant and blissfully normal.

"Let's start with something simple," Alex announced as she scanned the menu. "Was that you I felt earlier?"

"I lost my temper," I murmured, my eyes falling to the tabletop. It had been stupid and irresponsible. Now that I was calm, I could admit as much. My actions had been careless and irresponsible, just like when I convinced Tristan to help me attack the naturi in England. We had been outnumbered and outgunned. I knew that when we spotted them, but I went ahead anyway. As a result, I barely escaped with my life, endangering Danaus and Tristan unnecessarily.

I knew better than to take these stupid risks and risk the lives of those I had sworn to protect. Shame and guilt burned away in my stomach. Fear of the naturi was driving me to make one bad decision after another, and it couldn't go on. I had already lost Michael. I refused to lose anyone else in my life because of my stupidity.

Drawing in a steadying breath, I lifted my eyes from the glass tabletop to look over at Danaus, who sat to my right with his arms folded over his chest. "Do you eat?"

"Yes," he said, frowning at me.

"Then find something to eat," I said, tapping his untouched menu with the index finger of my right hand. "Order something big. I'm putting it on the Coven gold card."

"That's petty," he chided, but he still picked up his menu.

"I regret to say that I'm feeling very petty right now," I said with a dramatic sigh, relaxing in my chair. Alex chuckled, shaking her head behind her menu. Her dark hair cascaded over one shoulder, caressing her cheek.

We let the conversation die while Alex, Nicolai, and Danaus perused their menus. I contented myself with twirling the stem of my glass of red wine. After what had happened to Thorne, I wasn't going to even sip it. Ingesting anything other than human blood had effectively lost its appeal. After the server returned and the others placed their orders, I reopened the conversation.

"How did you get stuck with Coven duty? Piss off one of the big dogs?" I teased, looking at Alex. She was frowning at me but there was no real anger in her eyes.

"Just rotten luck, I guess," she confessed with a shrug. "I had been in London on business for the past week. When news hit of the strange piles of ashes, phones calls were made and e-mails were flying. I was sent to a small town outside of London to check it out. I swear, Mira, the second I saw it I thought of you, but I've never seen you do anything like that. Their bodies were reduced to ash, but the ground around them was completely untouched. Some are talking warlocks and spontaneous combustion, but there are still too many holes in the theories."

"They'll cover it up," I said indifferently. "In a few days they'll think of some very simple explanation and blast it across all the news agencies. It may have holes, but people will buy it because they want to. They need everything to make sense."

"You think?" she said skeptically. She stared down at her short but perfectly manicured nails. "I wish I had your confidence."

I shook my head, not liking to see her so shaken. Alex exuded confidence and strength in her own pack or when on her own, but when faced with issues outside her own control, her confidence and strength wilted like a flower with too little water. "Don't get me wrong," I said. "You were right when you said this moves up the timetable. Too many things have been happening lately, and science has gotten too far too fast to keep hiding."

"Damn it, Mira!" she suddenly exploded, shattering her mien of calm. "Fifty years was a nice number. I was hoping to be dead and buried before the Great Awakening. It's going to be ugly, and I don't want to be around for it." She leaned her forehead on her hands, her frame tense and her teeth clenched.

"It'll be fun!" I laughed, trying to cheer her up. "Just think of all the groupies we'll gain. These people are completely enamored of the idea of the occult."

"What about the Daylight Coalition?" she demanded. "What about him?" She jerked her thumb at Danaus.

"I'm not saying it'll be easy, but I don't think it will be that bad either. We've been preparing these people for a few centuries. It's not like it's going to come as a complete shock."

"Preparing? What's this Great Awakening you mentioned?" Danaus interrupted.

My gaze jerked over to the hunter and it was all I could do to keep from saying something incredibly rude, but I held back. Frowning, I shoved one hand through my hair, pushing it back from where it had fallen about my face. "You can't stay with them," I said in a low voice. I knew the others could hear me, but the comment was directed solely at Danaus. "Ryan should have told you a long time ago."

I wasn't the only one being kept in the dark by those I trusted and needed to trust. Themis was supposed to be a great society that studied the various other races, but they remained bogged down by archaic ideas and old myths that had no basis in reality. To make matter worse, the group was led by Ryan, an extremely powerful warlock who refused to set his flock straight, even if it meant the lives of my kind and the lives of members of the other races.

Danaus refused to meet my gaze, his dark blue eyes focused on the fountain at the edge of the square. But he didn't have to say anything. I could feel his frustration bubbling below his unmovable exterior of indifference. His time with me had proven on more than one occasion that he'd been operating under some false assumptions, and

Ryan—the man he relied on for correct information—hadn't done anything to see that Danaus knew the truth.

"A few centuries ago, the various groups got together—"

"What groups?" Danaus demanded.

"Warlocks, witches, nightwalkers, lycanthropes, and a few other heavy hitters," Alex supplied, counting off each group on her fingers.

"The naturi?"

"No!" we both shouted. I held up my hand before Alex could continue to berate him for what I'm sure Danaus thought was a valid question. After what we saw at the main hall, it was actually a valid question, but Alex didn't know that yet.

"No," I repeated calmly. "The leaders of the various groups met and came to the agreement that mankind isn't as stupid as we would hope. One day, people are going to figure out that this whole other world exists. So in an attempt to control the chaos, the various groups agreed that mankind would come to this realization on our terms. A timetable was designed, with a date set for what is being called the Great Awakening—the day mankind wakes up and realizes that it's not alone on this planet."

"Along the timetable there are several stages where we try to prepare man for the idea that vampires and lycans are real," Nicolai interjected. "Things have picked up in the past hundred years with stories in the tabloids, major motion pictures, books, and now a large number of Web sites."

"Propaganda?" Danaus asked, sounding absolutely horrified by the thought.

"Of course," I laughed. I stretched out my legs and crossed them at the ankles as I relaxed in my seat. "Nightwalkers own three major publishing companies and half a dozen small press companies. We also own more than a dozen movie production firms around the world. We are constantly churning out positive propaganda for the cause."

Frowning, he shifted in his chair, sitting on the edge of his seat. "Promoting vampires." Such a thing would not make his job of hunting us any easier if we succeeded in winning the support of a large portion of humans when the Great Awakening finally arrived.

"Not just nightwalkers," Alex quickly said, drawing his glare to her. "The various groups agreed that anything put out by one of our companies would not intentionally cast another race in a negative light. We're in this together. If one goes down, we all fall."

But then, even that lovely idea had fallen into question following the appearance of a lycan and a witch with a member of the Daylight Coalition.

Our conversation ground to an uneasy halt as the server arrived with several plates of food. Alexandra had ordered a medley of shrimp and linguine in red sauce, while Danaus settled on manicotti and an order of veal parmesan. Nicolai ordered some kind of seafood concoction that I couldn't identify. But that wasn't surprising. I hadn't eaten real food in more than six hundred years. After that long, it all started to look the same. Sometimes the smells would tantalize, but the actual appearance of food had become unappealing. It frequently reminded me of the aftermath of some of my more gruesome and bloody battles.

As my companions dug into their meals, I stared across the plaza, which had begun to empty. The night grew darker and deeper, but much of the inky blackness was held at bay by the warm glow of lamplights scattered about the square. The pigeons had left to find a roost for the night, the air filled with the bubbling murmur of conversation and the faint hint of a melancholy tune plucked on an acoustic guitar somewhere nearby.

"When is the big day?" Danaus asked between bites.

"There's no exact date," Alex said, cutting her food into delicate little bites. It was almost amusing. She was such a lady in public, but I'd seen her hunt. Nothing ladylike about running down and tearing the throat out of a twelve-point buck.

"It's tentatively set for sometime in 2055," I said, twirling my glass again. "Every once in a while a few of the groups get together and reevaluate the timetable." It had been a while since I'd sat this long out in the open with so many people. I was continually scanning the area for anything, but we were alone. "Sometimes science or technology jumps a little faster than we anticipated and stages have to be moved up. It's always a very liquid process with room for change, but there's no denying that it's coming."

Danaus went still beside me, drawing my gaze back to his solemn face. "Were you counting on Rowe?" he asked.

"No," I softly said, looking down at the deep red liquid in my glass. I laid my hand flat on the table, suddenly fearful I would unintentionally shatter the stem. The dark naturi with the leather eye patch was determined to free his queen and the rest of the naturi horde waiting on the other side of the seal. He was also determined to accomplish this feat with my help.

"Why do I get this horrible chill whenever someone mentions that word?" Alex said, laying a forkful of linguine back on her plate. "What's Rowe? Does it have something to do with the reappearance of the naturi?"

With a faint sigh my gaze drifted away from my friend and back out to the plaza as I mentally sorted through the events of the past several days, even the events that had taken place more than five hundred years ago. What to tell her? So much of it would horrify her, but I also knew that keeping secrets at this stage wouldn't protect her.

Reluctantly, I launched into the tale of the naturi, sparing her of as many of the grizzly details as possible. I stretched back to what little I knew of that horrible night more than five centuries ago and mentioned tidbits of what had happened to us during the past several days. I told her of the sacrifice at Konark and the failed sacrifice at Stonehenge. I mentioned the symbols we had found in the trees as the naturi sought to break the seal that bound them. I described the attack in Aswan, Thorne's pain-filled death, and holding Michael in my arms as his soul fought for freedom during the final seconds of his life.

Alex sat back in her chair and blinked a few times when I spoke of my lost angel. She had met Michael a couple of times and liked his easygoing manner. I appreciated her teary eyes . . . I had yet to shed my own tears for the young man. There was no time, as the naturi hounded us and I attempted to outmaneuver whatever plans Jabari and the Coven were apparently cooking up for the demise of my race.

However, I purposely omitted the fact that I was not actually a member of the triad that protected the seal, but its weapon. Nor did I voice the fact that the hunter who sat beside me could wield my abilities like a sword. While Alex and I were friends, her loyalty would always be to the pack, and anything I told her could eventually fall on their ears. I was already skating on thin ice by telling her about Rowe and his attempts to free the naturi. The handling of the naturi had always fallen to the nightwalkers, and it had become a tightly kept secret. But if we failed, I didn't want her to be blindsided.

Nicolai remained silent during my tale. I wasn't overly fond of the idea of this outsider hearing all of these details. But I was forced to trust him since Alexandra and the lycanthropes had to know what they were facing before it was too late.

The female naturi in the main hall was also omitted from my tale. If Alex and Nicolai didn't sense her, then it was better that they didn't know about it. I didn't know what was going on yet, and wasn't about to start a panic among the other races. If the lycans thought the nightwalkers had aligned with the naturi, a horrible war would sweep across the globe before the naturi ever managed to escape their prison.

When I was finished with my tale, Alex pushed her half-eaten meal away. "I've lost my appetite," she said weakly. She actually looked like she was going to be sick, her eyes taking on a glassy appearance as the scent of fear drifted from her to my nose.

"Finish eating," I prodded, pushing her plate toward her again. "How often do you get to eat real Italian? I mean, outside of a full moon, of course."

"That's not funny," she snapped. No, Alex didn't hunt humans, though a select few of her kind did. Even in animal form there was enough of Alexandra the human left behind to restrain her from attacking humans. She hunted only animals, and even then, only on the rare occasion when she gave in to the urge. "How can you make jokes? Don't you realize what could happen if they enter our world?"

"Trust me, Alexandra, I understand better than most," I said in a low, even voice, my eyes narrowing as I looked anywhere but at my companions. Alex didn't know about my captivity by the naturi—I'd left that out while recounting the events in Machu Picchu earlier—but she knew there was something dark and ugly in my past that left behind some deep emotional and physical scars. She took the hint. "There are a number of things going on that I don't understand, but I will soon. Panicking right now isn't going to help."

"It gets worse." Alex's usually strong voice dropped down to an unexpected whisper, drawing my gaze back to her lovely face. Shadows danced across her features, thrown up by the candle flickering in the hurricane glass in the center of the table.

A part of me wanted to ask her how it could possibly be any worse. The vampires were meeting with the naturi in secret. The witches and werewolves were meeting with the Daylight Coalition. Ancient enemies were suddenly allies, and old alliances with the lycans and witches were crumbling before us.

"They've starting calling us," she said.

"When?" I demanded, barely able to push the word from my constricted throat.

"About a week ago, but after last night I've heard that it has gotten worse. Most of the leaders have managed to hold their packs together, but a few here and there have gone missing. Most of them are younger, newer to lycanthropy. It seems like the call is worse the farther west you head," she explained.

I looked back over at Nicolai, who was staring straight ahead, his full lips pressed tight into a hard, unyielding line. "What about your pack?"

"I don't know. I've been out of contact with them for more than a month," he said stiffly, his eyes refusing to meet mine. I left the comment alone. A member of a pack was never out of contact from its members for long. Lycanthropes also never "belonged" to a vampire. Something dark was going on and I was willing to bet that it was rather painful and horrible for Nicolai. It would explain why Alex did nothing to even acknowledge the man's presence. She didn't look at him, didn't talk to him.

I frowned, turning this new bit of information over in my head. There were four different ancient holy sites in North and South America that the naturi could potentially use for their next sacrifice attempt: Old Faithful at Yellowstone Park, Mesa Verde in Colorado, Easter Island, and Machu Picchu in Peru. Would they dare to return to Machu Picchu after their horrible defeat there centuries ago? If it meant freeing Aurora, yes, without a doubt.

Turning my focus back to Alexandra, I struggled to keep my sympathy for her plight from showing on my face. It wouldn't help her when faced with the threat of suddenly becoming servants for a vicious race bent on the total extermination of humanity.

There were a couple theories as to how lycanthropy started. Some thought it was the result of a spell or curse woven by an old Native American god. Yet, some thought the root of shapeshifters was older than that. However, the darkest of the theories was that lycans were created by the naturi as a type of servant and soldier. Because of a lycan's close tie to nature, the naturi could call to a lycanthrope, summoning him or her across vast distances to do their bidding. Most viewed that as the future of man if the naturi entered this world—extermination or lycanthropy.

"So we'll be faced with both the naturi and lycans if the next sacrifice is to be held in the West," Danaus said grimly.

"Maybe even an assortment of Wiccans," I said. It was becoming a real party, and it appeared everyone was invited.

I turned my attention back to one of my few friends. Alex was nearly fifty, though she could still easily have passed for someone in her mid-twenties. Lycanthropy gave a person an amazing ability to heal from nearly every injury, except for those caused by silver. Particularly silver bullets and knives. Her "curse" also slowed down the aging process, usually doubling or tripling a human's average life span. I liked Alex. She had a good sense of humor and philosophy on life. I didn't want this future for her.

"When is your flight home?" I asked, battling to keep a frown from tugging on the corners of my mouth.

"Tomorrow morning." There was no mistaking the anxiety that crowded those two words. She lived in Portland, on the lovely West Coast. She was in danger of succumbing to the call and she knew it.

"Go back to London and stay until after the new moon," I ordered, sitting on the edge of my chair. My eyes jumped over to Danaus, who was watching the exchange with a worried look. "Could Themis protect her?"

"Mira," he softly said, his voice deep and weary. "Themis isn't an organization of bodyguards. We can't—"

"Damn it, Danaus!" I cried, hitting the heel of my palm on the table, rattling the nearly empty dishes. It was a struggle to bring my voice back under control, but I finally managed it before I continued. "I'm not asking your people to protect a pack of rabid vampires. Alex is still human—the race you're so desperate to protect. Call Ryan. Talk to him."

Alex shook her head, pressing her lips into a thin line. "I can't. My pack needs me. I have to go back."

"You have to take care of yourself. Go back to London. Your pack will manage."

"I have to go," she said, her smile as fragile as a cracked eggshell. "I'm an Alpha now."

My brows furrowed at this announcement and I sat back in my chair. "And you're still in Portland?"

"You don't need to sound so surprised." She stabbed her food with her fork, using enough force to cause the tines to scrape loudly across the ceramic plate.

"Forgive me," I said with a little bow of my head as I pressed my right hand to my heart. "Congratulations on your new position." It was quite an accomplishment. The Portland pack was large, with about forty members, last I'd heard. The packs out West were larger and there were more of them than on the East Coast in the States. Across Europe and throughout Asia, the packs had only twelve or fewer members and stuck to the rural areas.

With a shake of my head, I raised my left hand high in the air and snapped my fingers while my right hand dropped back to the arm of my chair. A server instantly appeared and placed the bill in my hand. I scratched out the name of an account on the bill and handed it back. It was the name of the Coven account and was known to all business operators across Venice. The bill would be sent to that account and immediately taken care of. I'd learned that trick when I started doing little odd jobs for the group not long after leaving Jabari. If you were going to do the dirty work of the Coven, they were willing to supply some basic perks while you were staying in Venice.

"With that said," I continued when the server walked away, "I still believe you should go to London for the next few days."

"You know I can't, Mira," she said, standing at the same time as Danaus and I.

I grabbed her elbow and squeezed it. "Don't go to them, Alex," I warned, dropping my voice so it was low and firm. The tone would leave my words burrowed into her brain like a swarm of ticks. I wanted those words to resonate within her mind during the coming months, hoping they would protect her against the siren song of the naturi. "I've enjoyed our friendship, but I won't hesitate."

Alex looked up at me with sad eyes. She knew that if she stood between me and the naturi, I wouldn't hesitate to kill her. Once she answered to the call of the naturi, she would be under their complete control.

"Just promise to make it quick," she said, a halfhearted smile lifting one corner of her mouth. "I don't want to think about being under the control of those bastards."

"I understand," I whispered, and pressed a kiss to her temple. "When it's over, come to Savannah and we'll go hunting."

Pausing beside the table, I looked down at Nicolai, still lounging in his chair, his glass of wine in his hand. We would meet again. Jabari might order the lycanthrope to kill me before I left Venice, and Nicolai would do it. Not because he bore any hatred for me and my kind, but because Jabari was holding something over him.

"It's been a pleasure," I said with a little smirk. Nicolai smiled in return and raised his glass to me. We both knew that we would meet again. It was a shame that it would be on opposite ends of the battlefield.

"Good luck, Mira," Alex whispered, grabbing my cool hand in both of her warm hands and squeezing it tightly.

I chuckled as I walked away, my hand slowly slipping from her grasp. "I don't need luck," I called, turning and walking backward so I could look at her as I departed. "I'm the Fire Starter."

I just wished I had a plan.

TEN

Danaus and I wandered down the dark streets in silence, slowly heading back to the speedboat. The sound of water lapping at the stone sides of the canal followed us throughout the winding city. The night was still in its infancy and I wasn't particularly eager to go back to the hotel suite where Sadira and Tristan were most likely cuddled. I paused on the sidewalk next to our boat and stared across the canal at the lights of the Doge's Palace and Piazza San Marco. The air was cluttered with the various thoughts and emotions of the people out enjoying the warm summer night.

"When was the last time you were in Venice?" I asked, looking over my shoulder at Danaus. He was also watching the lights reflect off the undulating waves.

"I've never been to Venice," he said. It was on the tip of my tongue to demand how that was even possible. He was Italian, or at least Roman, and more than a thousand years old. How could he have not visited the canals? But I knew I wasn't going to get an answer. He was still stingy about personal information regardless of the fact that he had popped into my thoughts on more than one occasion.

"Come on," I said, jumping onto the boat we had borrowed from Roberto. "I want to show you something." With a somewhat skeptical look, he climbed onto the boat and sat down while I started the engine. I rushed back out into the Lagoon, away from the bright lights and crowded canals. We cruised away from the tourist hot spots and the quaint neighborhoods, as I took him across the Lagoon and between the islands of Burano and Murano to the tiny island of Torcello.

I slowed the boat as I carefully maneuvered us past the swamps that surrounded the island. Navigating the *laguna morta* would have been treacherous at best during the middle of the day, let alone during the black of night when the moon had waned to a slender sliver in the sky. But I knew these waters and marshes. Torcello was my hidden sanctuary within the dark heart of the nightwalker world.

We glided down the main canal and pulled up near one of the few bridges that spanned the waterway. Danaus rose and tied the boat to an empty pole while I killed the engine. The only sound disrupting the silence was the break of the waves brushing against the side of the boat as we settled at the landing. In all of Venice, the island of San Michele would have been the only place more peaceful, but despite some of the popular myths about vampires, I didn't get any particular kicks wandering around a crumbling, mold-infested graveyard at night. The living were generally more interesting than the dead.

"Where are we?" he asked as we left the boat and wandered down the disintegrating *fondamenta* along the canal, toward the only cluster of buildings rising up in the darkness.

"The birthplace of Venice," I said. My voice hovered at a whisper, as if anything loud would break the spell. Lights began to appear as we reached the edge of the *campo* that was now more dirt and gravel than the original stonework. Grass crowded close to the road and weeds pushed their way between the cracks in the remaining paving. The main square was overgrown, with only a few bits of broken column and statues left to adorn the area like tombstone markers for the city that once was.

"The island is nearly deserted, but they say that this is where the Venetians first settled in either the fourth or fifth century," I said, running my hand over one of the stone columns. All its original marks were worn away, leaving what appeared to be a pale white, bonelike pillar rising up without the rest of the skeleton. "I've always liked it here. I love the island's sense of history and its peace."

"It's nice," he whispered. Danaus wandered over and stood before an odd chunk of white stone that resembled a chair. The locals referred to it as the throne of Attila the Hun, but no one actually believed he had ever sat on that hunk of rock. A light breeze stirred the leaves in some nearby trees, sending up their soft song into the night. Not far from the square, lights from the only restaurant on the island glowed in golden patches, but even they were beginning to dim under the lateness of the hour. The few inhabitants of the island were slipping off to bed, leaving Danaus and me alone.

"This city is almost as old as you, Danaus. Its memory is nearly as long as yours," I teased.

A faint smile lifted his features as he looked around the empty plaza. "A lot of Europe is," he reminded me. His voice was gentle, losing its usual gruff, angry edge. It was as if he had forgotten for a brief moment that I was a nightwalker; the enemy.

"True." I nodded, clinging to my smile though it was starting to fade. "I think it's one of the drawbacks to living in the New World; too new."

"No sense of history or identity," he murmured.

"Come on," I said. "I've got something else to show you."

I led him across the square and past the external colonnade to the front door of the church of Santa Fosca. The small structure was a mix of classical Byzantine and Greek. It took me only a moment to pick the lock and push open the dark wood doors. Pale slivers of moonlight shone through the open windows, revealing the high arching ceiling and wooden beams that crossed overhead. The forlorn coos of pigeons echoed off the walls as the birds settled in their roosts for the night. The interior was made of white bricks and a handful of white marble columns. There were no statues at the altar of the Blessed Mother, and only a single crucifix hung on the back wall. Tall white candles dotted the altar and filled the wall sconces that lined the walls. The center aisle was wide, but the intricate mosaic floor was cracked and broken, with a layer of dust veiling its former beauty. Only the old wooden pews still gleamed in the faint light, as if someone took the time to carefully wax each one at least once a week.

"Isn't it beautiful?" I said, spinning to look at my companion. "It's visited by only tourists now and hasn't been used as a church for a couple centuries. It's a shame. The architecture is as lovely as any of the churches in San Croce or even San Marco."

"How?" he asked breathlessly.

"How what?"

"How is it that you can be here? Has God abandoned this place?" I watched Danaus. His whole body was tensed, looking as if he expected one of us to be struck by lightning at any second. A faint sheen of perspiration glistened on his forehead in the moonlight.

"The magic is gone from this place," I replied. "It's not God, Danaus, but the faith of the people who go to a church that keeps me out. Faith is just another form of magic. If a human believes God will protect him, then he has cast a spell. And when people stop going to a church, the magic eventually fades."

Walking over to the pews to my right, I extended my hand, slowly moving it through the air. I could feel a light residue of energy. Someone had sat there during the day and whispered a prayer, a near-silent plea for hope or help, or maybe thanks or protection. There were other pockets in the air around me, thin and faint like a ghost, fading with the passage of time.

"I—I don't understand," he said, his voice faltering. I could taste his fear and horror in the air, but there was nothing enticing about it. From him, it was unnerving and even a little sickening, like a slow-working poison. It was as if the world was crumbling away beneath his feet and I was the cause.

"For some people, a cross doesn't work against nightwalkers." I lowered my hand back to my side and turned to face my companion. "These people believe that something about the shape of the metal keeps my kind at bay. They have faith in the cross, but not in the idea of a protective God, and that's never as strong. Your heart and soul aren't involved in that kind of faith, just your mind."

"I don't believe you," he said, his face hardening. If he had been armed, I think he would have drawn his sword to protect himself against my words. But instead he stood in the darkness of the church glaring at me.

"I'm not asking you to," I said with an indifferent shrug. "I'm just telling you what I've learned from experience. But you have to consider, I am standing in what has been a Christian church at one time."

Danaus remained quiet as I walked toward the altar. He was still uneasy, his emotions verging on frustration and anger. I stopped at the two small steps that led up to the remains of a marble altar. Behind it hung the tortured image of Jesus Christ still pinned to the wooden cross. His face and body was streaked and stained from time and water damage. His benevolent face appeared as if he had been crying tears, mourning the state of his home, or maybe just the state of man.

"Why did you do it, Mira?" Danaus asked, his voice strangely gentle.

"Do what?" I replied, trying to sound only mildly interested. Something twisted in my stomach; this was going to take an ugly turn.

"Why did you abandon God?"

"*What?*" My voice jumped above a whisper for the first time since we landed on Torcello, shattering the silence that had become suffocating. I spun on my right heel to gaze with confusion at my dark companion. His whole body was tensed, his hands balled into tight fists at his sides.

"Why did you abandon God?" he repeated. "Why did you choose to become a vampire?"

Plopping down on the two little stairs leading to the altar, I laughed. I tried to tell myself that it was an amusing point of view, but even I heard the thick layer of caustic bitterness in my voice. Danaus had been born centuries ago, long before Christianity took hold as the dominant religion in Europe, but he had obviously learned and clung to its teaching during his long years. I, on the other hand, had taken a slightly different route.

"Abandon God?" I repeated, pushing back to my feet. "I didn't abandon God; He abandoned me. Take a good look at me, Danaus. This isn't vampire enchantment—I was born looking this way." A ball of fire suddenly hovered beside my face as I walked toward him. "Red hair and violet eyes. I was born on the island of Crete in a small fishing village during the fourteenth century. Everyone had either brown or black hair and brown eyes. Do you know what they said when I was born? I was the spawn of Satan.

"I spent the first sixteen years of my life on my knees, begging God to forgive me for being born. And do you know what His reply was? This!" I held both of my hands out to my sides and they instantly became engulfed in flames. "A group of men from my village tried to rape me one night as I walked back home from church. In my terror, I accidentally set two of them on fire. Before that day, I had never harmed a single human being, but that night I killed two men."

"It was an accident," Danaus firmly said.

"Was it? How could it be an accident if that's what I was born to do?" I extinguished the flames I had created, letting the darkness flood the church again as I walked back toward the altar. My heels hitting the broken stone floor echoed through the heavy silence. The night moved close again, wrapping me in its cold arms, holding me, protecting me against Danaus's questions and memories I desperately wanted to forget.

"Choosing to be a nightwalker wasn't about abandoning God," I continued, the hard angry edge disappearing from my voice. "I lost my faith that night when those men died. Becoming a nightwalker was about power and gaining control of my life."

"You traded power for eternal damnation when you died." Hard accusation filled his voice. His footsteps scraped against the gritty dirt floor as he moved a few feet closer to me.

"Why do you cling to these archaic ideas?" I shouted, sending several of the pigeons overhead nervously into the air. Their wings beat against the wind as they darted out the open window in search of a quieter location to spend the night. "Not in all my six centuries have I run across this Satan that you are so confident I have sold my soul to. No one has ever spoken of him. Not the Coven, nor Sadira."

"You kill."

"I have yet to meet a race that didn't kill. The naturi, humans, lycans, witches, even God's precious angels kill. Why is my race suddenly different?"

"You drink blood."

"So what! I feed on the life of others. I take their blood, and under most circumstances, leave the life behind. Most carnivores can't claim that."

"It's not right!" he shouted at me. There was an underlying tremble in his voice, as if something small and frightened within him had finally lashed out at me. His ragged breathing filled the quiet of the church, and I could easily make out the frantic beat of his heart.

"Says who? Your religious leaders up in their ivory towers? I don't know whether there is truly a Heaven and Hell, but I believe you earn either place based on the choices that you make."

"And you chose to become a vampire," he hurled back at me.

"I also chose to save more lives in the past few days at the risk of my own than I care to count." I took a couple steps up the aisle toward him, barely suppressing the urge to create a fireball in defense against his callous comments. "I'm no innocent, but I'm not the embodiment of all evil that you want me to be. You want to kill me because you think I'm evil. Fine. Just make sure it's because of the things I've done and not because of what I am."

"Is that why you're doing this?" His whole demeanor suddenly changed. The tension that had pulled the shoulder muscles taut eased and his fists loosened so that his fingers now hung open at his sides. "Because you're trying to earn salvation?" he asked, his tone losing its harshness.

"Fuck Heaven!" I spat, my hands balled into fists so tight my knuckles had begun to ache. "I'm doing this because it's the right thing to do. If I don't, my people will die. If I don't, everything beautiful in this world will die."

I paced down the aisle again, stopping at the two little stairs, willing myself to calm. I couldn't fathom why this was still a sore topic with me. For more than six hundred years I had turned over ideas of God, Heaven, Hell, and the devil in my mind. I came up with theories for why my kind existed and our place in the great scheme of things. Sometimes my theories proved to be wrong and I threw them out for new ones. I didn't have many answers, but my mind was open to possibilities.

When I finally spoke again, I was surprised at how tired my voice sounded. As if the long centuries had been condensed into a single sound. "You've walked this earth for more than a millennium. How can you still cling to the idea that concepts like these are black and white?" I turned to look at him. He still stood near the head of the aisle, as if afraid to enter this place. "Good and evil are not black and white. Human doesn't automatically equal good and vampire doesn't equal evil. You've spent a lifetime slaughtering my people. Have you never paused for half a second to wonder if we really are what you want us to represent?"

"Once." His voice was little more than a summer breeze through a maple tree, soft and soothing.

"When?" He didn't answer me, but I knew when as soon as I asked the question. It had been the first night we met. He hesitated that night when we fought. I'd believed it was because of Nerian and the naturi, but there had been something else brewing in the back of his mind. "And what did you decide?"

"I don't have an answer. I don't know! For some reason, you throw everything into confusion. You make me question all the answers I thought I had," he raged, taking an angry step toward me. His powers surged out from him, hitting me in the chest with enough force to make me take a steadying step backward.

"There's nothing wrong with asking questions," I said with a half smile. The anger and frustration I felt earlier had dissipated, leaving only a fine trembling in my muscles.

"But these questions take away hope," he said. I could feel the anger draining out of him, to be replaced by a bone-deep despair that threatened to crush us both. For just this brief moment in time he looked lost, and it was my fault. Before meeting me, he had purpose and direction, he had a light to sail by, but I had destroyed that. I didn't like him killing, but I also didn't believe in taking away another creature's hope.

"I want to call in my debt," I announced after a heavy silence had filled the air.

"What do you want?"

"Tell me what you are." He turned and started to walk out of the church without a word. "Stop, Danaus. I've thought about this since I first laid eyes on you. You're at least part human, that can't be mistaken, but you're not a warlock or a lycan. I've mentally gone through the laundry list of every creature I've encountered and nothing seems to fit. What is it that you are so desperate to hide?"

"Let's go," he said. The hunter stopped walking but was still facing the entrance.

"Not until you tell me. What's so horrible? Can it top the fact that I am a monster among my own kind? Or that I can be used as a weapon by my enemy to destroy both naturi and nightwalkers? This secret is destroying you and my kind. You have to tell someone." I was grasping at straws but knew that his twisted outlook on the world had to be rooted somewhere. After more centuries that I cared to count, Danaus's mind and identity were still mostly human, but the secret of his existence was tearing him apart and destroying far too many of my own kind in the process. It also left him vulnerable to creatures such as Ryan, who were all too happy to use Danaus's desperation and confusion to their advantage.

"Why you?" he asked, glancing over his shoulder at me.

"Because us freaks got to stick together," I replied, flashing him a wicked grin.

He made a strange noise, almost like a strangled laugh, and shook his head. "Bitch," he muttered under his breath, but in the quiet church it was like he had shouted it.

"I pray you're not just figuring that out," I said blandly, but then quickly turned serious again. "What is this burden on your shoulders?"

Danaus turned around, resting one hand against the doorjamb as if to steady himself. When he finally spoke, his voice was low and rough, making me wonder how many times he had spoken these words aloud. "My mother was a witch. Before I was born, she made a deal with a demon to gain more power."

"And the price?" Those three words escaped my lips in a rough and ragged whisper. I already knew the answer. There was always a price for more power. I knew that personally. For my amazing abilities, I traded in my ability to be awake during the day and gained a complete dependence on blood for survival.

"Me."

My knees buckled and I landed on my butt on the edge of one of the marble steps leading up to the altar. Panic screamed in my brain as I struggled to comprehend the words he had uttered. A fierce shaking started in my hands and a sharp, biting chill swept through my body. There were no such thing as demons—not as humans comprehended them—but back in the beginning, when the world was young, there were two guardian races, the naturi who watched over the earth and the bori who watched over all souls.

The bori were an immensely powerful race that had come to represent both angels and demons in human mythology. And while the naturi had the ability to force all lycanthropes to do their bidding, the bori could easily subjugate the entire nightwalker race. The naturi wanted to destroy us, but the bori wanted to rule us. It was why both races had been banished from this world. Yet, something was off.

While we all knew some naturi were left on earth after the seal had been made, supposedly none of the bori remained. All the bori had been locked away for centuries. Had Danaus's mother found a way to partially summon a bori back to earth?

I couldn't raise my gaze to look at him, not when I knew my horror was clearly written across my face. My world was crumbling around me at an alarming rate. Jabari could control me, Rowe wanted to use me to permanently free Aurora, and Danaus, with his link to the bori, could use me to destroy both the naturi and the nightwalkers.

Closing my eyes, I drew in a deep breath as I pushed down the rising wave of panic filling my chest. I needed to think clearly. "You're a demon?" I finally said, lifting my gaze to look down the long aisle at the creature that had saved me on more than one occasion.

Danaus narrowed his beautiful blues, closely examining my face for my reaction to the news. "Half. Like you said, part of me is still human."

But it wasn't that simple. The bori weren't demons, and I had never heard of anyone being half bori. There was no cross-breeding with humans. The closest mix between a human and a bori was a nightwalker, and I knew without a doubt that Danaus was not one of us.

It sounded as if the bori that made the deal was more of a parasite attached to Danaus's soul, lending him power as the bori bided his time. And while the naturi clung to twelve wells of power from the earth, Danaus had potentially become a walking doorway for the entire bori race. They just had to figure out how to unlock him.

And yet, Danaus had never used the term bori. He didn't know, didn't understand, their long history. He was just clinging to the ancient definition of what a demon was and making his decisions based on that. He had no idea what he was.

"So you're trying to save your human half by ridding the world of evil, namely vampires," I said, trying to quell my rising panic before he sensed it. What could I tell him? That it wasn't a demon that owned a part of his soul, but something nastier and more complicated? I didn't have any answers for him. And what information I could give him would only make it worse. I needed time and more information before I opened my mouth.

"I have no desire to spend eternity in Hell because of my mother's need for revenge," he coldly said, taking a few steps toward me.

I ran a shaking hand through my hair, pushing it away from my eyes. "How do you know that is your destination?"

"It is the destination of all demons," he simply said. He stopped when he was a couple feet away from me, his eyes on the ground.

"Maybe. Maybe not. I've not seen any proof to sway me one way or the other."

"Have you known any demons?"

I could only smile weakly at my companion. There was nothing I could say that would help him. I hadn't had any personal encounters with the bori. My experiences in this lifetime had been limited to battling the naturi, which had always been more than enough for me.

"They're evil," he continued when I remained silent.

"Most probably are," I conceded, rubbing my hands together to brush off some dirt. "But every creature that slinks across this earth is given a choice. You've chosen not to be evil. You're also part human. That has to throw something into your favor."

Danaus slowly lifted his gaze, staring deep into my violet eyes, searching for something. He wanted to believe me. He truly wanted to grab onto the lifeline I was tossing him as he struggled out in the dark abyss, but he was also fighting centuries of religious theory and conditioning. He wasn't about to toss aside his faith so easily because it eased his mind and conscience.

"I'm not asking you to believe everything I've said. Just think about it. These ideas you've clung to are man-made ideas. They're narrow-minded and flawed. Earlier tonight we were discussing the Great Awakening. Mankind's concepts of God and redemption didn't take our kind into consideration," I said, threading a lock of hair that had come loose behind my left ear. "If you survive this nightmare, go talk to Ryan. I have a feeling you're willing to believe him a little more than me."

"You've lived longer. How could he know more?" he countered.

I didn't trust Ryan, but the white-haired warlock was a potential source of information. He represented a starting point for Danaus. And if I survived this mess as well, I hoped to do a little digging around myself. "Ryan's spent his life studying the other races and religions. I've picked up what I can along the way. A lot of it is myth and rumor. You sift through it as best you can and keep an open mind."

"And then what?"

"Nothing," I said with a shrug. I rose to my feet in my boneless manner. "You keep moving. Let's go."

I stepped around him and strolled down the aisle in my usual breezy, happy-go-lucky way, but my mind was churning. A bori. Well, a half bori sort of. That was not something I had expected. I had thought maybe he was a strange half warlock, half lycan mix that couldn't shift. No, Danaus was a half bori that had the ability to control me. It was enough to send shivers down my back, but somehow I had to bury my terror deep inside my chest. Of course, if I had lost it in front of my dark companion, Danaus would have been out the door.

"Mira . . ." he slowly called, sounding hesitant.

"Yeah, I know. It's a deep, dark Danaus secret," I said, spinning around so I could look at him as he walked up the aisle behind me.

"So you can read my mind now?"

"Not quite. It's the type of thing I would request. Beside, it's not like I want you bragging to your little cult about your nifty new Mira marionette."

"It seems we're on equal ground," he said, extending his hand to me.

"Always have been," I replied, slipping my hand into his. I was surprised that I didn't hesitate to take his strong hand in mine after the last three times we had touched. There was no rush of power pushing to enter my body this time, no thoughts that didn't belong to me. Just his usual warmth washing over my skin, soaking in and heating me like the sun. Despite what he was and the heritage that haunted him, Danaus still had a choice and still had his honor.

Standing in the silence of the church holding his hand, a dark thought flitted through my brain before I could stop it. Had I promised to protect something more dangerous to my kind than the entire naturi horde? Wasn't death better than an eternity of slavery? For a reason I had yet to understand, the Coven had struck a pact with the naturi, offering up some type of protection. I'd brought Danaus into the center of our civilization, a creature that was part bori and a vampire hunter. Despite my best intentions, had I betrayed my kind in the same way?

"Of course, you realize that this conversation won't stop me from hunting vampires," he coldly said, releasing my hand.

I forced myself to laugh as I turned to leave the church. "I wouldn't dream of stopping you," I replied, pushing open the heavy wood door. "I just want you to think about why." There was no forcing Danaus to do anything he didn't believe in. However, with enough time and knowledge, I believed he would choose to stop hunting nightwalkers.

We casually strolled back through the weed-infested main *campo*. Looking out across the Lagoon toward the glow of Murano and Burano, I could sense the other nightwalkers going about the usual nightly activities. They were hunting and feeding and laughing. De-

spite their dead bodies, they were as alive as the humans that surrounded them. I couldn't believe we were evil. Or more specifically,
that I was evil. Would I still be mourning the loss of my angel if I was
evil? Would I still cherish my sweet Calla and the life I once had if I
was evil? In the gathering darkness with Danaus at my side, those
questions were all I had left to cling to.

ELEVEN

A slow hiss slipped between my clenched teeth as I paused at the edge of the grassy courtyard. Jabari was playing a game. First, he demanded I come to Venice, where I was almost guaranteed to discover the Coven's plot with the naturi, and now this. We were no longer alone. My focus had been so completely locked on Danaus and our conversation that I didn't notice Nicolai until he stood watching us from the second floor window of a vacant building.

He was early. I hadn't expected Jabari to send his assassin at least until after the next sacrifice. Of course, this meant that the Ancient had broken his promise that he wouldn't send one of the court flunkies to see to my demise. But I knew Jabari's goal wasn't to kill me there. I was too old and experienced to be taken out by a lycanthrope. He wanted something else. Nicolai was simply a pawn that had been moved into play. Unfortunately, I wasn't the opponent Jabari was playing against; I was just another one of his game pieces. What was I supposed to accomplish in fighting Nicolai? Did Jabari expect me to kill the werewolf? Was he more important than I knew? I wanted to scream. Second-guessing myself and trying to predict Jabari's next move was going to get me killed.

Standing in the deep shadow thrown down by the building the werewolf occupied, I shoved my hand into my pocket and withdrew the silver ring that held the key to the boat. The little slip of metal jingled before I closed my fingers around it. "Take the boat back to the hotel," I murmured, not looking over at Danaus as he came to stand beside me.

"How will you get back?" he inquired, not yet reaching for the key.

"I'll swim." I extended my left hand and turned it over, waiting for him to put his open hand beneath mine so he could catch the key, but the hunter refused to budge.

"What's going on?" Tension tightened his words into hard little syllables that could barely squeeze past his clenched teeth. Before I had a chance to murmur *Nothing,* a wave of power swept away from his body and washed over the tiny island. I didn't know if he could sense werewolves as well as he could nightwalkers, but I was going to find out in a couple of seconds. There were only a couple dozen humans on the whole island, all of them older in age. Probably born on the island and determined to die there like so many of their ancestors.

"It's none of your business, hunter," I said sharply. "Get out of here."

"What does the lycan want?" he demanded as his powers were sucked back into his body. Their sudden absence made me feel chilled, as if a damp cold had found its way into my bones.

"Her heart." The words drifted down to us from the dark window, edged with a slight echo as they bounded briefly around the empty building before escaping into the night air. The tone held no menace, but sounded like the soft caress of a concerned lover wondering why his beloved companion was walking in the fading moonlight with another man.

Danaus stepped away from me and looked up at the building, his right hand unconsciously reaching for a knife at his hip, only to find that it wasn't there. After our audience with the Coven, neither of us had thought to go back into the hotel room to get our weapons. I had been too distracted by what happened on San Clemente to think about such a little thing as self-defense. The hunter pressed his lips into a hard thin line and let his hand drop back to his side, his fingers flexing in their irritation.

"What's going on?" he bit out.

"Mr. Gromenko has been sent to kill me," I calmly replied, lowering my hand to my side. The key was still tightly gripped in my fingers. I was beginning to get the feeling that Danaus wasn't going to leave. I didn't want him hanging around when Nicolai attacked. I didn't trust Danaus to keep his nose out of my business. The gods knew I couldn't.

Danaus jerked his gaze back to my face, his beautiful blues widened in surprise and confusion. I knew what he was thinking. We had eaten dinner with this man an hour earlier. We smiled, laughed, and traded worried looks about the dark days that lay beyond the horizon. And now he had come to collect my heart.

"Jabari wants me dead," I said with a shrug, as if that could explain everything. And in my world, it did. If an Ancient wanted something, it happened, regardless of what a person had to do to get it done.

Danaus opened his mouth to say something, maybe argue with what to me was a very logical statement, but before he could speak, Nicolai jumped down from his perch and lightly landed a few feet away. Danaus tensed and took a step closer, attempting to get between me and the lycan, but I laid a restraining hand on his arm. Beneath my cool fingers I could feel his muscles jump at my touch, and his energy arced through me, looking for a new home. He was tense and wasn't exactly trying to keep his powers under a tight wrap.

"Danaus!" I snapped. My fingernails bit into his warm flesh, while at the same time a part of me struggled to keep his powers from burrowing within me. "This is not your fight. I don't need your protection."

The two men stared at each other. Danaus's features were hard and unyielding, his jaw muscles tensed as he clenched his teeth. Nicolai's face was emotionless, as if a veil had come down between his mind and his emotions. I didn't know what he was thinking, and there were few ways more effective at starting a fight than rummaging around the mind of another creature who could sense it. Most humans wouldn't know, but magical creatures could, the same way a wolf could sense a coming storm.

"Can he kill you?" Danaus demanded, still refusing to back off.

"He can try," I replied, ignoring the shifter.

"Will you kill him?"

"Not if I can avoid it," I admitted. I had no desire to kill Nicolai. He seemed like a nice guy and I honestly had nothing against him. This whole hunting-me-down thing was Jabari's fault, not his. Of course, if killing him was the only way to save myself, I wouldn't hesitate.

Danaus's frowned deepened and he arched one thick eyebrow at me in question without his gaze wavering from Nicolai. Clenching my teeth, I shoved Danaus back a step. "I'm not some mindless killing machine," I snarled.

The hunter snorted, making it clear he didn't believe that bit of logic either. "Regardless, I can't just walk away. The naturi are trying to break free. We can't afford to risk your life needlessly."

"Your concern warms my cold blood." I thoughtlessly shoved the boat key back into my left pocket, irritated beyond rational thought.

"Mira—"

I didn't let Danaus get any further. Grabbing a handful of his shirt, I jerked him around and slammed his back into the nearby building, earning a grunt from him. "I did not survive more than six centuries because I had some human with a chip on his shoulder watching my back. I will handle this without your assistance."

"I'm not leaving. We promised to leave Venice together," he murmured.

That was when it finally dawned on me. Sometimes it's amazing how slow I can be to pick up on some of the little things in life. While we were flying to Venice, we promised that we would both get out of the city alive. I had taken that as an agreement on my behalf to keep him alive. It never occurred to me that he would attempt to protect my existence as well.

My grip in his shirt loosened and I took a half step away from him in surprise. Thoughts of Nicolai, the naturi, the Coven—they all slipped away for a couple of seconds. The air grew heavy with a strange silence that was broken only by Danaus's heartbeat. It was faster than usual; faster than during our fights and faster than during our arguments. The beat was hypnotic, trying to tell me another of his great secrets, but I couldn't understand what it was whispering to me.

"Fine," the lycanthrope said nonchalantly, jolting me back from our own private world. "You stay." The blond Adonis filled with rippling muscles reached around me and grabbed a handful of Danaus's black locks. Pulling his head forward slightly, Nicolai slammed the back of Danaus's head against the brick wall behind him before either of us could react. The hunter made no sound as he slid to the ground in a heap, pulling out of my grip.

I looked up at Nicolai, a smile wavering on my lips. "You better hope I kill you, because he's going to be seriously pissed when he wakes up."

"Then I guess we better get this done quickly," he replied, stepping away from Danaus's unconscious form. His dark brown eyes swept over the area, searching for something. His large, muscular frame was tensed, waiting for me to attack him. He would have been moving before I could flinch. But I wasn't going to start this fight.

"There," he said, with a jerk of his head. "The *campo*." My eyes followed his gaze to the overgrown square with the crumbling pillars and broken sidewalk. It was beyond the church Danaus and I had been in. It appeared as if the three sides of the square were surrounded by small, empty buildings, while the fourth side looked out onto the Lagoon.

I walked in that direction and paused at the edge of the square beside a tall pillar, my hands resting on my narrow hips as I looked over the proposed battlefield. My only warning was a slight shifting in the air just half a breath before Nicolai threw his body into mine. A grunt jumped from my throat as he crushed me against the column. The cool, rough stone scraped and scratched against my bare arms and back like coarse sandpaper, threatening to remove a layer of skin. Snarling, I pushed him off me before he could get his feet planted again, pitching him halfway across the square. Like a cat, he easily landed on his feet, sliding a bit on the rubble that littered the area.

With one hand braced on the ground and his feet spaced apart, the lycan was poised to jump at me again. His eyes glowed with power, a strange copperish light, as a low growl rumbled in his chest. He wouldn't risk changing. The process took too long and would leave him vulnerable to my attack.

A breeze stirred, pushing against the heavy wall of summer heat and thick moisture. The scent of the Lagoon teased my nose along with the musky scent of Nicolai. He was coated in the scent of fear, the scent of frustration.

With a sharp inhalation of air, he launched himself across the square at me. He was a dark blur, more wind than man as he moved. I darted to my right, only attempting to sidestep him, but I misjudged his speed. Pain exploded in my left forearm and I looked down to find three long, ragged cuts across my pale skin. Blood welled up and streaked down my arm before finally dripping to the ground. My eyes darted back to Nicolai, to find that his fingers were elongated and tipped with long black claws.

Frowning, I bit back a curse and slowly took a couple steps away, circling him. He could partially shift. That meant he was either a lot older than I initially thought or a lot more powerful. Shifting specific body parts was very difficult, demanding a great deal of energy and control. I had seen Alex do it only once, and it left her shaking and sweating afterward. I knew I could stretch out the fight in an attempt to wear him down, but I think we both preferred to have this done before Danaus woke up from his catnap.

Nicolai lunged for me again, but this time I remained still, my feet planted and legs braced. Ducking under massive arms that reached out to grab me, I punched him hard in the side, under his ribs. Air exploded from his lungs in a harsh grunt. His right heel scraped against the ground as he struggled to regain his balance against the unexpected blow. Before he could draw in a fresh lungful of air, I slammed my left fist into his jaw, wincing at the impact. I didn't want to hurt Nicolai, but I needed to knock him out so I could finally end this contest.

The punch knocked him on his ass. I immediately backpedaled a few steps as he rolled back to his feet, sucking in a couple ragged breaths.

"What are your orders?" I demanded. We circled each other, only a few feet of empty air separating us.

"Kill you," Nicolai evenly replied. The werewolf stepped forward in a blur, swinging his right fist at my stomach. I jumped backward, dodging the blow and landing balanced on the tips of my toes. He dipped down before I could land flatfooted again and swung one leg around. His foot and ankle connected with my toes, knocking me back.

Instead of landing flat on my back, I caught myself on my fingertips, continuing the flip over. It wasn't pretty, but I managed to land on one foot and a knee, ready to lunge at him.

Nicolai backed off a couple steps when he realized his attempt to knock me on my back had failed. Fists raised, he waited for me to rise to my feet again.

"Just kill me?" I continued. "What about Danaus? Or Tristan?" I needed to understand this game Jabari was playing. I knew the Ancient would send Nicolai after me, but what was his rationale for doing it? Did he want me to rid him of this pet? Or was Nicolai a greater threat than I was giving him credit for? My death here would put both Tristan and Danaus at great risk. And with the appearance of the naturi in the main hall, I was beginning to seriously wonder if Jabari truly needed me alive any longer. I knew my nights were numbered, but I now felt as if I had fewer of them than I had previously believed.

"He named only you," Nicolai stated. His heavy breathing and his fast heartbeat were the only sounds in the empty *campo*. No sound came from his footsteps as we started to circle each other again.

"Alex?" I swung at him, but he dodged it. Unfortunately, I had overextended, positive that the blow would connect. Off-balance and moving too slow, I swallowed a curse when I felt Nicolai's large hands wrap around my shoulders. White light exploded before my eyes when he slammed his head against mine. The pain was immediately followed by a second swelling of pain as his fist hit my chin, snapping my head around.

Somehow, I remained standing, though I had yet to open my eyes. I didn't need to see him. I could hear him. I could smell him. I could feel the heat pulsing off his massive frame. Gritting my teeth, I drilled my right fist into his side. The sound of at least two ribs breaking was unmistakable.

"Just you," he grunted.

Taking a couple unsteady steps backward, I blinked my eyes a couple times to clear my vision. Good grief, that man had a freaking hard head! Nicolai stood a couple feet away, still upright, but one hand was now pressed against his wounded rib cage.

I snorted softly. "I'm a lucky girl."

"Sorry." The single word escaped him in a nearly breathless whisper, causing a frown to tug at the corners of my mouth. We were all trapped in this collection of islands one way or another.

Nicolai came at me again, his talonlike nails aimed to remove more than one layer of flesh from my body. I didn't try to dodge him this time. Grabbing his upper arms, I used his momentum to help me throw him away from me. Unfortunately, the lycan was smart enough to wrap his long fingers around my wrists and pull me to the ground with him.

We landed in a heap with him beneath me. Both of us grunting, we slammed into the hard, stone-covered ground. Rolling several feet as we struggled for supremacy, our legs tangled in each other. When we finally settled in one spot, Nicolai was on top of me, his knees resting on either side of my hips as he struggled to keep my arms pinned on either side of my head.

A little golden flash of light caught my eye, and my gaze drifted down to find a gold cross dangling from his neck on a thick gold chain. The little piece of metal had caught a sliver of moonlight and winked at me. It didn't glow or heat up like so many of the movies liked to show. But I could feel it throbbing with power, beating against me as it fought to keep me back away from the werewolf. Nicolai's faith was strong. Without uttering a word, I knew he believed very deeply that God and the heavenly host would keep him safe from me.

A hiss escaped my clenched teeth and I pressed back into the cool, broken stone in an attempt to put some distance between me and the cross. Touching it would burn me, and since it was a spell-induced burn, I would never completely heal from it. And I preferred not to have a cross-shaped scar somewhere on my face.

"Thought of everything, didn't you?" I taunted. The words pushed past my lips in a harsh whisper since I couldn't unclench my teeth. Nicolai remained silent, focused on keeping me pinned, but even that was faltering. He was strong, but I was still stronger. I managed to lift my arms a couple inches off the ground, beginning to push him off me. With one last groan, he relaxed the pressure he was using to hold me down for less than a breath before slamming my arms back down to the ground. The sound of bones breaking shattered the silence.

I screamed, my back arching off the ground a little. He had brought my right forearm down on a rock, snapping the bones in half. My vision swam in the pain for a couple seconds. The thought of defeating him without killing him vanished. Instinctively, I brought my knees up between his legs. The surprise and pain was enough to finally push him off.

Before he hit the ground, a circle of fire sprang up around him, stretching more than six feet into the air. Scrambling to my feet, I cradled my broken arm against my chest as I darted off to the darkest niches of the *campo*. One of the far corners held a type of two-walled arbor, thick with vines. The shadows were deep, affording me some cover.

Mira!

I flinched at Danaus's sudden presence in my head. The touch was tentative and distant, making me think he was still leaning against the wall where I left him.

Go away! I mentally snarled at him. *I'm busy trying not to get killed.*

You're hurt.

Go away! I wasn't surprised that he could tell I was injured, since the pain seemed to fill my entire frame. Yet I stiffened when I suddenly felt the small wave of power sweeping through me. Danaus and his warm touch were slowly moving over my body, searching for the injury. *It's my right arm. It's broken.* Even the thoughts sounded shaky and frightened in my head. Nightwalkers couldn't do this. We could read one another's thoughts and emotions, but we could not reach out and touch each other like this.

I'm coming. The thought was firm and resolute in my head. I could feel him moving, drawing closer.

No, it's healing. Stay where you are. I—

I quickly ended the thought when I saw Nicolai leap through the fire, his arms raised to protect his face. A nightwalker would never have taken such a chance. We caught fire far too easily. When he landed on his feet, I immediately extinguished the fire, plunging the square back into utter darkness. I knew that the fire would have destroyed the lycan's night vision, and I had only a couple of seconds before he could pierce the gloom again.

Grabbing a rock the size of my left fist, I darted across the square to his side in silence. My goal had been to hit him on the back of the head. If it worked for Danaus, it would work for Nicolai. But the werewolf sensed me at the last second, whether by a stir in the air or the sound of my clothes as I moved, I don't know. He turned to face me and I ended up hitting him in the temple. He crumpled at my feet like a sack of wet noodles.

A scrape on the concrete snapped my gaze to the edge of the square, and I raised my left hand with the rock, ready to throw it at the intruder. Danaus stood in the shadows, his arms raised in surrender, a smirk on his lips.

"You're a mess," he murmured, earning a glare from me.

"Have a nice nap?" I sneered, dropping the rock.

The smirk dissolved from his lips, turning into a matching glare. I hurt too much to trade barbs with the hunter. There were more pressing concerns as the night continued to age.

I knelt down beside Nicolai but didn't touch him. His chest rose in deep, even breaths and I could hear the strong, steady rhythm of his heartbeat. He would recover. Blood leaked from his temple, but I was sure that would stop soon enough. When I stood again, Danaus was on the other side of the unconscious lycan. "Check to make sure he's still wearing his cross," I said.

Danaus furrowed his brows at me but knelt wordlessly and pulled the man's shirt collar away from his throat with one finger to reveal a gold chain and cross against tan skin.

"I don't want someone else picking up the scent of his blood and making a snack of him," I muttered as I turned and walked away. I once again cradled my arm against my stomach, the pain beginning to ease. The bone was mending, but the process was slower than healing a flesh wound.

"Why did Jabari send him?" Danaus asked, following behind me.

"I don't know."

"But the naturi—"

"I don't know, Danaus. I don't know what they're planning, but I'm beginning to wonder if Jabari has something else in store for me," I softly admitted. If I was needed to protect and make the seal that bound the naturi, it meant the Coven couldn't have me killed. But after Nicolai's attempt, it meant that either Jabari had finally made his replacement or the Coven no longer wanted to protect the seal. Or Jabari had plans for me that didn't include the Coven or the naturi.

Standing on the pavement beside the boat, I looked across the Lagoon toward the bright lights of San Marco. *Welcome back to Venice, Mira.* In this dying city, pain and horror skulked in every shadow and around each corner, all held beneath a veneer of elegant, Old World beauty and civilization.

Danaus stood behind me and unexpectedly laid his hand on my right shoulder. My head darted over to look at the large hand as his warmth seeped through my cold flesh. At the same time, he dipped two fingers from his free hand into my front left pocket. I tried to jerk away from him in shock but was effectively trapped between his larger body and the open canal. My narrowed gaze snapped to his face. Danaus smirked again and dangled the key before my face.

"You're in no shape to drive," he said, then stepped into the boat. Frowning, I said nothing as I hopped into the little speedboat and settled into one of the seats. My arm was mostly healed, but I didn't care. I was feeling ragged and worn from the encounter.

The engine roared to life as Danaus pulled us away from the island and back into the Lagoon, headed for Guidecca and our hotel. The sound of the wind and waves was relaxing, wiping the tension from my shoulders. I thought of Nicolai for a moment, wondering what it was that Jabari held over the werewolf.

I shook my head, not caring that no one was around to see it, lost to my own thoughts. Jabari was playing a game. I just didn't understand his goal. Mine was unmistakable. Protect the peace. And the only way to do that was to destroy the Coven's bargain with the naturi. I just had to figure out how.

TWELVE

Any reprieve I thought I might have earned after nights of running and fighting to stay alive had been adequately crushed. Now I just wanted a few minutes of quiet in which to think and try to anticipate Jabari's next move. A sigh knocked against the back of my teeth but never managed to escape as Danaus and I stepped into our suite at the Cipriani. Instead of being faced with the sweet, cuddly scene of Sadira and Tristan, the rooms were empty. I hadn't left explicit orders for them to remain in the rooms, but I didn't sense them out hunting in the streets when I scanned the hotel area before leaving Torcello.

A heavy tension hung bloated and ugly in the air, pressing against my chest. Standing in the middle of the black and gray parlor, I struggled to keep from clenching my fists. The beautiful room with its elegant furniture and shiny marble floors was untouched—indicating that they walked out on their own.

I started slowly, hesitant. My powers spread from my body in a circle, reaching outward until I had covered the main islands of Venice. There was no Tristan or Sadira. Reluctantly, I pushed out across the Lagoon to San Clemente, where I found Sadira in the Great Hall. She wasn't alone.

Her emotions were clear. She was calm, but sad. I still didn't sense Tristan, but I knew he was there too. Someone was blocking my ability to sense him, and there was only one person who could do that: Tristan's beloved maker, Sadira. A nightwalker could keep other nightwalkers from sensing him and his children as a type of defense mechanism. Only the older ones like Jabari could keep it up for nights on end. At best, Sadira could maintain the barrier for a couple of nights, but she didn't need to hide him for long. She was only buying the others some time. And maybe so had Nicolai. Jabari might not have truly believed that the werewolf could kill me, but he knew that Nicolai could stall me for a time.

"Can you go inside a church? A still functioning church?" I asked Danaus. My low voice crept through the tense silence that filled the suite. Standing next to the sofa, I leaned down so my right hand tightly gripped the corner of one of the dark end tables, causing my newly mended forearm to ache. Danaus stood behind my left shoulder near the double doors to the suite. I didn't bother to try to hide my frustration and anger. What was the point? He could sense my emotions if he wanted to.

"Yes," he said. "What's going on?" His heavy footsteps crossed the room to stop before his bag of weapons, which sat near the sofa. Placing the worn duffel bag on the coffee table, he unzipped it without looking up at me and started rummaging around for the one appropriate item that would destroy his enemy

My lips parted but my voice couldn't quite push past the lump in my throat. I licked my lips and tried again, forcing my fingers to loosen their death grip on the table because they were starting to throb and I didn't want to shatter the wood. "There's something I need to take care of." The words came out flat and emotionless despite the turmoil in my chest. I had to go back to San Clemente.

Looking over my shoulder at my dark companion, I found that his hard gaze never wavered from the flash of steel and leather as he dug through his bag of goodies. "Where's Sadira and Tristan?"

I ignored the question and stood erect again as I finally pried my fingers loose from the table. Silently, I removed the necklace and earrings I had been wearing, shoving them into my front pockets. They would only get in the way. "There's a small church just a couple blocks south of here. Go there and stay inside until dawn," I directed, staring straight ahead instead of at him.

"I'm going with you."

I spun around to face Danaus, standing a few feet away now. His black brows were drawn together over his nose, and his jaw muscles hardened as he clenched his teeth. His fingers deftly attached his leather knife sheath over his belt as he prepared for the coming fight. He had made his decision to follow me into whatever battle I now faced. My own frown eased from my lips and something light swelled in my chest, pushing aside the anger and fear that had been weighing me down during the past few nights. He didn't know what we faced or how bad our odds, but he was willing to follow me.

Unfortunately, he could not come with me this time. "That's not an option," I said with a slight shake of my head. "Our business is getting rid of the naturi." My voice had grown as cold and unyielding as the Russian tundra. I couldn't let him accompany me; both for Tristan's sake and my own. "This is nightwalker business. You're not going. Go to a church. I don't want to worry about someone coming after you while I'm gone."

He refused to be put off by my tone, and roughly grabbed my wrist when I tried to walk away from him. "What's going on, Mira? First Nicolai, and now this. Where are Tristan and Sadira?"

My gaze met his narrow blue eyes and for a moment I longed to sink into their cool depths. I wanted to forget about it all and go back to playing cat and mouse with him through the historical district of Savannah. I knew he would willingly walk in the main hall and protect me with his last breath.

Of course, his protection of me had nothing to do with me per se, but with the protection of the human race. I was the key—the weapon that would beat back the naturi. For half a breath I wondered if he hated me all the more for it. A creature he perceived as completely evil, now the savior of mankind. A vampire hunter forced to protect his chosen prey.

"Sadira has taken Tristan to the Coven," I whispered.

"Why?" His deep voice had also dropped to hushed tones, as if we were sharing secrets. But we had already done that tonight, and most of what we'd said shouted at the top of our lungs for all the heavens to hear.

"Punishment," I murmured, forcing the word past a clog in my throat. "I stole Tristan from her, so she must strike back at me." My gaze wavered and darted across the room to stare out the windows that overlooked San Marco Piazza. The warm yellow light glowed in the square, beckoning the late night revelers.

"Will they kill him?"

"Yes, but not until I get there." My voice hardened and my hands balled into fists as I stared blindly out the bank of windows. "She'll want me to see it; to know that I failed to protect him."

Danaus's thumb rubbed the inside of my wrist in a light caress, drawing my gaze back to his face. "Will they try to kill you?"

A half smirk tweaked the right corner of my mouth, pushing aside the concern that had undoubtedly drifted across my features. "They can try, but I doubt it. It's time for the Coven to bring me to heel. They will try to break me and remind me that I serve them."

"I can't go," Danaus whispered, releasing my wrist. His hand fell limp back at his side. He finally understood that I had to prove my strength. It was a test. If he walked in and guarded my back, it would be taken as a sign of weakness on my part. Any help he gave me would cause more damage than good.

"No." I walked toward the door, refusing to look back at my partner in crime. They were going to hurt me. They were going to make me wish I was dead, but they wouldn't kill me. Tonight was just a bit of fun. If I somehow managed to survive the next few nights and stop Rowe's plan to free the naturi, then it would be open season on my head.

With one hand on the open door, I looked over at my shoulder into the room, suddenly hating its opulence. My eyes still refused to find his face. "It'll be over before dawn."

I wasn't exactly sure what "it" was, but I was sure that before the dawn came, someone was going to be dead. I had known Sadira would strike back at me. Beyond the fact that it was her way, it was the way of all nightwalkers. I had stolen something that belonged to her in front of a member of the court. It would have been no different if I'd walked up to her and spat in her face. Of course, word of my theft spread like wildfire through the nightwalker legions.

But, stupidly, I had thought I would have more time. Sadira was usually an extremely patient creature. She toyed with her prey over decades if time permitted, letting them dangle on a thin strand of hope for years before finally crushing them. I thought she would wait until after we finally defeated Rowe. Apparently she didn't think she'd get another shot at me so she rushed things. That, or someone else was pulling the strings.

I shot across the Lagoon in record time. I knew these waters. Maybe not as well as the streets of my beloved Savannah, but enough that I could push the little boat to her limits as I sped to the island. Circling around to a small, attractive stone landing closer to the main hall, I eased the tiny speed boat to the dock. It was crowded with boats of different shapes and sizes, but there was still one spot open. They were waiting for me.

Still in the boat, before stepping onto the stone pier I scanned the island one last time. Everyone was pulled back to the Great Hall of the Coven. I could vaguely pick out Elizabeth in the lower levels that served as the daylight chambers. Macaire was also there, but he was moving, heading for the lower levels. Jabari, of course, was nowhere to be found. It had been years since I was last able to sense him. He kept his protective cloak up constantly now, hiding from something.

As I was pulling back, a scream of pain tore through my brain, sending me to my knees. Searing pain ripped along my flesh as if the claws of a thousand cats were using me as a scratching post. Muscles trembled and my stomach clenched and unclenched, quivering under the onslaught of pain with no source. I tightly clutched the steering wheel, trying to regain my balance as the last wave of pain and terror swept through me. I had found Tristan.

A knot of fear twisted in my chest, but it was melting under the heat of the rage building in my veins. Sadira had pulled back the veil blocking Tristan from my senses. They had been torturing him, waiting for my eminent arrival. I could feel the pain as it coursed through his lean frame and the crippling exhaustion as his body strained to heal the assortment of wounds that had been inflicted. I hopped off the boat and walked briskly up to the main hall. There was no need to rush. The assembled vampires had stopped their amusements as they waited for me.

The same pair of humans from earlier in the evening pulled the massive front doors open, their muscles jumping under the effort it required to move the thick combination of wood and iron. A nervous look danced in their dark eyes, which darted only briefly to me before returning to intently stare at the ground. They knew something was happening inside, something gruesome. They had heard Tristan's screams even through the thick doors and were simply grateful they weren't the focus of these grim activities. Yet, there were still several hours before the night finally withered away, plenty of time for them to fill in.

The chandeliers dangling overhead had been extinguished, the long hallway sparsely lit with a scattering of iron candelabras holding thick yellow candles. Even after living in the glory of the electronic age, there were certain things that would not be shed, particularly in the Great Hall. The little flames danced on their precarious perches, throwing long shadows that congregated in the deep corners, plotting their own secret schemes.

Before me the doors to the main audience chamber swung soundlessly open, pushed from the inside. I couldn't see who had opened them, but it didn't matter. My gaze didn't stray from Tristan, who knelt in the middle of the room. Naked and bleeding, he had a large manacle clamped around his neck, with a heavy chain running from it to a thick iron ring in the floor. His arms and legs were not chained, so he could fight back, but the chain running to his neck was so short that he could not fully stand up.

Tristan raised his head when he heard my footsteps echoing heavily across the marble floor, his body cringing at the sound as if the vibrations added to his pain. His beautiful face was covered in blood and his nose was broken. I could see the bite marks on his neck and on the inside of one of his arms. They had taken the time to drain him before beating him so his body wouldn't be able to heal from the wounds.

However, it was his eyes that finally drew an angry hiss out of me. Those haunted blue orbs would chase me for the rest of my existence. He wasn't pleading to be saved, but for me to finally end his pain. The physical pain was minor compared to what they most likely had done to his mind. I had a feeling Macaire had had some fun with him before he handed the young nightwalker over to the rest of the court.

Movement finally drew my eyes from Tristan and I caught sight of Sadira. She was sitting on the stairs before the chair Macaire had sat in earlier in the evening. Her face was expressionless and still, as if she carved out of white marble. Gritting my teeth, I dragged my eyes from her slender form and looked around the room. Nearly a dozen other nightwalkers were gathered. High-back wooden chairs and a couple chaise lounges now lined the walls; a little comfort while they watched the show.

Tristan was the warm-up act, and I was the main attraction. Turning my attention back to Tristan, I forced the anger to coil up in the pit of my stomach as I stood before him. I would deal with them. I would teach them to fear me. My days of facing the members of the court for my survival were centuries ago during my time with Sadira. Most of these vampires had not been reborn yet. To them I was a myth, a fanciful tale based on very little fact. I would remind them that I was a nightmare.

With my hands resting limply on my hips, I stared down at Tristan. The cold marble floor around him was smeared with his blood. I somehow swallowed my rage and revulsion, lightening my voice to one of irritated boredom. "What are you doing here?"

"I was told to come," he rasped. His beautiful voice was raw from his screams.

"By whom?"

"Sadira."

"I am your mistress now," I said, amazed at how steady my voice sounded. On the inside, my muscles were trembling and my throat had constricted. I had been half his age when I made my first appearance as the evening entertainment and I'd had to be carried out. Sleep dominated my nights for more than a week as my body struggled to recover. I never forgave Sadira for my time with the Coven. Many believed playing the part of the court's entertainment was supposed to be a rite of passage. It was not only supposed to make a night-walker stronger, but it also taught obedience. It had taught me to hate.

Looking at Tristan, I knew he was just chum. He wasn't meant to live a long existence and grow to be strong. Sadira had made him weak and kept him weak by chaining him to her side. I had slaughtered those stronger than him because they'd grown careless and could not take care of themselves. Without Sadira, he would become one of those nightwalkers, and it would be me hounding his steps one night like some dark angel of death. But I wouldn't let it happen to Tristan. He belonged to me now.

Maybe it was because there was something in his eyes that reminded me of Michael. It might have been the fact that in two nights I had failed to protect both Thorne and Michael. Or maybe it was that I saw too much of myself in those pain-filled eyes. I knew the horrors he had faced and the pain that still awaited him. But reasons why weren't important.

For once, I wanted to save someone instead of destroying them. I wasn't going to let these monsters have Tristan. But, unfortunately, we all had a part to play, a little pretense to portray before we could all go our separate ways. And I had to be sure I had Tristan's absolute obedience.

"I told you not to come here," I said. My hands slid from my hips to hang limp at my sides, even as tension hummed like an electric current through my taut body. "I should leave you here as punishment for your disobedience."

"Please, no! Mira, please! She's my maker. I had to obey," he pleaded. His soft voice barely jumped above a whisper. He lurched forward, grabbing my legs, a cry escaping his parted lips. When he leaned forward, I saw that his back was a bloody mess of tissue. They had peeled the skin from his body.

I leaned down and placed my hand gently under his chin, forcing him to look up at me. "After tonight, she is nothing to you. After tonight, I am your whole world," I said coldly.

"Yes, Mistress," he choked out past the throb of pain.

Cupping his face with both of my hands, I wiped the bloody tears away with my thumbs as they streaked down his cheeks. "Now tell me who touched you."

I slowly raised my eyes to sweep over the assembled masses as Tristan remained silent. No names left Tristan's cracked and trembling lips, but I hadn't expected him to tell me who his tormentors were. We all knew that I could pick the faces from his memories at any time. But I wouldn't even need to do that.

I didn't bother to look at Sadira. She hadn't touched him. It didn't matter if she had. It was enough that she handed him over to the court for its fun. Skimming over the faces, I noticed Valerio slumping in one of the high-backed chairs, his long pale fingers laced together over his stomach. One corner of his handsome mouth lifted in a smirk, daring me to challenge him, but his clothes were spotless, unlike some of his companions. He had watched the show. It was a neutral stance, not challenging, but he also wasn't on my side. It was the best I was going to get at the moment.

"I thought he was quite delicious," Gwen announced, rising gracefully from one of the chairs off to my left, near the dais at the end of the room. Her pale blue shirt and little white shorts were splattered with Tristan's blood. She would have looked like a tourist on vacation if not for the blood stains and the glow in her narrowed eyes.

"I was so hoping you would say that," I said, the words held in the embrace of a dark laugh. I stepped around Tristan so I was between him and Gwen. "I believe I said that he was not to be touched."

"The Elders promised him to us," she said. Her smile was triumphant, lighting up her blood-smeared face.

"I warned you," I carefully enunciated in Italian. The Italian came without thought as my mind slipped easily back into seemingly ancient memories of fights fought as the Elders watched. The violence, the brutality, the feral need to rend and shred had built in the air until it became a living, breathing creature.

As I spoke, candles around the room flared to life. The little teardrops of fire popped into existence, sending the shadows scrambling to the far corners.

"The Coven's word is law!" Gwen shouted, her gaze darting away from me as she noted the increased firelight. Lines of strain stretched from the corners of her mouth as she struggled to keep from frowning. "You're not above them, Fire Starter."

"A mistress has the right to deny the use of her pets if she so chooses," I said, quoting old law.

"His maker handed him over," Gwen argued, pointing at Sadira. Her smile had faded somewhat and there was no mistaking the trembling in her extended index finger. No one ever denied the use of his or her pet when an Elder wanted to use the poor soul as entertainment. If a master did, he would have to defend him against all comers. In all my years, I had heard of it being done only once. Jabari had denied Macaire when he made the request of me, driving the wedge even further between them. It also didn't help that during that time I was neither a Companion of Jabari nor was he technically recognized as my master.

"I am his mistress. I warned you," I repeated. My words were low and even, deceiving in their calm, but Gwen was not fooled.

"You're nothing!" she screamed, her hands balled into fists at her sides.

I chuckled, my voice sinking into lower, sultry depths. The sound stretched strangely across the room, echoing off the walls as I darted toward her. My fist collided with her jaw before I even stopped moving. She tried to dodge it but her reactions were a hair slower. I felt bone breaking beneath my hand as her head snapped back, the force of the blow throwing her backward into the wall.

Gwen tried to quickly push back to her feet, blood spilling from the corner of her mouth, but I was already there. Grabbing her by the throat, I lifted her off her feet. It was easy considering that she was several inches shorter than me. Her long nails clawed at my hand and down my arms as she struggled to get loose. Little rivers of blood rose to the surface and briefly streaked down my white skin. I smiled at her, pulling back my lips enough to expose my fangs before tossing her across the large room.

With a bone-crunching thud, she landed not far from the center of the room, near the foot of the dais. The sound of her collarbone shattering when she landed split the air, followed by the low squeal of her skin sliding a couple feet across the shiny marble floor.

I paused and looked down the line of vampires who stood watching the struggle. They had risen from their chairs and were eyeing me intently, trying to decide whether I would jump at them next or finish off my current prey. I growled low in the back of my throat, warning them to stay back. A couple hissed in return but backed off a few steps, giving me ample room. Valerio watched me with intent questioning eyes from his chair.

"Elizabeth will destroy you!" Gwen shrieked hysterically. Her jaw had healed enough for her to curse me.

"Where is she, Gwen?" I inquired, strolling back toward her as she struggled to sit up. The pain in her left shoulder from where she had hit the floor slowed her movements. Nightwalkers had the ability to heal with amazing speed, but that didn't mean we didn't feel excruciating pain just like every other creature. "She must know by now that you're in pain. I'll wait while you call to her."

I stood over her and pretended to inspect my nails. With a howl of pure rage, she pushed off the floor with her right hand, launching herself into me. She moved faster than I'd anticipated, knocking me to the floor with her on top. Her long nails raked down my face and tore a large hunk of flesh from my throat. I backhanded her with my right fist, throwing her off so I could roll to my knees.

"She's abandoned you to your fate," I taunted, easily rising to my feet as she struggled. She had fed on Tristan, but his blood wasn't strong enough to heal her. She should have fed on a human or two before facing me, not wasted her night with him. Broken bones slowed her down, and I'd dislocated her jaw when I backhanded her.

I kept my left hand pressed to my neck as I walked back to her side. The blood seeped through my fingers and trickled down my chest to soak into my shirt. "I warned you."

With no hesitation, I knelt before her and punched her in the chest. My hand tore through skin and muscle, shattering her sternum. It took only a second to open my hand in her chest and wrap my fingers around her motionless heart. She had enough time to mouth the word *No* before I yanked it from her chest. Her body slumped lifeless to the floor, the remnants of her soul brushing against me as it floated into the ether.

Clutching her heart tightly in my right hand, her blood ran down my arm and dripped from my elbow. The lukewarm muscle squished in my fist, pushing between my fingers. A wide smile split my pale face as I laid the heart on Elizabeth's chair, a gift from me to the Coven.

THIRTEEN

The monster roared in my chest, the sound causing my soul to tremble in the frail casing of my body. The same feeling that gripped me in the London alley tightened the muscles in my slim frame, screaming for release. I wasn't hungry, but the air was thick with the scent of blood. My limbs were splattered with it and the only sound in the vast room was the soft patter of blood dripping from my fingertips to the shining black marble floor.

But it was more than that. Killing Gwen awakened something within me, and it wanted more. An unexpected warmth rushed through me as if I were still alive and basking naked in the summer sun. My fangs throbbed, needing to be embedded in soft, tender flesh.

My head fell back and a laugh bubbled up from my chest. When it hit the air, the sound was frosted with ice and completely void of all humor. The world slipped away and time eased to a crippled limp. There were only the nightwalkers left within the hall and myself. My eyes lazily fell on the scattering off to my left. Several pairs of glowing eyes met mine and smiled. They were swept up in the same primal wave of blood and violence. I was more than happy to oblige. Tonight, the monster was unleashed.

We were in motion at the same time. Three nightwalkers lunged forward from the far wall as I took my first steps toward them. I was only vaguely aware of the others as they slipped off toward the exits. The wave had washed through these younger nightwalkers, and now they wisely backed off, willing to get their blood and violence from a safer source than me.

The dance was graceful, full of fluid movements, but a blur to any human who would have seen us. There was no thought anymore.

Just the need to kill. Or be killed. The first was young, barely through his first century. His wide green eyes glowed at me like sparkling emeralds a second before I ripped his heart from his chest. The second followed in much the same manner, but I earned a set of claw marks across my stomach for my trouble.

I turned to locate the remaining third when I was slammed to the hard floor, stars exploding before my eyes. Wincing and clenching my teeth against the pain that threatened to steal consciousness away from me, I rolled to the right. Half a breath later a heavy oak chair crashed to the exact spot I'd been, cracking the marble floor. The high-backed chair shattered, sending shards darting through the air under the force of it being thrown to the floor. Instinctively, I shielded my heart from the flying debris, though none of it had enough force to penetrate my sternum.

Rolling onto my back, I gazed up at my attacker. Standing barely over five feet, the nightwalker with the sandy blond hair and glowing blue eyes was holding one of the broken legs of the chair. I smiled up at her and the wooden leg burst into flames. All the wood from the chair scattered about the floor was instantly consumed with dancing flames. The nightwalker yelped in surprise, dropping the leg and stumbling a couple steps away from me.

The fire and pain cleansed me, washing away the blood lust and the need to kill. The monster had grown silent, pleased with my offering. My vision was blurred and my back protested any movement, begging me to lie still, but I couldn't. One remained. Pushing off the ground with my left hand, I bonelessly rose to my feet. The nightwalker paused, watching me, waiting for my next move.

Slowly, I waved my right hand, swallowing back the whimper of pain that slashed through my back. Chest-high flames sprung up around the nightwalker, completely encircling her. Her blue eyes widened, losing their unnatural glow. Frowning, I easily stepped through the flames and grabbed her by the throat, but she barely noticed me despite the fact that my long nails were digging into her cool flesh. Her eyes were locked on the fire that danced less than a foot away from her body. It was only after I gave her a rough shake that she finally met my hard gaze.

"Who am I?" I snarled, tightening my grip on the short nightwalker. Her wide eyes stared up at me, confused and terrified. There was a smear of blood on her small chin. She had fed on Tristan as well. She deserved to die, consumed in the flames that surrounded her, and she knew it.

"The Fire Starter," she whimpered in a strangled voice.

My frown hardened into a cold smile. "Tell them what I have done," I commanded in a low, grating whisper. "Tell them that if anyone touches what belongs to me, I shall hunt them down and collect their hearts for display in my domain. Remind them of who I am."

Still smiling, I shoved her away from me toward the far door on the left side of the room. A terrified scream escaped her as she threw up her arms to protect her face, fully expecting to be engulfed in the fire. But as she reached the ring of fire, I extinguished it so she would pass through untouched. She stumbled and fell to her ass. Quickly realizing she had escaped without being singed, she pushed back to her feet and disappeared through the side door.

My gaze slowly tripped around the room as my eyes adjusted to the lower levels of light. My brain took in the broken bodies and growing pools of blood as they spread about the room like small black lakes. After nearly a full minute, my eyes reached the far dais. Sadira remained on the stairs before Macaire's seat, never moving from the spot she'd occupied when I entered the main hall.

My face was void of all emotion and my thoughts a blank slate. I wasn't even aware that I was approaching her until I heard Tristan scream.

"No, Mistress!" he cried, twisting painfully so he could watch me, the chain still around his neck. His bleeding had stopped, for the most part, but he was weak. "She's our mother."

"My mother died centuries ago. She is nothing to me!" I shouted. Anger suddenly blossomed within chest and flowed through my veins like magma searching for an opening. I walked over to her, once again facing her soaked in the blood of others.

"You can't touch me," Sadira confidently announced. "I am part of the triad."

I licked my lips as a grim smile graced my features, still edging closer. "If I've learned anything during the past few nights, it's that you're replaceable. I'll find another."

The triad had been the ones to create the seal that kept the naturi locked away. And with the naturi threatening to break free, we needed to reform the triad, considering that Tabor had been destroyed nearly fifty years ago. While no one seemed pleased with the choice, Danaus had become Tabor's replacement. Maker or not, I had no doubt I could find a replacement for Sadira as well, if necessary.

"There's not enough time." Confidence still filled her voice, but she rose to her feet. "The new moon and the harvest holiday are in four nights, and they will use it to break the seal. You can't destroy me if you hope to stop the naturi."

"Please, Mistress!" Tristan begged. "It's my fault. I shouldn't have left the room. Punish me."

I paused, my teeth clenched in frustration. She was right that there wasn't enough time to find a replacement. And with my luck, it would turn out to be another Thorne fiasco. I couldn't risk it, no matter how much I loathed her.

"Why?" The single word came out strangled and fractured from the back of my throat.

"He's weak. He has to be taught what it means to be a nightwalker." Her shoulders straightened as she spoke, confident in her reasons for torturing one of her own precious children.

"Is this what it means to be a nightwalker?" I demanded, holding my bloody hands out to her.

"Yes," she hissed, her composure cracking. Her thin, bony hands clenched into fists before her stomach. An unhealthy glow rose from her wide brown eyes. "It's about power and not bowing to those weaker than you. I love Tristan, but he had to learn that."

I snorted, my fingers trembling, sending drops of blood to the black marble floor. "If you think that is what tonight was about, you're a fool. He was an appetizer and you let it happen. He relied on you for protection and you betrayed him. Tonight was about revenge. It was about striking back at me because you were too much of a coward to stand up to the court."

"They would have killed me," she argued, her voice wavering.

"Not yet. Like you said, you're part of the triad. They would have toyed with you, but you would have survived. Unfortunately, Tristan wasn't worth it for you. It was easier to hand him over."

Turning sharply on a heel, I stalked back over to Tristan, who had been silently watching the petite tête-à-tête between mother and daughter. I wanted her to attack my back. I longed for one more small reason to lash out at her, just so the tiny voice of my battered conscience could use the excuse of self-defense when I ripped her head off. But Sadira never moved.

"Don't come back to the suite," I called back to her without turning around. "If I ever see you again after Rowe is defeated, I will kill you. And trust me, I will be looking forward to that day."

"You're not free of me, my Mira," Sadira called, her sweet lilting voice burrowing its way under my skin: *You belong to me. Tristan belongs to me. I am your maker.* It was almost hypnotic, the way it drifted through my brain. There were no protective walls I could put up to guard against her intrusion into my mind. She was my maker; she would have access as long as she survived.

I spun on my heel to snarl at her, but as I turned, the Great Hall disappeared from around me. The massive stone walls and black marble floor were replaced by a worn wooden floor and uneven stone walls. Sadira had done the same trick before when I was severely wounded. She had mentally taken me to the dungeon I was reborn in. But this time I wasn't in the dungeon. I was in the small farmhouse I had inhabited briefly back in Greece before Sadira kidnapped me.

A small whimper escaped me as I looked around the crude house that had given me such joy for an extremely short period of time. For a few years I'd lived in a home, was loved by my husband and adored by my sweet daughter Calla.

"Stop this, Sadira," I commanded in the firmest voice I could muster. I struggled to hold onto the rage and violence that had driven me through my earlier fight.

"This is where it all started, my daughter," she patiently replied. She stood before me in the open doorway, though I wasn't sure if it was truly her or simply part of the illusion. Behind her, black night stretched in all directions. "This place was simply a dream. You were hiding. I set you free."

"You kidnapped me!" I shouted. "I had no choice." I took a step forward and swore I heard the floor creak beneath my feet.

"Mama," cried a low, sleepy voice.

"No," I gasped, taking another step toward Sadira, my arms wrapped tightly around my stomach. I moved away from the soft patter of little footsteps from the next room. "Don't do this, Sadira. She's not real. She's dead. She's been dead for centuries."

"I know that, Mira, but you refuse to let her go," Sadira gently said. Her voice was light, a caress, a soft touch on my cheek. This is your chance to say good-bye and then you can start over with me and Tristan. We will be your family. You won't have this horrible weight hanging on you."

I tried to close my eyes but it was all in my head. There was no escaping the images she wanted me to see. "It's not real. It's not real. It's not—" but my words became lodged in my throat when a girl about three years old entered the room. She wore a long white shirt that just missed covering her small bare feet. A wealth of sleep-tangled black hair fell down her back. She stared up at me with her father's brown eyes. But then, she got most of her looks from her father, and I was grateful about that. I didn't want my daughter to be cursed like me, but perfectly normal like her father.

"Mama," she repeated, stretching her arms up, her eyes pleading with me to pick her up and hold her close. My arms ached to hold her, finally filling the void that had haunted me for centuries. I wanted to feel her warmth against my body and to breathe her scent in so I could hold it forever in my lungs. I wanted to hold my daughter one last time.

Painfully, I took another step backward, trying to find a middle ground between Sadira's image and the image of Calla. I wanted to grab up my daughter, wrap her tightly in my arms, and run from this place. I wanted to run from Sadira, the Coven, and all nightwalkers. I wanted to run back to the life I could have had centuries ago in the sunlight.

But that chance was gone forever. It was shredding me on the inside, leaving me trembling. My legs shook and my knees threatened to buckle. I refused to give in to Sadira. She would not have me again.

"I won't go with you," I growled, tensing the muscles in my legs and clenching my teeth. "Calla is dead. That life I had is dead because of you. You and Jabari. I won't go back to you."

"You will or I will kill Tristan now," she calmly said, switching tactics when images of Calla couldn't make me cave.

"Ridiculous. You won't."

Sadira laughed lightly, reminding me faintly of a bird's song. "Of course I will. You are far more valuable to me than he could ever be."

"Mira?" The voice was soft and fragile, reaching me from beyond the nightmare I was trapped in. It was Tristan. I had forgotten about him. We were really in the Great Hall, and for now Tristan was alive and still mine.

It suddenly dawned on me to fully open my mind instead of closing everything down in an effort to block out Sadira. Tristan's pain and fear instantly flooded in. It was more than Sadira could effectively block out. The image of my home in Greece disintegrated. Calla faded away to only a ghostly memory.

I knelt on the ground beside Tristan, who was still chained to the floor. Reaching across, I took his hand and gently squeezed it as I slowly reduced our mental connection. His pain was draining me and I needed to be sharp against Sadira.

The rage from my earlier fight pumped in my veins again, and a new anger filled my trembling frame. I had packed my past away and left it to collect dust in the corner of my mind, but Sadira trotted it out as a way of controlling me. She had defiled the memory of my daughter; she sullied those precious few moments in my life when I'd felt human and whole and happy. I didn't need the monster dwelling inside of me to fire my need for violence. Sadira had already done that.

"I'm free now," I said, pushing back to my feet. "And Tristan belongs to me."

You can't have him, she snarled in my mind. I felt her pulling another veil over my mind, so I opened my thoughts to Tristan again. Trapping my mind between two realities, it stole away my sense of balance. I had no idea where Sadira was. Desperate, I threw up a ring of fire around Tristan and me.

Sadira's screams rang through the hall. She had been approaching and got trapped in the fire. With her out of my mind, I extinguished the flames, but she was already blackened to a crisp.

With a little effort, I broke the lock on the manacle around Tristan's neck and dropped it with a loud clang. Tristan leaned heavily on me as we moved away, his fingers digging into my forearm as he struggled to stay on his feet.

The smell of burning flesh filled the room, overpowering the scent of the Lagoon and lush gardens that wafted in through the open front doors. Tristan struggled against my hold on him, trying to look back at the creature that had spawned us both, but I wouldn't let him stop moving forward.

Sadira didn't die that night, but every nightwalker in Venice could feel her pain. At dawn she would fall into her deep sleep wrapped in that pain, and tomorrow when she awoke would still be drowning in it. Even if she gorged herself on blood, it would still take several nights to recover from those burns. I only needed to keep her alive until we defeated Rowe. No one had ever said anything about the condition she had to be in.

Tristan and I paused at the front doors long enough for him to feed off the two doormen. I knew they would come in handy sooner or later. Borrowing a pair of pants off one of the unconscious men, we slowly walked back to the boat. My back ached and my head throbbed from where I'd been hit with the chair. From the way my vision still blurred from time to time, it seemed that the nightwalker with the chair had cracked my skull. I needed to feed and sleep for a couple days, but I doubted I would get such a luxury.

Tristan moved more easily as his body healed with the fresh infusion of blood, but our progress was slow. We were several yards from the docks when I saw Nicolai walking toward us up the path. I pulled Tristan to a stop, my whole body tensed. If the werewolf attacked now, I knew I would kill him. My body hummed with pent-up energy from the fight. I might not intend to, but I would still kill him.

"Walk away, Nicolai," I called to him. Now was not the time to resume our fight. Jabari had ordered him to kill me, and I could only assume that Nicolai would pursue that task until he finally completed it or was dead. The golden shifter had stopped in the middle of the path more than twenty feet away, watching me. "Turn around, get back in a boat, and drive off."

"Why didn't you kill me?" The question was soft and reached me on the back of the breeze crossing the island.

"My fight isn't with you," I said. Beside me, Tristan tightened his grip on my arm. He wasn't so much looking for support as he was questioning me, seeking assurance. I placed my right hand over his and gently squeezed it. He had been through enough for one night.

Nicolai caught the movement and frowned at our hands. "He's the reason I was sent to kill you," he said, the words barely pushing past his clenched teeth. "A distraction?"

"Possibly."

Nicolai jerked his eyes away from us as a string of Russian curses rumbled from his chest like a freight train across the desert. His fists were clenched at his sides, trembling. He had been used so another could be tortured, and now he knew it.

"Please, Nico," I started again, hoping a nickname would get him to acquiesce to my request. "Walk away. I need to get him somewhere he can rest and recover."

Frowning, Nicolai walked toward us. I stepped forward, putting myself between the werewolf and Tristan. His expression instantly softened when saw my aggressive stance and he halted a few feet away from us.

"I only want to help you to the boat," he said, holding up his hands in surrender.

Nodding, I turned and put Tristan's hand back on my left arm. Nicolai took Tristan's other hand and placed it on his right arm. The werewolf got a glimpse of Tristan's back and swore softly, his jaw clenched in boiling anger.

"This has nothing to do with you," I murmured a while later, breaking the tense silence.

"But I didn't help matters. I held you up when you could have rescued him sooner," he grumbled.

I said nothing because it was true. He didn't know how he was being used. He didn't know he was aiding in the torture of another. I wondered if he would have followed orders if he'd known what the plan was. By the pained anger that filled his copper-brown eyes, I doubted it.

We didn't speak again until we reached the little speedboat. Nicolai helped me lower Tristan in. The nightwalker sighed deeply as he lay across the bench on his stomach.

"I could have killed you," Nicolai abruptly said, pulling my gaze back up to his handsome face. He stood on the dock with his hands shoved into the pockets of his dirty slacks. His left cheek was smudged with dirt, and a shadow of blond stubble outlined his hard jaw. A smear of blood stained his temple where I had hit him with the rock, but there was no lump or other discoloration. His stare was intense, holding me silent for a moment, unable to read the emotions that lay just below the surface.

"You have the ability," I conceded, a smile lurking on my lips. "But you couldn't have killed me tonight. You don't have a good enough reason, and you need a reason to kill." It was a guess, but I doubted that I was far from the mark.

Nicolai snorted and opened his mouth to argue, but I held up my hand and continued before he could speak. "Don't go back to the hall until after daybreak. I didn't leave its occupants in a good mood."

"Thanks for the warning," he said with a half smile.

With a nod, I turned on the engine and pulled away from the stone dock, eager to get Tristan back to the relative safety of our suite. By the time we reentered the Lagoon, the worst of his wounds had healed and he was beginning to relax.

My muscles were battered and the wind was chilling the blood that covered my body. We crossed those dark waters in silence, lost in our own thoughts. Even now I could still hear Sadira's screams, feel Gwen's warm heart squishing between my fingers. The soft touch of each soul as it left the bodies of the nightwalkers I had killed this evening pranced through my mind, and I smiled. I felt more alive with every existence I'd extinguished, and I loved it.

Maybe I'd been wrong about what I told Danaus. Maybe I *was* evil. I could argue that I had killed those nightwalkers of the Coven court to stop them from hurting another vampire. I could argue that I'd done it to protect Tristan. But that would have been a lie. I did it to prove my own power and exert my control over them. I killed them simply because I could.

FOURTEEN

The night closed in around me, warm and wet like a lover's lips on the hollow of my throat. But I wanted to shove the feeling away. I didn't want to be touched. I didn't want to hear another heartbeat or feel heat radiating from another human body. I didn't want to look up and meet Tristan's haunted gaze, asking questions I couldn't bring myself to answer.

For the first time in what seemed an eternity, I was alone. Gabriel, my guardian angel, was hundreds of miles away, and Danaus remained safely ensconced in a church—protected from me and my kind. Tristan had been left curled up on the bed. After a quick shower to remove the fresh coating of blood, I slipped down to the landing.

As I flew across the Lagoon, a roar rose up from the engine of the tiny speedboat and I could feel it rumbling through my bones. Waves slapped against the sides of the boat and the wind pulled at my hair, tangling it. The darkness crowded close as I headed away from the lights and sputtering heart of Venice.

I needed to be away from the pulse of humanity so I could think. Yet, something in me was afraid to plumb the dark depths of my feelings too deeply. I didn't regret the destruction I had brought at the hall. I didn't regret the lives that I took or the joy I felt in doing so. And it wasn't the act that was gnawing away at me—it was my complete lack of remorse. I don't know whether it was some wrinkled remnant of my humanity or if I truly believed it, but something was screaming inside of me that I should be horrified by the bloodbath I had created. But I wasn't.

Beyond the screaming, another, more insidious voice mocked me. Nearly two centuries ago Valerio had warned me there was no escaping what we were—heartless, cruel, and violent. I had left Europe professing that I could be different, I could avoid what he believed was fated. Less than twenty-four hours back in Venice and I was covered in the blood of my compatriots, basking in their terror, and laughing like a madwoman struck by the moon.

As I neared the dark island, I cut the engine and let the small boat glide into the dock. I had gone to the one island where I knew I would be completely alone. No human lived here, and no vampire would dare find rest here due to the constant traffic of people during the daylight hours. I had come to San Michele—the cemetery island.

The entire island was ringed with an enormous red-brick wall, and a pair of graceful white stairs and gates led into the sanctuary. The shadows were deeper on the island, thrown down by the countless cypress trees that reached up past the walls. Most of the island was thickly lined with graves, marked with headstones of varying size and decoration, from the traditional white cross to the more elaborate family crypts. The lanes were laid out in a neat grid, but due to the need for space, they were narrow, forcing visitors to walk single file in most places.

With my head down, I wove my way to the east. It had been a while since I last visited, but I remembered a small section that was left as a park. The scent of jasmine and roses drifted to my nose. The air, thick and humid, left me feeling I was pushing through wet cotton. As I turned the last corner, I allowed myself to release a soft sigh as my gaze fell on a small patch of earth that had yet to be turned into a resting place for the dead. The park had shrunk in size, but it was enough for me to sit in silence, surrounded by cypress and what appeared to be a pair of hybrid poplar trees.

Yet, something was wrong. I felt as if I wasn't alone, though I knew I was. No human lived here and nightwalkers had no reason to visit this place. Despite my logic, I still scanned the entire island with my powers, but I sensed no one. Shoving my fingers through my hair, I shook my head and forced myself to walk into the clearing. I was frazzled from the long night and the seemingly endless battles with the naturi.

I sat on the ground and threaded my fingers through the cool grass, wishing the silence of the island would seep into my soul and wipe away the pain caused by Calla's sweet memory. Behind the great stone walls, I could no longer hear the waves of the Lagoon and the clang of the buoy bells were faint. There was just me and the wind and the dead.

"I have grown very weary of you, little princess," someone above me announced.

Rolling over to balance on my hands and toes, I looked up into the poplar tree that had been at my back. But I didn't need to see him. Frustrated tears welled up in my eyes at the sound of Rowe's taunting voice. I was too tired both in body and spirit to fight the naturi now.

"Leave here," I snarled, the muscles in my calves starting to tremble from the awkward position I remained in. "I didn't come here looking for you."

He snorted and stood easily on the branch he had been sitting on. His large black wings brushed and scraped against leaves and branches as he resettled them. "You leave. I was here first."

Was it that simple? I wasn't surprised to find him in Venice after seeing the female naturi in the Great Hall. Hell, I was sure there were several other naturi wandering around the city or even swimming in the Lagoon. But he didn't honestly seem to be there for me, since his best weapon was the element of surprise.

Letting my knees fall so I was kneeling in the grass, I quickly glanced over my shoulder in the direction Rowe was facing. By my best guess, he was looking out toward San Clemente and the Great Hall.

I had to get off the island and find some way to alert Jabari or Macaire. Stopping the naturi meant stopping Rowe, but I couldn't accomplish that alone. I had no idea what the wind clan was capable of, but I was willing to bet there was more to it than just a nice pair of wings. Unfortunately, I had succeeded in pissing off everyone in the Coven, as well as angering and/or scaring the shit out of all the flunkies. I couldn't reach Jabari, Elizabeth would rather see me dead at the hands of Rowe after what I did to Gwen, and Macaire . . . well, the only way I could reach Macaire was through the flunkies, and that wasn't going to happen. My only potential contact inside the Great Hall was Sadira. I could have screamed. No matter what I did, I kept wading deeper and deeper into the mire until there was simply no escape.

With a shrug, I made a show of dusting off my hands as I rose to my feet. I was on my own. "Fine. You can have the island. I'm sure this is the only way you can tolerate being surrounded by humans."

"I have to know, Mira," Rowe began, halting me before I could take my first step. "Do you regret your decision?"

"No," I said, far too quickly to be convincing.

A low chuckle rippled from Rowe as he shook his head at me.

There was no question about what decision he was referring to. He had given me a chance to change sides, to help the naturi in exchange for their protection. I chose my kind without hesitation, but within minutes questioned whether it had truly been the wisest choice.

If anything, I realized that I should be searching for a third option instead of trying to figure out which was the lesser of the two evils.

"No? You're pleased, yet you run away to the one place in this wretched city where there's not a single vampire to be found?" he said. Rowe threaded a loose stand of hair behind his ear, keeping it from blocking his one good eye. Between his long black hair and the leather eye patch, he still reminded me of a pirate straight from a romance novel.

A smirk twisted on my lips as I looked up into the tree at my enemy. "I like the view of the city from here."

His head snapped up to look out across the island. Another low laugh drifted down from the tree to me. From the ground, the only thing that could be seen in all directions was the massive brick wall that edged the island like a piece of industrial strength lace. I wanted to keep him laughing. It meant that he wasn't trying to kill me. Rowe's laughter was better than Nerian's. My old tormentor's laughter haunted me, skipping back from memories that were sealed away under blocks of steel and concrete. Nerian's laughter was the sound of madness and pain.

"I made a mistake with you," Rowe unexpectedly announced, again stopping me from walking back toward the gate I'd used to enter the cemetery.

"What? When you helped Nerian torture me? Or when you tried to grab me in Egypt?" My indifferent, easygoing tone withered. "No, wait! You mean when you threatened to poison me in London."

"No, none of that was a mistake," he replied with a wave of his hand. "I mean when we first met."

"Machu Picchu," I supplied. I honestly didn't remember him being there, but he'd said on more than one occasion that he had. And maybe it was true. There were a lot of things that were blurry about my two-week captivity on that mountain. I might have blocked him out.

Rowe dropped down from the tree branch he had been standing on, landing only a few feet from where I stood. I immediately darted backward, putting more than twenty feet between us, and even that still felt too close. Surprisingly, he lifted both hands, palms out, giving the international sign that "It's all good." Of course, I was hoping that was what the gesture meant in naturi.

"You honestly don't remember me," he said softly, staring at me with a strange intensity. His large black wings were hidden now and he vaguely reminded me of a somewhat muscular elf, without the pointed ears, of course.

"No, I don't remember you," I snapped, pacing to my left then back again. The ground was sloped and the grass was slick under my feet. Not the best location for a fight. "There's a lot about Machu Picchu I don't care to remember."

"We met in Spain," Rowe corrected.

I jerked to a halt, my lips parting at this sudden bit of unexpected news. Had he been among those who kidnapped me from Spain and took me to Peru?

"It's been more than six centuries," he continued. "I looked different, but you haven't changed much. Your hair seemed longer, and you were human. Sort of."

"You're lying," I whispered, shaken to my very soul. He knew me when I was human. That didn't seem possible. Was I a magnet for these twisted creatures? Sadira had found me living on a small farm in Greece, the nearest village almost a day's walk away. And now Rowe claimed to have known me during my brief human years.

"It was four hours from sunset and you were sitting near the edge of a lake," Rowe stated. His voice grew harder and colder with each new detail. His hands fell limp back at his sides. "You sat in the sun wearing a green dress. A strand of black pearls was woven through your hair."

While my memory of that day had faded during the long stretch of years, his memory remained crisp and fresh. But there was no question of the day he was recalling. I had worn that dress just once and then burned it, destroying the last bits of my human life. Rowe had met me on the last day that I was human.

A fine trembling started in my fingers and a knot jerked tight in the pit of my stomach. I started to shake my head, denying what he was saying, when the fog around my own memory started to clear. A man had walked up out of the nearby woods. He was tall and lean, with bright green eyes, the same shade as wet grass after a summer storm. His shoulder-length hair was a pale blond almost like milky sunlight.

"I warned you . . . that the landowner didn't—"

"Like trespassers," Rowe finished. He leaned against the tree he had been perched in only moments ago. A soft laugh escaped him as he tilted his head back, staring up at the canopy. "I would never have guessed you were talking about a flock of vampires."

"I was only trying to keep you from being dinner," I replied. I couldn't raise my voice above a whisper as my mind struggled to comprehend this information.

"And I let you slip through my fingers," he muttered, looking at me again. "I came out of the woods because I sensed you. Something strange sitting on the edge of the lake. Not naturi. And yet, not quite human. A little bundle of energy as warm and sweet as a zephyr."

"Human," I firmly said. "I was human."

Rowe shrugged his broad shoulders at my comment. "Maybe." His eyes then narrowed on me and a frown pulled at his lips. "You managed to convince me back then. 'I wanted to see the sun one last time,'" he mimicked in a high falsetto voice that sounded nothing like me.

"It was the last time I ever saw the sun," I confirmed.

"I thought you were dying," he barked, pushing off the tree, but he didn't approach me. He stared at me, his fists clenched at his sides. "Humans were dropping dead all over the land. I thought you would too."

That was part of the reason Sadira offered to change me. The Black Plague had swept through Europe for several years, and she began to fear that I wouldn't be able to escape it. If I caught the illness, she could not heal me and would have had to watch me die. So she offered to change me into a nightwalker. I'd recently discovered that there was much more to it than that, of course, but none of that was a part of my own memories, so to me Sadira remained my maker alone.

"No, I had another kind of death in mind," I murmured.

"Aarrgh!" Rowe shouted, shoving both of his hands angrily through his hair as he took one step toward me then back over to the tree. "If I'd done something that day—anything—so much could have been different. If I had just killed you then, or taken you away from those vampires, everything would have been different," he ranted.

It was an interesting viewpoint that I had not considered. If I had not been at Machu Picchu, the naturi would have most likely opened the door and returned to the earth. Things would have been vastly different if I had not lived. After looking back on so many of my seemingly harmless decisions that had gone horribly wrong during the past several days, it was nice to be faced with someone dealing with the same horror. Six hundred years ago, if Rowe had killed a somewhat strange human, his wife-queen would be walking the earth beside him along with the rest of the naturi horde. They would not be facing the battle that was looming now. A broad smile danced across my lips and brightened my eyes. I wasn't the only one to royally screw up without realizing it until it was far too late to fix.

"We would be free," he said in a low voice full of wistful longing.

My smile withered. "And I would be dead. Countless humans and nightwalkers and lycans would be dead. The bori would be free.

The old war would start again," I said, my voice gaining strength for the first time since I had seen Rowe.

"You think the bori would be free if the naturi returned?" he countered, leaning against the tree again. He seemed to have gotten over his moment of frustration, but then, he'd been dealing with that little bit of truth for more than five hundred years.

"Of course. It's the only option any non-naturi would have left." I took a couple steps closer to him, shoving my fingers into the front pockets of my leather pants. "When the nightwalkers discover that we have no way of defeating you, we would find a way to set the bori free, your one and only equal in power."

"It's a sad future you paint," Rowe said with a shake of his head.

"It doesn't have to be that way," I said, a wide grin returning to my face. "You could walk away now. Give up these plans to break the seal forever and let the naturi return to obscurity."

To my surprise, Rowe snorted again and folded his arms over his chest. "You would protect me from my kind?"

I smiled. It was the same offer he had made to me nights ago. Change sides. Betray your own people. "Of course."

"I was serious, Mira. You don't belong with them."

"I am nightwalker, Rowe. It's the only place I belong."

He sighed, then frowned at me as if disappointed. "Regardless, getting rid of me won't solve your problems." I noticed that as he spoke, his eyes darted back toward the wall over my shoulder. Toward the Coven and the female naturi within the Great Hall.

"Probably not, but it would be a great starting point," I conceded. "Of course, I'm getting the feeling that I should start with the female on that island you keep looking at. A friend of yours? Or maybe she keeps you warm at night, considering the little woman is stuck on the other side."

There was no mistaking the snarl that jumped from the back of Rowe's throat. The light banter we had enjoyed early was over and it was now time to get down to business. I just hoped I survived the next few minutes. While I could comfortably contend that killing him would halt the naturi's attempts to break the seal, my death would also ensure that nightwalkers had no way of reforming the seal or closing the door again if the naturi actually succeeded.

"You know of her?" he demanded, to which my grin only grew. Rowe took a couple steps toward me, and I matched him by stepping backward. The air seemed to swell with energy. The wind picked up, causing the trees to violently sway. I chanced a glance up at the night sky to see the clouds churning and bubbling like witch's brew. The stars had been blotted out and a low roll of thunder growled in the distance.

"I can sense her on the island, yet I cannot reach her," he admitted, and it was more than a little reassuring to discover that at least the naturi couldn't break through our protective barriers. "Nightwalkers control that island."

"Venice belongs to us," I said. "It has belonged to us for centuries and it will remain ours. Are you surprised there are places in this world that you cannot go?" I was playing with fire when it came to taunting Rowe, but playing with fire was what I did best.

"Who do you hold on that island?" he demanded, ignoring my remarks. "She's a captive."

Something in his voice gave me pause. A slight hesitation or a breathless pause that could be easily overlooked. He had intended it to sound like a statement, but it didn't. Not only was he unsure of who was on the island, but he was also unsure whether she was actually a hostage.

"Now that is an interesting question," I slowly said. "Unfortunately, you're the only living naturi I know. The rest tend to die quickly upon meeting me."

Thunder rumbled again, louder this time, the storm drawing closer. Rowe growled as his arm shot up into the air. Less than a second later a bolt of lightning plummeted to the ground, striking no more than three feet from where I stood. I jumped away, landing in a heap before rolling back to my feet. The air still tingled with the electricity hanging in the atmosphere along with the scent of burnt ozone.

Rowe's hand shook slightly as he lowered it back to his side. There was no missing the intent look on his face as he watched me. I was getting a firsthand look at the powers of the wind naturi. Not only could they fly, but apparently they could also control the weather. I would never survive a lightning strike, and I knew he could kill me before I could incinerate him.

"Hmmm," I mocked, desperately trying to hide my mounting fear behind sarcasm. "Killing me may solve some of your problems, but it won't help you discover the identity of the little naturi hiding on the island."

"Hiding? What do you mean 'hiding'?"

I laughed at him, but swallowed the sound when Rowe started to raise his arm again. Lightning darted among the rolling clouds, illuminating each black giant for a blink of an eye before plunging all back into darkness again. Gritting my teeth, I took a desperate chance.

I ran straight at Rowe. The air tingled and the ground shook as another lightning bolt struck the ground directly behind me.

Slamming his back into the tree, I wrapped my fists in his red shirt and leaned in so my nose nearly touched his. "You may be able to control the lightning, but I am willing to bet you can't survive a lightning strike. So the question becomes, how badly do you want to see me dead?"

"That's an interesting wager," he replied. His green eyes narrowed on mine and a smirk twisted his lips.

There was no mistaking the surge of energy that crackled and snapped around us. He was pulling the energy from the earth and I could sense it; something that should not be happening. Nightwalkers lost all connection with the earth when we were reborn.

The sensation from the building power was both amazing and painful, biting at my flesh and gnawing on my bones. The energy was trying to find a way into my body, but it was at odds with what I was. Nightwalkers were creatures of blood magic. We couldn't do earth magic. Or at least that's what I had always been led to believe.

"Of course, we both know that killing me won't get you any closer to finding out about your missing female," I said, just trying to buy a few seconds. "And we've both seen what a joke kidnapping me is."

"I'm sure I can come up with some other options."

"While you're at it, why not try thinking of a reason as to why a naturi may be ensconced on an island filled with nightwalkers and not be threatened?" I pulled my face away from his so I could clearly look into his eyes without going cross-eyed myself. Some of the anger had slipped from his features as he thoughtfully stared at me. Standing so close, I could see the scars that snaked across the right side of his face and disappeared behind his eye patch. I remembered that when we met years ago, there were only a couple faint scars along his neck but nothing else. Once, he was pale and blond and nearly perfect, but now he stood before me dark and scarred. What had he been through that could possibly scar a naturi like this?

"I think you've got bigger problems than just me," I said, slowly releasing my grip on his shirt. I knew that the naturi on San Clemente was not a hostage, but part of some bargain the Coven was working out. Meanwhile, Rowe knew there was a naturi on the island but had no idea who it was or why she was there, which indicated that he had not sent her. He was not a part of whatever this other naturi and the Coven were cooking up. I wasn't the only one who was being betrayed in Venice.

I winked at him one last time as I backed away, hoping I had finally given him enough to think about so I could escape to a more populated location. "Just a word of advice," I said. "I'd get all your ducks in a row before trying again in four nights."

Before I could slip away, Rowe roughly grabbed both of my shoulders, holding me just inches from his body. A wicked grin split his mouth and laughter danced in his one good eye. "You say you don't remember me being at Machu Picchu," he murmured. "Let me see if I can jog your memory."

To my utter shock, he jerked me close and pressed his lips against mine. I stood frozen, my brain completely locked up in a mix of disbelief and revulsion. And something even worse happened. I realized that his touch, his smell, his taste were all too familiar. I pushed against him violently, pulling out of his grasp as I stumbled backward. His mocking laughter followed me, but I was only vaguely aware of it as my thoughts flew back to my time at Machu Picchu.

"You were in the cave," I choked out past the lump in my throat.

"You still thought I was human," Rowe taunted.

I had been exhausted, weighed down by pain and starvation after being tortured for more than a week. An hour before sunrise, they returned me to the caves that made up the Temple of the Moon. Only this time there was a pale blond human in there already. I didn't think about how or why. Through the fog of pain, I only saw the human I had met by the lake.

"You said they'd kill you," I whimpered, bringing a dark laugh from my companion. Rowe had told me they would kill him if I didn't do as the naturi ordered. He pleaded with me to save his life, but I couldn't betray my people to save the life of one human. When they came for him, I pulled on the chains that bound my hands behind my back. I tried to set them on fire, but I was too weak. All I could do was shout and kick as the naturi approached, tears streaming down my dirty face.

As they grabbed my blond-haired companion, he had leaned down and kissed me. I remembered the softness of his lips, the taste of sweetness in his mouth like ripe berries. I could smell him, a mix of earth and desperation. He pleaded with me one last time to save him, but all I could do was weep for him as they dragged him out, the words lodged behind the lump in my throat.

I stared horrified at Rowe now, all the memories rushing back with startling clarity. I had wept endless tears for him, guilt eating away at me like acid. I had forced myself to forget about him because his memory nearly destroyed me. I thought I had sacrificed an innocent man to save my own kind from extermination.

"You may have forgotten me, but I never forgot the taste of the tears you cried for me," he said in a low voice.

I wrapped my arms around my middle, nearly hunched over in pain. They had nearly destroyed me with a trick, nearly broken me. Even now, after so many centuries, the pain felt so fresh.

Rowe simply smiled at me, making no move to stop me as I backed away from him. "It was the will of the fates you survived our first two encounters so many years ago. Your life will benefit me one day."

Shaking my head, there was nothing I could say. I blinked back tears of humiliation as I slowly walked back toward the entrance. That night at Machu Picchu replayed in my head over and over again with each step, increasing my endless hatred for the entire race.

A low rumble of thunder followed me back to the boat, but the lightning remained locked within the clouds. Rowe was still laughing at me.

FIFTEEN

The sun slid back beneath the earth, its long rays of light clawing at the sky in a desperate attempt to find some last second purchase. The world sighed and shuddered, shaking off the day's tight grasp like shedding a skin it had outgrown. I didn't see the sun's steady descent into darkness, but I could feel the birth of a new night. The subtle shift of the nocturnal world as it yawned and stretched, ready for a night of hunting, rippled through me.

Tristan lay silent last night in the bed after returning from the Coven, lost somewhere between Sadira's betrayal and my failure to protect him. I'm sure his mind had replayed his time with the court in all its gory detail. He'd come so close to dying in that place of permanent night and horrors.

I should never have left him alone with Sadira, completely underestimating her need to strike out at me. The court could have easily destroyed him, and Sadira had already proven that he was dispensable if it meant breaking me. Protecting Tristan was going to be harder than I'd anticipated, and he had paid the price for my foolishness and ego. His encounter in the Great Hall was my fault. We both knew now that neither of us would ever be completely free until Sadira was dead and gone. But at the moment, he slept deeply beside me on the bed, curled up in the fetal position, the blankets twisted around his naked body.

Hesitantly, I reached over and smoothed some of the soft locks from his face. Full dark was still more than an hour away, and he was immersed in the deep, healing sleep of our people. Blissful darkness consumed his thoughts, and for a time the memory of Sadira's betrayal and my failure were no doubt wiped away. He would have to face those memories again all too soon, but for now there was only nothingness.

I stared down at his beautiful form, cool and limp. A knot lodged in my throat and I blinked back a swell of tears that blurred my vision. My sweet, beautiful Tristan with the fragile, playful smile. In him, I saw both a child and a brother. Brought into the darkness by the same nightwalker, we were of the same bloodline. Yet, he was so much younger and weaker. His very existence seemed so tenuous.

Jabari had saved me five hundred years ago from Sadira, bringing me out of the shadow of pain and despair. Was it my job to save Tristan now? How could I when I could barely protect myself? Both Michael and Thorne had died while I watched. Would the young nightwalker be next despite my best efforts?

Touching his hair again, I wished his peace would last. I wished for his wounds to heal, on the outside as well as the scars on the inside, but I feared it would all be for nothing. Just nights ago I had professed to James that nightwalkers were more than monsters. I told him that we felt joy and that we loved. Yet hadn't the bloody mess that they'd made of Tristan's back when they peeled the skin from his body proven that wrong? Hadn't the fact that I reveled in the bloodbath I created proven that wrong? How could one monster ever succeed in protecting another monster?

Sparing a glance to find that his back had healed from last night's debacle, I pushed off the bed. Never in my long existence had I risen so early. I had been called. I could feel Valerio in my head the second consciousness came flooding into my brain, and then he pulled away, leaving behind a faint impression on my lips, as if he'd kissed me. Standing in the silent room, I inhaled deeply, half expecting to catch a faint whiff of his scent, and my brain even told me for a second that I did, but I knew he had never been in the room. His presence in my thoughts had been so strong that it left a mark on all of my senses.

But that was Valerio, as silent as a shade and as ubiquitous as the wind. He was a ghost from my past that I could never quite shake off. But then, there was the question of whether I truly wanted to shed his long-reaching touch.

The sound of the door to the hotel room closing jerked me from my thoughts. I grabbed the ankle-length silk robe from where I'd tossed it over a chair and quickly pulled it on. I was still tying the sash of the hotel robe when I stepped into the main salon. Danaus was pushing in a cart covered with a white cloth, laden with dishes hidden under silver covers. A dozen scents of rich sauces, cooked meat, and hot coffee suddenly filled the air. It was time for dinner or breakfast. By the smell of it, I was convinced that the hunter was indulging in both.

Danaus abruptly halted, his eyes darting from me to the bay of windows that revealed the distant sunset. The sky was painted deep shades of red, orange, and a heavy purple. It had been centuries since I last looked on such colors in the sky.

"Did you have any problems last night?" I stiffly inquired. With my arms folded over my stomach, I walked over to the windows, ignoring the silent question resting in his narrowed eyes. The fading sunlight made my eyes burn, and I blinked back bloody tears but didn't move. I wasn't sure if I would ever see the sunset again, and I wanted to soak in the colors while I could.

"No. You?"

"Nothing important." I tried to sound nonchalant and indifferent about last night, but failed. Those two words came out sounding weary and ragged. My encounter with Rowe and the slaughter at the Great Hall had left me torn in two.

"Mira?" I hadn't heard him move, but he sounded closer now. Just a few feet away, standing directly behind me. The scent of him was strong, a soothing mix of soap and the sun, with a hint of spice from his cologne or aftershave. A part of me wanted to lean back and rest my shoulders against his strong chest as we shared the sunset in comfortable silence.

"Everything is well," I said, pushing aside the silly urge.

"It would be easier to protect each other if I understood what was happening," he firmly said. "Who took Sadira and Tristan?"

I opened my mouth to say that it was none of his business and that I had it all under control, but another set of words came tumbling out. "Sadira took Tristan to the court of the Coven to punish me. He was tortured until I arrived."

"Did you destroy Sadira?" The words escaped his throat, sounding matter-of-fact, his question holding no emotion or inflection. I couldn't decide whether he would condemn or praise me for my actions.

"She still exists, though I'm sure she wishes she didn't," I finally replied.

"And the Coven?"

"Who knows what they think? They weren't present at the time. They will only act when it is to their benefit." Biting back a sigh, I turned on my bare right heel to face him. I needed to get moving. Valerio had woken me for a reason. He wanted something, and I didn't want him showing up there. "I have another meeting tonight."

"Alone?"

"Naturally," I said with a little smirk, which faded almost as quickly as it appeared.

"What about the Coven and their arrangement with the naturi?" Danaus inquired.

"I haven't forgotten. We have to stop it, or it could mean war among all of the races, along with fighting a war against the naturi. No one would survive such a thing."

"Don't you find it odd that Jabari demanded we come here, risking us discovering their grand plot?"

A smile brightened my features and exposed my fangs briefly. "Yes, I do," I said, almost chuckling. "I'm beginning to think that not everyone is of one mind on the Coven."

"And it's our job to destroy the bargain," Danaus finished with a nod.

"Destroy the naturi trying to break the seal. Destroy the Coven's bargain with the naturi."

"It's what we do best," Danaus said. A fleeting smile slipped across his face.

"True, but we may need some help, hence the meeting." I glanced over my shoulder one last time as the colors in the sky continued to fade. "Stay close to Tristan while I'm gone. Don't let him out of your sight," I commanded, not caring how the hunter felt about my issuing orders to a creature more than three times my age.

"Do you think they'll come after him again?"

I cocked my head to the side as an odd thought skipped through my brain. "Would you protect him if they did?" I softly asked, my eyes drifting over his hard features. Danaus's eyes darted across the room and his frown deepened as he paced a few steps away from me. I doubt either one of us knew the answer to that question. I opened my mouth to push on when he suddenly spoke, his voice like a distant rumble of thunder in the quiet room. "I would protect him against the creatures that hurt him last night."

I wouldn't go into detail about what happened to the young nightwalker last night. That was Tristan's choice. But I had no doubt that Danaus felt my pain and rage. I had not attempted to shield him.

A slow smile grew on my lips, and my eyes glowed dark lavender with the memory of the bloodbath. "Those creatures no longer exist," I purred.

Danaus nodded, the frown disintegrating from his face. I was surprised. There was no disgust or disappointment in his eyes when he looked at me. All I could feel from him was a sense of peace and calm.

I blinked and the glow disappeared from my eyes, the swell of power slipping from my form as if caught up by a light breeze. "No, that is not why I want you to stay with Tristan. I fear the court may come after you next."

"And you expect him to protect me?" he asked incredulously.

"No," I said, a smile trembling on my lips. "Tristan and I are connected. I can feel his emotions and see through his eyes. I will know if you are troubled."

"Unlike our connection?" he asked, arching one thick brow at me.

"Our connection weakens with time and distance," I replied sharply. "It is also a connection I do not wish to cultivate, and would prefer it to die completely." I was still unnerved by the way his mind had touched mine last night, slowly scanning my body for the injury I'd sustained. But now the contact had dissipated, and I was only vaguely aware of his emotions, much like most humans.

Danaus simply nodded, wisely refraining from commenting on the fact that I hadn't known Tristan was in trouble last night until it was too late. But then again, I had taken care of that problem last night. Sadira wouldn't cause any problems for a long time.

As I turned to go back into the bedroom to throw on some clothes, Danaus pointed out a large box that had been delivered to the room a couple hours earlier. I shook my head as I carried it into the bedroom with me, knowing without opening it who had sent it. Valerio believed that appearance was everything in keeping up a facade.

Placing the large, white garment box on the bed, I pulled off the lid. Inside I found a black silk camisole and a white wrap made of antique lace. The straight, black skirt fell to my calves and was slit up the back. And of course, a pair of heels that had wide black ribbons that wrapped around my ankles. Quickly dressing, I decided at the last minute to leave my hair down. I took one last glance in the mirror and couldn't quite fight back the small smile that rose on my lips. The outfit was elegant and appropriately conservative. Yet, it still somehow managed to be sexy and alluring with its tiny flashes of pale skin. If Valerio could divert his attention long enough from fashion and keeping up appearances, he could be a truly dangerous figure.

I was still smiling when I strode out of the suite and rode the elevator down to the lobby. It had been on the tip of my tongue to warn Danaus that Rowe was in the area as I slipped from the room, but I knew if I mentioned the naturi's name, I would never be able to attend this meeting without his dark shadow. Besides, Danaus could at least sense the naturi, making him better protected. He didn't need my warning.

When I entered the large marble lobby to the hotel, the sun had finished its descent in the horizon and the night took over. My footsteps nearly stumbled at the sudden surge of power that rippled through the air. For a brief moment my body felt more awake and alive, connected to something larger than myself. But just as suddenly the feeling faded, leaving me aware and calm. I was back in my element.

A soft chuckle drew my gaze across the nearly empty room. Valerio folded the newspaper he was pretending to read and laid it aside as he pushed out of his chair.

Valerio was the classical image of a vampire. Not the rotting, shambling corpse with breath that smelled like death, but the Hollywood version with brown hair and pale blue eyes like a glacier kissed by the sea. His cadaverous white skin was stretched over lean muscle, created by a human life spent at hard manual labor and an undead existence filled with constant physical activity. He was shorter than me, but not by much. It was not something easily noticed either. When the nightwalker entered a room, his presence filled it in such an overwhelming way that you couldn't be aware of anyone or anything else. He became everything and was everywhere.

Handsome was an inadequate word to describe him. He was beautiful in the same fashion Michelangelo's David was beautiful or the Venus de Milo. He possessed the same type of beauty as a summer sunset on the Mediterranean with a full moon rising in the distance. Awe-inspiring. Breathtaking. The type of peaceful, exquisite beauty that made you want to believe in a God or that there was good left in the world. It was the kind of beauty that convinced you to hold on for just one more day.

But it was more than his appearance that fulfilled the image humans now clung to when it came to vampires. It was also his manner. Calm, unshakable confidence oozed from every pore and controlled the muscles in his lean frame. It was in his walk and the way he stood, poised and always aware of his surroundings. He possessed the same seductive beauty as a sleeping jaguar. Beautiful and infinitely deadly when awakened.

Sadira taught me concepts like power and control when dealing in the world of nightwalkers. Jabari gave me the concepts of loyalty and honor, instilling within me a sense of history for my kind. But Valerio taught me how to live as a nightwalker and how to live with myself. He opened my eyes to the world of pleasure and joy. I learned to laugh again. Valerio gave my kind a new reason to fear me. I learned how to play games with my prey, both physical and mental, to induce equal parts happiness and fear.

When I left both Sadira and Jabari, I had never looked back. I stepped from their shadow and pursued my own life, in a fashion. But I had yet to completely shed Valerio. Years withered away and I found myself once again seated in an elegant parlor or strolling down a rat-infested alley with Valerio smiling at my side. I'd leave him with unspoken words like "Never again" balanced on the tip of my tongue, but knew better than to say it. Our paths always found a way to cross.

I had no idea how old he was. Old enough. He had such a quiet, unobtrusive way about him that I couldn't begin to guess the extent of his powers, but none dared to cross him, and he gave few reason to do so. Was he born chum, or was he a First Blood? I couldn't even begin to guess.

I didn't fear him, and I knew that it might prove to be my greatest mistake. I didn't trust him and was extremely cautious around him, but my lack of fear could prove to be the end of me. If anything, Valerio had taught me to fear myself.

Walking over to where I stood, a patronizing smile lifted his full lips, revealing a hint of white teeth. "*Cara* Mira," he chuckled, an Italian accent faintly lacing his words. "I had forgotten you usually sleep late, missing out on the birth of the night."

"What is it you wanted to see me about?" I demanded, overcoming my momentary surprise that he had chosen to speak in English. It was a struggle to keep from crossing my arms over my chest. I didn't want him to see how tense I was, but I had no doubt he could read it in the stiffness of my shoulders and the frown that pulled at the corners of my lips.

"Where is your companion? The hunter?" he asked, shoving his hands in his pockets.

"In the suite. I assumed you wanted a private meeting."

"Oh, I do," he said, his smile widening. Valerio took one last step forward, the lapels of his jacket briefly brushing against my breasts. His left hand snatched up my right hand from where it dangled limp at my side and he placed his right hand on my waist as he forced me into a quick waltz around the lobby. If we hadn't been cloaked from the gaze of the people who lingered in the expansive entrance, I'm sure we would have earned more than a few strange stares. "I've been waiting to discuss a few things with you, sweet Mira."

Tilting my head down slightly so I could look him in the eye, Valerio took advantage of our closeness to press his lips to mine. My body reacted to the familiar contact before my brain had a chance to step in. We stopped moving and I leaned into his hard frame, relaxing at his touch as my eyes drifted shut. His right hand slid from my waist to my back, pulling me tightly against his frame. His familiar touch eased the tension from my shoulders and it drained from the muscles in my limbs. His scent teased my nose as if trying to call up some of the good memories I had packed away of him. For some strange reason, the nightwalker smelled of cinnamon.

But it was wrong. My thoughts finally surfaced above the sensations vibrating in my frame. Valerio was trouble. He was another manipulator and killer. And the kiss was no different than the one I had received from Rowe, leaving me feeling used and dirty. More of my nights with Valerio had been washed in blood than all my years with Sadira and Jabari. The only difference being that Valerio had made it fun, where his predecessors had turned it into a nightmare.

Breaking off the kiss, I pushed against his chest. The nightwalker didn't fight me, allowing me to take a few steps out of his embrace. Rubbing my eyes, I shook my head, marveling at how quickly I had been swept up in him. "Don't touch me," I said in a cold, hard voice.

"I've missed you, Mira," he murmured, drawing my gaze back to his face.

I snorted, stifling the bitter laugh that nearly escaped. "And last night you were calling me a traitor. I'm no fool, Valerio."

"Foolish, sometimes, but never a fool," he said. His smile widened to reveal a pair of perfect white fangs.

Waving my hand dismissively at him, I turned to pace away from him when the sound of my muffled footsteps caught my attention. I looked down at the thick white carpet that covered the floor. The hotel lobby was entirely filled with marble. My gaze jerked up to find that I was no longer standing in the lobby of the Cipriani, but in a salon with antique furniture.

"Damn it, Valerio!" I growled, stalking over to one of the curtained windows on the far wall. "Where the hell am I?" The decor was unlike anything I had seen in the Cipriani. In fact, it didn't remind me of anything I'd seen in Venice.

"Somewhere private," he replied.

Ignoring him, I grabbed the curtains in my fists and jerked them open to reveal concrete where the canals had once been. I glanced up and down the street but didn't immediately recognize any of the buildings. A knot of panic tightened in my stomach and I forced myself to release my hold on the curtains before I sent them up in flames. "Where the hell am I?" I snarled, turning back to face the nightwalker.

He still stood in the center of the room, his hands in his pockets again. My flare of temper had no effect on his mien of perfect calm.

"In my private apartment in Vienna," he said with a slight shrug.

"Vienna, Austria?" I shouted. "Send me back now." I was furious with him and myself. He had kissed me so I wouldn't notice the push through space, and I let it happen, hoping for a moment to erase the memory of Rowe's kiss. I wanted to ask when he had gained the ability to disappear and reappear across vast distances like Jabari. It was a skill I had never seen him display before, and it made me more than a little nervous. Only the Ancients had such a skill, and Valerio never admitted to being more than one thousand years old.

"We need to talk Mira and we cannot do that in Venice," he calmly said.

"I will not let the court hurt Tristan again or threaten Danaus. Send me back now," I said through clenched teeth, closing in on him. "First Nicolai, and now you. I always thought the role of distraction was beneath you."

"I am not acting on behalf of the Coven or its pets," he continued, unmoved by my rage. "I left the island last night shortly before you did and have not returned to San Clemente. I do not know what the Coven plans for you today, but I promise that my bringing you here is not an attempt to threaten those that belong to you."

"Then send me back," I stubbornly repeated. My anger was ebbing, but frustration was still evident in my voice. I was afraid Jabari or anyone else on the Coven would sense that I was no longer in Venice. They would jump at the opportunity to attack Danaus and Tristan. I had to protect them, but I couldn't do that when I was several countries away.

"I cannot. We must talk and I do not feel safe doing so in Venice," he finally admitted. I paused, noticing for the first time a tension around the corners of his eyes and an unusual brittleness in his smile. "Reach out and touch Tristan's mind. See that he is safe. Touch the hunter's mind."

I frowned but said nothing. Touching Danaus's mind was tricky and I doubted if I could do it from that distance. However, I did reach out and touch Tristan's thoughts. He was just awakening from his daylight slumber. His thoughts were sluggish and confused, but he was calm.

When I met Valerio's gaze again, my frown eased a bit. The nightwalker's shoulders slumped slightly as some of the tension flowed from his body. "So now you believe me?" he gently asked, a soft smile haunting his lips again.

"For the moment," I snorted, walking away from him. The door between my mind and Tristan's was left open a crack. I wasn't in his mind reading his thoughts because I wanted to give him some privacy, but the constant connection would allow me to know the second anything was wrong.

I returned to the far wall and pulled open the curtains on the three windows there, giving me the opportunity to look out on the grand old city. It had been a long time since I last visited Vienna, and my reason for leaving then had been grim. Yet, the long, endless years had dulled the pain and muted the memories. I was more disturbed now by the fact that the pain I thought I should be feeling was little more than a hollow ache.

"I haven't lied to you, Mira," Valerio continued. There was a whisper of cloth rubbing as he walked over to me. "I have missed you."

"You were never one to lie, Valerio. You just preferred to omit crucial information," I said, not bothering to turn to look at him, but continued to stare out the window. My hands rested on the smooth wooden windowsill, letting the tips of my fingers absently trace the fine lines created when the white paint dried.

Laying his hands on my shoulders, his strong fingers kneaded my tense muscles, rubbing away the several days' worth of tension. Slowly, he let his hands slide down my arms, pulling away the lace wrap to bare my shoulders. "We were so good together," he whispered, gently pressing a kiss to my right shoulder. "Remember our fun in Morocco? I don't think we stirred from that apartment for nearly two weeks."

"Or the bars after the bullfights in Pamplona," I volunteered with a little laugh. "It was a shame about the matador. I don't think he ever properly recovered."

"What's that American saying? He could have been a contender," he chuckled, pressing another kiss to my bare skin, only this time a slight whisper of teeth grazed my flesh. Only after his chuckles died did he speak again. His voice was heartwrenchingly soft, like an ex-lover's touch on my cheek. "Since traveling to the New World, you have not returned to visit."

"You could have come to the United States," I countered, twisting around slightly so I could look him in the eye. "You obviously have the ability to make it a quick trip."

"You never invited me."

My brows furrowed and my eyes narrowed at his strange comment. "My domain is a single city within the country. That's all. You don't need me to invite you into the country should you wish to visit."

"Most would question such a statement from you. It is well known that nightwalkers within that country defer to your judgment in most matters, particularly if they wish to continue their existence. Don't lie to me or yourself. You know your reach extends far beyond the boundaries of your quaint city."

Turning completely around to face Valerio, I stepped away from his touch. The fresh smile on my lips wilted and died in a breath. "I know the question without reading your mind: Do I plan to take the empty seat on the Coven? I'll tell you what I've told everyone else. No. I don't want the seat. I don't want anything to do with the Coven."

Valerio threw his head back and laughed. The noise seemed to echo and skip as he sped to the opposite end of the room and plopped down in a comfortable chair.

"Mira, my little firefly, maybe you should wonder why so many are asking you that question," he suggested with a chuckle. "You've set up your own little kingdom in the New World."

"My domain is only the city of Savannah," I interrupted.

"But you've hunted and destroyed nightwalkers who were a threat to the secret from one coast to the other in that darling country," Valerio countered. He folded his hands over his stomach as he rested his left ankle on his right knee.

"At the request of the Coven."

"A group you've never hidden your lack of respect for. And now you're back in Venice after being absent for more than fifty years—"

"Again, at the request of the Coven," I interjected, but my voice was losing strength and my fingers were shaking. I was beginning to see all my actions in a new, horrible light.

"Maybe so, but you walk in with your head held high and a nightwalker killer in tow, making no secret that he is under your protection." I had no argument to make against his words, so he continued, laughter filling his voice. "Then, as if to top it all off, the pièce de résistance, you steal one of your own maker's children from her and stage a bloodbath in the Great Hall I've not seen the likes of in more than a few centuries. Hell, probably not since you appeared before the court the last time."

"Valerio," I whispered, his words crushing my throat. "I don't want a seat on the Coven. I'm just trying to survive."

"Survive?" he gasped, sending him into new peaks of incredulous laughter. "Surviving would be keeping your head down and your mouth shut. Surviving would be allowing the court to have its fun with Tristan and the hunter. Surviving is not pissing off both your maker and members of the Coven."

He pushed out of his chair and was at my side in a flash. His large hands cupped my cheeks and his thumbs wiped away tears I hadn't realized were falling. "I have always marveled at the cautious way you've lived your life," he softly began again, his sweet voice a gentle caress on my frayed nerves and fractured thoughts. "But recently you've acted in such an impulsive fashion. I can't begin to fathom why you've acted with such a suicidal fervor unless you truly wish to die."

Lifting my haunted eyes to meet his confused gaze, I wet my lips and forced the two words past the lump in my throat. "The naturi."

I could feel the jerk in his muscles as he flinched at my whispered words, but his hands didn't fall from my cheeks as his gaze narrowed into cold blue slits of ice.

"The naturi are coming," I continued.

"What are you talking about, dearest?" he demanded. His deep voice was firm, but not as steady as I would have preferred, as his hands dropped from my face.

Closing my eyes, I drew in a deep breath, catching the hint of cinnamon mixed with the scent of roses in a crystal vase on the other side of the room. When I looked at Valerio again, I launched into my tale, starting with Nerian in my own domain and stretching through the attacks in Egypt and London. I told him of the massacre at Themis and the discovery that not only would Danaus be a part of the triad that would push back the naturi, but that I was also the weapon they would wield. I even told him of the female naturi that appeared to walk freely in the Great Hall. I talked until my throat was raw and choked with tears I was no longer willing to shed. I spoke of fear and blinding pain and night after night of death until I was sure that the grim reaper himself now hounded my every step.

I talked until there were no more words and I was on my knees, shaking and exhausted by just the memory of everything that had happened and the horror still to come. Looking up, I found Valerio standing on the opposite side of the room, one hand resting on the wall as if to steady himself. His beautiful face was blank except for the look of horror he could not push from his eyes. The distance between us made me feel as if my very presence carried with it a pestilence that would destroy all of our kind, and maybe it did. Those around me didn't seem to live long lives.

It suddenly dawned on me that he probably didn't believe me. If I hadn't lived through it, I would have claimed it all was madness. The naturi hadn't been seen in centuries, seeming content to fade into oblivion.

"Doors," he suddenly said, the word coming out ragged and breathless. Valerio turned his eyes to finally meet mine and he slowly pushed away from the wall. He took a couple steps closer to me but maintained a large distance. "In the lower levels beneath the hall, great iron doors were placed before the rooms where we sleep during the daylight hours. Another iron door was placed before one of the rooms, and guards stand at it during at all hours of the day and night. No one dared to ask the Coven why the doors were added, but everyone knows that iron affects only one creature. I spent one day at the Great Hall. At sunrise I no longer find rest within the shelter offered by the Coven. If the Coven does not feel safe on San Clemente, then none of us will be."

"The naturi are coming. The next new moon is in three nights, as well as an old pagan holiday. I think the naturi will try again to break the seal then," I explained. Placing my left hand flat on the floor, I tried to find the will to push back to my feet but couldn't. "I cannot begin to guess at what the Coven plans. You're older than most. I assumed that you might know more."

"I know nothing," he admitted with a shake of his head. "Most of the court is a witless bunch, prone to gossip. If any of them knew what was going on, I believe I would have heard by now."

"Macaire will try soon to meet with me privately," I murmured, dragging my gaze back up to his face. A new frown pulled at his full lips, drawing deep lines of worry in his cheeks. It somehow added to the distinguished age of his features.

"More games," he muttered, absently pacing the room. I had a feeling he was talking to himself more than to me.

"Jabari and I have had . . . a falling out," I said, fumbling for some phrasing to encompass my hatred for a creature I had once loved and respected. Everything fell short of what I needed, but it wasn't important.

"More games," Valerio repeated, sounding more confident.

"I will not be a pawn for the Coven," I firmly stated.

Valerio stopped pacing and looked down at me. A small sad smile slipped across his mouth and glittered in his eyes. "Firefly, that is all you have ever been."

"Even for you?"

His smile grew larger and more sheepish at my question. Extending his hand to me, I ignored it until he finally spoke. "I have never used you as such, but that doesn't mean I wouldn't or won't if the opportunity presented itself."

I hated his answer, but it was the truth, which was more than I was getting from anyone else. Struggling to keep from gritting my teeth, I placed my left hand in his so he could help me to my feet. Yet he paused unexpectedly, staring down at my hand. It was only when I felt his thumb run over my ring finger that I realized he was looking at the ring he had given me a few centuries ago. It was a silver band with ocean waves inscribed in it in an old Grecian style.

"You still have it," he whispered, not trying to keep the surprise from his voice.

"I like the memories," I admitted as he finally pulled me to my feet.

"And the creature those memories are tied to?"

"He's tolerable some nights," I teased, brushing a kiss across his cheek near his ear.

"I believe you found me more than tolerable some nights," he reminded me, his voice dipping down to a husky tone. He still held my hand in his, increasing the pressure slightly. I was being drawn back into him, his allure, his promise of happiness away from all the chaos that seemed to currently rule my life.

"Valerio . . ." I started, but paused when my voice threatened to fracture. When I could finally speak again, the words would drift no higher than a whisper. "What games are you playing?"

The nightwalker looked up at me, a smile back on his lips, but it somehow failed to reach his eyes. "I'm just trying to survive."

He tilted his head back and pressed a kiss to my jaw just below my ear. "We do not have to go back," he whispered, his lips skimming across my cool flesh. "Stay with me. Away from the naturi."

"And keep running from the Coven?" I asked, letting my eyes fall shut. For a moment the idea was truly tempting; more tempting than the fantasy Sadira had dangled before me last night because this one was real. To go back to my nights of hunting and pleasure with Valerio at my side. No more naturi. No more Coven Elders. No more worrying about whether a nightwalker could protect himself without me. No more horrid weight of responsibility dragging me down.

"In time, they will forget about you."

With a sigh, I took a step away from him and blinked back some unexpected tears. "No, they won't. And the naturi won't go away because I go into hiding with you."

"I blame Jabari for this silly noble streak in you. It certainly didn't come from me," Valerio teased before brushing his lips across mine. "But the offer still stands."

"I can't spend the rest of my existence running from Jabari."

"Facing him will only shorten your existence."

"I—"

Mira!

The sudden, unexpected shout from Tristan in my head nearly put me back on my knees. I was beginning to wonder if I would ever get adjusted to so many creatures stomping around in my brain.

No shouting, please. I briefly wondered if the sarcasm would translate this way. I never spent a great deal of time speaking with other nightwalkers that way. I never felt confident that they could see or hear only what I wanted them to, and I liked my privacy.

The naturi. They're here!

I didn't question him. At any other time I would have laughed and called him crazy, but not now. A naturi was already lounging in the catacombs of the Great Hall and Rowe was sulking on San Michele. Why couldn't more be strolling down the fractured sidewalks of Venice?

"We have to go back," I said, turning my attention to Valerio again.

"What's wrong?"

"The naturi are in Venice." Those words actually caused the vampire to backpedal a couple steps away from me, and I honestly couldn't blame him. A nightwalker did not go marching into any area where the naturi were known to be. It's why you never heard tales of vampires wandering the woods alone on a moonless night.

"No," I snapped, instantly closing the distance between us. I wrapped my fists in the lapels of his jacket, holding him close to me. "You and I are going back to Venice now or I will give you a nasty sunburn. You have to see them. You need to understand."

"Mira—"

"Now, Valerio!"

I didn't have a chance to make another argument when I felt the push of magic as it ran its hands through my body. There was only time to blink when I found us standing in my suite at the Hotel Cipriani. I opened my mouth to thank him when Valerio wrapped his arms around me, pressing my body tightly against his as he leaned forward. A second later there was the telltale thunk of a knife hitting wood.

Valerio stood, pulling me back into an upright position. We both looked around to find a silver knife with a black handle embedded in the door frame of one of the bedrooms. Our eyes then traveled over to Danaus, who stood frowning at us.

"Does he always try to kill you when you enter a room?" Valerio teased, slowly releasing his hold on me.

"We have a special relationship." I stepped away from the nightwalker. I didn't have to say anything to Danaus. The hunter had been startled by our sudden appearance and reacted. It was that kind of speed that had kept him alive for so long. I was even particularly pleased with the fact that Valerio obviously had the ability to come and go where he wanted. I'd always thought there were more rules and limitations to that type of travel. Unfortunately, asking Valerio directly was a waste of time. That wasn't the kind of information he would volunteer.

"Mira." Tristan's fragile voice pulled me back to why I had raced to the Venice in the first place. The young nightwalker was standing before the bay of windows dressed only in a pair of jeans that were too big for him. His heels were resting on the bottom of the pant legs and the waist hung low on his hips. I briefly wondered if they belonged to Danaus, considering he and I were the only ones to bring a change of clothes, but decided not to ask. My eyes briefly skimmed over Tristan's back to find only a few faint red marks.

Frowning, I joined him at the window, with Valerio standing behind me. I didn't need to follow where Tristan was pointing. The three black shapes were easy to make out despite the dark sky as they headed toward the island of San Clemente. The creatures flew like bats, with quick movements of their wings instead of gliding on the air. However, they were too big to be anything that humans were accustomed to seeing. These nightmarish figures were naturi.

"What are they?" I asked, unable to tear my eyes away from them as they drew closer to the distant island. The three figures circled once then finally descended into a pocket of trees. They were headed for the Great Hall. I placed my hand on Tristan's shoulder, meaning for the gesture to be reassuring, but removed it when I felt him flinch at the contact. His fear rippled through me, sapping my own reserve of strength, which had kept me going during the past few nights. We were all running low and this dance was far from over.

"Not sure," Danaus admitted, drawing my gaze to his face. He was standing a couple feet away from me, his features tight and drawn. After a couple of seconds he looked down at me. "But this isn't good."

"I agree. We need to get out of Venice soon. If they're going to make another attempt at breaking the seal, they'll try to do it during the harvest holiday and the new moon. That's only a few nights away, and we have no idea where the sacrifice is going to be. Delays aren't good."

A part of me wanted to know where the next sacrifice was now so we could grab my private jet and head off to that distant locale. We could stop whatever naturi were in that hot spot, but that wouldn't keep more from arriving from other parts of the world. It would be a nonstop battle for the next three nights. If one or both of us were killed before the new moon rose, there would be no way to stop the naturi from making the sacrifice.

"But . . ." A slow smile dawned on my face as I looked up at the hunter. "We could stop by the Coven and see what's happening." Jabari had brought us there for a reason, and I refused to believe it was because he wanted the naturi to destroy us. He wouldn't give up the opportunity to kill me himself if he was so desperate to have me dead. Danaus and I needed to be on the island to disrupt whatever plans the Coven and the naturi were cooking up.

A rare smile trembled on Danaus's full lips and jumped in his deep blue eyes, laughing at me. "Risky, don't you think?"

"Oh, it's definitely risky, but not as much as you would think. Besides, it could also be fun." I laughed.

"More risky than going after nearly a dozen naturi in the forest?" Danaus asked, raising one thick eyebrow at me.

"No," I said, my smile dwindling at the memory. Looking back on the hastily launched assault in the woods not far from Stonehenge, I realized that the plan had been stupid and highly flawed. I'd reacted out of fear and anger. I knew better than to launch an attack on the naturi in the woods with an inexperienced nightwalker at my side. The fact that all three of us hadn't been destroyed was a miracle in itself.

I shook my head, pushing away the memory and the need to berate myself for my impulsive stupidity. It would do no good now, and I assured myself that this time would be different. "The Coven still needs us both alive. That's our ace in the hole. You in?"

"Definitely. Weapons?" he asked, his right hand sliding down to the knife that was still strapped to his waist.

"Load up." My gaze slid over to find Tristan watching me with a blank expression. He was waiting to see if I would command him to accompany Danaus and me. And he would if I demanded it, regardless of the fear still trembling within him. "You're not coming along. Not old enough," I teased.

"Mira, I can—"

"No," I interrupted before he could continue, my hand tightening on his shoulder. "Danaus and I are the only ones going in. Makes it easier to get out again."

"Do you actually think they won't kill you for this?" Valerio demanded. I had forgotten that the nightwalker was still in the room. Looking over my shoulder at him, I was surprised to see his handsome features looking haggard. His full lips were pressed into a hard, thin line and shallow furrows now stretched from the corners of his eyes and crisscrossed his brow.

The naturi had become a garish ghost story we told all the new, little nightwalkers to give them chills, but now we were all waking up to discover that this nearly dead species was suddenly fighting back. Our nightmares were threatening to become real and expose us to the sun. Again.

"That's another question I'm hoping to answer," I admitted with a smirk. "Exactly how irreplaceable am I? Would they be willing to risk the door opening by killing me or Danaus? Would they damn all nightwalkers just to protect their schemes? Or is that their plan in the first place?"

"You're not that important, Mira," Valerio chided, his frown deepening.

That was probably true but I wasn't planning on being killed that easily. I still had an ace or two up my sleeve in the form of Danaus. Of course, this plan could just as easily slit my own throat as save it if I was reading Jabari's intentions wrong.

"I need your help," I started, turning to Valerio. I quickly grabbed the sleeve of his blazer, even though I couldn't hold him here if I wanted to.

"I'm not going with you to the Coven. They need me alive even less than they need you."

"True, but I need you alive," I countered. I took his left hand in both of mine. "Go east. Find others who are older than me. Tell them everything I told you. If the Coven succeeds with whatever it's planning with the naturi, our people have to be prepared."

"You want me to raise your army," Valerio said, trying to pull his hand free.

"No, if the Coven and the naturi succeed, it will be your army. Someone needs to protect the nightwalkers from the Coven."

"Mira, I'm not a leader."

"Bullshit. You just never wanted the responsibility. Fine. Then find someone else to give the job. Don't let the information stop with you."

Frowning, Valerio squeezed my hand. "You may not want a seat, but you're the only one that deserves to be on the Coven."

"For our sakes, I hope you're wrong."

SIXTEEN

Once I was back in a pair of leather pants and one of the few cotton tops that had survived my travels, Danaus and I quickly snatched up a speedboat and rushed out to the island. The hunter drove the boat, his large hands tightly gripping the steering wheel. His black hair danced in the wind, revealing his clenched jaw and narrowed eyes. Tension hummed through his muscular body and energy snapped silently around him. I wanted to remain in the far corner of the boat away from him, but it wasn't an option. We had to talk, come to some kind of understanding before we waltzed into the Great Hall.

Lounging in the other chair beside him, my eyes locked on the island as we approached. "Do you have any guesses as to what flew to the island?" I asked.

"Big bats," he muttered.

"Great. Are they the only ones?"

There was a pause as his powers jumped from his body and spread out toward the far reaches of the area. They washed through me like a warm wave. It was a feeling I wasn't sure I would ever become accustomed to, and always left me wishing I could wrap myself up for a minute longer before facing the cold reality of what loomed ahead of us.

"I won't be able to sense what is on the island until I reach it, but they're not the only naturi," he announced. His voice had a distant, dreamy quality, as if his attention was focused on a faraway point. I resisted the urge to take the steering wheel from him and remained seated. "There are another six naturi on the mainland, not far from Venice. It's hard to pinpoint. Maybe somewhere around Padua or Verona. And there's one alone in Venice. But I don't know the area, I can't tell you which island."

A chill slipped down my arms. "Rowe," I whispered, talking to myself, but I knew that Danaus heard the name the moment it left my lips. I occasionally forgot about his stronger than normal hearing.

"You think he's here?" Danaus demanded. The hunter turned his head briefly to look at me before returning his gaze back to the open waters before us.

"I know it," I admitted. "I ran into him last night after I got Tristan settled in the hotel. He knows there's a naturi on San Clemente, but he doesn't know who it is or why she's there."

"Doesn't he think she's a captive?"

"I may have disabused him of that idea," I said with a little smirk as I recalled his stunned expression last night. "At the very least, we know that he's not in on whatever the Coven is planning."

Danaus slowed up as we drew closer to the island. "How does that help us?"

"It creates turmoil within his own kind. Possibly a distraction, a weakness we can later exploit." I said, pushing some hair back from my face. "I think the other six on the mainland are to serve as backup in case something goes wrong. Together with the three we saw from the hotel window, these nine were either sent by Rowe to reclaim the missing naturi or are outside of Rowe's plans and aligned with the naturi already on San Clemente."

"Should I ask if you even have a plan?"

"Get out alive," I replied dryly, folding my hands over my stomach. The statement earned me a fresh frown as Danaus concentrated on pulling the speedboat into the dock. It wasn't the most difficult of tasks, considering there was only one other boat tied to the little stone structure. Apparently, the house had been emptied of the court before the Coven's guests arrived. The hunter had also chosen the dock the farthest from the Great Hall. With the court gone, we could quickly travel to the hall and still give me enough time to lay down a couple of ground rules. I wasn't sure Danaus was going to go for it, but I had to try.

Of course, I'd promised to keep him alive while in Venice, so I had to protect him no matter what happened with the Coven. Yet, nowhere in that agreement did I state in what condition he had to be in. If he became too much of a risk, I'd drain his stubborn ass in a heartbeat and keep him unconscious until we were out of Venice.

"We need information," I said. "We need to know what the Coven is planning, why the naturi are appearing in Venice, and what in the world they have agreed to. To get any of this information, it means no killing."

Danaus shut off the engine and stared at me as if I'd been babbling in ancient Celtic. "Your so-called leaders are making deals with the enemy and you don't want to kill them? After you were so eager to finish them just last night?" he demanded, shoving the keys into his pocket. His hands absently swept over the pair of knives attached to his belt at various locations and the sword strapped across his back. As a seeming last resort, a handgun was in a holster at the small of his back.

"You misunderstand me," I chuckled, rising bonelessly to my feet. Unfortunately, the motion wasn't as graceful as I had hoped— my sudden shift in weight made the boat rock, and I hadn't accounted for it. I wasn't meant to be on a boat for extended periods of time. Steadying myself with a hand on the back of the chair I had been sitting in, I continued, "I want each of them writhing in unbearable agony, their flesh slowly stripped from their dusty old bones, their eyeballs melting and oozing from their sockets as they beg for death. I want the Coven and the naturi dead in the worst way, but now is not the time. If the Coven is destroyed, their secrets die with them, and that does not help our plans."

"That didn't stop you from trying last night," Danaus tartly reminded me again as he stepped from the boat and onto the dock.

"That was a mistake," I conceded, jumping onto the dock beside him. "I wasn't thinking clearly and let my anger get the better of me. This time is different. I will need your help, but I need you to promise not to try to wipe out the Coven and the naturi without my agreement."

"Mira—"

"No, I'm serious," I quickly said when he sounded as if he would argue. "Do you think killing the Coven tonight will actually stop the naturi from entering our world? Will killing these winged monsters stop the sacrifices? If we're killed tonight, do you honestly think Ryan will be able to stop the naturi in three nights?"

"Then what's to keep them from killing us the second we walk into the Great Hall?" he asked.

"Fear." The hunter snorted and started to walk up the dock toward the path that wound its way through the tiny forest to the Coven. I jogged up to him and stood in his path, stopping him again. "They're scared, or at the very least wary of me, and they're terrified of you."

Danaus scoffed again and tried to step around me, but I quickly moved to block him, putting a hand on his broad chest. Beneath my fingertips I could feel his heartbeat pounding a mile a minute. It was a bit surprising to find him so anxious when none of it leaked out into his voice or expression. "You've killed countless nightwalkers, and I'm sure more than one of them was an Ancient. Jabari has also seen firsthand what we can accomplish together. By now the naturi would have heard what happened in England. Both sides may be willing to give us a little space."

"You're not afraid of me," Danaus said, catching me off-guard with the comment.

I stared into his intense crystalline eyes, forcing a smile onto my lips. "That's because I know you're a big pussycat at heart. Wouldn't hurt a fly," I teased, then turned and walked down the path before he could answer. Good thing I wore my boots, because it was getting deep. Afraid of Danaus? I was terrified. I tried not to surround myself with creatures that could destroy me with a thought. Or worse, destroy my whole kind with a thought while using me as a weapon.

The walk to the Great Hall was uneventful, but we were prepared the whole time with weapons in hand. I gripped the little dagger I had worn so tightly that my knuckles ached when the huge double doors finally came into view. Holding up my hand, I motioned for Danaus to follow me over to the tree line. The two human guards who stood at the front doors were missing, and I could sense only a handful of nightwalkers on the whole island. While we were by no means hidden, I felt a little better knowing we weren't standing out in the open.

"Who is on the island?" I asked, peering around a large oak to look up at the oppressive stone building.

"Five vampires," he began before I even felt him reach out with his powers. "A scattering of humans and four members of the naturi. Wait! The lycan is here too."

"Nicolai?" I demanded, my eyes swinging around to look at the hunter as I searched the grounds again with my powers. I had checked only moments before asking him, and picked up on the vampires and humans, but Nicolai was there now. A little faint, but definitely present. Damn Jabari! What was the point of having this ability if you couldn't get an accurate count when you really needed one?

"Why would he still be here?" Danaus asked, staring at the building.

"Oooh," I said as the pieces started to slowly fit together in my brain. "You think he might be the next sacrifice?" I suggested, pulling Danaus's eyes back to my face. One brow arched in question as he turned over the idea. "The new moon certainly isn't going to be working in their favor when they need to perform this sacrifice under a full moon. But I bet you would probably get a nice burst of energy from killing a lycan. Enough to bust through a magic seal that's holding shut a door between two worlds."

"Possible."

"And wouldn't it be a crying shame if they lost their sacrifice to me?"

A wide grin grew on my face as he turned over the idea. "You plan to steal another pet?" he asked, reminding me of how I neatly purloined Tristan while Sadira watched. If I stole Nicolai, it could turn into a full-time job keeping the werewolf alive, but that was more of a long-term worry. Right now my main concern was just getting off the island alive. Nicolai was the key to whatever bargain the Coven had set up. It explained why Jabari had sent him after me in the first place. I had the opportunity to disrupt the plan.

"Let's go get my prize," I announced, stepping out from behind the tree and starting up the path.

"They know we're here," Danaus stated, but I had a feeling that it was meant to sound more like a question.

"Without a doubt."

"We're never going to get through the door."

"Getting in won't be the problem." I forced myself to put my foot on the first step leading up to the double doors. Getting out alive was going to be the real trick.

SEVENTEEN

There was no one waiting to rip our heads off when we shoved open the double doors to the Great Hall. I tried to take that as a good sign. Leaving the heavy wood and iron doors open, we turned our attention to the other set of doors that barred the way into the throne room. The candles in the iron candelabras sputtered and danced in the light breeze, with a few snapping out with a wisp of gray smoke. Absently waving my hand in their general direction, I caused the teardrop flames to steady and grow brighter as I scanned the deep, shadowy corners for potential attackers. We might have sensed only five vampires and a scattering of humans, but I wasn't taking any chances.

We were about to proceed to the main audience chamber when one of the doors opened and Elizabeth slipped through the slim crack. She quickly shut the door behind her again before either of us could sneak a peek into the room. Her pale yellow dress with a high empire waist made her look like a spring tulip. She reminded me vaguely of Napoleon's Josephine, composed and regal, with her long dark hair artfully piled on her head and diamonds sparkling around her neck.

I halted, resisting the urge to reach for the dagger I had put back in its sheath at my waist. This was the first time I'd seen Elizabeth since I slaughtered Gwen and left her heart on the Elder's chair. Acts like that didn't particularly endear you to the Ancients, and I hadn't exactly counted on a direct confrontation with the nightwalker.

"You have no business here," she crisply said in English with a faint accent I couldn't quite place. French possibly, but older. She was a tiny figure, touching five feet only when her hair was piled high on her head in a series of twists and curls. Her hands were closed at her sides but not yet clenched into fists. It was on the tip of my tongue to make some comment that she had been sent like a messenger to stop me from entering the room, but I had enough trouble planned. Why go looking for a small, petty fight like that when I could thumb my nose at the whole Coven at once?

I gave her a slight bow of my head. Not quite the usual subservience I'm sure she'd grown accustomed to, but at least I didn't try to ignore her. "I have business with Jabari," I announced.

"And I still have business with you," she said, lifting her chin so she could look me in the eye. "You destroyed my property."

"Your property was warned to stay away from my property," I bit out, taking a step closer so I loomed over her. "Your property was warned of the consequences. If you didn't want your property damaged, you should have reined it in." With my heels, I had close to ten inches on this woman, and regardless of the power I knew she wielded, my physical presence and maybe even my reputation were enough to make her take one step backward. Around us, I let the candlelight flicker a bit, with some of the candles going out, breathing new life into the shadows. I hated talking about Gwen like a piece of chattel. I may have despised the creature, but she had been a "living," sentient creature.

"You owe me, Fire Starter," Elizabeth continued. Each word escaped her lips sharp and tight, as if she ground them between her teeth before releasing them.

"Then I suggest you start a tab, because it's going to get worse before I leave here tonight," I replied, enjoying the smirk that lifted the left corner of my mouth.

As I tried to step around her, I saw her swing her left hand toward my back from the corner of my eye. Spinning on my right heel, I slipped the dagger from its sheath on my hip and sliced at her throat. I hadn't expected her to directly attack me. It wasn't the typical style of the Elders. They had flunkies around to do their dirty work. Of course, I knew absolutely nothing about Elizabeth, which made her as dangerous as Macaire and Jabari.

However, Danaus had already stepped in, grabbing the nightwalker's wrist and holding it immobile above her head before I could even touch my blade to the Ancient's smooth skin.

"Should I kill her now?" he asked simply, his face blank. I looked down at Elizabeth, whose wide eyes were darting between me and Danaus. If she flinched, Danaus would snap her wrist without a thought. And if I said the word, he'd boil what blood filled her veins until it blackened her skin and turned her organs into a pool of stinking goo.

I slipped the knife back into its sheath. "Later," I said with a faint frown. If she thought we'd spared her life now, we might be able to buy her assistance later. Besides, I wasn't convinced that Danaus could destroy her that easily.

He nodded once and released her, giving the nightwalker a slight shove to precede us toward the doors that led to the Great Hall. The Elder said nothing, but stiffly walked toward the doors, which were pulled invisibly open when she approached. It was one of the abilities I envied the most. Nightwalkers didn't generally attain the ability of telekinesis until close to the thousand-year mark. I hoped to get it a little earlier. At the moment the best I could do was rattle a teacup and saucer—not exactly useful or intimidating.

The enormous three-story room was ablaze with candlelight, as if someone was afraid of the monsters that lurked in the dark corners. Along the east and west walls, close to twenty floor candelabras flickered, with more than a dozen large yellow candles in each. The chandeliers overhead also glowed with life, illuminating the various flags and banners that hung from the ceiling. Even the black marble floor reflected the light.

Only the dais, with the seats for the Coven and Our Liege, remained blanketed with shadows. Elizabeth returned to her seat on the dais next to Macaire. Jabari sat in the third Coven seat, and the fourth was still vacant, along with the seat of Our Liege. The three nightwalkers appeared to be alone, but Danaus sensed the presence of the naturi so they had to be lurking around somewhere. Had they left the hall when we appeared?

"I do not recall summoning your presence," Macaire declared when Danaus and I reached the center of the room. We stopped walking, preferring to maintain a little distance between us and the Coven, not that it would keep us any safer. I was just hoping to buy an extra second or two to react.

"I came to claim something that belongs to me," I replied, shoving my fingers into the back pockets of my pants, affecting a casual stance. I didn't know if it worked, because I was sure everyone in the room could smell my fear.

"A vampire is here we didn't agree on," said a hypnotic voice from somewhere near the ceiling. The melodious sound was like a dream in the way it bounced off the walls before finally drifting down to me. "A stranger who carries no value here. Should we return with the threat of dawn when we will find no unwelcome ears?"

"The werewolf we came for is near," countered a second voice, not far from the location of the first. This one was significantly softer, but just as seductive as its companion. "You know leaving isn't something we'd enjoy until they speak the words we must hear, and then back home we can take the wolf boy."

"Oh, forgive me," I quickly replied, giving a large sweeping bow to the three members of the Coven before me. "I had no idea you had guests. I'll be happy to leave once Jabari hands over Nicolai."

"Why would I do such a thing?" Jabari slowly inquired, his dark eyes narrowing on me while his long fingers tightened on the arms of his throne. I half expected to hear the wood cracking and groaning under the force of his grip.

"Do you deny you sent him with the order to kill me?" I asked, my tone sweeter than sugar. My head cocked to the left and I flashed him a toothy smile. I knew when he'd figured out exactly what I was doing there because at least one of the wooden arms made a large cracking sound. Some small part of me prayed it was all an act for the rest of the Coven, or I was in serious trouble.

"He was sent for your heart," Jabari admitted. His growing anger was causing his accent to thicken, pushing him closer to his traditional Egyptian. Sliding forward, he sat perched on his seat as if preparing to leap at me.

It was a fight for me to keep from taking a step back. The hairs on the back of my neck stood on end. Confronting Jabari was like baiting a tiger—I'd be lucky if he didn't rip my face off if I was wrong.

"Then I have come to claim the spoils of the fight. I spared his life, so it now belongs to me," I said, forcing a smile. It was a very old tradition of my kind and not one frequently enforced simply because we typically killed whoever attacked us.

"You can't have him," Jabari snarled.

"What is the meaning of this?" Macaire demanded. A frown marred his distinguished features while his eyes darted between me and the Elder.

"He sent the lycanthrope to kill Mira," Danaus replied, stepping forward so he was directly beside me. In no way attempting to hide his antagonism for the whole group, his right hand rested casually on the handle of one of the knives at his waist.

"*Mira?*" cried one of the female voices above my head. There was a sudden scrape of movement along the ceiling as if claws were scratching the stones overhead. There was a whisper of voices, words I couldn't quite make out despite my keen hearing. I took a step backward and craned my head up in an attempt to see the creatures that lurked on the ceiling, but they remained hidden behind the scattering of flags and banners. Taking another step back, I intentionally bumped my shoulder into the hunter's.

What the hell is up there? I sent the question directly into his brain, struggling to keep from sounding as terrified as I felt.

No idea.

I quickly stepped away from him at the sound of wings and a blur of shadow. One of the creatures swooped down from the ceiling and landed lightly on the floor directly between me and the Coven. I had to clamp down on my tongue to keep the scream from escaping when my eyes clearly took in the monster for the first time.

At close to five feet tall, the creature looked almost like a woman, though only by a stretch of the imagination. And that's if you erased the batlike wings that stretched from the inside of her thin arms and down along her body. At the end of the wings were three long bony fingers, tipped with black claws. Her skin was flesh-colored and appeared paper-thin since it sagged on her spindly body. However, it was her crowlike feet with their long talons clicking ominously on the marble floor that finally triggered a memory in my mind. This creature was the source of the ancient harpy mythology.

After encountering the two female naturi from the wind clan in the woods in England, I had assumed they were all the fairy-tale type, with elfin features and butterfly wings. Sure, Rowe looked different, but then everything about Rowe was different, from his black hair to his scars to his black wings. I never expected to find a naturi so horrifying to look upon.

"This is the monster who tamed the flame and reduced us to dusty ash," the naturi said, taking a hesitant step closer to me. She wrapped her wings around herself so that her hands lightly gripped her bony shoulders, concealing her naked body. "Once again fulfilling her birth name. Yet, behind her lurks a bit of trash." The creature's narrowed yellow eyes turned to Danaus and closely inspected him, creeping yet another step closer.

"What is he? Please, tell me," demanded a third voice from the ceiling. This one sounded younger, almost childlike in its pitch and impatient urgency. "He smells of sweat and weak human flesh, but carries behind him no shade of death. Not human born."

"Nor vampire made," chimed in a second from overhead.

"Nor wolf by moonlight torn," finished the other naturi standing a few feet away.

"And he's not for sale, so don't get too attached," I snapped, their strange rhyming grating on my nerves. I took a step sideways, to stand between Danaus and the naturi. The creature glared at me and retreated a step, keeping a comfortable distance between us. I was surprised they couldn't identify the origin of the hunter's powers. The naturi and bori were archenemies seemingly since the birth of time. You'd think they'd have recognized the presence of a bori no matter how faint. Then again, it had been more centuries than anyone could count since the last bori wandered the earth. Maybe they forgot what one felt like.

Struggling to tear my eyes off the creature with the stringy gray hair, I looked up at the Coven and said, "Just send out Nicolai, and we'll be on our way."

"We cannot," Macaire said. "We have other plans for him."

"Time to change your plans." I smiled, slipping my dagger from my waist. I reached my free left hand behind me to the hunter, who took it. "Or Danaus and I turn anything that stinks of naturi into ash. Send out the wolf."

Chaos erupted. The first harpy launched herself into the air with amazing speed and grace, disappearing among the flags hanging above. Again their voices swelled as they discussed something in their own language that I couldn't quite make out. They either didn't care for being threatened or had just figured out that the wolf I demanded was their soon-to-be sacrifice.

As I lifted my eyes to try to locate the three naturi that clung to the ceiling like overgrown bats, my brain filled with pain. At first Jabari had been the only presence pushing against my thoughts, but Danaus quickly shoved his way inside. Energy from both creatures surged through my frame, battling for dominance. The hunter was winning the battle, but I had a feeling it was only because he actually had physical contact with me, gripping my hand, while Jabari still sat several feet away on the dais. My scream shattered the air as the pain buckled my knees beneath me. I was only vaguely aware of the sound of my knife hitting the marble floor at the same time my knees came in contact with the cool stone.

My bones felt as if they were being ground into dust as Jabari and Danaus fought for control. Danaus still held my hand, and I tried to pull it free in a blind effort to stop the pain. Of course, if he released me, there was a chance that Jabari would win control and the hunter would die. There were no voices in my head this time. Just raw, angry power. I screamed again, wishing there was a way I could push them both out of my head, but there was nothing to grab onto, nothing to push against. They were both everywhere at once, separate but nearly indistinguishable in the various shades of pain they caused.

When I was sure I could take no more, Danaus finally won the battle, ejecting Jabari from my thoughts. Unfortunately, there was too much energy flowing in my painfully tense frame. I couldn't let it go. A ring of fire nearly twelve feet in diameter instantly burst into existence. The flames crackled for a second in bright yellow and orange before settling into a silent pale blue. No one had put the need to create fire in my brain, it just happened.

But the ring of eight-foot flames wasn't all that ignited. Candlelight around the room flared, the little tongues of fire stretching and elongating until they seemed to take on a life of their own. Two of the flags burst into flames overhead, shoving aside more of the darkness that cowered in the room. One of the chairs that survived last night's fight also burst into flames, crackling and popping with a growl that seemed to mimic the same anger burning through my soul. The flames were soothing despite the fact that Danaus skulked around in my brain as if he owned it, seeming to wait for Jabari to attack again.

Instead the attack came from above. I heard the near-silent flap of leathery wings only seconds before I was jerked backward. Danaus's hand was pulled from my grip as he was lifted from his feet. Twisting from where I sat on the floor, I saw two of the harpies lift him into the air, their taloned feet digging into his broad shoulders. The closer he moved to the ceiling, the weaker his presence grew in my thoughts, allowing Jabari to muscle his way in again.

Desperate, I tried to throw up mental barriers, not caring who was being pushed out. With both hands planted on the floor in front of me, I gritted my teeth and pushed against anything I was sure wasn't my own thought, but even that distinction was growing fuzzy. A snarl rippled up from my throat as I barely suppressed the urge to hurl fireballs at the harpies, but I couldn't risk it. There was a good chance I would hit Danaus as well.

Mira . . . Jabari's voice in my head was light and taunting as I kneeled on the floor. It wasn't strong yet, but he had the power to wear me down.

Give me Nicolai and call off the harpies. My demand sounded ragged and breathless even to me as I shoved the thought back at Jabari, wishing I could make him choke on it.

Let them have their fun. I could easily envision the shrug of his narrow shoulders as he sent me that thought. There was laughter woven around every word that danced through my brain. *Besides, don't you think you've collected enough pets you cannot protect?*

It dawned on me then that his thoughts were devoid of the anger or frustration he had shown just moments ago when we were speaking. Damn him! He had manipulated me. He knew I would come for Nicolai, but what was his goal? Danaus's death? Mine? Or was he manipulating me into killing the naturi for him? I didn't understand his game.

This deal with the naturi can't be allowed, I told him.

Stealing Nicolai won't stop it, he admitted

Will it help? I waited for his answer. After everything that had happened, I felt as if I was extending a desperate hand to him, begging for his help after he had manipulated me into this position in the first place. I hated what he could do to me, and I hated him more because I needed him.

They will fear you more, he finally said.

Overhead, a woman's voice sliced through the silence in a heart-shattering scream. Another voice was raised in pain a second later, followed by the sound of ripping cloth. I looked up in time to see Danaus fall to the floor. He landed as lightly as a cat, his knife in hand, stained with black-looking blood. One of the flags fluttered to the ground behind him, torn from where he had grabbed it in an attempt to slow his fall.

If you fight with Danaus for control over me again, it will destroy what little is left of my mind and potentially my body. That cannot help your goal. I sent the thought lashing out at Jabari as Danaus approached. *Hand over Nicolai and we will leave.* I had only seconds to get Jabari to acquiesce. The ring of fire wouldn't stop Danaus from returning to my side. If the hunter touched me again, I knew I wouldn't survive it. My arms were trembling and my stomach felt as if it had been flipped inside out and dipped in acid.

We're close.

I wanted to asked what he meant by that, but there wasn't time. In truth, it didn't matter if I understood. I was just the weapon, not the warrior.

"Enough!" Jabari roared, surging to his feet. What seemed like a child crying in pain was the only sound in the room. Apparently, Danaus had done some serious damage to one of the harpies. There was a brief scraping and clacking of claws on stone and then the crying grew softer and fainter.

I hesitantly lowered the flames so they were only a couple feet high and surrounded me more tightly, in a circle with a diameter of only a few feet. Danaus stopped a couple feet away from me outside the flames, his knife still in hand, as we waited to hear what Jabari had to say.

"Kill her, Jabari," Macaire ordered. His arms shook from where he tightly held the arms of the chair, barely managing to keep his seat. A horrid green light glowed in his eyes, burrowing into me through the flickering flames.

A deep chuckle rumbled from Jabari and a cold smile slithered across his lean, hard features. I had seen that expression once before. The warm, compassionate veneer had been stripped away at the Themis Compound when he told me I was the weapon wielded by the triad to stop the naturi. At least this time his icy amusement was directed at Macaire and not at me.

"You've cried for her death since the second she was reborn."

Jabari's words slithered like a poisonous snake into my ears and through the cells of my brain, sending an uncontrollable shiver through my exhausted body. He had switched to our language; the first language spoken by nightwalkers, which was written in our very blood. There was no learning it. A vampire was reborn fluent and afraid. No one spoke it without a good reason. Jabari most likely had something to say he didn't want the naturi to understand.

"If you wish her dead, you must dirty your hands, because I'm not through with her," Jabari continued, gracefully sitting back down in his chair. "But remember last night's bloodbath. She's not without her own skills. And beside her stands an experienced hunter of our kind."

"It sounds as if you are afraid to attack her," Macaire taunted, also using the same language. It didn't roll from his tongue with the same elegance, and I wondered if it was because he was afraid of me and Jabari.

"No."

And that was all he had to say. Jabari could destroy me without raising a finger and we all knew it. There was no fear, no hesitance. He would kill me when he was done using me.

"But she means to take your pet from you," Macaire said. There was no missing the desperation that colored each word. He wouldn't be able to convince Jabari to do anything he didn't want to do. If Macaire wanted me dead, he was going to have to do something about it himself.

"He was lost to me regardless of the outcome," Jabari said with an indifferent shrug. He had sent Nicolai knowing I would either kill him or claim him. Damn Jabari. After living with me for roughly a century, he had come to know me far too well.

With a wave of his hand, one of the side doors slammed open, banging against the wall. Nicolai stepped into the room, his eyes quickly taking in all the players. The handsome werewolf was wary, but exhaustion was starting to take its toll on him. His copperish-brown eyes were underlined with dark shadows and there was a day's growth of whiskers on his jaw and chin. He stood near the dais, not far from Jabari, struggling to stare blankly straight ahead. However, he could either sense or hear the harpies overhead, his eyes occasionally darting toward the dark shadows near the ceiling.

There was only the soft drip of blood leaking from one of the harpies as it hit the marble floor. Nicolai's and Danaus's heartbeats thundered in my head as I suddenly became aware of my growing hunger. My fight with Jabari and the other nightwalkers during the past two nights had pushed me too far and I needed to feed again.

Reluctantly, I doused the last of the flames, but remained kneeling on the floor, conserving the last of my energy should I need it to escape this nightmare.

"If you can protect him, you may have him," Jabari conceded. There was no missing the condescension in his tone. I'd already failed to protect Tristan and he certainly didn't believe I would be able to protect Nicolai when the Elder chose to attack him.

Pushing to my feet, I was surprised when I didn't sway once I was standing again, despite the fact that my thoughts were coated in a thick layer of fog and pain and my body screamed at every movement. If there had been an ounce of blood left within my frame, it seemed I would have heaved it onto the floor. I wanted to curl into a little ball and pray for the dawn to wipe away my mind. Instead I squared my shoulders and nodded. We both knew that without rising from his chair, Jabari had beaten me because he had the ability to control me. I was getting Nicolai because it was what Jabari wanted, not because I had won.

He smiled widely at me, revealing a glimpse of white fangs, and motioned with a couple of fingers for Nicolai to walk over to me. The lycan's eyes darted from the Elder to me in confusion and shock before taking a couple slow, hesitant steps toward me. My muscles tensed, waiting for one of the Coven to lurch forward and attack the werewolf, but none of the three even flinched. However, understanding finally dawned on the naturi that clung to the ceiling. There was a quick flap of damp, fleshy wings as they watched Nicolai stand near me.

"What is this, nightwalker?" exclaimed one of the harpies in melodious outrage.

"The lycan was not part of the original agreement," Jabari said in a harsh voice that made me flinch.

"No!" The screech reverberated through the room as one of the harpies swooped down from the ceiling, her taloned feet extended to grab the werewolf up by the shoulders. Without hesitation, I launched a fireball at the attacking monster at the same time an invisible hand slammed into the creature, crushing it against the far wall. The harpy screamed and pushed off from the wall, returning to the relative safety of the shadows that huddled in the corners of the ceiling. I didn't have to look up at the dais to know that Jabari had protected Nicolai. He hadn't been sure I had the energy to do it after my scuffle with him.

Turning to look at a scratched and bloody Danaus, I bit out an order, "Get him out of here." The hunter was smart enough not to argue with me. He knew I was running on empty. I couldn't keep fighting off the harpies all night and still hold my own against the Coven. Danaus grabbed a stunned Nicolai by the shoulder and pulled him out the door, his eyes continuously moving from the dais to the ceiling, expecting another attack.

If anything, the fact that Danaus and I were walking out with Nicolai indicated that the Coven still needed us alive for whatever dark plan they had in mind. So far I had not stepped too far out of line. Furthermore, I had potentially completed a task that Jabari always meant for me to accomplish. *Bastard.* I would have preferred to find out what the Coven was planning with the naturi, but felt lucky to be walking out at all. There was still a little time left to discover the Elders' plans.

My gaze returned to the dais and the Elders, who were each plotting my demise in their own special way, I was sure. Macaire was expressionless as he stared at me, but there was no hiding his white knuckles or tensed frame. He was less than pleased with both me and Jabari. Only at this point he wasn't sure which of us would be easiest to kill. Besides, I was still willing to bet that he wanted to meet with me. Macaire was the type to mentally manipulate you; try to win you over with "logic" and lots of seductive promises. He wasn't willing to get his hands dirty the same way Jabari was.

Elizabeth had been silent through this whole affair, which made me more nervous than when I considered Macaire. I could guess Macaire's and Jabari's motive, but I didn't know whose side she was on or if she had her own goal. All in all, I had no doubt she would rather see me staked out in the sun than standing in the Great Hall again.

At last my gaze settled on Jabari, who was watching me with amusement dancing in his dark eyes. I bowed my head to him, no longer wishing to know his schemes that involved me and no little amount of pain. I was about to turn and stride out of the room when my eyes caught on the empty chair at Jabari's right hand. Tabor's chair. A seat on the Coven. But to be a member of the Coven would mean being Jabari's puppet. At one time I would have followed the Elder's wishes simply because I believed in him. Now I would do it because I had no choice.

My gaze stumbled back to Jabari, to find him grinning broadly at me, guessing my thoughts. He would welcome me onto the Coven with open arms, as it solidified his power over the other two members. I smiled back at him before turning on my left heel and stiffly leaving the Great Hall. My heart would be in the hunter's hand before I took a seat on the Coven.

EIGHTEEN

Pulling the heavy doors closed behind me, I paused at the top of the old granite stairs and tipped my head up toward the stars that winked at me as if enjoying some great cosmic joke. The air was warm and moist, and the wind had begun to stir, whispering dark promises of a summer squall that would leave San Marco Piazza under a foot of water. The flood was usually reserved for later in the season, but was not unheard of during late July.

It was only standing in the summer air that I realized I was cold. The chill that had bit at my limbs finally began to permeate the aches and throbbing pains that dominated my consciousness. I couldn't remember the last time I'd fed. Had it been while I was in London? It seemed all so long ago, but only a couple of nights had passed. Despite that, I needed to feed again, and soon.

With a frown, I started to descend the stairs when my knees decided to no longer obey my wishes. My legs were made of seaweed and completely useless. I reached out to catch myself, briefly wondering if my arms would even work, when I found myself in Danaus's strong arms. I didn't see him move. In fact I hadn't been aware of him being so close, but I didn't care. I had enough to worry about.

Danaus carefully wrapped my left arm around his shoulders then swept me wordlessly up in his arms. His stride was steady and unhurried as he headed back to the boat. My eyes drifted closed as his warmth wrapped around me, helping to erase some of the aches and pains that filled my body. Beside us I heard Nicolai walking to Danaus's right.

"My hero," I murmured in a low voice, resting my head against Danaus's shoulder. He snorted in disgust, earning a breathless chuckle from me. I had no doubt he would have loved to drop me on my ass right there and let me crawl to the boat, but it wouldn't get us off this wretched island any faster.

"Was it worth it?" he asked. I could feel his turmoil and worry beating against me as if they were my own emotions. Our connection was still strong from earlier and I didn't have the spare energy to try to put up any mental walls to keep him out, not that it would have done me much good. Danaus and Jabari could waltz in whenever they pleased.

"Yes," I sighed. My right hand slid down from his shoulder to his chest, and I could feel his heartbeat beneath my palm. "We know the Coven is not of one mind about its plans and that Our Liege knows nothing of the Elders' plans. We also know that Jabari will keep us alive until after we've destroyed whatever they're cooking up with the naturi. At least he wants to keep the door closed."

"Unless you're wrong about Jabari," Danaus interjected.

"Thank you for that happy thought," I grumbled, cracking open one eye to look up at him. It wouldn't be the first time I had been horribly wrong about Jabari and paid a high price for it.

"What about him?" the hunter asked, jerking his head toward Nicolai. "He wasn't the sacrifice."

"Maybe he was, in a last minute change," I suggested.

"Sacrifice?" Nicolai finally chimed in. "What the hell are you talking about?"

"Did you know you were to be handed over to the harpies?" I inquired, letting my eyes drift shut again. Nicolai's agitation had caused his own powers to swell and brush against my skin. They weren't as soothing as Danaus's, and I found myself trying to huddle closer to the hunter.

"Harpies?" Nicolai's voice jumped from its usually deep, rough tones. "That's what was in the room with us? No, I didn't know anything about it."

"Why tell him when he might put up a fight ahead of their arrival?" Danaus said to me. "The naturi might not have been interested in damaged goods."

I fought back a snicker by biting my lower lip. It was a cold and heartless way of putting it, but it was also probably very accurate. "I think what Jabari said was true. Nicolai wasn't part of their original agreement. Maybe it was decided later that he would act as a deposit against any damage done to the female in the Coven's custody. Maybe he was a gift. I don't know. In the end the important thing was our appearance and us walking out with Nicolai. It implied that the

Coven couldn't stop us. The naturi now have a new reason to fear us.
Nicolai was just a pawn."

"Thanks," the wolf grumbled.

"Look at it this way," I countered, turning my head so I could
look at him. "If you had been truly important to the Coven's plans, I
would have never gotten you out of there. And don't worry. Once this
naturi uprising has been put down, Jabari will come to claim your
head the first chance he gets."

It was a grim and ugly truth. At best I extended Nicolai's life by a
matter of days. If he was good at hiding, maybe I gave him a few
months. But in the end we both knew that Jabari would eventually
hunt us down.

Turning my head back to Danaus's chest, I was suddenly overwhelmed by the scent of his blood. It wasn't only the smell of it pulsing beneath his skin, but it was dried on his skin and soaked into his
shirt from where the harpies had gouged his shoulders with their
claws. Clenching my teeth, his warmth and blood beat against me,
tempting me. The beast inside my chest shifted and pushed my soul
down into the dark shadows of my body, fighting for dominance. The
need for blood swelled within me until it nearly blotted out all thought.
My head fell back, my lips parted so I could feel a brush of air across
my tongue. It was only then I realized I was losing the struggle to stay
in control.

I violently shoved against Danaus's chest, tumbling out of his
strong arms. I hit the ground with a bone-jarring thud, which helped
clear my thoughts. Huddled in the grass beside the sidewalk that led
to the Coven, I dug my fingers in the dirt and clenched my eyes shut.
I wouldn't bite Danaus. I wouldn't drink from him if he was the last
creature that walked this earth. Wasn't it enough that he and Jabari
had control of me? I wouldn't be controlled by the hunger as well.

"Don't touch me!" I shrieked when I heard the two men draw
closer to me. "I—I just need a couple seconds." With my eyes clenched
shut, I drew my sore and protesting body into a tighter ball. "Go to
the boat. I'll be there in a minute."

"I'm not leaving you," Danaus firmly replied. "It's too dangerous."

"What's wrong?" Nicolai asked. I could feel the werewolf a couple feet away off to my right.

"She's starved," Danaus answered before I could open my mouth.
"She needs to feed." His words stunned me into silence. I forgot that
he could sense my emotions. I read his so clearly, but forgot that mine
poured into his mind just as easily. He knew I was fighting back the
hunger and had taken a chance carrying me anyway. Was he testing

me? I had no doubt that he would have cleaned my clock if I'd taken a nip at him.

Pushing down the hunger to more controllable levels, Danaus's emotions crept back into my brain. I could hear his heart pounding in his chest as if he had run a marathon, his emotions a chaotic mix of fear and . . . something else. Adrenaline? Hunger? His overriding fear and frustration were crushing the other emotion, so I couldn't clearly make it out. And in truth I don't think either of us wanted to know just yet the other emotion Danaus was feeling.

"Mira, can you drink from lycans?" Nicolai asked, kneeling beside me in the grass. Some nightwalkers could drink from lycanthropes. Most could not. I could. I had some guesses as to why I could, but the implications were not the sort of thing that would help extend my life span; not that much could at this point.

"Go away, Nicolai," I muttered, slowly untensing the muscles in my arms so I could move away from him quickly if he reached for me. I was in better control than a couple minutes ago, but it would be too easy to go back over that edge. "I didn't risk my neck saving your worthless butt just to drain you a few hundred yards from the hall."

"The offer stands," Nicolai said, and then returned to his feet without touching me.

Shuddering, I unclenched my fingers and pushed to my feet as well. The hunger still throbbed in my chest, but I was in control again. As long as I could keep a physical distance from the two men, I could fight back the urge to feed until we reached the main islands of Venice. There, I could blend into the crowd and choose my prey from the hordes that filled the city.

The trip back to the hotel was quick and silent, with Nicolai and Danaus keeping as much distance between me and themselves as humanly possible. I nearly sighed with relief when we landed at the docks next to the Cipriani, but Nicolai didn't give me a chance. The wolf stood in front of me as I tried to exit the boat, grabbing both of my arms in his large hands. My body instantly came alive with his energy and physical contact. I was holding on by a thread, only vaguely aware of what he was saying.

"Can you honestly hunt tonight without killing your prey?" he demanded, his voice like granite. His large hands loosened their grip on me when I didn't try to pull out of his grasp.

"Yes," I hissed, gritting my teeth. It was all I could do to keep from sinking my fangs in his neck right there. He was so warm, with his life and essence beating against me in endless waves. Danaus and

Nicolai were slowly driving me insane. I needed to feed before I did something truly stupid.

"You've saved my life twice," he said tightly. The least I can do is offer my services." Before I could come up with some witty reply, the lycan bent down and tossed me over his shoulder. I don't remember passing Danaus, going through the lobby, or even riding the elevator up to our suite. My mind was occupied with his tight rear end and wondering if it was worth trying to sink my fangs into one of his cheeks. I decided it wasn't—his blue jeans would probably absorb most of his blood before I could get it down my throat.

"Mira!" Tristan's shocked voice tore me from my preoccupation long enough to look up at the young nightwalker through thick strands of my red hair as we entered my suite.

"I'm fine," I called as Nicolai headed for one of the bedrooms. "Go play with Danaus. We'll talk before dawn." My last word was cut off by the door slamming shut.

Nicolai tried to dump me on the bed and take a step away, but I didn't let him. The second my back hit the bed, I reached out and grabbed a fistful of his dark burgundy T-shirt. I barely scooted out of the way in time before he fell backward onto the bed with a bounce. In the blink of an eye I was straddling his hips, one hand entangled in his long blond locks, pulling his head to one side to expose his beautiful neck.

I wanted to ask him one last time if this was what he wanted. I wanted to give him a chance to back out, but I couldn't. There was only the red haze of hunger filling my brain. Enough of me was left to be aware of the fact that I was in a safe location with a source of blood. Willing or not was no longer important. I would console myself later with the thought that having brought me up there, he supposedly knew what he was getting into.

The second his warm blood hit my tongue, the world faded away. There was nothing beyond the warm body lying beneath me and his beating heart. All the aches and pains subsided and the beast inside my chest sighed with relief. I relaxed against him, gentling my hold on his head. One of us moaned as he wrapped his arms around my body, pressing me against his hard length. Drinking his blood, I slipped into his mind, sending a hundred feelings of pleasure through his body. This time I was sure it was Nicolai who moaned, his fingers sliding down my back as they searched for the edge of my shirt.

The first touch of his hands on my skin sent me scrambling off his body. Crawling to the top of the bed, I sat with my back pressed against the wood headboard. With my head tilted back, I ran my tongue over my teeth, taking in the taste of him. His heartbeat and heavy breathing were the only sounds in the room. I hadn't taken much blood from him, nowhere near as much as I needed. I would have to feed again later, but his blood took the edge off my hunger and gave me back a measure of control.

Nicolai shifted on the bed, and I opened my eyes to find him lying on his stomach looking up at me, a wide grin playing on his lips. My eyes drifted to his neck to find that the wound was already healing on its own. That was one of the nice things about feeding on lycans—they healed so fast there was little chance of leaving behind any evidence you were ever there.

"You've not fed enough," he said, his voice a low, husky rumble.

Shoving my right hand through my hair, pushing it back from where it fell around my face, I smiled at my companion. "I've had enough to get me to my next meal," I murmured, feeling a little more relaxed for the first time in several nights. "I'll not drain you to satisfy my cravings."

Nicolai chuckled. "I'm not offering all of my blood," he said, a smile lightening his features, easing back some of the worry lurking around his eyes since I'd first met him. He slid his right hand up to lightly wrap around one of my ankles. "But I can take more than that little snack."

"For some reason, I get the impression you're offering more than just a meal," I hedged, my eyes pointedly slipping down to look at the long fingers wrapped around my ankle. This hadn't been a part of my plan when I sank my teeth into his neck.

"And you're opposed to the offer?" he inquired, making no effort to keep the sarcasm from his voice. Pushing to his knees, Nicolai sat up and pulled his shirt over his head, revealing acres of tanned skin and muscles pulsing with warmth and life. I think he dropped the shirt over the side of the bed, but I honestly couldn't drag my eyes from his chest or his arms.

I'd been with my share of handsome men during my extended lifetime; human, lycan, and nightwalker. I'd been with enough to think that my head couldn't be turned by a nice body or a handsome face. But Nicolai was putting my resolve to the test. He didn't have the same, almost frightening beauty that Valerio possessed. Nicolai had his flaws. There was a long white scar on his chest, stretching above his heart. His stomach seemed almost too thin for his frame, making me wonder if his meals recently had been too sparse or infrequent. But it was this perfect combination of frailty and strength that was intoxicating.

With considerable effort I closed my eyes, but the image of his chest seemed to have already been burned into the insides of my eyelids. "I don't want your body in exchange for your life." I had to force the words from my mouth because something in me simply ached to run my tongue over his chest.

His laugh caused my eyes to open my eyes and focus on his handsome face again. Slowly, he reached down and took both of my ankles in his hands, making me feel very small. With a quick jerk I slid down the bed toward him so I was laying flat on my back with my knees brushing against his hips. Planting his hands on either side of my head, he leaned down until his lips were inches from mine.

"The blood was in gratitude for my life," he whispered, his lips brushing against mine with each word. He moved his head, running his lips along my jaw as he spoke. "The sex is as much for me as it is for you. We've both had enough death and violence during the past few days to last a lifetime. And it's not over, is it?"

His question gave me pause, waking me up from the spell his husky voice was weaving. I met his eyes and found those large copper-brown orbs asking me the same question I had seen in the eyes of Tristan, Sadira, James, Alexandra, and, for even a fleeting moment, Danaus. Were we going to survive? Was I going to protect them? Was there a hope to cling to? And for some reason, they all looked to me to be their savior. A pariah among my own kind. The Coven's anathema.

Threading the fingers of my left hand through the golden wave of hair that cascaded down to frame his face, I pulled him closer so that my lips brushed against his. "It doesn't matter. There is only now," I whispered. Nicolai smiled against my lips as he leaned in to kiss me.

My eyes fell shut and there was only the feeling of his lips and his warmth wrapping around me like a wonderful cocoon, smothering all thoughts of the rest of the world. My tongue easily slid between his parted lips, and the taste of him reminded me of honey and fresh bread, memories of a home I was forced to leave years too early. My fingers left his hair to slide down along his massive shoulders, taking in skin that seemed impossibly soft. I turned my head and trailed kisses along his neck as I ran my hands down his back, lightly scratching him with my nails as I dragged my hands back up to his shoulders.

"Still looking for a bite?" he chuckled, nuzzling my neck before his lips finally settled on my earlobe. A sigh escaped me as the tip of his tongue ran along the edge of the sensitive piece of flesh. Tension that had hummed throughout my body for so many endless nights was beginning to unravel from each one of my muscles.

"Hmmmm . . . There are far more interesting places for me to snack," I teased. Planting my heels in the bed and wrapping my arms around his waist, I rolled us over so he was lying on his back and I was straddling his hips.

Surprise lit his eyes, but he quickly recovered. He didn't seem willing to relinquish control that easily. His hand shot out to snake around the back of my neck, pulling me back down so his mouth could reclaim mine in a long, deep kiss. His tongue slid along one of my fangs until finally pricking it. There was no fighting the moan that swelled up in my throat at the taste of his blood. Stretching out my legs on either side of him, I pressed the length of my body into his as I sucked blood from his tongue until the tiny wound finally healed on its own.

As a shiver ran through me, I broke off the kiss and slid my mouth down along his jaw near his ear. "You've done this before," I purred.

"Been with a vampire?" he asked, running his hands down my back to cup my rear end. As he pressed my body closer to his, he arched his hips, grinding his hardened body into mine. "Oh, yeah. Surprised?"

"No," I laughed, pushing up with my hands braced each side of his head so I could look down at him. But the laughter died when I thought about it. He had been held to Jabari's side while at the court. I knew the horrors the Coven's court were capable of. "While you were here?"

Nicolai cupped my cheeks with both of his hands and tried to pull me back down to him, but every muscle in my body had stiffened and he couldn't move me. "No," he said in a firm but gentle voice. "No one's touched me while I've been here. My experience came well before Jabari."

I sucked in a cleansing breath of air, trying to wipe away the moment of tension. I agreed that we both needed to heal, and sex would at least give us a moment of that. But doing something that mirrored anything he may have been forced to do with another nightwalker would not help him.

Nicolai pulled me back down and we got lost in another series of drugging kisses that only left us needing more, needing to be closer. The scent of his blood just below his warm skin beckoned to me. His blood was wonderful, better than pure human. It was richer and more potent, but my hunger for his blood was steadily being overpowered with the need to know every inch of his long body.

Nicolai had no problem with my intentions, and was already

pulling my plain cotton shirt up and over my head as I sat up. Once again straddling his hips, I reached back to unfasten my lacy black bra. He snatched the opportunity and, sitting up, pulled the bra down to free my breasts.

My eyelids fell shut as his tongue slowly circled the left nipple before taking it into his mouth. The fingers of my right hand fumbled with the clasp twice before I finally used both hands to undo the bra. The wonderful moist heat on my left breast and his strong, kneading fingers on my right had successfully scattered my thoughts to the wind. My hands fell to his shoulders, then of their own will slid into his hair, holding his head gently imprisoned as I arched my back, pressing closer to him. Lifting his mouth from my breast, his breath skimmed over the damp flesh, sending a chill dancing over my whole body before he shifted to the other breast, his tongue briefly dipping into the valley between them.

A soft sigh whispered past my parted lips. There was only Nicolai and his gentle hands and seeking mouth. How long had it been since I had last been touched like this? Weeks? Months? For a heartbeat the memory of the last time I'd had a moment like this drifted through my brain, but I quickly pushed it aside. So many mistakes made. So many lies and denials that only ended in death. I needed this now, a break from the ghosts that haunted me, to escape the pain that waited for me. To bask in gentle hands that didn't want to hit, stab, or tear.

Forcing his head up, I kissed him deeply as I pushed him back to the bed. "I need another snack," I murmured when I finally lifted my mouth from his. Inching my way lower, I kissed and licked a long trail down his chest to the waistband of his pants. I kissed the hard bulge at his groin as my fingers pulled at the button of his jeans. I kissed him again, but this time my teeth lightly scraped against the thick fabric. I wouldn't dare bite a man there. Any sane man would faint dead away in a heartbeat, but the tease had been enough to increase Nicolai's heart rate again.

"Mira," he said in a husky voice edged with warning.

"I wouldn't dream of it," I whispered, unzipping his pants. "I've got another place staked out."

Slipping my fingers inside the waistband of his pants and boxers, I slowly pulled them down, climbing down the bed as I went. I paused long enough to strip off his shoes and socks before letting my eyes travel back up his body. Nicolai now lay stretched out before me, all golden skin and hard muscle. Little blond hairs curled along his legs, and I ran my hands up his calves as I settled between his thighs. I kissed his right inner thigh, drawing an infinity sign with the tip of my tongue.

"*Mira.*" My name escaped him in a breathless whisper, holding an almost pleading tone. He knew what I was looking for; the large vein that ran along his inner thigh, pulsing with life. As my fangs pierced his skin, I wrapped my fingers around his hard length, stroking him as he arched against my hand, keeping him rock hard as I took a quick drink.

Closing the wound after a couple of seconds, I moved higher. I kissed the inside of his hip, running my tongue over the soft tender flesh there. I was drunk on the power I had over him. For once, it wasn't about physical strength or the power I had gained as a nightwalker. It was solely about being female and Nicolai wanting me as a female the same way I wanted every inch of him, because he was a very handsome male.

He allowed me to run my tongue along his engorged penis before entwining his fingers in my hair and hauling me back up to his mouth. Clamping his mouth on mine, he rolled me onto my back so he could more easily kiss me while pulling off my pants. I had no clear memory of it, just his tongue thrusting into my mouth as he fumbled with the button. In the next second, I simply wasn't wearing pants any longer. There was only his hot soft skin rubbing against mine, his hard body nudging against the entrance to mine.

"Mira?"

I blinked and forced myself to look into his eyes, which were now more copper than brown. His voice was thick and husky, but I didn't miss the question there. He was holding himself perfectly still, waiting for me. I wasn't sure if he was giving me one last chance to back out or if he needed to know if I was ready. It didn't matter. I was well beyond such thoughts.

"Please. Now," were the only words I could manage, and they escaped me as a shaken, desperate plea. It was enough.

Nicolai thrust into me, tearing a cry from my throat. He was larger than I expected, and my body hadn't been as ready as I thought, drowning me in equal parts pleasure and pain. It didn't matter. By his next thrust I was arching my hips to meet him, taking every inch of him I could get. We were beyond soft touches and gentle caresses. Now it was rough and fast, with strong, hard hands pushing and pulling us closer to that oblivion of pleasure that lay beyond the horizon.

My mind was overloaded with sensations. His heartbeat was pounding in my brain, mixing with the sound of his heavy breathing and a so-soft grunt as he thrust into me. I breathed him in, drawing his unique scent along with the smell of his sweat and sex into my lungs to hold him there as well. I leaned up and ran my tongue along his neck and up to his ear, needing the taste of him imprinted on me.

Nicolai reached down and cupped my bottom with both of his large hands, changing the angle slightly, grinding his body deep into mine. Pleasure finally edged ahead of pain in their battle for my body. One last scream was torn from my lips as my body imploded with the force of the orgasm that tightened every muscle. For a moment there was only blinding starlight and an intense pleasure that filled all of my pores. *Dear God, never let this end . . .*

It was minutes later when my brain started to function enough that I realized Nicolai was lying on top of me, his body still shivering inside me with the aftershocks of his orgasm. A silly grin lifted my lips as I briefly wondered if it was possible to destroy brain cells with a really good orgasm. Probably not, but I certainly didn't feel all that intelligent as my brain struggled to pull together a string of coherent thoughts.

Slowly, he began to stir, burrowing his face in my neck. He nipped at my earlobe, earning a chuckle from me before he finally lifted his head. His large eyes had returned to their normal shade of brown, with only a faint hint of copper. Staring at the shadows clinging to his smiling face, I realized neither one of us had bothered to flip on a light. Of course, we both had the night vision of cats, so why bother?

"Feeling better?" he inquired, a cute smugness filling his tone.

"Much." I smiled, pressing a gentle kiss to his lips. "Thank you."

"Thank you," he replied, kissing me back. "We make a good pair."

"You mean when you're not trying to kill me," I teased.

The easygoing smile slipped from his full lips. "I didn't have a choice," he firmly said before rolling off me. Then he lay on his back in silence, roughly running his hands over his face a couple times, as if it could help clear his thoughts. He finally dropped his hands back to his sides, staring up at the ceiling. "Besides, I'm apparently not the first murderous stalker you've tamed."

"Don't misunderstand my truce with Danaus," I said, turning onto my side. Leaning on one elbow, I brushed a lock of hair behind my ear. "If he gets the chance, he means to kill me when this is all over. That hasn't changed."

"Despite the fact that you've protected him?"

"It's a special relationship we have." I flashed him a wide smile, letting my fangs poke out from beneath my upper lips before I rolled off the bed.

"Like this?"

I couldn't stop the laugh that bubbled up as I snatched the black silk robe that lay draped over one of the chairs in the bedroom. "No, we've just called a truce until we can find an appropriate time to kill each other." I pulled the robe on as I strolled over to the window and jerked open the heavy curtains. The window faced San Marco Piazza and the Grand Canal. The large *campo* was aglow with lights, while stars winked in and out overhead. The waves in the Lagoon had grown during the past several minutes and were beginning to white-cap as a storm blew in.

"Speaking of special relationships," I slowly began, not bothering to look over at my companion. "What hold does Jabari have over you?" I waited for his answer, but there was only silence. With a frown, I turned away from the window and walked to the end of the bed with my arms folded over my chest. Nicolai lay as still as death, his golden body gilded with starlight that leaked through the window.

"Before the Coven, I took you into my keeping. I claimed you from an Elder," I said, stressing each word. "I have promised to protect you from any and all who would harm you, including the Coven. I don't know if lycans have an equivalent of such a vow, but it is not something to be taken lightly among nightwalkers. When Jabari comes to claim your head and I sacrifice myself to stop him, I would like to know exactly why he is ripping my heart out."

When Nicolai finally spoke, his voice was low and void of emotion, but his words nearly brought me to my knees. "Members of my pack were aiding the naturi."

"No," I gasped, my voice going hoarse. My mind stumbled forward, struggling to understand the concept. Why would anyone assist the naturi? They were horrid creatures whose only goal was to destroy anything that was not of their kind. "*Willingly?* Were they willingly helping the naturi?" I asked, grasping at my last few desperate straws to understand what he was saying. Maybe they had been forced, mind-control wiping away all choice.

"Yes."

I was moving without a thought. One second I was standing at the foot of the bed, and the next I was kneeling beside him, my hands reaching for his throat, my fangs bared. Nicolai caught my wrists at the last second and was struggling to hold me back. "Were you? Were you helping the naturi?" I snarled.

"No!" he shouted. "I would never help the naturi. I know what they've done. I know what they're capable of."

"Then why did Jabari want you?" I demanded, jerking my wrists from his grasp.

Nicolai pushed up so he was leaning back on his forearms and elbows. "There were three naturi sympathizers in my pack. Somehow Jabari found out and threatened to tell the other packs. Everyone in my pack would have been killed, no questions asked. Instead he killed two of the sympathizers immediately and wanted to keep the third as a pet. I bargained with Jabari to take me instead of her."

I sat back on my heels, hating his words, despising the fact that I sympathized with him. Of course, if I had been in Jabari's place, I have no doubt that I would have destroyed the whole pack without a second thought, and not feel an ounce of remorse about the deed. In this war, it was us against the naturi. There was no room for sympathy or betrayal. But betrayal seemed to surround me when it came to the naturi. Trust was a withering corpse in the sun. Vampires and lycans were siding with the naturi. Witches and lycans were with the Daylight Coalition. And I stood alone with a bori half-breed at my back.

"Girlfriend?" I asked after a long moment of silence, pondering the "her" he had mentioned.

"She was my sister," he softly replied.

With a growl, I climbed off the bed and strode back over to the window, my arms once again folded tightly under my breasts, as if to protect myself against the very idea. There was no questioning the "was" in his statement. We both knew his former pack would have killed his sister the second Jabari departed with him. She had betrayed not only her own kind, but also the pact made by all the other creatures to fight against the naturi. When given the choice between what could be a long, painful existence in servitude to a nightwalker and a quick death, Nicolai stepped in to give her the more merciful option. Would I be so forgiving of someone I loved?

I roughly ran my right hand through my hair, pushing it away from my eyes, trying not to think about the answer that came so quickly to mind. Despite my so-called noble actions in regard to Tristan, I didn't like myself much when it came to my dealings with the naturi. The blood flowed too easily and the joy too sweet.

What was also eating away at me was the idea that Jabari had discovered this betrayal within the United States. It wasn't my domain, but it felt too close. The Elders never came to the New World, and there only a handful of Ancients in the region. The idea that Jabari had come and gone without my knowledge had left me feeling . . . violated. Maybe the others were right. Maybe I had begun to see all of the New World as mine. Or at the very least, safe from direct interference of the Coven.

"I'm sorry," I whispered. We both knew her betrayal had left her with no other fate, but that knowledge did little to ease the pain of loss. "I have to get you to my domain," I said when the silence began to grow between us again. Turning away from the window, I walked over to the nightstand by the bed and picked up my cell phone. Nicolai covered my hand with his before I could pick up the phone, dragging my eyes to his face.

"You'll still protect me?" he asked, confusion furrowing his brow.

"I promised to protect you. I keep my word," I said solemnly with a nod of my head. "But I can't do that here. I have to get you and Tristan to my domain back in the United States. As repayment for this protection, you must guard Tristan during the daylight hours as you travel to my home. You must promise to guard him with your life."

"I swear I will. No harm will come to him." Nicolai squeezed my hand as he made his vow. I tried to smile at him, reassure him, but I couldn't. I believed him. He would die before he allowed anyone to lay a hand on Tristan, and that was reassuring. Yet when I looked at him, my mind now wondered if he had known what his sister was doing. Did he try to hide her actions? Protect her the same way he protected her from Jabari?

"Get some sleep. I have to make some arrangement. You'll be flying out in the morning." Picking up my cell phone, I wordlessly walked out of the bedroom into the main living area and shut the door behind me.

It was four hours until sunrise and I needed every minute of it to make my plans. I spent nearly an hour on the phone arguing with Barrett, the Alpha of the werewolf pack in Savannah. He was less than pleased with the idea of me bringing an unknown lycan into his territory; not that I could blame him. Naturally, I couldn't tell him the real reason as to how Nicolai came to be in my care. It didn't help matters that the Savannah pack was very peculiar since most of those in it were actually related by blood or marriage, and outsiders were very rarely permitted to move into the region. I think Barrett finally caved in to my request only because I promised him that it would not be a long-term arrangement.

Other than the brief, heated argument, it felt good to talk to him. Since leaving Savannah a week ago, the naturi had disappeared completely from my domain. There were no more attacks, no more deaths. Prior to my traveling to Egypt with Danaus, the naturi had attacked a human nightclub and a private nightwalker club, resulting in several deaths—some at the hands of werewolves being controlled by the naturi. Tension was still running high, but the area was otherwise quiet.

With Barrett reassured, somewhat, it was then on to my human assistant Charlotte, who would make the arrangements for the private flight from Venice to Savannah. She had received enough bizarre phone calls like this one to know not to ask too many questions. After talking to her, I contacted my bodyguard Gabriel, still recuperating in England following our last battle with the naturi. A lump grew in my throat at the sweet sound of his familiar voice. Closing my eyes, I could see his crooked smirk. Gabriel had protected me for years, knew my secrets. He would also grab a flight tonight and be waiting in Savannah when Tristan and Nicolai arrived. My angel would see to it that Tristan was properly taken care of when he arrived in my domain.

I wanted to call Knox. While relatively young, he had proven capable and intelligent enough to manage the region when I was out of town. I wanted to hear his voice, the touch of dry humor that laced his every comment. I needed to know from him that all the night-walkers I had left behind in my domain were still safe. But Tristan and Danaus returned as I ended my call with Gabriel and sank into the soft cushions of the sofa, forcing me to put aside my phone.

The nightwalker had been considerate enough to go hunting while I occupied myself with Nicolai. Neither said anything about how I had spent my evening because Tristan got it into his head to argue with me for the next hour over whether he would travel with me to the site of the next sacrifice and battle the naturi.

In the end I won and he agreed to travel to my domain. He had suffered enough, and I wasn't willing to lose him to the naturi. I prayed it was the start of a series of smart choices on my part.

Nineteen

If I had been human, I would have tossed and turned, twisting the smooth cotton sheets. I would have stared up at the ceiling as the minutes crawled by, imagining the hundreds of threats and dangers Tristan could potentially face while he lay helpless during the daylight hours. I would have laid there hating Danaus and Nicolai, fearing they would betray my desperate trust. Hell, if I was human, I would have accompanied Tristan's lifeless form down to the airport and personally secured him on the private jet.

But I wasn't human, and at times I wondered if I had ever been human, considering my horrid past. I was a nightwalker. When the sun finally tore at the horizon and the night gave its last shuddering breath, consciousness left me no matter how badly I wished to remain awake. There were no thoughts of Tristan, no bits of safeguard I could offer him. There was only the desolate blackness and an emptiness from which I could not pull away. In those last seconds, I hated the dawn and my weakness, not for the first time since being reborn.

Yet, my daylight hours weren't completely filled with undisturbed nothingness. In my final hour before waking, images of Tristan filled my brain, flashing in my mind like a demonic slide show. This was not like the nightmares I suffered in Egypt and England. Those grim plays had been a mix of my own memories and growing fears.

These garish images were from Macaire's memories of the night when Tristan was tortured by the court. But there was no order to the images, no linear progression. The Elder's memories flickered in my brain like a reel of film that had been badly spliced together. One moment Tristan was hunched over covered in blood, his back raw and his limbs trembling in pain. Yet, in the next moment, he was standing unharmed, surrounded by his kind as he anticipated his fate.

The only thing about the nightmare that was linear was Tristan's thoughts. They whispered through my head like a ghostly soundtrack, going from disbelief that his beloved maker would abandon him to his fate, to broken pleading for her to save him. Save him from the pain. Save him from the blackness that was swallowing up his hope. In the end his fragile, fractured mind clung to a single, unwavering word: Mira. He knew I would come and end the pain.

When I was finally released from the hellish nightmare and awoke, my body began trembling and I choked back a sob. Rolling onto my side in the bed, I curled into the fetal position as I waited for the shaking to pass. My thoughts were sluggish, as if a thick, tarlike film covered them, a disgusting residue left behind by Macaire's mental touch.

When I could finally unclench my fingers, which were twisted in the sheets, I mentally reached out for Tristan, but came up with only dead air. Instantly lurching into a sitting position on the bed, legs bent before me and eyes tightly closed, I concentrated again. All of my energy poured into the single act of touching his thoughts, being able to feel his presence. I needed to know he was safe.

When the sun had risen that morning, Tristan was laying beside me. Danaus and Nicolai had agreed to get him safely aboard the chartered jet. Either one of them had ample opportunity to stake him while he slept.

No. Shaking my head at the thought, I knew Danaus wouldn't kill a nightwalker when he or she slept. The hunter might hate my kind, but his sense of honor ran deeper than that. If he wanted Tristan dead, he'd take care of the matter while the nightwalker was awake and able to defend himself.

Nicolai, I didn't trust. He could have been lying. Maybe he was a naturi sympathizer and I'd left Tristan at his mercy. Damn it! I was an idiot.

Twisting on the bed, I snatched up my cell phone from the nightstand and pulled up Gabriel's number. My bodyguard answered after the second ring, and some of the tension in my stomach slowly unknotted at the sound of his voice.

"Do you have Tristan?" I quickly demanded, inwardly wincing at the harshness of my voice.

"Yes. Are you in trouble?" he asked.

I ignored his question. I was in all kinds of trouble, but there was nothing he or Tristan could do about it. "Let me speak to him."

"Mira," Gabriel started hesitantly, "he's still asleep. It's about two-thirty in the afternoon."

Falling back against my pillows, I gave a breathless chuckle, laughing at my own stupidity. All the chaos flying about me had scattered my thoughts. I was so worried about Tristan's safety that I forgot about the six-hour time difference.

"Sorry," I mumbled.

"He's safe," Gabriel reassured me, his voice growing soft. "Both he and Nicolai landed around one."

"Is Nicolai with you?"

"No. You didn't say anything about him staying with you, so I left him at your town house. He wasn't happy about it."

The thought brought a faint smile to my lips. Nicolai possibly didn't trust Gabriel with a vulnerable Tristan, but I had told the lycan that Gabriel was my bodyguard.

"I had to agree to have Tristan call Nicolai the second he was awake," he continued.

"Have you actually seen Tristan?"

"I opened the trunk after I pulled into the garage at your place. He's curled up with head and heart in their right places," he teased, and I couldn't blame him. My paranoia was worse than usual. "I won't leave him until he's in the house and knows how to set the alarms."

"Thank you, my angel," I sighed, letting my eyes drift shut. The security system for my house wasn't quite Fort Knox, but it would deter most humans and give Tristan enough warning if another creature was near at night. There was also a vault in the basement with a separate security system, which would keep him safe during the daylight hours. Not even Gabriel knew how to disarm the locks on the vault. I had given Tristan those codes before he fell asleep that morning.

"How bad is it?" Gabriel inquired when a comfortable silence had grown between us.

"Bad enough." I didn't want to say more. It would take too long and serve no good purpose. "Have you healed?" I asked, changing the subject. The last time I saw him, he had sustained a wound to his side and thigh, and was still nursing an injured arm from a fight in Egypt.

"Enough to be a threat." I could imagine one of his rare smiles flitting across his lips as he spoke.

As my own smile faded, I gave him instructions to contact my assistant, Charlotte, and have her arrange for a chartered jet to be ready to leave Venice that night. The new moon was in two nights. We had enough time to be at whatever location would be the site of the next sacrifice. Enough time to face the naturi for what I hoped would be the last time.

Rolling out of bed, I showered and dressed. Unfortunately, I was down to my last clean garment—a sleeveless cotton dress that hung down to my ankles. I had hoped to wear it in Egypt as I wandered around the decaying monuments, listening to the sound of the Nile splashing between its banks. The breezy, navy blue skirt would only hinder me in a fight, but I knew I wouldn't be fighting Macaire when he finally decided to appear. The Elder might be seriously pissed at me, but he also understood the value of a good weapon. And if I had proved anything during the long years, it was that I was an efficient killer.

I had hoped to slip out of the suite without being stopped, but Danaus was sitting in the living room drinking coffee. The remains of his dinner rested on a trolley brought up by room service. A ghost of a smile floated across my lips as I looked at the hunter settled comfortably on the sofa. It always amused me when I saw him doing such mundane things like eating or enjoying the warmth of a good cup of coffee. It kept my mind struggling to grasp hold of him, as he constantly shifted between ruthless killer and human in my thoughts.

He was dressed in a dark navy linen shirt with short sleeves that revealed his deeply tanned, muscled arms. His shoulder-length locks were pulled back, letting my eyes caress his strong features. The day's growth of dark stubble had been removed from his chin, but it did nothing to lessen the shadows that clung to the hollows of his cheeks. Danaus looked like a wealthy Italian gentlemen on holiday, but there was a seriousness, a dark shadow in his sapphire eyes, that no amount of expensive clothes could hide.

Had circumstances been different, I would have been content to spend the night staring at him, slowly memorizing his features. I would have happily passed the night curled in a chair, arguing philosophy, mythology, and our place in the universe with him.

"You're awake early," he said, setting his cup on the table before him. He rose from the sofa, slipping his hands into his trouser pockets. A knife was once again attached to his waist, and he was wearing a hard leather wrist guard on his right arm. The weaponry and guard were at odds with his clothes, reminding me that there was no escaping what he was—a hunter.

"Another meeting, I believe," I said. I was dead inside after all that had happened during the past several nights. Walking over to the wall of windows, I leaned against the wall and crossed my arms loosely over my stomach.

"Like last night's?"

"No."

"Alone?"

I stared out the wall of windows, admiring the pallet of colors washing across the sky. Since becoming a nightwalker, my skies had been limited to inky black and sickly shades of gray. Yet, while in Venice, I had been given two chances to add some color to my skies. Tonight, the sky was bathed in deep reds and oranges as the sun sank deeper beneath the horizon. "No," I said, a surprised smile dawning on my face. Danaus knew almost as much as I did at this point. Why should I try to hide this? He was also part of the triad. If Macaire wanted to talk to me about the naturi, then he would have to tell Danaus as well.

"We have to leave tonight," Danaus reminded me. I knew that. The new moon was in two nights. It was also Lughnassadh, the pagan preharvest festival. Ancient lore said the celebration was in honor of the god Lugh's wedding to Mother Earth. While I can't say that I put much stock in the old pagan tales, it would have been rather fitting if the naturi managed to break the seal on that night, erasing the one thing blocking the union of the two worlds.

"Do you know where the next sacrifice will be?" I asked, turning to look at him.

He shook his head, a grim smile lifting the corners of his mouth. "I was going to ask you the same question."

"Great," I muttered, walking over and plopping down in one of the chairs next to the sofa. "We're out of time."

"We should never have come here. We should have been looking for the next location, or at least trying to hunt down Rowe," Danaus growled, but to my surprise, he seemed as frustrated with himself as he was with me.

"I don't remember us having a lot of choice in the matter," I said, fixing my dark gaze on the hunter. "Or at least, I didn't. Jabari wanted me here. I wouldn't have been able to fight him. I'm a puppet, remember?"

Danaus sat down on the sofa again, leaning forward so he could rest his elbows on his knees. He stared off into space, lost in his own thoughts. Unfortunately, this arguing wasn't getting us anywhere.

"The naturi can't do anything for another two nights," I said with a sigh. "If we hadn't come here, we would have been jumping from place to place, chasing anything that looked suspicious. That would have been a waste of our time and extremely dangerous. Rowe could have attacked at any time during the day. At least here we were protected."

That comment finally made Danaus's head snap up, a frown pulling at his mouth. In this case, "protected" simply meant that we were safe from the naturi because this area was controlled by nightwalkers. And apparently because the Coven had struck up some kind of bargain with the naturi.

"Look at it this way, if we hadn't come, Tristan and Nicolai would most likely be dead. We wouldn't know the Coven has cooked up some scheme with the naturi, and we wouldn't know that Rowe is unaware of the alliance. Once we know what the Coven is planning, it will be easier to stop them," I argued.

"But that still leaves us with one very large problem," Danaus countered. The hunter picked up his coffee cup again and drank the last of its contents.

Pulling myself up using the arms of the chair, I sat up straight. "I think we have more than that, but which one are you referring to?"

"Where is the next sacrifice?"

"We should know tonight. I think Macaire will tell us," I said, causing Danaus's features to twist in confusion.

"And why do you think he will do that?"

"Call it a hunch." I shrugged my shoulders at the hunter as I smiled at him. "Have you talked to Ryan recently? Are your people looking as well?"

The warlock was the head of Themis, a research group that had spent centuries watching nightwalkers, lycanthropes, and any other creepy-crawly creatures the rest of the human race wasn't aware of. Their numbers were large enough that they could watch all twelve of the so-called holy sites and report back any kind of activity. And the one major advantage they had over nightwalkers was that they could keep an eye on things during the daylight hours. While I fully expected Macaire to tell us the site of the next sacrifice, I wanted Ryan to confirm the information for me. Macaire would tell us the location; I just wanted to be sure it was the real location.

"Ryan is looking into it," Danaus replied. "No word yet on the location."

"Gabriel is contacting Charlotte. She'll arrange for the flight out tonight," I said, pushing back to my feet. Forcing a smile onto my lips, I motioned with my head toward the door. "Ready?"

The hunter's muscular body was almost humming with energy as we headed down to the main landing. Pausing near the canal, I willed my body to relax, pushing the tension from my arms and down my legs until it flowed out of my toes. A light summer breeze stirred, dancing down the canals and threading its way between the buildings. Street lamps were popping on and the glow from Piazza San Marco was starting to swell.

"How do you like your rooms?" inquired a gentle voice from behind me in strangely accented English. I jerked around, stunned to find Macaire seated on a bench just a few feet from us. I hadn't felt him there a moment ago, hadn't even sensed his approach, but I guess that's what made him an Elder.

Danaus instinctively reached for his knife, but I gently laid my hand on his wrist, halting his movement. Macaire had done nothing yet to threaten us. I was willing to play it cool for now. No reason to start a fight. There would be plenty of time for that later.

"They're stunning, particularly the large wall of windows facing the east," I answered. His face split into a wide, almost malicious grin. "When did the Coven acquire the Cipriani?"

"A few years ago," he said, pushing to his feet and walking over to us. His English was perfect, but the accent was strange. I knew he wasn't as old as Jabari, making me doubt that his people were a dead civilization. Slavic, Eastern European, or maybe Russian? But even that seemed wrong.

Macaire wore a pale, mint green button-up shirt that contrasted nicely with his deep brown eyes. His white linen pants and supple brown loafers made him look so damn approachable and pleasant. He should have looked more predatory; something to indicate to the world that he was one of the most powerful nightwalkers on the planet.

When he was standing beside me, he offered his arm. With a great deal of effort, I managed to keep my face expressionless as I slipped my hand into the crook of his arm while I let my other hand drop from Danaus's wrist.

"The hall was receiving too many visitors, making sleeping arrangements uncomfortable," he continued, pleased to see that I was willing to play along. His eyes for a brief moment skimmed over Danaus as if weighing some thought. "We thought it wise if we started keeping some of our guests off the island."

"It's beautiful. I've always liked the quiet of Guidecca," I said, strolling down the street next to him. In the eyes of the world, we were a trio of tourists on an evening walk along the narrow street of the island, not enemies trying to find a way to accomplish our individual goals without dying in the process.

"How is Tristan?" Macaire abruptly asked as we crossed a small bridge, heading deeper into the island of Guidecca.

"I imagine he is faring much better than Sadira." I couldn't quite stop the smile that rose to my pale lips. Her screams echoed through

my memory for a brief moment, loud enough that I felt muscles twitch
in Macaire's arm. I figured he was listening to some of my thoughts.

"Yes, I fear she'll be in pain for quite some time," he said, his
voice hardening. "Not exactly a wise choice, considering that she
must be strong to help you with the naturi."

"Nor was her choice of enemies wise," Danaus darkly interjected.

I was pleased with the hunter's comments, but I didn't want to
worry about trying to separate the Elder and Danaus while I was still
trying to get information. "Are you concerned?" I asked quickly,
arching one brow as I looked down at him.

Macaire paused and turned his body so he was facing me. He laid
one of his hands over my hand, which was lightly resting on his arm.
"Of course I am."

"I had my doubts," I said with a frown. "Considering your new
business partner, I was under the impression that maybe the Coven no
longer wanted to keep the door closed."

"Ahhh," Macaire said, resuming our walk through the neighborhood. "You misunderstand, my young one." His condescending tone
made my teeth clench, but for now I knew it had to be tolerated.

"I can't imagine why." Hidden by the material of my dress, my
free hand clenched into a fist at my side. "What is going on, Macaire?
What has the Coven done?"

"We've struck a rather unique bargain."

"Has the Coven decided to destroy us all?"

Macaire stopped walking again. He reached up and placed his
hands on both of my cheeks, his eyes softening to a look of sweet
concern. The nightwalker looked older than many of the others. It
appeared that he was in his late forties to early fifties when he was
reborn. His dark brown hair was sprinkled liberally with gray, giving
him a wise and distinguished look. There was a cleft in his chin and
deep lines around his mouth and eyes. It was strange. He looked like
he was almost twice as old as Jabari, but the Egyptian was the older
of the two.

"What we have done is for the protection of our kind," he reassured me. His eyes pointedly moved from my face to stare at Danaus,
who stood behind my right shoulder. "What have you done for the
protection of our kind?"

I stepped backward out of his touch, my brows bunching angrily
over the bridge of my nose. "I'm not a fool. You can't make deals with
the naturi and expect them to live up to the agreement."

"Some would say the same about you," he ruefully stated, looking from Danaus to me again.

"Enough! What is going on?"

Smiling, Macaire lifted his arm, patiently waiting for me to place my hand back in the crook of his elbow. He liked the farce, and I knew he would say nothing until I complied with his wishes. Nearly growling in my frustration, I placed my hand back on his arm and we continued our walk.

"Several decades ago, the Coven was quietly approached by a handful of naturi," he began, sounding as if he was retelling a tale of misadventure at the office. "They told us of their queen's plans to open the door between our worlds. It seems that they had become content with the way things had gone since becoming separated from the rest of the host. They had no desire to fall back under the thumb of their illustrious ruler. This small group came to us requesting that we not only close the door, but that we also kill Aurora."

My legs stopped working as I listened to these words, as if the very idea had locked up my brain. I stood planted to the spot, blindly staring ahead at the large plaza we had entered. "Kill Aurora," I repeated dumbly.

"They wish to return to the peaceful existence they had found. Aurora will not allow that. She will continue with her plans for wiping out both humans and nightwalkers."

"I don't believe it." I shook my head, as if trying to clear the clutter of questions that had crowded in my brain. Macaire tried to continue walking, but I wouldn't move.

"You do not have to," he said patiently. "The Elders do."

"To kill Aurora, she has to come through the door, which means we have to allow them to open the door," Danaus reminded him. "It would be safer to stop them before they open it. It may be centuries before she has another chance to open the door again."

"We considered that, and there is one problem . . ." Macaire paused, moving his gaze from Danaus to my face. "You."

I lurched backward a step, putting a little distance between us. The sidewalk seemed to have narrowed, leaving me feeling trapped between Danaus and Macaire. This conversation had taken a strange, unexpected turn. "What do you mean?"

"You are needed to shut the door and form the seal. We also believe you are our best chance at destroying Aurora," he said. "Unfortunately, considering your reckless lifestyle and your unexpected alliance, the Coven doesn't feel confident that you will survive long enough to stop Aurora if she tries again a couple centuries from now."

"Best chance—don't you mean best weapon?" I snapped irritably.

"Yes," he said in a slow hiss. "You are an exquisite weapon, whether you act alone or are being wielded by another. The Coven thinks this is our best chance to stop Aurora once and for all. To finish it. And we're not sure we'll have another chance like this one."

"So we allow her to come through the door, close the door, and then kill her," I stated, frowning darkly at him. "After that, the naturi that hired us go free."

"Returning to their quiet lives," he said with a nod as he laced his stubby fingers behind his back and continued to walk along the sidewalk until it opened up into a large, open square.

"What do we get out of this?" I demanded, unable to keep the skepticism out of my voice. I folded my arms over my chest and stared hard at the Elder, but he ignored my dark looks.

"Besides the chance to destroy their queen and cripple their race?"

"Yes. We're the ones risking everything."

Macaire smiled and strolled into the center of the *campo*, his hands clasped loosely behind his back. Reluctantly, Danaus and I followed him into the center of the square. The area was mostly empty. At the far end of the *campo* a stage was being decorated by several people. They appeared to be preparing for a festival, though I wasn't sure which one. On the stage sat a row of five chairs with high backs, reminding me vaguely of the Great Hall dais. Obviously, Macaire had planned on walking to this part of the neighborhood. He had something else on his mind.

"What do you know of the Great Awakening?" he asked, his tone sounding as if he had just asked what the weather would be like tomorrow.

"A general outline of the plan. Why? It's not supposed to be for another fifty years and even that's still up for debate."

"It's the debate that has the Elders concerned," he said. His hands swung from his back and hung limp at his sides. He looked around, taking in the string of little lights overhead and the other tables that lined the edge of the square. Tomorrow they would most likely be overflowing with food while the square buzzed with conversation and laughter. "It seems Our Liege wishes to change the date of the Awakening."

"To what?"

"Next year."

"Is he mad?" Danaus blurted out, causing me to wince at his volume and tone. It was not the type of thing anyone dared to voice about Our Liege. You never knew who was listening. I had always been outspoken, but there were a few lines even I was hesitant to cross.

"That's not the word I would use," Macaire said, his grim voice a proper reprimand for my companion's unseemly outburst.

"It's too soon," I said to the Elder, resisting the urge to place my hand on Danaus's arm to steady myself. My world was spinning out of control and I desperately wanted to run away from them all. "The humans may be able to adapt, but there are still a few stages that are supposed to be implemented. It would make the transition easier. The timetable was developed to protect our kind. You can't throw it aside."

"You're not telling me anything the Coven has not already discussed." Macaire waved one hand absently at me. A frown dug deeper lines into his grim face.

I walked over to stand directly in front of him, lowering my voice. Our agitated conversation was drawing the confused gaze of those on the stage at the far aside of the square. "What about the other races? What have they said?"

"They wish to stick to the timetable."

I closed my eyes, not wanting to hear any more, but there was one other question that had to be asked. "Will Our Liege proceed without the rest of the races?"

"It is his intention."

"Then it will be war," I said wearily. The other races would attack nightwalkers around the globe to keep us from pulling aside the veil that protected our common secret. If I survived Aurora's planned assassination, I would be headed into a war against creatures I had been at peace with for centuries. And in the end, the humans would still discover us ahead of schedule. We wouldn't be able to hide the war from them forever, and they would discover us in the worst possible way.

"So now you understand our dilemma." The Elder sounded tired, as if the weight of centuries had trickled into his voice.

"What is the Coven's plan?"

Again Macaire smiled at me, sending a shiver skittering across my skin. Nightwalkers may not have been reborn evil, but there were moments when I thought something truly evil resided in Macaire's chest. "The naturi can move about during the day. They would be able to get past bodyguards."

"You plan to—"

"Do not even breathe the words!" he sharply said. Even the powerful Macaire had his fears. I knew what they planned to do. The Coven planned to have the naturi assassinate Our Liege while he slept during the day.

"And all of the Coven has agreed on this course of action?"

"Of course."

"Even Tabor?"

The Elder's gaze darted to Danaus before he could stop himself and then he stared silently at me for a long time. I could almost see the thoughts bouncing around in his head as he weighed my question. His lips twitched. It wasn't quite a smile, but it was something. Maybe a word that he had stopped at the last second.

"That is an interesting question," he said at last. "I think he would have if he had survived longer."

"But he didn't initially," I prodded. Something still didn't feel right about this. It might have just been my survival instincts telling me not to trust a word Macaire told me. I believed there was some kernel of truth to this tale, but I also knew there were a few other important tidbits he was leaving out. I had never met Our Liege and didn't feel any particular allegiance to the nightwalker. As far as I knew, he had done nothing for me and was generally indifferent to my existence. In truth, Our Liege and the Coven had little effect on the night-to-night life of a vampire.

"He had his doubts," Macaire said. "Why do you ask?"

"Just curious," I replied with a shrug.

I strolled through the *campo* then, heading toward the stage, when I abruptly stopped, my eyes locked on the five chairs. The people who were hanging the last of the deep purple cloth to hide the wooden beams supporting the stage had finished and left the plaza. Danaus and I were alone with the Elder.

"Another question if you please?" I called into the air, trying to lighten my voice of the fear coursing through my entire body.

"What is on your mind, my dear?" Macaire said, coming to stand beside me. His voice was sweet and pleasant. He already knew what thoughts were dancing through my head.

"Supposing Our Liege meets an untimely demise at the hand of the naturi. Then our kind will find itself without a clear leader for the first time in several millennia. That cannot be in the best interest of our people."

"No, that would not be," he said with a solemn shake of his head. "But our race wouldn't be without guidance. The Coven would remain."

"So the rule of one and four would be replaced by the rule of three," I said. That did not feel like an improvement.

"Until someone rose to power to reclaim the throne, and a fourth filled the empty seat on the Coven."

I was frowning again. The Coven was not an improvement over Our Liege if one used the court as any kind of example of what the future would hold for my race. The Elders did as they wanted, but Our Liege held their collective leash. I might not have been too keen on his plan to throw away the timetable and start a war, but I wasn't thrilled with my other option either.

Thick, heavy shadows had moved into the large plaza, and the voices of the people had dulled. Night was fully born. To my surprise, Macaire hopped up on the stage. The nightwalker sat down in the chair in the center, balancing his left ankle on his right knee.

"There is a belief among our kind that you will take the open seat on the Coven," he casually began, motioning toward the seat that would have been Tabor's.

It was a fight not to clench my teeth. I was doomed to hear this question repeated until it drove me mad. "I'm not an Ancient," I said carefully.

"That is more a tradition than a law," he said with a dismissive wave of his hand. I remained silent, waiting for him to finally say what was on his mind, but I should have known it wouldn't be that easy. "The rumor has begun to pick up steam now following your return to Venice and your little display the other night with Gwen. You were never one to adopt pets. I also heard what you told Valerio the other night about choosing sides. One might think that you are starting to build a following." All this was said with a great amount of indifference and a frosting of boredom, but I wasn't fooled. There was something he wanted to hear from me, and he was hanging on my every word.

"My actions during the past several days have nothing to do with the Coven and everything to do with defeating the naturi. That is all," I said sharply, folding my arms over my stomach.

"Even Nicolai?"

A wide grin spread across my face, exposing my fangs. I was wondering when he would get around to what had happened with the harpies. "That was only a bit of fun."

"As you wish. But the question remains . . ."

"Part of being on the Coven means being able to defend your position, and I am not strong enough to do that," I hedged.

"This, coming from the one who tried to destroy all three members of the Coven at once just nights ago," he scoffed, putting his foot back on the stage with a hollow thud as he leaned forward.

"That was a stupid move on my part. I lost my temper and did not think," I conceded. My eyes fell to look at the cobblestone plaza, an appropriate stance of subservience. I wasn't sorry about the whole thing. In fact, if Danaus hadn't stopped me, I might have been able to pick off one of them before my head was ripped off.

"True, but you do have a nasty past with the naturi. It was understandable and I have forgiven you."

I wanted to tell him to choke on his forgiveness but thought it better not to antagonize Macaire, since we were currently getting along so well. I decided to wisely ignore the comment and push ahead.

"Regardless of recent events, I know that there is at least one Elder who would not support my ascension to the Coven," I cautiously hedged, curious as to his opinion. "And after Gwen's demise, I have succeeded in upsetting another. Even you called for my death last night."

Macaire sighed dramatically, shaking his head slightly as he chuckled to himself. "You do have a way with people," he murmured, sitting back in his chair. "I acted rashly last night. The development with Nicolai was unexpected. Elizabeth is not pleased with you, but you did warn Gwen. She had to fight her own fights. Elizabeth accepts that."

"And Jabari?" Danaus asked, as he came to stand beside me. He placed his hand on my shoulder, but I could not feel his presence in my thoughts. I was suddenly wary of his new interest. Could he honestly want me on the Coven? I wanted to shake my head to clear it of the thought. The only place Danaus wanted me was staked and headless. Yet the new thought stuck like a worm in an apple's core.

"No, Jabari means to have Mira's head after the door is closed," Macaire said sadly as he returned his ankle to his opposite knee.

"I can't defeat him." There was no emotion in that statement. It was a simple fact I had known for as long as I'd been a nightwalker. As long as Jabari could control me, it was impossible for me to destroy him. And even without that ability, Jabari was extremely old and powerful. I wasn't sure anyone could actually defeat him.

"I think you underestimate your powers." I opened my mouth to argue, but Macaire held up his hand, stopping the words in my throat. "If half of what Ms. Brooks described is true, I think you could easily triumph with some help from your hunter."

"But that would not be on my own."

"No one else would know that." His words escaped his thin lips as a whisper, a grin reappearing on his face.

"No one but you," I corrected. Nicely done. He had found a way to not only get rid of Our Liege, but Jabari as well. Unfortunately, for him, I wouldn't let myself be used by him. "I won't be a puppet for you."

"How is that possible? I'm sure you have guessed by now that I cannot use you the way Jabari has," Macaire said, with no small amount of bitterness.

"I won't do it."

"Loyal to the end," he sneered, his mouth twisting so that I saw a flash of fangs. "Even after all that he has done to you. Even though he means to end your life."

"If I defeat Jabari, it will be on my own. Besides, I don't want a seat on the Coven." I didn't want to have anything to do with the group. I just wanted to go home and forget about them all. Of course, if I did somehow manage to kill Jabari after we defeated the naturi, it would mean leaving two seats on the Coven open and Our Liege standing in danger. It would be all too easy for Macaire to take the throne and create his own Coven.

"If that is what you wish," he said softly. He rose from the chair and jumped back down to the ground. I turned my back to him and stepped away from Danaus as I let my gaze sweep over the square. Lights in the shops and houses threw down a mismatch of golden squares on the plaza. Within the walls I could feel the humans going about their tasks, making dinner and talking to their loved ones. Just a few yards away their lives hung in the balance, being decided by creatures they didn't even know existed.

"Are you prepared to leave?" Macaire inquired, returning my thoughts to the most urgent problem.

"A jet will be ready to leave by midnight. Where are we going?" I asked, swallowing some of the horror and anger that were still crowding in on my thoughts. This was why I had been brought to Venice. Not so much for my protection, but to make sure I understood what was at stake. To Macaire, I was being called in for one last mission on behalf of the Coven. When the time came, he expected me to kill Aurora as if she was some rogue nightwalker reeking havoc in a tiny town half forgotten by the world. However, it seemed Jabari wanted something else from me. He'd brought me there for the sole purpose of discovering the bargain, and wanted the naturi to fear me. But I had no idea what his ultimate goal was. After the horrid tale Macaire told, could Jabari truly want me to disrupt this bargain when it could stop two wars?

"Crete," Macaire replied to my question.

A bubble of laughter escaped me as I shook my head. Oh yes, it could get worse. I hadn't been to Crete since I escaped that wretched island as a young woman hoping to elude the mob screaming for my head. More than six hundred years had passed since I touched that land, and I had no desire to revisit it and the ghosts that waited for me.

Danaus stepped close. He didn't touch me, but I could feel the warm brush of his powers against my bare arms. It was like a soothing embrace. "And what exactly do you want me to accomplish?" I bit out when I finally got control of my emotions again.

"Allow the naturi to complete the sacrifice," Macaire replied. "The seal must be broken if they are going to be able to open the door."

"Then why send me?" I demanded, taking a step closer to him. His unique brand of logic was starting to drive me crazy. "Why send anyone? If we take on the naturi again, there's a good chance we're going to end up dead."

A grim smile graced his lips, and he stepped closer, in no way intimidated by me or my reputation. "Because I need you to kill Rowe. He's their leader. He has the best chance of stopping us when we attack Aurora. He also has the best chance of keeping the naturi organized. The remaining naturi will most likely scatter and die off without a strong leader like Aurora or Rowe."

"Do your new business partners know about this part of the plan?" I inquired sweetly.

"No, but they have been made aware that it is very likely many will be killed during this campaign."

I nodded and took a step backward, my shoulder bumping into Danaus's chest. Very neatly done. I had trouble believing the Coven would agree to anything that would allow the naturi to walk away and live in peace. The hope was that if we wiped out those who comprised their monarchy, it would eventually result in the complete destruction of their race.

"Will Jabari and Sadira be joining us in Crete?"

"No."

"Are any others being sent?"

"A few others have been summoned and sent on ahead. They will be arriving tonight. They have been instructed to stay away from the site of the sacrifice and remain hidden until you have contacted them with the plan of attack. Remember, you can't act until after they complete the sacrifice," he instructed.

I frowned, staring off into the darkness. I still didn't know what I was going to do. Not that I had that much choice in the matter. I was just the weapon. While I agreed that we would all be better off with Aurora dead, it was a great risk to allow the door to open. The only other wild card in this disaster waiting to happen was Danaus, and I couldn't even begin to fathom what his thoughts would be on the situation.

"You have to bring that hunter to heel, Mira," Macaire said, not caring that Danaus was standing right behind me. He had obviously been listening in again. I wanted to laugh. Danaus wasn't controlled by anyone, least of all me.

"I'll do what I can. Danaus does as he pleases," I warned.

"We can't afford mistakes."

"I know," I whispered, but when I looked up at him, I discovered that he was gone. Bastard. I hated it when the Ancients did things like that.

As I started to shuffle out of the plaza, I paused and looked back at the stage where the five chairs loomed over the large stone square. Jabari kept the balance on the Coven, protected the calm. If I killed him, there would be no stopping Macaire, except possibly Elizabeth. Unfortunately, I knew nothing about her. In my experience, she had always been like Tabor, a silent partner who enjoyed a little entertainment from time to time but kept to the shadows for the most part. Did she actually believe this scheme would work, or was she worried that she would be crushed like Tabor?

I wished I could talk to her for a few minutes; find out if she stood with Our Liege or Macaire. But after I played doctor with Gwen, I didn't foresee that conversation being particularly productive. I also feared she wouldn't be willing to speak for fear of being heard by Macaire. After seeing Jabari's willingness to shake up the agreement with the naturi last night, I knew he wasn't too keen on this plan either. That would also explain why Jabari remained in constant hiding. It meant neither Macaire nor the naturi could find him.

Sighing softly, I folded my arms over my chest. What was I left with? Let Jabari kill me when I finally grew useless so the balance on the Coven would remain. Not exactly my first choice. If I killed Jabari, would I have to take a seat, and spend the rest my existence butting heads with Macaire until he finally had me killed? Should I try to warn Our Liege? Other than the fact that he was trying to destroy us all now, he was an improvement over Macaire. Of course, the whole story could be a lie.

To add to it all, I had never met Our Liege. I didn't know where he was or how to contact him if I wanted to warn him. Not to mention that there was no telling if he would actually believe such a ridiculous tale. As it had been pointed out on more than one occasion, I wasn't the most popular creature among my kind.

But all of that was secondary to the greater, more immediate problem: What was I going to do when I got to Crete? The command to kill Rowe wasn't a particular problem. I couldn't see any benefit to leaving him alive, since he either wanted to use me or kill me. Yet, allowing them to complete the sacrifice would allow them to open the door at a later date. If there were any mistakes when the door was opened, all of the naturi could come rushing back into the world along with Aurora. A very bad thing.

On the other hand, if the door never opened and Aurora was never killed, then the naturi would never fulfill their promise to assassinate Our Liege. While I might not want him dead, I definitely didn't want him to send us into a war with all the other races just to stop the Great Awakening from happening ahead of schedule. Another very bad thing.

It seemed I only had two choices: war with the naturi or war with creatures I had once called friends.

Shuffling back toward the hotel with a silent Danaus, my mind a jumble of thoughts, I realized that I missed my original plan. It had been a good, solid plan.

1. Kill Nerian.
2. Find Jabari or some other Elder.
3. Tell Elder of the naturi plan.
4. Return home.

Oh, and kill Danaus.

But even that had gotten fouled up along the way. To hell with plans. In less than twenty-four hours I was going to be standing in the remains of a place I had once called home, surrounded by the naturi. I doubted another one of my brilliant plans was going to see me through. May the fates forgive me, what I needed was to talk to Jabari

TWENTY

My skin crawled. I stepped onto the tarmac of the runway at the Nikos Kazantzakis Airport in Heraklion and my stomach lurched and churned within me. Clenching my teeth, I paused at the foot of the stairs leading down from my jet and wrapped my arms around my middle as if I could protect myself from the memories that seemed to rise up from the dead in the back of my brain.

I might never have lived in this town—my family had lived in a small house to the south of Chania, a port town west of Heraklion—but I was home. After standing on the runway for less than a minute, the familiar smells were already teasing at my mind. The wind swept up from the south, running over the island before finally reaching me. The warm breeze had skimmed through the valley and over the mountain ranges that bisected the island, carrying with it the rich scents of Jerusalem sage, Cretan bee orchid, and dark Cretan ebony from where it clung to the cliffs down at Siteia. Mixed in was the heady scent of olives and lamb roasting on a spit. *Oh God, I was home.*

Since leaving Crete as a young woman, I'd never looked back, never set foot on her sandy shore. My mother died when I was twelve and my departure to the mainland left my father alone in Chania. Laying under the stars in Greece, I cursed myself more than once for leaving my father, wishing I'd had the strength and courage to convince him to come with me. I should have demanded that he leave Crete behind and join me on the mainland. There had been nothing left for either of us on this island. But he returned. He went back to the same house I'd been born in, the house he'd been born in, because it was the only place he could ever call home.

"Mira?"

"I'm fine," I snapped at Danaus before I even thought about what I was saying. Straightening my spine, I resettled my bag on my left shoulder and took a few steps away from the jet so he could finish descending the stairs. "Do we have company?"

"There's a vampire headed this way, but other than that, I don't sense anyone else in the area," Danaus replied, coming to stand beside me. His bag of clothes and weapons was slung over his right shoulder. None of his usual weapons were visible, but I knew he had something lethal within quick reach.

During the short flight, we'd discussed possible scenarios that could occur at the airport when we landed. The naturi would expect us to show up at the Palace of Knossos, after I had stopped them at Stonehenge just a few nights ago. We would continue to thwart their every move until they finally gave up or we were all dead. I wasn't in the mood to contemplate which would happen first.

The night air was surprisingly quiet. I had expected them to attack us as soon as we stepped off the plane. The flight would leave us stiff and somewhat disoriented as we struggled to acquaint ourselves with our new surrounding. It was one of their best opportunities. Of course, the prime time to attack was going to be sunrise, and I still needed to come up with a good plan for that eventuality. A part of me wished I could climb back on the plane and fly to Greece, where I could spend my daylight hours in peace. I didn't want to sleep here. Were there stories of me in Crete? Old folklore of a demon child born with hair the color of Hell's fires? Were the children taught to fear me like other nightmarish creatures? Damn, I wanted to be gone from this island and her memories!

Forcing myself to concentrate, I scanned the area and picked up two nightwalkers, but only one was approaching us. This was not what I had expected. There were only two in the entire region. The palace was not far from the city. The whole area should have been teeming with nightwalkers. Two vampires was all the Coven had thought to send? *Bastards.* Every last one of them.

The nightwalker slowly sauntered across the tarmac from the nearby hangar, her heels clacking loudly on the hard surface. A wealth of black hair spilled over her left shoulder and down her back while a secretive smile played across her mouth. As she approached, her eyes never left Danaus. I couldn't decide what had caught her attention: his dark attractive looks or any of the rumors that had leaked from Venice.

"Who sent you?" I demanded before she could draw enough of a breath to speak. I was already on edge about being in Crete, and we still needed to come up with a plan to defeat the naturi. We were running out of time. Our flight out of Venice had been delayed, and it was now nearly 4:00 A.M. Dawn was drawing close.

"The Coven," she said, her lips twisting in a frown as she looked me over. My clothes were rumpled and wrinkled, appearing as if I had wadded them up in a tight ball before bothering to put them on. I looked like a lost vagabond next to her neat cream-colored slacks and pale blue blouse.

"My name is Penelope. Macaire requested that I meet you and aid you against the naturi."

"Where are the others?" I barely resisted the urge to run my hands over my dress in a senseless attempt to smooth out some of the wrinkles.

"Hugo waits at a distance, watching to make sure we are safe," she replied.

"And that's all?"

"Yes."

I had a few choice words to say about Macaire and the rest of the Coven. This was ridiculous. There was no way Danaus, a pair of nightwalkers, and I could defeat all of the naturi lurking on this island. With odds like these, the naturi were going to have little trouble breaking the seal, and I was going to get staked in the process. However, before I could vent my growing irritation, Danaus spoke up.

"We need to get moving." His deep voice pushed aside my anger. He was right. We were easy targets standing out in the middle of the landing strip.

Without any further discussion, Penelope led the way out of the airport and to a taxi she had waiting. At one time or another all three of us looked over our respective shoulders. It hung unspoken in the air. The naturi were out there and they were watching us. I wasn't sure why they hadn't attacked yet, and a part of me didn't want to know the answer.

Penelope took us to a small square house she was renting. The exterior was painted white and the roof was flat. It looked like there might be some kind of awning covering part of the roof, offering tenants a place to rest at the end of the day and look out over the city. Even after all the centuries, Venetian influence was still visible in most of the buildings. For a time, Crete had been controlled by the Venetians, who left behind their form of art and architecture as a pervading influence. The cities such as Heraklion and Chania still glowed with the beauty of that dying city.

The interior of the house was the typical Cretan structure, with windows along only the front wall, while the other walls were covered in colorfully woven cloths and painted plates. A rounded archway led from the main living room into the kitchen and dining room, while the bedrooms were at the back of the house, off the kitchen. A window air-conditioning unit filled one of the few windows, growling softly as it put out a steady stream of cold air. The evening air had cooled to the low seventies, but the house retained most of the balmy afternoon heat.

It was a considerably larger house than the one I'd grown up in, and obviously more modern, but there were too many similarities in the design and the use of color. My hands trembled and a knot seemed to be permanently lodged in my throat.

Dropping my bag of clothes on the floor, I once again tried to push the little reminders that I was in Crete out of my mind and focus on why I had come to the island now. "How long have you been here?" I asked, trying to sound polite despite my raw nerves and growing frustration.

"I arrived on the island a few hours after sunset," Penelope replied. She was watching me warily from the opposite side of the room. She stood underneath the tall archway, her arms folded over her chest. "I have been living in Athens for almost a century and I come to Crete during the summer season for the tourists."

"Does this Hugo belong to you or did Macaire send him too?" I walked over to sofa that faced a corner fireplace made of small stones placed in an interesting mosaic. I leaned against the back of the sofa so I could face the nightwalker, crossing my left ankle over my right.

"Macaire sent him," Penelope replied. "Is it true that you stopped the naturi at Stonehenge?" She made no attempt to hide her skepticism when she fired back at me before I could continue to interrogate her.

I smiled at her and rubbed the knuckles of my right hand on the front of my dress as if shining my nails. Holding my hand out in front of me, my fingers instantly became engulfed in blue fire. "I've got a few tricks up my sleeve." As I had expected, Penelope took one step backward, but she quickly stopped herself and returned to the spot she'd been standing, determined not to be bullied.

"You're going to need it," Danaus remarked.

"How many?" I asked him, instantly extinguishing the fire. My fun was over. We needed to get back down to business. We needed to figure out exactly what we were up against and how to defeat them.

Danaus's power brushed past me as it moved out of the house and across the island. His eyes remained opened as he searched Crete, but his focus was not on anyone in the room. "A couple dozen. Less than England," he said.

I was surprised. They had staged an enormous attack on the Themis Compound, throwing more naturi at us than I thought had lived on the entire earth. Had we seriously depleted their numbers to the point that they could no longer risk such a significant assault, no matter the importance of the event? One could only hope.

"Where are they?"

Danaus's gaze focused as he leveled his blue eyes on me. "I don't know this island."

"Would a map help?" Penelope inquired in a voice so sweet it grated on my nerves.

"Yes," I snapped before Danaus could answer. "Find one."

After throwing a nasty look at me, Penelope stomped out of the room, disappearing into the kitchen as she headed toward the back of the house. A snort from Danaus caused me to look back over at him.

"What put you in such a mood?" he asked.

"I just want to get this done and get the hell out of here," I snarled, no longer even trying to control my temper.

To my surprise, his expression softened. It annoyed me. I didn't want to see sympathy or pity from the hunter. I wanted him angry or annoyed or any of the other moods I had grown accustomed to seeing on his face. A moment later I felt a faint touch in my brain, like a hand feeling blindly about in the darkness.

Maybe it's time you faced your past. The sound of Danaus's thoughts echoed in my mind. He was getting too good at speaking to me telepathically. Just over twenty-four hours had passed since he had last pushed his powers into me, but our connection grew stronger each time he did it.

To hell with my past. This isn't the time to go all Freudian on me. We find the naturi and stop them. That's it, I mentally flung back at him.

Danaus didn't reply, but I could feel him laughing at me, some silent chuckle rumbling through his mind and slipping into mine.

But the feeling ceased at the sound of the front doorknob turning. A knife seemed to magically appear in Danaus's hand as he twisted around to face whoever was entering the house. I stood, my knees slightly bent, ready for anything. We both scanned the house at the same time to find the other nightwalker. However, neither of us relaxed when he stepped into the room with hands up and palms out and open.

Hugo was built like a freaking refrigerator. The nightwalker could have caused a lunar eclipse if he happened to step in front of the moon. His shoulders were wide, tapering down to a narrow waist and hips before splitting into legs that resembled tree trunks. He could have easily palmed a basketball with one large hand. I would have taken a step backward if my left thigh wasn't already pressed against the back of the pale yellow sofa. I'd never seen a vampire as big as Hugo. The only relief I felt was the fact that he wasn't very old; less than a century.

"Hugo?" I asked in a hard voice.

"*Ja,*" he grunted, lowering his hands.

A curse rose up the back of my throat but I swallowed it down again. I spoke only a sprinkling of German and it had been a long time since I had last tried. "*Sprechen Sie Englisch?*"

"*Ja,*" he replied, to my immediate relief. "Mira?"

"*Ja,*" I said, trying to match his low growl and not quite pulling it off. I guess I needed a set.

"Hunter." Hugo's mouth twisted into a sneer as he looked over at Danaus.

"I'm glad we've got the introductions out of the way. Now, if we can get back to business, we—"

The sound of Penelope's heels clicking across the floor as she returned to the kitchen halted me. She opened what appeared to be a travel guide for the island of Crete and unfolded a colorful map from the back.

"Have either of you seen or encountered the naturi since coming to the island?" I asked as I walked over to where she'd spread the map out on the table.

"No, but neither of us has been on the island that long," Penelope said, shaking her head, her black hair flowing down around her face, nearly blocking her eyes. For the first time since meeting her, I saw a flicker of fear cross her face.

"Danaus," I called, looking over my shoulder at the hunter so I didn't have to look at Penelope any longer. I put my finger over Heraklion, which was on the northeastern part of the island. "This is where we are. Where are the naturi hiding? In the city or farther away?"

He moved behind me so he could see the map, but at the same time he didn't have his back completely turned toward Hugo. I didn't particularly want to turn my back to the enormous vampire either, but if Hugo knew that I was unnerved by his great hulking mass, he'd never follow my orders. And right now I needed him to follow me without question.

Once again Danaus's powers flowed out of his body, passing

through me like a warm wind, threatening to sweep my soul out of my body and drag it across the entire island. "Farther away," he murmured. "None are in the city right now."

"He—He can sense them?" Penelope asked, her voice wavering.

"Mmmm . . . he knows all kinds of nifty tricks." A dark smile lifted the corners of my mouth. The nightwalker took a step back from the table, the fingers of her left hand curling into a fist. She glanced over her shoulder at Hugo, but I didn't catch his expression. Danaus had lifted his right hand, moving it from Heraklion toward the west.

"They're all gathered in one place," he continued, his hand hovering over a relatively broad part of the island.

I leaned in close to read the tiny print on the map. "Can you get a sense of the region? Does it have a green feel? Mountainous?"

"Mira, my powers aren't that exact," he bit out as his hand moved back a little, toward the west. "I don't sense the earth, just the naturi."

"What about humans?" Penelope inquired, taking a tentative step closer again. "If they are in the Amari Valley, there are other villages there. People would be close to the naturi."

"No, there are no humans. Not for a good distance."

"Then they are on Mount Idi," I said, straightening from where I was bent over the table. I looked up at Penelope as she straightened as well, a frown flattening her full lips into a thin line.

"That entire area is dotted with caves," she stated, waving one hand over that part of the map. "The naturi could be hiding anywhere, and it would take us several nights to flush them all out."

"We won't need to flush them out," I said. "They'll be at the Palace of Knossos in two nights."

"You want us to wait for two nights and then take on all the naturi at once?" Hugo asked from where he was still standing in the living room. "I was told that I was to kill a naturi called Rowe. How am I to get to him if he is surrounded by his brethren? There are only four of us."

Hugo's German accent was incredibly thick and it wasn't helped by his growing anger. It had actually taken me a couple seconds to figure out what he was saying.

"Wait! You mean, this is it? No one else is coming?" Penelope shouted, slamming both her open palms on the table. "I never agreed to a suicide mission. The tales of the battle at Machu Picchu told of hundreds of nightwalkers. Why are we the only ones?"

"Don't know. You piss off Macaire or the rest of the Coven recently?" I asked. I was about to say more but my cell phone started ringing, stunning everyone into silence. Stepping away from the rest of the group and walking into the living room, I hiked up my dress and got my phone from where it was strapped to my leg. No pockets.

The little LCD screen revealed that it was my home phone number back in Savannah. There were only a couple of people who could be calling me from that number. "Who is it?" I demanded.

"Gabriel said you wanted me to call," replied a soft voice that instantly made my hands begin to tremble in relief. It was Tristan. He was awake and safe. For once, something had gone right.

I turned my back to the group and hunched my shoulders as if I could disappear from their view. I even went so far as to lower my voice, though I knew they could all clearly hear me. It didn't matter. I needed this private moment with Tristan to settle my own nerves.

"Are you okay? Did Gabriel show you around?" I asked, cringing at my own questions. I sounded like a worried, overprotective mother. I sounded like Sadira.

"He said he would after I called you. Are you still in Venice? What about the naturi? I can still—"

"No, I'm in Crete," I interrupted, and instantly wished I hadn't used such a harsh tone. "We should have this all cleaned up in a few nights. I'll be home in three or four nights, and then we can . . . find a more . . . permanent arrangement for you."

A heavy silence filled the air. I couldn't guess at what he was thinking. He either doubted that I would be back at all or was insulted by the idea that I was already looking to unload him like a pile of unwanted baggage. I had never wanted a family for this very reason. I didn't want anyone underfoot and didn't know what to do with someone once he was in my life.

"I should let you go," Tristan murmured.

"Wait! I . . . If you don't hear from me within the next week, I . . . I want to you seek out a nightwalker called Knox. He . . . sort of helps me out and . . ." I stumbled awkwardly. It was like telling my next of kin where to find my will. I had no provisions set aside, no preparations made for Tristan should something happen to me. He would be on his own in a foreign country. But at least for now he'd be away from Sadira and the Coven.

"I understand. I'll be fine. Take care of Rowe," he said, then hung up before I could say anything truly idiotic.

After returning the phone to its place on my leg, I turned back around to find everyone staring at me. Hugo looked a little stunned, while Penelope was outright smug. On the other hand, Danaus's expression was blank. But then, he knew who had called. He knew why Tristan was half a world away.

"As I was saying," I stated, trying to ignore the blush that I was sure stained my cheekbones, "we don't need anyone else. The naturi numbers are fewer. We're chipping away at their ranks and we'll continue to do so until we finally get to Rowe."

"But—"

"We'll plan a series of incursions for tomorrow night based on their location," I pressed on, cutting off Hugo before he could argue. "We can try to wipe them out before the new moon."

"I can do some scouting during the day," Danaus offered. I opened my mouth to argue when my phone rang again.

"By the gods, Mira," sneered Penelope. "Hire a babysitter."

I turned my back to her, refusing to comment as I grabbed my phone. However, the number was different this time, not one I remembered seeing before. Few had my number, and those who did knew to only call in an emergency.

"Who is this?" I demanded.

"Mira?" answered a startled voice. "This is James. James Parker. We met a few days . . . er . . . nights ago. I'm with Themis."

"Yes, I remember you, James," I said as I turned to look at the only other Themis member in the room. I didn't have to ask how James had gotten my number. Danaus had used my phone to call him days ago. "I'm a little busy right now."

"Actually, I'm looking for Danaus. You see, we're here and we need to know where—"

"What?" I exclaimed, my thoughts coming to a screeching halt. "What do you mean 'here'? Where's 'here'? And who's this 'we'?" That's when I felt it. The first tear in the night. We had less than an hour before sunrise and I still needed a safe place against the daylight and the humans. "Never mind." Stalking across the room, I slapped the phone into Danaus's open hand.

Leaning against the wall with my arms crossed over my chest, I watched as he slowly paced away from us. The hunter quickly gave his assistant instructions to get settled in a hotel and told him he would go there after sunrise. We were all eavesdropping on the conversation. There was no such thing as privacy when a nightwalker was in the room.

I was shocked to hear that James had traveled to Heraklion with the intention of helping Danaus. We had contacted him before leaving Venice, wanting Themis to confirm that Crete would be the next location of the sacrifice, since I didn't trust the Coven to tell the truth. It was part of the reason we had delayed our flight, waiting for the little research society to hear from all its field operatives at the twelve locations.

But I was speechless when James revealed that Ryan had come to Crete as well. The gold-eyed warlock was trouble. I might have temporarily escaped the scheming and torture of the Coven, but I was now faced with an extremely powerful human with an agenda I had yet to understand.

"What's this Themis?" Penelope asked softly, taking a couple steps closer to me.

"The help you were looking for." My gaze returned to Danaus as he ended the call. I'd been with the hunter every moment since we had spoken with Macaire, heard both of his conversations with James. He had not yet spoken of the Coven's pact with the naturi. But he was now planning to meet with Ryan without me.

Will you tell him? I asked when his fingers brushed against my hand as he returned my phone.

I have to.

Don't. Not yet. Telling him will only start a war.

And if I don't, we could all be in danger, he argued, frowning at me. However, the look in his eyes told me a different story. He was worried and unsure. I could see it, and feel the emotions beating between us.

Just give me one more night.

Why?

I need more time to think. There has to be a better way. Please.

Postponing won't help us.

It buys us one more night without war among all the races. Isn't it enough that we're fighting the naturi?

After a moment, Danaus softly grunted and walked away from me. I had bought one more night. I trusted him to keep his word, even though he had not actually spoken at all. Chaos was swirling around us and we needed to tread carefully if we had any hope of protecting what we had all come to value in this world. And I had a dark suspicion that I would get only one shot at this.

TWENTY-ONE

No one was happy the next night when we finally left Ryan's hotel. Danaus didn't want me alone with Ryan; Ryan didn't want Danaus paired with Penelope; Penelope didn't want to be left alone with the hunter; and James didn't want to be left behind at the hotel. Only Hugo wasn't verbally complaining, but by his expression, I could tell he didn't want to go at all. By the time the bickering stopped, I was ready to leave them all behind. However, I wasn't that insane just yet.

After waiting for Ryan to change from his dress slacks into a pair of worn blue jeans, the warlock and I set out in a tiny taxi to the Palace of Knossos. Danaus had already confirmed that the naturi left the mountains and were approaching the city. However, due to his lack of familiarity with the area, he couldn't tell whether they had arrived yet at the Minoan ruins.

I rubbed my eyes, trying to push aside some of the tension humming through me. I didn't feel rested. Crete was eating away at my peace of mind. My sleep had been filled with nightmares of running from an angry mob, my father fighting to save me, only to be killed himself. To add to it, I knew very little about the warlock who sat beside me. We had met only a few nights earlier at the Themis Compound back in England. Sure, we were technically on the same side now, but he'd ordered Danaus to kill me some time ago. I wasn't completely confident that the order had merely been put on hold until this little naturi mess was cleaned up.

I was more than a little curious to discover why Ryan had come to Heraklion himself. Of course, from what I'd gathered during my brief visit to the Compound, Themis wasn't exactly crawling with magic users. He might have been the only one with enough power and skill to be of real aid—not that this made me feel any better. But for now I had a more pressing questions beating against the back of my brain.

"What possessed you to bring James along?" I asked him, trying not to sound too snide.

"Whatever do you mean?" Ryan asked, positively oozing faux innocence. His perpetual smile grew on his lips, mocking me.

"He's not like us. You're putting his life in danger," I bit out in a low voice. There was no doubt that the taxi driver could hear us; I was just hoping his English wasn't that good. Or at the very least, that he thought we were a pair of crazy tourists. "He doesn't need to be here."

"That's surprisingly sweet of you, Mira," Ryan said, his facade of innocence never wavering. "I wouldn't have expected that."

"Oh, shove it, Ryan!" I snarled, flashing my clenched teeth at him. "You're not this dense."

The smile remained on his lean, ageless face, but it faded from his golden eyes as they danced over my features. He watched me with a frightening intensity before he finally drew in a breath to speak. "I brought him for three different reasons. First, he is the assistant to both Danaus and me. He will be aiding us in any matters that we are unable to address while we are looking into our current problem."

It was a reason. I didn't think it was a particularly good reason. Charlotte Godwin was my human assistant back in Savannah and she took care of the day-to-day problems of managing my financial interests and seeing to my travel arrangements—things that generally needed to be addressed during the daylight hours.

"Second, James has been with Themis for several years," Ryan continued, "but he has had very little field experience. I thought this would be a good opportunity."

"You could have started him out on something a little less dangerous," I criticized, shaking my head at him. As we stopped at an intersection, I scooted forward in my seat so I could address the taxi driver. "How far to Knossos?" I inquired in broken Cretan Greek. Despite all the years I'd been gone, my knowledge of the language hadn't faded from my brain, as I would have expected. However, my dialect was archaic. It was unlikely anyone would be able to understand me. After listening to others, however, I'd picked up enough to get by. Undoubtedly, I sounded like a tourist.

"Less than a kilometer," he said, glancing over his shoulder at me. He was an older gentleman with white hair and a lined face weathered by time and the sun.

"Let us out here," I said, pulling a few euros out of the front pocket of my leather pants. I had converted the last of my Egyptian pounds into euros at the Cipriani before Danaus and I flew out. I didn't have much on me but figured it would get me through the next couple of nights. Beyond that, I had to survive our next encounter with the naturi before I worried about my cash flow.

The driver seemed about to argue, but swallowed his comment when he heard Ryan already getting out of the car. He hadn't been too sure about us heading to the palace at this late hour, but with a slight mental push, I managed to convince him to take us anyway.

We had left the city of Heraklion behind and entered into the hilly countryside filled with vineyards and olive orchards. From a quick scan of the region, I was relieved to find very few humans in the area. I didn't have to worry too much about being discovered or anyone stumbling into a deadly battle. The problem with many of the so-called holy sites was that they were now major tourist attractions, leaving the area thickly surrounded by shops, restaurants, and hotels for weary travelers burdened with far too much cash.

Ryan and I silently waited in the darkness until we saw the taxi driver head back toward Heraklion and the relative safety of the city before we turned and headed down the empty lane toward the Minoan ruins. Danaus and Penelope had taken a taxi ten minutes before us, to head south of the palace before getting out and walking back toward the ruins. Hugo took a separate cab and would be arriving at the palace from the east. If we couldn't stop them, our goal was to at least herd the naturi back toward the caves of Mount Idi and away from any of the large cities and towns in the immediate area. It was a temporary solution at best if we couldn't destroy them all.

For the first time since I'd become a nightwalker, the darkness felt like a physical weight pressing on my shoulders, rather than the soothing presence it had always been. Dark violent memories of fear and hatred lurked behind every tree. My mother's death, the men I killed—all ghosts waiting for a moment of weakness before they would strike. With my fists clenched at my side, I struggled to stay focused on the task that loomed before me and the potential adversary beside me.

"You said there were three reasons for bringing James," I said to Ryan, resuming our earlier conversation from the car after we'd walked in the dark for a few minutes. "What was the third reason?"

He remained silent for a long time, until I was sure he wasn't going to tell me at all. He drew in a deep breath and his hands stopped swinging loosely at his sides. "Something has happened, and James—being the responsible fellow that he is—feels he should be the one to tell you."

"Why do I get the feeling that you don't want him to tell me?"

"At the very least, I'd rather he not tell you in person. I fear that you're the type to shoot the messenger," Ryan stated, cocking his head to the side as he looked down at me.

"I didn't kill Danaus when he told me of the naturi. I would think that would be proof enough." I shoved my hands in my back pockets, my eyes sweeping away from the warlock beside me to the rows of trees and hills that rose up around the winding road. I had the Browning that Danaus had given me in a holster at my lower back, and I was ready if anything so much as twitched. The only one in the immediate area who I could sense was Ryan, and it was driving me crazy. The air was still, redolent of the earth and wildflowers. It felt as if the world was holding its breath in anticipation of the inevitable battle.

"You needed Danaus alive," Ryan countered. "Besides, I'm not entirely sure you could kill him."

I bit back the first sharp comment that rose to mind and pushed on. He was trying to distract me, but there was no reason to jump at the bait. "Are you going to tell me or do I have to drag it out of James later tonight?"

"Michael is missing," Ryan softly said.

I sighed softly, the sound barely rising above the scuff of my boots along some loose gravel on the road. "Michael isn't missing. He's dead."

"Yes, I know. Gabriel told us." Ryan stopped walking and I looked up at him. The tall man's white hair framed his narrow face, creating a strange outline to the shadows that filled the hollows of his cheeks. "We can't find his body."

My temper instantly flared and I took a step toward him. It was a struggle to keep my hands from closing around his throat, but I succeeded. There was a tingle of magic in the air coming from my powerful companion, and I had no doubt that he could send my flying across the road without blinking an eye.

But this horrible news diminished the danger of the warlock. Michael had been one of my guardian angels for several years. He'd been an able, dedicated bodyguard; a sweet, gentle man; and a considerate lover. He had watched over me during my daylight hours and stood with me against the naturi, who physically took his life. Recently, I realized that I'd been slowly stealing his life on another level, and the naturi had stolen away my chance to ever make it up to him.

But now this? Lost? A dead body lost?

"What do you mean? The night of the attack, I left him in the front hall. What did you do with him?" I shouted, not caring if I caught the attention of every naturi in the area. Michael deserved better than this. I needed to take him home where he could finally rest.

"We couldn't find him. I met him. James knew him. Gabriel was there. We searched every inch of the manor and all the area surrounding the Compound. He's not there," Ryan calmly said. He laid his large hands over my shoulders, squeezing lightly. The small comfort eased some of the tension from them, but I couldn't unclench my jaw.

"Who?" I whispered in a choked voice. "Who has him?"

"Mira . . ." Ryan paused again and licked his dry lips. "The naturi were all over the first floor of the manor—"

"No!" I jerked away from him, walking to the other side of the road while shaking my head in denial. My hands were shaking. The very idea of any naturi touching Michael's lifeless body fueled a mindless, irrational fire within me. "Absolutely not! No! They don't need his body. Why would they do it?"

"To get at you."

"No, I don't believe you. You have him."

"Why? So I can point the finger at the naturi and get you to hate them more?" he argued, his voice growing firmer. "That's impossible. According to Danaus, your hatred of the naturi is boundless and eternal. There's nothing I could do to increase that."

I paced back across the road toward Ryan, my fingers clenched into shaking fists. The urge to set the surrounding fields on fire was overwhelming, like a boiling kettle of water begging to blow off some of the steam before it overflows. "Why?" I growled.

"I don't know who has Michael, but it doesn't matter. As you said, he's dead. There's nothing they can do to him now."

Yes, logic said that Michael was in a better place and that his empty body was not important. But I needed this. I needed to bury him in the plot of land that had been put aside for my bodyguards. During my century in the United States, I had survived a few other bodyguards and seen to their burial since they had no other family. Michael belonged with them and me, back home in Savannah. In the one place where I could watch over him.

Turning away from Ryan, I resumed our walk toward the palace. He fell into step beside me after a couple seconds. I didn't know whether I believed him. To me, it didn't make sense for either Themis or the naturi to take Michael, but I knew it would come back to haunt me someday.

We had been walking uphill and could now see the valley spread out around us, dotted with farms and vineyards off in the distance. As the road curved to the left, the line of trees parted before us, revealing the first glimpse of the ruins of the palace. From what I could see, it was enormous, as if a city unto itself.

But something felt off. A few minutes later my steps slowed as we approached the Minoan ruins. I held my right hand out before me with my palm open. There was an energy growing in the air, unlike the tingling electric feel coming off of Ryan. This was different; hot and thick, as if it were a living thing growing in stature and substance.

"Can you feel that?" I whispered, my dragging feet finally drawing to a stop. I held up both hands before my body, feeling the air as if pressing against a solid creature, though the area was empty before me.

"Yes, an energy," he replied. He stood beside me, his left hand slowly waving through the air before him. "Did you feel this at Stonehenge?"

Did I feel this at Stonehenge? When I'd arrived at the ancient location, my body was still wracked with pain from Danaus stealing away my abilities and body for his own purposes. I couldn't stand and every inch of me had screamed in agony. There had been a layer of pain in the air, but my senses were so clouded that I wasn't sure which of the feelings was related to Stonehenge and the swell of power from the earth.

"I'm not sure. I think so," I hedged, finally forcing my feet to resume their steady approach. My hand fell back to my side, where I anxiously flexed my fingers a few times as if to loosen the muscles. The power in the air was building. "Can you tell if the energy will peak tonight or tomorrow night?" I asked, glancing over at him.

"No idea." He shrugged his wide, narrow shoulders before looking down at me. "I'm not an earth user."

Frowning, I paused before a set of cracked and crumbling stairs that led up to the palace. There were essentially two types of magic: earth and soul, which was also referred to as blood magic. Most magic users dabbled in both, but eventually everyone specialized in one side or the other. Both sides could do the same things, but each magic style had its own requirements and limitations.

And then there was Rowe. As a naturi, he was naturally a strong earth magic user, but he seemed equally adept at weaving blood magic, given that he'd gone to the trouble of arranging a harvest in Egypt less than a week ago. It would have been so much easier if the naturi stuck to earth magic and the bori stuck to blood magic. Then a person would know exactly where she stood when the shit hit the fan.

With one foot on the stairs, I reached out and scanned the area. Danaus and Penelope were roughly south of us, slowly approaching, while Hugo was in position to the east. Unfortunately, out of the five of us, only Danaus could sense the naturi. We were waiting for him to fire a shot to signal that they were here if no one else reacted first.

Creeping to the top of the staircase, I paused, squatting down, pressing my hands against the worn stones. The palace was mostly raised above the hill upon which it stood. If I walked onto the ruins, I would stand out as an easy target for any of the naturi. Despite the darkness of the night, I could easily see within the thick shadows. The only forms I could pick out were columns and bits of broken stone. The area appeared deserted, but I knew better.

I rolled my shoulders once and clenched my teeth. The push of the power in the area had grown a little stronger as I climbed the stairs. A throbbing had started in my temples and I could feel pressure building at the base of my skull. For a whole new reason, I had begun to hope that this battle wouldn't take too long. The pain was starting to become a distraction, and I wasn't sure how it would affect my ability to control my powers.

Ryan eased down so he was sitting opposite me on the stairs, his body held low to the ground. I wasn't sure how good his eyesight was in the pitch-black, but I assumed he knew a spell or two to make it better than the average human.

"Has Danaus told you about Rowe?" I whispered, drawing the white-haired warlock's attention back to my face. He nodded, so I continued to pick away at the thought that was nagging at me. How often would I find myself in the company of an ancient warlock with oodles of magic information crammed into his brain? "He's different. Scarred. Dark hair, dark eyes. Unlike the other naturi. It's from the magic?"

Ryan seemed to hesitate a moment before he nodded. "He's tainting the magic so it's tainting him," he finally replied in a low voice. "He's using the power of the earth to fuel blood spells."

I stared at him for a long minute in silence, taking in his snow white hair and gold eyes, features I'd never seen on another human being in all my six hundred years, before finally voicing the thought we both knew was floating through my head. "The opposite of what you've done. You've tainted earth spells by fueling them with blood magic."

The perpetual smile that seemed to haunt Ryan's face melted

away and his expression became completely unreadable. There were
no laws against what he and Rowe were doing. However, it was my
understanding that the mixing of styles was dangerous and frowned
upon.

"This isn't the time for this conversation," Ryan stated in chilled
tones.

"Actually, it is," I corrected, smiling broadly at him. I leaned
closer and lightly laid my hand over his wrist. "You know earth
spells. You've got an abundance of power flowing up from the earth
here. Use it. Cast something here and now. Anything."

He pulled back, his mouth finally slipping into a frown. "The
earth spells I know aren't to be used lightly, and my strength isn't in
using power from the earth. It would be too dangerous."

"More dangerous than allowing the naturi to complete their sacrifice here tomorrow night?" I demanded, my voice briefly spiking
higher. "If you cast something here now, won't it siphon off some of
the power? Couldn't it disrupt their ability to break the seal?"

The warlock looked away from me, staring off across the ruins.
His brow was furrowed in thought as he turned over my argument.
My understanding of how magic worked was pretty rudimentary, but
the logic seemed to fit. If we used the magic here before the naturi, the
power from the earth would dissipate and move on to the next location. It was extremely unlikely that the naturi would be able to find the
next location before the new moon tomorrow night. They would have
to wait until the Fall equinox more than a month away. That would
give us ample time to hunt down Rowe and destroy him.

"There's another problem," Ryan stated after a couple minutes.
"Regardless of which earth spell I cast, I'd have to start it with blood
magic and then switch to earth magic."

"Can you do that?" I asked, earning a very smug smile as laughter danced in his narrowed eyes. I rolled my own eyes in response.
"So what's the problem?"

"I don't use my own soul to fuel my magic," he admitted, his
smile never wavering.

Of course not. That kind of nonsense was for the novices. Why
waste the energy from your own soul when you could drain anyone
else's energy that happened to be near you? No wonder he was so
comfortable as the head of Themis. Not only was he tapped into an
excellent source of information regarding all the other races, but
he was constantly surrounded by an ample source of energy. Much
like nightwalkers, blood warlocks always stuck close to cities, while
the few earth witches in the world preferred wooded regions. You

have to stick close to your food source. Or in the case of magic users, your fuel source.

"I repeat: What's the problem?"

"No humans nearby."

It was on the tip of my tongue to remind him that Danaus was not far, but I swallowed the hunter's name. We both knew that Danaus wasn't entirely human, though I wondered if Ryan was aware that Danaus had some kind of bori connection. Obviously, the hunter was off limits, which was probably best for everyone involved.

"Can you use a nightwalker?" I asked. I wasn't exactly comfortable with the idea of Ryan highjacking some of the energy that kept me alive, but I was more afraid of facing the naturi here in another battle to protect the seal.

"I can't. You don't have a s—"

"That's bullshit and you know it," I hissed, tightening my grip on his wrist. "Nightwalkers have souls. Besides, we're pure blood magic. It's how we stay alive."

He moved his arm, twisting it so I would release him. "I can try. I've never done this so I can't be sure—"

"I'll be fine," I said, cutting him off. Turning my attention back to the ruins, I looked over the area, searching for any sign of the naturi. It remained quiet, with only the sound of the wind lightly rustling the leaves in the surrounding trees. Before we moved, I mentally reached out and told Penelope and Hugo what our plans were. They would keep us covered while Ryan cast his spell.

I pushed off the ground with both hands, climbed the last couple stairs, and walked across the stone floor, heading deeper into the ruins. Since Danaus had yet to fire a single shot, Ryan and I assumed there wasn't a naturi in the actual ruins. Of course, I checked more than once to make sure that Danaus was still alive and conscious. Not that I thought Penelope could kill Danaus, but I definitely didn't trust her. I needed the hunter alive much more than I needed her at that moment.

"Where are we going?" Ryan whispered, leaning close to me as he spoke. It seemed silly to me. We were completely out in the open, easy targets. If the naturi couldn't see us, I certainly wasn't going to worry about them hearing us. Of course, when I replied, I whispered too. Some things defy logic when fear is twisting like a knot in your stomach.

"There's a large courtyard in the center of the palace. I'm willing to bet the magic is strongest there," I replied. Danaus and I had spent most of the flight to Crete studying maps of the Palace of Knossos.

There was more than one place the naturi could use for the site of the sacrifice, which might be problematic with only five of us there. It would be better if we just got rid of the magic now and ruined their plans.

Pausing to edge around the corner of one of the few walls that was still standing, I saw Ryan closely examining the faint mural that had survived the centuries. Even in the darkness I could tell that the colors were relatively crisp despite the wear of the ages. I wished I could have taken the time to wander the ruins and marvel at what had obviously been an amazing structure. But for now the naturi dominated my thoughts.

"Mira," he said, laying his hand on my shoulder before I could walk away from the wall. "Those old myths about the labyrinth . . ."

"The labyrinth was supposedly found under the palace."

"And the minotaur?"

One of my eyebrows popped up in surprise at his question. I honestly couldn't tell if he was serious or joking. The minotaur? The half-man, half-bull creature that was supposed to be held captive in the center of the maze.

"They made the lycanthropes," Ryan reminded me when the silence had stretched for longer than he was comfortable.

"That has never been proven," I murmured, shaking my head. I had trouble accepting that supposed myth surrounding the lycans and the naturi because there was a second half to it that I found even more distasteful, which had to do with the origins of my own race. "There's no such thing as the minotaur. Just a fanciful human tale."

We continued on for another couple minutes before we came to a large clearing in the center of the palace. The space was rectangular, its edges marked off by broken rocks from what had been the walls, columns, and roof of the building centuries ago. I had heard old tales of the Palace of Knossos when I was growing up in Chania, but we never traveled far from our home.

"Do you have a spell in mind?" I asked, turning my back to Ryan as he stood in the center of the clearing. The power in the air was incredible, pushing against me as if it could force its way through my skin and into my organs. But at the same time, the energy felt thick and heavy. The very molecules felt too large to sink into me, but it didn't keep them from trying.

"Yes," he replied. Even his voice seemed more muffled here, as if the sound was fighting its way through energy. "I'm going to create a storm."

I suddenly spun around to face the warlock, my mouth falling open at his announcement. "Isn't that a rather big spell? With this much power in the air, you could destroy half the island, not to mention us."

"Actually, if I'm not extremely careful, I could destroy not only this island, but several others in the area," he said. His voice was calm and even, as if the notion of ending countless lives didn't ruffle his feathers in the least. "This is what you wanted."

"I want you to cast a spell, not cause mass destruction. Why such a big spell?" I might not have known much about magic, but I did know that weather spells were extremely complicated and took a great deal of energy. Very few could even cast them, and of those that could, even fewer had the ability to control them once they were started.

"I told you, I'm not an earth user. I don't know a lot of earth spells and the few I do know are very dangerous. Do you want me to do this?" he demanded. Both his hands were raised out to his sides, his palms facing out. It was as if he were about to grab the air around him and pull it in toward his body.

To my surprise, I hesitated only a moment. This was stupid. This was dangerous. And this might be our only chance to stop the naturi in Crete. If we could stop them tonight, I thought, we could spend the next few weeks hunting down Rowe, our main target.

"Do it."

Ryan drew in a deep, cleansing breath while his eyes fell shut. I was turning my back toward him again when a gunshot rang out. Damn it. We had company. The warlock was of no use to me now. He couldn't be distracted from the complicated spell he had committed himself to, and I needed to protect him no matter what.

Pulling the gun from the holster at the small of my back, I turned slowly around, holding the weapon before me with both hands as I scanned the area. I didn't see or hear anything yet. A second shot was fired, the bullet pinging off a stone behind me.

My stomach lurched and I spun around in time to see a naturi running toward me with a short sword raised above his head. I squeezed off three rounds before I finally managed to lodge a bullet in his chest. The naturi jerked at the impact before stumbling over some broken rocks, sending him to his hands and knees. With a loud clatter, the sword hit the ground while the naturi softly groaned.

A smile drifted across my lips, and then I was unexpectedly knocked to my knees. My arms fell and the gun almost slipped from my numb fingers. Nothing had hit me. From my back came a tugging sensation, as if something within me had been snagged or caught. My vision blurred and fatigue weighed on my shoulders.

Ryan had succeeded in tapping into my energy. I doubted that most humans would have even detected it, maybe only paused and yawned at the sudden wave of fatigue and then gone on with their day. However, my existence was pure soul energy, I could no longer generate my own, which was why I had to feed on the blood of others. If Ryan didn't release me soon, I would need to either feed or sleep. Not an option at the moment. As much as I wanted to drain the moaning naturi dry, their blood was poisonous to all nightwalkers.

A scrape of stone and a new voice jerked my attention back from my own fatigue. A second naturi knelt next to the one I had shot only seconds ago. With her right hand, she was helping him to sit up, while still holding a sword in her left.

I pushed to my feet at the same time she rose to hers. Gritting my teeth, I prepared to attack when I saw Danaus and Penelope appear out of the shadows to my right. They had finally come to join in the fun. I realized then that the naturi were attacking from the east. They had circled around to surprise us. But that also meant they had either slipped by Hugo undetected or silently killed the nightwalker before reaching the palace. Unfortunately, we couldn't go looking for him until the naturi were taken care of.

Turning back to Ryan, I found the warlock standing where I'd left him. His hands were stretched above his head, reaching toward the heavens he sought to control. His lips were moving quickly but I couldn't hear anything he was saying. The wind had picked up, dropping the temperature in the area several degrees. Overhead, dark thick clouds churned in the formerly clear sky, blotting out the stars. A massive storm was forming.

The weight on my shoulders suddenly lifted and the fatigue slipped away like a wave pulling back out to sea. Ryan had released my energy and started to use the earth energy that was rising up from beneath our feet. The warlock grunted, drawing my gaze back to him. Lines of strain deepened in his face. Above him, his long fingers trembled. I wanted to ask him if he was okay but knew better than to distract him. Regardless of what his answer would have been, there was no turning back now.

A whisper of cloth, a prickling of the hairs on the back of my neck—they were my only warning. Turning on my left heel, I spun around, raising the gun in both hands at the same time. I unloaded four shots in the naturi before he finally fell to the ground dead. Clenching my teeth, I hurried over and picked up the short sword he'd dropped.

Standing over the dead naturi, I took an extra moment to cut off its head. No reason to take silly chances. I wasn't a very good shot with a gun. Strangely, this naturi had been from the earth clan. From my experience, they weren't melee fighters. That was left to members of the animal clan. The earth clan preferred to use magic, letting the earth and plants do the fighting for them.

The naturi weren't using magic. Was it for fear of tapping into the earth magic that permeated the area? A smile lifted my lips as I turned back around to where Danaus and Penelope were battling four naturi. My guess could prove to be right.

Large drops of ice cold rain started to fall from the sky, landing on my head like small pebbles and instantly soaking into my T-shirt. A flash of lightning forked through the sky, darting from one black mass to the next before being followed by a loud bang of thunder. The storm was still building.

The wind gusted, blowing my hair in front of my face, momentarily blinding me. I pushed it back in time to see another earth naturi running toward Ryan and me, sword raised. Returning the gun to the holster at my back, I beat the creature back with the short sword in my right hand. I didn't think the worsening weather would help my aim, and I needed to save the last few bullets I had for an emergency.

It was a struggle to fight back the naturi as the storm continued to build. The wind roared while the rain fell in relentless sheets, blinding us. Lightning lashed at the sky, lighting up the area like a strobe light in a smoky nightclub. After finally dispatching my opponent by plunging my sword through his heart, I turned back to Ryan, pressing my left hand to my left thigh in an effort to stem the bleeding. The naturi had gotten in a lucky strike before I killed him. The pain was only a dull throbbing in the back of my mind.

The rain was coming down so hard I could no longer see Danaus and Penelope. All sounds of the battle had been drowned out by the rain and thunder. I couldn't see Ryan either. He had been only a few feet behind me. I took a few frantic steps forward, sucking in a lungful of air to shout his name when I nearly tripped over his foot. The warlock was seated on the ground, his arms resting on his bent knees before him.

Kneeling before him, I grabbed his slumped shoulder. Ryan jumped, his head snapping up. The tension instantly eased from his shoulder when he realized it was me. "It's done," he announced, wiping some of the water from his eyes. His clothes were plastered to his lean frame and he was trembling, either from the cold or exhaustion.

I glanced up at the sky. The storm was still building around us. The lightning that had been content to jump from cloud to cloud was now slamming to the earth with increasing frequency. A couple of trees had already exploded in a shower of sparks and wooden shards as they were struck.

"What do you mean it's done?" I shouted over the pounding rain. Water blurred my vision and dripped off the end of my nose. If I still breathed, I would have been afraid of drowning. "The storm is getting worse."

"The storm is getting its energy from this spot. It will continue to build until the energy runs out," Ryan shouted back.

I instantly released him and nearly lost my balance, as if the world had shifted beneath me. The storm was drawing its power from the well of the earth. It wouldn't run dry. "Are you insane?" I screamed. "You have to stop it!" If this storm left Crete, it would sweep up through the Aegean Sea, crushing one island after another before slamming into the mainland. Thousands of people were going to be killed.

He stared at me, his mouth soundlessly opening and closing a couple of times. "I can't," he finally said when he could use his voice again. "I released this spell. I can't call it back or control it."

"Are you insane?" I repeated. It was all I could think to say. Terror had locked up my thoughts.

"You said you wanted to use up the energy," he shouted angrily back at me.

"Yeah, but not destroy all of southern Europe in the process." I tightly gripped both of his shoulders and shook him. "You have to stop this." By the weight still in the air, the spell hadn't made a dent in the power swelling up from the earth. Ryan had to stop it before it got any worse.

Pain exploded in my cheek and jaw as I was thrown backward, Ryan's shoulders wretched out of my hands. I slid back across the broken rock until I slammed into a bigger, immovable rock. The sharp edge dug into my back, trying to insert itself between the vertebrae of my spine.

With a groan, I looked up to find Rowe standing next to a confused Ryan. Drenched, but entirely unfazed by the growing storm, the naturi smiled at me as he shoved the warlock aside. Planting his feet wide apart, Rowe casually raised his left hand above his head, his eyes never wavering from me as I pushed to my feet again.

Overhead, the storm calmed. The pounding rain lightened to a steady downpour and the wind stopped trying to push me across the clearing. Rowe had taken control of the storm with little effort and strain.

I shouldn't have been surprised. He had demonstrated his ability to manipulate the weather when we met in Venice. I just didn't expect it to be so easy for him. No struggle. No strain. He simply lifted his hand and the fury of the gods slipped into his palm.

While the naturi calmed the raging storm, I quickly looked around. There were still no humans, which meant they couldn't complete the sacrifice. And then my gaze stumbled back to the warlock, who had also pushed to his feet. They couldn't complete the sacrifice unless they grabbed Ryan. I needed to get him out of there. I didn't think Rowe would try to break the seal tonight, but I didn't want to take my chances and be proven wrong.

"Fancy meeting you here," I called, brushing my scraped-up hands on the legs of my leather pants. My body was battered, bruised, and thoroughly chilled. What I needed was a good soak in a tub of hot, sudsy water. Instead I got a naturi with an attitude.

"Ancient ruins. Middle of the night. It's where all the lovers meet," he taunted, his smile widening to a malicious grin.

I slowly stepped to my left, edging closer to Ryan. I wanted to get between him and Rowe, but the naturi guessed my plan. With a slight twitch of his fingers, a lightning bolt slammed into the ground between Ryan and me. We both dove in the opposite direction, the air around us crackling with energy.

When I looked back at Rowe as I regained my feet, he was closely watching Ryan. The warlock was preparing to cast something; I didn't have a clue what. I was just worried that he would draw the energy from me, leaving me weak and vulnerable.

"Stupid humans," Rowe growled, letting his arm fall back to his side. "You'll never gain the ability to control the weather. The earth is beyond your comprehension."

"Wow!" I mocked, luring his stare back to me. "I would never have guessed you to be an elitist prick." Gathering up my energy before Ryan could tap it, I created a fireball in each hand. Because of the ceaseless rain, I put a little more energy behind it.

But something unexpected happened. The energy that had been pressing against me finally found a way into my body. The softball-size fireballs I had attempted to create appeared in my hands larger than basketballs, crackling and spitting in horrific fury. I hurled both of them at Rowe before I could contemplate it any further. However, once the energy found a way into my system, I had no way of stopping it. The power continued to flow in, hot and biting.

I blinked, struggling to rise above the flow of power, watching as Rowe darted away from the fireballs. With the energy filling me, I had no choice but to continue to pitch fireballs at the dark naturi in hopes of setting the bastard on fire. Not the easiest of tasks even with the free flow of energy. I had an amazing source of power, but I didn't have the same level of control I had perfected over the long centuries.

As Rowe hit the ground, he swung one arm at me. A bolt of lightning plunged from the sky, striking a few feet from where I stood. I lurched backward, my onslaught of fire halted. Rowe took advantage of the pause to cause the storm to build again. Lightning bolt after lightning bolt hammered the earth, each striking closer and closer to me. He was driving me back, farther from him and the center of the clearing.

Keeping me on the run was also stopping me from using the power building within my body. I couldn't force it out. I couldn't stop it. The only relief I could find was to use the energy, but I couldn't concentrate on using my ability if I was dodging lightning bolts.

Mira.

The relief I felt at the sound of Danaus's voice within my mind was instantaneous. I had been so centered on taking out Rowe, I forgot that the hunter was lurking somewhere about.

What do you need me to do?

Get Ryan out of here. They could use him, I ordered in a brief respite between strikes. I quickly threw another fireball at Rowe, but it went wide of its mark and struck another naturi, bathing him in liquid orange flames. I hadn't had enough time to concentrate and aim.

Another lightning bolt. It hit far too close. I jumped but didn't look at where I would land. My right foot came down on a large chunk of rock and I fell backward, landing heavily on my back. I cried out as the pain shot through my spine and ribs. My control slipped on the energy that was vibrating through my body. A wall of fire whooshed up around me with an angry roar.

Laying on my back, I looked up to find a circle of fire surrounding me, reaching up more than ten feet into the heavens. The snapping orange and yellow flames encased me like an oven, drying my clothes and hair, sucking away cold that had chilled me to my bones. I hadn't thought of the wall of flames. After more than six hundred years, it was a reflexive move, like raising my hand to protect my eyes from a bright light.

Mira! The frantic shout in my head was my only warning. Danaus was there. More than just a presence in my head, he was inside me, his power burrowing down into me until I could no longer separate myself from him. Pain exploded in my frame. I thought my bones were going to splinter under the force of the energy he was pushing into me.

I nearly shouted at him to release me when I realized that as his energy filled me, the energy flowing into me from the earth was being pushed out. The circle of fire was shrinking back down into the earth. I lay still, letting my eyes fall shut as I concentrated on the war being fought within me, but without my influence.

"Mira!" Danaus shouted. He was still within me, but he was calling now. He was close.

"I'm fine," I muttered, but that was questionable. My body hurt in a hundred different ways, making me wish I'd let Rowe hit me with a lightning bolt. I couldn't imagine a nightwalker surviving such a thing. Of course, it would be just my luck that I would.

Release me, I said to Danaus, using our private connection. No reason to let everyone in on our little secret. We had enough problems. Slowly, I felt him pull his powers out of my body, leaving me feeling cooler, emptier. I immediately noticed that the power I had felt pouring from the earth into me didn't return, but went back to pushing against my skin.

A light rain splattered on my face and a grumble of thunder rolled in the distance, pulling me back to the present. I lurched back into an upright position, wincing at the pain in my back and in my head. Rowe had been firing lightning bolts at me only moments ago. But now he was gone. All the naturi were gone.

"Where?" I whispered in confusion, pushing back some hair that had fallen around my face.

"They left," Penelope answered as she hesitantly stepped closer. "When the wall of fire went up, they ran." I briefly wondered if this new cautious attitude was the result of the havoc Danaus and I had created when we destroyed so many naturi near Stonehenge.

"Should we follow?" Danaus asked. The hunter extended one hand to me, offering to help me back to my feet. I hesitated only a second, frowning at his hand. Before when he had pushed his powers into me, he needed to be touching me. But, much like Jabari, Danaus had learned to do it without touching me. I didn't want to know how far away he'd been at the time.

"No," I said, shaking my head as I regained my feet with his help. I had a feeling we had a new problem. "We need to find out what happened to Hugo first."

TWENTY-TWO

Penelope and I stumbled across the clearing, weaving through the crumbling remains of the ruins until we reached the far eastern edge of the Palace of Knossos. We could still sense the nightwalker's soul, but it was weak and thready. He wasn't going to last much longer if he didn't receive help very soon. The rain had slowed to a light drizzle, more annoying than anything, as it added a chill to the air we shouldn't have felt for a late summer evening.

Slipping in a patch of mud, I finally located Hugo lying under a couple of trees, covered in blood. I hadn't liked leaving him alone to face the naturi, but I was short on help. I had hoped that his enormous size would add some menace to his figure and deter the naturi without him needing to raise a sword or gun. Instead they had taken advantage of the fact that he was alone and overwhelmed him.

I knelt beside the wounded nightwalker. His eyelids fluttered as he attempted to open his eyes. I hadn't made a noise in my approach, but he could sense me. I laid a hand on his barrel chest and he flinched at my touch. There was a long cut on his throat and another across his middle. Shallow cuts covered his arms and legs. His face was bruised, with his left eye nearly swollen shut. Hugo was lucky they hadn't cut off his head or carved out his heart. They had left him to suffer as pints of blood slowly poured from his body. He was losing blood too fast for his body to heal the wounds and hold in the blood.

Looking over my shoulder at Penelope, who was staring white-faced down at Hugo, I ordered her to fetch a car. We needed to move the giant vampire. If we were going to be lucky enough to save him, we couldn't do it here.

"What should we do?" Ryan inquired, taking Penelope's place behind me.

I gritted my teeth, catching a whiff of his blood on the slight breeze. It wouldn't help Hugo. Ryan wasn't a candidate for a donation. Warlock blood didn't always go well with every nightwalker, and I didn't see Danaus allowing it even if Ryan agreed.

"Go gather up all the dead naturi," I said, putting my hand over the wound on Hugo's stomach in a desperate attempt to slow some of the bleeding. He let out a low moan as I applied pressure, sending a fresh wave of pain through his body. "Put them in one spot. I have to dispose of them before we leave."

I waited until the sound of Danaus's and Ryan's footsteps faded in the distance before turning my attention entirely back to Hugo. His body was ice cold to the touch, and if I hadn't felt the actual presence of his soul in the large body before me, I would have assumed he was dead.

I dipped into his mind and immediately got sucked into a swirling maelstrom of pain. Not that I could actually feel his pain. It came through to me as black chaos that permeated every thought and memory. It was difficult to locate Hugo within the chaos, and it didn't help that everything was coming through in German.

Can you tell me what happened? I asked, finally finding Hugo within the haze of pain and hunger.

Naturi . . . everywhere. There was a long pause and I could feel him pushing against the pain, fighting to focus his thoughts. *I heard something. Rocks shifting. I turned and they were beside me. Too many. Too close.*

It's okay, I murmured in his head, wishing I could lend him some of my strength.

They came from . . . southwest . . . I thought they killed you before reaching me.

No. We didn't see them. I closed my eyes, trying to ignore the scent of his blood. It was everywhere, coating my hands, filling the air with its oh-so-sweet smell. I was still achy and tired from our encounter with the naturi. I needed to feed myself, but it would have to wait.

My mind drifted. I didn't know how I was going to save Hugo. We needed to get him some blood, lots of it. We would need to keep pumping it into him until the wounds finally closed and he could hold it within his body. The wounds had to close before the sun rose or the blood would drain out of him during the day and he wouldn't reawaken with the setting of the sun.

The sound of a car motor approaching the ruins jerked me from my thoughts. A quick check revealed that it was Penelope and she wasn't alone. She was bringing two humans with her. I hadn't thought to ask her to round up a quick bite for Hugo, just something to buy him a little more time. Of course, no matter what my condition, I tended to be somewhat selective in my meals. Looking back down at Hugo and his gray pallor, I doubted I'd be picky if I was in the same state as he was.

Penelope parked the car not far from Hugo's location and made her way toward us as quickly as possible. A dark frown tugged at the corners of my lips when I saw the elderly couple preceding her to the site. They wouldn't survive a substantial blood loss, but I was willing to bet she'd simply grabbed the owners of the car. There was no time to go hunting down a pair of strapping young men who could stand to lose a couple pints of blood each.

The hiss of a sword being pulled from its scabbard sent a chill up my spine. With my hand still pressed to Hugo's stomach, I twisted around to see Danaus pointing the sword at Penelope, who had taken a step in front of the two humans as if to protect them from the hunter.

"Mira!" Danaus's hard voice landed heavy on my shoulders.

"Danaus, wait!"

"Hugo needs blood," Penelope argued, lifting her upper lip in a snarl that revealed a pair of perfect fangs. It was a warning.

"Hugo won't last much longer if we don't get some blood back into his system," I said, trying to keep my voice calm and even. The sound of Danaus's and Ryan's hearts pounding seemed to echo through the tree-lined area, rising above the rustling of the leaves. Everyone was tense from the fight with the naturi and tempers were short. I couldn't afford to have someone snap.

"She means for him to kill the humans," Danaus said, taking a step closer. The hunter lifted the point of his sword to the level of Penelope's throat. "Release the humans."

"No! Hugo needs them!" Penelope shouted. "Mira, control him! Hugo needs blood."

"Danaus! Stand down!"

"I won't let you kill humans," Danaus said. His grip on the sword shifted, tightening. It was my last warning.

Time slowed down and I sat on the ground, one hand on Hugo, frozen. Danaus swung his sword twice; first plunging it into Penelope's chest, then removing it and swinging it in a wide arc, slicing off her head. I watched it happen, unable to bring a single word of protest from my throat as he moved in a flawless, fluid swing. Shock halted any useful thoughts. In a span of just a few seconds everything had spiraled completely out of control.

The spray of Penelope's blood washed over all of us. With her death, the humans woke up from the trance she had been holding them under to keep them calm and quiet. Their screams rang through the valley, bouncing off the nearby mountains and waking me from my own morbid thoughts. The old man and woman stared down at their blood-covered hands and clothes, screaming and shaking. They had woken up to find themselves standing outside with two blood-covered bodies on the ground and three soaked, scary figures looming before them. Looking into their wide, horrified eyes, I briefly wondered what Our Liege was thinking when he decided to move up the Great Awakening. It was madness.

"Ryan!" I shouted, my voice shaking. Hugo was stirring, a new moaning rumbling through his brain. Danaus was denying him his only chance at survival. Fear had gripped the nightwalker, and I didn't want him to try to move, reopening wounds that had begun to heal.

"I've got it." The warlock's voice was remarkably calm despite the insanity reigning around us. With a wave of his hand, the two humans grew instantly silent. A dull, unfocused stare returned to their faces. They were no longer aware of where they were or what was going on. I had thought Ryan would know such a trick. We all had to learn to hide in the open and control the minds of others if we were going to survive in a world that demanded we keep such a big secret.

With a growl, I finally turned my attention to Danaus, who was putting his sword back to the scabbard on his back. "What the hell were you thinking? She was only trying to save Hugo. How could you kill her, you heartless bastard?" My voice was choked and broken, struggling to push past the lump in my throat.

"She was going to let him kill both the humans," Danaus said. "You know she was. She was going to sacrifice two humans in hopes of saving him." I looked up again to find him staring down at me, his blue eyes narrowed on my face. "I won't let you kill humans to save yourself."

"Yes she was! But did you ask me what I was planning? Did you ever wonder if I would allow such a thing to happen?" I had to close my eyes to keep the tears from falling. I felt so betrayed. Not until that moment did I realize how much I'd come to depend on Danaus. I had wrongly thought that he'd started to trust me, that he believed in me to do the right thing.

But even the idea of the right thing had begun to blur. Was sacrificing two humans such a bad thing when it came to trying to save the entire human race from the naturi? Keeping Hugo alive would give us one more fighter against the naturi. As it stood now, Penelope was dead and it was highly unlikely that Hugo would last the rest of the night. Any other nightwalker wouldn't have thought twice about draining those two humans dry, but I'd hesitated. No longer sure.

"I don't kill humans when feeding," I said in a voice that sounded broken and beaten. "And I won't allow those around me to do it either. I thought you knew that. You didn't think and you've damned us all." Shaking my head, I looked up at Ryan, who was standing next to the humans. "You and Danaus take the humans. Wipe their memories and send them home. Leave me the car. I'll take care of Hugo."

"But—"

"Just go," I interrupted Ryan before he could argue further. "I'll clean up here."

I sat still on the ground next to Hugo, my hand still pressed to his stomach as if it was my only anchor to sanity in this world. For the first time since becoming a nightwalker, I could feel the night pull in around me and a deep emptiness filled my chest. Even when I was being held captive by the naturi, I didn't give up hope that Sadira or another nightwalker would come to my rescue. But with one nightwalker dead by the hand of a man I had come to rely on, and another dying in my arms, I couldn't find any hope to cling to. The naturi would crush us all.

TWENTY-THREE

I sat with my back pressed against the stone wall of the mausoleum I hid in during the daylight hours. Exhaustion had settled deep within my bones, making it hard to even move, let alone crawl into the crypt so I could hide from the approaching dawn. Too much had happened in the past few hours, which left me struggling to find some good to cling to in the end.

When I moved Hugo to the car, I discovered that he had also been stabbed in the back, puncturing his heart, which explained why he was so weak. Stopping at the edge of Heraklion, I summoned a dozen inhabitants from their warm, comfortable beds. Hugo fed briefly from each of them before I sent them blindly back to bed again. The drain on my powers was enormous, forcing me to feed as well before I could deposit a sleeping Hugo in a dark crypt in a cemetery between Heraklion and Knossos. When I dropped him off, only the worst of his wounds was slowly seeping blood. I hoped he would last the day.

After leaving him, I returned to the palace ruins, where I burned the bodies of the naturi and Penelope. Guilt gnawed at me for burning her with the naturi, but I no longer had the strength to maintain several fires, and I didn't want to take any chances being so close to the swell of energy rising up from the earth. I'd been burned once; I couldn't afford for it to happen again. What bones I couldn't destroy were buried in a shallow grave. It was the best I could do. Daylight was approaching.

With all evidence of our existence eliminated from Knossos, I cleaned the blood and fingerprints off the car and left it in the heart of Heraklion. I checked on Hugo one final time before finding my own crypt, not far from his.

Now as I sat in the dark, my mind numb, I felt someone approaching me. I pulled the Browning from the holster at the base of my spine and laid it on the ground beside me, partially hidden in the shadows cast by my body. A quick scan revealed that my visitor was Danaus, but I was surprised when I found that I didn't want to put the gun away. I didn't trust him any longer. If push came to shove, I knew I wouldn't try to kill him with a gun. I'd just try to slow him down enough so I could rip his heart out with my bare hands.

"You shouldn't be here," I murmured wearily when the hunter finally came into view. He was still several yards off, but his hearing was nearly as good as mine. He heard me.

"I came to talk," he said in a low voice, as if he was afraid of waking some other graveyard occupant.

I snorted, but still loosened my grip on the gun at my side. My fingers didn't completely uncurl from around the butt, but stayed close just in case. "I can't image we have much to talk about. Everything has been cleanly laid out."

Danaus walked around the last tree separating us in the cross-dotted garden, coming into full view. From what I could see, he was completely unarmed. Both his guns were missing, along with the sword on his back and the two knives usually attached to his leg and waist. Even his leather wrist guards were missing. He stood before me as vulnerable as it was possible for him to be. Could he still kill me in a heartbeat? Without a doubt. He could boil my blood as quickly as I could set him on fire, but he was trying to come before me without weapons.

"I—I came to apologize," he admitted.

I sat in stunned silence for a moment before finally shaking my head to clear it. "I'm not the one you should be apologizing to. You should be apologizing to Penelope for taking her head off. You should be apologizing to Hugo for stealing away his one chance at survival," I bitterly snapped.

"I'm apologizing to you because I should have trusted you," he corrected, standing before me with his legs spread wide, his hands shoved in his pockets. I gazed up, my frown matching his. "I know you. You wouldn't have let Hugo kill those two people. But Penelope would have. Hugo would have. They wouldn't have thought twice about it, and I can't forgive them for that."

"You can't forgive them for wanting to survive?" I demanded, my hand reflexively tightening around the gun as my other hand balled into a fist in the dirt.

"I can't forgive them for killing innocent people," he said. What sympathy and compassion he may have felt drained from his voice, leaving it cold and hard like Siberian permafrost.

"But you have no problem with him dying for these people that you protect," I said, gritting my teeth as I sat up. "We're allowed to fight for them and die for them, but we're not allowed to do anything that might save our own lives."

"It's not like that," he said, hesitant. He took an unsteady step backward with one foot then shifted it forward again.

"Yes, it is." I rose to my feet in a boneless manner, using my powers instead of my muscles for the sole purpose of unnerving him and underscoring my otherness. I did nothing to hide the act of putting the gun back in the holster at my lower back. "You and I work great together so long as you forget what I am. When it's just you and me against the world with sword in hand, we work great together. But if I need to feed or give you some other small reminder that I'm a nightwalker, then you freak out. You can't understand that I'm something beyond *what* I am."

"Forget?" he said in a louder voice. "How could I ever possibly forget what you are? I sense you more clearly than I have ever sensed any vampire. When you're hungry, the feeling burns through me like a fire in my veins. When you use your powers, it's like a cool breeze on a hot summer day. You're in my head and I'm in yours. Do you think I didn't feel your horror and disappointment tonight? What am I supposed to do? I'm a hunter! I'm supposed to protect humanity from threats like nightwalkers."

"Maybe it's time to get a new job," I said, feeling myself softening toward him. I hadn't realized how strong our connection had been for him. I didn't want to forgive him. I didn't want to understand his point of view. I wanted to hold onto the anger so I could easily walk away from him when we finally finished our business with the naturi.

"Enough, Mira," he said in disgust. I had given him similar advice in the past, but this time I was serious.

"Do you believe in fate?"

"What?"

"Fate. That great cosmic force that leads us down particular paths during our existence to—"

"Yes, I know what fate is. No, I don't believe in it."

"Maybe you should," I suggested, sliding my hands into the back pockets of my leather pants. "I'm beginning to wonder myself. Maybe fate brought you to this point not to be a nightwalker hunter but a hunter of naturi. You have the strength, the speed, and the ability to sense them. You have an edge over every nightwalker in existence.

Maybe it's time to stop saving humanity from my kind and start saving them for the naturi."

"And who will protect mankind from you?" he demanded, shaking his head at me.

A weak smile twisted one corner of my mouth as I looked up at him. His hair fell forward around his face, hiding his features in dark shadows. "Nightwalkers? No one will need to. It looks like we're on the path to extinction without your help at all."

In fact, my people were on the fast track to extinction. Just on the off chance that we did succeed in stopping the naturi from opening the door and flooding the world with their kind so they could start a massive war, there was still Our Liege's plan. Pushing the Great Awakening ahead of schedule was going to start a war with every lycanthrope, warlock, and witch on the planet. The war would leak out and humans would discover us ahead of schedule in the darkest light. They would join Danaus in the hunt for nightwalkers. Our nights were numbered.

Danaus shocked me when he reached up and gently moved some hair from where it had fallen in front of my face. I looked up to find him faintly smiling down at me as two of his fingers rubbed a lock of my hair as if memorizing the feel. "Rowe won't get you. Remember, we still have to finish our dance. I won't let some dirty naturi kill you when I've promised myself that honor."

"We're overdue for that dance," I said, smiling back up at him.

He shrugged his large shoulders and dropped my hair, letting his hand fall limply back at his side. "Things have gotten in the way. There's still time."

"Is there? What have you told Ryan about the bargain?" I asked, abruptly changing topics. I knew this might have been my only chance to question the hunter while we were completely alone. I had to know if the warlock was looking for a way to stick a knife in my back at the first opportunity.

"Against my better judgment, I've said nothing to him."

"Really?" There was no hiding my surprise. I couldn't begin to fathom Danaus. He did trust me in some strange fashion, just not when it came to controlling the baser needs of my kind. I was beginning to wonder exactly what he felt when he sensed my hunger.

Danaus shoved both of his hands through his hair as he paced a few steps away from me. "I thought you might have a plan to stop this from turning into a war among the races. Ryan is viewed very highly among the warlocks. If he says one word about what is going on in Venice, there will be no stopping the war."

"I have been thinking about it, and no matter what we do, we're screwed. If we let the door open, so we can get our shot at Aurora, the naturi will spill out. There's going to be no hiding them or the war they start. The Great Awakening will happen regardless of anyone's wishes." I leaned back against the small crypt, folding my arms over my chest.

"And if we break the bargain?"

"Assuming we can, we stop the sacrifice and kill Rowe. Once that's done, I imagine that Macaire will hunt me down and cut my head off after he's done torturing me. The Great Awakening will happen within the next year and there will be war among the races, but then, I think we're building toward that already, considering we saw a witch and a lycan traveling with a Coalition member."

"One war or two. That's what we face. Fighting a war on one front or on two."

My head snapped up and I stared silently at him. I didn't need to read his mind to know that he was thinking of the same thing I was. At some point that war was going to put us on opposite sides. He would fight with my kind against the naturi, but he would fight against night-walkers if it meant protecting humans from us.

We had gotten accustomed to being on the same side. We fought well together, like two dancers in an intricate tango.

"We break the bargain," I said at last, shattering the growing silence. "No bargain should be made with the naturi. We may still find a way to stop Our Liege from pulling back the veil so early. The only problem is, how do we convince the naturi faction that the bargain has been broken?"

"Besides stopping them from breaking the seal?" Danaus said, walking back toward me.

I shook my head, shifting from one foot to the other. Night was wasting away and I was exhausted. I had fed enough, but I needed my rest. Unfortunately, we needed to have this settled before we went into battle tomorrow. "It needs to be more than that. There has to be no doubt in their mind that we are the enemy and they are not going to be permitted to open the door for any reason. They need to know that we won't allow anything to happen to Our Liege."

"You could kill the naturi we saw in Venice," Danaus suggested. "That could be pretty convincing."

"A little late for that now that we're in Crete. I can't go running back—"

"She's here," Danaus interrupted. "I saw her tonight and I noticed that she wasn't among the dead. She's here with Rowe. Apparently, she's making sure everything goes according to plan."

"Sounds like a good plan to me." I nodded, then moved my head to one side, cracking my neck. "Now get out of here so I can get some rest. We'll come up with a more definite plan tomorrow when we have Ryan with us."

"Hugo?" he asked hesitantly.

"Resting for now. If he's lucky, he'll make it through the day, but he won't be with us tomorrow."

Danaus nodded but didn't move from where he stood staring at me. "I can stay."

And a part of me desperately wished he would stay. While trapped at Themis, he'd sat outside the room where I slept helplessly through-out the day while surrounded by his brethren. He had hovered close on so many occasions while I slept that I now hated the idea of him not being there when the sun broke above the horizon. Danaus was my only sense of security in this world that was changing too fast. He threatened to destroy everything that I believed in and everything that I protected. But at the same time, he seemed to be the only one left trying to protect me.

"Get out of here. You'll attract too much attention. I'll be fine," I said, waving him off.

He hesitated a moment before turning around and wandering out of the cemetery back the way he had come in. I concentrated on him with my powers until I felt him just on the edge of the city, well away from the graveyard.

My whole body ached and felt like a giant bruise. I needed some rest, but even now with the approaching dawn, I wasn't tired. In fact, I was wide-awake with a new frightening thought. Killing the naturi wasn't going to be enough to convince the faction that some rogue nightwalker had the power to break a promise made by the Coven. I knew what had to be done. The only problem was, I needed either Jabari or Macaire's help to accomplish it.

TWENTY-FOUR

I didn't want the sun to set. The dawn had finally brought on a bliss-ful peace, sweeping me away from death, Danaus's betrayal, and the wars that were brewing. By the time I had settled into the windowless crypt, I was trembling from exhaustion that reached down to my very core.

Lying in the stone crypt at nightfall, ignoring the sound of bugs crawling around me, I tried to focus my thoughts. I needed to know how old the night was. I needed a plan for how to deal with the naturi. But instead I got the feeling I wasn't alone in my tiny mausoleum. I scanned the immediate area but didn't sense anyone—not human, vampire, or warlock. Regardless, I still couldn't shake the feeling.

My right hand tightened around the gun I'd left on my stomach while I slept. With the other hand, I pushed back the heavy stone lid to the crypt that had protected me from the sun. It was not the first time I'd slept in a cemetery, and no matter how distasteful I found it, I doubted that it would be the last. When desperate, it proved to be one of the safest places to hide without fear of being exposed to the sun.

Sitting up, I pointed the gun directly in front of me, swinging it back and forth, trying to find the creature my instincts were screaming was close. Fear and anger swelled in my stomach and I clenched my teeth. The sight of the gun wavered when my gaze fell on Jabari leaning against the wall near the door. I still couldn't sense him, but I had known he was there. All I could figure was that he had appeared the moment I awoke for the night, and I sensed the shift of energy in the air.

"You can lower the weapon now," he said, his dark eyes locked onto my face.

"Really? That doesn't seem like such a good idea to me," I sneered, more irritated with the fact that I couldn't get my hand to stop trembling than with him.

Jabari arched one eyebrow at me in mocking question as his gaze shifted to the gun. He didn't have to say anything. We both knew he could make me drop the gun at any time. Or if he was feeling particularly evil, he could make me raise the gun to my temple and pull the trigger.

With a growl I couldn't stop, I returned the gun to the holster at my lower back and climbed out of the crypt. "What are you doing here? I thought no one else was coming."

"I came to check on your progress," he said. "Things don't seem to be going so well. Hugo is barely clinging to life."

"He made it through the day?" I demanded before I could stop myself. Jabari's presence surprised me so much that I had forgotten to scan the cemetery to see if I could still sense the big nightwalker.

"Yes, but he will be of no use to you tonight. He will need to feed and sleep for a couple more nights and days before he will be of use to anyone." He paused as I slid the lid of the crypt back into place and leaned against the stone coffin. "And I can no longer sense the other nightwalker that was sent with you . . ."

"Penelope," I murmured. My head fell and I shoved one hand through my hair. I still had to face the nightmare that played through my head like a broken record. "She was killed. Danaus killed her. To stop her from killing two humans."

I waited for the Ancient to strike me, to break me in some horrible, painful way because I had failed to control the hunter. But it never came. After a few seconds I looked up to find him still watching me from where he stood near the door.

"I can't control him," I started, talking simply to fill the growing silence. "I never claimed to be able to control him, but we need him alive. Regardless of how we all feel about him, we need him."

"But you feel betrayed by him," Jabari said, taking a step forward. I took a quick step back, my spine slamming into the stone crypt that ran horizontally along the back wall of the mausoleum. Only a few feet of open, thick blackness separated Jabari and me. The Elder closed the distance as I remained trapped. "I can feel the pain rolling off you. He betrayed you. You trusted him and you thought he trusted you."

A bitter smile twisted my lips as I looked up at one of my three makers. "You'd think I would have learned not to trust powerful creatures."

Jabari leaned close, his eyes glowing faintly in the absolute darkness like a cat's eyes catching a car's headlights. There was no hiding my fear from him. My stomach clenched and my hands trembled despite tightly gripping the edge of the crypt. He might need me alive, but he could cause me severe amounts of pain.

"You still trust me," he whispered, his voice low and hypnotic.

I closed my eyes for a second, trying to quell the shaking that had gone from my hands to encompass my entire body. He couldn't be right. I wouldn't let him be. Clenching that thought between my gritted teeth, I opened my eyes to find him standing by the door on the opposite side of the tiny room. I hadn't even heard him move.

"Why are you here?" I demanded, summoning up my anger again. I knew better than to believe his line that he was just checking up on us. I was surprised by his appearance, but I shouldn't have been. The last time he had randomly appeared was at the Themis Compound, the night of the attack and the sacrifice at Stonehenge. "Afraid of missing out on another sacrifice?"

Jabari smiled this time, a dark and evil thing. "Just missed the last one." The smile slithered from his face and he turned serious again. "You know why I'm here. It's the same reason I commanded you to appear in Venice. The one place in the world where you could prove to be the greatest nuisance."

"Because of the naturi in the Great Hall," I said.

Jabari simply nodded, the smile returning to his lips.

My hands fell back to my sides and I leaned against the tomb that had served as my daytime bed. "Honestly, old friend, is what Macaire told me the truth? Just between you and me and the spiders."

"I do not know, but I have found that it's very rare for Macaire to speak the truth," Jabari replied, matching my mocking tone.

"Has the Coven truly made a bargain with the naturi?"

"A small group within the naturi, yes," Jabari corrected.

I bit on my lower lip for a second, trying to hold back a smile, as he carefully hedged. "They want us to kill Aurora."

"That is correct."

"And the Coven wants them to kill Our Liege."

To this, Jabari said nothing, but he did nod once.

Yeah, I was the only nightwalker insane enough to actually say those words out loud. But then again, I had lots of people trying to kill me, what was one more? "And this is because he's trying to move up the Great Awakening."

Again Jabari nodded.

"This is ridiculous!" I shouted, barely resisting the urge to start pacing in the tiny crypt. "This is nothing more than Macaire's power play. He has to know that allowing the door to open will bring about the Great Awakening. There will be no hiding a war with the naturi from the humans."

"That is true, but it is proving to be effective. Tabor was vocally against the plan, threatening to go to Our Liege."

"And he ended up dead," I said, finishing the thought. "I'm assuming this is the reason no one has been able to sense you for the past several years."

"I prefer my privacy, yes," Jabari murmured, as if this was all a lighthearted game. He leaned against the wall opposite me, crossing one leg in front of the other. His dark skin allowed him to nearly blend into the darkness, giving the night an almost velvety texture where he stood.

"But I don't understand." I shoved one hand through my knotted and dirty hair in frustration. "Why drag me into this? Kill Macaire and end the bargain. You didn't need me in Venice for that."

"I needed you causing chaos in Venice, threatening to spread our secret and disrupting our meetings with the naturi. It strikes fear in them, and we need them to fear us. Besides, you should never underestimate Macaire. He has been on the Coven longer than me. He is harder to kill than you would think."

"So I was brought to Venice to discover the secret?"

"With the hunter at your side, it was inevitable."

"And Nicolai?"

"We offered him as a sacrifice."

"So I was supposed to save him . . ."

"No, you were supposed to kill him, but everything still worked out in the end," Jabari admitted with a shrug of his broad shoulders.

"What's the next step in your master plan?" I demanded, my temper flaring. I had been used and manipulated since the moment I stepped off the plane in Venice. Jabari didn't have to use his powers to control me. He could do just fine with me running around on my own, creating chaos wherever I went.

"The same plan that I am sure you have already cooked up with the hunter," Jabari said, pushing off the wall. He slowly walked over to stand before me. Only a slender column of air separated us when he spoke again. "Kill the naturi called Rowe. Stop the sacrifice and protect the seal. We must make it clear to them that there is going to be no bargain between nightwalkers and naturi."

"The naturi from Venice. The one in the hall. She's here with Rowe," I said, trying to swallow back my fear. My anger had slipped away and now there was just the cold chill of the crypt as I stood alone with one of my makers, and one of my greatest betrayers. Once again we found each other as allies when I knew it was only a matter of time before we would find ourselves on opposite sides of the battle-field.

"Then we kill her. If the harpies appear, we kill them as well."

"Jabari, I—I . . ." I hesitated. I had some fears about our plan, but I didn't want to volunteer my solution unless it was absolutely neces-sary. "Do you still mean to kill me?"

Lifting one hand, he cupped my cheek as he leaned forward and brushed his lips against my other cheek. His lips strayed down my jaw to my bare neck, sending a chill sweeping through my entire body. "My fragile desert blossom," he murmured in my ear. "I want you dead in the worst way. But for now I have a use for you, so you live."

That's what I thought. I was trapped, surrounded by creatures that wanted me dead, but for now all seemed to have a use for me as some kind of weapon against the naturi. Except for Rowe. He wanted to use me as a weapon against the nightwalkers.

I bit back a sigh as Jabari stepped away from me. Our course was set. The big bad Ancient could make it sound easy all he wanted, but I knew the truth. When we walked back into the Minoan ruins that night, the naturi were going to throw everything they had at us to ensure that they completed the sacrifice. There was no way they were going to let us stop them a second time.

TWENTY-FIVE

Ryan and Danaus were waiting for us along the road to the Palace
of Knossos. Both of them looked surprised to find Jabari walking beside me, but neither one asked about Hugo, which was probably
the smartest course of action. His absence indicated that he either
hadn't made it through the day or was too weak to aid us tonight.

After last night's freak storm, summer had returned to the island,
leaving the air thick and heavy like a sweat-soaked blanket. The wind
was silent, allowing any noise we made to travel easily to our intended prey. But I didn't actually have much hope of sneaking up on
them anyway.

As we walked along the side of the road, bits of gravel crunching
beneath my feet, I completed my weapons check for the second time.
The weapons Danaus gave me when we flew into Venice had been
reorganized due to the unexpected arrival of James and Ryan. One of
my guns now rested with James, whom I suspected was once again
pouting alone in the hotel room. My sword had also been replaced
with a pair of knives that rested in holsters strapped around my legs.
I had more experience with close, hand-to-hand fighting, and my
speed made me more lethal with a knife. The sword had been handed
off to Danaus.

However, I still had one of the detested guns the hunter had given
me. I pulled the Browning from where it rested at my lower back and
ejected the magazine from the butt of the gun. The magazine wasn't
fully loaded.

"Here," Danaus said, walking up beside me.

I looked down at the spare magazine he extended toward me.
With a grunt, I accepted it, sliding it into my back left pocket. I hadn't

forgiven him. I wanted to spend several nights beating him senseless for what he'd done. A part of me also wanted to curl up into a ball and weep. But the naturi were gathering and I didn't have time for either, so I accepted the bullets and kept walking.

"What's the plan?" Ryan inquired from the rear of the line.

"Jabari," I quickly said, hoping the nightwalker would happily step up into the lead. He was, after all, an Ancient and an Elder member of the Coven.

"This is your dance, Mira. You may lead. I am here only to fill in for the fallen nightwalkers," Jabari called from behind me. I could almost hear his mocking laughter with each syllable. *Rat bastard.*

I hesitated, resisting the urge to look over at Danaus. Had he told Ryan about the Coven deal with the naturi?

"We have to face the fact that it is very unlikely the human they have selected for the sacrifice will survive," I slowly began. My stomach churned with each ugly word I uttered. "Even if we rescue this person, as long as he or she in the area of the palace, they can be used as the sacrifice. The only way to eliminate the risk is to eliminate all humans from the area."

"You're saying kill the human before the naturi get the chance?" Ryan said. There was no surprise or disgust in his tone. He had asked matter-of-factly, as if simply confirming what I'd said.

"Our main focus needs to be eliminating the naturi threat," I replied, aware of Danaus and evading a direct response. "Jabari and I will focus on Rowe. We will need you and Danaus to keep the naturi off our backs."

If anyone was planning to comment on my ultracrappy planning skills, they lost out on the opportunity because we had reached the edge of the palace. With the gun clenched in my right hand and a knife in my left, I moved onto the first step leading up to the palace and paused. There was no time for fear or anger now. It was time to just worry about killing Rowe and surviving the next hour or so.

The energy I had felt last night was nothing compared to what I felt beating against me now. Ryan had created a storm with the force to not only destroy all of Crete but also wipe out several of other islands in the region, and it hadn't even dented the energy I now felt vibrating in the air. It pushed against my skin, determined to once again find entrance into my body. I couldn't use my powers tonight. This energy would shred me.

"They're here," Danaus murmured.

My head jerked toward the hunter, forcing me from my dark thoughts. "How many?"

"About two dozen. Most are centered in the main clearing, but there are a few hanging back toward the south. Two more are in the air."

Before shifting my weight to take the next step, I scanned the area as well, looking for the exact location where the human was being held. The naturi would wait until the night was near its peak, but they would be preparing the human. I was willing to guess that Rowe was hovering close to the human as well. But the naturi managed to surprise me again.

"Damn it," I snarled in a low whisper. I stepped backward and lowered my gun.

"There are three," Jabari said from behind me, stating what I'd just discovered. I walked a few feet away from the entrance to the ruins, flipping the safety of the gun back on in an effort to keep from putting a bullet in my foot in a moment of frustration. There were three humans at the center of the ruins. Not one. Three.

"Decoys?" Danaus asked, drawing my gaze to his face for a flash.

I looked away just as quickly, my eyes darting from Danaus to Ryan before finally settling on Jabari. "Yeah, maybe," I softly said, holding the Elder's eyes.

"And one of those decoys is James," Ryan announced.

"What? How?" I gasped, feeling the need to point my gun at the warlock. Bringing the human along had always felt like packing live bait to me, and now the young man was caught.

"He was grabbed during the middle of the day," Danaus answered. "He ran down to the corner store and never returned."

I wanted to smack them both for letting James out of their sight. Hadn't my own mistake with allowing Michael to get involved in a fight against the naturi taught them anything? Humans only ended up dead when the naturi and nightwalkers were involved.

We needed to hurry now. It had been night for more than an hour already. They could have started the process. While they might not complete the sacrifice until the peak of the night, the naturi could spend several hours in the ritual, removing the human's various organs and burning them. They would keep James alive and conscious right up until the end. But we wouldn't have any hope of saving him if they had already cut him open.

"New plan," I announced, insanely hoping I could convince Danaus and Ryan to go along with my newest bout of insanity. "There are three humans but only one is the true sacrifice. I will go after Rowe and keep the bastard occupied. Danaus will focus on freeing James and getting him over to Ryan. Once Ryan has James, the two of them will return to Heraklion."

"Mira, I think I can—" Ryan started, but I quickly cut him off.

"No, you can't. You're still a human, Mr. Warlock, and can be used as a sacrifice. Both you and James have to be away from the site. Jabari will focus on the other sacrifices. Ryan, I need you to hang back until James has been freed. If Rowe or any of the other naturi tap into the weather again, I need you to stop it."

"Mira, that's earth magic. Not my strong suit," he argued.

"You have to try." I flipped the safety off the gun again and took a step toward the entrance. "Do whatever you can to interfere with the spell. We'll try to keep them away from you so you can work."

Turning, I walked toward the entrance and up the stairs without looking back at anyone. I knew that none of the humans were decoys. Rowe wasn't taking any chances. We had stopped him once, and now he was betting we wouldn't be able to stop all three sacrifices.

As I reached the top of the stairs, a high-pitched screech rent the silence of the night. I cringed, lowering my head as if I expected the wrath of the heavens to fall on me at that second. Not quite. Two of the harpies from Venice had come to Knossos to help Rowe with the sacrifice. And we had obviously been spotted.

Sneaking around one of the remaining walls, a smile lifted my lips. The idea was to let me protect the seal and kill Rowe. The positive aspect to the plan was that I could kill every naturi that stood between him and me. I knew I would find a bright side somewhere within this nightmare.

We edged closer to the central courtyard. Only a handful of naturi stepped forward to harry us. With Jabari tagging along, they were quickly dispatched with little trouble before any of them could fire up their special powers. I wasn't surprised. The main force of the naturi was pulled back to defend the sacrifices.

The wind suddenly picked up, shifting twice before it blew at my back, pushing me forward. Climbing over a low, broken wall that surrounded the courtyard, I tightened my grip on the knife and gun. Rowe stood a few yards away, legs spread and hands on his hips. He smiled at me. Behind him more than a dozen torches flickered and danced in the wind. Spread before us across the wide courtyard were the three humans; two men and one small child. They had been tied down, their bodies stretched out from east to west. Just like at Stonehenge not so long ago.

"Is this all you brought?" Rowe demanded, arching the eyebrow over his one good eye. "I thought last night was a little scouting party. But this is it?"

"Why waste the manpower when four is all we need?" I mocked. "We're ending this tonight."

"I agree."

A duet of screams filled the air above me. Reluctant to take my eyes off Rowe, I looked up in time to see the two harpies plunging toward me, their fleshy wings pulling in close to their bodies to increase the speed of their fall. I lunged forward, slamming against the rock floor while Danaus and Jabari dove in opposite directions. Pain exploded in my ribs as I hit the ground, but I pushed it aside and kept moving. Rolling onto my back, I lifted my gun, searching the black skies for the mythical nightmares. But they were gone.

Rolling to my knees, my head snapped back as pain exploded in my jaw and I cried out, falling to my back. Rowe was on me in a second. His fist connected with my cheekbone, both sides of my face now throbbing in pain. The naturi straddled me, his knees pressed against my hips.

"You should have taken my offer," he growled, and slammed his fist into my stomach. "We would be on the same side now."

I swung my right hand up, trying to aim the gun at him. "Never," I grunted.

Rowe easily knocked my hand away, but I was counting on it. I swung my left hand up, burying my knife up to its hilt in his side. He screamed, backhanding me as he pulled away. His blood covered my hand, causing the knife to slip out of my grip as he stumbled off.

I pushed back to my feet, the pain in my face beginning to subside. I tried to get my bearings as Rowe hurried away to heal the latest wound I had inflicted on him. But I didn't have a chance. They attacked silently this time and I wasn't watching the skies.

The winged naturi swooped down in a rush of wind, blotting out the meager starlight. I'd taken half a step back when impossibly long talons dug into my arms and shoulders. A scream was ripped from my throat as my feet left the ground, matched by the sweet sounds of their laughter as they carried me off.

I tried to twist from their taloned grasp, but the claws only dug deeper into my flesh and muscles until I could feel them scraping against bone. Blood streamed from my shoulders, soaking into my cotton shirt, still stained from last night's battle. Lifting the hand that held the gun, I tried aiming it at either of my two captors as we rose higher into the night sky. I managed to get off only two shots before the gun was ripped out of my hand, and looked down in time to see it plummeting to the earth, which was steadily receding farther and farther away. The ruins were drifting away too as the pair of wind naturi carried me to the north, toward Heraklion and the sea.

With each flap of their massive wings, a gust of wind hit me. A chill flashed across my body, cooling the blood that crawled across my stomach in a growing stream. A reflexive shiver shook me, causing their talons to dig deeper. I had to get free. Danaus and the others were outnumbered. James had to be saved. Rowe would complete the sacrifice soon, and the power . . . I couldn't feel the power any longer. The harpylike naturi had carried me far enough away.

My head fell back and a bubble of laughter jumped from my throat a second before both of the naturi holding me erupted into flames. Their screams echoed across the skies as their clawed feet opened, releasing me. I moved quickly, grabbing an ankle of each naturi before I could fall back to the earth. Pain burned in my shoulders, threatening to loosen my grip, but I held tight. If I lost sight of them or lost contact, I wouldn't be able to keep the fire going.

The flames ate at their flesh, burning holes in their fleshy wings until we were all plunging to the ground in a hideous heap of burning, melting flesh. The naturi in my grip twisted and screamed, not so much fighting me, but simply trying to escape the pain. I finally released my hold on their legs as the ground approached with surprising speed. I had made this mistake before, not paying attention to where I was falling. The last time it happened, I'd been impaled on a tree limb and barely survived the encounter. And Sadira wasn't around now to save my sorry ass.

Plummeting to the ground, I looked down to discover I was falling into an orchard. Damn it. Ready-made stakes. I lost sight of the two naturi, so the fire I had created instantly went out. Crossing my arms over my chest in a desperate attempt to shield my heart, I crashed through the smaller upper branches. My feet hit a larger branch, but I just as quickly slid off so that I landed across it. Something cracked. Whether it was my ribs or the branch, I don't know, but only a moment later both the large branch and I were laying on the soggy ground.

I wanted to stay there awhile. Pain throbbed in my body in half a dozen places, and I wanted to collect my thoughts before adding to the network of cuts and wounds that crisscrossed me. But a pair of low moans pulled me back. The two wind naturi had crashed through a tree right behind me.

Using the trunk of the tree I'd fallen through to help me to my feet, I hobbled over to where the naturi were writhing on the ground. Their pale pink skin was now black and flaking off in bits of ash.

Their wings had burned straight through, leaving them grounded. But then, we all knew they would never fly again even if I hadn't destroyed their wings.

Their screams lasted for less than a minute as I once again encased them in bright orange flames. I felt no remorse, no regret, no doubt. The naturi intended to do the same to every other creature soon enough.

When they were destroyed, their ashes left to dance in the wind, I summoned up my powers again and searched the island for Danaus. I had a vague idea where I was but couldn't waste time wandering around in the darkness. I located the hunter with ease. He was my beacon in the night.

Cutting across the open farmland, I ran as quickly as my wounded body would permit. I had lost blood and my body was trying to repair itself, but it wasn't an easy job, as I refused to stop and rest. Reaching the road again, I picked up speed, and returned to the ruins in a matter of minutes.

At the main courtyard, I found Jabari at the westernmost sacrifice. He was easily tearing through one naturi after another as each one bravely approached the Ancient. Danaus was to the east, holding his own with a sword in his hand while naturi formed a semicircle around the hunter. James was still staked to the ground, though one of his hands was loose and he was struggling to free his other hand.

Ryan was my greatest concern. The warlock stood opposite Rowe. As I approached them, I paused long enough to pick up a short sword from the ground. A lost weapon from a dead naturi. It wasn't my first choice, but I'd lost one of my knives in Rowe earlier and the harpies had stolen my gun. I had one knife left, and I was going to need that if Rowe pinned me again.

Overhead, the sky had begun to churn and the wind gusted, whipping my hair in front of my face. Rowe was calling up another storm. The ground around Ryan glowed a strange pale blue. The warlock had created some sort of protective circle to keep the naturi physically at bay. But I knew it wouldn't protect him from a bolt of lightning. At least, not for long.

"We're not finished!" I shouted across the courtyard. Rowe's head snapped up, and for a breath he actually looked surprised. Then the shock melted away, the fleeting emotion replaced with a grin that reminded me of my old tormentor, Nerian.

"Good to see you in one piece," Rowe replied. His one good eye jumped from me to Ryan and back again as he struggled to watch the warlock and me at the same time.

I was about to lunge at him when someone far more interesting captured my attention. "Rowe, you once said there was some great reason why I was left alive that day. Some role I had yet to play," I shouted over the gusting wind. "Call this me returning the favor."

Rowe genuinely looked confused as I sidled past him and moved toward the female naturi who stood nearby. She was the one who'd appeared within the Great Hall. She was the one with whom the bargain had been made. She held a sword in one hand and her lips were pressed into a thin line of worry. She knew I recognized her despite the fact that she now wore a pair of jeans and a black tank top.

"I see you got your playmate back," I taunted. "Did she enjoy her stay within the hall?"

The tip of Rowe's sword dipped as he looked from me to the other naturi at his side.

"She's insane," the female quickly said, shaking her head. "She's lying. I don't know what she's talking about."

"Hmmm . . ." Rowe said, taking a step away from her. "Maybe. But then, Mira's not one to lie."

"Jabari! Is this her?" I shouted across the courtyard, hoping to snag the attention of the Ancient as he tore apart another naturi. The Elder turned, his robes soaked in blood. He casually paused for a moment and looked at the naturi I had indicated.

"Yes," he said with a nod. "Kill her. The bargain is off."

"You can't call off the bargain!" she screamed without thinking. "A single member of the Coven can't call off the bargain. You promised us!"

I didn't think she would go for it so easily. I wasn't sure how many of the remaining naturi in the region were a part of this faction that wanted Aurora dead. I needed to not only convince Rowe that there was a deal, but those faction members also had to believe that the bargain was dead. I had dreaded this moment, but now that it was here, I didn't feel the panic I'd anticipated. Adrenaline pumped through my body and my hand tightened on the hilt of the short sword I held. I was ready to finally take matters into my own hands, ready to take back a measure of control of my life.

"I claim the open seat on the Coven," I announced, straightening my stance. "Jabari, do you recognize my claim?"

The smile grew across his face and I could feel him laughing in triumph. "I recognize your claim," he solemnly replied with a bow of his head. And then his voice changed to something darker, more insidious, as he finished, "Welcome to the Coven."

"Now, as we were saying," I continued, turning my attention back to the naturi, who stood before me with her face growing redder with anger. "The bargain is off. If you want Aurora dead, you can do it yourself. The door is staying closed."

"No!" she screamed. She came running at me with her sword raised above her head.

Grabbing a knife from my side with my free hand, I knelt down and threw it directly at her chest. The small knife buried itself in her heart. She paused, still standing, long enough for me to rise to my feet and remove her head with a single, fluid swing.

Her blood sprayed everywhere, pelting me in the face. I wiped it off with the back of my hand as I turned my full attention back to Rowe. "Obviously, you didn't have all your ducks in a row, but you do now."

"The same could be said about you and your young man," Rowe countered, motioning with his sword toward Danaus.

James was sitting up now, but the naturi were getting closer. Danaus was painfully outnumbered, while Jabari was trying to defend the two other humans at the same time. The bargain was dead, but we were stretched too thin to try to stop the sacrifice. Besides, there would be no combining our powers this time. Danaus and I were desperate, but what we'd done last time was too ugly to repeat. There had to be another way.

"I—"

Whatever Rowe meant to say was cut off when another naturi called to him. His whole body stiffened at the sound of her voice. He quickly stepped backward, putting some distance between himself and Ryan. But I also noticed he carefully positioned himself between me and the newcomer.

It drew my attention to her. She was shorter than me and her body was incredibly slender, as if she were only an animated skeleton in soft gray clothes. A mass of straight black hair hung down her back. She watched me with enormous eyes that seemed to be the same shade of pale gray as her clothes. In fact, the only thing that didn't seem to be monotone in this slim creature was her ruby red mouth, which at the moment held neither a smile nor a frown. I watched her until Rowe stepped into my line of sight, thinking insanely that she looked familiar.

Rowe shouted something at her and she responded. They spoke in their own language, which I couldn't understand. But Rowe's body language and tone spoke volumes. He pointed his sword at me with his right hand and waved his left hand at her, motioning her to stay back. Eyes narrowed and body bent forward, he was ready to attack me if I took a single step toward her.

Again he shouted some direction at her that I couldn't understand. Just over his shoulder, I saw her gaze up at the sky once. There was no moon to see, but I knew what she was doing. She wasn't looking for some celestial body or even a fresh wave of winged naturi to aid them. I knew her expression—she was gauging the night. We were out of time.

Something clenched in my stomach and my hands started to shake. Now was the moment, and I felt trapped. I was afraid to use my powers. I could kill us all. There was too much energy in the air and I wouldn't be able to control it.

"Danaus!" I screamed. I hoped the hunter heard me. I hoped he understood by the desperate plea in my voice what I was asking, because there was no more time for plans and explanations. "Kill the female! Stop her!" My voice rang out over the fighting, echoing across the valley. Jabari, Danaus, and Ryan heard me. They would stop her if I could not.

Rowe's face twisted in rage at my words, turning his whole body to face me. He raised his sword and came at me. I countered him, and his sword clashed with mine again and again, the impact sending sparks flying around him. We were both desperate, but Rowe was also afraid of something, which made him sloppy. Dodging a blow meant to remove my head, I punched him in the face, knocking him back a few steps. To my surprise, he fell backward over a piece of broken rock and didn't get back up.

Chaos surrounded me. Dropping the short sword, I reached inside of myself and tapped my own abilities. I was ready to summon up all the fires of Hell. No one would leave the ruins alive. The sacrifices had to be stopped. The seal had to be protected.

With the first flicker of fire, the energy came rushing into me, alive and crackling. For the first time in my life, I was fully in touch with the powers of the earth. There was no calm, sweet peace. No sound of babbling brooks or whispering winds. There was only crackling rage and the fury of a power long unused. Mother Earth was fucking pissed and I was now her outlet.

Each naturi that approached me burst into flames instantly, but it wasn't enough to relieve the pressure building in my body. The torches became engulfed in flames while giant basketball-size balls of fire hovered in the air, lighting the courtyard so it appeared as if daybreak had finally arrived. I located Danaus and James and quickly encircled them in a protective wall of fire. I did the same with Jabari, but it wasn't enough.

The power was building. It was going to destroy me, and I couldn't find the gray female Rowe had been so intent on protecting. The power was going to kill me before I could stop her.

Danaus. I reached out. My voice in my head seemed like a small whisper compared to the roar of power within me. I couldn't concentrate anymore. The fires were getting larger, brighter, stronger. I was going to kill the very people I was trying to protect.

I'm here. His voice in my brain was a cool balm against the burning inside me.

Can't concentrate. Can't find her. Don't know which sacrifice she's going after.

She's here.

"No!" I screamed. *James!*

Pain exploded within me. I didn't even have a chance to react. My whole body was thrown backward. I flew what felt like yards through the air in a terrifying blur of motion before my spine slammed into the hard stone ground. An incoherent scream of pain erupted from my throat as I writhed. Something was being torn deep within me, as if someone or something was attacking the fragile shreds of my soul, trying to pull them from my body. I curled into the fetal position, desperate to hold my soul within my battered frame. The pain burned within me. Nerve endings trembled and twisted. Organs sizzled. Agonizing pain ripped through my brain until there wasn't a single thought.

And then the blackness seeped in. It consumed everything, the pain, the tearing sensation in my chest, the outside world. The blackness blotted out everything and then it stole me away.

TWENTY-SIX

I jerked upright and gasped, which sent razor blades down my throat and through my lungs before the first clear thought rang through my brain. I didn't need to breathe, but there were some instincts that even death couldn't kill. When I awoke each night from a nightmare, my first reaction was always to gasp for air. But this wasn't a nightmare.

Blinking as I tried to clear my blurred vision, I felt a hand at my back and on my shoulder as someone eased me back to the ground. I coughed and tried to roll back onto my side as I pushed the unnecessary air out of my body. Something inside of me ached. My thoughts were fuzzy as I tried to remember what had happened. No one had touched me, but pain had exploded inside of me, frying every organ and brain cell.

"Rest, Mira." Jabari's deep voice swept over me from my right. I lay on my back and unclenched my eyes. Ryan was kneeling beside me on my left, one of his hands holding mine. Jabari was kneeling too. His clothes were torn and he was covered in blood, but a soft smile hovered on his lips. He had won. I was on the Coven, which only benefited him because he was able to control me.

"James?" I asked, fearing the answer when I looked up at Ryan. The warlock nodded over past Jabari. Twisting, I saw the young man seated against the wall, bloodied, bruised, and swollen, but still breathing.

"But Danaus—" I started, then slowly shook my head as I tried to clear the fog from my thoughts. "He said the naturi was by him. Is the seal still safe?"

"The seal was broken," Jabari confirmed, his smile falling into a dark frown.

"How?" I demanded in a raspy voice.

"The human male I freed. He jumped through the ring of fire you created and into the waiting arms of the naturi. It took them only a second to subdue him and complete the task."

"And the child?" I whispered.

"He sleeps," Ryan said. "He'll be returned to town tonight and will remember none of this."

I pressed my right hand to the center of my chest. Was the seal breaking what I had felt? Had the seal been tied to my soul? The pain had been excruciating, as if something were being torn from me. Even now there was a hollow, ragged sensation throbbing within me.

"I . . . felt . . . pain," I said. My voice wavered and sounded rough to my own ears.

Jabari nodded. His large hand swept over my forehead and down as he moved some hair from my face in a surprisingly comforting gesture. "You created the seal. It's natural that you felt its destruction."

Ryan's hand tightened at Jabari's words. "You created the original seal?"

I pulled my hand out of his grasp and rolled away from him. I couldn't look at the warlock. Getting my knees beneath me, I slowly sat up. However, all thoughts of standing left me when I looked around the area. The carnage was gut-wrenching. Blood and bodies were strewn everywhere, bringing back images of the battle at the Themis Compound less than a week earlier. There was nowhere I could go. Destruction seemed to hound my every step. Chaos followed in my wake.

And now the seal was broken. The naturi would soon determine a time to open the door between our two worlds, and the war would officially begin. What lay before me was simply a minor skirmish.

"I'm a monster," I whispered, shaking my head as tears slipped unchecked down my scratched and dirty face. Burned corpses filled the area, with smoke still rising from their bodies. "I'm a monster with this kind of power and yet still I fail."

"The bargain has been broken. Our Liege is safe," Jabari patiently reminded me. "We succeeded."

"No, the seal was broken," I moaned.

Kneeling before me, he placed his hands on either side of my face and forced me to meet his dark gaze. "We failed because we didn't work together. We separated when our greatest strength is to work together through you. This will be for the best. This is the only way to end this permanently. We will kill Aurora and destroy the naturi for all time. No more seals and no more gateways to other worlds. We end it for all time."

"But—"

"To protect our way of life, to protect the humans, we have to destroy the naturi. And the only way to do that is to destroy their queen."

I wanted to believe Jabari. I couldn't remember ever wanting anything more. And he might have been right—the only way to destroy the naturi could be through Aurora. But all I could see was this black shadow of death stretching across the earth. To get to Aurora, so many would have to die; vampire, lycanthrope, and human.

But at least now we had some time. We had time to plan. We had time to hunt.

I pulled back, removing my face from his grasp. "You had better be right."

Painfully, I pushed to my feet. The sound of Jabari and Ryan rising as well drifted to my ears, but my attention was on the carnage around me. Danaus was slowly approaching. He was covered in blood and scrapes. A long cut ran along the right side of his face, blood dripping from the end of his chin. His deep blue eyes glittered in the fading torchlight.

"Rowe?" I asked.

"Unknown," Danaus said with a slight shake of his head. "He was badly wounded. They carried him out of here."

I knew better than to hope. Centuries ago I had left Nerian for dead at the top of Machu Picchu, confident the naturi would never be able to pull his intestines back into his body before he bled to death. I had been wrong. I wouldn't believe that Rowe was actually dead until I saw his cold, lifeless body lying on the ground before me. And even then I'd incinerate him to white hot ashes just to be on the safe side.

But for now I wanted Rowe alive. He knew there was a faction within his happy family that wanted his wife-queen dead. That division within the naturi could work to our advantage in the coming nights. Rowe would be forced to conduct a witch hunt within his own people to find out who wanted Aurora dead. It would create chaos, and creating chaos was what I did best.

Turning, I looked over at one of the nightwalkers who was rumored to have created me. Something deep inside of me hated Jabari for using me, for making me his own powerful plaything. But I didn't have the memories of those horrible moments to keep the fires of hatred burning brightly. All the memories I had of him were of loving companionship and trust. Even now, knowing the truth about my creation and past, some part of me still trusted him, needed to believe that what he'd told me was the truth.

Regardless of my feelings for Jabari, I didn't want to be on the Coven, but for now, my presence struck a balance against Macaire and maybe even Elizabeth. And until Macaire was either broken or dead, Jabari would be content to leave me alive. I had bought myself and Our Liege some time.

"I'm leaving," I announced.

"You're to go back to the Coven," Jabari ordered. "You belong with the Coven."

I smiled at him. "No," I simply said. "I'm going where I am needed. I'm going home. When the time comes to fight Aurora and the naturi, you know where to find me."

I walked toward the northern entrance, but stopped after only a few feet. Looking over my shoulder, I stared at Danaus for a few seconds in silence. So many unanswered questions, confused emotions, and ugly mistakes. A bori wrapped in human trappings. A hunter who was no longer sure who the enemy really was. And a nightwalker who was no longer sure where her loyalties lay. There was only one thing I knew for sure when it came to Danaus: We weren't finished yet.

"Are you coming?" I called.

He arched one thick black brow at me. His lips twisted and one corner of his mouth quirked in a mocking smile.

"It'll be easier to kill you if I don't have to hunt you down," I said, answering his unspoken question, *Why?*

Without a word, Danaus slid his blood-smeared sword back into the sheath on his back and followed me out of the Minoan ruins. For now, we could both say to hell with the Coven, Themis, and the naturi. I was headed home, where Danaus and I could focus on more important things. Like trying to get back to the business of killing each other.